"*My Secret Life* is by far the most famous and the longest sexual autobiography written in the nineteenth century. It has in it invaluable material for social and cultural historians, literary scholars, students of manners and morals — and it has more of what we might call 'encounters' than any narrative ever penned in English. . . . The question of its authorship wallows in the land of rumor."
— From the Introduction by James Kincaid

The Anonymous Author of *My Secret Life* has never been identified. Rumors have suggested he was a prominent scholar, the eccentric son of an earl, even a titled woman. All we do know is evident in the text: that he was raised by nursemaids and governesses, surrounded by servants, and educated at a good boarding school. His young adulthood was spent not in learning a trade, but in exploring the world of sex and recording every encounter.

James Kincaid is Aerol Arnold Professor of English at the University of Southern California and the author of *Child-Loving: The Erotic Child and Victorian Culture* as well as books on Dickens, Trollope, and Tennyson.

My Secret Life

Anonymous

*Edited, Abridged, and with
an Introduction by James Kincaid
with Richard Tithecott*

Ⓒ
A SIGNET CLASSIC

SIGNET CLASSIC
Published by New American Library, a division of
Penguin Putnam Inc., 375 Hudson Street,
New York, New York 10014, U.S.A.
Penguin Books Ltd, 27 Wrights Lane,
London W8 5TZ, England
Penguin Books Australia Ltd, Ringwood,
Victoria, Australia
Penguin Books Canada Ltd, 10 Alcorn Avenue,
Toronto, Ontario, Canada M4V 3B2
Penguin Books (N.Z.) Ltd, 182–190 Wairau Road,
Auckland 10, New Zealand

Penguin Books Ltd, Registered Offices:
Harmondsworth, Middlesex, England

Published by Signet Classic, an imprint of New American Library,
a division of Penguin Putnam Inc.

First Signet Classic Printing, April 1996
10 9 8 7 6 5

 REGISTERED TRADEMARK—MARCA REGISTRADA

Library of Congress Catalog Card Number: 95-74999

Printed in the United States of America

BOOKS ARE AVAILABLE AT QUANTITY DISCOUNTS WHEN USED TO PROMOTE PROD-
UCTS OR SERVICES. FOR INFORMATION PLEASE WRITE TO PREMIUM MARKETING DIVI-
SION, PENGUIN PUTNAM INC., 375 HUDSON STREET, NEW YORK, NEW YORK 10014.

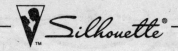

Silhouette®

SPECIAL EDITION™

Emotional, compelling stories that capture the intensity of living, loving and creating a family in today's world.

Silhouette®
Desire

Modern, passionate reads that are powerful and provocative.

Silhouette®
nocturne

Dramatic and sensual tales of paranormal romance.

Romances that are sparked by danger and fueled by passion.

SDIR07

Harlequin® Historical
Historical Romantic Adventure!

Imagine a time of chivalrous knights and unconventional ladies, roguish rakes and impetuous heiresses, rugged cowboys and spirited frontierswomen— these rich and vivid tales will capture your imagination!

Harlequin Historical… they're too good to miss!

INTRODUCTION

My Secret Life is by far the most famous and the longest sexual autobiography written in the nineteenth century. Its eleven fat volumes contain invaluable material for social and cultural historians, literary scholars, students of manners and morals — and I believe it has more of what we might call "encounters" than any narrative ever penned. Since the book's publication around 1902, this astounding document—narrated by the otherwise anonymous "Walter"—has been notorious as an energetic, entertaining narrative of one man's tireless sexual activity.

Since only scholars and the mentally tangled could read the original in its entirety, nearly everyone who knows *My Secret Life* has read it in an abridged form. These abridgements have generally taken care to present a somewhat expurgated and sanitized image of Walter, a Walter who (apart from his insatiable sexual appetite) is a safe, agreeable, and somehow recognizable individual. None, until now, has shown us Walter in anything like his full range of poses and postures. But the Walter in the volume you are holding, much more like the Walter who grinds through the original eleven volumes, is a more varied, indiscriminate, and often disturbing protagonist. This new Walter is not simply rollicking through life but also, we will see, raping; reveling not only in flesh, but in pain; not only in lust, but in fear. Take care.

The Walter presented here seems to me also the first Walter who has behind him a coherent story, who can be said to be recognizable as a man with a background and a life. This version actually has something like a plot; not much of a plot, to be sure, since even our more well-rounded Walter seems only to do one thing. Like a good Victorian, he has listened to the sage Thomas Carlyle: "Find your work and do it." Walter has found what he's good at—sex—and he is determined to lunge into it and never leave off, which may not be exactly what Carlyle had in mind. But it's probably what readers of *My Secret Life* have in mind; otherwise, they'd do as well reading Carlyle, where at least they'd not find things like:

" 'Oho—oho' she said with a prolonged sigh, 'do—oh, take away—oh—your hand, Walter dear,—oh I shall be ill, —oho—oho.' " As descriptions of such things go, this seems conventional enough—though we ourselves may never have found "oho" coming so often to mind when we reached for the perfect word on such occasions.

In fact, *My Secret Life* contains so little of what we have learned to recognize as conventional for writing on sexual activity that it may seem more like a journal than fantasy, more social history than pornography. There is less panting, sighing, and swooning than there is sweating, flopping, grunting, elbowing, washing, and attending to unromantic bodily details: " 'Get up love, I want to piddle,' said she. I rolled off her belly." Walter takes such pleasure in absolutely all things bodily—after skidding off her belly, he probably goes and watches her piddle—that he can't get enough of it. "I liked flesh," he says agreeably; "a woman's bum could not be too big for me." A bum the size of the Ritz: that's his dream.

He nearly finds it in one of his sweetest partners, Big Sarah: "Her bum was vast, but she was thick up to her waist, and had large breasts as firm as a rock. Her thighs were lovely, but her knees so big, that no garter would remain above them." Sarah is no Harlequin heroine, and not just in appearance. She is desperately poor but generous, not easily shocked but sadly innocent. Walter likes her so much and is so appreciative of that lovely, boundless flesh that he gives her a ten-pound note. Sarah had never in her life even seen a bank note, and she asks Walter just what it can be. When he tells her, Sarah, large in heart as in body, vows to share some with her old mother, and goes off into the night, calculating the exact extent of her delight: "I had two pounds, and now I've twelve."

With all this emphasis on class, and money, and on who has the power to do what to whom, Sarah starts to look like a heroine from Zola or Stephen Crane. We may begin to wonder what kind of book we have entered. *My Secret Life* may be seen as pure social history, absurdist (or erotic) fantasy, or some mixture of the two. It has but one subject, the oft-repeated and remarkably successful search for and the performance of sexual intercourse or something like it; yet this is no hack-work piece of porn. Single-minded as it is, it presents us with a mind capable of reflecting on the world about him, those with whom he comes in (very close) contact, his own obsessions, even his follies. One thing is clear: This strange and compelling book, perhaps the strangest to come down to us from those mysterious, devious Victorians, is unlike anything else produced then—or now.

———————————

My Secret Life, probably written in the 1880s, made its inaugural public appearance as a tease, the first six chapters being published in 1901 as *The Dawn of Sensuality* by the publisher "Charles Carrington," who followed this up the next year with a catalogue announcing the whole book, a whopping eleven volumes, for sale. According to Carrington, who seems never to have said a truthful thing in his life if he could help it, the work was printed in Amsterdam around 1880 in an edition limited by the author to six copies (though more may have been run off by an unscrupulous printer, Carrington claimed). Since that time the work has been issued in many different forms and titles, some of which have been seized by police and, predictably, made the subject of periodic legal/moral battles. Imitations have appeared, and also "Supplements," one nearly as long as the original written for an Oklahoma oil-baron whose thirst for new matter was such that he needed a couple of hundred fresh pages a week and was willing to pay what it took to get them. All in all, *My Secret Life* is hardly a pure text, which would have pleased the decidedly impure "Walter."

But who is Walter? As with most other things connected with this book, the question of its authorship wallows in the land of rumor. We will never know who wrote this; who (if anyone) experienced all, some, or any of these adventures; who chose to publish such intimate accounts (or lies) and why. There is an intriguing possibility, floated by some experts, that the author was one Henry Spencer Ashbee, a fascinating scholar, bibliographer, collector, and tweaker of the righteous. It is my guess that Ashbee knew more about printed erotica than any man who ever lived: He published a remarkable three-volume listing (with details and copious selections) of nineteenth-century arousing material called *Bibliography of Prohibited Books* and he possessed a good deal of erotica himself, willing it at his death to the British Museum, on condition that they make it available to one and all. This was a brilliant piece of satiric blackmail, since the Museum's acceptance of the racy books that they did not want was a condition for the receipt of innumerable other valuable materials that they very much did want and that Ashbee also proposed to donate. But there really is no evidence to confirm his authorship, outside of Ashbee's undeniable devilishness, knowledge, and interest in the subject; all areas in which he was extraordinarily proficient but hardly alone.

So what we do have in *My Secret Life*: An arty sexual autobiography that will remind us of Henry Miller; a cynical bit of pornography; an accurate and serious (if quickening) peek at the habits of our far-from-starchy forebears; or a novel? What mask are we to put on when we read *My Secret Life*? It all depends on what we think we're reading—and that's not easy to decide. First of all, do we regard what Walter's telling us as plain fact? Walter says he has had intercourse with twelve hundred women and manually manipulated the genitals of "certainly three hundred others." That number, which modestly excludes the men and boys with whom he had fun, gathers into its fold women of twenty-seven "empires, kingdoms or countries and eighty or more different nationalities, including every one in Europe except a Laplander."

On the other hand, the matter-of-fact tone of the work and the mundane details that the narrator includes seldom suggest Casanova–style boasting, parody, or mad fantasy. Maybe Walter just had a way about him, but he says he didn't: He insists that he was an average guy who just happened to be persevering; as if fifteen hundred different sexual partners would fall into the lap of anyone who wasn't a slacker. He suggests that women are really as anxious to have sex as men and that they'll do just that, given reasonable encouragement and opportunity. He says further that what he's doing is nothing very remarkable: "What I have done, thousands of others are doing."

Sure. Perhaps others will simply nod in agreement at this observation, but my own experience and perhaps gaunt sense of the probable cause me to abandon at just this point the idea that Walter is an historical character, at least in the usual sense, though he is a brilliant fictional narrator, a novel-writer. It's a novel whose plot is, I grant, formed as a set of variations on a single theme. Here we have a picaresque (or post-modern) novel which invites us playfully to participate in all the episodes—or the single repeated episode. Dickens's *Great Expectations* opens with Pip recalling his first memory of "the identity of things," of the whole cosmos; but Walter's first words take a more limited world for his survey: "My first recollection of things sexual . . ."

Walter's focus (one could say his artistic integrity) is so intense that he makes sex the measure of all things, even time: When he is young, he orders events not by the calendar but by the size of his penis. This novel operates as a subversive version of genteel fiction and its main motor: How sheer tenacity and good luck can overcome the odds, master the obstacles created by class, modesty, and money. As in many other novels, from Defoe to Horatio Alger to Joseph Heller, Walter overcomes them again and again, and yet again.

This work takes as its subject the Inexhaustible and poses as its main artistic goal the representation of recurrence. Now, recurrence is a different thing from blunt repetition, to be sure, but not much different; and how does an author make us feel that each going-at-it is indeed a new dawn and not just another slog through the same old routine? Walter knows he has a problem on his hands: "fucking is always much the same," he says, and fucking, he admits, is his major (only) subject. "The roads to copulation are like the act, very much the same everywhere." There is, in fact, "nothing mysterious about it excepting in the psychology." Only that—but that "psychology," which he elsewhere terms "imagination," is everything, transforming dull routine into heady new exploration. For Walter, as for any artist, "novelty always stimulates my salacity," and he can always, literally always, find novelty by exercising his imagination, the secret of all art and, we gather, sexual bliss.

It is true that, especially in the second half of the novel, Walter does seem to locate variety not simply through ingenious imaginative contemplation, but through more and more direct recourse to external stimulants: including boys, flagellation, partners with unusual body formations, and group play. He decides at about midpoint in the novel that his life (sex-life that is, but they seem the same) has been "simple, commonplace, and unintellectual," so he vows to cut down the amount of "simple belly to belly exercise," charming as it has been, and to add a lot of, as he puts it (and who could say it better?), "suck and fuck all around." One could see this welcoming of variety as an act of sad desperation, an attempt to hide from himself the emptiness of his life, an addiction he cannot rid himself of.

But Walter himself sees his life in grandly heroic terms: He was "determined to know everything, and to do everything once in my life." Everything! And he's not talking about skydiving, snorkeling, and safaris. He's not some timid Ernest Hemingway sort. He really means everything that is personal, vulnerable. Walter has a literal mind, and he has a literal courge: He means to make his body available to pleasure at the risk of ridicule, failure, and pain. The very opposite of Hemingway in this respect, he throws himself into the most sensitive and dangerous tests of all. He doesn't need to shoot a lion as a substitute for sex. Walter has no truck with substitutes and thus is like a bedroom-Faust—unsatisfied with less than All. Walter laments his failure not simply to sleep with a Lapland woman but with the entire population of Lapland. But he's a comic Faust, of course, since, there's so little that he doesn't get at the finish. At the end, Walter says, "Eros adieu," but this is just a way to stop the book, not conclude it. Nobody believes him when he says adieu to anything, certainly not eros. Even if Walter were to be stricken with a fatal disease, he'd make love to the ambulance drivers, the entire emergency room, the undertaker, the grave diggers—his erotic urge would not stop for death.

Whether we regard the work as a comic novel or not, we will notice about it some very striking and unusual features. It is, for one thing, the least sexually squeamish work to come down to us from the past. Walter is apparently incapable of censoring anything, even when we might like him to do so. Walter is wildly excited by many things most of us might regard as uninteresting or actively unattractive. For instance, nothing excites him more than the sight or sound of a woman peeing: "seeing them piddle became a taste I kept all my life," he says right off the bat. (page 27) He carries an auger with him to foreign hotels, eagerly drilling holes so he can catch others at play or at the chamber pot.

Not that this peculiarity blocks him from more conventional engagements, though even these are sometimes portrayed as more than a little grotesque: "I had to pull open this one's sausage lips and hold back the dark fringe, which got into my eyes and tickled my nose. . . . Then her thighs closed round my head tightly enough to squeeze it off." The Rabelaisian humor is not lost on the narrator, who can even laugh at the vagaries of his mind-of-its-own penis, and the difficulties he has in choreographing the more complex figures in group sex, at one point having so many arms and legs blocking the essential organs that he resorts to a series of ceiling hooks, pulleys, and ropes to hoist the excess out of the way. We sometimes feel we are in the middle of an X-rated *Night at the Opera*.

But just as often we glide over from the grotesque to the lyrical, especially to passionate celebrations of the woman he's near—or near to engaging. He often says that he has little interest in faces or bodies (apart from one area, on which he is a connoisseur), that he simply likes best of all in the world the woman with whom he is about to copulate, no matter what she looks like. Sometimes he falls in love, and he often seems to develop considerable affection for women he knows, even when their relationship is decidedly short-term. Indeed, one of the most attractive features of Walter is the respect he has for prostitutes and the easy and quite convincing friendships he forms with them. He can move us most strongly when he is talking to these women, inquiring after their interests and needs, wondering how it is they get by. Such passages are probably more affecting than the self-conscious apostrophes to "cunt" or, even worse, the celebration of the power (untold) of the penis. All his life, he nourishes the belief that once he gets his penis—"What a persuader!"—into a woman's hand or even into her line of vision, she is a goner: "Powerful organ which all women worship!" I like him better myself when he is talking about pleasure rather than worship; for instance, when he tells us how much fun he and a very early partner named Charlotte had together, totally unable to keep their hands off one another and going at it in halls, privies, on tables, in a schoolroom, in fields, in the rain, standing up and kneeling—hanging from the ceiling, probably. He reflects on all this with an unusual note for him, understated and simple lucidity: "Nothing in my career since is so lovely as our life then was."

I have held off talking directly about the character of this "Walter," since there is so much about him that will assault modern sensibilities, and perhaps any sensibilities. Except for the time with prostitutes, he is pretty much devoting his life to a career of sexual harassment; when he isn't, that is, actually committing rape. There is probably no other way we can view all this, though we ought to remain aware that such terms would not be altogether meaningful then. Still, Walter clearly believes that he knows what women want and what they mean much better than they do; that he is, always and without exception, doing them a favor by fulfilling what, if they only knew it, is their own will and deep desire. His scientific curiosity, while sometimes amusing to us and

[xi]

perhaps even commendable, also leads him inevitably to wonder what it would be like to deflower ten-year-olds.

For some readers, there is no more to be said; and to point out that Walter is also honest, often compassionate, and without conceit would be as wrongheaded as insisting on the Marquis de Sade's good grooming habits. Still, it is worth noting, though not as an apology, that Walter does not see himself as exceptionally endowed (in any way) or even exceptionally successful with women; that he is invariably generous in his financial dealings, and that he never imagines that he is seeking or finding some kind of higher truth. He knows very well that the search for pleasure will get you, if you're lucky, pleasure—but not enlightenment. The wisdom he picks up on the way he does give to us, but it amounts to no more than a few (dubious) tips on how to use "the persuader" to best effect in the seducing game and a long essay on the genitals, offered for the naive of all ages.

The best that can be said for Walter is that, for all his occasional brutality, he does certainly, by his lights, respect and like women. He believes that they love what he loves and that their pleasure in it is every bit as intense as his. Walter has in mind an organization of our (male *and* female) being in which will and consciousness are more or less superficial, in which libido, once awakened and released, can give us a taste of bliss in a cold and careless world. Walter can be hard-nosed and callous about money and class (most of his relationships are with poor women), but he rarely makes the error of believing that women are demeaned by being poor, or that poor women are any different from those more fortunate. He is, in this sense, a liberal, a democrat.

But let's not stretch the point: Walter is not a social philosopher, but a party boy. He's writing the book not to instruct or entertain us, but to keep the party going: "The writing indeed completed my enjoyment." Readers may find that a disturbing thought—Walter writing all this down and then reading it back to himself in order to relive the excitement. What room is there for us in such a closed circuit? Going through this book, we might feel a little like voyeurs; as if, like Walter, we had taken out our auger, bored through the wall, and started peeking at someone else's "enjoyment."

Still, what a lot of enjoyment there is; and how ingeniously it is renewed, over and over again. It is this comic energy, I think, which is most evident. Walter is hospitable, after all; he has a kind of affable and daffy confidence that his pleasure will give us pleasure; and he welcomes us to take what we like. Not everyone will choose to accept his invitation, and even those who do, may well hold on to some outrage and a fair number of ethical and political objections. But raising objections before Walter is like trying to dodge killer bees. And many readers—"oho, oho"—will not—"oho, oho,"—I guess—"oho, no"—be too much—"oh, oho"—interested—"ahhhhh"—in escaping anyhow—"oho, oho."

—JAMES R. KINCAID

A NOTE ON THE ABRIDGEMENT

This abridgement of the original eleven-volume edition is carefully selected to catch such continuous narrative strands as exist and to be faithful to the range of Walter's experiences and views as they develop over time. Since this often meant using parts of and sometimes splicing consecutive chapters, we felt that it would be clearer to number our chapters consecutively, without regard to the original volume and chapter designations. The key below will indicate, for those interested, how our chapters correspond to the original and how this abridgement is fashioned.

SIGNET CLASSIC EDITION/11-VOLUME 1902 EDITION

* Chapter abridged

My Secret Life

INTRODUCTION

In 18— my oldest friend died. We had been at school and college together, and our intimacy had never been broken. I was trustee for his wife and executor at his death. He died of a lingering illness, during which his hopes of living were alternately raised, and depressed. Two years before he died, he gave me a huge parcel carefully tied up and sealed. "Take care of but don't open this," he said; "if I get better, return it to me, if I die, let no mortal eye but yours see it, and burn it."

His widow died a year after him. I had well nigh forgotten this packet, which I had had full three years, when, looking for some title deeds, I came across it, and opened it, as it was my duty to do. Its contents astonished me. The more I read it, the more marvellous it seemed. I pondered long on the meaning of his instructions when he gave it to me, and kept the manuscript some years, hesitating what to do with it.

At length I came to the conclusion, knowing his idiosyncrasy well, that his fear was only lest any one should know who the writer was; and feeling that it would be sinful to destroy such a history, I copied the manuscript and destroyed the original. He died relationless. No one now can trace the author; no names are mentioned in the book, though they were given freely in the margin of his manuscript, and I alone know to whom the initials refer. If I have done harm in printing it, I have done none to him, have indeed only carried out his evident intention, and given to a few a secret history, which bears the impress of truth on every page, a contribution to psychology.

PREFACE

I began these memoirs when about twenty-five years old, having from youth kept a diary of some sort, which perhaps from habit made me think of recording my inner and secret life.

When I began it, I had scarcely read a baudy book, none of which, excepting *Fanny Hill,* appeared to me to be truthful: that did, and it does so still; the others telling of récherché eroticisms or of inordinate copulative powers, of the strange twists, tricks, and fancies of matured voluptuousness and philosophical lewedness, seemed to my comparative ignorance as baudy imaginings or lying inventions, not worthy of belief; although I now know, by experience, that they may be true enough, however eccentric and improbable, they may appear to the uninitiated.

Fanny Hill's was a woman's experience. Written perhaps by a woman, where was a man's written with equal truth? That book has no baudy word in it; but baudy acts need the baudy ejaculations; the erotic, full-flavored expressions, which even the chastest indulge in when lust, or love, is in its full tide of performance. So I determined to write my private life freely as to fact, and in the spirit of the lustful acts done by me, or witnessed; it is written therefore with absolute truth and without any regard whatever for what the world calls decency. Decency and voluptuousness in its fullest acceptance cannot exist together, one would kill the other; the poetry of copulation I have only experienced with a few women, which however neither prevented them nor me from calling a spade a spade.

I began it for my amusement; when many years had been chronicled I tired of it and ceased. Some ten years afterwards I met a woman, with whom, or with those she helped me to, I did, said, saw, and heard well nigh everything a man and woman could do with their genitals, and began to narrate those events, when quite fresh in my memory, a great variety of incidents extending over four years or more. Then I lost sight of her, and my amorous amusements for a while were simpler, but that part of my history was complete.

After a little while, I set to work to describe the events of the intervening years of my youth and early middle age, which included most of my gallant intrigues and adventures of a frisky order; but not the more lascivious ones of later years. Then an illness caused me to think seriously of burning the whole. But not liking to destroy my labor, I laid it aside again for a couple of years. Then another illness gave me long uninterrupted leisure; I read my manuscript and filled in some occurrences which I had forgotten but which my diary enabled me to place in their proper order. This will account for the difference in style in places, which I now observe; and a very needless repetition of voluptuous descriptions, which I had forgotten and had been before described; that however is inevitable, for human copulation, vary the incidents leading up to it as you may, is, and must be, at all times much the same affair.

Then, for the first time, I thought I would print my work that had been commenced more than twenty years before, but hesitated. I then had entered my maturity, and on to the most lascivious portion of my life, the events were disjointed, and fragmentary and my amusement was to describe them just after they occurred. Most frequently the next day I wrote all down with much prolixity; since, I have much abbreviated it.

I had from youth an excellent memory, but about sexual matters a wonderful one. Women were the pleasure of my life. I loved cunt, but also who had it; I like the woman I fucked and not simply the cunt I fucked, and therein is a great difference. I recollect even now in a degree which astonishes me, the face, colour, stature, thighs, backside, and cunt, of well nigh every woman I have had, who was not a mere casual, and even of some who were. The clothes they wore, the houses and rooms in which I had them, were before me mentally as I wrote, the way the bed and furniture were placed, the side of the room the windows were on, I remembered perfectly; and all the important events I can fix as to time, sufficiently nearly by reference to my diary, in which the contemporaneous circumstances of my life are recorded.

I recollect also largely what we said and did, and generally our baudy amusements. Where I fail to have done so, I have left description blank, rather than attempt to make a story coherent by inserting what was merely probable. I could not now account for my course of action, or why I did this, or said that, my conduct seems strange, foolish, absurd, very frequently, that of some women equally so, but I can but state what did occur.

In a few cases, I have, for what even seems to me very strange, suggested reasons or causes, but only where the facts seem by themselves to be very improbable, but have not exaggerated anything willingly. When I have named the number of times I have fucked a woman in my youth, I may occasionally be in error, it is difficult to be quite accurate on such points after a lapse of time. But as before said, in many cases the incidents were written down a few weeks and often within a few days after they occurred. I do not attempt to pose as a Hercules in copulation, there are quite sufficient braggarts on that head, much intercourse with gay women, and doctors, makes me doubt the wonderful feats in coition some men tell of.

I have one fear about publicity, it is that of having done a few things by curiosity and impulse (temporary aberrations) which even professed libertines may cry fie on. There are plenty who will cry fie who have done all and worse than I have and habitually, but crying out at the sins of others was always a way of hiding one's own iniquity. Yet from that cause perhaps no mortal eye but mine will see this history.

The Christian names of the servants mentioned are generally the true ones, the other names mostly false, tho phonetically resembling the true ones. Initials nearly always the true ones. In most cases the women they represent are dead or lost to me. Streets and baudy houses named are nearly always correct. Most of the houses named are now closed or pulled down; but any middle-aged man about town would recognize them. Where a road, house, room, or garden is described, the description is exactly true, even to the situation of a tree, chair, bed, sofa, pisspot. The district is sometimes given wrongly; but it matters little whether Brompton be substituted for Hackney, or Camden Town for Walworth. Where however, owing to the incidents, it is needful, the places of amusement are given correctly. The Tower, and Argyle rooms, for example. All this is done to prevent giving pain to some, perhaps still living, for I have no malice to gratify.

I have mystified family affairs, but if I say I had ten cousins when I had but six, or that one aunt's house was in Surrey instead of Kent, or in Lancashire, it breaks the clue and cannot matter to the reader. But my doings with man and woman are as true as gospel. If I say that I saw, or did, that with a cousin, male or female, it was with a cousin and no mere acquaintance; if with a servant, it was with a servant; if with a casual acquaintance, it is equally true. Nor if I say I had that woman, and did this or that with her, or felt or did aught else with a man, is there a word of untruth, excepting as to the place at which the incidents occurred. But even those are mostly correctly given; this is intended to be a true history, and not a lie.

SECOND PREFACE

Some years have passed away since I penned the foregoing, and it is not printed. I have since gone through abnormal phases of amatory life, have done and seen things, had tastes and letches which years ago I thought were the dreams of erotic mad-men; these are all described, the manuscript has grown into unmanageable bulk; shall it, can it, be printed? What will be said or thought of me, what became of the manuscript if found when I am dead? Better to destroy the whole, it has fulfilled its purpose in amusing me, now let it go to the flames!

I have read my manuscript through; what reminiscences! I had actually forgotten some of the early ones; how true the detail strikes me as I read of my early experiences; had it not been written then it never could have been written now; has anybody but myself faithfully made such a record? It would be a sin to burn all this, whatever society may say, it is but a narrative of human life, perhaps the every day life of thousands, if the confession could be had.

What strikes me as curious in reading it is the monotony of the course I have pursued towards women who were not of the gay class; it has been as similar and repetitive as fucking itself; do all men act so, does every man kiss, coax, hint smuttily, then talk baudily, snatch a feel, smell his fingers, assault, and win, exactly as I have done? Is every woman offended, say "no," then "oh!" blush, be angry, refuse, close her thighs, after a struggle open them, and yield to her lust as mine have done? A conclave of whores telling the truth, and of Romish Priests, could alone settle the point. Have all men had the strange letches which late in life have enraptured me, though in early days the idea of them revolted me? I can never know this; my experience, if printed, may enable others to compare as I cannot.

Shall it be burnt or printed? How many years have passed in this indecision? why fear? it is for others' good and not my own if preserved.

CHAPTER I

Earliest recollections. — An erotic nursemaid. —
Ladies abed. — My cock. — A frisky governess. —
Cousin Fred. — Thoughts on pudenda. — A female
pedlar. — Baudy pictures. — A naked baby.

My earliest recollections of things sexual are of what I think
must have occurred some time between my age of five and
eight years. I tell of them just as I recollect them, without attempt to fill in what seems probable.

She was I suppose my nursemaid. I recollect that she
sometimes held my little prick when I piddled, was it needful to do so? I don't know. She attempted to pull my prepuce
back, when, and how often, I know not. But I am clear about
seeing the prick tip show, of feeling pain, of yelling out, of
her soothing me, and of this occurring more than once. She
comes to my memory as a shortish, fattish, young female,
and that she often felt my prick.

One day, it must have been late in the afternoon for the
sun was low but shining — how strange I should recollect
that so clearly — but I have always recollected sun-
shine, — I had been walking out with her, toys had been
bought me, we were both carrying them, she stopped and
talked to some men, one caught hold of her and kissed her,
I felt frightened, it was near a coach stand, for hackney
coaches were there, cabs were not then known, she put what
toys she had onto my hands and went into a house with a
man. What house? I don't know. Probably a public-house,
for there was one not far from a coach stand, and not far
from our house. She came out and we went home.

Then I was in our house in a carpeted room with her; it
could not have been the nursery I know, sitting on the floor
with my toys; so was she; she played with me and the toys,
we rolled over each other on the floor in fun, I have a recollection of having done that with others, and of my father
and mother being in that room at times with me playing.

She kissed me, got out my cock, and played with it, took
one of my hands and put it underneath her clothes. It felt

rough there, that's all, she moved my little hand violently there, then she felt my cock and again hurt me, I recollect seeing the red tip appear as she pulled down the prepuce, and my crying out, and her quieting me.

Then of her being on her back, of my striding across or between her legs, and her heaving me up and down, and my riding cockhorse and that it was not the first time I had done so; then I fell flat on her, she heaved me up and down and squeezed me till I cried. I scrambled off of her, and in doing so my hand, or foot, went through a drum I had been drumming on, at which I cried.

As I sat crying on the floor beside her, I recollect her naked legs, and one of her hands shaking violently beneath her petticoats, and of my having some vague notion that the woman was ill; I felt timid. All was for a moment quiet, her hand ceased, still she lay on her back, and I saw her thighs, then turning round she drew me to her, kissed me and tranquillised me. As she turned round I saw one side of her backside, I leant over it and laid my face on it crying about my broken drum, the evening sunbeams made it all bright, it had at some time been raining, I recollect.

I expect I must have seen her cunt, as I sat beside her naked thigh. Looking towards her and crying about my broken drum, and when I saw her hand moving no doubt she was frigging. Yet I have not the slightest recollection of her cunt, nor of anything more than I have told. But of having seen her naked thighs I am certain, I seem often to have seen them, but cannot feel certain of that.

The oddest thing is that whilst I early recollected more or less clearly what took place two or three years later on, and ever afterwards on sexual matters, and what I said, heard, and did, nearly consecutively, this, my first recollection of cock and cunt, escaped my memory for full twenty years.

Then one day, talking with the husband of one of my cousins, about infantine incidents, he told me some thing which had occurred to him in his childhood; and suddenly, almost as quickly as a magic lantern throws a picture on to a wall, this which had occurred to me came into my mind. I have since thought over it a hundred times, but cannot recollect one circumstance relating to the adventure more than I have told.

My mother had been giving advice to my cousin about nursemaids. They were not to be trusted. "When Walter was a little fellow, she had dismissed a filthy creature, whom she had detected in abominable practices with one of her children"; what they were my mother never disclosed. She hated indelicacies of any sort, and usually cut short allusion to them by saying, "It's not a subject to talk about, let's talk about some thing else." My cousin told her husband, and when we were together he told me, and his own experiences, and then all the circumstances, came into my mind, just as I have told here.

I could not, as the reader will hear, thoroughly uncover my prick tip without pain till I was sixteen years old, nor well then when quite stiff unless it went up a cunt. My nursemaid I expect thought this curious, and tried to remedy the error in my make, and hurt me. My mother, by her extremely delicate feeling, shut herself off from much knowledge of the world, which was the reason why she had such implicit belief in my virtue, until I had seen twenty-two years, and kept, or nearly so, a French harlot.

I imagine I must have slept with this nursemaid, and certainly I did with some female, in a room called the Chinese room, on account of the color of the wall papers. I recollect a female being there in bed with me, that I awoke one morning feeling very hot and stifled and that my head was against flesh; that flesh was all about me, my mouth and nose being embedded in hair, or some thing scrubby, which had a hot peculiar odour. I have a recollection of a pair of hands suddenly clutching and dragging me up on to the pillow, and of daylight then. I have no recollection of a word being uttered. This incident I could not long have forgotten, having told my cousin Fred of it before my father did. He used to say it was the governess. I suppose I must have slipped down in my sleep, till my head laid against her belly and cunt.

Some years afterwards, when I got the smell of another woman's cunt on my fingers, it at once reminded me of the smell I had under my nose in the bed; and I knew at a flash that I had smelt cunt before, and recollected where, but no more.

How long after I have no idea, but it seems like two or three years, there was a dance in our house, several relations were to stop the night with us, the house was full, there was bustle, the shifting of beds, the governess going into a servant's room to sleep, and so on. Some female cousins were amongst those stopping with us; going into the drawing-room suddenly, I heard my mother saying to one of my aunts, "Walter is after all but a child, and it's only for one night."

[25]

"Hish-hish," both said as they saw me, then my mother sent me out of the room, wondering why they were talking about me, and feeling curious and annoyed at being sent away.

I had been in the habit then of sleeping in a room either with another bed in it or close to a room leading out of it, with another bed, I cannot recollect which; I used to call out to whoever might have been there when I was in bed: for being timid, the door was kept open for me. It could not have been a man who slept there, for the men-servants slept on the ground-floor, I have seen their beds there.

The night I speak of, my bed was taken out, and put into the Chinese-paper room, one of the maids who helped to move it sat on the pot and piddled; I heard the rattle, and as far as I can recollect it was the first time I noticed anything of the sort, tho I recollect well seeing women putting on their stockings and feeling the thigh of one of them just above her knee. I was kneeling on the floor at the time and had a trumpet, which she took angrily out of my hand soon afterwards, because I made noise.

I recollect the dance, that I danced with a tall lady, that my mother, contrary to custom as it seems to me, put me to bed herself, and that it was before the dance was over, for I felt angry and tearful at being put to bed so early. My mother closed the curtains quite tightly all round a small four post bed, and told me I was to lie quietly and not get up till she came to me in the morning; not to speak, nor undo my curtains, nor to get out of bed, or I should disturb Mr. and Mrs. *** who were to sleep in the big bed; that it would make them angry if I did. I am almost certain she named a lady and her husband who were going to stay with us; but can't be sure. A man then frightened me more than a woman, my mother I dare say knew that.

I dare say, for it was the same the greater part of my early life that I went to sleep directly I laid down, usually never awaking till the morning. Certainly I must have gone fast asleep that night; perhaps I had had a little wine given me, who knows; I have a sudden consciousness of a light, and hear someone say, "He is fast asleep, don't make a noise"; it seemed like my mother's voice. I rouse myself and listen, the circumstances are strange, the room strange, it excites me, and I rise on my knees, I don't know whether naturally, or cautiously, or how; perhaps cautiously, because I fear angering my mother, and the gentleman; perhaps a sexual instinct makes me curious, though that is not probable. I have not in fact the slightest conception of the actuating motive, but I sat up and listened. There were two females talking, laughing quietly and moving about, I heard a rattling in the pot, then a rest, then again a rattle and knew the sound of piddling. How long I listened I don't know, I might have dozed and awakened again, I saw lights moved about; then I crawled on my knees, with fear that I was doing wrong, and pushed a little aside the curtains where they met at the bottom of the bed. I recollect their being quite tight by the tucking in, and that I could not easily make an opening to peep through.

There was a girl, or young woman, with her back to me, brushing her hair, another standing by her, one took a night gown off the chair, shook it out, and dropped it over her head, after drawing off her chemise. As this was done I saw some black at the bottom of her belly, a fear came over me that I was doing wrong and should be punished if found looking, and I laid down wondering at it all; I fancy I again slept.

Then there was a shuffling about, and again it seems as if I heard a noise like piddling, the light was put out, I felt agitated, I heard the women kiss, one say "Hish! you will wake that brat," then one said, "Listen" then I heard kisses and breathing like some one sighing, I thought some one must be ill and felt alarmed and must then have fallen asleep. I do not know who the women were, they must have been my cousins, or young ladies who had come to the dance. That was the first time I recollect seeing the hair of a cunt, though I must have seen it before, for I recollect at times a female (most likely a nursemaid) stand naked, but don't recollect noticing anything black between her thighs, nor did I think about it at all afterwards.

In the morning my mother came and took me up to her room, where she dressed me; as she left the room, she said to the females in bed they were not to hurry up, she had only fetched Wattie.

But all this only came vividly to my mind when, a few years after, I began to talk about women with my cousin, and we told each other all we had seen, and heard, about females.

Until I was about twelve years old I never went to school, there was a governess in the house who instructed me and the other children, my father was nearly always at home. I was carefully kept from the grooms and other men servants;

once I recollect getting to the stable yard and seeing a stallion mount a mare, his prick go right out of sight in what appeared to me to be the mare's bottom, of father appearing and calling out, "What does that boy do there?" and my being hustled away. I had scarcely a boy acquaintance, excepting among my cousins, and therefore did not learn as much about sexual matters as boys early do at schools. I did not know what the stallion was doing, I could have had no notion of it then, nor did I think about it.

The next thing I clearly recollect, was one of my male cousins stopping with us, we walked out, and when piddling together against a hedge, his saying, "Shew me your cock, Walter, and I will shew you mine." We stood and examined each other's cocks, and for the first time I became conscious that I could not get my foreskin easily back like other boys. I pulled his backwards and forwards. He hurt me, laughed and sneered at me, another boy came and I think another, we all compared cocks, and mine was the only one which would not unskin, they jeered me, I burst into tears, and went away thinking there was some thing wrong with me, and was ashamed to shew my cock again, tho I set to work earnestly to try to pull the foreskin back, but always desisted, fearing the pain, for I was very sensitive.

My cousin then told me that girls had no cock, but only a hole they piddled out of, we were always talking about them, but I don't recollect the word cunt, nor that I attached any lewd idea to a girl's piddling hole, or to their cocks being flat, an expression heard I think at the same period. It remained only in my mind that my cock and the girl's hole were to piddle out of, and nothing more, I cannot be certain about my age at this time.

Afterwards I went to that uncle's house often, my cousin Fred was to be put to school, and we talked a great deal more about girls' cocks, which began to interest me much. He had never seen one, he said, but he knew that they had two holes, one for bogging and the other to piddle from. They sit down to piddle said he, they don't piddle against a wall as we do, but that I must have known already, afterwards I felt very curious about the matter.

One day, one of his sisters left the room where we were sitting. "She is going to piddle," he said to me. We sneaked into a bedroom of one of them one day and gravely looked into the pot to see what piddle was in it. Whether we expected to find any thing different from what there was in our own chamber pot I do not know. When talking about these things my cousin would twiddle his cock. We wondered how the piddle came out, if they wetted their legs and if the hole was near the bum hole, or where; one day Fred and I pissed against each other's cocks, and thought it was excellent fun.

I recollect being very curious indeed about the way girls piddled after this, and seeing them piddle became a taste I have kept all my life. I would listen at the bed room doors, if I could get near them unobserved, when my mother, sister, the governess, or a servant went in, hoping to hear the rattle and often succeeded. It was accompanied by no sexual desire or idea, as far as I can recollect; I had no cock-stand, and am sure that I then did not know that the woman had a hole called a cunt and used it for fucking. I can recall no idea of the sort, it was simple curiosity to know something about those whom I instinctively felt were made different from myself. What sort of a hole could it be, I wondered? Was it large? Was it round? Why did they squat instead of stand up like men? My curiosity became intense.

How long after this the following took place I can't say, but my cock was bigger. I have that impression very distinctly.

One day, there were people in one of the siting rooms; where my mother and father were I don't know; they were not in the room, and were most likely out. There were one or two of my cousins, some youths, my big sister and one brother, besides others, our governess, and her sister, who was stopping with us, and sleeping in the same room with her. I recollect both going into the bed room together, it was next to mine. It was evening, we had sweet wine, cake, and snap-dragon, and played at something at which all sat in a circle on the floor. I was very ticklish, it nearly sent me into fits, we tickled each other on the floor. There was much fun, and noise, the governess tickled me, and I tickled her. She said as I was taken to bed, or rather went, as I then did by myself, "I'll go and tickle you." Now at that time, when I was in bed, a servant, or my mother, or the governess took away the light and closed the door; for I was still frightened to get into bed in the dark, and used to call out, "Mamma. I'm going to get in to bed." Then they fetched the light, they wished to stop this timidity, often scolded me about it, and made me undress myself, by myself, to cure me of it.

I expect the other children had been put to bed. My mother keeping all the younger ones in the room near her.

The nursery was also upstairs; my room, as said, was next to the governess.

When in bed, I called out for some one to put out the light, up came the governess and her sister. She began to tickle me, so did her sister, I laughed, screeched, and tried to tickle them. One of them closed the door and then came back to tickle me. I kicked all the clothes off and was nearly naked, I begged them to desist, felt their hands on my naked flesh, and am quite sure that one of them touched my prick more than once, though it might have been done accidentally. At last I wriggled off bed, my night-gown up to my armpits, and dropped with my naked bum on to the floor, whilst they tickled me still, and laughed at my wriggling about and yelling.

Then what induced me heaven alone knows; it may have been what I had heard about the piddling-hole of a woman, or curiosity, or instinct, I don't know; but I caught hold of the governess' leg as she was trying to get me up on to the bed again, saying, "That will do, my dear boy, get into bed, and let me take away the light." I would not; the other lady helped to lift me, I pushed my hands up the petticoats of the governess, felt the hair of her cunt, and that there was something warm, and moist between her thighs. She let me drop on to the floor, and jumped away from me. I must have been clinging to her thigh, with both hands up her petticoats, and one between her thighs, she cried out loudly — "Oh!"

Then slap-slap-slap, in quick succession, came her hand against my head. "You ... rude ... bad ... boy," said she, slapping me at each word. "I've a good mind to tell your mamma, get into bed this instant," and into bed I got without a word. She blew out the light and left the room with her sister, leaving me in a dreadful funk. I scarcely knew that I had done wrong, yet had some vague notion that feeling about her thighs was punishable. The soft hairy place my hand had touched, impressed me with wonder, I kept thinking there was no cock there, and felt a sort of delight at what I had done.

I heard them then talking and laughing loudly thro the partition. "They are talking about me; oh, if they tell mamma, oh! what did I do it for?" Trembling with fear, I jumped out of bed, opened my door, and went to theirs, listening; theirs was ajar; I heard: "Right up between my thighs. I felt it! He must have felt it; ah! ah! ha! would you ever have thought the little beast would have done such a thing!" They both laughed heartily. "Did you see his little thing?" said one. "Shut the door, it's not shut"; — breathless I got back to my room and into bed, and laying there heard them through the partition roaring with laughter again.

That is the first time in my life I recollect passing an all but sleepless night. The dread of being told about, and dread at what I had done, kept me awake. I heard the two women talking for a long time. Mixed with my dread was a wonder at the hair, and the soft, moist feel I had had for an instant on some part of my hand. I knew I had felt the hidden part of a female, where the piddle came from, and that is all I did think about it, that I know of, I have no recollection of a lewed sensation, but of a curious sort of delight only.

It must have been from this time, that my curiosity about the female form strengthened, but there was nothing sensual in it. I was fond of kissing, for my mother remarked it; when a female cousin, or any female, kissed me, I would throw my arms round her and keep on kissing. My aunts used to laugh, my mother corrected me and told me it was rude. I used to say to the servants, "Kiss me." One day I heard my godfather say: "Walter knows a pretty girl from an ugly one doesn't he?"

I had a dread of meeting the governess at breakfast, watched her and saw her laugh at her sister, I watched my mother for some days after, and at length said to the governess, who had punished me for something, "Don't tell mamma." "I have nothing to tell about, Walter," she replied, "and don't know what you mean." I began to tell her what was on my mind. "What's the child talking about? You are dreaming, some stupid boy has been putting things into your head, your papa will thrash you, if you talk like that." "Why, you came and tickled me," said I. "I tickled you a little when I put your light out," said she, "be quiet." I felt stupefied, and suppose the affair must have passed away from my mind for a time, but I told my cousin Fred about it afterwards. He thought I must have been dreaming, and I began to wonder if it really had occurred, I never thought much about it until I began to recall my childhood for this history.

I must have been twelve years old when I went to an uncle's in Surrey and became a close friend of my cousin Fred, a very devil from his cradle, and of whom much more will be told: before then I had only seen him at intervals. We were then allowed, and it seems to me not before that time, to go out by ourselves. We talked boyish baudiness. "Ain't you green," said he, "a girl's hole isn't called a cock, it's a cunt, they fuck with it," and then he told me all he knew. I don't think I had heard that before, but can't be sure.

From that time a new train of ideas came into my head. I had a vague idea, though not a belief, that a cock and cunt were not made for pissing only. Fred treated me as a simpleton in these matters and was always calling me an ass; I had quite a painful recollection of my inferiority to him in such things, and of begging him to instruct me. "They make children that way," said Fred. "You come up and we will ask the old nurse where children come from, and she'll say 'out of the parsley-bed,' but it's all a lie." We went and asked her in a casual sort of way. She replied. "The parsley-bed," and laughed. The nurse at my house told me the same when I asked her afterwards about my mother's last baby. "Ain't they liars?" Fred remarked to me. "It comes out of their cunts, and it's made by fucking."

We both desired to see women piddling, though both must have before seen them at it often enough. Walking near the market-town with him, just at the outskirts, and looking up a side-road, we saw a pedlar woman squat down and piss. We stopped short and looked at her: she was a short-petticoated, thick-legged, middle-aged woman; the piss ran off in a copious stream, and there we stood grinning. "Be off, be off, what are you standing grinning at, yer damned young fools," cried the woman. "Be off, or I'll heave a stone at yer," and she pissed on. We moved a few steps back, but, keeping our faces toward her, Fred stooped and put his head down. "I can see it coming," said he jeeringly. He was rude from his infancy, bold in baudiness to the utmost, had the impudence of the Devil. The stream ceased, the woman rose up swearing, took up a big flint and threw it at us. "I'll tell on yer," she cried. "I knows yer, wait till I see yer again." She had a large basket of crockery for sale, it was put down in the main-road at the angle; she had just turned round into the side lane to piss. We ran off, and, when well away, turned round and shouted at her. "I saw your cunt," Fred bawled out; — she flung another stone. Fred took up one, threw it and it crashed into the crockery, the woman began to chase us, off we bolted across the fields home. She could not follow us that way; it was an eventful day for us. I recollect feeling full of envy at Fred's having seen her cunt. Though writing now, and having in my mind's eye exactly how the woman squatted, and the way her petticoats hung,

I am sure he never did see it; it was brag when he said he had, but we were always talking about girls' cunts, the desire to see one was great, and I then believed that he had seen the pedlar woman's.

Then one of Fred's companions shewed us a baudy picture, it was coloured. I wondered at the cunt being a long sort of gash. I had an idea it was round, like an arse-hole. Fred told his friend I was an ass, but I could not get the idea of a cunt not being a round hole quite out of my head, until I had fucked a woman. We were all anxious to get the picture, and tossed up for it, but neither I nor Fred got it, some other boy did.

Soon after that, Fred came to stop with us and our talk was always about women's privates, our curiosity became intense. I had a little sister about nine months old, who was in the nursery. Fred incited me to look at her cunt, if I could manage it. The two nurses came down in turns, to the servants' dinner, I was often in the nursery, and, soon after Fred's suggestion, was there one day when the oldest nurse said: "Stop here, master Walter, while I go downstairs for a couple of minutes, Mary (the other nurse) will be up directly, and don't make a noise." My little sister was lying on the bed asleep. "Yes, I'll wait." Down went the nurse, leaving the door open; quick as lightning, I threw up the infant's clothes, saw her little slit, and put my finger quite gently on it, she was laying on her back most conveniently. I pulled one leg away to see better, the child awakened and began crying, I heard footsteps and had barely time to pull down her clothes, when the under nursemaid came in. I only had had a momentary glimpse of the outside of the little quim, for I was not a minute in the room with the child by myself altogether and was fearful of being caught all the time I was looking.

There must have been something in my face, for the nursemaid said, "What is the matter, what have you been doing to the baby?" "Nothing." "Yes, you are colouring up, now tell me." "Nothing, I have done nothing." "You wakened your sister." "No, I have not." The girl laid hold of me and gave me a little shake. "I'll tell your mamma if you don't tell me, what is it now?" "No, I have done nothing, I was looking out of the window when she began to cry." "You're telling a story, I see you are," said the nursemaid; and off I went, after being impudent to her.

I told Fred, and he tried the same dodge, but don't recollect whether he succeeded or not. His sisters were some of them older, and we began to scheme how to see their cunts, when I was on a visit to his mother's (my aunt), which was to come off in the holidays. The look of the little child's cunt, as I described it, convinced him that the picture was correct, and that a cunt was a long slit and not a round hole. That cast doubt on males putting their pricks into them, and we clung somehow to the idea of the round hole, and we quarrelled about it.

It must have been about this time that I was walking with my father and read something that was written in chalk on the walls. I asked him what it meant. He said he did not know, that none but low people, and blackguards wrote on walls; and it was not worth while noticing such things. I was conscious that I had done wrong somehow, but did not know exactly what. When I went out, which I was now allowed to do for short distances by myself, I copied what was on the walls, to tell Fred, it was foul, baudy language of some sort, but the only thing we understood at all, was the word cunt.

Just then being out with some boys, we saw two dogs fucking. I have no recollection of seeing dogs doing that before. We closed round them, yelling with delight as they stuck rump to rump, then one boy said that was what men and women did, and I asked, did they stick together so, a boy replied that they did; others denied it, and, all the remainder of the day, some of us discussed this; the impression left on my mind is that it appeared to me very nasty; but it seemed at the same time to confirm me in the belief that men put their pricks up into women's holes, about which I seem at that time to have had grave doubts.

After this time my recollection of events is clearer, and I can tell not only what took place, but better what I heard, said, and thought.

CHAPTER II

My godfather. — At Hampton-Court. — My aunt's backside. — Public baths. — My cousins' cunts. — Haymaking frolics. — Family difficulties. — School amusements. — A masturbating relative. — Romance and sentiment.

My godfather (whose fortune I afterwards inherited) was very fond of me; somewhere about this time he used perpetually to be saying, "When you get to school, don't you follow any of the tricks yourself that other boys do, or you will die in a mad-house; lots of boys do." And he told me some horrible tales; it was done in a mysterious way. I felt there was a hidden meaning and, not having knowledge of what it was, asked him. I should know fast enough, said he, but mark his words. He repeated this so often that it sunk deeply into my mind, and made me uneasy, something was to happen to me, if I did something — I did not know what — it was intended as a caution against frigging, and it had good effect on me I am sure in various ways in the after time.

One day talking with Fred, I recollected what I had done to the governess. I had kept it to myself all along for fear. "What a lie," said he. "I did really." "Oh! ain't you a liar," he reiterated, "I'll ask Mis Granger." The same governess was with us then.

At this remark of his, an absolute terror came over me, the dread was something so terrible that the recollection of it is now painful. "Oh don't, pray, don't, Fred," I said, "oh, if Papa should hear!" He kept on saying he would. I was too young to see the improbability of his doing anything of the sort. "If you do, I'll tell him what we did when the pedlar woman piddled." He did not care. "Now, it's a lie, isn't it, you did not feel her cunt?" In fear, I confessed it was a lie. "I knew it was," said Fred. He had kept me in a state of terror about the affair for days, till I told a lie to get quit of the subject.

I was evidently always secret, even then, about anything amorous, excepting with Fred (as will be seen), and have continued so all my life. I rarely bragged or told anyone of my doings; perhaps this little affair with the governess was a lesson to me, and confirmed me in a habit natural to me from my infancy. I have kept to myself everything I did with the opposite sex.

We now frequently examined our pricks, and Fred jeered me so about my prepuce being tight that I resolved no other boy should see it; and though I did not keep strictly to that intention, it left a deep-seated mortification on me. I used to look at my prick with a sense of shame and pull the prepuce up and down, as far as I could, constantly, to loosen it, and would treat other boys' cocks in the same way, if they would let me, without expecting me to make a return; but the time was approaching when I was to learn much more.

One of my uncles, who lived in London, took a house in the country for the summer near Hampton-Court Palace. Fred and I went to stay there with him. There were several daughters and sons, the sons quite young. People then came down from London in vans, carts, and carriages of all sorts, to see the Palace and grounds (there was no railway), they were principally of the small middle classes, and used to picnic, or else dine, at the taverns when they arrived; then full, and frisky, after their early meal, go into the parks and gardens. They do so still, but times were different then, so few people went there comparatively, fewer park-keepers to look after them, ankles of what is called delicacy amongst visitors of the class named.

Our family party used to go into the grounds daily, and all day long nearly, if we were not on the river banks. Fred winked at me one day, "Let's lose Bob," said he, "and we'll have such a lark." Bob was one of our little cousins, generally given into our charge. We lost Bob purposely. Said Fred, "If you dodge the gardeners, creep up there, and lay on your belly quietly, some girls will be sure to come and piss, you'll see them pull their clothes up as they turn round, I saw some before you came to stay with us." So we went, pushing our way among shrubs and evergreens, till a gardener, who had seen us, called out, "You there, come back, if I catch you going off the walks, you'll be put outside." We were in such a funk, Fred cut off one way, I another, but it only stopped us for that day. Fred so excited me about the girls' arses, as he called them, that we never lost an opportunity of trying for a sight, but were generally baulked. Once

[36]

or twice only we saw a female squat down, but nothing more, till my mother and Fred's came to stop with us.

Fred's mother, mine, the girls, Fred and I went into the park gardens, one day after luncheon. A very hot day, for we kept on the shady walks, one of which led to the place where women hid themselves to piss. My aunt said, "Why don't you boys go and play, you don't mind the sun," so off we went, but when about to leave the walk, turned round and saw the women had turned back. Said Fred, "I'm sure they are going to piss, that's why they want to get rid of us." We evaded the gardeners, scrambled through shrubs, on our knees, and at last on our bellies, up a little bank, on the other side of which was the vacant place on which dead leaves and sweepings were shot down. As we got there, pushing aside the leaves, we saw the big backside of a woman, who was half standing, half squatting, a stream of piss falling in front of her, and a big hairy gash, as it seemed, under her arse; but only for a second, she had just finished as we got the peep, let her clothes fall, tucked them between her legs, and half turning round. We saw it was Fred's mother, my aunt. Off aunt went. "Isn't it a wopper," said Fred, "lay still, more of them will come."

Two or three did; one said, "You watch if anyone is coming," squatted and piddled, we could not see her cunt, but only part of her legs, and the piddle splashing in front of her. Then came the second, she had her arse towards us, sat so low that we could not even see the tips of her buttocks. Fred thought it a pity they did not stand half up like his mother. On other occasions, we went to the same place, but though I recollect seeing some females' legs, don't recollect seeing any more. Nevertheless the sights were very delightful to us, and we used to discuss his mother's "wopper" and the hair, and the look of the gash, but I thought there must be some mistake, for it was not the idea I had formed of a cunt.

Fred soon after stopped with us in town, we had been forbidden to go out together without permission, but we did, and met a boy bigger than either of us, who was going to bathe. "Come and see them bathing," he said. My father had refused to take me to the public baths. Disregarding this, Fred and I paid our six pence each, and in we went with our friend; we did not bathe, but amused ourselves with seeing others, and the pricks of the men. None, as far as I can recollect, wore drawers in those days, they used to walk about hiding their pricks generally with their hands, but not always. I was astonished at the size of some of them, and at the dark hair about them and on other parts of their bodies. I wondered also at seeing one or two, with the red tip shewing fully, so different from mine. All this was much talked over by us afterwards, it was to me an insight into the male make and form. Fred told me he had often seen men's pricks in their fields, and in those days, living in the country as he did, I dare say it was true, but I don't recollect ever having seen the pricks of full grown men, or a naked man, before in my life.

It must have been in the summer of that same year that I went after this to spend some days at my aunt's at H***dfs***l***, Fred's mother. We slept in the same room and sometimes got up quite at daybreak to go fishing. One morning Fred had left something in one of his sisters' rooms, and went to fetch it, though forbidden to go into the girls' bed-rooms. The room in question was opposite to ours. He was only partly dressed, and came back in a second, his face grinning. "Oh! come Wat, come softly. Lucy and Mary are quite naked, you can see their cunts, Lucy has some black hair on hers." I was only half dressed, and much excited by the idea of seeing my cousins' nudity. We both took off our slippers and crept along through the door half open, then went on our knees! but why we did so, to this day I don't understand, and so crept to the foot of the bed, then raising ourselves, we both looked over the footboard.

Lucy, fifteen years old, was laying half on her side, naked from her knees to her waist, the bed-clothes kicked off (I suppose through heat), were dragging across her feet and partly laying on the floor; we saw her split, till lost in the closed thighs, she had a little dark short hair over the top of her cunt, and that is all I can recollect about it.

Mary-Ann by the side of her, a year younger only, laid on her back, naked up to her navel, just above which was her night-gown in a heap and ruck; she had scarcely a sign of hair on her cunt, but a vermillion line lay right through her crack. Projecting more towards the top, where her cunt began, she had what I now know was a strongly developed clitoris; she was a lovely girl and had long chestnut hair.

Whilst we looked she moved one leg up in a restless manner, and we bobbed down, thinking she was awaking; when we looked again, her limbs were more open, and we saw the cunt till it was pinched up, by the closing of her buttocks. In fear of being caught, we soon crept out, closed the door ajar, and regained our bed-room, so delighted that we danced with joy as we talked about the look of the two cunts; of which after all we had only had a most partial, rapid glimpse.

Lucy was a very plain girl, and was so as a woman. She had, I recollect, a very red bloated looking face as she lay (it was so hot); she it was, who in after-life my mother cautioned about leaving her infant son to a nursemaid.

Mary-Ann was lovely. I used afterwards to look and talk with her, thinking to myself: "Ah! you have but little idea, that I have seen your cunt." She was unfortunate; married a cavalry officer, went to India with him, was left at a station unavoidably by her husband, who was sent on a campaign, for a whole year; could not bear being deprived a cock, and was caught in the act of fucking with a drummer boy, a mere lad. She was separated from him, came back to England, and drank herself to death. She was a salacious young woman, I think, from what I recollect of her, and am told was afterwards fucked by a lot of men; but it was a sore point with the family, and all about her was kept quiet.

One of Lucy's sons, in after years, I saw fucking a maid in a summer-house: both standing up against a big table; I was on the roof. Many years before that I fucked a nursemaid, she laying on that table in the very same summerhouse, as I shall presently tell.

Fred and I used to discuss the look of his sisters' and mother's cunts, as if they had belonged to strangers. The redness of the line in Mary-Ann's quim astonished us. I do not recollect having even then formed any definite notion of what a girl's cunt was, though we had seen the splits, but had still, and till much further on, the notion that the hole was round, and close to where the clitoris is, having no idea then of what a clitoris was, though we had got an Aristotle and used to read it greedily; the glimpses of the two cunts were but momentary, and our excitement confused our recollections.

Fred and I then formed a plot to look at another girl's cunt; who the girl was I don't know, it may have been another of Fred's sisters, or a cousin by another of my aunts, but I think not; at all events, she was stopping in aunt's house, and from her height, which was less than that of Fred and myself, I should think a girl of about eleven or twelve years of age. I scrupulously avoid stating anything positively unless quite certain. Some years afterwards when we were very young men, we did the same thing with a female cousin (but not his sister), as I shall tell.

There was haymaking. We romped with the girl, buried each other in hay, pulled each other out, and so on. I was buried in the hay and dragged out by my legs by Fred and the girl. Then Fred was; then we buried the girl, and as Fred pulled her out he threw up her clothes, I lay over her head, which was covered with hay. Fred saw, winked, and nodded. It came to my turn again to be buried, and then hers; I laid hold of her legs and pulling them from under the hay, saw her thighs, I pushed her knees up, and had a glimpse of the slit, which was quite hairless. My aunt and others were in the very field, but had no idea of the game we were playing, the girl romping with us had no idea that we were looking at her cunt, and an instantaneous peep only it was.

What effect sensuously these glimpses of cunt had on me, I don't know; but have no recollection of sexual desire, nor of mine nor Fred's cock being stiff. I expect that what with games and our studies, that, after all, the time we devoted to thinking about women was not long, and curiosity our sole motive in doing what we did. I clearly recollect our talking at that time about fucking, and wondering if it were true or a lie. We could repeat what we had read and heard, but it still seemed improbable to me that a cock should go up a cunt, and the result be a child.

Then a passionate liking for females came over me; I fell in a sort of love with a lady who must have been forty, and had a sad feeling about her, that is all I recollect. Then I began to follow servants about, in the hope of seeing their legs or seeing them piddle, or for some undefined object: but that I was always looking after them I know very well.

Then (I know now) my father got into difficulties, we moved into a smaller house, the governess went away, I was sent to another school, one of my brothers and sisters died; my father went abroad to look after some plantations, and after a year's absence came back and died, leaving my mother in what, compared with our former condition, were poor circumstances, but this in due course will be more fully told.

I think I went to school, though not long before what I am going to tell of happened, but am not certain; if so, I must have seen boys frigging; yet as far as I can arrange in my mind the order of events, I first saw a boy doing that, in my own bed-room at home.

I was somewhere, I suppose, about thirteen years of age when a distant relative came from the country to stay with us, until he was put to some great school. He was the son of a clergyman, and must have been fifteen, or perhaps sixteen, years old, and was strongly pitted with the small-pox. I had never seen him before and took a strong dislike to him; the family were poor, this boy was intended for a clergyman. I was excessively annoyed, that he was to sleep with me, but in our small house there was just then no other place for him.

How many nights he slept in my bed I don't recollect, it can have been but few. One evening in bed he felt my prick; repulsing him at first, I nevertheless afterwards felt his, and recollect our hands crossing each other and our thighs being close together. Awakening one morning, I felt his belly up against my rump, and his feeling or pushing his prick against my arse, putting my hand back, I pushed him away; then I found it pushing quickly backwards and forwards between my thighs, and his hand, passed over my hips, was grasping my cock. Turning round, I faced him; he asked me to turn round again, and said I might do it to him afterwards, but nothing more was done. An unpleasant feeling about sleeping with him is in my memory, but as said, I disliked him.

The next night, undressing, he showed me his prick stiff, as he sat naked on a chair; it was an exceedingly long but thin article; he told me about frigging, and said he would frig me, if I would frig him. He commenced moving his hand quickly up and down on his prick, which got stiffer and stiffer, he jerked up one leg, then the other, shut his eyes, and altogether looked so strange that I thought he was going to have a fit, then out spurted little pasty lumps, whilst he snorted, as some people do in their sleep, and fell back in the chair with his eyes closed; then I saw stuff running thinner over his knuckles. I was strangely fascinated as I looked at him, and at what was on the carpet, but half thought he was ill; he then told me it was great pleasure, and was eloquent about it. Even now, as it did then, the evening seemed to me a nasty, unpleasant one, yet I let him get hold of my prick and frig it, but had no sensation of pleasure, He said, "Your skin won't come off, what a funny prick"; that annoyed me, and I would not let him do more, we talked till our candle burnt out; he stamped out the sperm on the carpet, saying the servants would think we had been spitting. Then we got into bed.

[*41*]

Afterwards he frigged himself several times before me, and at his request I frigged him, wondering at the result, and amused, yet at the same time much disgusted. When frigging him one day, he said it was lovely to do it in an arse-hole, that he and his brother took it in turns that way: it was lovely, heavenly! would I let him do it to me. In my innocence I told him it was impossible, and that I thought him a liar. He soon left us and went to college. I saw him once or twice after this, in later years, but at a very early age he drowned himself. I told my cousin Fred about this when I saw him; Fred believed in the frigging, but thought him a liar about the arse-hole business, just as I did. This was the first time I ever saw frigging and male semen, and it opened my eyes.

Though now at a public school, I was shy and reserved, but greedily listened to all the lewed talk, of which I did not believe a great deal. I became one of a group of boys of the same tastes as myself. One day some of them coaxed me into a privy, and there, in spite of me, pulled out my cock, threw me down, held me, and each one spat upon it, and that initiated me into their society. They had what they called cocks-all-round: anyone admitted to the set was entitled to feel the others' cocks. I felt theirs, but again, to my mortification, the tightness of my prepuce caused jeering at me; I was glad to hear that there was another boy at the school in the same predicament, though I never saw his. This confirmed me in avoiding my companions, when they were playing at cocks-all-round; being a day scholar only, I was not forced at all times into their intimacy, as I should have been had I been a boarder.

We had a very large playground; beyond it were fields, orchards, and walks of large extent reserved for the use of the two head-masters' families, many of whom were girls. On Saturday half-holidays only, if the fruit was not ripe, we were allowed to range certain fields, and the long bough-covered paths which surrounded them. Two or three boys of my set told me mysteriously one afternoon that when the others had gone ahead we were to meet in the playground privy, in which were seats for three boys of a row, and I was to be initiated into a secret without my asking. I was surprised at what took place, there was usually an usher in the playground in play-hours, and if boys were too long at the privy, he went there, and made them come out. On the Saturdays, he went out with the boys into the fields: there was no door to the privy; I should add, it was a largish building.

One by one, from different directions, some dodging among trees which bordered one side of the playground, appeared boys. I think there were five or six together in the privy, then it was cocks-all-round, and every boy frigged himself. I would not, at first. Why? I don't know. At length incited, I tried, my cock would not stand, and vexed and mortified, I withdrew, after swearing not to split on them, on pain of being kicked and cut. I don't think I was one of the party again, though I saw each of the same boys frig himself in the privy when alone with me, at some time or another.

After this a boy asked me to come to a privy with him in school time, and he would show me how to do it. Only two boys were allowed to go to those closets at the same time, during school time. There were two wooden logs with keys hung up on the wall by string: A boy, if he wanted to ease himself, looked to see if a log and key was hanging up, and if there was, stood out in the centre of the room; by that the master understood what he wanted. If he nodded, the boy took the key and went to the bog-house (no water-closets then), and when he returned, he hung up the log in its place. Those privies were close together, and separate, there were but two of them.

You wait till there are two logs hanging up, and directly I get one, you get up and come after me. Soon we were both in one privy together. "Let's frig," said he; we were only allowed to be away five minutes. Out he pulled his prick, then out I pulled mine; he tried to pull my skin back, and could only half do it, he frigged himself successfully, but I could not. He had a very small prick compared with mine. How I envied him the ease with which he covered and uncovered the red tip. I frigged that boy one day, but finding my cock was becoming a talk among our set, I shrunk from going to their frigging parties, which I have seen even take place in a field, boys sitting at the edge of a ditch whilst one stood up to watch if anyone approached. When they were frigging in the privy, a boy always stood in the open door on the watch, and his time for frigging came afterwards. With this set I began to look through the Bible and study all the carnal passages; no book ever gave us perhaps such prolonged, studious, baudy amusement; we could not understand much, but guessed a good deal.

Before I had seen anyone frig, I had been permitted to

read novels, not a moment of my time when not at studies was I without one. My father used to select them for me at first, but soon left me to myself, and, now he was dead, I devoured what books I liked, hunting for the love passages, thinking of the beauty of the women, reading over and over again the description of their charms, and envying their lovers' meetings. I used to stop at print-shop windows and gaze with delight at the portraits of pretty women, and bought some at six pence each, and stuck them into a scrapbook. Although a big fellow for my age, I would sit on the lap of any woman who would let me, and kiss her. My mother in her innocence called me a great girl, but she nevertheless forbade it. I was passionately fond of dancing and annoyed when they indicated a girl of my own age, or younger, to dance with.

These feelings got intensified when I thought of my aunt's backside, and the cunts of my cousins, but when I thought of the heroines, it seemed strange that such beautiful creatures should have any. The cunt which seemed to have affected my imagination was that of my aunt, which appeared more like a great parting, or division of her body, than a cunt as I then understood it; as if her buttock parting was continued round towards her belly, and as unlike the young cunts I had seen as possible. Those seemed to me but little indents. That the delicate ladies of the novels should have such divisions seemed curious, ugly, and unromantic. My sensuous temperament was developing, I saw females in all their poetry and beauty, but suppose that my physical forces had not kept pace with my brain, for I have no recollection of a cockstand when thinking about ladies; and fucking never entered into my mind, either when I read novels or kissed women, though the pleasure I had when my lips met theirs, or touched their smooth, soft cheeks, was great. I recollect the delight it gave me perfectly.

After having seen frigging, it set me reflecting, but it still seemed to me impossible, that delicate, handsome ladies, should allow pricks to be thrust up them, and nasty stuff ejected into them. I read Aristotle, tried to understand it, and thought I did, with the help of much talk with my schoolfellows; yet I only half believed it. Dogs fucking were pointed out to me; then cocks treading hens, and at last a fuller belief came.

I began then, I recollect, to think of their cunts when I kissed women, and then of my aunt's; I could not keep my eyes off of her, for thinking of her large backside and the gap between her thighs; it was the same with my cousins. Then I began to have cock-stands and suppose a pleasurable feeling about the machine, though I do not recollect that. I then found out that servants were fair game, and soon there was not one in the house whom I had not kissed. I had a soft voice and have heard an insinuating way, was timorous, feared repulse, and above all being found out; yet I succeeded. Some of the servants must have liked it, who called me a foolish boy at first; for they would stop with me on a landing, or in a room, when we were alone, and let me kiss them for a minute together. There was one, I recollect, who rubbed her lips into mine, till I felt them on my teeth, but of what she was like I have no recollection, and I did not like her doing that to me.

My curiosity became stronger, I got bolder, told servants I meant to see them wash themselves, and used to wait inside my bed-room till I heard one of them come up to dress. I knew the time each usually went to her bed-room for that purpose, the person most in my way was the nurse: she after a time left, and mother nursed her own children. "Let's see your neck; do, there is a dear," I would say. "Nonsense, what next?" "Do, dear, there is no harm; I only want to see as much as ladies show at balls." I wheedled one to stand at the door in her petticoats and show her neck across the bed-room lobby. The stays were high and queerly made in those days, the chemises pulled over the top of them like flaps. One or two let me kiss their necks, a girl one day said to my entreaties, "Well, only for a minute"; and easing up one breast, she showed me the nipple, I threw my arms round her, buried my face in her neck and kissed it. "I like the smell of your breast and flesh," said I. She was a biggish woman, and I dare say I smelt breasts and armpits together; but whatever the compound, it was delicious to me, it seemed to enervate me. The same woman, when I kissed her on the sly afterwards, let me put my nose down her neck to smell her. We were interrupted, "Here is some one coming," said she, moving away.

"What makes ladies smell so nice?" said I to my mother one day. My mother put down her work and laughed to herself. "I don't know that they smell nice." "Yes, they do, and particularly when they have low dresses on." "Ladies," said mother, "use patchouli and other perfumes." I supposed so,

[45]

but felt convinced from mother's manner that I had asked a question which embarrassed her.

I used to lean over the backs of the chairs of ladies, get my face as near to their necks as I could, quietly inhale their odours, and talk all the time. Not every woman smelt nice to me, and when they did, it was not patchouli, for I got patchouli, which I liked, and perfumed myself with it. This delicate sense of the smell of a woman I have had throughout life, it was ravishing to me afterwards when I embraced the naked body of a fresh, healthy young woman.

From about this time of my life I recollect striking events much more clearly, yet the circumstances which led up to them or succeeded them I often cannot. One day Miss Granger, our former governess, came to see us. I kissed her. Mother said: "Wattie, you must not kiss ladies in that way, you are too big." I sat Miss Granger on my lap in fun (my mother then in the room), and romped with her. Mother left us in the room, and then, seating Miss Granger on my lap again, I pulled her closely to me. "Kiss me, she's gone," I said. "Oh! what a boy," and she kissed me, saying, "Let me — go — now — your mamma is coming." It came into my mind that I had had my hand up her clothes, and had felt hair between her legs. My prick stiffened; it is the first distinct recollection of its stiffening in thinking of a woman. I clutched her hard, put one hand on to her and did something, I know not what. She said: "You are rude, Wattie." Then I pinched her and said: "Oh! what a big bosom you have." "Hish! hish!" said she. She was a tallish woman with brown hair; I have heard my mother say she was about thirty years of age.

A memorable episode then occurred. There were two sisters, with other female servants, in our house. My father was abroad at that time; I was growing so rapidly that every month they could see a difference in my height, but was very weak. My godfather used to look at me and severely ask if I was up to tricks with the boys. I guessed then what he meant, but always said I did not know what he meant. "Yes, you do; yes, you do," he would say, staring hard at me, "you take care, or you'll die in a mad-house, if you do, and I shall know by your face, not a farthing more will I give you." He had been a surgeon-major in the Army, and gave me much pocket-money. I could not bear his looking at me so; he would ask me why I turned down my eyes.

About this time, I had had a fever, had not been to school

for a long time, and used to lie on the sofa reading novels all day. Miss Granger had come to stop with my mother. One day I put my hand up her clothes, nearly to her knees; that offended her, and she left off kissing me. One of my little sisters slept with her, in a room adjoining my mother's room; I slept now on the servants' floor, at the top of the house. Again I recollect my cock standing when near Miss Granger, but recollect nothing else.

I was then ordered by my mother to cease speaking to the servants, excepting when I wanted anything, though I am sure my mother never suspected my kissing one. I obeyed her hypocritically, and was even at times reprimanded for speaking to them in too imperious a tone. She told me to speak to servants respectfully. For all that, I was after them, my curiosity was unsatiable, I knew the time each went up to dress, or for other purposes, and if at home, would get into the lobby, or near the staircase, to see their legs, as they went upstairs. I would listen at their door, trying to hear them piss, and began for the first time to peep through keyholes at them.

CHAPTER III

A big servant. — Two sisters. — Armpits. — A quiet feel. — Baudy reveries. — Felt by a woman. — Erections. — My prepuce. — Seeing and feeling. — Aunt and cousin. — A servant's thighs. — Not man enough.

A big servant, of whom I shall say much, had most of my attention; she went to her room usually when my mother was taking a nap in the afternoon; or when out with my sisters and brother. When I was ill in bed, this big woman usually brought me beef-tea; I used to make her kiss me, and felt so fond of her, would throw my arms round her, and hold her to me, keeping my lips to hers and saying how I should like to see her breasts; to all which she replied in the softest voice, as if I were a baby. I wonder now if my homage gave the big woman pleasure, or my amatory pressures made her ever feel randy. She was engaged to be married, but I only heard that at a later day, when my mother talked about her; her sister was also with us, as already said.

The sister was handsome, according to my notions then (I now begin to remember faces clearly); both had bright, clear complexions. I kissed both, each used to say, "Don't tell my sister," and ask, "Have you kissed my sister?" I was naturally cunning about women, and always said I had done nothing of the sort. The two were always quarrelling, and my mother said she must get rid of one of them.

The youngest was often dancing my little sister round in the room, then swinging herself round, and making cheeses with her petticoats. As I got better, I would lay on the rug with a pillow, and my back to the light reading, and say it rested me better to be on the floor, but in hope of seeing her legs as she made cheeses. I often did, and have no doubt now that she meant me to do so, for she would swing round, quite close to my head so that I could see to her knees, and make her petticoat's edge, as she squatted, just cover my head, immediately snatching her petticoats back and saying: "Oh! you'll see more than is good for you."

It used to excite me. One day as she did it, and squatted, I put out my hand and pulled her clothes, she rolled on to her back, threw up her legs quite high, and for a second I saw her thighs; she recovered herself, laughing. "I saw your thighs," said I. "That you didn't." One day she let me put my hand into her bosom; I sniffed. "What's there to smell?" said she. I have some idea that she used to watch me closely when I was with her sister, as she was always looking after her, and before she kissed me would open the door suddenly or go out of the room and then return. I've seen the other sister just outside the door of the room, when suddenly opened.

The big sister must have been five feet nine high, and large in proportion; the impression on my mind is that she was two and twenty: that age dwells in my recollection, and that my mother remarked it. She had brown hair and eyes, I recollect well the features of the woman. Her lower lip was like a cherry, having a distinct cut down the middle, caused she said by the bite of a parrot, which nearly severed her lip when a girl. This feature I recollect more clearly than anything else. My mother remarked that, though so big, she was lighter in tread than anyone in the house, her voice was so soft; it was like a whisper or a flute, her name was I think Betsy.

I had none of the dash, and determination towards females, which I had in after life; was hesitating, fearful of being repulsed or found out, but was coaxing and wheedling. Betsy used to take charge of my two little sisters (there was no regular nursery then), and used to sit with them in a room adjoining our dining room; it had a settee and a large sofa in it, we usually breakfasted there. She waited also at table, and did miscellaneous work. I am pretty certain that we had then no man in the house. I used to lie down on the sofa in this room. One day I talked with her about her lip, put my head up and said: "Do let me kiss it." She put her lips to mine, and soon after, if I was not kissing her sister, I was kissing her regularly, when my mother was out of the way.

One day when she went up to her bed-room, I went softly after her, as I often did, hoping to hear her piddling. Her door was ajar, one of my little sisters was in the room with her, I expect I must have had incipient randiness on me. She taught the child to walk up stairs in front of her, holding her up, and in stooping to do so, I had glimpses of her fat calves. At the door, I could not see her wash, that was done at the other side of the room, but I heard the splash of water and, to my delight, the pot moved, and her piddle rattle. The looking-glass was near the window. Then she moved to the glass and brushed her hair, her gown off, and now I saw her legs, and most of her breast, which looked to me enormous.

Then I noticed hair in her armpits; it must have been the first time I noticed any thing of the sort, for I told a boy afterwards, that brown women had hair under their armpits; he said every fool knew that. When she had done brushing, she turned round, and passing the door, shut it: she had not seen me.

I fell in love with this woman, an undefined want took possession of me, I was always kissing her, and she returned it without hesitation. "Hush! your mamma's coming"; then she would work, or do something with the children if there, as demurely as possible. I declare positively as I write this that I believe I gave that woman a lewed pleasure in kissing me, her kisses were so much like those I have had from women I have fucked in after years, so long, and soft, and squeezing.

One day I was in the sitting-room laying on the sofa reading, she sitting and working; where the children were, where my mother was, I can't say: they must have been out; why this servant was in the room with me alone, I don't know.

On a table was something the doctor had ordered me to sip from time to time. "Come and sit near me, I like to touch you, dear" (I used to say "dear" to her). She drew her chair to the sofa, so that her thighs were near my head, she handed me my medicine, I turned on one side, put my head on her lap, and then my hand on her knee. "Kiss me." "I can't." I moved my head up and she bent forward and kissed. "Keep your face to mine, I want to tell you something." Then I told her I had seen her brushing her hair, her breasts, her armpits. "Oh! you sly boy! you naughty boy! you must not do it again, will you?" "Won't I, if I get the chance; put your head down, I've something more to tell you." "What?" "I can't if you look at me; put your ear to my mouth." I was longing to tell her, and could not do it whilst she looked at me. I recollect my bashfulness perfectly, and more than that, my fear of saying what I wanted to say.

She bent her ear to my mouth. "I heard you piddle." "Oh! you naughty!" and she burst into a quiet laugh. "I'll take care to shut the door in future." I let my hand drop by the side of the sofa, laid hold of her ankle, then the calf of her leg (without resistance); then up I slid it gently, and gradually above her garter, and felt the flesh; she was threading a needle. As I touched the thigh, she pressed both hands down on to her thighs, barring further investigation. "Now, Wattie, you're taking too much liberty, because I've let you feel my ankles." I whined, I moaned. "Oh, do, dear, do, kiss me dear; only for a minute." I tried very gently to push my hand (it was my left hand) further. "What do you want?" "I want to feel it, oh! kiss me — let me, — do, — Betsy, do," and I raised my head.

Sitting bent forward towards me as I lay, until she was nearly double, she put her lips to mine and, kissing me, said: "What a rude boy you are, what do you expect to find?" "I know what it's called, and it's hairy, isn't it, dear?" Her hands relaxed, she laughed, my left hand slid up, until I felt the bottom of her belly. I could only twiddle my fingers in the hair, could feel no split, or hole, was too excited to think, too ignorant of the nature of the female article; but of the intense delight I felt at the touch of the warm thighs, and the hair, which now I knew as outside the cunt, somewhere, I recollect my delight perfectly.

She kept on kissing me, saying in a whisper, "What a rude boy you are." Then I whispered modestly, all I had read, told of the Aristotle I had hidden in my cupboard, and she asked

[50]

me to lend her the book. I touched nothing but hair, her thighs must have been quite closed, and a big stay-bone dug into my hand and hurt it, as I moved it about. I have felt that obstacle to my enterprise in years later on, with other women.

Then came over me a voluptuous sensation, as if I was fainting with pleasure, I seem to have a dream of her lips meeting mine, of her saying oh! for shame! of the tips of my fingers entangling in hair, of the warmth of the flesh of her thighs upon my hand, of a sense of moisture on it, but I recollect nothing more distinctly.

Afterwards she seems to have absorbed me. I ceased speaking to her sister, and could think of nothing but her neck, legs and the hair at the bottom of her belly. I was several times in the same room with her, and was permitted the same liberties, but no others. I lent her Aristotle, which I had borrowed, and one day recollect my prick stiffening, and a strange overwhelming, utterly indescribable feeling coming over me, of my desire to say to her "cunt," and to make her feel me, and at the same time a fear and a dread overtook me, that my cock was not like other cocks, and that she might laugh at me. After that, I used to pull the skin down violently every day, I bled, but succeeded; it became slightly easier to do so, yet I have no recollection of having a desire to fuck that woman, all that I recollect of my sensations I have here described.

I was still ill, for there was brought me to my bed at nights a cup of arrowroot. My mother usually did this, but sometimes the big woman did; I was so glad when my mother did not. Then I would kiss her as if I never wanted to part with her, but my hand out of bed, scramble it up her clothes, till I could feel the hair. Then she would jut her bum back, so that I could not touch more. One night my prick stood, "Take the light outside," I said, "I've something to say to you." The door was half open when she had complied; the gleam of the light struck across the room, my bed was in the shade, "Do let me feel you further, dear and kiss me." "You naughty boy!" but we kissed. Again I felt her thighs, belly, and hair. "What good does it do you, doing that," she said. I took hold of her hand, and put it under the bed-clothes on to my prick. She bent over me, kissing and saying, "Naughty boy," but feeling the cock, and all around it, how long, I can't say, "Oh! I'd like to feel your hole," I said. "Hish!" said she, going out of the room, and closing the door.

She felt me several times afterwards. When my mother brought me the arrowroot, she having an idea that I liked her to do so, I would not take it, saying it was too hot. She said, "I can't wait, Wattie, while it cools." "Don't care, mamma, I don't want it." "But you must take it." "Put it down then." "Well, don't go to sleep, and I'll send Betsy up with it in a few minutes." Up Betsy would come, and quickly and voluptuously kissing, keeping her lips on mine for two or three minutes at a time, she would glide her hand down and feel my cock, whilst my fingers were on her motte, her thighs closed, then she would glide out of the room. I never got my hand between her thighs, I am sure.

I used to long to talk to her about all I had heard, but don't think I ever did more than I have told, for I had a fear about using baudy words to a woman, though I already used them freely enough among boys. I used to talk only of her hole, my thing, of doing it, and so forth; but what made her laugh was my calling it pudendum, a word I had got out of Aristotle and my Latin dictionary. In spite of all this, and of the voluptuous sensations which used to creep over me, I have no clear, defined, recollection of wishing to fuck her, nor did I ever say anything smutty, if I could see her face.

I got better. Then she refused either to feel me, or let me feel her, on account of my boldness. One day, just at dusk, she was closing the dining-room shutters, I went behind her, and after pulling her head back to kiss me, stooped and pulled up her clothes to her waist; it exposed her entire backside. Oh how white and huge it seemed to me. She moved quickly round not hollering out but saying quietly: "What are you doing? Don't, now!" As she turned round, so did I, gloating over her bum, then laid both hands on it, slid them round her thighs, and rapidly kneeling down, put my lips on to the flesh, her petticoats fell over my head. She dislodged me, saying she would never speak with me again. She never either felt me or permitted me any liberties afterwards, and soon left. One or two years after that, she came to see my mother with her baby. She smiled at me. I don't recollect what became of her sister, but think she soon left us also.

My physique could not then have been strong, nor my sexual organs in finished condition, because I am sure that up to that time, I had not had a spend; perhaps my growing fast and the fever may have had something to do with it. My father came home broken-hearted I have heard, and ill. Soon after we only kept two female servants, a man outside the house, and a gardener. Father was ordered to the sea-side, my mother went with him, taking the children and one servant (all went by coach then). One of father's sisters, my aunt, a widow, came to take charge of our new house, and brought her daughter, a fair, slim girl, about sixteen years old.

I remained at home, so as to go to school; the servant left in the house was a pleasant, plump young woman, dark haired, and was always laughing; she was to do all the work. My godfather, who lived a mile or two away from us and whose maiden sister kept house for him, was to see me frequently, and did so till I was sick of him. Every half-holiday, he made me spend with him in walking, and riding; he insisted on my boating, cricketting, and keeping at athletic games when not at my studies. The old doctor I expect guessed my temperament, and thought, by thoroughly occupying and fatiguing me, to prevent erotic thoughts. He wanted me to stay at his house, but I refused, and it being a longer way from school, it was not persisted in.

My aunt slept in my parents' bed-room, my cousin in the next room. I was taken down, during my parents' absence, from the upper floor to sleep on the same floor as my aunt. They had not been in the house a week before I had heard my cousin piddle, and stood listening outside her bed-room door, night after night, in my bed-gown, trying to get a glimpse of her charms through the keyhole, but was not successful.

I made up to the servant, beginning when she was kneeling, by putting myself astride on her back. It made her laugh, she gave her back a buck up, and threw me over; then I kissed her, and she kissed me. She and my aunt quarrelled, my aunt was very poor and proud, and wanted a hot dinner at seven o'clock, I my dinner in the middle of the day. The servant said she could not do it all. The girl said quietly to me, "I'll cook for you, don't you go without, let her do without anything hot at night." She did not like her. My aunt said she was saucy and would write to my mother and complain that she wasted her time with the gardener. Godfather then renewed his offer for me to stay with him, but I would not, for I was getting on very comfortably with the servant in kissing, and things settled themselves somehow. I learnt the

[53]

ways of my aunt, and tried to get home when she was out, so as to be alone with the servant; but to escape both aunt and godfather was difficult. I did so at times by saying I was going out with the boys somewhere, on my half-holidays, or something of the sort, but was rarely successful.

The servant went to her bed-room, one afternoon; with palpitating heart I followed her, and pushed her on to the bed. She was a cheeky, chaffing, woman, and I guess knew better than I did, what I was about. I recollect her falling back on to the bed, and showing to her knees. "Oh! what legs!" said I, "Nothing to be ashamed of," said she. Whatever my wishes or intentions might have been, I went no further. My relations were of course out.

Another day we romped, and pelted each other with the pillows from her bed, she stood on the landing, I half way down the stairs, and kept when I could, my head just level with the top of the landing on which she was, so that as she whisked backwards and forwards, picking up the pillows to heave at me, I saw up to her knees. She knew what she was about, though I thought myself very cunning to manage to get such glimpses. On the landing I grappled with her for a pillow, and we rolled on the floor. I got my hand up her clothes, to her thighs, and felt the hair. "That's your thing," said I with a burst of courage. "Oh! oh!" she laughed, "what did you say?" "Your thing!" "My thing! what's that?" "The hole at the bottom of your belly," said I, ashamed at what uttered. "What do you mean? who told you that? I've no hole." It is strange, but a fact, that I had no courage to say more, but left off playing, and went down stairs.

On occasions afterwards, I played more roughly with her and felt her thighs; but fear prevented me from going further up. She gave me lots of opportunities, which my timidity prevented me from availing myself of. One day she said, "You are not game for much, although you are so big," and then kissed me long and furiously, but I never saw her wants, nor my chances that I know of, though I see now plainly enough that, boy as I was, she wanted me to mount her.

About that time, — how I got it, I know not, — I had a book describing the diseases caused by sacrificing to Venus. The illustrations in the book, of faces covered with scabs, blotches, and eruptions, took such hold of my mind, that for twenty years afterwards, the fear was not quite eradicated. I showed them to some friends, and we all got scared. I had no definite idea of what syphilis, and gonorrhea were, but that both were something awful we all made up our minds. My godfather also used to hint now to me about ailments men got, by acquaintance with loose, bad, women; perhaps he put the book in my way. Frigging also was treated of, and the terrible accounts of people dying through it, and being put into straight waistcoats, etc., I have no doubt were useful to me. Several of us boys were days in finding out what the book meant by masturbation, onanism, or whatever the language may have been. We used dictionaries and other books to help us, and at last one of the biggest boys explained the meaning to us.

One evening, my aunt being out (it was not I think any plan on my part), I had something to eat and then went into the kitchen, where the servant was sitting at needle-work by candle-light. I talked, kissed, coaxed her, began to pull up her clothes, and it ended in her running round the kitchen, and my chasing her; both laughing, stopping at intervals, to hear if my aunt knocked. "I'll go and lock the outer gate," said she, "then your aunt must ring, if she comes up to the door, she will hear us, for you make such a noise." She locked it and came back again.

The kitchen was on the ground-floor, separated from the body of the house by a short passage. I got her on to my knees, I was now a big fellow, and though but a boy, my voice was changing, she chaffed me about that; then my hand went up her petticoats, and she gave me such a violent pinch on my cock (outside the clothes), that I hollowed. Whenever I was getting the better of her in our amatory struggles, she said, "Oh! hush! there is your aunt knocking," and frightened me away, but at last she was sitting on my knees, my hand touching her thighs, she feeling my prick, she felt all around it and under. "You have no hair," she said. That annoyed me, for I had just a little growing. Then how it came about I don't recollect, but she consented to go into the parlor with me, after we had sat together feeling each other for a time, if mine could be called feeling, when my fingers only touched the top of the notch. I took up the candle. "I won't go if you bring a light," said she, so I put down the candle, and, holding her by the arm, we walked through the passage across the little hall to the front parlour; she closed the door, and we were in the dark. And now I only recollect generally what took place, it seems as if it all could but have occupied a minute, or two, though experience tells me it must have been longer.

We sat on a settee or sofa, she had hold of my prick, and I her cunt, for she now sat with thighs quite wide open. It was my first real feel of a woman, and she meant me to feel well. How large and hairy and wet it seemed; its size overwhelmed me with astonishment, I did not find the hole, don't recollect feeling for that, am sure I never put my finger in it, all seemed cunt below her belly, wet, and warm, and slippery. "Make haste, your aunt will be in soon," said she softly, but I was engrossed with the cunt, in twiddling it and feeling it in delighted wonder at its size and other qualities. "Your aunt will be in," and leaving off feeling my cock, she laid half on, half off the settee. "No, no, not so," I recollect the words, but what I was doing, know not; then I was standing by her side, my cock stiff, and still feeling her cunt in bewilderment. "I can't . . . stop . . . get on to the sofa." I laid half over her, my prick touched something — her cunt of course. Whether it went in or not, God knows, I pushed, it felt smooth to my prick, then suddenly came over me, a fear of some horrible disease, and I ceased whatever I was doing. "Go on, go on," said she, moving her belly up. I could not, said nothing, but sat down by her side, she rose up, "You're not man enough," said she, laying hold of my prick. It was not stiff, I put my hand down, and again the great size — as it seemed to me — of her cunt, made me wonder.

What then she did with me, I know not, she may have frigged it, I think she did, but can't say, a sense of disgrace had come over me as she said I was not man enough, disgrace mixed with fear of disease. "Let me try," said I; again she laid back, I have a faint recollection of my finger going in somewhere deep, again of my prick touching her thighs and rubbing in something smooth, but nothing more. "You're not man enough," said she again. A ring . . . "Hark! it's your aunt, go!" and it was.

I went into the adjoining room, where my books were and a lamp, she went to the street-door. My aunt and cousin came in and went up to their bed-rooms, I sat smelling my fingers; the full smell of cunt that I had for the first time. I smelt and smelt almost out of my senses, sat poring over a book, seeming to read, but with my fingers to my nose and thinking of cunt, its wonderful size and smell. Aunt came down. "Have you got a cold, Wattie?" "No, aunt." "Your eyes look quite inflamed, child." Soon after again, she said: "You have a cold?" "No, aunt." "Why are you sniffing so, and holding your hand to your mouth?" Suddenly the fear of the pox came over me, I went up to the bed-room, soaped and washed my prick, and had a terrible fear on me.

I was overwhelmed with a mixed feeling of pride, at having had my prick either touch or go up a cunt, fear that I had caught disease, and shame at not being man enough. Instinct told me I had lost, in the eyes of the woman, and my pride was hurt in a woeful manner. I tried to avoid seeing her, instead of as before getting excitedly into a room where she was likely to be alone for a minute. I did that for three days, then fear of disease vanished, and my hopes of feeling her cunt again, or of poking — I don't know which — impelled me towards her.

During those three days I washed my prick at every possible opportunity, and thought of nothing else but the incident; all seemed to me hurry, confusion, impossible; I wondered, and wonder still, whether my prick went into her or not; but above all, the largeness of the cunt filled me with wonder; for though I had had rapid glimpses of cunts as told, and had now seen a few pictures of the long slit, I never could realise that that was only the outside of the cunt, until I had had a woman. My fingers had no doubt slipped over the surface of hers, from clitoris to arse-hole; the space my hand covered filled me with astonishment, as well as the smell it left on my fingers, I thought of that more than anything else. This seems to me now laughable, but it was a marvel to me then.

When I sneaked into the kitchen again, I was ashamed to look at her, and left almost directly, but one day I felt her again. Laughing she put her hand outside my trowsers, gave my doodle a gentle pinch and kissed me. "Let's do it!" I said. "Lor! you ain't man enough," and again I slunk away ashamed.

CHAPTER IV

My first frig. — My godfather. — Meditations on
copulation. — Male and female aromas. — Maid and
gardener. — My father dies. — A wet dream. —
Bilked by a whore.

The frequency of my cock-stands up to this time I don't
know. Voluptuous sensation I have no clear recollection of;
but no doubt during that half swooning delight, which I had
when big Betsy allowed me to lay my head on her lap and
feel her limbs, that impulse towards the woman was accompanied by sensuous pleasure, though I don't recollect the
fact, but soon my manhood was to declare itself.

Some time after I had felt this servant's quim, I noticed a
strong smelling, whitish stuff, inside my foreskin, making
the underside of the tip of the prick sore. At first I thought
it disease, then pulling the foreskin up, I made it into a sort
of cup, dropped warm water into it, and working it about,
washed all round the nut, and let the randy smelling infusion
escape. This marked my need for a woman, I did not know
what the exudation was, it made me in a funk at first. One
day I had been toying with the girl, had a cock-stand, and
felt again my prick sore, and was washing it with warm water, when it swelled up. I rubbed it through my hand, which
gave me unusual pleasure, then a voluptuous sensation came
over me quickly so thrilling and all pervading that I shall
never forget it. I sunk on to a chair, feeling my cock gently,
the next instant spunk jetted out in large drops, a full yard
in front of me, and a thinner liquid rolled over my knuckles.
I had frigged myself, without intending it.

Then came astonishment, mingled with disgust, I examined the viscid, gruelly fluid with the greatest curiosity,
smelt it, and I think tasted it. Then came fear of my godfather, and of being found out; for all that, after wiping up my
sperm from the floor, I went up to my bed-room and, locking the door, frigged myself until I could do it no more from
exhaustion.

I wanted a confidant and told two schoolfellows who were

brothers, I could not keep it to myself, and was indeed proud though ashamed to speak of the pleasure. They both had bigger pricks than mine, and never had jeered at me because I could not retract my prepuce easily. Soon after they came to see me, we all went into the garden, each pulled my prepuce back, I theirs, and then we all frigged ourselves in an out-house.

Then I wrote to Fred, who was at a large public school, about my frigging. He replied that some fellows at his school had been caught at it and flogged; that a big boy just going to Oxford had had a woman and got the pox badly. He begged me to burn his letter, or throw it down the shit-house directly I had read it, adding that he was in such a funk for he had lost mine; and that I was never to write to him such things at the school, because the master opened every day indiscriminately one or two letters of the boys. He knew my mother was away and so did not mind writing to me. When I heard that he had lost my letter I also was in a funk; the letter never was found. Whether the master got it, or sent it to my godfather or not, I can't say, but it is certain that just after I had one night exhausted myself by masturbation, my godfather came to see me.

He stared hard at me. "You look ill." "No, I am not." "Yes, you are, look me full in the face, you've been frigging yourself," said he just in so many words. He had never used an improper word to me before. I denied it. He raved out "No denial, sir, no lies, you have, sir; don't add lying to your bestiality, you've been at that filthy trick, I can see it in your face, you'll die in a mad-house, or of consumption, you shall never have a farthing more pocket-money from me, and I won't buy your commission, nor leave you any money at my death." I kept denying it, brazening it out. "Hold your tongue, you young beast, or I'll write to your mother." That reduced me to a sullen state, only at times jerking out: "I haven't!" He put on his hat angrily, and left me in a very uncomfortable state of mind.

I knew that my father was not so well off as he had been, my mother always impressed upon me not to offend my godfather, and now I had done it. I wrote Fred all about it, he said the old beggar was a doctor, and it was very unfortunate; he wondered if he really did see any signs in my face, or whether it was bounce; that I was not to be a fool and give in, and still say I hadn't, but had better leave off frigging.

From that time my godfather was always at my heels, he waited for me at the school-door, spent my half-holidays with me, sat with me and my aunt of an evening till bed-time, made me ride and drive out with him, stopped giving me pocket-money altogether, and no one else did; so that I was not very happy.

The pleasure of frigging, now I had tasted it (and not before), opened my eyes more fully to the mystery of the sexes, I seemed at once to understand why women and men got together, and yet was full of wonder about it. Spunking seemed a nasty business, the smell of cunt an extraordinary thing in a woman, whose odour generally to me was so sweet and intoxicating. I read novels harder than ever, liked being near females and to look at them more than ever, and whether young or old, common or gentle, was always look-ing at them and thinking that they had cunts which had a strong odour, and wondering if they had been fucked; I used to stare at aunt and cousins, and wonder the same. It seemed to me scarcely possible, that the sweet, well dressed, smooth-spoken ladies who came to our house, could let men put the spunk up their cunts. Then came the wonder if, and how, women spent; what pleasure they had in fucking, and so on; in all ways was I wondering about copulation, the oddity of the gruelly, close-smelling sperm being ejected into the hole between a woman's thighs so astonished me. I often thought the whole business must be a dream of mine; then that there could be no doubt about it. Among other doubts, was whether the servant's quim, which had made my fingers smell, was diseased, or not.

Fear of detection perhaps kept me from frigging, but I was weak and growing fast, and have no recollection of much desire, though mad to better understand a cunt. It does not dwell in my mind now that I had a desire to fuck one, but to see it, and above all, to smell it; the recollection of its aroma seems to have had a strange effect on me. I did not like it much, yet yearned to smell it again. Watching my op-portunity one day, I managed to feel the servant; it was dusk, she stood with her back up against the wall, and felt my prick whilst I felt her; it was an affair of a second or two, and again we were scared. I went to the sitting-room, and passed the evening in smelling my fingers and looking at my cousin. This occurred once again, and I think now, that the servant must just have been on the point of letting me fuck her, for she had been feeling my prick and in a jeering way

saying, "You are not man enough if I let you," I embold-
ened, blurted out that I had spent, I recollect her saying,
"Oh! your story," and then something put us to flight. I
don't now know what. I certainly was not up to my opportunities, that I see now plainly.

I had a taste for chemistry, which served my purpose, as
will be seen further on, and used to experimentalise in what
was called a wash-house, just outside the kitchen, with my
acids and alkalis; that enabled me to slip into the kitchen on
the sly, but the plan of the house rendered it easy for my
aunt to come suddenly into the kitchen.

My bed-room window overlooked the kitchen yard, in
which was this wash-house, a knife-house, and a servant's
privy, etc., etc., the whole surrounded by a wall, with a door
in it, leading into the garden. Just outside on the garden side,
was a gardener's shed; the servant in the morning used to let
the gardener in at the kitchen entrance; and he passed
through this kitchen yard into the garden. I was pissing in
the pot in my bed-room early one morning, and peeping
through the blind, when I saw the servant's head just coming
out of the gardener's shed, she passed through the kitchen
yard into the kitchen in great haste, looking up at the house,
as if to see if anyone was at the windows. Then it occurred
to me, that if I got quite early to the kitchen, I could play my
little baudy tricks without fear, for my relatives never went
down till half-past eight to breakfast, whilst the servant went
down at six.

The next morning, I went down early to the kitchen, did
not see the wench, and thinking she might be in the privy in
the kitchen yard, waited. The shutters were not down, after
some minutes delay, in she came; she started. "Hulloh! what
are you up for?" I don't think I spoke, but making a dash,
got my hand up her clothes and on to her cunt. She pushed
me away, then caught hold of the hand with which I had
touched her cunt, and squeezed it hard with a rubbing motion, looking at me as I recollected (but long afterwards), in
a funny way. "Hish! hish! here is the old woman," said she.
"It is not." "I'm sure I heard the wires of her bell," and sure
enough there came a ring. Up I went without shoes, like a
shot to my bed-room, began to smell my fingers, found they
were sticky, and the smell not the same. I recollect thinking
it strange that her cunt should be so sticky, I had heard of
dirty cunts, — it was a joke among us boys — and thought

hers must have been so, which was the cause that the smell and feel were different.

Two or three days afterwards my mother came to town by herself, there was a row with the servant, I was told to leave the room; the servant and gardener were both turned off that day and hour, a char-woman was had in, a temporary gardener got, and my mother went back to my sick father. Years passed away, and when I had greater experience and thought of all this, concluded that my aunt had found the gardener and the servant amusing themselves too freely, had had them dismissed, and that the morning I found my fingers sticky the girl had just come in from fucking in the gardener's shed.

With all the opportunities I had, both with big Betsy and with this woman, I was still virgin.

When I saw Fred next, he told me he had felt the cunt of one of their servants. I told him partly what I had done, but kept to myself how I had failed to poke when I had the opportunity, fearing his jeers; and as I was obliged to name some women, mentioned one of my godfather's servants. He went there to try his chances of groping her as well, but got his head slapped. We talked much about the smell of cunt, and he told me that one day after he had felt their servant, he went into the room where his sisters were, and said, "Oh, what a funny smell there is on my fingers, what can it be? Smell them." Two of his sisters smelt, said they could not tell what it was, but it was not nice. Fred used to say that he thought they knew it was like the smell of cunt, because they colored up so.

I had noticed a strong smell on my prick, whenever the curdy exudation had to be washed out. Fred's talk made me imitative, so I saturated my fingers with the masculine essence one evening, and, going to my female cousin, "Oh, what a queer smell there is on my fingers," said I, "smell them." The girl did. "It's nasty, you've got it from your chemicals," said she. "I don't think I have, smell them again, I can't think what it can be, what's it like?" "I don't think it's like anything I ever smelt, but it is not so nasty, if you smell it close, it's like southern wood," she replied. I wonder if that young lady when she married, ever smelt it afterwards, and recognized it. I did this more than once, it gave me great delight to think my slim cousin had smelt my prick, through smelling my fingers; what innate lubricity comes out early in the male.

Misfortunes of all sort came upon us, the family came back to town, another brother died, then my father, who had been long ill, died, and was found to be nearly bankrupt; then my godfather died, and left me a fortune, all was trouble and change, but I only mention these family matters briefly.

My physique still could not have been strong, for though more than ever intensely romantic, and passionately fond of female society, I don't recollect being much troubled with cock-standings, and think I should, had I been so. My two intimate school-friends left off frigging, the elder brother, who had a very long red nose, having come to the conclusion with me that frigging made people mad, and worse, prevented them afterwards from fucking and having a family. Fred, my favorite cousin, arrived at the same conclusion — by what mental process we all arrived at it I don't know.

When I was approaching my sixteenth year, I awakened one night with a voluptuous dream, and found my night-shirt saturated with semen, it was my first wet dream; that set me frigging again for a time, but I either restrained myself or did not naturally require much spending at that time, for I certainly did not often do so.

But our talk was always about cunt and women, I was always trying to smell their flesh, look up their petticoats, watch to see them going to piddle; and the wonder to me now is that I did not frig myself incessantly; and can only account for it on the grounds, that though my imagination was very ripe, my body was not. The fact of hair under the arms of women had a secret charm for me about that time. I don't recollect thinking much about it before, though it had astonished me when I first saw it; and why it came to my imagination so much now I do not know, but it did. I have told of the woman under whose arms I first saw hair.

One afternoon after my father's death, and that of my godfather, Fred was with me, we went to the house of a friend, and were to return home about nine o'clock. It was dark, we saw a woman standing by a wall. "She is a whore," said Fred, "and will let us feel her if we pay her." "You go and ask her." "No, you." "I don't like." "How much money have you got?" We ascertained what we had, and after a little hesitation, walked on, passed her, then turned round and stopped. "What are you staring at, kiddy," said the woman. I was timid and walked away; Fred stopped with her.

"Wattie, come here," said he in a half-whisper. I walked back. "How much have you got?" the woman said. We both gave her money. "You'll let us both feel?" said Fred. "Why of course, have you felt a woman before?" Both of us said we had, feeling bolder. "Was it a woman about here?" "No." "Did you both feel the same woman?" "No." "Give me another shilling then, you shall both feel my cunt well, I've such a lot of hair on it." We gave what we had, and then she walked off without letting us. "I'll tell your mothers, if you come after me," she cried out. We were sold; I was once sold again in a similar manner afterwards, when by myself.

These are the principal baudy incidents of my early youth, which I recollect, and have not told to friends; many other amusing incidents told them are omitted here, for the authorship would be disclosed if I did. One or two were peculiar and most amusing, yet I dare not narrate them; but all show how soon sexual desires developed in me, and what pleasure early in life even these gave me and others.

I now had arrived at the age of puberty, when male nature asserts itself in the most timid and finds means of getting its legitimate pleasure with women. I did, and then my recollection of things became more perfect, not only as to the consummations, but of what led to them; yet nothing seems to me so remarkable as the way I recollect matters which occurred when I was almost an infant.

CHAPTER V

Our house. — Charlotte and brother Tom. — Kissing and groping. — Both in rut. — My first fuck. — A virginity taken. — At a baudy house. — In a privy. — Tribulations. — Charlotte leaves. — My despair.

After father's death, our circumstances were further reduced. At the time I am going to speak of, we had come to a small house nearer London; one sister went to boarding-school, an aunt (I had many) took another, I went to a neighboring great school or college, as it was termed, my little brother Tom was at home; but reference henceforth to members of my family will be but slight, for they had but little to do with the incidents of this private life, and unless they were part actors in it, none will be mentioned.

Our house had on the ground-floor a dining-room, a drawing-room, and a small room called the garden parlour, with steps leading into a large garden. On the first floor, my mother's bed-room and two others; above were the servants' room, mine, and another much used as a lumber-room; the kitchens were in the basement, outside them a long covered way led to a servants' privy, and close to it a flight of stairs leading up into the garden; at the top of the stairs was a garden-door leading into the fore-court, on to which opened the street-door of the house. This description of plan is needful to understand what follows.

I was about sixteen years old, tall, with slight whiskers and moustache, altogether manly and looking seventeen or eighteen, yet my mother thought me a mere child, and most innocent; she told our friends so. I had developed, without her having noticed it, love of women, and the intensest desire to understand the secrets of their nature had taken possession of me; the incessant talk of fucking with which the youths I knew beguiled their leisure, the stories they told of having seen their servants or other girls half, or quite, naked, the tricks by which they managed this, the dodges they were up to, inflamed me, sharpened my instinctive acuteness in such matters, and set me seeking every opportunity to know women naked, and sexually. Frigging was now hateful to me; I had never done so more than the times related, that is as far as I now can recollect, frightened, as said, by my godfather telling me that it sent men mad and made them hateful to women. So although boiling with sensuality, I was still all but a virgin, and actually so in fucking.

A housemaid arrived just as I came home from college; the cook stood at the door, she was a lovely woman about twenty-five or -six years old, fresh as a daisy, her name was Mary. The housemaid was in a cart, driven by her father, a small market gardener living a few miles from us. I saw a fresh, comely girl about seventeen years old in the cart as I passed, and when I got inside our fore-court, turned round to look, she was getting down, the horse moved, she hesitated. "Get down," said her father angrily. Down she stepped, her clothes caught on the edge of the cart, or step, or somehow; and I saw rapidly appear white stockings, garters, thighs, and a patch of dark hair between them by her belly; it was instantaneous, and down the clothes came, hiding all. I stood

[65]

fascinated, knowing I had seen her cunt hair. She, without any idea of having been exposed, helped down with her box, I went into the parlour ashamed of having, as I thought, been seen looking.

I could think of nothing else, and when she brought in tea, could not take my eyes off her, it was the same at supper (we led a simple life, dining early and having supper). In the evening my mother remarked, "That girl will do," I recollect feeling glad at that.

I went to bed, thinking of what I had seen, and stared whenever I saw her the next day, until, by a sort of fascination, she used to stare at me; in a day or two I fancied myself desperately in love with her, and indeed was. I recollect now her features, as if I had only seen her yesterday, and after the scores and scores of women I have fucked since, recollect every circumstance attending my having her, as distinctly as if it only occurred last week; yet very many years have passed away.

She was a little over seventeen years, had ruddy lips, beautiful teeth, darkish hair, hazel eyes, and a slightly turn-up nose, large shoulders and breasts, was plump, generally of fair height, and looked eighteen or nineteen; her name was Charlotte.

I soon spoke to her kindly, by degrees because free in manner, at length chuckled her under her chin, pinched her arm, and used the familiarities which nature teaches a man to use towards a woman. It was her business to open the door, and help me off with my coat and boots if needful; one day as she did so, her bum projecting upset me so that as she rose from stooping I caught and pinched her. All this was done with risk, for my mother then was nearly always at home, and the house being small, a noise was easily heard.

I was soon kissing her constantly. In a few days got a kiss in return, that drove me wild, her cunt came constantly into my mind, all sorts of wants, notions, and vague possibilities came across me; girls do let fellows feel them, I said to myself, I had already succeeded in that. What if I tell that I have seen it outside? will she tell my mother? will she let me feel her? what madness! yet girls do let men, girls like it, so all my friends say. Wild with hopes and anticipations, coming indoors one day, I caught her tightly in my arms, pulled her belly close to mine, rubbed up against hers saying, "Charlotte, what would I give, if you would ..." it was all I dared say. Then I heard my mother's bed-room door open, and I stopped.

Hugging and kissing a woman never stopped there, I told her I loved her, which she said was nonsense. We now used regularly to kiss each other when we got the chance; little by little I grasped her closer to me, put my hands round her waist, then cunningly round to her bum, then my prick used to stand and I was mad to say more to her, but had not the courage. I knew not how to set to work, indeed scarce knew what my desires led me to hope, and think at that time, putting my hand on to her cunt, and seeing it, was perhaps the utmost; fucking her seemed a hopelessly mad idea, if I had the expectation of doing so at all very clearly.

I told a friend one or two years older than myself how matters stood, carefully avoiding telling him who the girl was. His advice was short. Tell her you have seen her cunt, and make a snatch up her petticoats when no one is near; keep at it, and you will be sure to get a feel, and some day, pull out your prick, say straight you want to fuck her, girls like to see a prick, she will look, even if she turns her head away. This advice he dinned into my ears continually, but for a long time I was not bold enough to put his advice into practice.

One day, my mother was out, the cook upstairs dressing, we had kissed in the garden parlour, I put my hand round her bum, and sliding my face over her shoulder half ashamed, said, "I wish my prick was against your naked belly, instead of outside your clothes." She with an effort disengaged herself, stood amazed, and said, "I never will speak to you again."

I had committed myself, but went on, though in fear, prompted by love or lust. My friend's advice was in my ears. "I saw your cunt as you got down from your father's cart," said I, "look at my prick (pulling it out), how stiff it is, it's longing to go into you, 'cock and cunt will come together.' " It was part of a smutty chorus the fellows sang at my college; she stared, turned round, went out of the room, through the garden, and down to the kitchen by the garden stairs, without uttering a word.

The cook was at the top of the house, I went into the kitchen reckless, and repeated all I had said. She threatened to call the cook. "She must have seen your cunt, as well as me," said I; then she began to cry. Just as I was begging pardon, my friend's advice again rang in my ears, I stooped and swiftly ran both hands up her clothes, got one full on to her bum, the other on her motte; she gave a loud scream, and I rushed off upstairs in a fright.

The cook did not hear her, being up three pairs of stairs; down I went again, and found Charlotte crying, told her again all I had seen in the court yard, which made her cry more. She would ask the cook, and would tell my mother — then hearing the cook coming downstairs, I cut off through the passage up into the garden.

The ice was quite broken now, she could not avoid me, I promised not to repeat what I had said and done, was forgiven, we kissed, and the same day I broke my promise; this went on day after day, making promises and breaking them, talking smuttily as well as I knew how, getting a slap on my head, but no further, my chances were few. My friend, whom I made a half confidant of, was always taunting me with my want of success and boasting of what he would have done had he had my opportunities.

My mother just at that time began to resume her former habits, leaving the house frequently for walks and visits. One afternoon she being out for the remainder of the day, I went home unexpectedly; the cook was going out, I was to fetch my mother home in the evening; Charlotte laid the dinner for me; we had the usual kissing, I was unusually bold and smutty. Charlotte finding me not to be going out, seemed anxious. All the dinner things had been taken away, when out went the cook, and there were Charlotte, my little brother and I alone. It was her business to sit with him in the garden parlour when mother was out, so as to be able to open the street-door readily, as well as go into the garden if the weather was fine. It was a fine day of autumn, she went into the parlour and was sitting on the huge old sofa, Tom playing on the floor, when I sat myself down by her side; we kissed and toyed, and then with heart beating, I began my talk and waited my opportunity.

The cook would be back in a few minutes, said she. I knew better, having heard mother tell cook she need not be home until eight o'clock. Although I knew this, I was fearful, but at length mustered courage to sing my cock and cunt song. She was angry, but it was made up. She went to give something to Tom, and stepping back put her foot on the lace of one boot which was loose, sat down on the sofa and put up one leg over the other, to relace it. I undertook to do it for her, saw her neat ankle, and a bit of a white stocking.

"Snatch at her cunt," rang in my ears, I had never attempted it since the afternoon in the kitchen.

Lacing the boot, I managed to push the clothes up so as to see more of the leg, but resting as the foot did on one knee, the clothes tightly between, a snatch was useless: lust made me cunning, I praised the foot (though I knew not at the time how vain some women are of their feet). "What a nice ankle," I said, putting my hand further on. She was off her guard; with my left arm, I pushed her violently back on to the large sofa, her foot came off her knee, at the same moment, my right hand went up between her thighs, on to her cunt; I felt the slit, the hair, and moisture.

She got up to a sitting posture, crying, "You wretch, you beast, you blackguard," but still I kept my fingers on the cunt; she closed her legs, so as to shut my hand between her thighs and keep it motionless, and tried to push me off; but I clung round her. "Take your hand away," said she, "or I will scream." "I shan't!" Then followed two or three loud, very loud screams. "No one can hear," said I, which brought her to supplication. My friend's advice came again to me: pushing my right hand still between her thighs, with my left I pulled out my prick, as stiff as a poker. She could not do otherwise than see it; and then I drew my left hand round her neck, pulling her head to me, and covered it with kisses.

She tried to get up and nearly dislodged my right hand, but I pushed her back, and got my hand still further on to the cunt. I never thought of pressing under towards the bum, was in fact too ignorant of female anatomy to do it, but managed to get one of the lips with the hair between my fingers and pinch it; then dropped on to my knees in front of her and remained kneeling, preventing her getting back further on the sofa, as well as I could by holding her waist, or her clothes.

There was a pause from our struggles, then more entreaties, then more attempts to get my right hand away; suddenly she put out one hand, seized me by the hair of my head, and pushed me backwards by it. I thought my skull was coming off, but kept my hold and pinched or pulled the cunt lip till she hollowed and called me a brute. I told her I would hurt her as much as I could, if she hurt me; so that game she gave up; the pain of pulling my hair made me savage, and more determined and brutal, than before.

We went on struggling at intervals, I kneeling with prick out, she crying, begging me to desist; I entreating her to let me see and feel her cunt, using all the persuasion and all the baudy talk I could, little Tom sitting on the floor playing contentedly. I must have been half an hour on my knees, which became so painful that I could scarcely bear it; we were both panting, I was sweating; an experienced man would perhaps have had her then; I was a boy inexperienced, and without her consent almost in words would not have thought of attempting it; the novelty, the voluptuousness of my game was perhaps sufficient delight to me; at last I became conscious that my fingers on her cunt were getting wet; telling her so, she became furious and burst into such a flood of tears that it alarmed me. It was impossible to remain on my knees longer; in rising, I knew I should be obliged to take my hand from her cunt, so withdrawing my left hand from her waist, I put it also suddenly up her clothes, and round her bum, and lifted them up, showing both her thighs, whilst I attempted to rise. She got up at the same instant, pushing down her clothes, I fell over on one side, — my knees were so stiff and painful — and she rushed out of the room upstairs.

It was getting dusk, I sat on the sofa in a state of pleasure, smelling my fingers. Tom began to howl, she came down and took him up to pacify him, I followed her down to the kitchen, she called me an insolent boy (an awful taunt to me then), threatened to tell my mother, to give notice and leave, and left the kitchen, followed by me about the house; talking baudily, telling her how I liked the smell of my fingers, attempting to put my hand up her clothes, sometimes succeeding, pulling out my ballocks, and never ceasing until the cook came home, having been at this game for hours. In a sudden funk, I begged Charlotte to tell my mother that I had only come home just before the cook, and had gone to bed unwell; she replying she would tell my mother the truth, and nothing else. I was in my bed-room before cook was let in.

Mother came home later, I was in a fright, having laid in bed cooling down and thinking of possible consequences; heard the street-door knocker, got out of bed, and in my night-shirt went half way downstairs listening. To my relief, I heard Charlotte, in answer to my mother's enquiry, say I had come home about an hour before and had gone to bed unwell. My mother came to my room, saying how sorry she was.

For a few days I was in fear, but it gradually wore off, as

I found she had not told; our kissing recommenced, my boldness increased, my talk ran now freely on her legs, her bum, and her cunt, she ceased to notice it, beyond saying she hated such talk, and at length she smiled spite of herself. Our kissing grew more fervid, she resisted improper action of my hand, but we used to stand with our lips close together for minutes at a time when we got the chance, I holding her to me as close as wax. One day cook was upstairs, mother in her bed-room, I pushed Charlotte up against the wall in the kitchen, and pulled up her clothes, scarcely with resistance; just then my mother rang, I skipped up into the garden and got into the parlour that way, soon heard my mother calling to me to fetch water, Charlotte was in hysterics at the foot of the stairs — after that, she frequently had hysterics, till a certain event occurred.

My chances were chiefly on Saturdays, a day I did not go to college; soon I was to cease going there and was to prepare for the army.

I came home one day, when I knew Charlotte would be alone — the cook was upstairs — I got her on to the sofa in the garden parlour, knelt and put my hands between her thighs, with less resistance than before, she struggled slightly but made no noise. She kissed me as she asked me to take away my hand; I could move it more easily on her quim, which I did not fail to do; she was wonderfully quiet. Suddenly I became conscious that she was looking me full in the face, with a peculiar expression, her eyes very wide open, then shutting them "Oho — oho," she said with a prolonged sigh, "do — oh, take away — oh — your hand, Walter dear, — oh I shall be ill, — oho, — oho," then her head dropped down over my shoulder as I knelt in front of her; at the same moment, her thighs seemed to open slightly, then shut, then open with a quivering, shuddering motion, as it then seemed to me, and then she was quite quiet.

I pushed my hand further in, or rather on, for although I thought I had it up the cunt, I really was only between the lips — I know that now. With a sudden start she rose up, pushed me off, snatched up Tom from the floor, and rushed upstairs. My fingers were quite wet. For two or three days afterwards, she avoided my eyes and looked bashful, I could not make it out, and it was only months afterwards, that I knew, that the movement of my fingers on her clitoris had made her spend. Without knowing indeed then that such a thing was possible, I had frigged her.

Although for about three months I had been thus deliciously amusing myself, anxious to feel and see her cunt, and though I had at last asked her to let me fuck her, I really don't think I had any definite expectation of doing it to her. I guessed now at its mutual pleasures, and so forth, yet my doing it to her appeared beyond me; but urged on by my love for the girl — for I did love her — as well as by sexual instinct, I determined to try. I also was quickened by my college friend, who had seen Charlotte at our house and not knowing it was the girl I had spoken to him about, said to me, "What a nice girl that maid of yours is, I mean to get over her, I shall wait for her after church next Sunday, she sits in your pew, I know." I asked him some questions, — his opinion was that most girls would let a young fellow fuck them, if pressed, and that she would (this youth was but about eighteen years old), and I left him fearing what he said was true, hating and jealous of him to excess. He set me thinking, why should not I do it if he could, and if what he said about girls was true? — so I determined to try it on, and by luck did so earlier than I expected.

About one hour's walk from us was the town house of an aunt, the richest of our family and one of my mother's sisters. She alone now supplied me with what money I had, my mother gave me next to nothing. I went to see aunt, who asked me to tell my mother to go and spend a day with her, the next week, and named the day. I forgot this until three days afterwards, when hearing my mother tell the cook, she could go out for a whole holiday; I said, that my aunt particularly wished to see mother on that day. My mother scolded me for not having told her sooner, but wrote and arranged to go, forgetting the cook's holiday. To my intense joy, on that day she took brother Tom with her, saying to Charlotte, "You will have nothing to think of, but the house, shut it up early, and do not be frightened." I was as usual to fetch my mother home.

In what an agitated state I passed that morning at school, and in the afternoon went home, trembling at my own intentions. Charlotte's eyes opened with astonishment at seeing me. Was I not going to fetch my mother? I was not going till night. There was no food in the house, and I had better go to my aunt's for dinner. I knew there was cold meat, and made her lay the cloth in the kitchen. To make sure, I asked if the cook was out, — yes, she was, but would be home soon. I knew that she stopped out till ten o'clock on her holidays. The girl was agitated with some undefined idea of what might take place, we kissed and hugged, but she did not like even that, I saw.

I restrained myself whilst eating, she sat quietly besides me; when I had finished she began to remove the things, the food gave me courage, her moving about stimulated me, I began to feel her breasts, then got my hands on to her thighs, we had the usual struggles, but it seems to me as I now think of it that her resistance was less and that she prayed me to desist more lovingly than was usual. We had toyed for an hour, she had let a dish fall and smashed it, the baker rang, she took in the bread, and declared she would not shut the door unless I promised to leave off. I promised, and so soon as she had closed it, pulled her into the garden parlour, having been thinking when in the kitchen how I could get her upstairs. Down tumbled the bread on the floor, on to the sofa, I pushed her, and after a struggle she was sitting down, I kissing her, one arm round her waist, one hand between her thighs, close up to her cunt. Then I told her I wanted to fuck her, said all in favour of it I knew, half ashamed, half frightened, as I said it. She said she did not know what I meant, resisted less and less as I tried to pull her back on the sofa, when another ring came: it was the milkman.

I was obliged to let her go, and she ran down stairs with the milk. I followed, she went out, and slammed the door, which led to the garden, in my face; for the instant, I thought she was going to the privy, but opened and followed on; she ran up the steps, into the garden, through the garden parlour, and upstairs to her bed-room just opposite to mine, closed and locked the door in my face, I begged her to let me in.

She said she would not come out till she heard the knocker or bell ring; there was no one called usually after the milkman, so my game was up, but nothing makes man or woman so crafty as lust. In half an hour or so, in anger, I said I should go to my aunt's, went downstairs, moved noisily about, opened and slammed the street-door violently, as if I had gone out, then pulled off my boots, and crept quietly up to my bed-room.

There I sat expectantly a long time, had almost given up hope, began to think about consequences if she told my mother, when I heard the door softly open and she came to the edge of the stairs. "Wattie!" she said loudly. "Wattie!" much louder, "he has," said she in a subdued tone to herself, as much as to say that worry is over. I opened my door, she gave a loud shriek and retreated to her room, I close to her; in a few minutes more, hugging, kissing, begging, threatening, I know not how; she was partly on the bed, her clothes up in a heap, I on her with my prick in my hand, I saw the hair, I felt the slit, and not knowing then where the hole was or much about it, excepting that it was between her legs, shoved my prick there with all my might. "Oh! you hurt, I shall be ill," said she, "pray don't." Had she said she was dying I should not have stopped. The next instant a delirium of my senses came, my prick throbbing and as if hot lead was jetting from it, at each throb; pleasure mingled with light pain in it, and my whole frame quivering with emotion; my sperm left me for a virgin cunt, but fell outside it, though on to it.

How long I was quiet I don't know; probably but a short time; for a first pleasure does not tranquillise at that age; I became conscious that she was pushing me off of her, and rose up, she with me, to a half-sitting posture; she began to laugh, then to cry, and fell back in hysterics, as I had seen her before.

I had seen my mother attend to her in those fits, but little did I then know that sexual excitement causes them in women and that probably in her I had been the cause. I got brandy and water and made her drink a lot, helping myself at the same time, for I was frightened, and made her lay on the bed. Then, ill as she was, frightened as I was, I yet took the opportunity her partial insensibility gave me, lifted her clothes quietly, and saw her cunt and my spunk on it. Roused by that, she pushed her clothes half down feebly and got to the side of the bed. I loving, begging pardon, kissing her, told her of my pleasure, and asked about hers, all in snatches, for I thought I had done her. Not a word could I get, but she looked me in the face beseechingly, begging me to go. I had no such intention, my prick was again stiffening, I pulled it out, the sight of her cunt had stimulated me, she looked with languid eyes at me, her cap was off, her hair hanging about her head, her dress torn near her breast. More so than she had ever looked was she beautiful to me, success made me bold, on I went insisting, she seemed too weak to withstand me. "Don't, oh pray, don't," was all she said as, pushing her well on the bed, I threw myself on her and again put my doodle on to the slit now wet with my sperm. I was, though cooler, stiff as a poker, but my sperm was not so ready to flow, as it was in after days, at a second poke, for

[74]

I was very young; but nature did all for me; my prick went to the proper channel, there stopped by something it battered furiously. "Oh, you hurt, oh!" she cried aloud. The next instant something seemed to tighten round its knob, another furious thrust, — another, — a sharp cry of pain (resistance was gone), and my prick was buried up her, I felt that it was done, and that before I had spent outside her. I looked at her, she was quiet, her cunt seemed to close on my prick, I put my hand down, and felt round. What rapture to find my machine buried! nothing but the balls to be touched, and her cunt hair wetted with my sperm, mingling and clinging to mine; in another minute nature urged a crisis, and I spent in a virgin cunt, my prick virgin also. Thus ended my first fuck.

My prick was still up her, when we heard a loud knock; both started up in terror, I was speechless. "My God, it is your mamma!" Another loud knock. What a relief, it was the postman. To rush downstairs, and open the door was the work of a minute. "I thought you were all out," said he angrily, "I have knocked three times." "We were in the garden," said I. He looked queerly at me and said, "With your boots off!" and grinning went away. I went up again, found her sitting on the side of the bed, and there we sat together. I told her what the postman had said, she was sure he would tell her mistress. For a short time, there never was a couple who had just fucked, in more of a foolish funk then we were; I have often thought of our not hearing the thundering knocks of a postman, whilst we were fucking, though the bed-room door was wide open; what engrossing work it is so to deafen people. Then after unsuccessfully struggling to see her cunt, and kissing, and feeling each other's genitals, and talking of our doings and our sensations for an hour, we fucked again.

It was getting dark, which brought us to reason; we both helped remake the bed, went downstairs, shut the shutters, lighted the fire which was out, and got lights. I then, having nothing to do, began thinking of my doodle, which was sticking to my shirt, and pulling it out to see its condition, found my shirt covered with sperm smears, and spots of blood; my prick was dreadfully sore. I said to her that she had been bleeding, she begged me to go out of the kitchen for a minute, I did, and almost directly she came out and passed me, saying she must change her things before the cook came home. She would not let me stay in the room whilst she did it, nor did I see her chemise, though I had followed her upstairs; then the idea flashed across me that I had taken a virginity; that had never occurred to me before. She got hot water to wash herself. I did not know what to do with my shirt; we arranged I should wash it before I went to bed. We thought it best to say I had not been home at all, and that I should go and fetch my mother. After much kissing, hugging, and tears on her part, off I went, hatching an excuse for not having fetched mother earlier, and we came home with Tom in my aunt's carriage, I recollect.

Before going to bed, I ordered hot water for a footbath. How we looked at each other as I ordered it. I washed my shirt as well as I could, and looked sadly at my sore prick, I could not pull the skin back so much as usual, it was torn, raw, and slightly bleeding.

Awake nearly all night, thinking of my pleasure and proud of my success, I rose early and, looking at my shirt, found stains still visible, and that I had so mucked it in washing that an infant could have guessed what I had been doing. I knew that my mother, who now did household duties herself, selected the things for the laundress; and in despair hit on a plan: I filled the chamber-pot with piss and soap-suds, making it as dirty as I could, put it near a chair and my shirt hanging over it carelessly, so as to look as if it had dropped into the pot by accident; left it there, and put on a clean shirt. After breakfast my mother, who usually helped to make my bed and her own as well, called out to me; up I went with my heart in my mouth, to hear her say she hoped I would be a little more careful and remember that we had no longer my poor father's purse. "Look," she said, "a disgraceful state you left your shirt in, I am ashamed to have it sent to the laundress, have been obliged to tell the housemaid to partly wash it first, you are getting very careless." Charlotte afterwards told me that, when mother gave her the shirt to rough wash, she felt as if she should faint.

I need not repeat about my prepuce, which as said I could now pull down with a little less difficulty. Lacerated and painful over night, it was much more swollen and sore the next morning, when I pissed it smarted, the thinking and smarting made me randy: risking all, whilst my mother was actually in the adjoining room, the poor girl in horrid fear and looking shockingly ill, I thrust my hand up her clothes and on to her split. She whispered, "What a wretch you are!" I went to college, came back at three o'clock, thinking always on the same subject; my prick got worse, I took it into my head, that Charlotte had given me some disease, and was in a dreadful state of mind. I washed it with warm water and greased it, having eased it thus a little, got the skin down, then could not get it back again; it got stiff; as it did so, sexual pleasures came into my mind, and worse got the pain. I greased it more, my pain grew less, I touched the tip with my greasy finger, it gave a throb of pleasure, I went on without meaning, almost without knowing, the pleasure came, and spunk shot out. I had frigged myself unintentionally again.

I watched my penis shrink, its tension lessen, its high colour go, then came the feeling of disgust at myself that I have always felt after frigging, a disgust not quite absent even when done by the little hands of fair friends, to whose quims I was paying similar delicate attentions. I was able to pull up the skin again, but the soreness got worse, I told the poor girl that my prick was very sore, and that I thought it strange. It did not wound her feelings, for she did not know my suspicions. The next morning being no better, I with much hesitation told a college friend, he looked at my prick, and thought it either clap or pox. Frightened to go to our own doctor, I at his advice went to a chemist, who did a little business in such matters; we dealt there, but my friend assured me that the man never opened his mouth to any one, if youths consulted him, and many he knew had.

With quaking I said to the chemist, that I had something the matter with my thing. "What?" said he. "I don't know." "Let me see it." I began to beg him not to mention it to my mother, or anyone. "Don't waste my time," said he, "show it to me, if you want my advice." Out I pulled it as small as could be, but still with the skin over it. "Have you been with a woman?" said he. "Yes." He looked at my shirt, there was no discharge, then he laid hold of my prick with both hands, and with force pulled the skin right down, I howled. He told me there was nothing the matter with me, that the skin was too tight, that a snip would set me to rights, and advised me soon to have it done, saying, "It will save you trouble and money if you do, and add to your pleasure." I declined. "Another day, then." "No." He laughed and said, "Well, time will cure you, if you go on as you have begun," gave me a lotion, and in three days I was pretty right; warm water I expect would have had the same effect. I had simply torn the skin in taking the virginity.

Of course I wanted Charlotte again, she seemed in no way to help me, and used to cry, still there was a wonderful difference between then and before the happy consummation: she tried to prevent my hands going up her petticoats, but, once up, objection ceased, and my hands would rove about on the outside and inside of all, we stood and kissed at every opportunity. "When shall we do it again?" She replied, "Never!" for she was sure it would bring punishment on us both.

I neglected my studies absolutely; all I thought about was her, and how to get at her, it must have been a week or more before I did. Ready for any risk, that day my mother was out, I came home, had the early dinner; the cook after that always went up to dress, or, as she said, clean herself, and there she always was an hour. Waiting till I heard her go up, I went into the garden parlour, where as usual Charlotte was with my little brother. Going at her directly, I was refused, but now how different, once she would not rest until my hand was altogether away from her. Now I begged and besought her, with my hand up her clothes, my fingers on her quim. No — if we had not been found out, we were fortunate, but never, never, would she do it again; was I mad, did I wish to ruin her, was not the cook upstairs, might she not come down, whilst we did it? How light the room was, the sun was coming in. I dropped the blinds, her resistance grew less, as her cunt felt my twiddling. "No — now no — oh, what a plague you are; hush! it is the cook." I open the door, listen, there is no one stirring. "What will she think if she finds you here?" "What does it matter? Now do — let me, — I'll bolt the door, if she comes I will get under the sofa, you say you don't know how it got bolted." Such was my innocent device, but it sufficed, for both were hot in lust. I bolt it. My prick is out, I pull her reluctant hand on to it, my hands are groping now, but too impatient for dallying, I push her down on the sofa — that dear cunt. "Don't hurt me so much again, oh, don't push so hard." Oh! what delight! in a minute we are spending, together this time.

I unlock the door, go back to the dining-room, she strolls out into the garden, cook speaks to her out of the window. "Where is master Wattie?" "In the dining-room, I suppose." Soon out I stroll into the garden, play with Tommy of course, she can scarcely look me in the face, she is blushing like a rose. "Was it not lovely, Charlotte, is not your thing wet?" In she rushes with Tom, soon I follow, cook is still upstairs. "Come, be quick." Again the bolt, again we fuck, she walks off into the garden with Tommy, her cunt full, and cook and she chat from the window. How we laughed about it afterwards.

Modesty retired after this, we gave way to our inclinations, she refusing but always letting me if we got a chance! We were still green and timid, at the end of three weeks we had only had done it a dozen times or so, always with the cook in the house, always with fear. I was longing for complete enjoyment of all my senses, had never yet seen her cunt, except for a minute at a time, was mad for "the naked limb entwined with limb," and all I had read of in amatory poetry. I had gained years in boldness and manhood, and, although nervous, began to practice what I had heard.

I heard of accommodation houses, where people could have bed-rooms and no questions were asked; and found one not far from my aunt's, although she lived in the best quarter of London. Just before Charlotte's day out, I went to my aunt, complained of my mother's meanness, and she gave me a sovereign. On my way home, I loitered a full hour in the street with the baudy house, marked it so as to know it in the day, and saw couples go in, as my knowing friend who had told said I should. The next day, instead of going to college and risking discovery, I waited till Charlotte joined me, took a hackney coach to the street, and, telling Charlotte it was a tavern, walked to the door with her; to my astonishment it was closed. Disconcerted, I nearly turned back, but rang the bell. Charlotte said she would not go in. The door opened, a woman said, "Why did you not push the door?" Oh! the shame I felt as I went into that baudy house with Charlotte; the woman seemed to hesitate, or so I fancied, before she gave us a room.

It was a gentleman's house, although the room cost but five shillings: red curtains, looking-glasses, wax lights, clean linen, a huge chair, a large bed, and a cheval-glass, large enough for the biggest couple to be reflected in, were all there. I examined all with the greatest curiosity, but my curiosity was greater for other things; of all the delicious, voluptuous recollections, that day stands among the brightest; for the first time in my life I saw all a woman's charms, and exposed my own manhood to one; both of us knew but little of the opposite sex. With difficulty I got her to undress to her chemise, then with but my shirt on, how I revelled in her nakedness, feeling from her neck to her ankles, lingering with my fingers in every crack and cranny of her body; from

[79]

armpits to cunt, all was new to me. With what fierce eyes, after modest struggles, and objections to prevent, and I had forced open her reluctant thighs, did I gloat on her cunt; wondering at its hairy outer covering and lips, its red inner flaps, at the hole so closed up, and so much lower down and hidden than I thought it to be; soon, at its look and feel, impatience got the better of me; hurriedly I covered it with my body and shed my sperm in it. Then with what curiosity I paddled my fingers in it afterwards, again to stiffen, thrust, wriggle, and spend. All this I recollect as if it occurred but yesterday, I shall recollect it to the last day of my life, for it was a honey-moon of novelty; years afterwards I often thought of it when fucking other women.

We fell asleep, and must have been in the room some hours, when we awakened about three o'clock. We had eaten nothing that day, and both were hungry, she objected to wash before me, or to piddle; how charming it was to overcome that needless modesty, what a treat to me to see that simple operation. We dressed and left, went to a quietish public-house, and had some simple food and beer, which set me up, I was ready to do all over again, and so was she. We went back to the house and again to bed; the woman smiled when she saw us; the feeling, looking, titillating, baudy inciting, and kissing recommenced. With what pleasure she felt and handled my prick, nor did she make objection to my investigations into her privates, though saying she would not let me. Her thighs opened, showing the red-lipped, hairy slit; I kissed it, she kissed my cock, nature taught us both what to do. Again we fucked, I found it a longish operation, and when I tried later again, was surprised to find that it would not stiffen for more than a minute, and an insertion failed. I found out that day that there were limits to my powers. Both tired out, our day's pleasure over, we rose and took a hackney coach towards home. I went in first, she a quarter of an hour afterwards, and everything passed off as I could have wished.

From that day, lust seized us both; we laid our plans to have each other frequently, but it was difficult: my mother was mostly at home, the cook nearly always at home if mother was out; but quite twice a week we managed to copulate, and sometimes oftener. We arranged signals. If, when she opened the door, she gave a shake of her head, I knew mother was in; if she smiled and pointed down with her finger, mother was out, but cook downstairs; if it pointed up, cook was upstairs; in the latter case, to go into the garden parlour and fuck was done off hand. If cook was known to be going out, Charlotte told me beforehand, and if mother was to be out, I got home, letting college and tutors go to the devil. Then there was lip kissing, cunt kissing, feeling and looking, tickling and rubbing each other's articles, all the preliminary delights of copulation, and but one danger in the way: my little brother could talk in a broken way; we used to give him some favorite toy and put him on the floor, whilst we indulged voluptuously. On the sofa one day, I had just spent in her when I felt a little hand tickling between our bellies, and Tommy, who had tottered up to us, said, "Don't hurt Lotty, der's a good Wattie." We settled that Tom was too young to notice or recollect what he saw, but I now think differently.

Winter was coming on, she used to be sent to a circulating library to fetch books, the shop was some distance off; a few houses, long garden-walls, and hedges were on the road. I used to keep out, or go out just before she went, and we fucked up against the walls. I took to going to church in the evening also, to the intense delight of my mother, but it was to fuck on the road home. One day, hot in lust, we fucked standing on the lobby near my bed-room, my mother being in the room below, the cook in the kitchen. We got bold, reckless, and whenever we met alone, if only for an instant, we felt each other's genitals.

At last we found the servant's privy one of the best places. I have described its situation near to a flight of steps, at the end of a covered passage which could be seen from one point only in the garden; down there, anyone standing was out of sight. If all was clear, I used to ring the parlour bell, ask for something, and make a sign; when she thought it safe, there she would go, I into the garden, to where I could see into the passage by the side of the garden stairs. If I saw her, or heard "ahem," down I went into the privy and was up her cunt in a second, standing against the wall and shoving to get our spend over, as if my life depended on it; this was uncomfortable, but it had its charm. We left off doing it in the privy, being nearly caught one day there.

We thought cook was upstairs, mother was out, I was fucking her, when the cook knocked saying, "Make haste, Charlotte, I want to come." We had just spent, she was so frightened I thought she was fainting, but she managed to say "I cannot." "Do," said cook, "I am ill." "So am I," said

Charlotte. Said cook, "I can sit on the little seat." "Go to misses' closet, she's out." Off cook went, out we came, and never fucked in that place again; one day I did her on the kitchen table, and several times on the dining-room table.

We in fact did it everywhere else, and often enough for my health, for I was young, weak, and growing, and it was the same with her. The risks we ran were awful, but we loved each other with all our souls. Both young, both new at the work, both liking it, it was rarely we got more than just time to get our fucking over and clothes arranged before we had to separate, for her to get to her duties. Many times I have seen her about the house, cunt full and with the heightened colour and brilliant eyes of a woman who had just been satisfied. I used to feel pleasure in knowing she was bringing in the dinner, or tea, with my spunk in her cunt; not having had the opportunity to wash or piddle it out.

When she had another holiday, we went to the baudy house, and stayed so long in it that we had a scare; just asleep, we heard a knocking at the door. My first idea was that my mother had found me out, and, although I ruled her in one way, I was in great subjection to her, from not having any money. She thought her father was after her. What a relief it was to hear a voice say: "Shall you be long, sir, we want the room?" I was having too much accommodation for my money. That night we walked home, for I had no money for a coach, and barely enough to get us a glass of beer and a biscuit; we were famished and fucked out; my mother had refused to give me money, and another aunt whom I had asked said I was asking too often, and refused also.

Although we went to this baudy house, I always felt as if I was going to be hanged when I did, and it was with difficulty I could make her go: she called it a bad house, and it cost money. Something then occurred which helped me, penniless as I was.

At the extreme end of our village were a few little houses; one stood with its side entrance up a road only partially formed, and without thoroughfare; its owner was a pew-opener, her daughter a dressmaker, who worked for servants and such like; they cut out things for servants, who in those days largely made their own dresses. Charlotte had things made there. At a fair held every year near us, of which I shall have to tell more, my fast friend, who had put me up to so much and who, I forgot to say, tried to get hold of Charlotte, I saw with the dressmaker's daughter. Said he, talking to me next day, "She is jolly ugly, but she's good enough for a feel. I felt her cunt last night and think she has been fucked (he thought that of every girl); her mother's a rum old gal too, she will let you meet a girl at her cottage, not whores, you know, but if they are respectable." "Is it a baudy house?" I asked. "Oh, no, it's quite respectable, but if you walk in with a lady, she leaves you in the room together, and, when you come out, if you just give her half a crown, she drops a curtsy, just as she does when she opens the pew-doors and anyone gives her six pence, but she is quite respectable — the clergyman goes to see her sometimes."

Charlotte asked to go out to a dressmaker, I met her as if by chance at the door, the old pew-opener asked if I would like to walk in and wait. I did. Charlotte came in after she had arranged about her dress. There was a sofa in the room, and she was soon on it; we left together, I gave two or three shillings (money went much further then), and the pew-opener said, "You can always wait here when your young lady comes to see my daughter."

When we went a second time, she asked me if I went to St. Mary's Chapel (her chapel). We went to her house in the day that time. When we were going away, she said, "Perhaps you won't mind always going out first, for neighbours are so ill-natured." The old woman was really a pew-opener, her daughter really a dressmaker, but she was glad to earn a few shillings by letting her house be used for assignations of a quiet sort; she would not have let gay women in, from what I heard. She had lived for years in the parish and was thought respectable. She had not much use of her house in that way, wealthy people going to town for their frolics, — town only being an hour's journey — and no gay women being in the village that I knew of.

At this house, I spent Charlotte's third holiday with her, in a comfortable bed-room. We stopped from eleven in the morning, till nine at night, having mutton chops and ale, and being as jolly as we could be. We did nothing the whole day long but look at each other's privates, kiss, fuck, and sleep outside the bed. It was there she expressed curiosity about male emissions. I told her how the sperm spurted out, then discussing women's, she told me of the pleasure I had given her when fingering her in the manner described already; we completed our explanations by my frigging myself to show her, and then my doing the same to her with my finger. I bungled at that, and think I hear her now saying, "No, just

[*83*]

where you were is nicest." "Does it give you pleasure?"
"Oh, yes, but I don't like it that way, oh! — oh! — I am
doing it — oh!" I had no money that day, Charlotte had her
wages, and paid for everything, giving me her money to do
so.

One day we laughed at having nearly been caught fucking
in the privy. "She must have a big bum, must Mary," said I,
"to sit on that little seat at the privy," Said Charlotte, "She
is a big woman, twice as big as me, her bottom would cover
the whole seat." This set us talking about the cook, and as
what I then heard affected me much at a future day, I will
tell all Charlotte said, as nearly as I can recollect.

"Of course I have seen her naked bit by bit — when two
women are together they can't help it, why should they
mind — if you sit down to pee, you show your legs, and if
you put on your stockings you show your thighs, then we
both wash down to our waists, and if you slip off your chemise or night-gown you show yourself all over. Mary's
beautiful from head to foot; one morning in the summer, we
sleeping in the same bed, were very hot. I got out to pee, we
had kicked all the clothes off, Mary was laying on her back
with night-clothes above her waist fast asleep, I could not
help looking at her thighs, which were so large and white —
white as snow." "Had she much hair on her cunt?" said I.
"What's that to you?" said she, laughing, but went on: "Oh!
twice as much as I have, and of a light brown." "I suppose
her cunt is bigger than yours?" said I reflectively. "Well,
perhaps it is," said Charlotte, "she is a much bigger woman
than me, what do you think?" I inclined to the opinion it
must be, but had no experience to guide me; on the whole
we agreed that it was likely to be bigger.

"Then," said she, "I suppose some men have smaller
things than yours?" I told her that as far as I knew they varied slightly, but only had knowledge of youthful pricks, and
could not be certain whether they varied much when full
grown or not. We went on about Mary. "I know I should like
to be such a big, fine woman." "But," said I, "I don't like
light hair, I like dark hair on a cunt, light hair can't look
well, I should think." "I like her," said Charlotte, "she is a
nice woman, but often dull, she has no relatives in London,
never says anything about them or herself, she used to have
letters, and then often cried; she has none now; the other
night she took me in her arms, gave me a squeeze and said,
'Oh! if you were a nice young man now,' then laughed and

[84]

said, 'perhaps we would put our things together and make babies.' I was frightened to say anything, for fear she should find out I knew too much; I think she has been crossed in love."

I was twiddling Charlotte's quim, as I was never tired of doing, something in the sensation I suppose reminded her, for, laughing, she went on: "You know what you did to me the other night?" "What?" said I, not recollecting. "You know, with your finger." "Oh! frig." "Yes, well, Mary does that; I was awake one night, and was quite quiet, when I heard Mary breathing hard, and felt her elbow go jog, jog, just touching my side, then she gave a sigh, and all was quiet. I went to sleep, and have only just thought of it." She had heard or felt this jog from the cook before, so we both concluded that she frigged herself; Charlotte knew what frigging was.

"Do you recollect your mamma's birthday?" said Charlotte. "She sent us down a bottle of sherry, the gardener was to have some, but did not; so we were both a little fuddled when we went to bed. When Mary was undressed she pulled up her clothes to her hips, and looking at herself said, 'My legs are twice as big as yours.' Then we made a bet on it and measured; she lost, but her thigh was half as big again round as mine; then she threw herself on her back and cocked up her legs, opening them for a minute. I said 'Lord, Mary, what ever are you doing?' 'Ah!' said she, 'women's legs were made to open,' and there it ended. I never heard her before say or do anything improper, she is most particular." If Charlotte had been older or wiser, she would have not extolled the naked beauties of a fellow servant to her lover, for the description of the big bum, white thighs, and hairy belly bottom, the jog, jog of the elbow, and all the other particulars, sank deep into my mind.

We fucked more than ever, recklessly — it is a wonder we were not found out, for one evening, it being dark, I fucked her in the forecourt, outside our street-door; but troubles were coming.

Her father wrote to know why she had not been home at her holidays, she got an extra holiday to go and pacify him; then we had a fright because her courses stopped, but they came on all right again. One of my sisters came home and diminished our opportunities; still we managed to fuck somehow, most of the time they were uprighters. The next holiday she went home by coach (the only way), I met her on the return, and we fucked up against the garden wall of our house. A month slipped away, again we spent her holiday at the pew-opener's; no man and woman could have liked each other more, or more enjoyed each other's bodies, without thinking of the rest of the world. I disguised nothing from her, she told me all she knew of herself, the liking she took for me, her pleasure yet fear and shame when first I felt her cunt, the shock of delight and confusion when, on my twiddling it, she had spent; how she made up her mind to run out of the house when the milkman came, the hysterical faint when I first laid my prick between her slit and spent, the sensation of relief when I had not done, as instinct told her I should, in spending outside, the sort of feeling of "poor fellow, he wants me, he may do as he likes," which she had; I told my sensations. All these we told each other, over and over again, and never tired of the conversation; we were an innocent, reckless, randy couple.

We had satisfied our lusts in simple variety, but I never put my tongue in her mouth, nor do I know that I had heard of that form of lovemaking — but more of that hereafter. I did her on her belly, and something incited me to do it to her dog fashion, but it was never repeated; we examined as said each other's appendages, but once satisfied, having seen mine get from flaccid to stiff, the piddle issue, the spunk squirt, she never wanted to see it again, and could not understand my insatiable curiosity about hers. She knew, I think, less than most girls of her age about the males, having never, I recollect, nursed male children, and I don't think she had brothers.

How is it that scarcely any woman will let you willingly look at her cunt after fucking, till it is washed? Most say it is beastly, gay or quiet; it is the same. Is it more beastly to have it spurted up, to turn and go to sleep with the spunk oozing on to a thigh, or an hour afterwards to let a man paddle in what has not dried? They don't mind that, but won't let you look at it after your operations, willingly — why?

A modest girl lays quietly after fucking, and does not wash till you are away. A young girl who has let you see her cunt and take her virginity, won't wash it at all until you point out the necessity. A gay woman often tries to shove back her bum just as you spend, gets the discharge near the outlet, uncunts you quickly, and at once washes and pisses at the same time. A quiet young girl wipes her cunt on the outside only. A working man's wife does the same. I have fucked several, and not one washed before me. I incline to the opinion that poor women rarely wash their cunts inside, their piddle does all the washing. "What's the good of washing it?" said a poor but not a gay girl to me, "it's always clean and feels just the same an hour afterwards, whether washed or not." Is the unwashed cunt less healthy than one often soaped and syringed? I doubt it. An old roué said to me he would not give a damn to fuck a cunt at night which has been washed since the morning.

About sexual matters each of us knew about as much as the other, and we had much to learn. A girl, however, in the sphere of life of Charlotte, usually knows more about a man's sex than a youth of the same age does of a woman's; they have nursed children and know what a cock is; a girl is never thought too young to nurse a male child, no one would trust a boy after ten years of age to nurse a female child; but she had never nursed. From Charlotte I had my first knowledge of menstruation and of other mysteries of her sex. Ah! that menstruation was a wonder to me, it was marvelous, but all was really a wonder to me then.

After Christmas, my sister went back to school, our chances seemed improving, we spent another holiday at the pew-opener's. I had got money and we were indiscreet enough to go to see some wax-works. Next day her father came to see her; he ordered her to tell where she had been. She refused, he got angry, and made such a noise that mother rang to know what it was. He asked to see her, apologized, and said his daughter had been out several holidays without his knowing where she had been. My mother said it was very improper, and that he ought. A friend was with us in the room, and I sat there reading and trembling. My mother remarked to the lady, "I hope that girl is not going wrong, she is very good looking." Mother asked me to go out of the room, then had Charlotte up, and lectured her; afterwards Charlotte told me, for the first time, that her father was annoyed because she would not marry a young man.

A young man had called at our house several times to see her; she saw him once and evaded doing so afterwards. He was the son of a well-to-do baker a few miles from Charlotte's home, and wished to marry her; his father was not expected to live, and the young man said he would marry her directly the father died. Her mother was mad at her refusing such a chance. Charlotte showed me his letters, which then came, and we arranged together the replies.

She went home, and came back with eyes swollen with crying; some one had written anonymously to say she had been seen at the wax-works with a young man, evidently of position above her, and had been seen walking with a young man. The mother threatened to have a doctor examine her to see if she had been doing anything wrong; no one seemed to have suspected me; her father would have her home, her mother had had suspicion of her for some time, "The sooner you marry young Brown the better, he will have a good business and keeps a horse and chaise, you will never have such a chance again, and it will prevent you going wrong, even if you have not already gone wrong," said her mother.

It was a rainy night, I had met her on her return, and we both stood an hour under an umbrella, talking and crying, she saying, "I knew I should be ruined; if I marry he will find me out, if I don't they will lead me such a life; oh! what shall I do!" We fucked twice in the rain against a wall, putting down the umbrella to do it. Afterwards we met at the dressmaker's, talked over our misery, and cried, and fucked, and cried again. Then it was nothing but worry, she crying at her future, I wondering if I should be found out; still, with all our misery, we never failed to fuck if there was a clear five minutes before us. Then her mother wrote to say that old Brown was dead, and her father meant to take her away directly; she refused, the father came, saw my mother, and settled the affair by taking back Charlotte's box of clothes. I had not a farthing; at her age a father had absolute control, and nothing short of running away would have been of use. We talked of drowning ourselves, or of her taking work in the fields. I projected things equally absurd for myself. I tended in her agreeing to go home, — she could not help that, — but refusing to marry.

Charlotte wrote me almost directly after her return. My mother had reserved the right of opening my letters, although she had ceased to do so. That morning seeing she had one addressed to me, in fear I snatched it out of her hand. She insisted on having it back, I refused, and we had a row. "How dare you, sir, give it me." "I won't, you shan't open my letter." "I will, a boy like you!" "I am not a boy, I am a man, if you ever open a letter of mine, I will go for a common soldier, instead of being an officer." "I will tell your guardian." "I mean to tell him how shamefully short of money I am; Uncle *** says it's a shame, so does aunt." My mother sank down in tears; it was my first rebellion; she

[88]

spoke to my guardian, never touched my letters again, and gave me five times the money I used to have; but, to make sure, I had letters enclosed to a friend, and fetched them.

Charlotte was not allowed to go out alone and was harassed in every way; for all that, I managed to meet her at a local school, one Saturday afternoon when it was empty; some friendly teacher let her in, and she let me in. We fucked on a hard form, in a nearly dark room, about the most difficult poke I ever had, it was a ridiculous posture. But our meeting was full of tears, despondency, and dread of being with child. She told me I had ruined her, even fucking did not cheer her. A week or so afterwards, having no money, I walked all the way to try to see her, and failed. Afterwards, in her letters, she begged me never to tell anyone about what had passed between us. Her father sent her away to his brother's, where she was to help as a servant; for somehow he had got wind that she had met some one at the school-house. There she fell ill and was sent home again. Then she wrote that she should marry, or have no peace, wished I was older, and then she could marry me; she did not write much common sense, although it did not strike me so then. She was coming to London to buy things, would say she would call on my mother on the road, but would meet me instead. How she humbugged the young woman who came to town with her, I don't know, but we met at the baudy house, cried nearly the whole time, but fucked for all that till my cock would stand no longer; then, vowing to see each other after she was married, we parted.

She married soon, my mother told me of it; she lived twelve miles from us, and did not write to me. I went there one day, but, although I lingered long near their shop, I never saw her. I did that a second time, she saw me looking in, and staggered into a back room. I dared not go in for fear of injuring her. Afterwards came a letter not signed, breathing love, but praying me not to injure her, as might be if I was seen near her house. Money, distance, time was all against me; I felt all was over, took to frigging, which, added to my vexation, made me ill. What the doctor thought I don't know; he said I was suffering from nervous exhaustion, asked my mother if I was steady and kept good hours. My mother said I was the quietest and best of sons, as innocent as a child, and that I was suffering from severe study — she had long thought I should; the fact being that for four months I had scarcely looked at a book, excepting when she was near me, and had, when not thinking of Charlotte, spent my time in writing baudy words and sketching cunts and pricks with pen and ink.

Thus I lost my virginity, and took one; thus ended my first love or lust; which will you call it? I call it love, for I was fond of the girl, and she of me. Some might call it a seduction, but thinking of it after this lapse of years, I do not. It was only the natural result of two people being thrown together, both young, full of hot blood, and eager to gratify their sexual curiosity; there was no blame to either, we were made to do it, and did but illustrate the truth of the old song, "Cock and cunt will come together, check them as you may," and point to the wisdom of never leaving a young male and female alone together, if they were not wanted to copulate.

In all respects we were as much like man and wife as circumstances would let us be. We poked and poked, whenever we got a chance; we divided our money, if I had none, she spent her wages; when I had it, I paid for her boots and clothes — a present in the usual sense of the term I never gave her; our sexual pleasures were of the simplest, the old fashioned way was what we followed, and altogether it was a natural, virtuous, wholesome, connexion, but the world will not agree with me on that point.

One thing strikes me as remarkable now: the audacity with which I went to a baudy house; all the rest seems to have begun and followed as naturally as possible. What a lovely recollection it is! nothing in my career since is so lovely as our life then was; scarce a trace of what may be called lasciviousness was in it; had the priest blest it by the bands of matrimony, it would have been called the chaste pleasure of love and affection — as the priest had nothing to do with it, it will be called, I suppose, beastly immorality. I have often wondered if her husband found out that she was not a virgin, and, if not, whether it was owing to some skill of hers, or to his ignorance? I heard afterwards that they lived happily.

CHAPTER VI

At the Manor house. — Fred's amours. — Sarah and Mary. — What drink and money does. — My second virgin. — My first whore. — Double fucking. — Gamahuching. — Minette.

One aunt as said lived in H***shire, a widow; her son, my cousin Fred, was preparing for the Army. I wanted a change and went by advice to stay there. Fred was a year older than me, wild and baudy to the day of his death, he talked from boyhood incessantly about women. I had not seen him for some time, and he told me of his amours, asking me about mine. I let him know all, without disclosing names; he told me in nearly the words that it was "a lie," for he had heard my mother say that I was the steadiest young fellow possible, and she could trust me anywhere. This, coupled with my quiet look and the care I took not to divulge names, made him disbelieve me; but I disclosed so many facts about women's nature that he was somewhat astonished. He told me what he had done, about having had the clap, and what to do if I got it; then he had seduced a cottager's daughter on the estate; but his description of the taking did not accord with my limited experience. One day he pointed the girl out to me at the cottage door, and said he now had her whenever he wanted.

She was a great coarse wench, whom he had seen in my aunt's fields. He had caught her piddling on one side of a hedge; she saw him looking at the operation from a ditch, and abused him roundly for it; it ended in an acquaintance, and his taking her virginity one evening on a hay-cock, — that was his account of it.

Her father was a labourer on my aunt's estate, the girl lived with him and a younger sister, her name was Sarah; he expatiated on her charms from backside to bubbies, but it was soon evident to me that with this woman it was no money, no cunt; for he borrowed money of me to give her. I had squeezed money out of my aunt, my guardian, and mother, and had about ten pounds, — a very large sum for me then, — so I lent him a few shillings.

He had his shove, as he called it, and triumphantly gave me again such account of his operations and the charms of the lady that I, who had been some time without poking, wondered if the girl would let me; arguing to myself, he gives her money — my girls never wanted money, — why should his? He had been dinning into my ears that all women would let men for money, or presents, or else from lust. "Kiss and grope, and if they don't cry out, show them your prick and go at them." These maxims much impressed me.

"Fred," said my aunt at breakfast, "ride over to Brown about his rent, you will be sure to find him at the corn market," and she gave him other commissions at the market town. I promised to ride with him, but had been tortured with randiness about this great wench of his; so made some excuse and, as soon as he was well off, sauntered towards the cottage, which was about half a mile from the Hall.

It was one of a pair in a lane. Scarcely anyone passed them, excepting people on my aunt's lands. One was empty. The girl was sweeping in front of the cottage, the door was wide open. I gave her a nod, she dropped a respectful curtsey. Looking round and seeing no one, I said, "May I come in and rest, for it is hot and I am tired?" "Yes, sir," said she, and in I went, she giving me a chair; then she finished her sweeping. Meanwhile I had determined to try it on. "Father at home?" "No, sir, he be working in the seven-acre field." "Where is your sister?" "At mill, sir," — meaning a paper mill. I thought of Fred. It was my first offer, and I scarcely knew how to make it, but, chucking her under the chin, said, "I wish you would let me — " "What, sir?" "Do it to you," said I boldly, "and I will give you five shillings," producing the money; I knew it was what Fred gave her usually.

She looked at me and the five shillings, which was then more than her wages for a week's work in the fields, burst into laughter and said, "Why, who would ha' thought a gentleman from the Hall would say that to a poor girl like me." "Let me do it," said I hurriedly, "if you won't I must go — I will give you seven and six pence." "You won't tell the young squire?" said she — meaning Fred. "Of course not." She went to the door, looked both ways, then at the clock, shut the door, and bolted it without another word.

The house consisted of a kitchen, a bed-room leading out of it, and a wash-house. She opened the bed-room door, there were two beds which almost filled the room; at the foot of one was a window, by its side a wash-stand. She got on to the largest bed saying, "Make haste." I pulled up her clothes to her navel and looked. "Oh! make haste," said she. But I could not, it was the third cunt I had seen, and I paused to contemplate her. Before me lay a pair of thick, round thighs, a large belly, and a cunt covered with thick brown hair, a dirty chemise round her waist, coarse woollen blue stockings darned with black, and, tied below the knees with list, thick hob-nailed boots. The bed beneath was white and clean, which made her things look dirtier; it was different to what I had been accustomed to. I looked too long, "Better make haste, for father will be home to dinner," said she.

I put my hand to her cunt, she opened her thighs, and I saw the cleft, with a pair of lips on each side like sausages, a dark vermillion strong clitoris sloped down and hid itself between the lips, in the recesses of the cock-trap; the strong light from the window enabled me to see it as plainly as if under a microscope. I pushed my finger up, then my cock knocked against my belly, asking to take the place of my finger, and so up I let it go. No sooner was I lodged in her, than arse, cunt, thighs and belly, all worked energetically, and in a minute I spent. Just as I pulled out, her cunt closed round my prick with a strong muscular action, as if it did not wish the pipe withdrawn, a movement of the muscles of the cunt alone, and it drew the last drop of lingering sperm out of me.

I got on my knees, contemplating the sausage lips half open, from which my sperm was oozing, and then got off sorry it had been so quick a business. She laid without moving and looking kindly at me said, "Ye may ha me again an yer loike." "But your father will be home?" "In half an hour," said she. "I don't think I can," said I. Such coolness in a woman was new to me, I scarcely knew what to make of it. She got hold of my tool, I had not had a woman for some time, soon felt lust entering my rod again, and sought her cunt with my hands. She opened her legs wider in a most condescending manner, and I began feeling it. I was soon fit, which she very well knew, for immediately with a broad grin on her face she pulled me on to her and put my prick in her cunt herself, lodging it with a clever jerk of her bum, a squeeze, and a wriggle.

I fucked quietly, but it was now her turn; she heaved and wriggled so that once she threw my prick out of her, but soon had it in again. "Shove shove," said she suddenly, and I shoved with all my might, she clipped my arse so tightly that she must have left the marks of her fingers on it, then, with a close wriggle and a deep sigh, she lay still, her face as red as fire, and left me to finish by my own exertions.

I felt the same squeeze of the cunt as I withdrew, one of those delicious contractions which women of strong muscular power in their privates can give; not all can do it. Those who cannot never can understand it. Those who can will make a finger sensible of its clip, if put up their cunts.

She got up and tucked her chemise between her legs to dry her split, she did not wash it. "I am always alone," said she, "between eight and twelve just now," and as any woman just then answered my wants, I made opportunities, and I had her again two or three times, till a rare bit of luck occurred to me.

We were in the bed-room one hot day; to make it cooler I took off trowsers and drawers, laid them on a chair, carefully rolled my shirt up round my waist, so as to prevent spunk falling upon it, and thus naked from my boots to waist, laid myself on the top of my rollicking, belly-heaving, rump-wriggling country lass.

I always gave her five shillings before I began; she had taken a letch for me, or else, being hot cunted and not getting it done to her often, dearly liked my poking her; and, seeming to want it that day unusually, began her heaving and wriggling energetically. We were well on towards our spend, when with a loud cry of "Oh! my God!" she pushed me off and wriggled to the bed-side. I got off and saw a sturdy country girl of about fifteen or sixteen years standing in the bed-room door, looking at us with a broad grin, mixed with astonishment, upon her face.

For an instant nobody spoke. Then the girl said with a malicious grin, "Pretty goings on Sarah, if fearther knowed un — " "How dare you stand looking at me?" said Sarah. "It's my room as well as yourn," said Martha, for that was her name; and nothing further was said then. But Martha's eyes fixed on me as I sat naked up to my waist with my prick wet, rigid, red, throbbing, and all but involuntarily jerking out its sperm. I was in that state of lust, that I could have fucked anything in the shape of a cunt, and scarcely knew, in the confusion of the moment, where I was, and what it was all about. Sarah saw my state, and began pulling down my shirt. "Go out of the room," said she to her sister. "Damn it I will finish, I will fuck you," said I making a snatch at her cunt again. "Oh! for God's sake, don't, sir," said she. With a grin out went young sister Martha into the kitchen, and then Sarah began to blubber, "If she tells fearther, he will turn me out into the streets."

"Don't be a fool," said I, "why should she tell?" "Because we are bad friends." "Has she not done it?" "No, she is not sixteen." "How do you know she has not?" "Why we sleep together, and I know." "Who sleeps in the other bed?" "Fearther." "In the same room?" "Yes." "Don't you know anything against her?" "No, last haymaking I seed a young man trying to put his hands up her clothes, that's all; she has only been a woman a few months." If she tells of her, she will tell of me, I thought. It might come to my aunt's ears, Fred would know, and I should get into a scrape.

"It is a pity she has not done it," said I, "for then she would not tell." "I wish she had," she replied. One thing suggested another. "She knows all about what we were doing?" Sarah nodded. "Get her to promise not to tell, and get her to let me do it to her, and I will give you two pounds," said I, taking the money out of my purse.

It was more money than she had ever had in her life at one time, her eyes glistened; she was silent a minute as if reflecting, then said, "She has always been unkind to me, and she shan't get me turned out if I can help it." Then, after further talk, some hesitation, and asking me if I was sure I would give her the money, she said, "I'll try, let's have a jolly good drink, then I'll leave you together," and we went into the kitchen. I saw her dodge.

Martha was leaning, looking out of the window, her bum sticking out, her short petticoats showing a sturdy pair of legs; she turned round to us, it was about eleven o'clock in the day, the old man was at work far off and had taken his dinner with him that day, Sarah had told me.

"You won't tell fearther," said Sarah in a smooth tone. No reply but a grin. "If you do, I will tell him I saw young Smith's hand up your clothes." "It's a lie." "Yes, he did, and you know you have seen all he has got to show." "You are a liar," said Martha. Sarah turned to me and said, "Yes, she did, we both saw him leaking, and a dozen more chaps." "She saw their cocks?" said I. "Yes." "You took me to see them, you bitch," said Martha, bursting out in a rage. "You

[95]

did not want much taking; what did you say, and what did you do in bed that night, when we talked about it?" "You are a wicked wretch, to talk like that before a strange young man," said Martha and bounced out of the cottage.

In a short time she came in again; the eldest told me scandals she knew about her sister and made her so wild that they nearly fought. I stopped them, they made it up, and I sent off the eldest to fetch shrub, gin and peppermint; it was a good mile to the tavern in the village.

When she had gone, I told Martha I hoped she would do no mischief. She was nothing loath to let me kiss her, so there was soon acquaintance between us. She had seen me half naked, how long she had been watching I knew not, but it was certain she had seen me shoving as hard as I could between the naked thighs of her sister, and that was well calculated to make her randy and ready for the advances of a man. "Here is five shillings, don't say anything, my dear." "I won't say nothing," said she, taking the money. Then I kissed her again, and we talked on.

"How did you like him feeling you?" I asked, "was he stiff?" No reply. "Was it not nice when he got his hand on your thigh?" Still no reply. "You thought it nice when in bed, Sarah says." "Sarah tells a wicked story," she burst out. "What does she tell?" "I don't know." "I will tell you my dear; you talked about Smith's doodle and the other men's you saw pissing." "You are the gentleman from London stopping at the Hall," she replied, "so you had better go back and leave us poor girls alone," and she looked out of the window again.

"I am at the Hall," said I, putting my hand round her waist, "and like pretty girls," and I kissed her until she seemed mollified and said, "What can you want in troubling poor girls like us?" "You are as handsome as a duchess, and I want you to do the same as they do." "What is that?" said she innocently. "Fuck," said I boldly. She turned away looking very confused. "You saw me on your sister, between her thighs, that was fucking; and you saw this," at the same time pulling out my prick, "and now I am going to feel your cunt."

I put my hand up her clothes and tried to feel, but she turned round, and after a struggle half squatted on the floor to prevent me. The position was favorable, I pushed her sharply half on to her back on the floor, got my fingers on to her slit, and in a moment we were struggling on the floor, she screaming loudly as we rolled about.

She was nimble, got up, and escaped me, but by the time her sister came back I had felt her bum, pulled her clothes up, and talked enough baudiness; she had hollowed, cried, laughed, abused, and forgiven me, for I had promised her a new bonnet, and had given her more silver.

Sarah brought back the liquors; there was but one tumbler and a mug, we did with those; the weather was hot, the liquor nice, the girls drank freely. In a short time they were both frisky, it got slightly into my head; then the girls began quarrelling again and let out all about each other, the elder's object being to upset the younger one's virtue and make her lewed. I began to get awfully randy, and told Sarah I had felt her sister's cunt whilst she had been out. She laughed and said, "All right, she will have it well felt some day, she's a fool if she don't." We joked about my disappointment in the morning, I asked Sarah to give me my pleasure then. "Aye," said she, "and it is pleasure; when Martha has once tasted it, she will like it again." Martha, very much fuddled, laughed aloud, saying, "How you two do go on." Then I put my hands up Sarah's clothes. "Lord how stiff my prick is, look," and I pulled it out, Martha saying, "I won't stand this," rushed from the room. I thought she had gone, and wanted to have Sarah; but she thought of the two pounds, and, shutting Martha's mouth, "Try her," said she, "she must have it some day, she'll come in soon." When the girl did, we went on drinking. What with mixing gin, peppermint, and rum shrub, both got groggy, and Martha the worst. Then out went Sarah saying she must go to the village to buy something, and she winked at me.

She had whilst the girl was outside told me to bolt the front door, and if by any chance her father came home, which was not likely, to get out of the bedroom window, and through a hedge, which would put me out of sight in a minute. Directly she was gone I bolted the door and commenced the assault. Martha was so fuddled, that she could not much resist my feeling her bum and thighs, yet I could not get her to go and lie down; she finished the liquor, staggered, and then I felt her clitoris.

I was not too steady, but sober enough to try craft where force failed. I wanted to piss, and did, holding the pot so that she could see my cock at the door, but she would not come into the bed-room. Then I dropped a sovereign, and pretending I could not find it, asked her to help me; she staggered into the bed-room laughing a drunken laugh. The bed was near, I embraced her, said I would give her two sovereigns if she would get on the bed with me. "Two shiners?" said she. "There they are," said I laying them down. "No — no," but she kept looking at them. I put them into her hand, she clutched them saying, "No — no," and biting one of her fingers, whilst I began again titillating her clitoris, she letting me. From that moment I knew what money would do with a woman. Then I lifted her up on to the bed and lay down besides her. All her resistance was over, she was drunk.

I pulled up her clothes; she lay with eyes shut, breathing heavily, holding the gold in her hand. I pulled open her legs, with scarcely resistance, and saw a mere trifle of a hair on the cunt; the novelty so pleased me that I kissed it; then for the first time in my life I licked a cunt, the spittle from my mouth ran on to it, I pulled open the lips, it looked different from the cunts I had seen, the hole was smaller. "Surely," thought I, "she is a virgin." She seemed fast asleep, and let me do all I wanted.

In after life, I should have revelled in the enjoyment of anticipation before I had destroyed the hymen; but youth, want, liquor, drove me on, and I don't remember thinking much about the virginity, only that the cunt looked different from the three others I had known. The next instant I laid my belly on hers. "Oh! you are heavy, you smother me," said she rousing herself, "you're going to hurt me, — don't, sir, it hurts," all in a groggy tone and in one breath. I inserted a finger between the lips of her quim and tried gently to put it up, but felt an impediment. She had never been opened by man. I then put my prick carefully in the nick, and gave the gentlest possible movement (as far as I can recollect) to it.

Her cunt was wet with spittle, I well wetted my prick, grasped her round her bum, whilst I finally settled the knob of my tool against it, then, putting my other hand round her bum, grasped her as if in a vise, nestled my belly to hers, and trembling with lust, gave a lunge — another, — and another. I was entering. In another minute it would be all over with me, my sperm was moving. She gave a sharp "oh!" A few more merciless shoves, a loud cry from her, my prick was up her, and her cunt was for the first time wetted with a man's sperm; with short, quiet thrusts I fell into the dreamy pleasure, laying on the top of her.

Soon I rolled over to her side; to my astonishment she lay quite still with mouth open, snoring and holding the two sovereigns in her hand. I gently moved to look at her; her legs were wide open, her gown and chemise (all the clothing she had on) up to her navel, her cunt showed a red streak, my spunk was slowly oozing out, streaked with blood, a little was on her chemise; but I looked in vain for that sanguinary effusion which I saw on Charlotte's chemise and on my shirt when I first had her; and, from later experience, think that young girls do not bleed as much as full grown women, when they lose their virginity.

Fred went up to London next day, and I was at the cottage soon after; the girls were there, the elder grinned, the younger looked queer, and would not go to the bed-room. "Don't be a fool," said the elder, and soon we were alone together there. Half force, half entreaty got her on to the bed, I pulled up her clothes, forced open her legs, and lay for a minute with my belly to hers in all the pleasure of anticipation, then rose on my knees for a close look. My yesterday's letch seized me, I put my mouth to her cunt and licked it, than put my prick up the tight little slit and finished my enjoyment.

Afterwards when I had her she was neat and clean underneath, although with her every day's clothes on. She was frightened to put on her Sunday clothes She was a nice plump round girl, with a large bum for her size, with pretty young breasts and a fat-lipped little slit; the lining of it, instead of being a full red like Charlotte's, Mary's, and Sarah's cunts, was of a delicate pink. I suppose it was that which attracted me. Certain it is that I had never licked a cunt before, never had heard of such a thing, though "lick my arse" was a frequent and insulting invitation for boys to each other.

I saw her nearly every day for a week, and her modesty was soon broken. Sleeping in the same room with her father, accustomed to be in the fields or at a mill, such girls soon lose it; but she seemed indifferent to my embraces, and all the enjoyment was on my side. "I've not much pleasure in that," said she, "But more when you put your tongue there." I could not believe that was so in a young and healthy lass, but being always in a hurry to get my poking done lest her father came home, used to lick, put up her, spend quickly, and leave; but she soon got to rights. I licked so hard and long the next time I had her, at the side of the bed, that all at once I felt her cunt moving, her thighs closed, then relaxed, and she did not answer me. I looked up, she was laying with eyes closed and said, that what I had done was nicer than anything. I had gamahuched her till she spent.

After that she spent like other women, when I had her. I tell this exactly as I recollect it, and can't attempt to explain. She worked at a paper mill; slack work was the reason of her being at home, now she was going back to work; I feared a mill hand would get her and offered to pay her what she earned; but if she did not go to the mill her father would make her work in the fields, and she dare not let him see she had money.

Indeed the two sisters did not dare to buy the finery they wanted, because they could not say how they got the money. So back to the mill she went, it being arranged that she should stay away now and then, for me to have her. "Oh! won't she," said Sarah, "She takes to ruddling natoral, I can tell you." Sarah said she told her everything I had done to her, including the licking, and I felt quite ashamed of Sarah knowing that I was so green, as I shall tell presently.

Fred returned, and I had difficulty in getting her often. My cousins walked out in the cool of the evening, I with them; often we passed the cottage, and I made signs if I saw the girls. I sometimes then had her upright in a small shed or by a hay-stack in the dark, where the hay pricked my knuckles.

Fred was soon to join his regiment, was always borrowing money of me "for a shove," and never repaid me; but he was a liberal, good-hearted fellow; and when in after life I was without money and he kept a woman, he said, "You get a shove out of ***," meaning his woman, "she likes you, and I shan't mind, but don't tell me." I actually did fuck her, nor did he ever ask me, — but that tale will be told hereafter. Nothing till his death pleased him more than referring to our having looked at the backside of his mother and at his sisters' quims, he would roar with laughter at it. He was an extraordinary man.

One day we rode to the market-town, and, putting up our horses, strolled about. Fred said, "Let's both go and have a shove." "Where are the girls?" said I. "Oh! I know, lend me some money." "I only have ten shillings." "That is more than we shall want." We went down a lane past the Town-Hall, by white-washed little cottages, at which girls were sitting or standing at the doors making a sort of lace. "Do you

see a girl you like?" said he. "Why, they are lacemakers."
"Yes, but some of them fuck for all that; there is the one I
had with the last half-a-crown you lent me" Two girls were
standing, together; they nodded. "Let's try them," said Fred.
We went into the cottage; it was a new experience to me. He
took one girl, leaving me the other; I felt so nervous; she
laughed as Fred (who had never in his life a spark of modesty) put his hands up her companion's clothes. That girl
asked what he was going to give her, and it was settled at
half-a-crown each. Fred then went into the back-room with
his woman.

I never had had a gay woman. A fear of disease came over
me. She made no advances, and at length, feeling my quietness was ridiculous, I got my hands up her clothes, pulling
them up and looking at her legs. "Lord! I am quite clean,
sir," said she in a huff, lifting her clothes well up. That gave
me courage, I got her on to an old couch and looked at her
cunt, but my prick refused to stand; her being gay upset me.
She laid hold of my prick, but it was of no use. "What is the
matter with you?" said she, "don't you like me?" "Yes, I
do." "Have you ever had a girl?" I said I had. Fred who had
finished, bawled out, "Can't we come in?" This upset me
still more, and I gave it up. In Fred and his girl came, and
he said, "There is water in the other room." I went in and
feigned to wash myself, and hearing them all laughing, felt
ashamed to come out, thinking they were laughing about me;
though such was not the case, it was because Fred was beginning to pull about my woman.

I had more money than I had told Fred, and when he said
he was thirsty, offered to send for drink, thinking my liberality would make amends for my impotence. Gin and ale
was got; then I began to feel as if I could do it. "She's got
a coal-black cunt," said Fred, and I seemed to fancy his
woman; then he said to mine, "What colour is yours?" and
began to lift her clothes; "let's change and have them together," and we went at once into the back room, whither the
two girls had gone. One was piddling, Fred pulled her up
from the pot, shoved her against the side of the bed, bawling
out, "You get the other," and pulled out his prick stiff and
ready. An electric thrill seemed to go through me at this
sight, I pulled the other in the same position by the side of
Fred's; then the girls objected, but Fred hoisted up his girl
and plunged his prick into her. Mine got on to the bed, leaving me to pull up her clothes. The same fear came over me,

and I hesitated; Fred looked and laughed, I pulled up her clothes, saw her cunt; fear vanished, the next moment I was into her, and Fred and I, side by side, were fucking.

All four were fucking away like a mill, then we paused and looked at our pricks, as they alternately were hidden and came into sight from the cunts. Fred put out his hand to my prick, I felt his, but I was coming; my girl said, "Don't hurry." It was too late, I spent, laid my head upon her bosom, and opening my eyes, saw Fred in the short shoves. The next instant he lay his head down.

I believe now that really all four felt ashamed, for directly after we were all so quiet, one of the girls remarked, "Blest if I ever heard of such a thing afore, you Lunnon chaps are a bad lot." A long time afterwards, I again had the girl for two and sixpence; Fred was then in Canada; she recollected me well, and asked me whether gals and chaps usually did such thing together in London.

Fred and I used to examine our pricks for a few days after, to see if there were any pimples on them. Fred soon forgot his fear and shame and offered to bet me the fee of the gals that he would finish first, if we went and repeated the affair, but we did not

Martha became very curious about me and my doings with Sarah. New to fucking as she was, she got jealous at the idea of anyone sharing my cock with her. She was curious too to know about her sister's pleasures; the elder had, I think, got all she wanted to know from the younger, and had made but little return for it in information.

Then my amatory knowledge was increased by an event unlooked for, unthought of, unpremeditated; I am quite sure I had neither heard nor read of such a thing before, and should, at that period of my life, have scouted the idea as beastly and abominable, though I had done it. How I came to lick Martha's cunt even then astonished me, I thought that it was the small size, the slight hair, and youthfulness of the article; but I used to lick it very daintily, wiping my mouth, spitting frequently, and never venturing beyond the clitoris. It occurred to me one day instead of kneeling, to lay down and lick; so I laid on the bed, my head between her thighs, my cock not far from her mouth, and indulging her in the luxury; for it was much the idea of pleasing her which made me do it. She played with my cock and wriggled as my tongue played over her clitoris, then grasped my prick hard, which gave me a premonitory throb of pleasure. "Do to me what I am doin to you," said I, "put it in your mouth," scarcely knowing what I said and without any ulterior intention. She with her pleasure getting intense, impelled by curiosity, or by the fascination of the cock, or by impulse, the result of my tongue on her cunt, took it in her mouth instantly. How far my prick went in, whether she sucked, licked, or simply let it enter, I know not, and I expect she did not either; but as she spent I felt a sensation resembling the soft friction of a cunt, and instantly shot my sperm into her mouth and over her face. Up she got, calling me a beast. I was surprised and ashamed of this unlooked for termination, and said so to her.

I had as said arranged signs, as I passed the cottage, about our meetings, yet had difficulty now in getting at her without being found out, and never should, excepting for the elder sister, to whom I gave every now and then money. She took care of the house, rarely went out, but worked at a coarse sort of lace and earned money that way. She used to sit outside the cottage door if fine, working, and curtseying when we, who were called the Hall folks, passed. My aunt said one day, "What a strapping wench that is, don't you think so, Walt? you always look at her as you pass." I might have replied, "Yes, she is, and her arse is remarkably like yours," but I did not and was after that more on my guard.

CHAPTER VII

Fanny Hill. — Masturbation. — Friend Henry. — Under street-gratings at the gunmaker's. — A frigging match.

I went back to London and resumed my preparations. Penniless, I tried to get money from my mother, but could not. I tried to feel our ugly housemaid, who threatened to tell. Just then a friend lent me *Fanny Hill,* how well I recollect that day, it was a sunshiny afternoon, I devoured the book and its luscious pictures, and although I never contemplated masturbation, lost all command of myself, frigged, and spent over a picture as it lay before me. I did not know how to clean the book and the table-cover.

Fascinated although annoyed with myself, I repeated the act till not a drop of sperm would come; and the skin of my prick was sore. The next day I had a splitting headache, but read at intervals, and again frigged; and did this for a week, till my eyes were all but dropping into my head. In a fever and worn out; the doctor said I was growing too fast and ordered strong nourishment; but I used to take the infernal book with me to bed, and lay reading it, twiddling my prick, and fearing to consummate, knowing the state I was in. It was indeed almost impossible to do it, and when emission came it was accompanied by a fearful aching in my testicles.

My friend had his book back; my erotic excitement ceased, I grew stronger, felt ashamed of myself, and soon found a new excitement.

I had a friend who, like me, was intended for the Army, his father was a gun manufacturer. The eldest son died, and the old man saying that five thousand a year should not be lost to the family, made his other son — my friend — go into the business. He resisted, but had no alternative but to consent. Their dwelling-house was just by ours, but the old man now insisted on his son residing largely at the manufactory, where he invited me to stay at times with him; which I did.

Several houses adjoining belonged to the old man, at the East-End of London, where the manufactory was. Some faced an important thoroughfare, the rest faced two other streets, and at the back, a place without a thoroughfare, on one side of which was the manufactory and workmen's entrance; on the other side, stables. The whole property formed a large block.

The house faced the better street; the family had for forty years lived in it before they became rich, and it was replete with comfort. The old man had since lived there principally, for his love was in his business, and he had made all arrangements for his convenience. He had a private staircase leading from a sitting-room into the manufactory, and could go into the warehouse, or the back street, or out of the front door of the house unnoticed. The people employed never knew when to expect him. He was a regular Tartar, but for all that a kind-hearted man.

There now lived in the house an old servant with her sister, who had been many years in the family. One was married to a foreman, in whom his master had much confidence; these three were in fact in charge of the premises, although nominally the keys were given up to my friend, whom we will call Henry. The old man wished his son to be happy, allowed friends to visit him, there was good wine, put out by the old man in small quantities from time to time, good food, good attendance, and all to make things comfortable; but the old man resolutely forbade his son to be out later than eleven o'clock, and kept him, as my mother kept me, almost without money. I expect that the old servants were told to keep an eye on the doings of Henry.

The basement was used as store-room for muskets, put into wooden boxes which stood in long rows upon each other like coffins. It was a large place and originally only went under the factory, but the old gentleman gradually, as he acquired the adjacent houses, let them, but retained most of the basements, so that his stores ran not only under the premises he occupied, but largely under half a dozen other houses of which he only let the shops and upper portions. On four sides this large basement had glimpses of light let into it, by gratings in the footways of the streets.

At one end and on the principal street was a row of windows, beneath what was then a first-class linen draper's shop — first-class I mean for the East-End — a large place for those days, and always full. Women used to stand by dozens at a time, looking into the shop windows, which were of large plate-glass — a great novelty in those days — people waiting for omnibusses used also to stand up against the shop.

Henry and I were old school friends; I had seen and felt his cock, he mine; I had not been with him an hour before he said, "When the workmen go to dinner, I will show you more legs than you ever saw in your life." "Girls?" said I. "Yes, I saw up above the garters of a couple of dozen yesterday in an hour." "Could you see their cunts?" "I did not quite, but nearly of one," said he. I thought he was bragging, and was glad when twelve o'clock came.

At that hour, down we went, through the basement stored with muskets; it seemed dark as we entered, but soon we saw streams of light coming through the windows at the end; they had not been cleaned for years. We rubbed the glass and looked up. Above us was a flock of women's legs of all sizes and shapes flashing before us, thick and thin, in wonderful variety. We could see them by looking up, it being bright above; but, dark and dusty below, they could not, by looking down, see us through the half cleaned windows, or notice round clean spots on the glass, through which two pairs of young eyes almost devoured the limbs of those who stood over them.

As our only way lay through the work-shop and we did not wish it known that we were there (there was no business done there, unless arms were being stored or taken out), we went back before the workmen returned from their meals; but for several days did we go into the place, gloating over such of the women's charms as we could discern; legs we saw by the hundreds, garters and parts of the thighs we saw by scores: quite enough to make young blood randy to madness, but the shadowy mass between the thighs we could not get a glimpse of.

"There are vaults," said I, "if there, we could see right up, and be at the back of the women." We tried unused keys to find one to open the door, and at length, to our intense delight, it unclosed. We stepped across the little open space under the gratings into the empty vaults, and, there arranging to take our turns of looking up at the most likely spots, we put out our heads and took our fill at gazing. We were right under the women, who, as they looked into the shop windows, jutting out their bums in stooping, tilted their petticoats exactly over our heads. If there was no carriage passing, we could at times hear what they said, but that was rarely the case.

In those days even ladies wore no drawers Their dresses rarely came below their ankles, they wore bustles, and, standing over a grating, anyone below them, saw much more, and more easily, than they can in these days of draggling dresses and cunt-swabbing breeches, which the commonest girl wears round her rump. For all that, so close to the thighs do chemise and petticoats cling, that it was difficult to see the hairy slits, which it was our great desire to look at. Garters and thighs well above the knees we saw by scores. Every now and then, either by reason of scanty clothing or short dresses, or by a woman's stooping and opening her legs to look more easily low down at the window, we had a glimpse of the cunt; and great was our randiness and delight when we did. On the whole we were well rewarded. Many as the legs and thighs are that I have since seen, I doubt whether I have seen so many pairs of legs half-way up the thighs, and all but to the split, as I saw in the times we stood under that big linen-draper's shop window. Old and young, thin and fat, dirty and clean, ragged and neat; there was every possible variety and number of legs and their coverings.

There were two states of the weather which favoured us: if muddy, women lifted their clothes up high. Having no modern squeamishness, all they cared about was to prevent them getting muddy; and then, with the common classes, we got many a glimpse of the split. But a brilliant day was the best. Then the reflected light being strong, we could see higher up if the lady was in a favourable position. We could see if they had clouts round their cunts, and had some strange sights of which I will only tell one or two.

One day, quite at the end of the gratings, two women, neat, clean, plump, and of the poorer classes (for we could soon tell the poorer classes from their legs and underclothing), stood close together. It was my five minutes. Henry was at my back. They had been standing talking, close together, not seeming to be looking at the shop, in fact they were at the spot where the shop window finished. One put her leg up against a ledge, keeping the other on the grating; it was a bright day, and I saw the dark hair of her cunt as plainly as if she were standing to show it to me. The next minute she gathered up her clothes a little high, and squatted down on her heels as if to piddle, her bum came down within four or five inches of the grating, and I saw through the bars, her cunt open just as a woman does when she pisses. I thought she was going to do so, when a plaintive cry explained it all; she had a baby, and all the movements were to enable her to do something to it conveniently. At the same time her companion dropped on one knee, pulling her clothes a little up, and arranging them so as to prevent soiling them, she put the other leg out in front, and sat back on the heel of the kneeling leg. Then was another split, younger and lighter-haired, partly visible from below, but not so plainly as the dark-haired one; and they did something in that position for five minutes to the squalling child.

I lost all prudence, whispered to Henry; and together we stood looking, till they moved away. "My prick will burst," said I. "So will mine," said he. The next instant both our pricks were out, and, looking up at the legs, stood we two young men, frigging till two jets of spunk spurted across the area. It would have been a fine sight for the women had they looked down, but women rarely did. They stood over the gratings usually with the greatest unconcern, looking at the shop windows, or only glanced below for an instant, at the dark, uninhabitated-looking area.

This was the beginning of a new state of things. We got reckless; Henry had business to attend to, I none, — I ceased to think about what might be said of our being so much in the store-house; and used to go by myself and stay there two or three hours at a time. Then I gave way to erotic excesses. My prick would stand as I went down the stairs. I used to wait prick in hand, playing with it, looking up and longing for a poke until I saw a pair of thighs plainly, then able to stand it no longer, frigged, hating myself even whilst I did it, and longing to put my spunk in the right place. I used to catch it in one hand, whilst I frigged with the other, then fling the spunk up towards the girls' legs. It was madness; for although the feet of the women were not three feet above my head, yet the smallness of the quantity thrown (after what stuck to my fingers), and the iron bars above, seemed to make it impossible that any of it should reach its intended destination; but I think it did one day. A youngish female was stooping, and showing part of her thighs. I flung up what I had just discharged; suddenly her legs closed, she stepped quickly aside, looked down and went away. I am still under the impression that a drop of my sperm must have hit her naked legs.

We both also grew more lascivious, having frigged before each other, we took to frigging each other. I went to my home; on going back, I found he had taken other young men to see the legs. One night five of us had dinner, we smoked and drank, our talk grew baudier and baudier; we had mostly been schoolfellows, and dare say we had all seen each other's doodles, but I cannot assert that positively. We finished by showing them to each other now, betting on their length and size, and finished up by a frigging sweepstakes for him who spent first.

At a signal, five young men (none I am sure nineteen years old) seated on chairs in the middle of the room began frigging themselves, amidst noise and laughter The noise soon subsided, the voices grew quiet, then ceased, and were succeeded by convulsive breathing, sighs and long-drawn breaths, the legs of some writhed and stretched out, their backsides wriggled on the chairs, one suddenly stood up. Five hands were frigging as fast as they could, the prick-knobs standing out of a bright vermillion tint looking as if they must burst away from the hands which held them. Suddenly one cried "f — fi — fir — first," as some drops of gruelly fluid flew across the room, and the frigger sank back in the chair. At the same instant almost the other jets spurted, and all five men were directly sitting down, some with eyes closed, others with eyes wide open, all quiet and palpitating, gently frigging, squeezing, and titillating their pricks until pleasure had ceased.

Afterwards we were quiet, then came more grog, more allusion to the legs of women, their cunts and pleasures, more baudiness, more showing of pricks and ballocks, another sweepstakes, another frigging match, and then we separated.

I do not think that, excepting to Henry, that baudy evening ever was referred to by me.

I got up I recollect next day ashamed of myself, and felt worse, when he remarked, "What beasts we made ourselves last night." What changes since then. Two of the five found graves in the Crimea, the third is dead also; Henry and I alone alive. He with a big family, with sons nearly as old as he was at the time of the frigging matches I wonder if he ever thinks of them, wonder if he ever has told his wife.

CHAPTER VIII

Of age. — Camille my first French woman. —
Lascivious delights. — Harlots by the dozen. — Baudy
books. — Tribades.

I came into my property, and, to the great horror of my mother and family, soon gave up my post at the *** and my intended career, and determined to live and enjoy myself. I had been all but posted to a regiment; that commission I resigned, though all my youth desiring it. I lost much money by doing so. What I did between the time that I had the two sisters until I went regularly on the town is not worth telling of more than already done. Frig myself I did not; gay women since my last clap I was shy of, but I used to shag a servant of a family close by, and rather think one of our own servants; but if so, all circumstances made small impression on me, and nearly escaped my mind, excepting those of a comely woman of about thirty, with black curls, of a wall not far from a church and of fucking her up against it, of her being so anxious to get indoors by nine o'clock, and scuffling off with her wetted cunt directly she had finished with me. Her name, or who she was, I quite forget.

This I know, that I had no other woman at home and had no liking for gay women, nor is it to be wondered at, since my experience with them was confined to one I had with my cousin Fred, women by the road-side who would take a shilling, and others of a queer class in the confines of the Waterloo Road (two debauches there told of) then filled me with horror, and three claps; yet I was to leave off giving my passion to quiet women and bestow all my attention for a time on gay women.

Walking up Waterloo Place one evening, with plenty of money in my purse and lust in my body, I met a fine, clear-complexioned woman, full twenty-five years of age, who addressed me in French, and then in broken English. She had an eye and manner which fascinated me, her dress was quiet yet elegant, as unlike the French woman of Regent Street of the present day as a duchess is to a milkmaid; but she was the ordinary French whore of the day, of whom there were then but few in London (there was no railway to Paris), and who were exclusively supported by gentlemen at the West End. I went home with her to a house at the corner of G*l**n Square, after fearing and hesitating

As I got to the door my fear returned, and, but for shame, I would not have gone in. "I have but little money," said I, "have you not a Victoria?" said she. "No," "You will find one, I am sure." By that time the door was opened, and in I went. "You will find one Victoria," said she in broken English as she closed the room-door, "but if not, shall you not give me what you shall find." The room was nicely furnished, out of it was a nice large bed-room and a smaller one (she paid twenty shillings a week for all, as you will soon hear). Four wax candles were lighted, down she sat, so did I, and we looked at each other. I could say nothing.

"Shall I undress?" said she at length. "Yes," I replied, and she began. Never had I seen a woman take off such fine linen before, never such legs in handsome silk stockings and beautiful boots. I had had the cleanest, nicest women, but they were servants, with the dress and manners of servants. This woman seemed elegance itself compared to them. A fine pair of arms were disclosed, a big pair of breasts flashed out, a glimpse of a fine thigh was shown, and as her things dropped off, and she stooped to pick them up, with her face towards me, her laced chemise dropped, opened, and I saw darkness at the end of the vista between her two breasts.

A pull up of the stockings and garters disclosed other glimpses of the thighs and surroundings. Then she sat on the pot, pissed and looked at me, whilst I sat in fear, saying nothing, doing nothing, my cock shrivelled to the size of a gooseberry, and longing to go away. The whole affair was unlike anything I had seen or dreamed of; a quiet, business-like, yet voluptuous air was about it, which confused me; it affected my senses deliciously in one way, but all the horrors about gay women were conjured up in my imagination at the same time. I was intensely nervous.

She, seeing me so quiet, sat herself on my knee and began unbuttoning my trowsers. I declined it. "Are you ill?" said she. I told her no, scarcely knowing what she meant. Then she unbuttoned me in spite of my objection, laid hold of my little doodle, and satisfied herself that it was all right I sup-pose; for she hurt me; I could not tell why she squeezed it, for I did not know then the ways of gay women. The squeeze gave me a voluptuous sensation, although fear had still hold of me; then she kissed and fondled me, but it was useless. Then she said, "You have never had a woman be-fore, I see." My pride was wounded, and I told her I had had many. "Are always you like this with them?" she asked. "No, but I really did not want it." "Oh! yes you shall. Come to the bed." She got off my knee, went to the bed, laid down on one side, one leg on, one dropping down to the floor, drew up her chemise above her navel, and lay with beautiful, large limbs clad in stainless stockings and boots, her thighs of the slightly brown color seen in Southern women, be-tween them a wide thicket of jet-black hair, through which a carmine streak just showed. She raised one of her naked arms above her head, and under a laced chemise showed the jet-black hair in the armpit. I had never seen such a luscious sight, nor any woman put herself unasked into such a seduc-tive attitude.

"Come," she said. I obeyed and went to the side of the bed, my prick not yet standing. She took my hand and put the finger on to her clitoris, pulled my prick towards her and kissed it, and at the double touch up it rose like a horn. "Ah!" said she, moving on to the middle of the bed, "take off your clothes." I was on to her without uttering a word and had plugged her almost before I had said "no," which I had meant to say.

What a cunt! what movement! what manner! I had till then never known what a high-class, well practised professional fucker could do. How well they understand the nature and wants of the man who is up them; hers was the manner of a quiet woman, who had been some time without a prick, it was so like baudy nature in a lady that I was in the seventh Heaven. My crisis came whilst she kept murmuring, "Don't hurry"; but the wriggle and heave, and the tightening of the cunt, kept hurrying me, as well she knew.

I had scarcely finished my spend when curiosity took possession of me. She yielded in the way a French woman does to all a man wishes, almost anticipating them. The black hair under her arm-pits first came in for my admiration, then her eyes, her bubbies came in for their share, as raising myself on an elbow, my prick still up her, I looked and felt all over her, I even opened her mouth and felt her teeth, which were splendid. Then, rising on my knees, I looked between her legs, at the splendid thicket of black hair. Far from attempting to get up, or prevent me, she opened her thighs wider, I pulled aside the cunt-lips, there rolling out from a dark carmine orifice was my essence. At the sight of it, up came my prick, still dripping, and up it went into the sperm-lined passage.

My second fuck over, she washed. No sooner was that done than I wanted to see it all over again. "You are very fond of women," she said, "I thought you had never had a woman before." Then I explained, gave her the Victoria, and, scarcely daring, said (for she was dressed again), "How I should like to do it again." "You take up much time of me, but you may, if you like, at side of de bed." Out came my prick, up it went, her duff and belly in sight now, till I spent in her, and, promising to see her again, I left. One does not get silk stockings, laced chemise, four wax lights, and three fucks for a pound now, if rooms be well furnished or not.

I saw her the next day, then saw her almost daily. Little by little I took to calling at all times, and sleeping with her. The more I had her, the more I liked her. She was a very nice woman in most ways, I scarcely ever found her untidy, dirty, or slammerkin. If not dressed, she had a clean wrapper on, had nearly always silk stockings on, and a clean chemise; and therefore, call when I might, she was ready to be fucked at a minute's notice. She was a good cook, and would

[*112*]

cook omelettes and nice things in her room. I used to fuck, get out of the bed, eat, and fuck again with the food almost in my mouth. I used to have little dinners in her room, sent in by a French cook, which were excellent, and then, with stomach full and with nice wine, would spend the evening in baudy joys.

What astonished and delighted me at the same time was the freedom and the way she lent herself to all my voluptuous inclinations. The gay women I had had I had fucked as fast and got away from them as soon as I could; my spend even scarcely finished at times. With my mother's servants (my first love Charlotte excepted, and for a time with Susan), my enjoyments were mostly hurried, a fingerstink, a frig on their cunt, and a hurried look were all my amatory preliminaries for the most part; because I was too impatient for the spend, was mostly obliged to seize opportunities in a hurry, or because the girls were impatient at being pulled about. When I had tried with them some of the little amatory amusements which were beginning to suggest themselves to my voluptuous imagination, they resisted, or only half lent themselves to my will. With Susan I had tried the most, because I knew she had had a bumbasting before, and she had been more willing; she liked pulling my prick about, but even she made a fuss one night when I wanted to fuck her with her bum towards my belly, and never let me look at her belly. Thus my baudy longings had never been satisfied. With Charlotte I did a little variety, from curiosity; now I began to want it from voluptuousness. The natural impatience of my age, and my few opportunities, had led me to bring my women to the bed, throw up their clothes, pull open their legs, give a rapid glance at their thighs, belly and cunt-fringe, by which time my prick was nodding and throbbing. Then followed a grope, and the next minute I was fucking as hard as I could.

With Camille all came like new to me. She even anticipated me. If I pushed her to the side of the bed, she fell on her back and opened her legs gently, disclosing her slit in the most voluptuous manner, without speaking. If I strove to pen her thighs, open they went as wide as she could make them, leaving me to open, shut, pinch, frig, or probe her cunt, as I listed. At a hint, she with two fingers would spread open the lips to enable the fullest inspection. If I turned her round, she would fall on the bed arse upwards, like a tumbler. If I cocked up a leg, there she kept it till I pulled it down. I scarcely ever said what I wanted, she guessed my desires from the way I turned her about. It was only at a later time, when my baudiness grew whimsical and invented strange attitudes, or singular caprices of love, that I had to tell her what I wanted; but at first I was too timid for that. She once said to me, laughing, "I am a born whore, for I like it, and like to see a man amuse himself with me."

Her every movement, even when I was tranquil, was exciting. If she sat down, her limbs were in some position which by contemplation stirred my lust and made me rush to stroke her, and was gratified in any form and manner I liked. With her, all forms of copulation were wholesome and natural, so that I had enough variety.

I was constantly with her until pretty well fucked out, then I stayed away a while. When I recommenced she, I expect, thought I was weary of her and set to work to keep me, by putting into my head things I had not heard or thought of, asking if I would like to sate my lust in such and such ways; and then procuring for me what she had suggested.

I was indeed worth treating so, for though I only gave her a sovereign at first, my money quickly began to go into her pocket from mine. The more variety I had, the more I paid, which was but natural and fair.

She had a book full of the baudiest French pictures; there was not an attitude depicted in it that I did not fuck her in. That done, she asked me one day if I would like another woman to feel whilst I had her. She came, and I fucked Camille feeling the other's cunt, longing to fuck it, but fearing to propose it. Camille guessed what I wanted and proposed it herself. With what joy my prick entered the stranger's split, Camille looking on, holding her cunt open for inspection at the same time and going through the motions of frigging herself whilst I was shoving. Then came endless variety. I had two other French ladies and fingered their cunts whilst I fucked a third, then two more, laying cunt upwards, legs in the air, and arses meeting over Camille's head. At last I had six altogether at once, and spent the evening with them naked, fucking, frigging, spending up or over them, making them feel each other's cunts, shove up dildoes, and play the devil's delight with their organs of generation, as they are modestly called.

Then came other suggestions. "I know such a little girl, not above this high," she said. I ballocked that little girl. Then she knew one six feet high. She also I had. Then she knew one with an immense duff of hair on her cunt. Of course I had her. Then one with none at all; and mightily pleased was I, as my doodle rubbed in and out of that hairless cunt, the owner laying at the side of the bed, I standing up, and Camille holding a candle over the hairless quim, to enable me fully to see and enjoy the novelty, I was pushing up.

At intervals, when worn out with spending, or disinclined to find the money needed for this endless variety of women and cunt-hunting, I frequently spent evenings quietly in Camille's society. I got from her information about habits of women in a way which is not often given to young men by gay women; learned that women thrust sponges up their cunts, to prevent men finding out they had their courses on. For the first time with her, I understood that women could, and did, frig themselves; and on her own cunt, placing herself my finger there, I first knew the exact spot where a woman rubs for her solitary pleasure. She told me of women rubbing their clitorises together so as to spend, — what the French call tribadism, — and two women of her acquaintance did this. All of us half spoony with champagne after a jolly little supper; she set the two girls rubbing their cunts together. The two girls on the top of each other I thought a baudy amusement, and did not believe until after years that flat fucking was practicable, and practised, with sexual pleasure.

Then should I like to see a man? Now it was not many years since I had frigged two or three, and seen a frigging match, which did not please me, so I declined it. Yet one night she expatiated so much about the wonderful size of a young man's prick, and what a lot he spent, and how respectable he was, and what gentlemen had him, etc.; that I, who had a dislike to men being near me, consented, and a fine young Frenchman came. I could not for half-an-hour go near him, but my temptress meant I should, and I frigged one of the largest pricks I have ever seen, and saw his spunk squirt over Camille's arse, which the Frenchman requested her to turn upwards for him to spend on; indeed he said he could not make his cock stand until he saw her arse. Directly afterwards I had the most ineffable disgust at him, myself and all, and never saw him again.

I would not again be in the room with a man, but she arranged to let me see, through a hole made in the door, herself fucked by another man, which I immensely enjoyed, but had not the sight repeated. I even used to hate the idea of her being fucked by any one but myself; not that I had anything in the way of love or liking for her, which might have been termed affection.

So time went on, I paying handsomely, trying to see and do anything she suggested, and glorifying myself at being in the lucky way of doing and knowing everything. I told much to some special friends, some of whom wanted to find out my sources of such enjoyments; others thought I was a mere braggart.

Nearly a year ran away, and four thousand pounds, leaving me with infinite knowledge and a frame pretty well worn; but I never had a love ailment, nor have I ever taken one from a French woman yet.

She never suggested arse-hole work. In her book were pictures of buggering, and she asked me if I would like such a thing. I frightened at what I knew, which seemed like a horrible dream, said, "certainly not," and asked if it was possible. She told me it was, but was *"villaine,"* and the matter was never again referred to.

CHAPTER IX

Used up. — Wanting a virgin. — Camille departs. — The Major's opinion. — Camille returns. — Louise. — Louise fatigues me. — Fred on the scent. — A cigar-shop. — Three into one. — A clap. — Serious reflexions. — The sisters disappear. — Enforced chastity. — A stricture. — Health restored.

At last having done as great a variety of ballocking, and learnt more baudiness than most men of my age, I was knocked up, fucked out. My mother with whom I still nominally lived, was in despair. My guardian, alarmed at the rate I was spending my money, remonstrated, so I left Camille and her bevy of women, and went to the sea-side. There I renovated, and then spent my time on the sands, trying to see the women in the water. As I grew better my randiness returned, I got hold of gay women, but my old timidity clung to me, I used to pay them to piss, and had a grope up them; but do not recollect having anything more. I came back to London, and for two or three days afterwards Camille's cunt had no rest. Then I temporarily got into another servant, and ceased to see Camille much. She tried all sorts of inducements to continue it on the old footing.

Then although she knew every incident of my life, she took to asking if I had ever had a virgin, saying, "Are you sure, did you see her cunt before you had her? Would you not like one again, if I can get you one, a young virgin French girl, one sure to be a virgin?" — and so on until she made me doubt if I had ever had one. At last I thought that I should like to have another. Well, she could get me a young French girl, but would have to go to France, it would cost a large sum of money. This talk went on for some time, and little by little I agreed to give her fifty pounds to pay her journey, and also to keep her lodgings on. She postponed the journey for a long time, but at length she went. She made me promise to do something for the girl besides paying her, — which meant something or nothing, — but I promised to pay the journey of the virgin back to France, should she want to go; and also whenever I had the girl, to pay Camille a Victoria, "because," said she, "you will have my rooms and prevent my bringing friends home."

So I came down with fifty pounds. Off she went in quiet dress, and looked a quiet lady or middle-class woman. She advised me to keep myself steady, and the very moment before she left, whilst the cab was at the door, I turned with bonnet and travelling dress on, bum outwards, and fucked her; she hurrying me all the time for fear she should loose the coach, she had not time to piss, or wipe, or wash. "It will give me good fortune perhaps," said she, laughing, "or make you wish me back, it is lucky for me."

There was but a slow rail to Dover then, nothing but tidal boats, and to Paris, the way I thought she was going, no rail at all, and it was a long journey. Whether she went to Paris or not I don't know, but from later experience think not, that she was a Southern woman, and went straight home. She was to be back in a month. It came, but not she; another week, another, and I began to think I had been sold; another, and I gave her up altogether, and experienced a little relief, for the habit of seeing her had so got hold of me that I could not shake it off, and yet I was tired of her, but I wanted the virgin.

There was a middle-aged man with whom I chummed much at my Club, a major retired, and a most debauched individual. He borrowed money of me, and did not repay it. His freedom of talk about women made him much liked by the younger men; the older said it was discreditable to help younger men to ruin. Ordinarily very careful how I spoke about women (for my loves having lain much in my mother's house, caution had become habitual to me), I one night talked about virgins and of getting them. He said such things were done; that Harridans got a young lass, if well paid for it, but that they generally sold the girl half-a-dozen times over, "and," said he, "they train the young bitches so, there is no finding them out; you may pay for one who was first fucked by a butcher boy, and then her virginity sold to a dandy; you may pay for it, my boy, and not find out you have been done." I pondered much over this, and the next night returned to the subject. His opinion was that an old stager like him was not to be done; but that any randy young beggar would go up the girl, and flatter himself he had had a virgin, if the girl was cunning. "When you see the tight covered hole with your eye, find it tight to your little finger, and then tight to your cock my boy; when you have satisfied your eye, your finger, and your cucumber, and seen blood on it, you may be sure you have had one, — and not otherwise."

Thought I, "I am going to be humbugged." Another week, no letter, I went to her lodgings, and found she had taken away everything she had with her. That night I told a little of my hopes to the Major, not telling him who the kind lady was, or where she was gone; but it made him laugh. "You are done brown my boy, done brown; that woman will never turn up again." He joked me so that I avoided him, and kept the subject to myself afterwards.

Again to the lodgings; the landlady could not keep them vacant any longer; I paid the rent, but she got no perquisites; I increased the allowance. Then again I went; the landlady said she did not expect to see her again. I had now set my heart on having this virgin; ten weeks nearly had gone; I said if Camille was not back next week she might let the rooms. It passed; a bill was put up in the window, and the next morning calling as a forlorn hope, there was a letter for me, — she would be back in a week. I was in a state of excitement that week and kept myself chaste, with the idea of the virgin cunt, and Camille's well paced rogering in anticipation.

The day came. I was so impatient that I was there quite

early; she arrived some hours earlier than she had said, and seemed surprized at finding me; my impression is that she did not want me to be there when she came back. She came in a hackney-coach; a stoutish full-sized young woman with a funny bonnet and long cloak on, got out of the coach with her, and in a free-and-easy way helped the things upstairs. She called her Louise. The wench put down a big box, and, on my turning round after giving Camille a kiss, I saw she had seated herself on it and, hands on her knees, was looking at me. "Uncord the box," said Camille. Said the girl, "I am tired." She uncorded it, again sitting down and looking at me said, "Is that your young man? — He's a good-looking fellow." Camille told her to hold her tongue, to go on unpacking, and that I understood French, eyeing her at the same time in a savage way and looking at me at times very uneasily. She was a rough sort of girl, she said, a relative of a friend of hers, had come as her servant, and in a short time would understand her place; smiling at me in a knowing way as she said that. Camille always addressed her servant in French, me in English; but I understood French tolerably well.

Louise did as she was told, but bounced about in an independent way, threw off her cloak and bonnet and, putting her hands on her hips, stared at me again. I stared at her, thinking of the virginity I was destined to break up. Certainly she was appetizing; her cloak off showed a thick woollen dress of dark brown, striped with blue, a fine big figure, a couple of big breasts; her arms naked nearly to her shoulders, as French peasants usually wore them, were large, fleshy, and brown; the petticoats were half-way up to her knees, and showed the thickest woollen black stockings on a stout pair of legs, and feet in thick shoes with brass buckles; she had immense gilt earrings, and was in fact in the dress of a Bordeaux peasant woman.

I did nothing but stare at her, Camille nothing but scold her, talking to me at intervals. The girl got the boxes ready for opening, then walked about, taking up poker and tongs, chimney ornaments, and everything in the room with curiosity. Camille and I had so much to say that we took little notice of her; then she threw up the window and looked out. As she bent forward, her short petticoats showed her legs up to her knee-backs; Camille was about to stop her looking out when I winked and, stooping, saw a thick roll of stockings just beneath the knees, and the flesh just above. Camille understood. "Madame, madame," said the girl, "come here, here is fun." I heard Punch squeaking in the streets; she was delighted; her mistress went to the window, giving me a knowing look, and, looking out of the window with the girl, put her hands over the girl's petticoats and lifted them up slightly. Louise took no heed of this, being so engrossed with Punch; I dropped on my knees and saw half-way up the girl's thighs. I had been chaste for a few weeks, or nearly so; the sight of Camille had fired me, the thighs finished me; I shoved my hands up Camille's petticoats on to her arse, got her into her bed-room, and with her clothes in a lump on her belly, drove up my prick, spending directly I got up her cunt.

With half my spendings outside, half inside I lay with throbbing prick, which only came out when it had spent again. Camille vowed she had not had a man for weeks, and took it out of me, perhaps fearing if I went away with stiffening left, some other cunt would take it out. The ballocking over, I went home.

I was early there the next day; Louise had been installed in the little room leading out of the sitting-room. Camille told me a great deal about the distance she had gone, and the trouble and expense she had been put to in getting the girl's relatives to let her come; she hoped I would pay the additional expenses; and that I did at a cost of about twenty pounds. What with that and paying for her journey, and for lodgings while absent, Louise had cost me nearly ninety pounds already. Then I undertook to pay for the additional room, in which a bed having been put, an extra was charged; cooking now being done downstairs. Then Louise must have a new gown; then Camille thought I ought to give her something for herself, because whilst away for me she had made no money. That I refused and blazed up about it; for all that agreed to pay for a new silk dress for her, and a lot of little odds and ends on the second day of Camille's return, for all of which outlays I had only had a peep up the girl's petticoats.

Then I had talk about her. The girl was the daughter of a small grape-grower, a friend of Camille's; they thought Camille was in London as a dressmaker, making a lot of money, because she sent money home to her father. Camille offered to take her, saying she would be sure to get on, if not in one way, then in another; that good-looking girls always did well in London. The girl was mad to come and persuaded her parents to let her do so, believing that Camille got her living honestly; she was to be her servant until she could be put in the way of doing well.

"What are you going to tell her now? What are you going to do with her? What will she say when she finds out?" I asked.

Camille did not know. The girl would find out, and then she must excuse herself as well as she could, would say it was better, and jollier, and more money making than to make dresses. Besides, the girl could not help herself and would have to make the best of it.

When was I to have her? I asked. As soon as I could get her; there she was, and I might try when and how I liked; help me more she could not, she could not insist on Louise letting me; but no doubt she would in time, no one else should have her.

I was not so sure of that. Camille was gay, and although I had for more than a year excluded most men from the house, yet she did have other men there, and I knew they would see the girl, might like her, might pay Camille; all the remarks of the retired major came strongly before me, and I thought I was going to be sold, and said so.

She replied that I was not; she would leave me with the girl when I liked; if the girl spoke to her she would advise her to let me, but would have nothing to do with influencing her beyond that; and when the event came off, she meant to be out, so that Louise's friends could not say anything. If she went gay it was no fault of hers, young women would have it done to them, it was natural. That was the game she meant to play.

I saw that I had paid her only for bringing a girl, and must take my chance of getting into her; all she would do was to keep the coast clear. I don't know what I really did expect Camille to do, but think I imagined that she would have got the girl in bed with her some night, let me get into bed with them, and helped to make her fuck, if she would not. This was dissipated; I was to have the chance I should have had with a servant in my mother's house, or less, for this girl I should not see so often, and could not be sure she would be so well looked after.

So Camille went out, leaving me alone with the servant whenever I wished. I expect she went with other men at houses of friends, and so got her time paid for twice over and made a good thing of it; perhaps she thought the longer this lasted the better it would be for her. I think now that that was her game.

I began going about elsewhere, sleeping with Louise at times; but she was always pestering me about being in the family way, which annoyed me; and wanted such a lot of ballocking, that that annoyed me also. My cousin Fred wanted me to go to Paris with him, Louise said I was going to forsake her. One night after dining with her, coming out we met my cousin Fred, nothing put him off, and he would walk with us. The next day he said in his old unchaste way, which some years in India had not improved, "So that is the woman your mother says she fears has got hold of you." It was the first time I had heard that my mother had any such suspicion, for although she had spoken to me about my wildness, she had never referred to a woman; but she had told my aunt, who told my cousin my mother was awfully astonished. For that six years I had shagged all our servants under her very nose, yet she had not the faintest suspicion of it, my pranks now coming to her ears, shocked her extremely. I told Fred, that I had had Louise's firsts, to which he replied, that he should like to rattle his stones against her arse. "Is she a good fuck? Where does she live?" I did not mean his stones to knock against her arse as long as mine did, I replied. "Oh! You are fond of her then?" "No," but I preferred her to myself. "Lord, what does it matter?" said he, "white women are scarce in India, there was one that all in my regiment were fond of, there was not an officer who did not stroke her, none of us minded; we say, 'the more a cunt's buttered, the better it grinds.'" I did not see it in that light, so with the remark from him, that she was a damned fine piece, we parted.

Two or three days afterwards he spoke of her again, said he knew where she lived, so I thought he was hunting after her which annoyed me; not seeing that if he had got into her, I could have left her with good excuse.

I had tried to learn from Louise if she knew where Camille went all day, but could learn nothing, one night in bed with her however, whilst handling each other's privates, and under the sympathy generated by the rub of my fingers on her clitoris, she on my solemn promise of secrecy told me that an old friend of Camille's had opened a glove and lace shop in O*f**d Street with Camille's money, and that he was going to marry her. In O*f**d Street I saw a small shop, there was a Frenchman in it whose face I seemed to know. I waited near it one night, and saw Camille leave the shop closely veiled, and take the best way towards G**d*n Sq***e. Madame Boileau was like an oyster. I could get nothing out of her, although she took my money. I was sure that Camille went to the shop daily, or nearly so, and as no man came to the house, suppose she got her cunt plugged in the shop parlour.

Afterwards Fred talked so much about Louise, that I said I kept her. "There are two there, do you keep both?" "Yes." "Then you are a fool, you can't be sure of one woman's cunt if you are not with her always, but two together are sure to make a couple of whores, — no wonder your tin goes so fast."

Meanwhile I went out with him of a night, and we had different women. One night three of us went to a cigar-shop kept by two women just by ***, it was not an unusual thing then for two to have a cigar-shop, with a big sofa in a back parlour, one keeping shop whilst the other fucked. From talking we got to business without intending it. Fred began joking the girls, we went into the back parlour, and had wine, one asked my cousin if he did not want to lie down and rest himself. He said "Yes," but wanted warmth to his belly when he rested. "You may have my belly to warm you," said she. "What, here?" "Oh! They can wait," said the girl, "and your quiet friend can find his tongue with my sister. (The other girl.) I had not spoken, being at times timid at first with a woman, and especially a gay one.

We said jokingly, that we had no money. "I will take you all for a sovereign," said she, "and the one who I say is the best poke shall give me another half-sovereign." It was agreed, we tossed up for the order of the fucking, two went outside while the other had his pleasure. My turn came last, the excitement in thinking of what was going on made me in such a state, that I was no sooner up her than I spent; when I went out the other girl said, "You have been in a hurry." My cousin was pronounced the best fucker. Whilst the strumming was going on in the parlour, people bought cigars, and tobacco — for it was really sold there, — little did they guess the fun going on behind that red curtain of the shop-parlour.

A night or so after, I slept with Louise, felt uneasy in the tip of my prick, and saw unmistakably that it was the clap. It was not Louise's gift, for great was her surprize when I saw her twice afterwards, and never attempted to have her. She was annoyed, and said she supposed I had another friend, and put herself in such luscious attitudes, that I got a cock-stand, and could scarcely resist putting it up her, but saying I was ill went away. Fred said he should go to Paris without me, I was to join him in a fortnight. What with being indifferent to Louise, annoyed with her randiness, her vulgarity, and temper, being in fact tired of her and the expense, and now having the clap, I determined to break off; so wrote to Camille to meet me.

I told her I had the clap. "I thought there was something wrong," said she, "but Louise, I can swear, has never had any other man than you, take her to any doctor you like." Then she told me that in three weeks she meant to leave England, and Louise must do the best she could, she had taken means to bring on the girl's courses, would I send her back to France, or must she go gay in London.

I could not bear the idea of the girl being gay, so agreed to give her money to take her abroad with her, and she accepted. By her advice I wrote to Louise, said I had the clap, and feared I had given it to her, that she would not forgive me I was sure, and so never meant to see her again.

I sent a cheque to Louise, it passed through my bankers, and suppose the girl had it. Then went to Paris, my illness kept to me, so returned to London, got a little better, longed for Louise, stood opposite the house one night, nearly crossed over to have her, but resisted, and seeing a nice woman in Regent Street went home with her. I was so impatient, that I pushed her to the side of the bed directly I was in the room, felt for her cunt, and spent in her in a minute, she had not taken her bonnet off. My spending hurt me, my doctor had told me I could go with a woman without fear of injuring her, but that for my own sake I had better abstain. She got up, and took off her bonnet, to see if lying down had hurt it. "I'll have you again," said I. "Let me wash, you've spent such a lot, it's all running down my thighs." Again I fucked her; and next morning my ailment came back. My doctor said it served me right.

Shortly after, "lodgings to let" was posted up in Camille's windows. On calling, Madame Boileau came to the door. The two women had left, the shop in Oxford Street was shut up, and I never heard of the women afterwards.

I am astonished now, that I was wheedled out of so much money for a French virgin. How I could have done much that

I did makes me now laugh, I must have been very green, and Camille very cunning; but I was also rich, and generous, which accounts for much. I see now how largely I was hum-bugged, but cannot explain or reason about it. I am telling facts as they occurred, as far as I recollect them, it is all I can do. Certainly I had a splendid full-grown virgin for my money, the toughest virginity I yet have taken, a regular cock-bender, and had an uninterrupted honey-moon. Camille was a most superior harlot, genteel, clever, and voluptuous, such as are not usually found; with her and her findings I had a year's enjoyment, leaving me lax, blasé, and a half-cured clap. What with women, horses, carriages, cards, dinners, and other items, I was a few thousands poorer than at the beginning of my ac-quaintance with Camille.

It's my fate to have sisters, — how curious! — and thrice to have had the clap, and yet not three-and-twenty, — how hard!

I was very much used up, and needed rest for body and mind; never had I been so much so before. Up to the time of getting my fortune, want of money curbed my lascivious tastes, and although I had servant after servant in my moth-er's house, the difficulties of getting them gave me frequent rests, and prevented me generally from exhausting myself; perhaps I got just enough fucking to keep me in health. The year's rioting with Camille and her troupe would have tired a strong man; I never counted them, but think that in that year I must have poked something like sixty or seventy dif-ferent women; I poked every one of Camille's acquain-tances, I am sure, — so it was time I had a rest.

My clap brought on a stricture, obliging me to have a bougie passed every other day to stretch the pipe open, and causing me to piss clots of gruelly blood about an hour af-terwards. I dared not fuck, but once frigged, and it brought on the inflammatory stage again. At length I got better, but with a gleet which wetted the tail of my shirt through daily; doctors advised me to get a change of air, I went to my aunt's place in H**tf***d-shire where I took cold baths, and did all I could to get myself well, — I was forbidden to touch a woman until permitted by the doctor.

Touch women I did not, think of them I did eternally, and deplored the time that I was wasting. I used to look at my female cousins, and long for them; my aunt whose flabby, brown-haired, thick-lipped furrow glanced at in my boyhood I used to think about, and should not have hesitated in getting a pleasure up it, had no other cunt been ready for me. I eyed the farm-women (coarse, strong, healthy bitches) with lust that made them look beauties in my longing eyes, I was boiling over with spunk, at the closet one day my turds were hard, and hurt me; the irritation affected my ballocks, my prick stiffened rigidly, I could not piss for it, the tip looked dry, as if gleet had ceased, I merely touched the top (not frigged), and out shot my sperm as I sat on the privy seat. What a relief! But what a loss of pleasure not to have injected some dear little cunt nicked in some smooth white bum! My prick seemed quite well, and I went into the fields to get hold of some girl doing field-work, or any woman, old or young, who had a cunt available, when with a throbbing my gleet returned; so I went to town to see my medical man about it. He pointed out to me how needful it was to restrain myself, I followed his advice, in two weeks was much better, and had determined to go to town to see him again about it, when I got well without him.

CHAPTER X

Fred at home. — Smith, the field-foreman. — A rape of a juvenile. — Funking consequences. — Nelly consents. — Fred looks on.

A wide-awake fellow was Fred. When my aunt said how delighted they all were to see me so steady, and had never seen me enjoy myself so much at the Hall before, he stared. "He goes often," said aunt, "with me to the dairy." "Yes, and pats the cows," said a cousin. Fred winked at me, and when we were alone said, "What's your little game Walter, where are you cunting now old fellow?" "Cunt," said I, "is of no use, my clap's not gone; but thank God I think it's getting all right again." He was quite taken in. "You have done the best thing you could," said he, "there is nothing here much to excite you, no woman worth having, is there?"

One morning we walked into the fields, the foreman came up and saluted us. He had been on the farm before Fred and I were born. "Well, Smith," said Fred, "still at the old games, — any bastards lately?" "Oi am tow ould for that now, Master." "Perhaps the girls don't like poking now?" "Oi they do, but they doon't like me as they did." Smith (my cousin told me), had had the credit all his life of poking all the agricultural laborers, and had been threatened with dismissal on account of it. "He might have had a worse berth," said I, "there are half-a-dozen girls in the field I would not mind sleeping with." "Why don't you have them?" said Fred. "I don't want to lose my character here." "That be damned, you can always have a field-girl, nobody cares, — I have had a dozen or two."

I turned this over in my mind. We were again in the fields, on the way there he gave me a long account of how old Smith used to wink at his having the field-girls; and indeed I had often heard him tell it. "You tell him you would like any one, and see what will come of it." There was a pretty sun-burnt girl about fifteen years of age that had given me a cock-stand. "That's a pretty girl Smith, I'd give a sovereign to have her, — is she loose?" "Don't think so yet squire, she be skittish; her sister's not fourteen, and they say she be in the family way, when one sister takes to it squire, the others generally do." "Where do you pay their wages?" I asked. The old fellow leered at me. "Why you be a taken a leaf out of young squire's book sir (it was Fred's advice); I pays them next at the root-stores," a shed about a quarter of a mile from the farm-yard, and in which he had a desk. The women waited outside the shed, each being called in and paid in succession. They were paid every night, excepting in haymaking times.

At pay-time I strolled into the shed. One by one he paid. The girl I wanted came last. He told her he wanted her to take a parcel to the village. "Yes sir," said she. Off old Smith went to fetch the parcel, — it was the dodge, Fred told me afterwards, the old goat always adopted to get a girl left alone with him.

Very randy but nervous I went out with Smith, then strolled back into the shed. The girl had seated herself on some loose straw, she got up and curtsied. "Sit down my dear," said I, "you may have some time to wait," and talked to her. "You are very pretty, — you will keep your sweetheart waiting." Smiling, she said, "I ain't got no sweetheart sir." Another look or two, and my randiness getting the better of me, I began chaffing suggestively, she sat down besides me, then I talked for a quarter of an hour warmer and warmer, then kissing, tickling, and pinching her legs. This

[*127*]

did not seem to affect her, she enjoyed it; then out I pulled my prick, and all changed at once. "Oh!" said she, rising up scared to go. I pulled her back.

"Let's do it to you." "I won't." "You've been fucked." "I ain't, — I am only fifteen years old (she did not affect ignorance of my meaning), — leave me alone." I threw her down, and got my hand up her clothes. She loudly screamed, and that is all I recollect clearly: I know that I struggled with her, offered her money, told her I knew her sister had been fucked, and a lot more. I was so much stronger that she had no chance, I rolled her over, she screamed, and screamed again (there was no one nearer than the Hall), I exposed her bum, her thighs, her cunt, and all she had. I was furious with lust, determined to have her; at last she was under me, panting, breathless, crying, and saying, "Now don't, — oh! pray don't," but I lunged fast, furiously, brutally, and all I heard was, "Oh! Pray, — pray now, — oh! — oh! — oh! Pray," as I was spending in her holding her tight, kissing her after I had forced her. Her tears ran down. If I had not committed a rape it looked uncommonly like one, and began to think so as I lay with my prick up her.

I got off her, saw for an instant her legs wide open, cunt and thighs wet and bloody, she crying, sobbing, rubbing her eyes. I was now in a complete funk, I had heard field-women so lightly spoken of, that they were so accessible, that I expected only to go up a road that had often been travelled. This resistance and crying upset me, the more so when at length rising, she said, "I'll tell my sister, and go to the magistrate, and tell how you have served me out."

I really had violated her, saw that it would bear that complexion before a magistrate, so would not let her go, but retained her, coaxed, begged, and promised her money. I would love her, longed for her again, would take her from the fields, and every other sort of nonsense a man would utter under the circumstances. She ceased crying, and stood in sullen mood as I held her, asking me to let her go. I took out my purse, and offered her money which she would not take, but eyed wishfully as I kept chinking the gold in my hand. What a temptation bright sovereigns must have been to a girl who earned ninepence a day, and often was without work at all.

In an hour and a half I suppose, old Smith came back, he had really got a parcel for her to take. She began again to cry, and blurted out that the gentleman had insulted her. "What, has he kissed you?" "More than that, — boo hoo." "What has he done?" "Been dirty with me, — and I'll tell my sister, and go to the justice."

"Pough, child," said Smith, "he arn't done you any harm, — a gent like him, — don't make a fuss, — make it up, — it's all fair yer know twixt a young man, and a maid — daresay yer wanted him to be dirty with you, — a gent like him, you ought to be proud of sich a one making love to you, — here, take this parcel, and be off."

"Take the sovereign (she had refused it before), I'll give you more another day; it will help to keep you a while, — hold your tongue, and no one will know," said I. She hesitated, pouted, wriggled her shoulders, but at last took the sovereign, and took up the parcel, saying she would tell her sister. Then said the foreman, "None o' that, gal, an I hears more on that, you won't work here any more, nor anywheres else in this parish, — I knows the whole lot on you, I knows who got yer sister's belly up, — she at her age, she ought to be ashamed on herself, and I knows summut about you too, — now take care gal." "I've done nothing to be ashamed on," said the girl, "you're a hard man to the women, they all say so, — ohe! — ohe!" "Well there," said he, dropping his bullying tone, "the square won't harm you; I think you be in luck if he loikes you, — say you nought; — that be my advice." The girl, muttering, went her way.

I followed her (it was getting dark), was so kind and coaxing, promised her so many fine things (I'm not sure I didn't say I'd marry her), that as we neared the village, the little lass let me pull her into a convenient grassy corner, and fuck her again. She promised she'd say nothing to anyone about it.

Next morning I had a fear, and was annoyed with myself. If the girl said anything it would be all over the parish in the afternoon, and in my aunt's ears the next day; all that for a dirty little farm-laborer. I had had none of that sensuous delight which both mentally and physically is found in getting into a virgin, had never thought of having her as one, nor did I recollect much cunt resistance to my penetration: but she certainly was a virgin. In my furious lust, and with my unbendable stiff prick I must have hit the mark, and burst through it at one or two cunt-rending shoves. She had given a loud cry in the midst of it, "Oh! Pray now, — oh! Pray," — but I had heeded it not. What excited me was her youth, her size, and the idea of having a little cunt with but little hair on it. In bed, thinking of, and funking consequences, I longed for a girl still smaller, for one with no hair on her cunt at all. On further reflection I calmed. She had taken the money, and let me do it a second time; it was all right, and I rose, and went to the scene of my exploit.

The girl was not at work in the fields, and my funk returned. "Smith," said I, "is Nelly (let's call her Nelly) here?" "No, nor her sisters." "Sisters?" "Yes, there are two: one a woman called ***, very much older, the other younger than Nelly, and the young un they says be with kid."

Next day the two sisters were at work again. I told Smith that after his dinner I wished to speak to the girl. The old cock-bawd told me to wait at the root-shed; and the girl came there to fetch his handkerchief which he left purposely. When she saw me, how she started. No, she had told no one, but was not going to let me do what I liked. A kiss. "I don't like your hand on my legs, — oh! Now you said you would not, — take your hand away."

My finger was on her cunt, I was feeling what little hair she had, my finger went up it, oh! How tight it was! "Now darling, let me, I won't let you go till you do, — there, what a dear little belly, — let me kiss it." "They will wonder why I am gone so long, — my sister will be asking me questions, — do let me go." "No." "Oh!" I had her on the straw. "Be quiet, dear, — my prick's up you, — be quiet — ah! — ah!"

CHAPTER XI

In a few days Fred went to London. I, for a change, went with him.

Theatre every night, heavy lunches, heavy dinners, much wine, and cigars never out of my mouth, that was the first few days' proceedings. Fred was keeping a woman named Laura of whom I shall say more; she was always with us. I don't recollect having a woman for a few days, but it may have been otherwise. On the fifth or sixth night we went to Vauxhall Gardens to a masquerade. It was a rare lark in those days. A great fun of mine was getting into a shady walk, tipping the watchman to let me hide in the shrubs, and crouching down to hear the women piss. I have heard a couple of hundred do so on one evening, and much of what they said. Such a mixture of dull and crisp baudiness I never heard in short sentences elsewhere. Although I had heard a few similar remarks when I waited in the cellars of the gun-factory, it was nothing like those at Vauxhall, and it amused me very much. There were one or two darkish walks where numbers of women on masquerade nights went to piss, and many on other nights.

At supper Laura said, "Where have you been the last hour?" I laughed. "Tell us." "Hiding in the shrubs where ladies go by ones, twos, and threes without men." Laura understood. "Serves them right, they should go to the women's closets; but you are dirty." "Well, it was such a lark hearing them piddle and talk." Fred, always coarse, said he never knew a woman piss off so quickly as Laura. Laura slapped his head. She had not been gay, and was very modest in manner and expressions; but loved a baudy joke not told in coarse language.

The signal sounded for fireworks. Off we ran to get good places. I cared more about women than fireworks, and lagged behind, seeing the masques and half-dressed women running and yelling (fun was fast and loose then). I passed a woman leading a little girl dressed like a ballet-girl, and looked at the girl who seemed about ten years old, then at the woman who winked. I stopped, she came up and said, "Is she not a nice little girl?" I don't recollect having had any distinct intention at the time I stopped; but at her words ideas came into my head. She — what a small cunt, — no hair on that. "Yes, a nice little girl." I replied. "Would you like to see her undressed?" "Can I fuck her?" I whispered. The little girl kept tugging the woman's hand and saying, "Oh! Do come to the fireworks." "Yes, if you like, — what will you give?" I agreed to give I think three sovereigns, a good round sum for a common-place poke then.

She told me to go out of the gardens first, get a cab, and stop at a little way from the entrance. In three minutes the woman and child joined me. At about five minutes drive from Vauxhall we stopped, walked a little way, turned down a street, and after telling me to wait one or two minutes, she opened the door of a respectable little house with a latch-key, went in and closed it. A minute afterwards she opened the door, and treading lightly as she told me, I found myself in a parlour out of which led a bed-room, both well furnished. Enjoining me to speak in a low tone I sat down, and contemplated the couple.

The woman was stout, full-sized, good-looking, dark, certainly forty, and dressed like a well-to-do tradeswoman. The girl's head was but a few inches above my waist, and she certainly was not more than ten years, but for such age as nice and fleshy as could be expected. She had an anxious look as she stared at me, and I stared at her. The last month's constant desire to have a cunt absolutely without any hair on it was to be realized, I was impatient but noticed and remarked, "Why, you have gas!" — a rare thing then in houses. "Beautiful, is it not?" said the woman, and in a voluptuous and enticing manner began undressing, until she stood in a fine chemise, a pair of beautiful boots, and silk stockings. Engrossed with the girl whom I was caressing, I scarcely had noticed the woman; but as she pulled up her chemise to tighten her garter, and showed much of a very white thigh, I said, "I've made a mistake, I did not mean you." "No," said she, "but it's all the same." She came to me, pinched my cock outside saying "oho" as she found it stiff, and then undressed the child to her chemise. I had white trowsers and waistcoat on, and was anxious about rumpling them. At my request she drew my white trowsers off over my boots with great care; then divesting myself of coat and waistcoat I stood up with prick spouting. "Look there, — feel it Mary." The girl not obeying she took her little hand, and made her feel it. Sitting down I lifted the girl on to my knees, and put my hand between her little thighs.

"Give me the three pounds," said the woman. All my life I have willingly paid women before my pleasure; but thought I was going to be done, so demurred, and asked if she supposed I was not a gentleman, took out my purse, showed I had plenty of money, gave her one sovereign, and promised the others directly I had the child, — and then pulled off my boots.

We went into the bed-room, she lighted candles, the gas streamed in through the open door. "Lay down Mary," said she. "Oh! He ain't going to do it like the other man, — you said no one should again," said the girl whimpering. "Be

quiet you little fool, he won't hurt you, — open your legs."
Pushing her back, or rather lifting her up, there I saw a little
light-pink slit between a pair of thighs somewhat bigger than
a full-sized man's calves; the little cunt had not a sign of
hair on it. To pull open the lips, to push up my finger, to frig
it, smell it, then lick it was the work of a minute. I was wild,
it was the realization of the baudy, dreamy longings of the
last few weeks. I was scarcely conscious that the old one had
laid hold of my prick, and was fast bringing me to a crisis.

Pushing her hand away I placed my prick against the little
cunt which seemed scarcely big enough for my thumb, and
with one hand was placing it under the little bum, when the
girl slipped off the bed crying, "Oh! Don't let him, — the
other did hurt so, — he shan't put it in."

"Don't do it to her, she is so young," said the woman in
a coaxing tone. "Why, that is what I came for." "Never
mind, it hurts *her*, have *me*, I am a fine woman, look," and
she flung herself on the bed, and pulled up her chemise, disclosing a fine form, and to a randy man much that was enticing. "Look at my hair, how black it is, — do you like
tassels?" said she, and throwing up her arms out of her chemise, she showed such a mass of black hair on her armpits
as I have rarely seen in other women, and rarely in an English woman at all.

"What the devil did you bring me here for? — it was for
her, not you, I have hair, — I like a cunt without hair."

"Have me, and look at her cunt whilst you do it, — here
Mary," and she pulled the young one on to the bed, cunt upwards. But disappointed, lewed, and savage, I swore till she
begged me not to make a noise, and saying "Well, — well, —
well, — so you shall, — hold your tongue (to the girl), he
won't hurt you, — look, his cock is not big." She pulled the
girl on to the edge of the bed again, and brought her cunt up
to the proper level with the bolster and pillows. Then said the
woman, "Let me hold your cock, you must not put it far in,
she is so young." I promised I would only sheath the tip; but
she declared I should not unless she held it. "Wrap your handkerchief round it," said she. I did so, and that left only half its
length uncovered. Impetuously I tore the white handkerchief
into pieces, wrapped round about an inch of the stem of my
prick with it, which then looked as if it was wounded, and
bound up; then hitting the little pink opening I drove up it. I
doubted whether I should enter, so small was it. It held my
prick like a vice, but up her cunt I was, the woman promising

the child money, to take her to Vauxhall again, and so on, and then put her hand over her mouth to prevent her hollowing, — she did not hollow at all really.

I spent almost instantly, and coming to my senses held her close up to my prick by her thighs, — there was no difficulty so light a weight was she. There I stood for a minute or two. "My prick is small now," said I, "unroll the handkerchief." "No," said the woman. "I will give you ten shillings extra if you do, my prick can't hurt now." The oddity of a woman attempting to unroll from a prick a slip of white rag, whilst the prick was up a cunt! But out came my prick from the little hole before she could accomplish it.

Desire had not left me, holding her thighs open I dropped on my knees, my prick flopping, and saw the little cunt covered with thick sperm. There lay the girl, there stood the woman, neither speaking nor moving, till my eyes had had their voluptuous enjoyment. "I will give you another sovereign now, and then fuck her again." "All right," said the woman. "But she must not wash." "All right." I gave it, then took the girl up like a baby, one hand just under the bum, so that the spunk might fall on my hand if it dropped out, and laid her on the sofa in the parlour, where the gas flared brightly, opened her thighs wide, gloated, and talked baudily till my prick stood again.

Then I lifted her back on to the bed, and rolled the strip of handkerchief round the stem again; but I longed to hurt her, to make her cry with the pain my tool caused her, I would have made her bleed if I could; so wrapped it round in such a manner, that with a tug I could unroll it. The woman did not seem so anxious now about my hurting her.

Sperm is a splendid cunt-lubricator, my prick went in easier, but still she cried out. Now I measured my pleasure. With gentle lingering pushes I moved up and down in her. Under pretence of feeling my prick, I had loosened the handkerchief, then tore the rag quite away, and afterwards lifted her up, and then with her cunt stuck tight and full with my pego, and both hands round her bum tightly, I walked holding her so into the sitting-room to a large glass. There seeing my balls hanging down under little arse, I shoved and wriggled, holding her like a baby on me, her hands round my neck, she whining that I was hurting her, the woman hushing, and praying me to be gentle, till I spent again. I held her tight to me in front of the glass, her thighs wide apart, my balls showing under her little buttocks, till my

[*134*]

prick again shrunk, and my sperm ran from her cunt down my balls. Then I uncunted, and sat down on a chair. We were both stark naked.

The girl sat down on a foot-stool, the woman sat in her chemise. I gave her the remaining money, and to the little one some silver. Although I had had her twice, I scarcely had looked at her; both fucks must have been done in ten minutes. Now I longed to see the little cunt tranquilly. "Let me wash her cunt," said I. "You can," said the old one. I took the girl into the bed-room, she left a large gobbet of sperm on the stool, which the old one wiped off. I washed her cunt, threw her on the bed, looked at the little quim. It seemed impossible I could have been up it; but from that day I knew a cunt to be the most elastic article in the world, and believed the old woman's saying, that a prick can always go up where a finger can.

Then after cuddling her, straddling between her legs and feeling my balls hanging between her thighs by passing my hand round her arse, I laid her on the bed, took a glance at the little cunt from a slight distance, and saw the old one in an exciting posture. She had thrown herself on the bed, and resting her head on one hand was watching me. Her chemise had slipped from her shoulders showing big white breasts, and the black thicket of hair in one armpit. Her chemise was up to her waist, one leg was bent up, the fat calf pressed against a fat thigh, the other extended along the bed, the thighs wide open, the middle finger of her left hand on her cunt, whose mass of black hair creeping up her belly and along the line of junction with the thighs could not be hidden by her hand. She was frigging her clitoris with her middle finger, and she smiled invitingly. "Come and do it to me, I do want it so, — I have not had a poke for a fortnight."

My love of a fat arse and a big hairy cunt returned suddenly. I stood turning my eyes, first to the little hairless orifice, then to the full-lipped split, then to the little pink cunt, and then back again to the matured cunt. "Come, do me." "I must go." "Why?" "I came to have her." "So you have, — now have me, — you can have her again if you like after." "Can I?" "Yes, — oh! Come, I am so randy." "It's late." "Stop all night." I said I would. Off the bed she got, put a night-gown on the child, laid her on the sofa, told her to go to sleep, and throwing off her boots and stockings, got on to the bed again.

I threw off my socks. "Shall I be naked?" said she. "Yes,

it is very hot." Off went her chemise, and the next instant cuddling up to me, she was tugging at my prick, kissing me, and using every salacious stimulant.

Though a hot night, naked as we both were, we felt a chill, so covered ourselves with a sheet.

"How old are you?" said I. "Guess." "More than forty." "I am not thirty-eight, although I am so stout, — feel how firm my flesh is, — how my breasts keep up." I threw down the sheet to see her fully. She was delighted, turned round and round, opened her thighs, pulled open her cunt, exposed herself with the freedom of a French whore, and by the time I had seen all my prick was at fever heat, and I fucked her. Our nakedness was delightful.

We talked afterwards. She was not the mother, nor the aunt, though the child called her so; the child was parentless, she had taken charge of her and prevented her going to the work-house. She was in difficulties, she must live, the child would be sure to have it done to her some day, why not make a little money by her? Some one else would, if she did not. So spoke the fat middle-aged woman.

I was sleepless. After an hour or two I longed to see them side by side, that strange contrast in age and size, and to try the difference with my finger as I had with my prick. She brought in the child, sleepy and peevish, I plunged my prick in the little one, took it out, and put it into the woman. It was a delight to feel the difference — the room in one, the confinement in the other's cunt.

The aunt annoyed me by putting her hand between our bellies to prevent my penetrating too far. It was not the stretching, nor the plugging, it was the boring too deeply which hurt the little one, she said.

I laid on my back and put the little one's belly upon me; stretching her little thighs I felt round them, and guided my prick up her, then the aunt put her fingers round my prick and squeezed my balls. How funny to have that little creature on the top of me; how funny to be able to feel at the same time a big hairy cunt at my side. Such thoughts and emotions finished me, and after spending in the little one, she again went to the sofa, then with my arse to the aunt's arse we went to sleep.

She was the youngest I ever yet have had, or have wished to have. We laid abed till about mid-day. I fucked as much as I ever did in my life, and found that a tiny cunt although it might satisfy a letch, could not give the pleasure that a fully developed woman could. Tight as it was, it had not the peculiar suction, embrace, and grind, that a full-grown woman's or girl's has. When I was getting drier and drier, the old one stiffened my prick, and I put it into the child; but oscillate my arse as I might, I could not get a spend out of me; then in the aunt's clipping though well stretched cunt, I got my pleasure in no time. A fuck is barely a fuck if a man's prick is but half up a girl, it wants engulfing. A very young girl never has the true jerk of her arse, nor the muscular clip in her cunt; so if languid prick be put up it, it will slip out, unless the letch be strong; whereas a flabby, done-for prick, once in the cunt of a grown woman may be resuscitated, and made to give pleasure to both, if she uses the muscular power which nature has given her between bum-hole, buttocks, and navel.

We eat and drank, I paid liberally, and with empty ballocks and a flabby tool went away. White trowsers and a black tail-coat were then full evening dress at Vauxhall; but ludicrous in the day. I recollect feeling ashamed as I walked out in that dress in the sun-shine. She would not fetch a cab as she was most anxious about noise. She gave me full instructions where to write and have the girl again. About a fornight afterwards I made an appointment, but she did not keep it. I went to the house and asked for her; a woman opened the door. "Do you know her?" said she. "Yes." "She is not here, and I don't know where she has gone, — perhaps you're as bad as she is," and she slammed the door in my face. A few years passed away before I took a letch for a hairless cunt again, — and then I was a poor man.

We went to Vauxhall on an ordinary night, and I showed Fred where I had heard and seen the girls make water. Laura I got to like, and she to like me which led to something at a later date. In about three weeks or more I went back to my aunt's, through an indefinable longing to poke, in a quiet intriguing way, the women I had had there. In London I had changed my women twice a day, and fucked every nice French woman who walked in Regent Street.

Then Fred and I went to town, he to see Laura, I to get promiscuous fucking, and other amusements. Laura who was one of the few women of her class whom I have found to be well educated, had a female friend stopping with her from her native place Plymouth. Her name was Mabel, a pretty, modest-looking girl. Laura had given out that she had married Fred, and this girl had been entrusted to keep her company. I tell the tale as it was told me. I dined with them daily, and in fact all but lived there.

One night we went to the theatre, and back to Fred's, had a jolly supper, and got as merry as sand-boys. It was a cold, foggy night, I said I would not go home as it was about three a.m., and would sleep on the sofa. Our conversation had been pretty warm. Fred remarked that I had better sleep with Mabel. Laura was surprized at Fred. Mabel laughed, and baudy insinuations passed without baudy words. Fred said he should go to bed, and off he went. Laura expected Mabel to go to bed, but she put it off laughing and joking. Laura got angry, Fred came out in his night-gown swearing if Laura did not come, he would go out, and get a woman; and off Laura went. Fred wanted a fuck before he went to sleep.

Mabel and I sat talking, both heated and randy. It got colder, she got sleepy, I would not let her go, so she laid on the sofa. I drew a chair to her side, and both drinking whisky and water time rolled on. "Oh! I wish I were Fred," said I. "Why?" "Because he is between Laura's thighs, belly to belly, how warm, how delicious, this cold night." "Oh! For shame!" "Nonsense my dear, quite natural and proper, we are made to keep each other warm, and give each other pleasure." "When we're married," said she. "Married, — pough! — then millions would never taste the pleasure." My words grew warmer, I kissed, and was kissed, edged myself on to the sofa, little by little felt my way from her ankles to her thighs, and behold me smothering her with kisses, with my hand on her cunt, her hand on my prick.

A modest woman will let you take liberties much more readily if you kiss her whilst taking them. Sit at the foot of a girl on a sofa, and try to force your hand up her clothes, she may resist you; sit close by her side, bend over her, kiss her, and at the same time your hand may find its way to her cunt, almost without hindrance.

So it was now. Mabel was scarcely modest. I recollect the conviction coming over me that she was no virgin, and if I had doubts before, the way my finger slipped from her clitoris up the love-pit and plugged it, confirmed them. She lay with her eyes fixed on me, palpitating gently with voluptuousness. Her petticoats up to her knees, I saw legs in black stockings, one in wrinkles, the other half-way bagging down the calf, and her feet in shabby slippers.

I had at that time a horror of black stockings, which affected me at times so much as to deprive me of all desire.

Once with a gay woman who had black stockings I was unable to poke her, spite of her blandishment, till she put white ones on. As I now saw Mabel's legs a disgust came over me, desire left me, and my prick began to shrink; I may have been tired, or had had my sperm drawn too much the night previously; that is likely enough, I don't recollect; but know I got nervous, a fear lest she should doubt my manhood, a sense of shame overcame me. I tried to rally, but in vain, for once that nervousness on me, it vanquished me. I ceased to probe her quim with my finger, my prick shrunk out of her hand, and the titillation ceasing, Mabel turned away her eyes, repulsed my hands, and drew her clothes down, looking at me full. I sat speechless.

"Are you ill?" said she. "Yes," said I, overjoyed with the suggestion, "a faintness came over me, and a giddyness, — I shall be better directly."

She believed it, gave me cold water, and we sat for a time. I looked at her beautifully white neck, thought how white her bum must be, tried to get the black stockings out of my head, but could not. It must have been past four o'clock in the morning when I asked her to lie down again, but she refused; the spell had been broken, the weakness gone, and she said she should go to bed.

"Is your bum as white as your neck?" said I. "Laura says I am the whitest-fleshed woman she ever saw, all the girls at school used to say so."

In my mind's eye I saw the white bum and thighs, my lust came back at a rush. "Let me see it," I said, and I laid hold of her. The flood-gates of my bawdiness were loosened, and as she afterwards told me, I let fly a torrent of voluptuous words, enough to have excited the passions of all the women in London. I had forgotten the stockings. She kept refusing, denying, and evading me. "Hish! Hish! Laura will hear you." Laura did, and came in in her night-gown. "I came to see if you had gone to bed," said she. "You need not have troubled yourself," said Mabel. "As long as you're here I shall look after you; when you're at home you can do as you like." "I'm quite old enough to take care of myself." They quarrelled. Mabel resented her interference. Fred roared out from his bed-room, "What the devil are you going in there for?" and Laura not replying, came in in his night-shirt. After an altercation Fred and Laura went back to bed.

Then Mabel said she should go to bed, must go up for five minutes, but would be down again. "To piddle eh?" Taking off my boots I blew out one candle, took the other, followed her, and opened the door. She was on the piss-pot. I closed the door, and locked it. Five minutes afterwards I was on the bed fucking her with her legs in black stockings, and five minutes afterwards uncunting, the first words I said were, "I loathe black stockings."

"I can't bear them myself," said she, "but I am in mourning." People in mourning wore black stockings then.

She was anxious for me to go, so that Laura could say nothing positive, whatever she might think. I would directly I had her again. We got into the bed together, and I had her, and then again. That is all I recollect, and that after the fuck we both fell asleep, and were awakened by a knock at the door. It was late in the morning, and broad daylight, Laura was knocking. I opened the door. Laura looked at me, and then at Mabel, and said, "Well, the sooner I send you back the better." There was a somewhat bitter row between them, short but sharp, in which Mabel gave as good as she got. Laura went away. Mabel turned round and wept; then we fucked, and went to sleep again.

This is the only point in my history with Mabel much worth noting, except that when I knew her from top to bottom, and found she got out of bed, and washed her cunt after my sperming it, I asked her, "Why did you not wash the first night?" "Because it's unlucky," said she, and I never got any more out of her; but she had known the sensation of a prick in her cunt before mine, that I found out the first night.

CHAPTER XII

A frolic at Lord A***'s. — After dinner. — Newspaper readings. — A strange rape. — Bets on pricks. — Pricks felt. — Fred on his head. — Beds on the floor. — Free fucking. — End of the orgie.

For brevity I compress the events of the next few months; it is a pity, but it would print to three the length otherwise. I was mostly in London. One or two funny whoring incidents I must leave out altogether, and for the same reason: brevity.

An intimate friend of Fred's was Lord A***, he lived with a lady who was called Lady A***. I don't think she had been gay, and in that respect resembled Laura and Mabel. The three women were much together. We often saw Lord A***, and all became friends. Lord A*** was not very true to his lady. He lived in B*t*n Street, where he had at that time the whole of a handsomely furnished house, but only could half occupy it. His in-door servants were a middle-aged woman who cooked, a maid who was her niece, and his valet, who waited at table as well. A woman who did not sleep in the house came daily. He had grooms and a coachman, but not in the house. Lord A*** had quarrelled with his father. He had been in the Guards, and drank very freely.

He invited us one night to dinner, and gave a splendid one. By the time we had finished, we were all noisy. It was never our custom to use baudy language when in each other's company, Laura had a great aversion to it. Mabel liked me to talk baudy to her, but did not talk it herself. Fred always after dinner would let out a warm word or so, and was at once snubbed by Laura. For all that our conversation after dinner was generally warm with *double entente*.

On the night in question our conversation got to open voluptuousness. Fred and Lord A*** went in for it, Mabel laughed, Laura hished and hished, said she would leave, but at last gave way, as did Lady A***; then we men got to lewedness. Whenever any sensuous allusion was made, my eyes sought Laura's, hers seeking mine; we were both thinking of the quiet and quick fuck we had, with Mabel snoring by our side. We compared our thoughts on that night, but at a future day.

Just at that time a case filled the public journals. It was a charge of rape on a married woman, against a man lodging in the same house. She was the wife of a printer on the staff of a daily paper, who came home extremely late; she always went to bed leaving her door unlocked, so that her husband might get in directly he came home. The lodger was a friend of her husband's, and knew the custom of leaving the door unlocked, — in fact he was a fellow-printer.

She awakened in the night with the man between her thighs, had opened them readily, thinking it was her husband. It appears to have been her habit, and such her husband's custom on returning home, or so she said. The lodger had actually all but finished his fuck, before she awakened sufficiently to find out that it was not the legitimate prick which was probing her. Then she alarmed the house, and gave the man in charge for committing a rape. The papers delicately hinted that the operation was complete before the woman discovered the mistake, — but of course it left much to the reader's imagination.

Fred read this aloud. I knew more, for the counsel of the prisoner was my intimate friend. He had told me that the prisoner had had her twice, that she had spent with him; that he had often said he meant to go in, and have her, that she had dared him to do it, and that she only made a row when she thought she heard her husband at the door on the landing, although it was two hours before his usual time of return. His prick was in her when she began her outcry.

With laughter and smutty allusions we discussed the case. "Absurd," said Laura, "she must have known it was not her husband." "Why?" "Why because — ," and Laura stopped. "If you were asleep, and suddenly felt a man on you of about my size, and his prick up you, very likely you would not tell if it were mine or not," said Fred. Laura threw an apple at his head. Decency was banished from that moment, a spade was called a spade, and unveiled baudiness reigned.

"I should know if it were not you," said Lady A*** looking at Lord A***. "How?" "Ah! I should, — should you not know another woman from Laura, if you got into bed with two women in the dark?" said she to Fred. "I am not sure for the moment if with a woman just for size, and as much hair on her cunt," said he. "I tell you what Fred, I won't have it," said Laura ill-tempered, "talk about someone else, I won't have beastly talk about me." "I'll bet," said I, "that if the ladies were to feel our pricks in the dark, they would not tell whose they each had hold of." Roars of laughter followed. "I should like to try," said Mabel. "So should I," said another. "Would you know, if you felt us?" said one woman. "If I felt all your cunts in the dark, I'll bet I should know Marie's," said Lord A***. "That is, if you felt all round and about," said Fred, "but not if she opened her legs, and you only felt the notch." "I think I should." "Why? — Is she different from others?" Lord A*** was going to say something, when Marie told him to shut up.

So we went on, the men in lascivious language, the women in more disguised terms, discussing the probabilities of distinguishing cunts or pricks by a simple feel in the dark. Each remark caused roars of laughter, the women whispered to each other, and laughed at their own sayings. Lewedness had seized us all, the women's eyes were brilliant with voluptuous desire. More wine was drunk. "Call it by its proper name," said Lord A*** when Marie remarked that a woman must know her own man's thing. "Prick then." "I will bet five pounds that Mabel would not guess my prick in the dark, if she felt all of us," said I. "And I'll bet," said another. "Shall we try?" said Fred. "Yes," said Mabel, more fuddled than the rest. Baudier and baudier, we talked, laughed, and drank, and at length set to work to make rules for trying, all talking at once.

One proposed one way, one another. "I can't tell unless I feel balls as well," said a woman. "Will they be stiff when we feel?" said another. "Mine will," said Fred, "it's stiff already." "So is mine," added I.

"How shall we know where to put our hands, if we are in the dark?" said Lady A***. "If a man is in front of you, you will find it fast enough," answered someone. Laura had now yielded to the baudy contagion, and made no objection, though Mabel and Lady A*** were the most forward. Then Lord A*** rang the bell, and told his valet he might go out for the night, and his house-keeper and maid they might go to bed, which they did at the top of the house, as we supposed. The sequel proved that to be doubtful, and that they must have had a most edifying night.

After lewed squabbles we arranged that each man was to give the woman if she guessed the prick right, ten pounds; the men were to be naked, the women to feel all the men's cocks, and give a card to him whose prick she thought she knew. The room was to be dark. No man was to speak, or give any indication by laughing, coughing, or any other way, under penalty of paying all the bets. The women were to lose if they spoke, or gave indications of who they were.

I took three cards, and wrote the name of a lady on each of them. Then each lady took her card, and they went upstairs to the bed-room pell-mell and laughing. The women were to stand of a row in a certain order against a side of the room, we to follow in an order they did not know. They were to feel all pricks twice, each giving her card to the man at the second feel, if she knew the prick. We undressed to our shirts, took off our rings, so as to leave no indications, and in that condition entered the room. The dining-room door we closed, there was no light on the first-floor lobby, nor in the bed-room, for we had put out the fire there. So holding each other by the shoulder, we entered, closed the door, and we were all in the room together in the dark.

We lifted our shirts, and closed on the women, each of whom in her turn felt our pricks. One felt mine as if she meant to pull it off. On the second feeling, we got somehow mixed, a slight tittering of women began, some one hished, and the tittering ceased Two hands touched me at the same time, but one withdrew directly she touched the other's hand. A card was put into my hand, afterwards another card touched me, and was withdrawn. After waiting a minute I nudged the man next me. "Have you all given cards?" shouted out the man. "Yes," shouted the three women at once. Then we all burst out laughing, and the men went downstairs, leaving the women all talking at once like Bedlam broke loose.

Looking at our cards, we found that each woman had guessed rightly her man's prick; but we changed our cards, and called out to the women who came rushing down like mad. "Not one of you has guessed right," said I, "you have all lost your bets." "I'll swear I'm right," said Lady A***, "it's Adolphus that I gave my card to." This set us all questioning at once. "What makes you so sure?" "She says it's very long and thin," said Mabel, "and so it is." "Hold your tongue," said Marie. "I felt it," said Mabel. "They all seemed the same to me," said Laura, "and one of you pushed my hand away." "It was I," said Fred, "you wanted to feel too much, you nearly frigged me." "Oh! What a lie." Then we told the truth, and that each woman had won, which caused much noisy satisfaction, then we had more wine, we men still with naked legs.

I have told all I can recollect with exactitude, but there was lots more said and done. Fred pulled up Lord A***'s shirt, his cock was not stiff. "That's not as it was when I felt it," said Mabel. "You've guessed pricks, but for all that you would not know who fucked you in the dark." "We should," cried out all the women. "Let's try," said Lord A***. "All right," said Mabel. "We are not prostitutes," said Laura. "A little free fucking will be jolly, let's take turns about all round," said Fred. Then the room resounded with our laughter, all spoke baudily at once, every second, "prick," "cunt," "fuck," was heard from both men and women, — it was a perfect Babel of lasciviousness.

"I'll bet ten pounds a woman doesn't guess who fucks her," said Lord A***. We echoed him. The women laughed, but led by Laura, refused, and squabbled. All wanted the bet to come off, but did not like to admit it. We had more champagne, the men put on their trowsers, we kissed all round, and talked over the way of deciding such a bet, the women got randier, one showed her leg to another, and at length all the women agreed to take part in the orgie.

The rest I shall tell as truthfully as I can. The drink and excitement I was under makes it difficult; but I will tell nothing I am not quite sure of. We arranged a plan with such noise and talking, that God knows how it was arranged at all. Where were we to poke? — in the bed-room? Impossible, there was but one large bed in Lady A***'s room, and one in the back-room. How were we to fuck all together? We all rushed upstairs, took all the beds and pillows from both rooms, and from the upper rooms, and put them on the floor in the large room, making one long bed, after moving aside the furniture. The fire had been put out. All this was done with shouts and yells, a fearful lascivious riot.

The women were to lie down in an order known to us, Lady A*** nearest to the door, and so on. There was to be absolute silence. Each man as he knelt between the woman's legs was to put a card with a number on it under her pillow. We men knew which number each had, the women were not to know which man was to have her, directly we had fucked we were to return, each woman was to produce her card, and guess who had been up her, they were to be in their chemises, we in our shirts. I never shall forget the looks of the women as they went upstairs to arrange themselves for the fucking, but think that they scarcely knew the rules of what they were to do.

The women undressed quickly enough, for we had scarcely had time to tie up our faces in napkins to prevent our whiskers being noticed (Lord A*** had none), before a voice shouted out, "We are ready." Then with shirts on only, up we men went. I only recollect kneeling down between Lady A***'s legs (we had agreed among ourselves how to change our women), giving a card, feeling a cunt, and putting my prick into it, then hearing the rustling of limbs, hard breathing, sighing, and moans of pleasure of the couples fucking fast and furiously; of my brain whirling, of a maddening sensuality delighting me as I clasped the buttocks of Lady A***, and fucked her.

We must have spent nearly all together, none when we compared after recollected more than his own performance. All were quiet. I was feeling round my prick which was still in Lady A***'s cunt, when a light flashed powerfully through the room. That devil Fred had risen, and lighted several lucifers, which then was done by dipping them in a bottle, — they were expensive. What a sight was disclosed at a glance!

All three women lay with chemises up to their navels, Lady A*** on her back, I on the top of her (rising rapidly at the light). Next to her Mabel seemingly asleep with thighs wide open. Fred kneeling between them, holding the lighted matches, Laura on her back with open thighs, eyes closed, Lord A*** cuddling, but nearly off of her by her side, and his prick laying on her thigh. The women shrieked, and began pulling down their chemises. I swore at Fred, the women joined chorus. "Most ungentlemanly," said Laura, getting up. That got up Lord A***. Mabel lay still on her back as if ready to be stroked again. But all was said. In a minute the lucifers burnt out, and it was dark again. Scuffing up, we men went downstairs, leaving the women chattering. Soon after, down they came, looking screwed, lewed, and annoyed that the bets were off, and all chattering at once.

Mabel was quarrelsome. "You," said she, turning to Lady A***, "said that your husband's thing was long and thin, you tried to mislead me in the bet, you wanted to make me lose." They had evidently been discussing their men's pricks.

"So you have been telling how each of us fucks," said Fred. Laura denied it. "We did," said Mabel. "It's a lie, Mabel, if you say it again, I'll tell something more than you will like to hear about yourself." Mabel retorted, Lady A*** chimed in. It was a Babel of quarrelsome lewed women, with their cunts full.

I feared a row, and that Mabel might after all know more about my having had Laura, the night we all three slept in the same bed, than I cared for; so I pacified them. Fred said we had better try again, Laura objected. "Oh! Yes, Mrs. Modest," said Mabel. "When you found it was not Fred, why didn't you cry out?" "I didn't know," said Laura. "Ah! Ah! the printer's wife," we shouted, then more baudy talk, recriminations, and squabbling. Laura said she should go home, Fred said she might go by herself. Lord A***, who had half fallen asleep, said it was too late, and we had better stop. Some one said we could soon again make the beds comfortable in the upper rooms. "That be damned," said Fred, "we will all sleep on the floor as they are now." "Free fucking forever," said I. Laura said I was a blackguard, Mabel said she should like it,

Lady A*** said she didn't care, if Adolphus didn't, Adolphus said any cunt would suit him. He was reeling drunk as he spoke.

All this time we were in shirts and chemises. One woman had thrown a shawl over her, one a petticoat, but their breasts flashed out, their arms were naked, their legs showing to their knees, the men were naked to their knees in their shirts. The scene was exciting, the women hadn't washed their cunts, Fred said so. Mabel asked him if he was sure of it. No, he would feel. Laura told him he must be drunk, and was a beast. "Drunk?" said he, "look here." He turned a somersault, and stood on his hands and head, his heels against the wall, his back-side in the air, his prick and cods falling downwards over his belly, his shirt over his head. Lady A*** took up a bunch of grapes, and dashed it on his ballocks. Then we chased the women round the room, tried to feel them, and they us. It was like hell broke loose, till we agreed to sleep on the floor together anyhow.

No lights; lights and piss-pots were put in the back bedroom, — a woman suggested that. "You're frightened of farting," said someone. The women went up to make the beds more comfortable, took blankets, etc., from the upper rooms, whilst we men fetched candles from the kitchen, the others being well nigh burnt out. The women had washed their cunts, we had more wine, and then we all were pretty well screwed, and Lord A*** pretty drunk when we went up to them.

Up to that time I was sufficiently sober to know all I have written, and plenty more. Surely I could tell a lot more of our conversation, but it would prolong the tale too much. After the last bottle of champagne I was groggy, recollect less clearly, was in a half-sleepy, feverish, excited, and bawdy state, my sleep was broken by others, but when awake my prick stood immediately, and I moved all night from one woman to another, fucking, and then dozing.

To satisfy Laura, and keep up a sort of appearance, we had said we would only have our own women, who were again to lay in a certain order. Directly they had left the room, we agreed to change. A*** doggedly insisted on having Mabel, so I was to take Laura, and Fred Lady A***. It was such a lark. My prick was up Laura when she cried, "It's not you, Fred." Then were simultaneous exclamations, "I'm not Mabel," — "What a lovely cunt!" — "Leave me alone," — "Feel my big prick," — "Damn, a cunt's a cunt," hiccupped

Lord A***. "Oh! — ah!" — "Ha! My love fuck, — My darling, oh!" — kiss, kiss, — spending, — "aha!" — sighs of delight, — "cunt," — "fuck," — "Oh!" — "Ah! Ah!" And I fell asleep on Laura amidst this.

Awake again. By my side a wet cunt, a heavy sleeper. Turning round, my legs met naked legs. I stretched out my hand, and felt a prick, perhaps Fred's, I don't know. Getting up, I felt my way, stumbling over legs to the wall to the furthest woman, and laid myself on her. "Don't Adolphus, I'm so sleepy," said she. The next instant we were fucking. Others awakened. "Where are you?" said someone. Then all moved, one man swore, a hand felt my balls from behind. I was spending, and rolled off the lady, turning my bum to her. Then I touched Mabel, and put my hand to her cunt. A man dropped on her, and touched my hand with his prick. Ejaculations burst out on all sides, the couples were meeting again, then all was quiet, and the fucking done. Then all talked. All modesty was gone, both men and women told their sensations and wants. "You fuck me, — Feel me, — No, I want so and so," Laura as lewed as the rest.

Again awaking. A hand was feeling my prick. "Is it you, Laura?" "Yes." I felt her cunt. "Oh! Let me go and piddle." But I turned on to her, and we fucked, "How wet your cunt is." "No wonder."

Again I awakened, someone got up, and fell down. "Hulloa! Who is that?" "I want to piss, and can't get up," said Lord A*** in a drunken voice. Someone opened the door, a feeble light came across from the back-room, we helped him up and he stumbled along with us men to piss. Then he insisted on going downstairs. He could scarcely stand, so we helped him to the dining-room, we lighted more candles, he swilled more wine, tumbled on to the sofa, where we left him drunk and snoring, and found him snoring the next morning with the hearth-rug over him. We two went back to the women. "I've fucked all three," said Fred. "So have I." "Laura's a damned fine fuck, ain't she?" Someone shut the room-door opposite, as we reached the landing. We pushed it open. Two ladies were pissing; Marie and Laura. "Where is Mabel?" "Drunk," replied one. The two were past caring for anything, pissed and went back with us to the bed-room. I took a light there. Mabel was on her back nearly naked, we covered her up, for it was cold. Then I fucked Laura, and Fred, Lady A***. The light we left now on the wash hand-stand, so we looked at each other fucking and enjoyed it, and then we changed women. There was no cunt-washing, we fucked in each other's sperm, no one cared, all liked it, all were screwed, baudy, reckless, Mabel snoring.

I awakened after a heavy sleep, chilly, feverish, headach-ing, and thirsty. I drew aside the curtains; it was late, light, but foggy; a nasty winter's morning. Fred and the three la-dies lay snoring, some covered, others partially so, the floor looking as if every article of bed-furniture had been thrown down with a pitch-fork. I drank water, and fucked out as I was, my lubricity was unsatiated. I could not resist gratify-ing it.

Moving stealthily, I uncovered the sleepers one by one. It was easy enough, as the clothes lay loose and in shapeless heaps. I saw Fred's prick touching Mabel's haunch, contem-plated Laura's thick-haired quim, saw spunk on her chemise. She looked lovely. Lady A*** on her back, her hand over her cunt, red stains about her, and on the sheet which I pulled off her, — her poorliness had come on. Mabel on her back looked ready for a man. My cock stiffened, I laid my-self on Laura, and awakened her. That awakened Fred who mounted Mabel. Both couples took to the exercise in the foggy day-light, and a long time we were in consummating. "Oh! Do leave off," said Laura, "I'm so sore." My prick was excoriated, it had not been so for many a day.

Never have I been in such an orgie before, never since, and perhaps never shall be; but it was one of the most deli-cious nights I ever spent. So said Fred, so said Mabel; and Laura admitted to me at a future day that she thought the same, and that since, when she frigged herself, she always thought of it, and nothing else.

I thought of nothing else for a long time. Nothing has ever yet fixed itself in my mind so vividly, so enduringly, except my doings with my first woman, Charlotte. At the beginning of my writing these memoirs, this was among the first de-scribed. The narrative as then written was double its present length, and I am sorry that I have abbreviated it, for the oc-currences as I correct this proof seem to come on too quickly. Whereas we dined at seven o'clock, and it was one o'clock I guess before we all went to bed together, and the stages from simple voluptuousness to riotous baudiness and free-fucking were gradual. At eight o'clock not one of us would have dared to think of, still less to suggest, what we all did freely at midnight.

CHAPTER XIII

Morning headaches. — An indignant housekeeper. — A saucy valet. — Consequences. — Fred leaves England. — Lady A***'s invitation. — Laura a widow. — Farewell Laura. — Adieu Mabel. — My guardian's remonstrances. — Parental advice. — Ruined. — Reflexions. — My relations.

With headaches, heated, irritable, thirsty, worn out, we arose; the men quiet, the women quarrelsome. The women began to dress, some where they had slept, some in the other room. We went down to Lord A***, and awakened him. He went upstairs, and bawled out to the housekeeper (he had rung the bell violently several times without her appearing). "Make us some tea directly," said he. She answered, "I shan't, — make it yourself." "I'll dismiss you if you don't." "I ain't going to make tea for prostitutes," said she, "and we are not going to keep in such a house." Fred said the wine was bad, or his head would not ache so. A*** said Fred knew nothing about wine. Mabel who had heard what the housekeeper said, bawled out that she would go up, and tear her eyes out. The free-fucking tone was gone, each man seemed jealous, and spoke harshly to his woman. At a remark of Marie's, Lord A*** told her to go to another room. No, she should not till Mabel was out of the house. Mabel, not quite sober, told me I had better go home with Laura. Fred said Laura would go home with him. Laura was quiet, and tried to get Fred to leave with her, and told Mabel she would be better if she took less liquor. At length we separated. We four were going to the same house, but went in separate cabs, then to our own rooms, and had breakfast separately there, — a thing we never had done before. We always lived in Laura's apartments, and shared the expenses.

After breakfast Mabel and I went to bed, late in the day we awakened. I was refreshed, for then a long sleep restored me from any excess. Although I did not like Mabel's behaviour, and did not care about her having had the other men as I thought, yet it annoyed me; but it had the effect of giving me a strong letch for her for some time. I used to think as I fucked her, of my prick rubbing where Fred's and Lord A***'s had rubbed, it delighted me to say, "Should you know it was my prick if you had just awakened?" — "Did his hurt you, when he pushed like this?" — shove, shove, — "Tell me how Fred goes just before he spends." We used to fetch each other by talking over that night; but she did not recollect very clearly, and declared she was sure I had not had her, although I certainly had her once that night, and when the spunk of Lord A*** and Fred's was in her. It used to horrify me when I thought of that, such was my masculine inconsistency then.

We all four dined together, but were a little reserved until wine was in us, then we laughed about the night; but Laura, saying we had better forget it, we agreed not to talk about it again, nor did we with the women. Fred and I used often to do so, he never seemed so happy as when he was asking me if Laura was not a damned fine fuck, but directly I said yes, he was silent.

The frolic brought about a great deal of mischief. Lord A***'s housekeeper and maid left that day, they would not stop. I dare say they had seen and heard enough to tell them the games we were up to, for we were not particular about shutting doors. Lord A*** regretted the cook, because she was such a good one. She told the valet, and soon after he was insolent to Lady A***, so Lord A*** kicked him out. He summoned A*** before a magistrate for an assault, and A*** was fool enough to compromise it. The man told a lot. The owner of the house gave Lord A*** notice to quit, and he and Lady A*** went to lodgings, and the publicity embroiled Lord A*** still more with his family.

Neither was the friendship between us all quite the same. Laura and Mabel quarrelled. Lord A*** would not let his mistress visit them unless he was with her, Laura would never leave Mabel in the room alone with Fred. Occasionally we still dined together, and went to the theatre. One night when we had had much wine, we joked about the night, and the women got quarrelling. Laura said the affair was disgraceful, and had it not been for Mabel, it never would have happened. Mabel bounced off to her own rooms. Soon after, I took separate lodgings for Mabel. There she was always in tears, if I left her long, and if away a day or two, she wanted to know if I had been with Laura. Lady A*** visited Mabel, and was frightened to let her Lord know it. Then Lord and Lady A*** quarrelled, he had the clap, and gave it to his mistress. Fred and I were always excellent friends, and at some annoyance through the women, suggested we should go to Paris, and leave them alone in London.

Before going, I met Lady A*** walking out, who asked me in, saying Lord A*** would be glad to see me. As I had not quarrelled with him, I thought a chat might heal our coolness. When in-doors, she called out to him, and professed to be surprized at his not being there. If I would wait, he would be in soon. We got nearer and nearer to each other on the sofa, began talking about the free-fucking night, of the good aim she had made with the bunch of grapes on Fred's balls as he stood on his head. We got very lewed, I kissed her, she me. Would she know it was I who was up her, if I came in the dark to her? She could not say, but should know it was not A***, — a beast. "Beast, why? — have you quarrelled?" Then she told me that A*** was often drunk, and stayed away from her for days. "He has got a disease from a beastly gay woman, and hasn't slept with me for weeks." "And not had you?" "Of course not." "Oh! don't you want it?" "No wonder if I do." At once I put my hands up her petticoats, felt her nice plump thighs, my fingers rubbed on the smooth quim. "Oh! Don't, — I can't bear it." I pulled out a stiff prick, and put it into her hand, we toyed with each other's genitals for a minute, then she sunk back on the sofa, I on her, and we copulated.

I stayed the whole evening with her, fucking at intervals. A*** did not come back. I am sure she knew he would not, and had asked me in because she wanted me to have her. She did not tell me she had had the clap, nor I her, — it was Mabel who had told me.

She hinted she should like to meet me again, and I made some half-sort of promise, but never did. Mabel became more and more expensive, discontented, lushy, and quarrelsome, and she was not clean. She would feel my wet prick after it had left her cunt, and then cut bread and butter without washing her hands. We had rows, and I left her, giving her a handsome sum of money. Laura said she had gone back to Plymouth with Lord A***, who had left Lady A***. Then Fred, I, and Laura were just as we used to be. He seemed to have forgotten everything, and I never presumed on having poked Laura. We went to Paris, leaving Laura in

[152]

London with her sister, who came up to stay with her, — a nice girl.

Though short of money now, Fred and I at Paris took no heed, but rattled away as if our purses were inexhaustible. His furlough was nearly up. We had no end of women. "Old *** (naming a relative) will leave you all his money," said he, "he's fond of you, and has no one else to leave it to." I and all my family thought that; my mother had repeatedly warned me that he was discontented with my goings on; but I counted on his love for me, love since I was a baby; so I played at Paris a jolly game, regardless of money.

When I came back from Paris, I tried to retrench, but found it all but impossible. I got rid of Mabel, spent five shillings for my dinner, where I used to spend twenty, went to live with my mother, put down my horses and carriage, and discharged my man and grooms. But as I diminished my amusements and extravagances generally, so I seemed more and more to need women. My cock stood all day, and half the night. Women I had by dozens. I tried to reduce their fees, and did to a little extent, but for some years I had been accustomed to a liberal expenditure in that article, and though to a country girl I could give five shillings, to a Londoner I could only give gold, and never refused more if they pleased me, and were not satisfied.

Fred then went abroad to his regiment. He made arrangements for Laura to have a small income, not a tenth of what she had had, but enough to keep her in a quiet way. I at first was to pay it to her. She was to have it as long as she remained steady, and he hoped she would go home, hoped she would keep steady till his return, — his return which was not probable in less than seven years at the least.

One night when together, we laughed at the absurdity of expecting it. "Walter, is it probable that a fine woman like that will be content with frigging herself?" "No." "She will be fucked, — I would if I were she, — it's a shame to wish her to go without fucking. If I were married to her, she would go with me, but a man can't take a mistress to India, he could not live with her, and all the regiment would be smelling at her tail, — she will be fucked, and I can't help it." Tears stood in his eyes. "You give her a grind, old boy, if she must have it, I'd rather you did it than anyone, and it will keep her quiet. You have had her, — do you recollect that night? — Oh! God, what a spree! I never had such a spree before in my life, and never shall again." I said I

[*153*]

would take care of her as if a sister, as to having her, he might dismiss such an idea from his head, and I meant what I said. He went abroad, and was killed in battle. I loved him.

Laura went into humbler lodgings, I saw her often, but never made the slightest advances. Soon she could not make her money do. Her mother came up to stay with her, and she had then partly two to keep. She dressed plainer, sold or pawned her best things, told me all, and how it was impossible to make the money do. Then I made her a present, she kissed me, and that set my blood boiling. Her mother wanted her to go back to the country, I advised it also; it was agreed she should, and her mother went back. A day or two afterwards I called on her, she got me a chop for dinner, and sent for wine. We talked about Fred, she cried about him, I kissed her to comfort her, she kissed me again as we sat on the sofa, my arm went round her, I pulled her hand on to my shoulder; and that spree at Lord A***'s came into my head.

"You miss a bed-fellow Laura, don't you?" "Oh! No, but I miss poor Fred, he was so kind." "Do you recollect that night?" "Don't mention it, I am ashamed of it, — oh! don't look at my boots, they are so shabby now." I had begun at the ankles, as I always did, it was on the road. "You are not so stout as you were, my dear." "There is not any difference in me." I pinched her thighs outside her clothes. "Ah! I'm no thinner there, I'm sure." "Let me feel." "Oh! Now don't, — it's a shame." My darling, you are as smooth and plump as ever, — I know the feel of those beautiful thighs, I've laid on them." Soon my hand was between them, my finger on the clitoris. "Poor Fred," said she, still crying, her head on my shoulder. In another instant her hand was round my prick, her thighs open, my hand restless, and roving all about her cunt. "Lay down." "I won't." "It won't hurt him poor fellow, he is far away." For a few minutes we coaxed and fondled, kissed and cried, saying it was not fair, and we never would. Then cock and cunt getting hotter and more sensitive, I pushed her flat on the sofa, and we fucked ecstatically. Rising, she sat looking at me; her clothes half-way up her thighs, I looking at her with my wet prick hanging its head. Then we hugged, kissed, and did it again.

"It was to be," said she (as if poking her was fate). "Quite true dear, but let's go to the bed, the sin is no greater if we do it ever so many times." Into bed we got, and there I think we laid for sixteen hours. Laura was a lovely bed-fellow. I had a good look at the hair on her cunt, it was very long, curled round, and completely hid her cunt, even when standing with her legs slightly open; and when she pissed, she left drops of piddle on the hair. On her that bush was handsome, but very long hair is not generally handsome on a cunt, and I have disliked it on others; but it is not often found. I am describing here what I saw more coolly, and often on future occasions, rather than what I saw and recollect of her cunt, on that night of exhausting pleasure.

I had now but little money to spare, but gave her a little from time to time, and a great deal of bumbasting. One day she said, "I'm in misfortune again." She was in the family way, had been so before by Fred, but had managed a miscarriage. She now got one, but was seriously ill, and sent for her mother, and when she got better she went home. I sent Fred's money to her there for some time, then she wrote me to send it to a post-office, and afterwards to send no more, as she was going to be married. She hoped I would never tell Fred, that I would burn her letters, and if I ever saw her, would not notice her. I never saw her again. She wrote to Fred about her marriage, and he was delighted at it, as well as at saving his money. I have finished her history, so far as it was connected with me; and must now take up my narrative at a time before this.

Friends were going to Paris, I went with them, and a jolly loose time we had for a few weeks. I made acquaintance with six or eight of the best baudy houses, and had women galore. Theatres, excursions, high feasting, unlimited whoring were the characteristics of my trip. I returned empty in pocket, and knocked up with copulating, yet had had none of the excitants with women that I have had there since. I rushed at cunt directly I saw it; my physical enjoyment was so intense, that I could not dally with my prick, but let it satisfy itself as soon as it liked. The varieties that Camille had given me left no taste for them. Cunt, belly, and thighs, seen, felt, and fucked in regular fashion, was my delight. Heaps of bills met me on my return. The thought of becoming bankrupt horrified me. I disposed of my remaining property, paid all, and was left with a few hundred pounds. I pass now over a short time of which there is nothing to be said, but that I was economical in all but women.

My remaining guardian and my mother had been always at me with advice, which I entirely disregarded, and flung away money in all directions. Had I only spent it on women it would have lasted years longer. That which women had I do not regret, they have been the greatest joy of my life, and are so to every true man, from infancy to old age. Copulation is the highest pleasure, both to the body and mind, and is worth all other human pleasures put together. A woman sleeping or waking is a paradise to a man, if he be happy with her, and he cannot spend his money on anything better, or so good.

Soon after, almost dependent again on my mother, who did nothing but upbraid me, my hopes centred in my old relative, who had promised to make me his heir. He was not so gracious to me as he used to be; he murmured at my extravagance, and supposed that any money I had would go down the same sink, by which he meant women. He died suddenly, just as he was in greatest wrath with me, and left me nothing.

All hopes were dashed to the ground. Laura was my consolation till she left. For a year of my life I was needy and discontented, but not so miserable as I was fated to be. I pass over that period, there was not much in the amatory line to tell of. Fucking is a common-place thing, the prince and the beggar do it the same way, it is only the incidents connected with it that are exciting. Voluptuous, reckless, youth and beauty together, make the vulgar, shoving, arse-wagging business poetical for the time, but it is animalism.

Then I committed a more fatal error than spending a fortune in jollity; what it was will be guessed, it is only referred to here to connect my history. I was then in my twenty-sixth year.

I add a few observations which on reading this written many years ago, seems now needful to explain even to myself.

Most of my relatives lived in the provinces, and were wealthy. We visited each other periodically, but distance (there were few railways then) prevented them from entering into my daily life, still less my secret life. Fred's mother was nearest to us, and as the episodes show, she and her family were most mixed up with my affairs. An aunt in London, childless and rich, gave me the most money, and afterwards left me a good sum. I cared but little about those living at a distance. With a cousin from the North I had some rousing debauches, which were at the time known to many of my family. He is still alive, but pious, and with a large family, and would not like to know I am writing this. Jolly old Ben,

I won't narrate our sprees, for you may live to read this, — who knows?

CHAPTER XIV

Married, and miserable. — Virtuous intentions. — Consequences. — Mary Davis. — Low-class fucksters. — A concupiscent landlady. — Reflexions on my career. — On the sizes of pricks. — My misconception. — My misery — Reflexions.

My life was now utterly changed; I was quite needy, with a yearly income (and that not my own) not more than I used to spend in a month, sometimes in a fortnight. Every shilling I had to look at, walked miles where I used to ride, and to save sixpence, amusements were beyond me, my food was the simplest, wine I scarcely tasted, all habits of luxury were gone, but worse than all I was utterly wretched. I tried to make the best of my life and could when by myself be cheerful, even in the recollection of the past fun; but there was that about me now which brought sorrow over to me. The instant I saw her, she checked my smile, sneered at my past, moaned over my future, was a nightmare to me, a very spectre.

I tried to like, to love her. It was impossible. Hateful in day, she was loathsome to me in bed. Long I strove to do my duty, and be faithful, yet to such a pitch did my disgust at length go, that laying by her side, I had wet dreams nightly, sooner than relieve myself in her. I have frigged myself in the streets before entering my house, sooner than fuck her. I, loving women, and naturally kind and affectionate to them, ready to be kind and loving to her, was driven to avoid her as I would a corpse. I have followed a woman for miles with my prick stiff, yet went to my wretched home pure, because I had vowed to be chaste. My heart was burning to have an affectionate kiss, a voluptuous sigh from some woman, yet I avoided obtaining it. My health began to give way, sleepless nights, weary days, made me contemplate suicide. It seemed as if I never could have happiness again, yet my physical forces, or so much of them as lay in my gener-

[*157*]

ative organs, seemed unimpaired. I neither drank nor debauched, and my prick stood incessantly; neither random frigs nor night-dreams stopped it.

My only relief from misery was in thinking over the pleasures I had had, yet all seemed such a long time past, that it was like a dream. Then a desire to have other women became invincible. I had no means to get those I had been accustomed to, and seemed to have no idea of going economically to work for my pleasures, but at length began to walk through streets inhabited by very poor gay women, in a neighbourhood I had known in my early youth. Then I found out other poor quarters, and one night with but a few shillings in my pocket, after thinking of throwing myself into a canal, I found myself at a spot where women of a somewhat better class lived in its centre, and on its outskirts very poor harlots.

"I will, — have I the money? — can't help it, — if one won't another will," and I slunk into a street, half ashamed of entering it. Saw girls standing at doors, never paused for selection, nor to see if one looked nicer than another, it was cunt I wanted. The moment I turned the corner of the street, I cared not who or what, as long as she had a petticoat, and what it hid from sight. I took the nearest.

"Will you let me have you for five shillings?" was all I uttered. I recollect it as well as possible, hanging my head, ashamed of my offer, and not looking at the girl, ashamed of being seen in the neighbourhood.

"All right," said she, turning round. I followed her through the little narrow passage of a four-roomed house into a little room with a bed on one side of it. I looked at her, and she at me for an instant only. "Here are the five shillings," said I. "Shall I undress?" "No." "Shall we get on the bed?" "No, at the side," — and whilst speaking I had half lifted her on to it. Laughing with a peculiar chuckle she fell back, pulling up her clothes. I saw plump thighs, dark hair, felt giddy, could not see, recollect opening the lips, and began to spend as the tip of my prick touched her cunt. Following the spunk as it shot up the passage as it opened its way with one thrust I was up her, and had finished. Fifty times in my life up to the time I pen this, has a similar rapid ejaculation occurred to me when randy.

"Didn't you want it!" said she. They were the first words I recollect being uttered as I bent over her. How divine she seemed. "Let me do it again." "Oh! You ought to give me a little more." "I'll give you a shilling, it's all I have, I fear; but more if I have it." "Very well then," said a soft voice. Oh! What a heavenly few minutes they seemed to me, — they still seem to me, — as I fucked her again. First and second fuck must have been all over in five minutes. I had not uncunted.

"Pull it out," said she, after an interval, my cock still keeping in her; but I kept close to her, and up her. "Be still dear, do, pray, — I'll see what money I have." My hat and my great-coat were on, it was cold, I had only unbuttoned my trowsers enough to get out my prick. Keeping still up her, I thrust my hand into my trowsers pocket, pulled out all the money I had, and put it on the bed beside her. "See, it is all I have, every farthing, a little more than I said, — let me do it again, — there is more than seven shillings," — and pressing well on to her haunches, I began wriggling my prick.

She turned her head, looked at the money, but did not touch it. "Very well," said she, in a low voice, "but take it out, — don't make my chemise in a mess, I have not another clean, — don't make a mess on the bed if you can help it." "I shan't." "Yes you will, you have spent such a lot, it's running out now."

I withdrew. She took a towel which was close at hand, wiped her cunt, and spread another for her bum. I threw off hat and coat. Soon now we were both on the bed, I up her, and leaning on my elbow, for the first time really looked at her. Up to that moment cunt, cunt, nothing but cunt was in my mind. Now I saw that her eyes were blueish, her hair dark and wavy, I recollect our staring in each other's faces for a minute or two without speaking. A candle on a little table close to the bed showed a strong light on us sideways; then we both fucked with vigor, and Mary Davis spent with me, — she spent with me, that poor little gay woman.

"You are a nice poke," said the girl. I got off the bed, sat on a chair by the fire, and looked at the merry face of the little gay woman as she smiled at me whilst washing her quim. The pleasure I had just had, the entrancement of the carnal pleasure contrasted so strongly with my misery at home, that I burst into tears, and sobbed like a child. She rubbed her quim dry, then silently came up to me, put her hand on my shoulder, and stood without uttering a word till my passion was over. "Are you unhappy?" said she in a gentle tone. Yes

[*159*]

I was. "Never mind, I dare say it will be over some day, — we have all got unhappinesses."

Having broken my virtuous resolution, I never regained it, and for a week fucked Mary from six in the evening till two the next morning. My week's amusement cost me about two pounds, but then that modest sum was too much for my pocket, so I left off for a while, and gave Mary a chance of keeping her other friends. They were mostly poor clerks, she told me, and married men better off, who gave her a pound, or at times paid her rent if in arrear. She paid I think but twenty-five shillings a week for her board and lodging together. My too exclusive attentions for a week had prevented her regulars from coming. There was lots of cheaper cunt in the neighbourhood so to send them away with full balls was dangerous.

The house was kept by an old man and woman, he a carpenter almost too old, yet who went to daily work. He used to fetch gin and beer for us. There was no other lodger in the house. They were a decent couple, and after a time I used to talk to the old woman, and when Mary once went away ill, she got me a beautifully shaped girl. I had offered her money to get me a girl of about fourteen years of age, a virgin. The streets about there swarmed with girls and boys who played about at night, I could hear their smutty language as they ran after each other yelling, laughing and quarrelling. She tried, but never could; she was not a woman who undertook that sort of thing, but the money tempted her. "There are lots of girls about," said she, "their mothers don't care what they do, but you want a virgin, — Lor! Where's she to be found? — when they's about thirteen or fourteen years old they won't be kept in, they is about the dark streets at night and Lor! If you heard what I have in the streets where the costers' barrows is, of a night!" And so the old woman intimated that all the young girls of that select neighbourhood, were got into by the coster boys, and that a virginity was a rarity at fourteen years old. I afterwards groped several young girls in those dark streets, and there was certainly no obstacle to my fingers searching their cunts.

Lots of children were about, who played in the streets at day, but disappeared if quite young towards dusk. If a man stopped and talked to a gay woman at the door, the children of the house usually went in, always did if more than about ten years old. They drew back as if they knew that a bargain for fucking was to be struck, and I believe knew all about it. They were mostly girls who sleeping in the same room with their parents, I dare say had seen the game of mother and father played often enough. The bigger girls frisked about the streets of an evening with boys of the same age, or not much older.

If a woman could get you to enter the passage, she almost pulled you into her room. "Come in, — don't stand there, — come out of the way of the lodgers, — I'll tell you if you come in, — well, make it half-a-crown, — I've got such a nice cunt, — such a fat arse, — feel my bubbies, — look here, — come in, and let me feel your prick."

My experience with this poor class of women was soon considerable. Satiated, sick of them, yet I continued to frequent them for the simple carnal pleasure of coition. There was no sentiment about it, no liking for the women, for though their manners sometimes amused me, they more frequently shocked me, and the poverty of some distressed me; but I had no money for choicer entertainment. My vigor was great, my pleasure in copulation almost maddening, a cunt was a cunt, and I got my pleasure and relief up it, whatever its owner might have been. A sensuous imagination aided me. When once my prick was up a woman she was for the time more or less invested with charms, and her imperfections forgotten. I used to shut my eyes, and fancy I was stroking a houri with the finest limbs and ivory flesh, and could fancy all this up to the moment of ejaculation, the woman I was enjoying was then to me some one I had had before and elsewhere, and I fancied thighs and cunt which were not those of the woman who was at that moment doing her best to please me.

There were occasions when the women when naked revolted me, my prick refused to stand, and I departed without copulating, but those occasions with this class of women are not worth noting. I have been subject to this sudden revolt and prostration, sometimes even when the woman was most beautiful. Nervousness, fear, some sudden dislike, and even most ridiculous reasons have caused it.

I should have mentioned that gradually it had taken hold of my mind that my prick was a very small one. How this notion first arose I cannot quite trace, I certainly had it in a degree when a youth, and it became stronger owing to the remarks of some French women. The men I saw fucking at Camille's had very large pricks, and no doubt they were selected on that account for exhibition; but I did not know that then, and used mentally to compare mine with theirs, and also with those of some of my former schoolfellows, and to my disadvantage.

With many harlots of both high and low class I had talked about size; each told me of men who had big pricks, rarely of those who had small ones. Experience has since taught me that harlots like talking about big pricks, for size affects their imagination agreeably. Of ridiculously small ones they make mention for a laugh, the average sizes pass without their notice. I used to ask them how mine compared with the big ones they spoke of, and got at last into my head the erroneous opinion about my own machine. At times I would produce it with an apologetic remark. "My prick's not a very big one, is it?" — and was much pleased when the woman's reply was complimentary. I know now from the inspection of many men's, that mine compares very favourably with the average, and is larger than most; but for many years I was of a very different opinion, and at times was almost ashamed of my prick, so much so that when a woman said it was as large as most, and many said that, I did not believe them, still less did I believe them when they said it was a handsome prick; then I thought they were humbugging me.

Now as I add these few words written years after the foregoing, and after having seen some dozens of pricks, both languid and erect, I know what they said was true, and I know that there is a size, a form, a curve, and a colour in pricks which makes some handsomer than others, just as undoubtedly there are ugly and handsome cunts.

These are the most noticeable events which occurred during the period of my narrowest means. In that time I must have seen the privates of fifty women, and copulated with nearly that number. Had it not been for their pleasures, coarse as they were, I think I should have made away with myself, so miserable was I. How I accommodated myself to the class I can't imagine; for although a few were nice, prettyish, healthy women, the majority were low coarse creatures, living in poor single rooms which were often not clean; but both rooms and women were as good as could be expected for the few shillings I gave for their pleasures.

Up to this period I had tailed a neighbourhood of free cunts, as far as trifling sums would get them to me. A shilling a feel, or a look at the nudity, and for half-a-crown to five shillings at the outside for complete enjoyment was a tariff generally accepted.

Then a remnant of my former fortune which had been in litigation was settled in my favour, and I had a little ready money. Immediately I left off frequenting the poor Doxies of whom I have told, and went to a higher class, in a better neighbourhood. My money was soon gone, for I had debts among other things to settle out of it. Whilst it lasted I had some very nice women, among whom I shall always recollect a tall, superbly shaped creole, with dazzling white teeth (a feature in women which always has had a great attraction for me), and who was one of the most voluptuous women in her embraces I ever yet have had; but she was plain almost to ugliness. In the rest of my amours there was nothing to need special notice, they were all fugitive, and the women were changed frequently.

It is difficult to narrate more without divulging my outer life. I would fain keep that hidden, but it is impossible, I shall however tell as little as may be and obscure it, but without falsifying or distorting any facts relating to my amorous pranks, some of which were not sought by me. I fain would have led a steadier life, and wished a home with a woman I could love; but I had an unquiet home, and a woman there whom I hated in bed and at board. I tried at times to overcome my antipathy, abstained from women for weeks at a time, so that sexual want might generate a sort of love, but it was useless, without reward, and a life of misery was before me. I broke out under it, wonder I did not break down, and should have done so, had it not been for whores. Cunt came to my rescue, and alone gave me forgetfulness, a relief far better than gambling or drinking, the only other alternatives I could have had recourse to.

CHAPTER XV

The garden privies. — Our neighbor's daughters. —
Effects of a hard turd. — Masturbation. — Bum-
trumpeting. — Seeing and hearing too much. — A
pock-marked strumpet. — A neighbour's servant. —
Don't wet inside. — On the road home. — Cheap
amusements. — Bargains. — Watching brothels. —
Cunt in the open. — Clapped again. — French letters,
and effects. — Income improved. — Piddle in the by-
streets. — An uprighter. — My pencil-case. — A
female bilker. — A savage frig. — A silk dress soiled.

I was still poor, but had got into an employment, and was
living in a small eight-roomed house. I kept one servant
only, but was pinched to keep up appearances. None of the
outside world could have known how much I was pinched.
I went home regularly, sat for hours by myself reading,
brooding, fretting, and even crying bitter tears, at the time I
take up my narrative.

Our old-fashioned house was one of a row with a narrow
frontage, and four stories high, had a long narrow garden,
and a privy about thirty feet from the back-door, hidden by
some evergreens, the common mode of building in London
at that time. On the first floor was my own little sitting-room
and a drawing-room, and above two bed-rooms, the back
one serving as a dressing-room for me, above those a servant's attic. With one servant only we helped ourselves a
good deal as may be supposed.

The privies of the houses in our terrace were built in pairs,
the garden wall divided them and partly the cess-pool which
was common to the two. I used to take pleasure in watching
to see these girls go to the privy, and although the idea of a
female evacuating revolted me, yet used to try to get to our
privy when one of the girls went to theirs, and would stand
smoking just inside the passage by the backsteps of my
house, tip-toeing to catch a glance of their heads, and stopping myself from bogging sometimes, so that I might get
there at the same time. Directly I saw a head off I followed

quietly, and if the weather was quite still we could hear footsteps in each other's gardens too well.

The cess-pool had at the time I write of just been emptied, the turds dropping and flopping down could be heard, it was not nice, but it did not shock me. I liked to hear the girls' piddle splashing, and used to push my prick back, and sit back on the seat, so that my piddle might drop straight, and make much noise. It pleased me to hear the joint rattle and splash we made if we pissed at the same time. I did this so constantly, that I could tell which girl was there, for the piddle of one always made twice as much splash as the other's. Up would stand my prick, and often I could not piss for its stiffness, directly I heard the girls splashing.

One day I had a hardish motion, and was randy that morning almost to pain. One of the girls was there. I strained, my cock got stiff, and began to throb violently, and shot out its spunk as I strained. I went back to the house, and just entering it saw the other daughter go towards the privy. Back I went and sitting down frigged myself as I heard her evacuations drop, so randy and charged with sperm was I.

After that I occasionally frigged myself at the privy, and used to picture to myself the girls sitting there, their clothes up round their rumps, and slightly up in front showing their limbs, and piddle squirting. After a time we knew a little of the girls, and when talking to them I used to think of the same thing. The idea used to fascinate me, and they used to say (I am told), that I was a strange man, for I always stared at them as if I had never seen a woman before. They little knew what was in my mind when I was staring.

Just after the emptying I could not only see their wax as it fell to the bottom, but the paper with which they wiped their bums, and could hear them fart. Sometimes the two came together. One day by a sudden whim I let a fart as loud as I could, and heard a suppressed titter, they I think never knew I could hear, for usually I tried to be as silent as possible. I never coughed when there, and used to pull open my arse-hole to lessen the noise of my trumpet, and singular as it may seem did this out of a feeling of delicacy. Soon the cess-pool was half-filled with water, and I could only indistinctly hear. Then I grew tired of the fun, and again let off my sperm up cunts instead of spilling it on the privy-floor, for sorrow always came over me as I saw it on the floor. A few months after this I took a dislike to the girls through thinking of what I had seen and heard of them, it seemed to shock my sentiment of the beauty and delicacy of a woman.

A confused number of random whorings and miscellaneous fuckings took place about this time, I cannot tell to a month or two, but it began directly after Mary had gone. I tell of one or two of them.

At the back of the Lowther Arcade one night I took a poor girl seemingly about sixteen years old to a house. She had a nice but thin form, and was as white as driven snow. When I had had her, I wanted to see her face more clearly, but she held a handkerchief to it, and half turned it away from the light, her privates she allowed to be inspected as I liked.

She was marked badly with the small-pox, and was nevertheless handsome, but with that sad expression which the pock-marks often give. Gents did not like it, she said. It was a dreadfully sloppy, snowy night. "Don't go yet," she said, "it is so warm here." So I sat a while feeling her quim and talking. "Do me again, I want it now, I did not when you did it before." So we fucked again. "Do I please you?" said the girl putting her hand to my face. "Yes my dear." "Will you see me again? — do." I was always careful about promising that, and hesitated; but at length said yes. Again I rose to go, again the girl asked me to stay, it was so warm. "Pay the woman again and say you are going to stay till ten o'clock." There was such simplicity about her that I consented. The woman put coals on the fire, and we sat by it warming ourselves.

After a time she said, "I don't think you like me." "Why?" "Because you don't feel me about." I laughed, and said I had been feeling her. Time ran out. "Won't you do it again?" "I can't dear." "Let me try to make you." "You may, but I can't." She came to me, knelt down, played funnily, but awkwardly with my cock till it stiffened, and again we fucked. "You won't see me again, though you say you will." "Why not?" asked I wondering at her sad manner. "They all say they will, but they never do, — it's the smallpox marks they can't bear, I know it is, — I'm tired of this life." Then suddenly she laughed and said she was only joking.

I never did see her again. Such a young white-fleshed girl, and so fond of the cock, or else she had had but little of it, I have rarely met with. She said she had only been out two months. "The other girls tell me what to do with men, and the old woman where I live tells me; but I always does what a gentleman asks me, I can't do more, can I?" said she.

[166]

"Other gals say they have regular friends, I haven't." I shall never forget that poor little girl.

On a cold evening a week or two after this, I saw a short-ish, dark-eyed girl going along the Strand. She walked slowly, and looked in at almost every shop. I could not make up my mind if she was gay or not. She was warmly wrapped up, her style that of a well-to-do servant. I passed and re-passed her, looked her in the face; her eye met mine and dropped, then she stopped and looked round several times after unmistakably gay women as they passed her, then went on again. Opposite the Adelphi she paused and looked at the theatre for a long time, a gentleman spoke to her, and seemed to importune her, she took no notice of him, and he left her. After walking on for a minute quickly she loitered and looked in the shops again.

Near Exeter Hall my cock which was in want of relief giv-ing me impudence, and liking her looks I spoke to her about the things in the windows. At first I got no reply, and she walked on. "Come with me, and I'll give you a sovereign. You can buy it then." What it was I don't recollect. She seemed uneasy and wavering, yet made no reply. I repeated my offer (it was just then money beyond my means, but I had hot desire on me). She looked up the street in both di-rections, and asked, "Will it be far?" I took her at the in-stant for a sly gay one. "You know I am sure, it's close by." "It's getting late, I'm in a hurry." Looking both ways quickly and uneasily she placed her arm in mine, and hang-ing her head down pressed close to me. We walked quickly, and soon were in a snug room in a house at the back of Exeter Hall.

"This is not a public-house," said she looking round. "No, but you can have drink if you like." "A little warm brandy and water then." I ordered it. "Take off your bonnet and cloak." She hesitated. "Tell me the exact time." I did, and then she took them off, sat down, and soon sipped brandy and water looking at me. Thought I, "You must be a servant after all."

I began to caress her, and got my hand on her thighs ask-ing her to come to the bed. "I must go soon, let me go soon." "I will, but let me see your legs and feel them." She let me pull the clothes up to her knees, then pushed away my hand but I thrust one up, and just felt the cunt. She gave me a shove, and nearly pushed me over, for I had dropped on to my knees, a favorite attitude at such times.

Savagely I got up. "Don't be a fool; if you mean to let me do it come to the bed." She hesitated. "Give me the money first." "Oh!" thought I, "she is a whore diseased, and a bilk," so I refused. "You really will give it to me, won't you?" "Of course, but I'm not to be done that way." Then I got her on the bed, and threw up her clothes. She resisted. "What do you take me for?" "Why a whore," said I savagely. It was a word I rarely used *of* a woman, still rarer *to* a woman. She pushed my hand angrily away and sat up.

"I am not, and wish I had not come here, and would not, only I want money for my poor mother, I thought you a gentleman, — I'm not the sort of woman you say, I'm a servant, I am indeed." "Well if you are, you have been fucked." "That is neither here nor there, I'm not what you call me," — and she pouted. "Lay down dear, — let's fuck if you mean it, if not let's go, — let me feel you, and you feel me." I pulled her back on to the bed, laying down by the side of her, and put my prick into her hand. It was persuasive, for soon I was having that delicious rub, probe, and twiddle. Then I got a sight of all but the cunt itself, the inspection of that she resisted. A fine pair of limbs, a fat backside, lots of hair on her split I could feel. My friction told, she began grasping my prick like a vice, — she was going to spend.

Nice to her that, but I wanted my pleasure. Again I got savage. At length quietly, and feeling my prick all the time she said, "Promise me something." "What?" "Don't you wet inside if I let you." I promised, and turning on to her belly fucked her, and forgot my promise, even if I ever meant to keep it. We were soon near the crisis. "Don't — now, — oh! — wet." "No dear." "T — aake — care." "I'll pull it out just as it comes dear." "Don't — we — wet, oh! — ah! — wet," she gasped out as clutching her arse my prick went fiercely up her and spent every drop against her womb-tube, my spend made doubly pleasurable, because she did not wish it in her cunt.

Said she with a long-drawn sigh, "You've done it all inside, — you should not." "I could not help it, you are so charming, I could not pull it out and make your clothes or bum wet," said I ramming on, and keeping my prick tight up her lubricated cunt. "Let me get up." "Not yet." "Oh do, I'm in a hurry." "Lay still dear." "No, I'm in such a hurry, — what o'clock is it? — do tell me what o'clock it is, — it will make me lose my place if I'm very late."

I uncunted, told her the time, and she washed her cunt.

"Let us do it again." She was wanting it. "I've such a long way to go." "Where?" She told me, and it was my way home. "I will take you home in a cab." On the bed she got, I overcame her scruples, kissed her knees, her thighs, all the way up to her cunt. The thighs opened widely, a second's inspection of a cunt at that time of my life made me think of immediate pleasure, and after promising not to wet in her again, she reminding me of that, till she lost all care or heed in her pleasures. I spent up her as before.

We went home in a cab, and felt each other all the way. She said she was keeping her mother who was poor, she feared, dying. At the end of the road she got out begging me not to follow her. I did not, and never saw her again. She had hazel eyes, spoke with a country accent, and I quite believe was a servant.

Although soon after this a little better off, I had difficulty in keeping out of debt, and the cost of amatory amusements prevented my having women as often as I otherwise should have done. I used to try the cheap at times, and often successfully. Would walk backwards and forwards between Temple-bar and Charing Cross for hours, looking at the women, thinking which I should like, and whether I could afford one. Sometimes I would follow the same woman, stop when she stopped if a man spoke to her, cross over, and wait till she moved off by herself, or if with the man, would follow them to a brothel, return to watch for her coming out, and wait till she did so. This pleased me much.

Then I began to feel women in the streets; they frequently came out of the E**t*r Street houses, and round by the side-entrance to Exeter Hall. That end of the street then was all but dark.

Stopping a woman, this was a frequent dialogue. "A nice night dear." "Yes." "Been taking a walk?" "Yes." "Been to piddle?" "Yes." They usually when I knew they had come out of a house, said they had been to piddle if I asked them. "A shilling to feel your cunt." "All right, give it me." With the left hand I gave the shilling, with the right I fingered their quims. "Open your legs dear, — a little wider, — let me feel up, — have you been fucked to-night?" "No." It was always no. I delighted in hearing them tell that lie. "Come with me." "How much?" "Give me a sovereign." "No." "Ten shillings then." "I can't afford more than five shillings." "No, not for that"; but they more often said yes. Sometimes I went with them, more frequently not. The lesson I learned was that most women denied that they had fucked more recently than the day before (it was always the day before), and that a little bargaining reduced the price of their pleasures.

If intending to have a poke I waited for a girl known by sight, and then often could not find her, then I saw those so dressed that I could not offer them a small sum. On other nights I went up to the girl with the fattest legs, and made advances. In this way I shagged many of all sorts and sizes, many of them poor creatures, others plump, fine, strong, healthy women, whom I was surprised took the small sum for their professional exertions. The end of this promiscuity was that again I took the clap, which laid me up some weeks, and made it again needful to open my piss-pipe by surgical tubes.

Then I was timid, used French letters, and took to carrying them in my purse again, but always hated them. Often my tool stiff as a boring-iron would shrink directly the wet gut touched it, and compelled me to frig up to near the crisis before I could insert it in the skin. Sometimes it would not stiffen completely till up the woman. I used to drop my tool in a state of partial rigidity into the letter, then thumb it slowly up the lady's orifice; there the warmth, the clip, the buttocks wagging, and the look at the belly and thighs between which I was working brought it to the proper stiffness. I usually had the ladies at the side of the bed, when wearing these condoms.

Sometimes my passions overcame my prudence, and a fair lady for her favours got her price. Then I was filled with regrets, and had to content myself with a feel for some time, or wait days till I could afford the full gratification of my senses with another woman, because I had not the money. Then I fell again on my five shilling offers. About this cunt-feeling there was something very peculiar in me: unless I liked the look of the woman I did not like to feel her cunt, and after I had been groping used to spit on my fingers, and rub them dry, and the smell off of them on to my handkerchief.

Some little time after my clap however I came into a better income through the death of a relative. It was small, but made a difference to me of great importance. I spent it all on myself, that is to say on cunt, and although some of my country relatives must have known I had come into the property, those most interested in knowing it I believe never did.

I now longed for nice women whom I could talk and spend the money with. The rapid business-like fucking in the baudy houses was not to my taste, I had scarcely gone to the Argyle Rooms, then not many years opened, for fear that my taste for nicety of manner and something more than mere cunt might lead me into an expenditure still far beyond my means.

CHAPTER XVI

A friend's maid-servant. — Jenny. — Initial familiarity. — A bum pinched. — Jenny communicative. — Her young man. — An attempt, a failure, a faint, a look, and a sniff. — Restoratives.

I knew an elderly couple who were childless and lived in a nice little house in the suburbs with a long garden in front, and one at the back as well; they were in comfortable but moderate circumstances, and kept two servants only. Every year they went to the seaside, taking one servant with them, and leaving the other at home to look after the house; and usually some one to take charge of it with her. This year they asked if I would, when I passed the house (as I frequently did), call in and see if all was going properly, for the housemaid left in charge was young, and her sister, a married woman, usually only stopped the night with her, leaving early each morning for work in which she was daily engaged. She was an upholstress.

I knew the servant whose name was Jane. She had been with the family some months. I often dined at the house; and once or twice when she had opened the garden-gate (always locked at nightfall) to let me out, I had kissed her, and tipped her shillings. She was a shortish, fat-bummed wench. Not long before this time I gave her bum such a hard pinch one night, that she cried out. A day or two afterwards I said, "Was it not black and blue?" "I don't know." "Let me see." "It's like your imperance," she replied.

After that I used to ask her when I got the chance, to let me see if the finger-marks were there, at which she would blush a little, and turn away her head, but nothing further had come of the liberty.

When I called at the house I had no intention about the girl, as far as I can recollect. She opened the door, and heard my errand and questions. Yes all was right. Did her sister come and sleep there? Yes. Was she there now? No, she would not be there till nearly dark. I stepped inside, for then I thought of larking with her. "I am tired, and will rest a little," and stepped into the parlour, sat down on a sofa, began questioning her about a lot of trifles, and in doing so thought of the pinch I had given her bum, and my cock began to tingle. Then I thought she was alone in the house. Oh! if she would let me fuck her! — has she been broached? — she is nice and plump. Curiosity increased my lust, and unpremeditatingly I began the approaches for the attack, though I only meant a little amatory chaffing.

"Is it black and blue yet, Jenny?" She did not for the instant seem to recollect, for she asked me innocently enough, "What sir?" "Your bum where I pinched it." She laughed, checked herself, coloured up, and said, "Oh! don't begin that nonsense sir." I went on chaffing. "How I should like to have pinched it under your clothes, — but no I would sooner kiss it than pinch it." "Oh! if you're agoing on like that I'll go to the kitchen." I stood before the door, and stopped her going out. "Now give me a kiss." I caught and kissed her, then gave a lot, and got a return from her. "I won't, — Lor there then, — what a one you are," and so on. "Well, Jane one kiss, and you may afterwards kiss whenever you want, you know." And so she seemed to think, for I got her to sit down on the sofa, and we gossiped and kissed at intervals, till my cock got unruly. "What a fat bum you have," said I. Then she attempted to rise, I pulled her back, we went on gossiping, and kissing at intervals. She got quite interested in my talk as I sat with one arm round her waist, and another on her thigh, outside her clothes of course.

So for a while; but I was approaching another stage, was getting randy, and reckless. "Lord how I'd like to be in bed with you, to feel that fat bum of yours, to feel your c — u — n — t," spelling it, "to f — u — c — k it I'd give a five pound note," said I in a burst, and stooping, got my hand up her clothes on to her thigh. She gave a howl. "Oh! I say now, — what a shame! — oh! you beast." I shoved her back on the sofa upsetting her, got my lips on her thighs, and kissed them. Then she escaped me, and breathing hard,

[*172*]

stood up looking at me after her struggle. "Oh! I wouldn't have believed it," said she panting with the exertion. What a lot of women I have heard say they would not have believed it, when I first made a snatch at their privates. I suppose they say what they mean.

Begging her pardon, "I could not help it," I said, "you are so pretty and nice, — I'd give ten pounds to be in bed with you an hour." "Well I'm sure." "Think what it is not to have a woman you like." "Well I'm sure, sir, you are a married man, — you've got a partner, and ought to know better, — missus would not have asked you to call if she'd a know'd you, — she thinks there's no gent like you, — what would she say if I tell her?" "But you won't my dear." "She thinks you a perfect gentleman, and most unlucky," the girl went on to say, "and she is sorry for you too."

"Oh! she does not know all, but you've heard, have you Jenny?" I tried to make her sit on the sofa again, and promising that I would not forget myself any more, she did so. We kissed and made it up, and talking I soon relapsed into baudiness.

The quarrelsome life I led with the oldish woman at home was, I knew, well understood by the old couple. "I lead a miserable life," said I. "Oh! yes I know all about it," said the girl, "master and missus often talk about you, — but you're very gay, ain't you?" Then I told this girl a lot. "Think my dear what it is not even to sleep with a woman for two months, — for two months we have never slept together, — I've never seen her undress, — never touched her flesh, — you know what people marry for, — I want a woman, — you know what I mean don't you, — every night what am I to do? — I love laying belly to belly naked with a nice woman, and taking my pleasure with her, — so of course I can't keep from having other women at times, — you don't know what an awful thing it is to have a stiff prick, and not a nice woman to relieve it." She gave me a push, got up, and made for the door at the word prick. Again I stopped her. She had sat staring at me with her mouth wide open, without saying a word, all the time I had been telling the baudy narrative of domestic trouble, as if she were quite stupefied by my plain language, until she suddenly jumped up, and made for the door without saying a word.

I was as quick as she, caught her, put my back against the door, and would not let her go, but could not get her to look me in the face, I had so upset her. There we stood, I begging her to sit down, and promising not to talk so again, she saying, "Now let me go, — let me out." "No, — sit down." "No." But in about a quarter of an hour she did, and then again I told her of my trouble, avoided all straightfoward allusions to my wanting other women, but hinted at it enough. She got interested, and asked me no end of questions. "Lord, why don't you separate? — if I quarrel with my husband so, I'm sure I will, — I tell my young man so." "Oh! you have a sweetheart." Yes she had, — a grocer's shopman, — he lived at Brighton, came up third class to see her every fortnight, starting early, and going back late. She was flattered by my enquiries, told me all about him and herself, their intention to get married in a year; and I sat and listened with one hand outside her clothes on her thigh, and thinking how I could best manage to get into her.

"He goes with women," said I, to make her jealous. "He don't I'm sure, — if he did, and I found out, I'd tear his eyes out, and break off with him, though he says Brighton is a dreadful place for them hussies." She got quite excited at the idea. "When he comes up, you and he enjoy yourselves, — his hands have been where mine have to-night." "No he hasn't, — if he dared I'd — now I don't like this talk, — you said you wouldn't, — leave me alone, — you keep breaking your word." Another little scuffle, a kiss, and a promise. "Why should you not enjoy yourselves? — who would know anything about it but yourselves, — it's so delicious to feel yourselves naked in each other's arms, your bellies close together." "Get away now," — and she tried to get up. I got my hand up her clothes, pulled her on to the sofa, and holding her down with one hand, pressed myself sideways on her, and kissed her, pulling out my prick with the other.

Then she cried out so loudly that I was alarmed, for the window at the back was open. "Hush, — be quiet, — there, — I've touched your cunt." I pulled one of her hands on to my prick. "Oh! for shame Jane you touched my prick." Again she got up, and made for the door; so did I, and stood there with my back to it, and my poker out in front of me. "Come and open the door my dear, and you will run against this." She turned her head away, and would not look. "Why don't you come on? — if you run up against it, it won't hurt you, — it's soft though it's stiff." "I'll write to my mistress tonight," she said, and turned away. "Do my pet, — tell her how stiff it was, and the old lady will want to see it when she comes back." "It's disgraceful." "No, my

[*174*]

dear, it's to be proud of, — why you're looking at it, I can see."

Then she turned quite away. "That's right dear, — now I can see where I pinched your bum, — it was not far from your little quim, — oh! if that could talk, it would ask to be introduced to this, — it's hot, isn't it Jenny?" I said, this and a lot more. She had walked to the back window, and stood looking into the garden whilst I rattled on. "You're laughing Jenny." "It's a story," said she, "I'm insulted," — and turned round with a stern face. I shook my tooley-wagger. "How ill-tempered you look, — come and feel this, and you'll be sweet-tempered at once." She turned round to the window again.

"I *will* write my missus, — that I *will*." "Do dear." "My sister will be here directly." "You said she comes at dusk, — it won't be dark for three hours." "I wish you would go, — what will people say if they know you're here?" "Don't be uneasy, — they will know no more than they know of your doings with your young man." "There is nothing to know about, but what is quite proper."

So we stood. She looking out of the window, and turning round from time to time. I standing by the door with my prick out; then I approached her quietly. "Feel it Jenny, — take pity on it." "Oh! for God's sake, sir, what are you doing?" She turned, and pushed me back, then retreated herself, keeping her face to the window as she stepped backwards. "Oh! there is Miss and Mrs. Brown walking in the next garden." Sure enough there were two ladies there; they could have seen everything close to the window over the low wall which separated the gardens; and had they been looking, must have seen Jane, me, and my prick. "Oh! if they have seen, they will tell my missus, and she'll tell my young man, and I shall be ruined, — oh! — oh! — oh!" she said sinking back into an armchair with a flood of tears, — half funk and shock, and perhaps randiness, causing it.

I was alarmed. "Oh!" she sobbed, "if they saw you, — hoh! — ho! — and it was no fault of mine, — you're a bad man, — oho! oho!" She sat with her hands to her face, her elbows on her knees. I dropped on my knees imploring her to be quiet, was sure no one had seen me, and tried to kiss her. The position was inviting, I slid my hands up her clothes between her thighs, she took no notice, was evidently in distress, not even conscious of the invasion. A bold push, and my fingers touched her cunt. I forgot all the intensity of my enjoyment, at feeling my fingers on the edge of the soft, warm nick. No repulse! I looked up, she sank back in the chair, seemingly unconscious and deadly white.

I withdrew my hand, then came a mental struggle; my first impulse was to get cold water, the next to look at her cunt. I went towards the door, turned round to look at her. Her calves were visible, I ran back, and lifted her clothes, so that I could just see her cunt-hair, gave her thighs a kiss, and then rushed downstairs, got water, and as I entered the room she was recovering. She knew nothing, or next to nothing of what had occurred, nor that my fingers had touched her clitoris, though she had not actually fainted.

"I wish I had some brandy," she said, "I feel so weak." "Is there any in the sideboard?" "No." "I'll go and get a little." A few hundred feet from the house down a side-street, was a public-house. As I was going, "You will let me in again?" I said. "If you promise not to touch me." She looked so pale that I fetched brandy, but put the street-door key in my pocket as I went. "If she don't let me in," I thought, "she shan't have the key, — and what will she tell her sister about that?" It was a key almost as big as a shovel; she never noticed that I had taken it away. She thought by her dodge that she had got rid of me, and told me so afterwards.

I brought back the brandy and knocked. "Let me in." "I won't." "Then you shan't have the street-door key." This was spoken to each other through the closed door. A pause, then the door opened. "You are coming Jenny." We went downstairs into the kitchen, she had brandy and water, and so had I. It was a hot day, the pump-water was deliciously cool, I made hers as strong as she would take it, — it was an instinct of mine. She got her colour back, and became talkative, we talked about her fainting, but she tried to avoid talking about it, and did not want me to refer to what had led to it. I did, and was delighted to think that it was owing to what is called "exposing my person."

"I don't think the ladies saw it, so you need not have been so frightened Jenny, — but you saw it, did you not?" No reply. "I saw you looking at it." "It's a story." "Why did you faint?" "I always feel faint if I am startled." "What startled you?" "Nothing." "You saw it, and you put your hand over it to hide it, and you touched it." "It's a story, — I wish you'd go." "You ungrateful little devil, when I've fetched you brandy." "It's through you that I felt ill." "Why?" No reply. "Don't be foolish, — it was for fear that the ladies should have seen my prick so near you, — now look at it," and I pulled it out, it was not stiff. "It was twice the size when you saw it, — feel it, and it will soon be bigger."

The girl rose and said she would go and remain in the forecourt till her sister came, if I did not leave, but I prevented her going out of the kitchen. She began to cry again, and had a little more brandy and water. My talk took its old channel.

"Do you know how long you were fainting?" "I didn't faint, but only a minute or so." "Do you know what I did?" She was sitting down, then got upright, looked at me full in the face, her eyes almost staring out of her head. "What did you do! — what? — what? — what?" She spoke hurriedly, anxiously, in an agitated manner. "I threw up your clothes, kissed your cunt, and felt it."

"It's a lie, — it's a lie." "It's true, — and the hair is short, and darker than the hair of your head, — and your thighs are so white, — and your garters are made of blue cloth, — and I felt it, the dear little split, — how I wish my belly had been up against it! — what a lovely smell it has!" (putting my fingers to my nose).

"Oho! — oho! — ono!" said she bursting into tears, "what a shame to take liberties with a poor girl when she can't help herself, — oho! — oho! — you must be a bad man, —missus had no business to send you to look after me, as if she could not trust me, — she don't know what sort of man you are, — and a gentleman too, — oho! — and married too, — it's a shame, — oho! — oho! I don't believe you though, — oho — o — o." And when I told her again the colour and the make of her garters, she nearly howled. "You mean man, to do such a thing when I was ill."

I kissed her, she let me, but went on blubbering. "I've a good mind to tell my young man." "That will be foolish, because you and I mean to have more pleasure than we have had, — and he'll never be any the wiser but if you tell him, he'll think it's your fault."

This had occupied some hours, it was getting dark, but it seemed only as if I had been there some minutes, so deliciously exciting are lascivious acts and words. The charm of talking baudily to a woman for the first time is such, that hours fly away just like minutes.

I got her on to my lap and kissed her. She was so feeble that I put my hands up her clothes nearly to her knees before she repulsed them. Then I feared her sister coming home;

she promised to hide the brandy, and we parted. She kissed me, and let me feel to her knees, to induce me to go. "Oh! for God's sake sir, do go before my sister comes." My last words were, "Mind you've felt my cock, and I've felt your cunt." "Pray go," — and I departed, leaving her tearful, excited, and in a state of exhaustion which seemed to me unaccountable.

Probably had I persisted a little longer I should have had her, such was the lassitude into which she had fallen; but I felt that I had made progress, and went home rejoicing, and forming plans for the future. When I had had some food, and thought over the matter, I came to the conclusion that I had been a fool in leaving her, and that had I pushed matters more determinately at the last moment, I should have certainly fucked her before I had left. I was mad with myself when I reflected on that, and the opportunity lost, which might not occur again.

Jenny had not fainted quite, but though unable to speak, resist, or indeed move, she must have been partially conscious. I think this from what I knew of her nature afterwards.

CHAPTER XVII

When are women most lewed. — Garters, money, and promises. — About my servant. — The neckerchief. —Armpits felt. — Warm hints. — Lewed suggestions. — Baudy language. — Tickling. — "Fanny Hill." — Garters tried. — Red fingers. — Struggle, and escape. — Locked out. — I leave. — Baudy predictions, and verification.

I have a confused recollection of thinking myself the next day an ass, for having missed a good opportunity of spermatizing a fresh cunt; yet for some reason or another it must have been three days before I went to try my luck again.

I had about this time of my life begun to frame intentions, and calculate my actions towards women, although still mostly ruled by impulse and opportunity in love matters. My philosophy was owing to experience, and also in a degree to

my friend the Major, to whom some years before I had con-
fided my having commissioned a French woman to get me
a virgin. He was older, poorer, and more dissolute than ever.
"He is the baudiest old rascal that ever I heard tell a story,"
was the remark of a man at our club one night. Ask him to
dinner in a quiet way by himself, give him unlimited wine,
and he would in an hour or two begin his confidential advice
in the amatory line, and in a wonderful manner tell of his
own adventures, and give reasons why he did this or that,
why he succeeded with this woman, or missed that girl, in a
way as amusing and instructive to a young listener as could
be imagined.

"If you want to get over a girl," he would say, "never
flurry her till her belly's full of meat and wine; let the grub
work. As long as she is worth fucking, it's sure to make a
woman randy at some time. If she is not twenty-five she'll
be randy directly her belly is filled, — then go at her. If
she's thirty, give her half-an-hour. If she's thirty-five let her
digest an hour, she won't feel the warmth of the dinner in
her cunt till then. Then she'll want to piss, and directly after
that she'll be ready for you without her knowing it. But
don't flurry your young un, — talk a little quiet smut whilst
feeding, just to make her laugh and think of baudy things;
then when she has left table, go at her. But it's well," the old
Major would say, "to leave a woman alone in a room for a
few minutes after she has dined, perhaps then she will let
slip a fart or two, perhaps she'll piss, — she'll be all the better for the wind and water being out. A woman's cunt
doesn't get piss-proud like a man's prick you know, they're
differently made from us my boy, — but show any one of
them your prick as soon as you can, it's a great persuader.
Once they have seen it they can't forget it, it will keep in
their minds. And a baudy book, they won't ever look at till
you've fucked them? — oh! won't they! — they would at
church if you left them alone with it." And so the Major instructed us.

About three days afterwards, taking a pair of garters, two
small showy neckerchiefs, and *Fanny Hill* with me, I
knocked at the door. "Oh! you!," said she colouring up.
"Yes, — is everything right?" "Yes! all right, what should be
the matter sir?" She stood at the street-door holding it open,
though I had entered the hall. I turned, closed the door, and
caught hold of her.

"Now none of that pray sir, you insulted me enough last

time." "I could not help it, you're so lovely, it's your fault, — forgive me, and I won't do so any more, — here is a sovereign, take it, kiss me, and make it up." "I don't want your money," said she sulkily. "Take it, I give it with real pleasure, — what I had the other day was worth double."

"I won't be paid for your rudeness, if that's what you mean." "Lord, my dear, I've no occasion to pay for that, I took it without pay, — I wish I could get what I told you yesterday, — I'd give ten times the sum." "You are going on again." "Don't be foolish, — take it, buy a pair of silk stockings." "I don't want silk stockings." "Your plump legs would look so nice in them," — and I forced her to put the money into her pocket.

Then I got her to the parlour, to sit down, to allow me to kiss her, and then to talk about me and my "missus," as she called her, a subject which seemed to excite her, for she began asking me question after question, and listened to all I said with breathless attention about my daily habits, rows, and fast doings. Once I stopped at some question. "I won't tell you that." "Oh! do, — do." "No it's curious." "Do, — do." It was about a pretty servant-girl whom I had noticed in my house. "It will offend you if I do." "No it won't." "Well give me a kiss then."

She kissed me. She had stood up a moment, now she sat down again by me on the sofa. I went on with my story, every now and then I stopped till she kissed me, it came to a kiss every minute, as I sat with my arm round her waist, talking.

Said I, "It was a servant whom my wife turned out at a day's notice, — a pretty girl, — I had taken to kissing her, and then I nudged her somewhere you know. One night when she opened the door, I saw by the light that my wife was in our bed-room. 'Is your mistress upstairs?' 'Yes sir.' 'And the cook?' 'Yes.' Then I closed with her. 'Don't sir, missus will hear.' I hugged her closer, shoved her up against the wall, got my hand on to her cunt, felt her, and gave her half a sovereign. How delicious it was to get the fingers on to the wet nick of that pretty girl, and say, 'How I should like to fuck that, Mary.' " I told it in words like that to Jenny, as she sat listening. At the word "fuck" up she got.

"You are a going on rude again." "You asked me." "Not for that." "But that's what I had to tell, what you kissed me to tell." "I didn't think you would say rude things." "Sit down, and I'll tell you without rude words." And so I did,

[*180*]

telling all over again with additions, but instead of saying "cunt," "fuck," and so on, said, "I got my hand you know where," — "and then she let me you know what," — "she was frightened to let me do, you guess what I wanted."

"Luckily, though she foolishly told her fellow-servant, she did not say who had been feeling her. That sneak told my wife, who told me about it, or she knew, and said she could not keep such an improper girl in the house as that. 'But the other servant may have told a lie to spite her.' 'Perhaps, but I'll turn her out too,' — and so she did, both left."

Thus I talked to Jenny till I expect her quim was hot enough; then said I, "Here is a pretty neckerchief, — put it on." "Oh! how pretty." "I won't give it you unless you put it on." She went to the glass and unbuttoned the top of her dress, which was made to button on the front. I saw her white fat bosom, she threw the kerchief round the neck, and tried to push it down the back. "Let me put it down, — it's difficult." She let me. "You are not unbuttoned enough, — it's too tight." She undid another button, I pushed down the kerchief, and releasing my hand as I stood at the back of her, put it over her shoulder, and down in front, pushing it well under her left breast. "Oh! what a lovely breast you have, — let me kiss it."

A shriek, a scuffle. In the scuffle I burst off a button or two, which exposed her breast, and getting my hand on to one of the globes began feeling and kissing it. Then I slid my hand further down, and under her armpit. "Oh! what a shame, — don't, — I don't like it." "How lovely, — kiss, kiss, — oh! Jenny what a lot of hair I can feel under here." "Oh!" — screech, — screech, — "oh! don't tickle me, — oh! — oh!," — and she screeched as women do who can't bear tickling. I saw my advantage. "Are you ticklish?" "Yes, — oh! — (screech, — screech). — Oh! leave off."

Instead of leaving off I tickled harder than ever. She got my hand out, but I closed on her, tickling her under her arm, pinching her sides, and got her into such a state of excitement, that directly I touched her she screeched with wild laughter; the very idea of being touched made her shiver. We were on the sofa, she yelling, struggling, whilst I pinched her, she trying to get away from me, but fruitlessly; I buried my face in her breasts which were now largely exposed, and she fell back I with my face on her, holding her tight. Then I put one hand down, feeling outside for her notch; that stopped her screeching, and she pushed me off as she got up.

[*181*]

I soothed her, begged pardon, spoke of the hair in her armpits, wondered if it was the same colour that it was lower down. Now she shammed anger, boxed my ears, and we made it up. I produced the garters. "Oh! what a lovely pair." "They're yours if you let me put them on." "I won't." "Let me put one half-way up." "No." "Just above the ankle." "No, my stockings are dirty." "Never mind." "No." Then she made an excuse, said she must see to something, and left the room. I thought she was going to piddle.

She came back. I found afterwards she had been out to lace up her boots, they were untidy. It was coquettishness, female instinct, for she wanted the garters, and meant to let me try them on, though refusing. "Where do you garter, above knee?" "I shan't tell you." "I've seen, — let me put them on below the knees." "No." "Then I'll give them to another woman who will let me." "I don't care." I threw the garters on to the table after some fruitless attempts. I was getting awfully lewed with our conversation.

"Do you like reading?" "Yes." "Pictures?" "Yes." "I've a curious book here." "What is it?" I took the book out, *The Adventures of Fanny Hill.* "Who was she?" "A gay lady, — it tells how she was seduced, how she had lots of lovers, was caught in bed with men, — would you like to read it?" "I should." "We will read it together, — but look at the pictures," — this the fourth or fifth time in my life I have tried this manœuvre with women.

I opened the book at a picture of a plump, leering, lecherous-looking woman squatting, and pissing on the floor, and holding a dark-red, black-haired, thick-lipped cunt open with her fingers. All sorts of little baudy sketches were round the margin of the picture. The early editions of *Fanny Hill* had that frontispiece.

She was flabbergasted, silent. Then she burst out laughing, stopped and said, "What a nasty book, — such books ought to be burnt." "I like them, they're so funny." I turned over a page. "Look, here she is with a boy who sold her watercresses, is not his prick a big one?" She looked on silently, I heard her breathing hard. I turned over picture after picture. Suddenly she knocked the book out of my hand to the other side of the room. "I won't see such things," said she. "Won't you look at it by yourself?" "If you leave it here I'll burn it." "No you won't, you'll take it to bed with you." There I left the book lying, it was open and the frontispiece showing. "Look at her legs," said I, for we could see the picture as we sat on the sofa; and I began to kiss and tickle her again.

She shrieked, laughed, got away, and rushed to the door. I brought her back, desisted from tickling and lewed talking, though I was getting randier than ever. "Now have the garters, — let me put one round the leg, just to see how it looks, — just half-way up the calf." After much persuasion, after pulling up my trowsers, and showing how a garter looked round my calf, she partly consented. "Promise me you won't tickle me." I promised everything.

I dropped on one knee, she sat on the sofa. "Put one foot on my leg." She put one foot there, and carefully raised her clothes an inch or two about the boot-top. "A little higher." She raised it holding her petticoats tight round the leg, and I slipped the garter round it. "It's too loose, raise a little more." "I won't any higher, — I can see how it looks." "Won't they look nice when they are above the knee! and won't your young man be pleased when he sees them there." "My young man won't see them any more than you will." "Let me slip on the other." The same process, the same care on her part. She bestowed all her care on the limb I was gartering, lest I should slip the garter higher up. The remainder of her clothes were loose round her other leg. Then I pushed my hand up her clothes and herself back on the sofa, relinquishing the leg I was gartering.

Rapidly my hand felt thighs, hair, cunt. How wet! What is this which catches my fingers? — what is it they are gliding between? With a yell she pushed me away, and got up as I withdrew my fingers. She had a napkin on, my fingers were stained red. "Oh you beast," said she bursting into tears. I caught hold of her, and began to tickle her; she pushed me violently away, and escaping, rushed downstairs, slammed the kitchen-door in my face, and locked herself in. I have been accustomed to this behaviour on similar occasions.

I stood outside begging pardon, talking baudiness, I tried to burst open the door, and could not. I was not fond of poorliness in women, had a keen nose, and oftentimes could smell a woman if poorly, even with her clothes down; how it was I did not smell *her*, considering how near my nose had been to her split and her breasts, I can't say, but suppose randiness overcame my other senses. I played with my prick which was in an inflammatory state, feeling it made me much randier, I called through the door how I wanted to fuck her, how my prick was bursting, how I would frig myself if she did not let me. "What a hard-hearted girl, — I'll give you ten pounds to let me, — who will know it, but you and me?" and a lot more; but it was of no use, and at length I went upstairs, determining to wait, and thinking that in time she might follow me.

On the sofa I sat thinking of what I had done. There lay one garter, I took it up, and rolled it round my pego, I rubbed the tip with it, thinking it might be a spell. I took up *Fanny Hill,* got more excited by reading the book, looking at its salacious pictures, and feeling my prick at the same time. Then the sense of pleasure got beyond control, and laying down the book on the floor just beneath me, where I could see a baudy picture, I turned on my side on the sofa, and frigged till a shower of spunk shot out.

Then down I went. The door was still locked, my senses were calmed, but I talked baudy, and offered her money without a reply; growing tired I bawled out, "I'm going, — you will let me in a day or two, and get the ten pounds towards the new shop, — you won't be so unkind when I come again." "I'll take good care never to let you in," said she. They were the only words I could get out of her. I went upstairs, took a slip of paper, and wrote on it, "I have wrapped the garter round my prick, it is a charm. Directly you put it on I shall know, for my prick will stiffen, — you will put it on I am sure; and directly my prick stiffens, your cunt will long to have it up it, even if I am miles away. You will put the garter on, for you can't help doing so, — I'm sure to fuck you, neither you nor I could avoid it if we would. Why should we deny ourselves the pleasure, — no one will know it, and you will be ten pounds the richer." I wrote that or something nearly like it, and charmed with my own wit, rubbed the garter over the top of my prick till I left the smell on it, then laid it on the table over the paper I had written, and went away, taking *Fanny Hill* with me.

It is a positive fact, that about two hours afterwards I had a violent randy throbbing in my prick, and found out later on that just at that very time she had put that garter on.

[And now for the complete understanding of what follows, it must be stated that the house was in plan nearly like that which I inhabited when I had my beautiful servant Mary. Kitchens in the basement, two parlours with folding doors between them, nearly always open; and rooms back and front over the parlours; and that my absent friend did with those rooms whilst absent at the seaside, what was not un-usual with people of their class in those days, lock most of them up, leaving only sufficient for the servant, or caretaker, to inhabit.]

CHAPTER XVIII

"Fanny Hill" sent to Jenny. — My next visit. — Thunder, lightning, sherry, and lust. — A chase round a table. — The money takes. — Tickling and micturating. — A search for "Fanny Hill." — A chase up the stairs. — In the bed-room. — Thunder, funk, and lewedness. — Intimidation and coaxing. — Over and under. — A rapid spender. — Virginity doubtful. — Fears, tears, and fucking.

I waited for a few days to ensure her poorliness being over. I had not left her *Fanny Hill*, but why I cannot tell, for I knew how baudy books excited a woman. The night before my next attack I wrapped up the book, directed it to her, gave a boy sixpence to deliver it, hid myself by a lilac which was in the front-garden close to the road, and saw the boy give it to her, and go off quickly as I had told him. It was just dusk, and too dark inside the passage of the house to see; for Jenny stepped outside the house so as to get light, and stripped off the envelope. I saw also that she opened the book, closed it, looked rapidly on both sides, then stepped inside, and closed the door. I expect that her cunt got hot enough that night. I saw her sister who slept with her nightly, going through the front-garden soon afterwards, and Jenny open the door for her. I had then moved off to a safe distance, the other side of the road.

Jenny was fond of finery, and I had heard the old lady of the house declaiming about it. Her pleasure at the showy neckerchief and garters was great, so I bought a pretty brooch, and filling my purse with sovereigns determined to have her at any cost, for my letch for her had got violent. The next day I had a good luncheon, went to the house just after her dinner-time, and took with me a bottle of sherry. I recollect the morning well. It was a sultry day, reeking with moisture; it had been thundering, the clouds were dark and threatening, the air charged with electricity. Such a day makes all creation randy, and you may see every monkey at the Zoological Gardens frigging or fucking. I was resolute with lustful heat, the girl was, I expected, under the same influence, and taking her as I did after a lazy meal, everything was propitious to me. How shall I get it? — if I knock she may not open; and if she sees me go up the front-garden she won't open. But I had to try, so walked up to the door, and gave one single loud tradesman's knock.

There was a little porch and a shelter over the street-door. Standing flat up against the door, so that I might be hidden from her sight if peeping, I heard an upper window open. She looked out, but where I was she could not see me. There was delay, so again I knocked, and soon the door began to open, I pushed it and stepped in. The front-shutters on the ground-floor to my wonder were closed.

"Hoh! sir, — you," said Jenny amazed, "what do you want?" I pushed the door to, and caught hold of her. "I've come to have a chat and a kiss." She struggled, but I got her tight, and kissed as a randy man then kisses a woman, it is a magnetizing thing. "Oh! there it is again," she cried as a loud thunder-clap was heard, "oh! let me go, — oh! it do frighten me so." "Where are you going?" "Oh! into the parlour, — I've closed the shutters." The girl was in a panic, and did not know what she said. The parlour-door was open, the room nearly dark, which suited me. She went just in, and then turned round to go out, but I pulled her to the sofa. A flash of lightning showed even in the darkened room, the girl cowered and hid her face with her hands. I took her round the waist. "Shut your eyes, and lean your head against me." Mechanically she did, she was utterly unnerved. I felt down with my right hand the form of her thighs and haunches through her clothes. My prick began to stand. Pulling it out, and taking her near hand I put it round my prick just as the thunder roared. She kept her hand unconsciously on it for a time, then with a start took it away and jumped up. "Oh! it's wicked," said she, "when God Almighty is so angry," — and just as she got to the door a terrific flash made her turn round again. I caught her, and sitting down on a chair pulled her on to my knee; she hid at once her face on my shoulder in terror.

Coaxing and soothing, and exciting her, in her fear she listened, at times twitching and oh-ing. I was sorry I had

touched her cunt the other day I said. "Oh! now don't."
"Feel my prick again, — do dear." "Let me go, — you've no
business here." Another flash came, I put my hand up her
clothes, the tip of my fingers just touched her quim. She
struggled and got away, and in doing so upset the chair
which fell down and broke. "Oh! now what will my missus
say!" said she. Then a screech, and she got to the other side
of the table.

This went on a little longer, a gleam of sunshine came
through the shutters. Then she opened one shutter, and said
if I did not go she would open the window and call out. The
light showed my pego, stiff, red-tipped and ready. "Look
what your feeling has done for this Jenny," said I shaking
my tooleywag at her.

But her resoluteness daunted me, so I promised not to do
so again. "Here is some sherry that I was taking home to
taste, — let's have a glass, — it will do both of us good after
this thunder, — you look white, and as if you wanted a
glass." I had got out of her on a previous day that she liked
sherry. "I'll go and get you a glass," said she. "No you
shan't, — you will lock the door," said I, — I knew that was
in her mind. No she would not. "We will go together then."

We did, and returning to the parlour under my most solemn promise of good behaviour, down she sat, and we began
drinking sherry. One glass, — two, then another she swallowed. "No I dare not, it will get into my head, — no more."
"Nonsense," — after your fright it will do you good." "Well
half a glass." "Isn't it nice Jenny?" "It is." "Does not your
sweetheart give it you?" "At Christmas, but only one glass."
The sherry began to work. "Only another half-glass," — and
I poured it out nearly full. Soon after I got up after filling
my own, and standing before her again filled up hers which
she had sipped without her seeing me. "Finish your glass
dear." "No I can't, — it's making me so hot." "Just another
half-glass." "I won't." But she began to chatter and told me
again all about her young man, of their intending to open a
grocer's shop when they had two hundred pounds; that he
had saved a certain sum, and when he had a little more his
father was to put fifty pounds to it. She also had put money
in the savings bank. I got closer to her, and asked for a kiss.
"Well I'll kiss you if you promise not to be rude again." A
kiss and a promise. She was one of the simplest and most
open girls I have ever met with, and once a half-feeling of
remorse came over me about my intentions, whilst she was

talking on quite innocently about her future but my randy prick soon stopped that.

"What nonsense dear, your young man won't know that I have felt your thighs, and you my thing, nor any one else what we do, — I have thought of nothing else since I touched you, — kiss; — now let me do it again, — just feel it, — only where my hand's been before, — I swear I won't put my hand up higher, just above your garters, — have you got those garters on?" "No." "Oh! you have." "Well I have." "Let me just see." "I shan't." "I'll give you a sovereign to let me." "Shan't." I pulled out the sovereign, put it on the table, and spite of her resistance pulled up her clothes just high enough to see one garter; then clutching her round the waist I pushed my hands up, and touched a well-developed clitoris. She struggled, but I kept my hand there, kissed her rapturously, and frigged her; her cap fell off in her struggle. "Oh! I — can't — bear — it — now — sir; — I — don't — oh! — like it, — oh!" Then with a violent effort she got my hand away, but I held her fast to me.

"What a lovely smell your cunt has," said I putting the fingers just withdrawn from her thighs up to my nose. I have always noticed that nothing helps to make a woman more randy than that action; it seems to overwhelm them with modest confusion; I have always done that instinctively to a woman whom I was trying. "Oh! what a man, oh! let me pick up my cap." Just then I noticed her hair was short, and remarked it. She was annoyed, her vanity hurt, it turned her thoughts entirely. "Yes," she said. "I had a fever two years ago, — but it's growing again." "Well it has grown enough on your cunt dear, — did it fall off there?" "Oh! what a man! — oh! now what a shame!" My hand was on her thighs again, and I managed another's minute frig, and kept her close to me.

The heat had become excessive. What with struggling, and the excitement, sweat was on both our faces. Her thighs by her crack were as wet as if she had pissed them, her backside again to wriggle with pleasure, which I knew I was giving her; but again with a violent effort she freed herself from me, and as I put my hand to my nose she violently pulled it away. The sherry was upsetting her wisdom.

"There is the sovereign," said I as she stood looking at me, "that will help you." "Don't want it." Seeing where her pocket-hole was I pushed it into it. "Oh! what a lucky sovereign, to lay so close to your cunt Jenny," — and pushing my hand into her pocket I touched the bottom of her belly through the linen. Again a struggle, a repulse, then she put her hand into her pocket. "You're feeling your cunt Jenny," said I. "O — oh!" said she taking it out quickly, "I was feeling for the money, — I wont have it."

Then I kissed her till the sweat ran off my face on to hers. "Oh! my goodness," said she as it grew darker, "it's going to thunder again." "Have another glass." "No it's gone into my head already." But she took a gulp of mine. "Let's fuck you Jenny dear." "What?" "Fuck." "Shan't." "Oh! you know what I mean." "No I don't, but it's something bad if it's from you." I pulled out my prick, and tried to push her on the sofa. She got away, and then with my prick out I chased her round the table. "Leave off," said she, "a joke's a joke, but this is going too far." She was getting lewed, and was staring at my prick which showed above the table as I chased her. Quick as me she managed to keep just on the side of it opposite to me.

"I'll swear I wont touch you again if you will sit down." "I won't trust you, — you've been swearing all the afternoon." "So help me God I will," said I, and meant it. "Well then not when you are like that." I pushed my prick inside my trowsers, and then she sat down. What a long time this takes to tell, what repetition! but there are not many incidents I recollect more clearly.

Then I took out ten sovereigns, all bright, new ones, laid them on the table, and then the brooch. "Do you like that Jenny?" "Yes." "It is for you if you will let me, and those ten sovereigns also." "You are a bad man," said the girl, "and would make me forget myself and be ruined, and without caring a bit," — and she began rocking her head about, and rolling her body as she sat beside me, and looking at the money. "Who will know? — you won't tell your young man, — I shan't tell my wife, — let me." "I shan't, — never, — never, — never, if it was fifty pounds," said she almost furiously. "He wont find it out." "Yes he would." "Nonsense, — half the servants do it, yet marry," — and then I told her of some I had had who had married. "No, — no, — no," she kept repeating, almost bawling it out, as I told her Mary So-and-So who married a butler, and Sarah So-and-So who married my greengrocer, though I'd fucked them over and over again. "No, — no," looking at the money; then suddenly she took up the brooch, and laid it down again.

Before running round the table after her, I had thrown off my coat and waistcoat. "It's so hot, I've a good mind to take off my trowsers," I had said; but I had another motive. She seemed weaker, and was so, for gradually she had got inflamed and lewed by heat, the electrical condition of the atmosphere, the titillation of my finger on her seat of pleasure, and the sight of my stiff penis. She had I expect got to that weak, yielding, voluptuous condition of mind and body, when a woman knows she is wrong, yet cannot make up her mind to resist. Just then it came into my mind to tickle her; and then followed a scene which is one of the most amusing in my reminiscences.

She shrieked, and wriggled down on to the floor. I tried to mount her there. She kicked, fought, so that though once my prick touched her cunt-wig, I could not keep on the saddle. She forgot all propriety in her fuddled excitement, and whilst screeching from my tickling, repeated incoherently baudy words as I uttered them. "Let me fuck you." "You shan't fuck me." "Let's put it just to your cunt." "You shan't, — you're a blackguard, — oh! don't, — leave me alone, — well I will feel it, if you'll let me get up, — oh! — he! hi! hi! — for God's sake don't tickle, — hi! — I shall go mad, — you shan't, — oh! don't, — oh! if you don't leave off." "I shall, — I must." "Oh! pray, — you shall if you leave off tickling then, — oh! don't pray, — oh! I shall piddle myself, — he! he!" She was rolling on the floor, her thighs exposed, sometimes backside, sometimes belly upwards with all its trimmings visible. "Oh! it's your fault," and as she spoke actually piddle began to issue. I had my hand on her thigh, and felt and saw it.

Randy as I was I burst out laughing; and she managed to get up, began to push in her neckerchief which I had torn out of the front of her dress, and arranged her hair.

"Oh! look at me, — if any one came, what a state I am in," said she looking in the glass, and there she stood her breast heaving, her eyes swollen, her mouth open, and breathing as if she had just run a mile, but attempting nothing, saying nothing further, awaiting my attack. What randy, pleasurable excitement she must have been in, though unconscious of it, whilst only thinking of how to prevent my fucking her against her will.

"You began piddling." "Didn't." "I felt the piddle on my hand." She made no reply, but passed on, and wiped her face. When I said more she merely tossed her head. "Don't

be a fool Jenny, — let us, — you want it as bad as me."
Then I rattled out my whole baudy vocabulary, "prick,"
"cunt," "fuck," "spunk," "pleasure," "belly to belly," "my
balls over your arse," "let my stiff prick stretch your
cunt," — everything which could excite a woman; to all of
which she merely said, "Oho! — oh!" and tossed her head,
and never took her staring eyes off me, nor ceased swabbing
up her perspiring face, and at the same time looking at my
throbbing, rigid cunt-stretcher.

Finding she took to yelling, and even hitting me, I desisted a moment. "Where is the book I sent you last night?"
I had till then forgotten it. That opened her mouth. "Have
not had a book." "I saw the boy give it you, and you open
it." "He didn't." "He did." "I burnt it, — a nasty thing, — I
would not let my sister see it." An angry feeling came over
me for the moment, for I thought it probable, and should
have had difficulty in replacing it. Then came an inspiration
to help me, — a man always gets somehow on the right track
to get into a woman if he has opportunity. Nature wills it.
The woman was made to be fucked, and the sooner for them,
the better for them.

"You have not burnt it, — I'll bet it's in your bed-
room, — in your box." "It isn't." "I'll swear it's there, —you
have been reading it all night, — I'll go up and see." She
started as if electrified into life as I made for the door. She
got there before me, and stood before me. "You shan't
go, — you've no business up there, — I've burnt it, — it's
not there." "It's in the kitchen then." "No, I've burnt it," he
went on rapidly and confusedly. "I'll go and see," said I
pulling her from the door, she screeching out, "No you
shan't go up, — that you shan't, — you've no business
there." Then I pulled up her clothes to her belly, she got
them down, but still she kept her back to the door. I kept
pulling her till her cap was off again, and felt sure she was
getting weaker and weaker.

Then she turned round suddenly, opened the door, and ran
up the stairs rapidly like a lapwing, I after her. Once she
turned round, "You shan't come up," said she, and tried to
push me back; and then again on she went, I following. I
stumbled, that gave her a few steps ahead; I sprang up three
stairs at a time, recovered the lost distance, and just as she got
into the bed-room, and slammed the door to, I put my foot in
it, — it hurt me much. "Damn it, how you hurt my foot, — I
will come in," — and pushing the door my strength prevailed;

the door flew open, I saw her running round the bed, and there on the very pillow of the unmade bed lay *Fanny Hill,* open at one of the pictures. I threw myself across the bed, and clutched the book. She then stood motionless, panting and staring at me, she had clutched at it, and failed just as I caught it. She would have got it, but for having to go round the bed.

I laughed. "Have you not had a treat Jenny dear!" Her face was a picture of confusion. I was stretched half across the bed, and now went right across. Then to escape me she ran away, and had nearly reached the door when throwing myself over the bed again I grasped her petticoats under her arse, and managed to pull her back. "Damned if I don't fuck you," said I, "by God I'll shove my prick up your cunt if I'm hanged for it," — and pushing a hand up behind I clasped her naked buttocks. She turned round, I pulled her petticoats clean up, she yelling, struggling, panting, imploring. I dropped on my knees, kissed her belly, and buried my nose between her thighs. The petticoats dropped over my head, her belly kept bumping up against my nose and lips, which were covered with her cunt-moisture.

I rose up, pushed and rolled her against the bed, my hand still up her clothes. "Oh! don't, don't now, — you are a great gentleman they say, and ought to think of a poor girl's ruin, — oh! if it was found out I should be ruined." "It won't darling," I had got my fingers well over the whole slit. "Pray don't, — well I'll kiss you, — there." "Feel it." "Will you let me get up if I do?" "Yes." "There then," and she felt me. "Oh! I must fuck you." "Oh! pray don't, — oh! let me go now, and I'll let you another day, — I will indeed sir, — oh! you hurt, — don't push your fingers like that." "Kiss me my darling." "You shan't." "Then there." Another struggle. "Oh! I can't — be — bear it." Her arse began to twist again, her head sank on my shoulder, her thighs opened; then with a start, "Oh! my God it's lightning (it began to thunder and lightning badly), — oh! I'm so frightened, — oh! don't, — another day, — it's wicked when it's lightning so, — oh! God almighty will strike us dead if you are so wicked, — oh! let me go into the dark, — oh! don't, — I can't be — bear it." Her arse was shaking with my groping and frigging.

"Now don't be a fool, — damned if I don't murder you if you are not quiet!" "Oh! oh!" I had got her somehow on to the bed, she was helpless; with fear, liquor, and cunt-heat. I threw myself on to her. A feel between thighs reeking with

[*192*]

sweat, with her cunt in a lather, with the sweat dropping in great drops from my face, with sweat running down my belly on to my prick and my balls; I shoved. One loud "aha!" and my prick-tip was up against her womb-door. A mighty straight thrust; and the virginity was gone at that one effort.

Right up there with but a shove or two as far as I recollect, and without trouble, my sperm spouted directly my tool rubbed through the wet, warm cunt-muscles. Then I came to my senses; where was I? had she let me, or had I forced her violently?

She laid quietly under me with closed eyes and open mouth, panting; I was upon her, up her, pressing heavily upon her rather than holding her; then thrusting my hands under her fat bum I recommenced thrusting and fucking. She lay still, in the enjoyment of a lubricated cunt, distended by a stiff, hot prick. Soon she was sensitive to my moments, her cunt constricted, a visible pleasure overtook her, her frame began to quiver, and the soft murmurs of spermatic effusion came from her lips. She spent. On I went driving as if I meant to send my prick into her womb, fell into a half dreaminess, and became conscious of a great wetness on my ballocks; it was her discharge more than mine, the most copious I recollect, excepting from one woman. Then I dropped off on her side. She lay still as death, the thunder rolled over us unheeded by her in the delirious excitement and delight of her first fuck.

She turned on her side slightly, her thighs and backside were naked, she hid her face, and shuddered at the thunder unheeding her nakedness, then buried her face in a pillow, and so we both dozed for a minute or two. Her backside was still naked, when I looked at her in all ways as she lay, and saw traces of sperm on her thighs and chemise. A little lay on the bed, but no trace of red, no signs of a bloody rupture of a virgin cunt. My shirt and drawers were spermed, but had not a trace of blood. The light fell full on her backside, I could see lightish brown hair in the crack of the parting of her buttocks; a smear of shit on her chemise. Her flesh was beautifully white. She had on nice white stockings, and the flashy garters; she had a tolerable quantity of hair on her quim on the belly side. I sat at the side of the bed, got off boots, trowsers, and drawers; then laying down gently inserted my longest finger and delicately began rubbing her clitoris which I could see protruding of a fine crimson color.

Then she moved; she was not asleep, but dazed by the fuck, fear of the lightning, the excitement, the heat, and the fumes of the wine combined.

She stared at me, pulled down her clothes, and tears began to run down her cheeks. What a lot of women I have had cry at such times! "Don't cry my darling." She turned on to her face, and hid it. For a quarter of an hour, I talked, but she did not answer. I told her she had spent, that I knew she had had pleasure. Then I pushed my fingers up her cunt; still she did not speak, but let me do just what I liked, keeping her eyes shut. So soon as my rammer was up to the mark, up her it went fucking, and again I felt its stem well wetted. She was a regular streaming spunker.

After that, "I am going downstairs," said she. "I'll come." "No don't." "You only want to piddle." "Yes," said she faintly. "Piddle here, — what will it matter?" "I can't." "I'll go out if you won't bolt the door." "It's no good bolting the door, — you have ruined me." I went outside, closed the door, and heard the rattle in the pot. When I re-entered she was sitting at the side of the bed crying quietly; she did nothing but look at me, but without speaking. "Arrange yourself in case any one comes to the door." "No one will come." "The milkman?" "He will put it down inside the porch." She sat down the picture of despair. Never had I felt more lewed, I was mad that day with lewedness. "Let's feel your cunt," said I, "I have spent in it three times." "I don't care what you do, you may do what you like, — it's of no consequence." I felt up her cunt, she hung her head over my shoulders whilst I paddled my fingers in the wet. "Don't hurt me," said she. "I have not hurt you." "Yes you have." "Let's look." That roused her. "Oh! no, — no, — no, — you shan't." "Wash your cunt." I fetched the sherry, but she had not washed her cunt. "You should wash it out." "Oh? — oh!" said she. "If I should be with child I shall never be married."

She drank more sherry, and promised to wash. Then I went downstairs, fetched up the brooch and the ten sovereigns, and gave them to her. "How shall I say I got it?" "Does he know how much you have saved?" "Yes." "Is it a year's wages?" "Yes," — and she began to cry again. "What shall I say about the brooch?" "That you bought it, — let's lay down and talk." She yielded instantly, I threw up her clothes, she pushed them down. Then I lay feeling her quim, and got out her bubbies, she submitted, laying with her eyes

[*194*]

closed, till my rubbing on her clitoris made her sigh. Then up her, I felt her wetting my prick-stem, and shot my sperm into her at that intimation of her pleasure.

It was about seven o'clock, I had been nearly five hours at my amusements, and was tired; but had that day an irrepressible prick. It began to stiffen almost directly it left her cunt. I went down with her to tea, there I pulled her on to my lap, and we began to look at *Fanny Hill*. I could not get a word out of her, but she looked intently at the pictures. I explained their salacity. "Hold the book dear, and turn over as I tell you." Then I put my fingers on her cunt again. How sensitive she was. "Let's come upstairs." "No," said she reluctantly, but up we went, and fucked again. Then she groaned. "Oh! pray leave off, — I'm almost dead, — I shall have one of my fainting fits." "Lay still darling, I shall come soon," — but it was twenty minutes hard grinding before my sperm rose.

Then she laid motionless and white through nervous exhaustion, excitement, and loss of her spermatic liquor, which I kept fetching and fetching in my long grinding. She told me afterwards that she could not tell how often she spent. I had never been randier or stronger, nor enjoyed the first of a woman more.

She was a most extraordinary girl. After the first fuck she was like a well-broken horse; she obeyed me in everything, blushed, was modest, humbled, indifferent, conquered, submissive; but I could get no conversation out of her excepting what I have narrated. She cried every ten minutes, and looked at me. After each fuck she laid with her eyes closed, and mouth open, and turned on her side directly, putting her hand over her quim, and pulling her clothes just over her buttocks. Then after I had recovered and began to talk, a tear would roll down her cheek.

CHAPTER XIX

A big maid-servant. — A peep up from below. — Home late, dusty and stupid. — Chastity suspected. — Consequences. — Dismissed. — My sympathy. — The soldier lover. — Going to supper. — At the Café de l'E*r**e. — In the cab returning. — Wet feet. — On the seat. — Mutual grasping and gropings.

I have forgotten to say that I had been again much better off, but by extravagance had to draw in, and now lived in a larger house, but kept only three servants. A charwoman came to do rough work; but why this temporary arrangement took place need not be told.

She was a big country woman quite five feet ten high, and speaking with a strong provincial accent. When she was alone in the house I used to cross the streets to see her kneel, and clean the door-steps. She had such a big arm, and her bum looked so huge that I wondered how much was flesh, and how much petticoats. She cleaned the windows on the ground-floor, which in the house I then inhabited were got at by an iron balcony with open bars beneath. Seeing her cleaning them one day I went stealthily to the kitchen, and then into the area, and peeping cautiously up her petticoats, saw her legs to her knees. They were big and suited to her buttocks; but though the sight pleased me much, I never thought of having her, for I avoided women in my own house and neighbourhood. She was plain-faced, sleepy, and stupid-looking; the only thing about her nice, was bright rosy flesh. She looked solid all over. Her hair was a darkish chestnut colour, her eyes darkish, and one day she lifted a table as heavy as herself. There was not the slightest amorousness in her face or manner, and she dressed like a well-to-do country woman. Give her lots of nice, good, white under-clothing; it was better than a sham outside, I heard she had said. She was about twenty-two years old, but she looked older.

About two months after she came (and just then when without other servants), on arriving home one Sunday night at about ten o'clock, I found she had been allowed to go out as usual, but had not returned. Another hour crept on. Savage, I thought of locking her out. About half-past eleven she returned. I let her in, and asked why she was so late. She looked dazed, muddled, had a very red face, muttered she was sorry, she had fallen down and hurt herself, and without waiting to answer me properly went downstairs. My wife went after her, and when she came up, told me she thought she was in drink, and that her dress and bonnet were covered with dust. "She had been up to some tricks with a man," said she.

Next day I heard she had told as an excuse, that as she was walking along a lane up which she turned to piddle, a man laid hold of her, and had taken liberties with her; that in the scuffle she had fallen down, had screamed, tried to catch him, had failed, and a lot more to similar effect. One or two days later I was told the woman had been dismissed. That I quite expected, for it was the mistress' custom to coax out the facts from poor devils in a kind way, and then to kick them out mercilessly; any suspicion of unchastity was enough for that. Middle-aged married women are always hard upon the young in matters of copulation.

"What is she going for? — a few days ago she was so beautifully clean, strong, and serviceable that none were like her!" "Oh! she has got a sweetheart, and is up to no good with him I'm sure." "How do you know?" "She told me so." "It's hard to dismiss on suspicion only, a poor girl who came up to us from the country." "You always take the part of those creatures." "I know nothing for or against her, nor you." "She is no better than she ought to be. — I have noticed a soldier idling about here for some time past." "As you like, — it's your business — but she came to us with an excellent character."

I pitied the woman, but more than that from the time I heard that a man had assaulted her, a slightly lecherous feeling had come over me towards her. I wondered what he had done, — had he felt her? — had he fucked her? — had she ever been fucked before, even if the man had recently done it to her? I began looking closely at her, getting in the way on some pretext or another, and always wondering if this and that had been done. I looked at the broad backside, so broad that a prick must look a trifle by the side of it. "Have the male balls banged up against it?" I thought. When I heard of her being turned adrift I thought I would just like to have her once or so, and that her leaving us gave me a chance. Curiosity was I believe at the bottom of my desire for her, — it was her huge fleshy form, and that spanking arse. Oh! to look at it naked, and feel it, if I did nothing more.

Finding the charwoman was not coming one day, and that the big servant would be a short time alone in the house, home I went; and on some pretext went down to the kitchen.

"So you are going to leave us." "Yes sir." "Why?" "I'm sure I don't know, — Missus says I don't suit, — yet only a few days ago she said I suited well." Here she broke into tears. I spoke kindly to her, said she would get another place soon, — she must take care not to go up dark lanes again with a man, nor go home late and dirty. She could not help it, — it was no fault of hers. What liberties did he take with her? I asked. The woman coloured up, and turning her head away, said he did what was very improper. "Did he put his hands up your petticoats?" "What was very improper," she repeated. "But how did you get so dirty?" They struggled, and she slipped. "I wish I'd been him, — I'm sure when he felt, he got his hand close up, — I'd give a sovereign to have mine there." That remark threw her into a distressing state of confusion.

I talked on decently, alluding to what I thought had taken place, and wishing I had been the man; but got nothing from her excepting that the man had taken liberties with her, — yes most improper liberties.

I told her I was sorry she was going, and thought she was hardly used, but I could not help it, — how was she off for money?

Very badly off, — she had come straight from the country to better herself, and had bought nice, good, underlinen, knowing she was coming to a gentleman's house, and now before she could turn herself round she was sent off. She had had to pay for her coach to London, and when she had her wages, and paid for a cab to lodgings, she would not have twenty shillings left. What was she to do if she could not get another place? Here the big woman blubbered, left off cleaning, sat down on a chair, and hid her face.

"Don't cry, you're used badly, — I'll give you a little money until you get a place, — it won't be long." "You're a good kind master," said she, "everyone says so, — but Missus is a beast, she ain't no good to any one, — I don't wonder you are out so much, and don't sleep with her." I gave a kiss and a cuddle. "What lovely limbs you have, — how firm your flesh is, — you are delicious, — I should like to sleep with *you*, — come into the lane with *me*, and tell me when you are going to piddle again, and let *me* take a liberty."

"Who told you I went up the lane?" "Your mistress," — and then I left, telling her on no account to let it be known that I had been home.

After this I heard that she had said it was a soldier. Now I knew that a soldier who took liberties with a woman, took no little ones, and generally got all he tried for; so made up my mind that she had been fucked on the night she came home late.

A day or two after I was surprised with the following. "I've got another servant, — she will come the day after to-morrow, so I mean to send Sarah away at once, — of course she will be paid her month's wages, but I shall get rid of her, for I am sure she is an unchaste woman."

"Poor devil! — it's enough to make her unchaste, — but it's your business." "Are you going out to-night?" "Why?" "Because if you are I'm going round to my sister's." "I am," — and off I went after dinner; but waited in a cab not far from the end of the street, watching to see if she really did go out. She did, and directly I spied her I drew myself back, and told cabby to follow her to the sister's house. Then I drove back part of the way, and went home.

"So you are going?" said I to the servant. "Yes, I'm turned out, sir." "A soldier and you went up a dark lane, —what a fool to tell your mistress." "Ah! she has told *you*, —what a bad un, she sneaked it out of me, — but I'm not to blame, he is my sweetheart, and is going to marry me." "Have you got lodgings?" "Yes sir, I'm going out to-morrow to see them, and I've written telling my sister (a servant also), and she has taken them." "Wait for me when you go, and on no account say I've been home, — I mean to help you, — you are badly used, — what can I do for you?" "If you would help me to go to the Tower, — my young man's name is ***, he is a Grenadier, — I've written him, but he has not replied, and I want to know if he is there." "I will wait for you to-morrow night outside, when you go to see the lodgings." A kiss, a hug, and out of my house I went again, after having ascertained where she was going to, and the time she was to go out.

Next evening I waited outside her lodgings, she came in

a cab with her box, and told me that her mistress had bundled her out. She had had nothing to eat since mid-day, and was sick and weary. "Make haste then, — arrange your things, and we will go and have something to eat, and you shall see your soldier to-morrow." "God bless you, I do feel grateful sir," said she.

In half an hour she came out. I did not know where better to go to, and knew that it was just the time when the place would be empty, so took her to the Café de l'Europe in the Haymarket. It was a long drive, but I wanted to be with her in the dark cab. She was wonderfully struck with the place, but I was ashamed of being seen with her. She was anxious to go home early, because she lodged with poor people who went to bed early. She had never tasted champagne, so I gave her some. Oh! her delight as she quaffed it, and oh! mine as I saw her drink it, — it was just what I wanted. "A cock has been into her I am sure," I thought, "so another can't do her much harm, — if she'll fuddle she'll feel and be felt, or fuck, or frig, they always go together," my old instructor in the ways of women used to say.

I arranged to take her the next day to the Tower; our talk naturally was about the affair. "He did it to you," I said. She wouldn't or didn't see my meaning. "I could not help it if he did, or what he did, — he took unproper liberties." "He took them more than once, I'll bet!" She did not like such joking, she remarked. All this was when we were going out to supper.

Going home in the cab I began to say a baudy word to her. "He felt your cunt," said I, "did you feel his prick?" She bounced up and hit her bonnet against the top of the cab. "Oh! my! sir," — but she kept on in her excitement, letting out bits of the history, saying at intervals, it was not her fault, — she was fuddled, — fuddled with beer and gin, — a little fuddled her. I saw that pretty clearly from the effect of the champagne; and unbuttoned so as to have my prick handy. It was a wet night, the bottom of the cab was wet straw. "My feet are quite wet," said she. "Put them on the seat, my dear." She did so; I felt them as if solicitous for her comfort, putting my hand higher than above her ankle, just to see if her ankles were wet also.

"Why your ankles are wet." "Yes they are." With a sudden push up went my hand between her thighs, — a yell and a struggle, but I had felt the split before she dislodged my fingers. She was stronger than me, but my hands roved

[200]

about her great limbs, searching under her petticoats round her huge backside. "Oh! don't, — you're a beast." "Oh! what a backside! — what thighs! — what a lovely cunt I'm sure you have! — let me keep my hand just on your knee, and I swear I won't put my hand higher." To ensure my keeping my hand there, she held my wrist as well as a vice would have done. She had by sheer force got it down to there.

I pattered out all my lust, my desire to have her, incitements, and baudy compliments on her form. "Let me fuck you." "You shan't." "You know what it means." "I know what you mean." "What harm could I do? — who would know?" And then the old, old trick. Taking her great fist in mine, I put my stiff prick into it. What a persuader! Though she kept up a show of struggling she did not get it away from that article instantly.

I suppose unless utterly distasteful to each other, that a man and woman cannot feel each other's privates, without experiencing reciprocal baudy emotions. They get tender to each other. The woman always does, after she has got over the first shock to her modesty, and her temporary anger. If after a man has felt her, a thermometer could be applied to her split, I believe it would be found to have risen considerably in temperature. After struggling and kissing, trying to feel her quim, trying to keep my hand on her thighs, it ended in our having our mouths together and my hand being pinched between her two great thighs, whilst the knuckles of one of her hands, with sham reluctance touched my doodle, just as the cab reached her dwelling, and there we parted. All the rest of our conversation was about her soldier, her being dismissed, and is not worth writing.

CHAPTER XX

*The next day. — At the Tower. — In tears. — "The
wretch is married." — At T***f***d Street. — After
dinner. — On the chamberpot. — My wishes
refused. — An attack. — Against the bed. — A stout
resistance. — I threaten to leave her. — Tears and
supplications. — On the sofa. — Reluctant
consent. — A half-virgin.*

Next day she met me early, and we drove to the Tower. On
the road I instructed her what to do when there (it was full
six miles off). I tried my best to get her passions up in a delicate way, but amatory fingerings I avoided whilst the poor
woman was in search of her lover. The feeling of each other's privates on the previous night, had opened her heart to
me. She let out a little more of the history of her escapade
with the soldier, and asked my advice how to act in certain
eventualities, which could only be applicable to a woman
who had been rogered. She was painfully anxious as she approached the Tower. I stopped in the cab just in sight of the
entrance, and after instructing her carefully again who to ask
for, and what to do, in she went.

In half an hour she came back with wet swollen eyes, got
into the cab, and began to bellow loudly. The cabman had
opened the door for her, and stood waiting for orders. For
a few seconds I could get nothing out of her, then told the cabman to drive to a public house near. There I gave her gin,
but still could learn nothing. All she said was, "Oh! such a
vagabond!" Into the cab again. I told the man where to drive
to, for I had laid my plans. "Tell me, — it's not fair after all
the trouble I've taken not to tell me," — sob — sob — sob.
Soon after it all came in a gush. "Yes he was there, that is,
he was two days ago," but the regiment had gone to Dublin, and would not be back for eighteen months, — a letter
would be sent him of course, but his wife would be there in
a day, for, — "Oh! — hoh! — hoh! — the wretch is a married man, and he's deceived me." "You should not have let
him do it." "I didn't mean to." "You let him do it more than

[*202*]

once I'll swear." "He did it twice to me, when in the house, — he swore he'd marry me three days after, if I let him, — and so I d — did, — ho! — her — ho!"

Thus I heard in snatches the whole history, which she told me more plainly afterwards. She had been fucked twice on the eventful night, once on the ground in a lane, and once in a bed-room.

I drove to T***f***d Street. It was not much more than mid-day. I got a comfortable little sitting-room, out of which was a large bed-room. A dinner was sent in by an Italian restaurant close by. After her first grief had subsided, the wine cheered her, and she made a good dinner, talking all the time of her "misfortun." When we had finished for a while I sat caressing her. Then I said, "I want to piddle," — and pulling my prick out before her went into the bed-room and pissed.

"Don't you want to?" "No." "Nonsense, — do you suppose I don't know? — now go." She went into the bed-room. I quietly opened the door ajar directly she had closed it. There was she sitting on the pot, one leg naked, adjusting her garter, and pissing hard.

Then raising her clothes that side she scratched her backside in a dreamy fashion, looking up at the walls. The rattle of her piddle went on. She had been out all the morning, had had gin and champagne, and her bladder must have been full. The side she scratched was towards me. She finished piddling, but still she sat scratching her rump. Then rising she turned round, looked in the pot, put it under the bed, pushed her clothes between her thighs, and looking round saw me at the half-opened door. She gave a start, I rushed up to her.

"What lovely thighs, — what a splendid bum" (though I hadn't seen it). "What a shame, — you've been looking at me." "Yes my darling, — what a lot you have pissed, — what a bum, — I saw you scratch it, — let's feel it, as I did last night, and you know what you felt." I got my hands on to her naked thighs, pushing her bum up against the bedside.

"What a shame to think you have been looking, — leave me alone, — pray do, — now you shan't, — no — you sh — han't."

I closed with her. I had pulled my stiff-stander out. I shook it at her. "Look at this my darling, — let me put it in you, — up your cunt." "No, — leave off, — I won't, — I have had enough of you men, — you shan't."

For a long time the game went on, I begging her to let me

have her, she refusing. We struggled and almost fought.
Twenty times I got her clothes up to her belly, my hand between her thighs. I groped all round her firm buttocks, and
pinched them, grasped her cunt-wig, and pulled it till she
cried out. All the devices I had used with others, all I could
think of, I tried in vain. Then I ceased pulling up her clothes;
but hugging her to me besought her, kissing and coaxing,
keeping one of her hands down against my prick, which she
would not feel, — but it was useless. Then stooping and
again pulling up her petticoats, letting loose every baudy
word that came into my mind, — and I dare say the choicest
words, — I threw myself on my knees, and butting my head
like a goat up her petticoats, got my mouth on to her cunt,
and felt her clitoris in my lips; but I could not move her. She
was far stronger than me. Then rising I tried to lift and
shove her on to the bed. I might as well have tried to lift the
bed itself. I tried to drag her towards a large sofa, big
enough for two big people to lay side by side, and made for
easy fucking. All was useless. Her weight and her strength
were such that I could not move her. There she stood with
her backside against the edge of the bed, her hair getting
loose, one of her stockings pulled by me down to her ankle,
and the upper part of her dress torn open, but no, she would
not let me. She was frightened, — she would not, — I was as
bad as the soldier. In the excitement she no longer cared
about her legs showing to her knees, but her cunt she fought
for, and get my prick against it I could not.

So we struggled I don't know how long, and then breathless, fatigued, I got into a violent rage, — a natural rage, not
an artificial one, — and it told as brutality often tells with a
woman.

We stood looking at each other. She kept one hand on her
clothes just outside her quim, as if to defend it. I with my
prick out, felt defeated and mortified. I had been so successful with women, that I could not understand not getting my
way now. "You damned fool," I said, "I dare say fifty have
fucked you, and you make a sham about your damned cunt,
and your fears, — what did you come here for?" She opened
her eyes with astonishment at my temper. "I didn't know I
was coming here, — I didn't know you meant me to do
that, — you said you'd be kind to me, and give me something to eat, sir, — I'd not eaten since last night, — you said
you would be kind to me, sir." It was said in the deferential
tone of a servant.

"So I will, but if I'm kind, you must be kind to me, —why should it be all on one side?" "I'm sure I don't know," she whimpered. "You know he fucked you, and I dare say a dozen others have." "No one's ever done it but he, and he only did it twice," said she blubbering. "Let me." "No I won't, — I'm frightened to." "Go and be damned." I put in my prick which had drooped, went into the adjoining room, put on my hat and coat, took up my stick, and returning to the bed-room, there was she still with her arse against the bed, crying. She started up when she saw me dressed to go out.

"Oh! don't leave me here alone sir, — you won't, will you?" "Yes I shall, — you can find your way out." "Oh! let me go with you sir." "I shan't, nor see you again, — why should I? — you won't let me have you, not even feel you!"

"I would let you, but I'm frightened. — I've got my living to get, and I've been ill-treated enough by that vaga-bond, — I didn't think you brought me here for that." "What did you think then?" "I didn't think about it at all, — I was all along thinking of him." "You didn't think of him when I felt your cunt in the cab last night, — good-bye."

"Oh! stay only a minute, — do stay sir, — don't leave me here." She still stood against the bed. "Will you let me? — what a fool you are." "Oh! don't call me names, — I would, but I'm frightened, — I've got my living to get." "Haven't you been fucked?" "Y — hes, — y — hes," she sobbed out, "but it wasn't no fault of mine, — I was — aho! — fud — dled," — and she blubbered as loud as a bull roaring.

A sentiment of compassion came over me, for I never could bear to see a woman cry. I threw off my hat and coat, and going up to her as she stood, kissed her. "There then, — let me feel your cunt, — that can't hurt you."

She did not struggle any more. I lifted her clothes, and placed my fingers on her quim. I frigged hard at the right spot, but could get my fingers no further towards the sacred hole. Her massive thighs shut me off from the prick-tube as closely as if it had been a closed door—I could not get my hand between them.

But my fingers were between the cunt-lips, twiddling and rubbing. "Don't cry, — you'll let me I know, — who will know but we?" I fetched a tumbler of champagne from the sitting-room, and she took it like a draught of water. Up went my hand again, and with fingers rubbing her clitoris we talked and kissed side by side. Then turning myself more towards her, up went my other hand round her big bum, which felt as hard, and smooth, and cold as marble.

This went on a long time. She began gradually to yield when she felt the effects of titillation. She then grasped my fiery doodle. Then frigging her harder, her head dropped over my shoulder, and I got my fingers under the clitoris, and there to the hole. "Oh! (a start) you are scratching me, — you're hurting me there."

Taking away my had. "Come here, — don't be foolish," said I, "let us do it, — you will enjoy it, — come," — and I pulled her. Her big form left the bed, and slowly she came with me to the sofa. "Sit down, — there, dear — kiss me, — put up your legs, there's a darling." Slowly, but with much pushing and begging there at last she lay, and the instant she was down I threw her petticoats up, and myself on to her.

I saw the great limbs white as snow. A dark hairy mass up in her thigh-tops. "Oh! don't hurt." "Nonsense I don't." "You do indeed, — oh!" My hands are roving, my arse oscillating. I'm up a cunt, — all is over, — she is fucked.

"Did you have pleasure (I always asked that if I had doubt), — answer me, — did you? — do say, — what nonsense to hold your tongue, — tell me." "Yes I did, after you had done hurting me." "Did I really hurt you?" "Yes." "Impossible." "You did." What a sham, I thought to myself, a woman always is, — a Grenadier has fucked her twice, yet she says my prick hurts her.

I turned off on my side, the sofa being large enough. We had done the trick, and the recklessness of the woman who has tasted the pleasure, and feels the man's spunk in her quim, had come over her. The champagne added its softening influence. She pulled her dress half-down, we laid and talked. I felt her quim. "Don't." "What is it?" "I'm sore." "Why, you are bleeding." "You've hurt me." Out stood my prick, then rose upright again in a moment. Her blood on my finger and her pain gave me a voluptuous shiver. My trowsers were in my way. I tore them off, and stood by her side. "Let me see your cunt." She resisted, but I saw her big thighs closed, and the dark-haired ornamentation. Then getting between her thighs kneeling, I pulled open the lips from which blood-stained sperm was oozing; then I dropped on to her, and again drove my prick up her. A glorious fuck it seemed as I clutched her huge, firm buttocks, and felt her grasping me round my arse. All women, and even girls without any instruction put their arms round the men who are tailing them, the first time they feel the pleasure, but not before. Then we dozed in each other's arms. Then we got up, she confused, I joyous and filled with curious baudiness. "Wash, — won't you?" "You go then." I did, but back I went soon. She had just sluiced it. "You are not bleeding." "I am a little." "You are poorly." "I am not."

I brought her back into the sitting-room. We drank more wine, she got fuddled, not drunk, or frisky, or noisy, but dull, stupid, and obedient. We fucked again and again, and stayed at the baudy house, drinking and amusing ourselves till nine at night. How that big woman enjoyed the prick up her! And the opening of her cunt opened her heart and mouth to me as well.

CHAPTER XXI

The big servant's history. — The soldier at the railway station. — Courting. — In the village lane. — On the grass. — At the pot-house. — Broached partially. — Inspection of her privates refused. — Lewed abandonment. — Her first spend. — A night with her. — Her form. — Sudden effects of a looking-glass. — The baud solicits her. — Sexual force and enjoyment. — She gets a situation. — We cease meeting. — The butcher's wife. — An accidental meeting. — She was Sarah by name.

This was her history. As she came up from the country to us, her box was missing at the station. A big soldier seeing she was a stranger made some enquiries for her, saw her into a cab, invited her to have a glass of gin, which she took, and told him the place she was coming to. The next night he showed himself there, he made love to her, wrote to her, met her on Sunday nights, and at other times when allowed to go out. He offered to marry her, and she had written to her sister to tell her about it all.

On the notable Sunday night, he took her to a tavern, and they had gin and beer till she was fuddled. She knew partially what she was doing, and thought it unwise to go up the lane in the dark with him; yet spite of herself she did. He would marry her that day month, then they would sleep together. He cuddled and kissed her, then began to take liberties. She resisted. Then if she would not let him, she might go home by herself, — why not let him? when soon they would be one in holy matrimony, — and so on. She felt as if she could not struggle. He tried to get into her upright against some railings. Then asking her to lay down on the grass, and she refusing, he pulled her down, and got on to her. She struggled and cried, but felt so frightened, that he seems to have had his way. For all that, he did not, she thought, broach her; he pushed and hurt her, and must have spent outside, she could not be at all certain about that. Steps were heard, they got up, she was crying. Her clothes were, she knew, dirty (though it was dry and fine), her bonnet was bent. She was frightened to go home; he said she must get brushed up, and took her to some low tavern to do so. Terrified at what had been done, and about losing her place and character, she scarcely knew what she did. She had more gin, went into a bed-room with him to wash and brush, and then he persuaded her that now he had done it once, he might as well do it twice. Then he fucked her on the bed. Now the man had turned out to be (there was no possible mistake about his identity) a married man — a sergeant — with two or three children.

"Are you sure he got right into you?" "Quite when on the bed, but I scarcely know what he did or said in the lane, — a little fuddles me, — yes I did bleed, for it was on my smock when I got home, and he did hurt me very much."

I wanted to see her cunt, for her blood-stains made me wonder, and the rather hard pushing I had had, though only for a second or two, set me thinking. I felt her cunt, she winced, — it hurt her. An almost imperceptible stain was on my finger. "You *are* poorly." "I'm not really, — I was so last week." "Let me see your cunt." I coaxed, caressed, tried to pull her thighs open. It was useless. She was much stronger than me, and when she laid hold of my wrist to free herself from my rovings, she removed it easily. Force could do nothing, — she was what had been said of her, as strong as a horse.

So again I got savage. I had conquered by my anger two hour before, and now took to damning and cursing her mock modesty. Then she began again to whimper. "Oh! you do frighten me, — you do 'bust' out so, — I'm quite afeared, — it's not nice to have your thing looked at." "You damned

fool, I've fucked it, — I dare say your soldier looked at it."
"He didn't, — he didn't, — not that I know of." By abusing
I got her consent. Pulling open her thighs I saw her quim.
Had she been gay, she would have taken care to turn her
bum from the light; but she laid with her arm across her
eyes, as if to hide from herself, the sight of man investigating her love-trap.

There was the ragged jugged-edged slit of a recent virginity, and near the clitoris the jagging seemed fresh, raw, and
signs of blood just showing on it. I touched it, she winced,
and nipped my hand with her great thighs, which set me
damning again. Again they opened, I probed deep with my
fingers up her cunt. There was no stain from the profundity,
and the blood came from the front. I looked till my cock
stood, and then fucked her again.

I could never make this out, and we never met without
talking about it. She was perfectly sure the soldier had been
up her, and spent in her when in the bed-room. As to his
prick, whether it was short or long, thick or thin, she knew
not, for she had never seen it, though he had put her hand to
it in the lane. His prick must have been a very small one,
and only split up enough for its entry, and I had finished her
virginity, that is my conclusion.

What is more remarkable, is that her cunt was one of the
tightest I ever met with in a full-grown woman. It felt more
like the cunt of a girl of fourteen, excepting in its depth. It
was a full size outside, and handsome to look at between
huge white thighs and huge globular bum-cheeks. It was
fledged like a young woman's. I expected to find it hairy up
to her navel, but it was only slightly haired, which helped to
satisfy me that she was what she said, only turned twenty-
one years of age.

She was great in bulk, but poor in symmetry. Her bum
was vast, but she was thick up to her waist, and had large
breasts as firm as a rock. Her thighs were lovely, but her
knees were big, that no garter would remain above them,
and she was clumsy in ankle and foot. She had a lovely skin,
and smelt as sweet as new milk, sweet to her very cunt. I
recollect noticing that in her, because some time before I had
been offended with the smell of Fisher's, a woman I fucked,
as already told.

I spent the rest of the day with Big Sarah, told her I would
keep her as long as she was in her lodgings, and advised her
to live well, and to enjoy herself. But she did not need idle-

ness and feeding to make her randy, she was a strong fucker, now that her passions had been once gratified.

I made her twice or thrice stop out all night. She told at her lodgings that she was going to stay with an aunt. I took her to J***s Street, which I liked better than T***f***d Street, for that though the quietest, and only frequented by swells of middle-age, was old-fashioned, dingy, and dull; whereas J***s Street had looking-glasses, gildings, red satin hangings, and gas-lights. We had a supper at the Café de l'Europe, and at nine p.m., we were in the room in which I had poked many a woman. I was delighted to see her white flesh under a bright light. "Now drop your chemise — look at me," — and I stripped to the skin. I exposed her bum, belly, and breasts in turn, whilst she laughing tried to prevent me. Flattery of her beautiful form did it. "Am I so beautifully made?" "A model my darling," — and she stood naked excepting stockings and boots. I had shifted the cheval-glass, and we laid on the sofa. "Look at your thighs and cunt my darling in the glass, — see how my prick looks in it." "Law! to think there be houses with all this, — are there many such?" she asked.

I placed her on the sofa, kneeling, her head against the bed, her backside towards me, and introduced my penis dog-fashion. How randy I had made her! — how randy I was as I felt my belling pressing against those two stupendous globes. "Turn your head there, and look in the glass." "Oh!" said she wriggling her backside, "what a shame for us to be looking like that." The sight made her breathless, and wriggle her cunt closer on to the peg, — how soon a woman learns to do that.

There was a large glass against the wall, so placed that those on the bed could see every movement, — I drew the curtain aside. We fucked enjoying the sight of our thrustings, heavings and backside wrigglings, and passed the night in every baudiness which then I practised. "Do you like looking?" "Yes I like it, — but it makes me do it all of a sudden." It was true, for I found that when fucking her, if I said, "Look at us, — look at me shoving," directly she looked it fetched her; her big arse quivered, and her cunt squeezed my prick like a vice. It was the same always on future days, or when if not in the same room I placed the cheval-glass at the side of the bed. The sudden squeeze and jerk of her arse as she looked amused me, and I always arranged for the spectacle with her. I did not usually do this with women.

It was a delicious night. We were both start naked. Her lower limbs looked so much better when quite naked, than when she had stockings and boots on. The room got hot, we threw all the clothes off. She was a juicy one, and the sheets in the morning were a caution, — I wondered whether it could have all come out of one cunt and one cock. "What will they think?" said she.

I showed her in the evening where she would find the closet, and advised her strongly if spoken to, not to reply to any one. We had breakfast in bed, then fucked. Her need to evacuate came on, and half dressing herself she went down. When she came back, out I went on similar errand. She had washed, and I found her on my return anxiously looking at the seminal stains on the bed-linen. We got on the bed again. Questioning her, she told me that the woman of the house had said to her, "What a splendid woman you are, — I wish you would tell me your address. — I could make your fortune." She had made no reply. I had her as already said several times after, at J***s Street, but took care never to let her out of my sight.

She went after a situation. Such a strong, big, fresh-looking woman was sure to get one, I knew. The next time I saw her afterwards she was in low spirits. "I've boiled myself a pretty kettle of fish," she said, "I could have married well in the country, but thought I should do better in Lunnun, — and now what am I?" "My dear, your cunt can't speak, and if you hold your tongue, no one will know anything about our little amusements, and you will marry well."

I soon tired of her. She was a good-natured, foolish, stupid, trusting creature, and my wonder is that she had lived twenty-one years in the country, without having had a prick up her. As a lovely-cunted fuckstress she left nothing to be desired. She had her fears about consequences, for her courses stopped, but she somehow managed to set that to rights, and at last went to her situation. Once afterwards I fucked her, — my God how she enjoyed it! She was in service not far from me. A butcher's man very soon after married her. They opened a shop, and did very well, then they moved some distance away, and I lost sight of her for years. Then I met her walking with two or three children, I suppose her own. We passed, only looking at each other.

But I almost spoke, for she came upon me so unexpectedly, and my first impulse was to speak. She stopped short, threw her head back, and her lower jaw dropped, so that her mouth opened wide, and it would have been ludicrous, had it not been for the expression of fear and pain which came over her face. I recovered myself, passed on, and never saw her more.

I paid her expenses at her lodgings, and gave her a ten-pound note as a present. It was very economical, — but I never knew a woman so delighted with my liberality. "I had two pounds, and now I've twelve," said she, "I shall send a pound to my mother." When I gave her the ten pounds she asked what it was, never having seen a bank-note in her life before. One or two country-women of the same class whom I have had, were just as ignorant of a bank-note.

CHAPTER XXII

A gap in the narrative. — A mistress. — A lucky legacy. — Secret preparations. — A sudden flight. — At Paris. — A dog and a woman. — At a lake-city. — A South American lady. — Mrs. O*b***e. — Glimpses from a bed-room window. — Hairy armpits. — Stimulating effects. — Acquaintance made. — The children. — "Play with Mamma like Papa." — A water excursion. — Lewed effects. — Contiguous bed-rooms. — Double doors. — Nights of nakedness. — Her form. — Her sex. — Carnal confessions. — Periodicity of lust.

I pass over many incidents of a couple of years or more, during which I was well off, had a mistress whom I had seduced, as it is stupidly called, and had children; but it brought me no happiness, and I fled from the connection. All this was never known to the world. My home life at length became so unbearable, that I at one time thought of realizing all I had, of throwing up all chance of advancement and a promising career which then was before me, and going for ever abroad I knew not where, nor cared. My mother had died, one sister was married, and was not much comfort to me; the other was far off, my brother nowhere. Just then a distant relative left me a largish sum of money, it was scarcely known to any one of my friends, quite unknown at home, and to none until I had spent a good deal of it. I kept the fact to myself till I had put matters in such train that I could get a couple of thousand pounds on account, then quietly fitted myself out with clothes. One day I sent home new portmanteaus, and packed up my clothes the same day. "I am going abroad," I said. "When?" "To-night." "Where to?" "I don't know, — that is my business." "When do you come back?" "Perhaps in a week, — perhaps a year." — nor did I for a long time. I never wrote to England during that time, excepting to my solicitors and bankers who necessarily knew where I had been at times.

I went first to Paris, where I ran a course of baudy house amusements, saw a big dog fuck a woman who turned her rump towards it as if she were a bitch. The dog licked and smelt her cunt first, and then fucked. He was accustomed to the treat. Then I saw a little spaniel lick another French woman's cunt. She put a little powdered sugar on her clitoris first, and when the dog had licked that off, somehow she made it go on licking, until she spent, or shammed a spend, calling out, "Nini, — cher Nini, — go on Nini," — in French of course.

I could make a long story out of both of these incidents if it were worth while, but it is not, and only notice that the Newfoundland, whose tongue hung out quite as long as his prick as he was pushing his penis up the French woman's quim, turned suddenly round when it had spent, seemed astonished to find he was not sticking arse to arse with her, and then licked the remains of the sperm off the tip of his prick. It was not a nice sight at all, nor did I ever want to see it again.

There were few large cities of Central Europe I did not see, and think that the best baudy houses in most large cities saw *me*. It was a journey in which my amatory doings were especially with the priestesses of Venus. Beautiful faces and beautiful limbs were sufficient for me, if coupled with ready submission to my wishes. Although I learnt no doubt a great deal, and had my voluptuous tastes cultivated in a high degree, yet they developed none of those outside tastes which ordinarily come with great knowledge and practice in the matters of cunt. I shall only tell the most remarkable fornicating incidents.

I was at the Hotel B*** in a Swiss town by a great lake, had arrived late, and was put into the third story, in a room overlooking a quadrangle. It was hot. I threw up my window when I got out of bed in the morning, and in night-gown looked into the quadrangle, and at the walls and windows of the various bed-rooms opening on to it on three sides. Looking down on my right, and one story below me, I caught sight over the window-curtain of a bed room, of a female head of long dark hair, and a naked arm brushing it up from behind vigorously. The arm looked the size of a powerful man's, but it was that of a woman. She moved about heedlessly, and soon I saw that she was naked to below her breasts; but I only caught glimpses of that nakedness, for seconds, as she moved backwards and forwards near the window. Then she held up the hair for a minute, and seemed to be contemplating the effect of the arrangement of it, and showed what looked like a nest of hair beneath one armpit. Her flesh looked sallow or brown, and she seemed big and middle-aged. My window was near the angle of the quadrangle, so was hers, on the adjacent side of it. Perhaps from the window where I was, and that above mine only, could be seen all what I saw.

The armpit excited me, and I got lewed, though the glimpses were so few and short. Now I only saw the nape of the neck, and now her back, according to the postures which a woman takes in arranging her hair, and so far as the looking-glass and blinds and my position above let me. Once or so I saw big breasts of a tawny color. Then she looked at her teeth. Then she disappeared, then came forwards again, and I fancied she was naked to the waist. Then I lost sight of her, and again for an instant saw just the top of her naked bum, as if she were stripped, and in stooping down had bent her back towards the window. When she reappeared she was more dressed. She looked up at the sky, approaching the window to do so, caught sight of me, and quickly drew the blind right down.

I went down to breakfast, met some friends, and sitting down to table with them in the large breakfast-room, saw close to me this very lady. I had seen so little of her face that I did not recognize her at first by that; but the darkness of the eye and hair, the fullness of bust, and the brown-tinted skin left me in no doubt. We were introduced to each other. "Mrs. O*b***e, a lady from New Orleans, a great friend of ours, — been travelling with us for some weeks, with her two little children," — and so on.

I found out from my friends as we smoked our cigars in the gardens after breakfast, that she, with another American lady, and themselves, were going for a long tour, and had been touring for some weeks in Europe. She was the wife of a gentleman who owned plantations, and had gone back to America; intending to rejoin his wife at Paris at Christmas. The lady with the very hairy armpits and her husband were intimate friends of my friends.

I found this party were travelling my road, and I agreed to wait at **** as long as they did. We met at meals; I joined in their excursions, and took much notice of her children who got quite fond of me. She seemed to avoid me at first, but in two or three days showed some sympathy. I guessed that my history had been made known to her, and found out at a latter day that it had. "A married man travelling without his wife is dangerous," said she to me one day when we were a merry party. "A married woman without her husband is a danger to me," I replied, and our eyes met, and said more than words.

I objected to my room, and in a few days the hotel-keeper showed me some better rooms. I had then ascertained which hers were, and pointed out the room next to them. "That," said he, "won't do — it's large, and has two beds." "Oh! it's so hot, I want a large room, — show it me." He did. "It's double price." "Never mind," — and I took it at once. Luck, thought I. Her own room was next, and adjoining it a room in which her two children slept. A half-governess, half-maid who travelled with her, was on another floor, — why I don't know, — perhaps because the next room to the children's was a sitting-room.

My new room had as usual a door communicating with hers. I listened one or two nights and mornings, and heard the slopping of water and rattle of pots, but with difficulty; and nothing sufficiently to stir my imagination or satisfy my curiosity. There were bolts on both sides of the doors, and double doors. I opened mine, and tried if hers was fastened. It was. But I waited my opportunity, intending to try to have her, thinking that a woman who had not had a man for months, and might not for some months more, would be ready for a game of mother and father if she could do so safely.

She was not very beautiful, but was fine, tallish, handsomely formed, with a large bust, and splendid head of hair. Her complexion had the olive tint of some Southerners. One might almost have supposed there was a taint of Negro blood in her, but her features were rather aquiline and good.

The face was coldish and stern, the eyes dark and heavy, the only sensuous features of her face was a full, large-lipped mouth, which was baudy in its expression when she laughed. I guess she was a devil of a temper.

After a day or two I gave up all hope, for she would not understand double entendres, coldly returned my grasp when I shook hands with her, and gave no signs of pleasure in my company, excepting when I was playing with her children. Yet when she looked into my face when laughing; there certainly was something in her eye, which made me think that a pair of balls knocking about her bum would delight her. I used to think much of what a friend of mine, a surgeon in a crack regiment in which I had some friends, used to say, which was this.

"All animals are in rut sometimes, so is a woman, even the coldest of them. It's of no use trying the cold ones, unless they have the tingling in their cunts on them; then they are more made for it than others, but it doesn't last. If you catch a cold woman just when she is on heat, try her; but how to find out their time, I never knew, — they are damned cunning." So said the surgeon.

I must have caught Mrs. O*b***e on heat I suppose, and it came about soon. We went out for some hours on the lake in a boat. She was timid, and when the boat rocked I held her, squeezed her arm, and my knees went against hers. Another time my thigh was close against hers. I put one of her children on to her lap. The child sat down on my hand, which was between her little bum and her mother's thighs. I kept my hand there, gradually moving it away, creeping it up higher and higher, and gripping the thigh as I moved it towards the belly, but so delicately, as to avoid offence, and I looked her in the face. "Minnie is heavy, isn't she?" I said. "She is getting so," she replied, looking with a full eye at mine.

Now I felt sure from her look, that she knew I was feeling her thigh. I had stirred her voluptuousness. The water got rougher. "I shall be sick," said she. "What! on such a lake!" "Oh! I'm a bad sailor." Placing my arm round her for a minute I pulled her close to me. It became calm, and lovely weather again. The water always upset her, it seemed to stir her up, she said. "I'd like to see you stirred up," said I. Then to avoid remark I changed sides with a lady, and sat opposite to Mrs. O*b***e. We faced each other, looking at each other. I pushed my feet forward, so as to rub my foot against her ankle. She did not remove her foot, but looked at me.

Arrived at *** we dined, and sat afterwards in the garden. It grew dusk, and we separated into groups. I sat by her side, and played with her children. One child said, "Play with me like Papa, — play with Mamma like Papa does." "Shall I play with you like Papa?" said I to Mrs. O*b***e. "I'd rather not," said she. "I'd break an arm to do so," I replied. "Would you?" said she. "Oh! put the children to bed Margaret," — and the governess with the children and Mrs. O*b***e walked off. I for a minute joined my friends smoking, then cut off by a side-path leading to that through which Mrs. O*b***e would pass. She had just bid the children good night. "I shall come up to see you directly," said she to them, — and to me, "I thought you were going into town." "Yes I think I'll make a night of it, — I'm wild. — I want your company." "Fine company it will be, I dare say." "Let me keep you company then." No one was near, I kissed her. She took it very quietly. "Don't now, you'll compromise me." It was now quite dusk. I kissed her again. "I'm dying to sleep with you," I whispered. "You mustn't talk like that, — there now, they will see you," — then I left her.

I had noticed her habits, and knew that usually she went up to her children soon after they had gone to bed, so I waited at the foot of the stairs. Soon she came. "What, you here?" "Yes, I'm going to bed like you." It was a sultry night, everybody was out of doors, the hotel servants lolling at open windows. No one met us as we went upstairs. "Why that's not your room, — it's next to mine." "Yes it is, — I've been listening to you the last two nights." "Oh! you sly man, — I thought you were sly." "Look what a nice room it is," said I opening the door. There was a dim light in the corridors, none in my room. She looked in, I gave her a gentle squeezing push, and shut the door on us.

"Don't shut the door," said she turning sharply round. I caught and kissed her. "Stop with me, my darling, now you're here. — I'm dying for you, — kiss me, do." "Let me go, — there then, — now let me go, — don't make a noise, — oh! if my governess should hear me, what would she think!" "She is not there." "Sometimes she stays till I go up to the children, — oh! don't now, — you shan't." I had her up against the wall, my arm round her, I was pressing my hand on her belly outside her clothes. She pushed my hand away, I stooped and thrust it up her clothes on to her

[*217*]

cunt, and pulling out my prick, pushed her hand on to it. "Let me, — let's do it, — I'm dying for you." "Oh! for God's sake don't, oh! no — now, you'll compromise me, — hish! if she should be listening." For a moment we talked, she quietly struggled, entreating me to desist; but my fingers were well on her cunt, frigging it. I don't recollect more what she said, but I got her to the side of the bed, pushed her back on it, and thrust my prick up her. "Oh! don't compromise me — don't now." Then she fucked quietly till she gasped out, "Oho — oho," as a torrent of my sperm shot into her cunt.

Off and on until daybreak we fucked. After the second she gave herself up to pleasure. The randiest slut just out of a three months quodding could not have been hotter or readier for lewed fun with cunt and ballocks. I never had a more randy bed-fellow. She did not even resist the inspection of her cunt, which surprised me a little, considering its condition. Our light burnt out, our games heated us more and more, the room got oppressive, I slipped off her chemise, our naked bodies entwined in all attitudes, and we fucked, and fucked, bathed in sweat, till the sweat and sperm wetted all over the sheet, and we slept. It was broad daylight when we awakened. I was lying sweating with her bum up against my belly, her hair was loose all over her, and the bed. Then we separated and she fled to her room, carrying her chemise with her.

Oh! Lord that sheet! — if ten people had fucked on it, it could not have been more soiled. We consulted how best to hide it from the chamber-maid, and I did exactly the same trick as of former days. Have not all men done it I wonder?

I got a sitz-bath in my room, which was then not a very easy thing to get. I washed in it, wetted all my towels, then took off the sheet, wetted it nearly all over, soiled it, then roughly put it together in a heap, and told the chamber-woman I had used the sheet to dry myself with. She said, "Very well." I don't expect she troubled herself to undo or inspect the wet linen, or thought about the matter.

I went to breakfast at the usual time. "Where is Mrs. O*b***e?" I asked. The governess appeared with the children saying the lady had not slept owing to the heat. She showed up at the table d'hôte dinner. I avoided her, knowing I should see her soon afterwards, and said I should go and play billiards; but instead, went to my bed-room and read;

nursing my concupiscent tool, and imagining coming pleasures.

I heard the children, having opened the door on my side
and found that the key of her door was luckily so turned as
to leave the key-hole clear. The doors connecting all the
rooms were as is often the case in foreign hotels, opposite
each other, and I could see across into the children's bed-
room. They were putting their night-gowns on in their own
room. Then the governess came into her mistress' room and
I heard her pissing, but could not see her. To my great
amusement, for the slightest acts of a woman in her privacy
give me pleasure, she then came forward within range of my
peep-hole, and was looking into the pot carefully. Then Mrs.
O*b***e came in and the governess left. Mrs. O*b***e
went to look at her children and returned, opened our doors,
and then we passed another amorous night, taking care to
put towels under her bum when grinding. We did not want
the sheets to be a witness against us again.

Mrs. O*b***e was not up to the mark, and began to talk
that sort of bosh that women do, who are funky of consequences. After a time she warmed, and yielded well to my
lubricity. I would see her cunt to begin with. It was a pretty
cunt, and not what I had expected, large, fat-lipped, and set
in a thicket of black hair, from her bum-hole to her navel;
but quite a small slit, with a moderate quantity of hair on her
motte, but very thick and crisp. I told her again how I had
seen her from the window. The recital seemed to render her
randier than either feeling my prick, or my titillation of her
quim. The hair in her armpits was thicker, I think, than in
any woman I ever had. Her head-hair was superb in its quantity. I made her undo it, and spread it over the bed, and
throw up her arms, and show her armpits when I fucked her.
She was juicy-cunted, and spent copiously; so did I. The
heat was fearful. We fucked start naked, again.

Later on she told me that she cared about poking but once
a month only, and about a week before her courses came on.
At other times it annoyed her. Going on the water always
upset her stomach, and made her lewed, even if in a boat on
a river, and however smooth it was, it upset her that way. At
sea it was the same. It made her firstly feel sick, then giddy,
then sleepy, but that always two or three hours afterwards,
randiness overtook her. After a day or two, the lewedness
subsided whether she copulated, or frigged, or not. She told
me this as a sort of excuse for having permitted me to sper-

matize her privates, the night of her excursion on the water with us.

She was curious about my history. I told her I had women at every town I came to. She declared that no other man but I and her husband had ever had her.

CHAPTER XXIII

At the town of A***n*n. — At the railway. — The station rebuilding. — Diarrhœa. — The closet-attendant. — The temporary shed. — Ladies' closets. — A peep-hole. — Women on the seat. — Peasants. — Piddlers outside. — At the peep-hole again. — Onanism. — A male intruder. — The letter-box. — An infantine pudenda. — An impatient male. — The soiled seat. — Sisters. — A succession of backsides. — The female attendant. — Bribed and kissed. — Her husband's occupation.

Then I saw a sight that I never wish to see again, for though it was exciting, it was nasty, and for some time afterwards came offensively into my mind, even in my most voluptuous moments with women; destroying the sense of their beauty, and what of romance there is in the conjunction of cunt and prick. However my mind came round to its right balance at last.

I was at A***n*n in the south of France, and went up with my luggage to the station which was being rebuilt. A branch-line had been opened the day before, and all was a chaos of brick, mortar, and scaffolding. The water-closets were temporarily run up in wood, in a very rough manner. A train had just brought in many passengers. I was taken with violent belly-ache, and ran to the closets. They were full. Fearful of shitting myself I rushed to the woman's which were adjoining the men's. "Non, non Monsieur," screamed out the woman in charge, "c'est pour les dames." I would have gone in spite of her, but they were also full. Foul myself I must. "Oh! woman I am so ill, — here is a franc, show me somewhere for God's sake." "Come here," said she, and going round to the back of the wooden structure, she opened the door of a shed. On the door was written "Control, private, you don't enter here." In I went rapidly. "Shut the door quite close," said she, "when you come out." It had been locked. I saw a half-cupboard, and just in time to save my trousers made myself easy on a seat with a hole in it.

It was a long compartment of the wooden shed and running at the back of several privies. No light was provided for it, excepting by a few round holes pierced here and there in the sides; but light came also at places through joints of the woodwork roughly and temporarily put together. There were chests, furniture, forms, cabinets, lamps, and shelves and odds and ends of all sorts in the shed, seemingly placed there till the new station was finished. The privy seat on which I sat was at one end. The privy enclosure had no door, and looking about when my belly-ache had subsided, and I could think of something else, I heard on my right, rustlings, and footsteps, as of females moving, and a female voice say, "Make haste." Then doors banged and opened, and just beyond my knee I saw a round hole in the woodwork through which a strong light came into my dark shed. Off I got in a trice, and kneeling down looked. It was a hole through which I could have put my middle-finger, a knot in the wood had fallen or been forced out, in the boarding which formed the back of one of the women's closets, and just above the privy-seat. What a sight met my eyes as I looked through it!

A large brown turd descending and as it dropped disclosing a thickly haired cunt stretched out wide between a fat pair of thighs and great round buttocks, of which I could see the whole. A fart followed, and a stream of piddle as thick as my finger splashed down the privy-hole. It was a woman with her feet on the seat after the French fashion, and squatting down over the hole. Her anus opened and contracted two or three times, another fart came, her petticoats dropped a little down in front, she pulled them up, then up she got, and I saw from her heels to above her knees as she stood on the privy-seat, one foot on each side of the hole. Off the seat then she got, pulling her petticoats tightly about her, and holding them so. Then she put one leg on to the seat, and wiped her bum with two or three pieces of paper which she held in one hand, taking them one by one from it with the other, wiping from the anus towards the cunt, and throwing each piece down the hole as she had done with it. Then looking at her petticoats to see if she had smirched them, she let them fall, gave them a shake, and departed.

She was a fine dark woman of about thirty, well dressed, with clean linen, and everything nice, though not looking like a lady. The closets it must be added, had sky-lights and large openings just above the doors for ventilation, so they were perfectly light. The sun was shining, and I saw plainly her cunt from back to front, her sphincter muscle tightening and opening, just as if she had arranged herself for me to see it. I recollect comparing it in my mind to those of horses, as I have seen many a time, and every other person must have seen, tightening just after the animals have evacuated.

The sight of the cunt, her fine limbs, and plump buttocks made my cock stiff, but my bowels worked again. I resumed my seat, and had no sooner done so than I heard a door bang. Down on my knees I went, with eye to peep-hole. Another woman was fastening the closet door. It was a long compartment. When near the door, I could see the women from head nearly to their ankles; when quite near the seat I could not see their heads, nor their knees which were hidden by the line of the seat; but I saw all between those parts.

It was a peasant-girl seemingly about twenty years old, tall, strong, and dark like the other. She took some paper out of her pocket, then pulling her petticoats well up, I saw the front of her thighs and had a momentary glimpse of the motte. She turned round, mounted the seat, and squatted. She then drew up her petticoats behind tighter, and I saw buttocks, turds and piddle. She did not lift up her petticoats quite so much in front, yet so light was it that the gaping cunt and the stream were quite visible. She wiped her bum as she sat, then off she went, leaving me delighted with her cunt, and annoyed at seeing what was behind it.

Then I found from looking around and listening, that there were several women's closets at the back of all of which the shed ran. It was a long building with one roof, and the closets were taken out of it. Through the chinks of the boards of one closet I could see the women enter, and leave, could hear them piss, and what they said in all of them; but in the one only could I see all their operations. I kept moving from one to the other as I heard their movements, their grunts, and their talk, but always to the peep-hole when there was anything to see, — and there was plenty.

I had now missed my train, the two women I expect must have gone off by it, and for quite an hour the closets were all empty. I began to think there was no chance of seeing more unless I stayed longer than an hour when I knew an express train arrived. I resolved to wait for that, wondering if any one would come into my shed for any purpose, but no one came in. I had eased myself, and covered up the seat; but a strong stink pervaded the place, which I bore resolutely, hoping to see more female nakedness.

There had been a market at A***n*n that morning. Some of the farm-people had come by the train for the first time, the junction railway only having just been opened. I had heard them say so on the platform before I was taken short. Hearing voices just outside my shed, I cautiously opened the door ajar and peeped. Groups of market people had arrived, and were standing outside the station, mostly women with baskets. The eaves of the shed-roof projecting much, gave a little shade from the sun, and they were standing up against it. That told me there would be another train soon; so I shut the door.

In a few minutes close to my door I heard two female voices. "I want to do caca," said one of them (in French of course). "They charge you a penny," said the other. "I won't pay a penny, — we shall be home in twelve minutes when the train starts." "I shall piss," said one in broad French. She was close up against the spot where I stood, a board only between us. I heard a splash, then two splashes together. I opened the door ajar again, and peeped. They were both standing upright, but pissing. Both laughed. "I must do it somewhere," said one. "Go over there then, — they won't see you." "No I'll go to the woman, and say I haven't any money when I come out." The next minute she came into the privy with the peep-hole. On my knees I went, and saw the operation complete. Such a nice little girl. She sat some minutes after she had dropped her wax, pulling her petticoats well up from time to time. I had such gloat over her cunt. Once or twice she put her hand under, and felt it.

Spite of my diarrhœa, my prick got so stiff, and I was so randy, that with my eye to the hole and gazing on her round bum and gaping cunt, I frigged myself. My sperm fell on the partition in front of me. I sat looking at it, when I was shitting again. The girl went back to her companion by the shed, and said she had been obliged to pay, and it was a shame. I opened the door, feeling as if I must see the girl's face again. They saw me. "There's some one in there," said one, and they moved away.

After that the woman in charge wiped the privy-seat, which I suppose was dirty. Then two or three women came in. Old, and dirty were one or two of them, who sat on it English fashion. I saw their skinny buttocks, and the back-view of their cunts. It sickened me, for they all of them shit, which revolted me. Yet the fascination of the cunt made me look at all of them, — I could not help it. One woman had her courses on, and moved aside a rag to do her needs, — that nearly made me vomit. That woman squatted on the seat.

For a quarter of an hour or so no one came. A trumpet, a railway-bell, and a hubbub, then told me the express train was coming in. Then was hurry, and confusion, a jabber of tongues in many languages. All the closet-doors banged at once, and I heard the voices of my country-women.

Pulling her clothes up to her hips a fine young English woman turned her bum on to the seat. It came out of a pair of drawers, which hid nearly her buttocks. As she sat down her hand eased her drawers away from her cunt. Splash, trump, and all was over. The hair of her cunt was light-ish. She was gone. Another came who spoke to her in English, and without a moment's delay pissed, and off she went.

Then a lady entered. As she closed the door I saw a man trying to enter. She pushed him out saying in suppressed voice, "Oh! for God's sake are you mad? — he can see from the carriage-window." "Not there sir," I heard the woman in charge cry out. The door was shut, and bolted.

The lady, young and handsome, stood quite still, facing the seat, as if overcome with anxiety; then feeling in her pocket, took out some letters, and selecting some, tore them in half, and threw them down the privy. That done she daintily wiped round the seat with a piece of paper, lifted up handsome laced petticoats, and turning her rump towards the seat daintily sat down. She had no drawers on. She must have fancied something, for she rose again directly, and holding her clothes half-way up her thighs looked carefully at the seat. Then she mounted it, but as if she scarcely knew how to do it, stumbled and bungled. She stood upright on it for an instant, and then I could only see half-way up her legs. At length the bum slowly descended, her petticoats up, and adjusted so as to avoid all chance of contamination. I saw the piss descending, but she was sitting too forward, and the piss fell splashing over the edge of the seat. She wriggled back opening her legs wider, and a pretty cunt with dark hair up to her bum-hole showed. My cock stood again.

She jumped off the seat, looked down the privy, gave her clothes a tuck between her thighs, and went off.

Then came others, mostly English, pissing in haste, and leaving, and bum after bum I saw. Then came a woman with a little girl. She was not English, she mounted the seat, and cacked. Whilst doing so she told the child to "pi-pi bébé" on the floor, which she did not. When she had finished she wiped her arse-hole with her finger, — how she cleaned the finger I didn't see. She then took up her child, held her up over the seat with her clothes up to her waist, her cunt to-wards me, and made her piss. The tiny stream splashed on the seat, and against the hole through which I was looking — a drop hit me on the eye. How funny the hairless little split looked to me. To think that her little split might one day be surrounded with black hair like her mother's, and have seven inches of stiff prick up it! Her mother's hair was black, and she had a moustache.

Again a row. "Not there Monsieur, — l'autre côté." "It's full God damn it, — I am not going to shit myself," said a man in English. "Vous ne pouvez pas entrer," — but he would. A big Englishman — a common man — pushed the woman in charge aside, and bolted the door muttering. "Damned fool, — does she think I'm going to shit myself!" He tore down his trowsers, and I moved away, but heard him let fly before he had sat on the seat (he had the squitters), and muttering to himself, he buttoned up and left. I heard him wrangling with the woman in charge.

Instantly two young ladies entered, — sisters seemingly, and English, — nice fresh-looking girls, both quite fair. One pulled up her clothes. "Oh! I can't sit down, — what a beastly place, — what beasts those French are," said she, — "dirty beasts, — call the woman, Emily." Emily looked out-side. "I can't see her, — make haste, or the train will be leaving." "I can't sit down." "Get on the seat as those dirty French do, and I'll hold your petticoats up. Take care now, — take care."

"I shall get my feet in it," said she. "No you won't." She stood fronting me, and pulling up her petticoats till they looked as if tied round her waist in a bundle, showing every part from her motte, to her knees, (my eye just at the level of her bum), and saying, "Don't look and laugh" — but laugh-ing herself, she got on the seat. A prettily-made creature, not stout, nor thin, with a cunt covered with light-brown hair. She squatted. I saw the bum-hole moving. "I can't do it like this," she cried, "with all this nastiness about me, — are my clothes falling down?" "No, — make haste, — you won't have another opportunity for two hours." Out and in went the anus again, the pretty fair-haired quim was gaping, the piddle began to fall. She wanted to piddle badly enough. I said aloud in my excitement at seeing her beauty, "Cunt, cunt."

The girl got upright, I could now only see half her legs. "Hish! did you hear?" said she. Both were silent. "It must be the woman in the next place." "It sounded like a man." Then she spoke in a whisper. "No it can't be." She squatted again laughing. "It's no one." Her evacuations dropped and off she got. "You go, Mary," said the other. "I only want to pee, and I'll do it on the floor." "The dirty creatures, why don't they keep the place clean?" Squatting I watched her face. It was all I could see then, and suppose she pissed. I only saw her hitch up her clothes, but nothing more.

Then the closet-woman came, and wiped the seat grumbling, women opened the door whilst she was doing so, then others came in, and for half an hour or so, I saw a succession of buttocks, fat and thin, clean and dirty, and cunts of all colours. I have told of all worth noting. The train went off, and all was quiet. I had again diarrhœa, and what with evacuating, the belly-ache, and frigging excitement, felt so fatigued that I was going away. As I opened the door the woman was just putting the key in. She started back as she saw me.

"Are you ill?" she said. "Yes." "What a time you have staid, — why did you not go?" Then all at once, as if suspecting something, she began looking at the backs of the women's closets, and found the hole, and looking half smiling, half angry, "You made that," said she. "No." "Yes you did." I declared I had not. "Ah! méchant, — méchant," said she (looking through the hole), and something about the chef de la gare. "You have been peeping through." "Certainly." I was so excited, so full of the adventure, that I had been bursting to tell some one, and talk the incident over. So in discreet words I told her about the man, and the woman, and her letters, and other incidents, till she was amused, and laughed. Then spite of my illness my lust got strong as I looked at her, for she had a cunt. She was a coarse sun-tanned, but fine stout sort of tall peasant woman about thirty-five years old. So I told her of the pretty little splits, and nice bums I had seen, all in select language. And I so longed, Madame. "Oh! if I had had them in here." "Ah! no doubt." "Or if you had been here, for I wished for you." "For me? — ah! ah!" — and she slapped both her thighs and laughed. "Mais je suis mariée, moi, — ah! méchant, — méchant." "Here is another five francs, but I must have a kiss." She gave it seemingly much flattered. I said I should come the next day. "Ah! non!" she must tell the Chef, it was her duty, — it would be useless if I came for that hole.

We talked on. She was the wife of a workman who it seems travelled up and down the line almost continually with officers of the railway, and only came home about once a week, or ten days. She had no children. Whilst talking my diarrhœa came on. My paper was gone, she produced some from her pocket, and simply turned her back whilst I eased myself (the enclosure had no door), as if it was the most natural thing in the world. Finally after saying that she would not dare to let me in the next day, yet on a promise of ten francs she said she would, and volunteered the information, that by an early train many farmers' wives would probably arrive for the market, that many would come by the line just opened. She must report the hole to the Chef, — it might cost her her place if she did not, and it would be stopped. I kissed her again, and whispered in her ear, "I wish I had seen you sitting, and that you had come in here afterwards." "Ah! mon Dieu que vous êtes méchant," she replied laughing, and looking lewdly in my eyes — and I went off. I had been there hours.

At the time I speak of I was travelling easily from place to place, without trouble or worry, eating, drinking, and living in the open air, and getting the chance of women every three or four days only. Then I could fuck them every two hours comfortably, and even five times in a night, but never more. Three times was my usual number, twice at night, and if I slept with them, once again in the morning. I did nothing, or but rarely anything to exhaust myself, and was always ready for a woman. What a delightful time it was. Soon after I returned to England.

CHAPTER XXIV

Camille the second. — Stripping. — The divan. —
Cock-washing. — Camille's antecedents. — Face,
form, and cunt. — Mode of copulating. —
Avaricious. — Free fucking offered. — Gabrielle. —
Cunt, form, and face. — Minette.

Since I had finished with Camille, her sister Louise, and the
French artistes in letchery whom she introduced to me when
I was twenty-one years old, I do not recollect having gone
with a French woman excepting when abroad, my tastes ran
on my own countrywomen. Now in the year 18**, a year of
national importance, and one in which strangers came from
all parts of the world to London, I was to have a French
woman again.

Was it for the sake of change only, or because they were
more willing, salacious, enterprising, and artistic in Paphian
exercises? — was it my recollection of having that when I
did not want it? — I cannot say.

At quite the beginning of the month of June, about four
o'clock in the afternoon, I saw a woman walking slowly
along Pall-Mall dressed in the nicest and neatest way. I
could scarcely make up my mind whether she was gay or
not, but at length saw the quiet invitation in her eye, and
slightly nodding in reply, followed her to a house in B**y
Street, St. James. She was a French woman named Camille.

I named my fee, it was accepted, and in a quiet, even
ladylike way she began undressing. With a neatness unusual
in gay women, one by one each garment was folded up, and
placed on a chair, pins stuck in a pin-cushion, &c., with the
greatest composure, and almost without speaking. I liked her
even for that, and felt she would suit my taste. As each part
of her flesh came into view, I saw that her form was lovely.
When in her chemise, I began undressing, she sitting looking
at me. When in my shirt, I began those exquisite preliminaries with this well-made, pretty woman, feeling her all over,
and kissing her; but my pego was impatient, and I could not
go on at this long. Smiling she laid hold of my prick. "Shall

we make love?" this was in the bed-room. "Yes." "Here, or in the salon?" "I don't like a sofa." "Mais ici," said she pushing the door open wide, and pointing to a piece of furniture which I had not noticed, though noticeable enough.

In the room was a sort of settee or divan, as long, and nearly as wide as a good-sized bed; so wide that two people could lie on it side by side. It had neither head nor feet, but presented one level surface, covered with a red silky material, and a valance hanging down the sides. At one end were two pillows, also red, and made flat like two bed-pillows. "There, on that," said I at once.

I never saw any divan or piece of furniture like it in my life since, neither in brothel, nor in private house, here or on the Continent, excepting once when quite in the extreme East of Europe.

It was a blazing hot day. "Shall I take off my chemise?" "Yes." Off she took it, folded it up, and took it into the bed-room. "Take off your shirt." Off I drew it, and we both stood naked. She laid hold of my stiff prick, gave it a gentle shake, laughed, fetched two towels, spread one on the divan for her bum, laid the other on a pillow for me, went back to the bed-room, poured out water in the basin, then laid herself down naked on the divan with her bum on the towel. I kissed her belly and thighs, and she opened them wide for me to see her notch without my having asked her to do so. To pull it open, have a moment's glance at the red, kiss and feel her rapidly over, mount her, fuck and spend, was only an affair of two or three minutes, so strongly had she stirred my lust for her.

I laid long up her, raising myself on my elbow to talk with her whilst my prick was still in her sheath. At length it slipped out. Gently she put her hand down, and caught it, taking off the excess of moisture. Delicately she raised the towel, and put her hand on her cunt, and saying with a smile, "Mon Dieu, il y en a assez," went to the bed-room, I following her.

She wiped her cunt with the towel, half squatting to do so, then rose up quickly saying, "Shall I wash you?" I had begun, but the offer pleased me. I have no recollection as I write this, of any gay woman having made such an offer since the first French Camille, and one or two of her set, excepting yellow-haired Kitty, who liked doing that to me. "Yes wash it." "Hold the basin then," — and talking it up she placed it under me, so that my testicles hung into it whilst I held it. She washed me. "Soap?" "Yes." "Inglis sop" (laughing), — the first English words I heard her speak. My prick washed, she performed a similar operation on herself. All was done so nicely, cleanly, and delicately that I have never seen it excelled by any woman.

"Causons-nous?" said she leading the way to the divan. Then both laying down naked we gossiped. She was from Arles, in France, eighteen years ago, had been in London a fortnight, had been tailed six months and lived with her father most of the time. A month ago had been persuaded to go to Lyons by an old woman who there sold her pleasures, and kept her money. Another old one snapped her up there, and brought her to London, to a house in B**n**s Street, where a young French woman more experienced than Camille induced her to work on her own account. They two got away, Camille set up in B**y Street, her friend elsewhere. That was told me laying naked with her on the divan.

[She was alone in London, and still exercising her occupation the other day, thirty-one years after I first had her. I have known her, and had her occasionally during all that time, though sometimes two or three years have elapsed between my visits to her. She has been in poor circumstances for years past, and oftentimes I have gone out of my way purposely to meet her, and give her a bit of gold, out of regard for her.]

We lay during her narration (which was soon told) naked. Hot as it was I felt a slight coolness, and drawing myself closer up to her, "It's cool," I said. Without reply, she put one hand over me to help my embrace of her, with the other handled gently my prick, the next instant kissed me, and I felt her tongue peeping out of her pretty lips, seeking my tongue. My fingers naturally had been playing gently about her cunt all the time of our talk, and her hand rubbing gently over my naked flesh. So for a minute in silence our tongues played with each other, and then without a word and with one consent, and like one body we moved together gently, she on to her back, I on to her belly, my prick went up her, and with slow probing thrusts, with now and then a nestle and a pause, till the rapid clip-clip of her cunt drove me into more rapid action, to the rapid in and out and the final short thrusts and wriggle against her womb, till my prick with strong pulsations sent my sperm up her again. "Ah! chéri, — mon Dieu, — a — h — a!" she sighed as she had spent with me. "You fuck divinely," said she, but in chaste words, afterwards.

A wash as before, and then with chemise and shirt on, we talked about France, London; beer, wine, and other topics. "Let me look at your cunt." I had scarcely looked at it. Without reply she fell back, opened her thighs, and then I saw all, all, — and so for two hours we went on, till it was time for me to dine, and with a parting fuck which we both enjoyed, we parted. I added another piece of gold to what I had already put on the mantel piece before she began to undress. A custom of mine then, and always followed since, is putting down my fee, — it prevents mistakes, and quarrels. When paid, if a woman will not let me have her, be it so, — she has some reason, — perhaps a good one for me. If she be a cheat, and only uses the money to extort more, be it so. — I know my woman, and have done with her henceforth.

Camille was a woman of perfect height, above five foot seven, and beautifully formed, had full, hard, exquisite breasts, and lovely legs and haunches, though not too fat or heavy. The hair on her cunt, soft and of a very dark chestnut colour, was not then large in quantity, but corresponded with her years. Her cunt was small, with small inner lips, and a pretty nubbly clitoris like a little button. The split of her cunt lay between the thighs with scarcely any swell of outer-lips, but had a good mons, and was altogether one of the prettiest cunts I have ever seen. I am now beginning, after having seen many hundreds of them, to appreciate beauty in cunts, to be conscious that there is a special, a superior beauty in the cunts of some women as compared with others, just as there is in other parts of their body. She had pretty hands and feet.

Her skin had the slightly brown gipsy tint found in many women in the South of Europe. I never saw a woman in whom the colour was so uniform as in her. From her face to her ankles it was the same unvarying tint without a mottle, even in any cranny. It had also the most exquisite smoothness, but it neither felt like ivory, satin, nor velvet, it seemed a compound of them all. I have scarcely felt the same in any other woman yet. That smoothness attracted me at first I expect, but it was only after I had had her several times, that I began to appreciate it, and to compare it with the skin of other women. She had with that, a great delicacy of touch with her hands.

Her face was scarcely equal to her form. The nose was more then *retroussé,* it bordered on the snub. She had small, dark, softly twinkling eyes, and dark hair; the mouth was ordinary, but with a set of very small, and beautifully white, regular, teeth. The general effect of her face was piquante rather than beautiful, but it pleased me. Her voice was small and soft, — an excellent thing in a woman.

[Such was the woman I have known for thirty-one years, but of whom there is scarcely anything to be told. No intrigue, nothing exciting is connected with her and myself. I cannot tell all the incidents of our acquaintance right off as I do those of many of my women, who appeared, pleased me, and disappeared; but she will be noticed from time to time as I had her, or sought her help in different erotic whims and fancies, which took hold of me at various periods. I write this now finding that her name appears in my manuscript a long way further on. She was moreover a most intelligent creature, clean, sober, and economical, and saving with a good purpose and object, to end alas! for her in failure.]

I never had a more voluptuous woman. Naked on that divan, or on the bed when the weather was warm, I had her constantly during that summer. I know nothing more exciting, than the tranquil, slow, measured way in which she laid down, exposing her charms; every attitude being natural yet exciting by its beauty and delicate salacity. She always seemed to me to be what I had heard of Orientals in copulation. She had the slowest yet most stifling embrace. There was no violent energy, no heaving up of rump, as if a pin had just run into her, nor violent sighs, nor loud exclamations; but she clung to you, and sucked your mouth in a way I scarcely ever have found in English women, or in French ones; but the Austrians and Hungarians in the use of tongue with tongue, and lips with lips are unrivalled in voluptuousness.

Beyond a voluptuous grace natural to her, she had not at first the facile ways of a French courtesan, they came later on. I saw the change, and from that and other indications feel sure she had not been in gay life long before I had her. I could tell more of her history, but this a narrative of my life, not of hers.

[I have destroyed some pages of manuscript solely relating to her.]

She soon got a good clientele, picked up English rapidly,

dressed richly, but never showily, and began to save money. She made affectionate advances to me which I did not accept. After a time she used to pout at what I gave her, and got greedy. So one day saying, "Ma chère, here is more, but adieu, — I don't like you to be dissatisfied, but cannot afford to come to see you." — she slapped the gold heavily down on the table. "Ah! mon Dieu, don't say so, — come, — come, — I am sorry, — you shall never pay me, — come when you like, — I did not want you to pay me, but you would, — come, — do come, — that lovely prick, — do me again before you go, — don't go, — my maid shall say I have not come home" (she expected some man), — and she never pouted about my compliment, till many years afterwards.

I suppose that having had this charming fresh French woman, made me wish for another; for spite of my satisfaction and liking for her, I made acquaintance with another French woman, as unlike Camille as possible. Her name was Gabrielle, a bold-looking woman with big eyes and a handsome face, very tall and well-made, but with not too much flesh on her bones, with a large, full-lipped, loud-looking cunt in a bush of hair as black as charcoal. I never told Camille about her, and think it was the great contrast between the two which made me have her. That woman also seemed later on to have taken some sort of fancy to me.

She had all the ready lechery of a well-practised French harlot, I saw it from the way she opened her thighs, and laid down to receive my embraces. About the third visit she brought water, and made me wash my prick, on which the exudation of healthy lust was showing whitish, before she let me poke her. I liked her cleanliness, but to my astonishment no sooner were we on the bed, then she reversed herself laying side by side with me, and began sucking my prick. I had no taste for that pleasure, nor since a woman in the rooms of Camille the first did it to me, had my penis been so treated that I recollect, though I had made ladies take it into their mouths for a second. I objected. "Mais si, — mais si," — and she went on. My head was near her knee, one leg she lifted up, showing her thighs, which opened and showed her big-lipped cunt in its thicket of black hair. She played with my prick thus till experience told her she could do it no longer with safety, then ceasing her suction, and changing her position, I fucked her in the old-fashioned way.

[233]

The amusement seemed not to have shocked me as much as I thought it should have done, and it was repeated as a preliminary on other days, without my ever suggesting it. After I had had my first poke, the delicate titillation of the mouth seemed vastly pleasant, my prick then being temporarily fatigued by exercise in its natural channel; but I felt annoyed with myself for relishing it at all.

I had not overcome prejudices then, though evidently my philosophy was gradually undermining them. Why, if it gives pleasure to the man to have his prick sucked by a woman, who liked operating that way on the male, should they be abused for enjoying themselves in such manner? A woman may rub it up to stiffen it, the man always does so if needful, — that is quite natural and proper. What wrong then in a woman using her mouth for the same purpose, and giving still higher, more delicate and refined pleasure? All animals lick each other's privates, why not we? In copulation and its consequences, we are mainly animals, but with our intelligence, we should seek all possible forms of pleasure in copulation, and everything else.

CHAPTER XXV

Explanations. — Reflexions, and observations about myself. — My private establishment. — Easy circumstances. — My new house. — James the footman. — Lucy the parlour maid. — Love exercises in the dining room. — Two dismissals. — The cook and James. — Kitchen and housemaid. — A general turn-out. — Lucy's despair. — My kind intentions. — At her lodgings.

[I have not looked through and corrected the foregoing manuscript. — The abbreviations may damage the narrative but there is no help for it, if it is to be printed; yet but few incidents having any novelty have been erased, and the conversations with my women are just as I wrote them originally — the excisions excepted. — How delightfully the episodes come back to my memory as I read the manuscript. Incidents fading into forgetfulness come out quite freshly to me, and I almost seem to be living my youthful life over again. Would that I were going to do so, for it was a lovely time with women; and was only cursed by that one lasting, deep, irremediable error.

[I am not sure about ages in one or two instances, nor the exact order of two or three of the more fugitive amours. I could perhaps set these quite right by reference to books now hidden and dusty, but it is not worth the trouble to do so. — None are of any real importance. I write for my pleasure alone, and if I print, shall print for my pleasure alone, so let the manuscript stand as it is paged.

[I notice now in reading it, that some of my raciest adventures, those which being unsought, those which fell to my lot as it were by accident, and which tho brief were among the most voluptuous, occurred whilst I had other and more enduring liaisons on hand. Such was my weakness and fondness for the sex, that I never could keep faithfully to any one woman absolutely, however much I loved her. I have wished and intended to do so, have tried hard, so hard, to avoid infidelity, but surrendered at last to the temptation. The idea of seeing another woman naked, of piercing a fresh cunt, seemed to foreshadow to me voluptuous pleasures never tasted before with any other woman. As my prick entered the cunt it had never touched before, the sensation always seemed to me more exquisite than that I had ever had with others. Yet many a time after such pleasures I have been disgusted with myself for my weakness, and tried to atone for it, without the object ever having been aware of the reason for my ultra kindness.

[The quantity of manuscript still left for revision, alas, is long. Amongst it is an essay on copulation, written I think somewhat earlier than some I have revised, and written with such knowledge of the subject as I then had, as well as with some ignorance which I now see. It has that freedom of expression which I at once adopted in my narrative, and leaves no doubt in my own mind about what I meant then, and at all times. — It pleased me much when I wrote it, yet it must be sacrificed to time, money, and expediency — for it is not an incident, and forms no part of the history of my private life, tho it illustrates well my frame of mind and knowledge of things sexual, at the period of my life when I wrote it.

[This perusal brings prominently before me all my acts, deeds, and thoughts for full twenty years, and I perceive clearly, that altho I had done most things which were sexually possible once, and almost out of curiosity, or else on sudden impulse (up to about this period), yet that my habits with women in my lust were for the most part simple, commonplace, and unintellectual; and that I had not sought for out of the way lascivious postures and varied complex delights in copulation or its preliminaries, which a fervid, voluptuous, poetical imagination has since gradually devised for my gratification. This desire for variety seems to have commenced some time after I became acquainted with the second Camille.

[But by that time I was evidently no longer displeased with that which, in years previously, would have shocked me. My prejudices have now pretty well vanished with the approach of middle age. I have conquered antipathies and reaped the reward, in seeing before me a great variety of frolics, suitable to my maturity, but which I am glad I did not have prematurely in my youth when I did not need them, and should not have appreciated them as I do now. — It is amusing now to notice the gradual change from simply belly to belly exercise, which contented me, to the infinitely varied amusements since indulged in.

[No doubt in this I tread but in the ordinary footsteps and ways of male-kind. What I have done, thousands of others are doing. It is only when lustful impetuosity is weakened that reflexion and experience begin to devise new pleasures to aid it. As we get older we invent them as a stimulus, and women thus become more and more charming, needful, and important to us; and just at a time when our responsibilities towards them become greatest. So by aiding and administering to us in our salacious devices, they reward us. In the end they are more and more needful to us, and we repay them by our generosity, our care of them, and our sacrifices for them. Nor are they behind us in desire to participate in these frolics, for they have lust as well as we. In a quiet, hidden way, they like lasciviousness if taught it gradually. But lust is mainly in we men — women are the ministers to it, it is the law of nature. — No blame attaches to women for liking or for submitting to such frolics, abnormal whims, and fancies, which fools call obscene, but which are natural and proper, and perhaps universally practised, and which concern only those who practise and profit by them. In my experience many women delight equally in them, when their imaginations are once evoked. Nothing can perhaps be justly called unnatural which nature prompts us to do. If others don't like them, they are not natural to *them*, and no one should force them to act them.

[The foregoing and similar paragraphs, written long after the manuscript, are to be enclosed in brackets thus [ ] so that I may identify them when I see them (if I do) at a future day in print, and this writing is destroyed.

[The headings of the chapters are now written for the first time. — They will be needful if this be printed. Now I resume my narrative.]

Whilst away I arranged it, and directly on my return to England gave up a snug, quiet, illicit establishment elsewhere, and to the satisfaction of both parties. Both agreed to it, and thought it was for the best. We had no quarrel. It cost much money down, and an annuity paid still, but no one was injured, no one wronged. All interested were provided for. I wonder if this will ever meet her eyes, or if so if she will know that it refers to her. It is not probable, for neither names, places, nor initials are given, and no clue afforded; yet nothing is impossible.

I had not returned to England a fortnight before a domestic turn-out took place, which caused me much annoyance but led me to unlooked for pleasure.

It has, I think, been said before that I had been for some time in better circumstances, had a larger house, more servants and so on. Among the servants whom I found on my return, was a parlour maid, a lovely girl with a superb pink and white complexion, and a skin which looked like ivory. She had darkish chestnut hair, soft hazel eyes, and a lovely set of teeth, was well grown, plump, and altogether a most desirable creature, and who looked a lady. Her name was Lucy. It passed through my mind that she would be an exquisite sweetheart, but I resisted incipient desire, avoiding by prudence and custom all intrigues with my own household.

Suddenly this girl was dismissed, and I was requested to dismiss my man, who had lived with us before I had left England, indeed had been in my service nearly two years. He was the best man I ever had, and was moreover a fine, handsome fellow, five feet ten high, and pleasant to look upon. He had been caught in loving familiarities with Lucy, who it was said also was with child by him; the poor girl had let this out to the cook or some one else, and the cook split

[237]

upon her. James was impudent and denied it all, but I think the case was proved. It would not have done to have passed over open fornication. Had I done so, the habit would have spread throughout the household; so I reluctantly gave him notice. The poor girl went off very quietly in tears. I never felt so sorry for a woman, especially as whilst denying that she had let him have her, she said that he had promised her marriage, which James, when I told him, said was a lie. But this statement of hers confirmed me in the belief that he had tailed her. Lucy was however promised a character, and that nothing should be said about her *faux pas,* unless a question leading to it were asked. It was an unusual piece of charity of my old woman.

So nice a looking girl was of course sought after, and in two or three days ladies applied for her character, but none would take her. James had not gone because I could not get suited with another man. I spoke to him again, and accused him of cruelty and wickedness in promising marriage, but he still denied it altogether. "But the cook asserts she has seen you on the sofa in the dining room more than once." "She's a liar," said James, "but I've several times had *her,* and on that sofa too, and because I'd have no more of her, she's got up this tale." — James got then insolent.

Now in my dining-room was a sofa, tho not an usual piece of furniture in a dining-room; but I liked to lay there by myself and read after dinner at times, so as to avoid the drawing-room and all that was usually in it. The footman and parlour maid laid the dinner things, waited at table, and cleared away, and as no other servant had any right in that room usually at those times, they had a nice chance and had availed themselves of it, I quite believed.

I wished the cook at the Devil for causing me to lose two nice servants, and immediately told my wife what I had heard about her.

She turned up into a high state of moral indignation, and had the cook up, and told her what James had said, I was asked to be present. Cook was fattish but had a pleasant face, was under forty — and I have fucked many a less tempting bit of flesh. — Never did a woman turn so red as she did. She was almost speechless, then almost choked, denied it, and dared the villain to say so to her face. I called him up. My wife said she could not have such investigations before her — yet she stayed. James repeated that he had been "very familiar" with her. — Cook howled, shed tears, and said he lied. He retorted that the kitchen maid knew it. The kitchen maid was called up and questioned in a most delicate way. — She first denied knowing anything about it, but catechised by James, said that the cook and he had certainly been to the top of the house together at times when missus was out. She didn't know why, it wasn't her business to spy her fellow servants, and so on. And then said that the housemaid who slept with Lucy knew more than she did about Lucy and James. A regular shindy ensued among the servants, and it ended in the whole lot being discharged, excepting the lady's maid. Altho by no means sure that the footman had not accused the cook out of spite, I felt sure that he had got into Lucy under promise of marriage.

At the end of a week the poor girl came crying to us, and imploring that nothing should be said to prevent her getting a place. Then I found out her lodgings and went really and truly to comfort her. It was about ten o'clock in the morning. "Three pair front," said the landlady, not looking very pleasantly at me, and directly I had gone, as I heard afterwards, said "I ain't a going to have any of them games here. You take yourself off if swells like him visit yer." — So as I really was much interested in the girl, and had determined to help her, I arranged for her to meet me at Charing Cross that afternoon. I declare I had no intention of trying to have her, tho I had felt a desire for her. But I meant to try to get her married to my man. That was my vague notion.

She was a little late, and as I could not well talk with her in the street, I took her to the Cafe de P**v**e and ordered a little dinner in a private room. — She had had very bad food since she had left my house, and this nice dinner delighted her. Like all women of her class she refused it at first, was nervous, said she could not eat before gentlefolks, and was most uncomfortable, but it gradually wore off as the food warmed and the wine cheered her. Her lovely eyes began to sparkle and her tears dried up. Then cheered myself, a sudden throb of desire went through me. She has had it up her cunt, has been spent in, has clasped a man in her arms, has felt his prick. — I wonder if she has a pretty cunt, much hair on it, and a group of cognate thoughts came on and my prick was standing, and was within a couple of yards of that cunt. Did my lust communicate itself to her by subtle magnetic influence? how can that be known? But I became silent for the moment, and so did she, staring intently and, as I thought afterwards, voluptuously at me.

The dinner was not long about. Whilst eating I told her that I meant to help her out of her difficulties. "How?" she asked. Well I must feel my way, try if I could get James to marry her, or send her home, or get her a place, or a doctor if she wanted one. But I must know more than I did, must feel sure I was on the right path, she must tell me the truth, or I could do nothing. — This was varied by talk about myself and household, and I heard much that had taken place, and what had been said, during my absence; for this girl had become our servant just after I went abroad. The talk however always got back to the subject of her *faux pas* with James, and there was an undercurrent of lewedness, for it all referred to cock and cunt; tho not a word of smut had I used, as we sat eating so close together, with my legs touching hers under the table.

The dinner was removed, but wine left, it was only sherry. Unnoticed I bolted the door, and down I made her sit with me on the sofa. "Now, Lucy," said I, "let us talk quite seriously about you and your belly; before I can do you any service, you must tell me the truth. Has James done it to you or not?" — After long hesitation she said slowly, "No." "And you're not with child?" "No." She did not look me in the face and became quite cast down. "He has never put it up you?" said I, revelling in the idea of evoking voluptuous recollections in the girl. "No sir," "Then if that be so, I don't see what use I can be to you. I was going, had you been fucked, and had you been with child, to have helped you to get rid of it, or to have sent you to your parents, till you were confined, or to some where else, and to pay for it all, for I much pity you. But now all you have to do is to get another place, which you are sure to do in time, so give me a kiss for my good intentions." I watched her closely as I said fucked, and saw her blush and wince, with a sense of modesty, and I felt a delicious lust creep through me when uttering the lewed words, and calling to her mind sexual pleasure.

For a minute she sat looking down speechless, and I repeated all I had said. She seemed to be struggling with herself, and at length raised her face to mine and kissed me. Then I kissed her passionately, and hugged her to me and kissed every part of her face, her ears, and eyes, and neck. — Her eyes filled with tears, she broke from me, buried her face in her hands, began crying violently, and saying that I was very kind. I tried to comfort her, putting my arm round her, kissing her, asking what it was all about, repeating, "Has he fucked you, has he? tell me, now tell me," but getting no reply for some minutes. Then her tears subsided and she sobbed out, "I told you a story, I'm past two months with child by James." And having made the confession she came to herself, kissed me whenever I asked her, and told me the history of her seduction (for that it was), whilst I cuddled her to me affectionately, making her sip sherry at times to comfort her, and keep her spirits up.

James had promised to marry her. One night he took her to the theatre, and then to have some drink in a house, and there he induced her to let him have her. Since then he had her repeatedly, and nearly always on the sofa in our dining room. For half an hour I questioned her and she told me all the detail, as if I were her confessor.

Then I repeated my promise. She was to consider what would be the best for her to do, but perhaps James would marry her. No he would not for she had written him, and he had not answered her letter. — I told her on no account was she ever to mention me to him, that she might be easy about money, for I would pay for all she needed, till she was out of her trouble. She said she didn't want money, having by her two or three pounds. I gave her more saying, "That will prevent your fretting." She was deeply grateful, and cried and kissed me again and again.

I can do her no harm thought I, for she is with child, and my prick swelled proudly. Voluptuous thrills passed through me as I thought of her cunt being within reach of my fingers, and I resolved to try for it. We finished the wine, she was heated. I again began talking about her love affair, and now in burning words of lust. My embraces, kisses, and lewed words excited her. Did he hurt her, when his prick first went up her cunt? Wasn't it pleasure to her, doing it. "Kiss me, Lucy." She kissed but did not answer. "How exquisite the sensations are just when the prick stiffens to its utmost when up the cunt, aren't they?" "Oh don't, sir, talk so," she burst out. "Why not, love? You know." Then my hand began moving about. "Have you much hair there, Lucy?" "I won't tell you, now leave off." "You garter above knee, don't you?" "Yes, sir." I pulled her further on the sofa, and still closer to me. "Let me feel." "Oh, sir, you mustn't now." But pressing her closely to me, kissing her, telling her of my desire for her, in a few minutes my hand was on her thighs and roving up and down, then round her haunches as far as I could reach, it went over her smooth, sweet flesh; and then the fingers nestled between her notch, and when half hidden by the plump lips and the thick, silky hair which curled over my knuckles — there they rested — "I'm feeling your cunt, Lucy, I don't hurt you, do I now?" She replied not, but our kisses met, and we laid in silent enjoyment. I am feeling her, she is being felt. The fingers of a man, even if motionless, on a woman's cunt, inflame her.

Now I got burning with fierce desire, as my fingers played delicately with a well-developed clitoris. "Fucking is lovely, isn't it dear Lucy, feel my prick, love." Removing my hand from her cunt, I got out my prick, and placed her hand on it. Back went my hand between her thighs and recommenced its delicate fingering. "Open your thighs dear, and let me feel lower down." "Oho," she gasped, as they widened apart, and softly with a burrowing motion, two fingers buried themselves in her vagina.

"How wet your cunt is, love — you want a fuck." Not a word she said, her breath seemed short, her eyes closed, she kissed me when ever I asked her, she was swooning with voluptuous feelings. "Let me do it, I want it so badly. You are so lovely and it can't hurt you now, let me," and I kissed her rapturously. "No," she whispered but almost inaudibly, holding my prick still in her hand. I took no denial, gently pushed her back, lifted her legs up, without resistance mounted her, and the next instant my pego was sheathed in a most heavenly cunt. With deep drawn sighs, Lucy clasped me to her and we fucked. "It's lovely, isn't it, dear?" "A-ho, o-ho," she whispered, and the next instant we were both spending in ecstasy.

What voluptuous, triumphant joy I had as, raising my self up partly, I looked at that lovely face. — My prick still buried up her. Then in tranquil enjoyment I lay kissing her, till my prick slipped out. How uncomfortable the sofa suddenly seemed to be. I have had scores of women on sofas, but how few sofas gave full comfort in copulating. That which we were on now was a miserably small one. I got up, so did she. "Wasn't it lovely, Lucy?" "Did you bring me here to make me do that?" said she sorrowfully.

I swore that I had not, — that it was only the result of her beauty, — an accident — that I suddenly had lusted for her. She shook her head as if she doubted me.

"I wish I could wash," said she. — I rang the bell, the chambermaid showed her a room. When she came back we had more wine. "I'm fuddled," said she, but she wasn't. "Never mind, I'll see you home, but come with me, we have some hours before us, and we will go where we can be more comfortable, finish your wine." In ten minutes I was in the room which I first entered with Sarah Mavis.

"It's a bad house," said she. "So they call it, my love, but it's good to us, so why is it bad? Take off some of your things, and we will talk about your troubles lying down." She was docile. Soon we were on the bed half undressed. — "Now don't be foolish dear. Let me look at it. I've fucked it, what can be the harm in looking at it?" In half an hour I had seen all, and we fucked as often as we could, till it was time to go. I took her to within sight of her lodgings in a cab.

CHAPTER XXVI

Lucy without place. — Fausse couches. — Goes home. — James leaves. — A confession. — Lucy's marriage. — My wedding gift. — An anonymous letter. — James' amourous exploits. — The use of a dining-room table. — Camille again. — Erotic literature. — Erotic anticipations. — Camille's opinion thereon. — Ill. — Memoirs arranged. — Frail fair ones. — My gratitude.

She could not get a situation, for her uncharitable brute of a mistress, always after giving her a good character, some how let out about this *faux pas*, so Lucy and I both agreed that she should get an abortion. — I told her to spare no money, and put her in the way of getting the thing done. She took other lodgings and got relieved (at her third month), and then went home to her parents. I gave her twenty pounds the day she left, and told her to write at any time to me at a club if she wanted any more; but never to mention me, or any thing about our connection, or her miscarriage, to any living soul as long as she lived, even if she married, or was dying. I never told her about the general turn out of servants in my house, or what James said he had done to the cook, thinking the less I said about those things the better.

I had got a new set of servants, for even the lady's maid it was thought desirable to send off, but James remained for I could not get suited. I took a dislike to him for his brutality in not answering the girl's letter; and taking no notice of her when out of place. So one morning, "James," said I, "what has become of that poor Lucy, has she got a place? She has ceased coming here about her character." He replied that he didn't know. "Well, it's no business of mine, but I have an impression that you have wronged her. Poor creature, and such a nice young woman. If it be really true that you seduced her by a promise of marriage, you will some day regret it, it will be on your conscience heavily. She would make a good wife to a man of your class, and a man even far above you. I never felt more for a poor creature, than I did when I saw her going away crying." "How am I to keep a wife?" said he. "Set up a shop for her, or let her take in washing, and you can work as either indoor or outdoor servant, you are both strong and healthy." "Where does she live?" "I don't know, I can find out; but I know where her parents live in the country, and dare say she's gone home." I noticed all this time that James had ceased to deny having had her. Then impulsively I said, "Poor thing. I'd give fifty pounds to help her, and prevent her become a street walker, for that will be the end, if it be not already." Then turning away I said sharply, "That will do, you will leave on Wednesday." — "Are you suited, sir?" "No, but I won't have you about me any longer." The man retired — crest fallen — he had been, I know, flattering himself that I would after all still keep him on as my servant. He liked me I must add. On Wednesday he left.

A fortnight elapsed before I heard anything of him, and was surprized he had not applied for his character. Then he came to me. He was trying for a place in the country, would I give a written character as footman or valet. It was a place where he was to live out. Yes, if I was certain all was square. — Where was it? At **** near the village where Lucy lived. Then he volunteered that she was with her parents, and that he had been down to see her. I was startled, and began to think about my own little games in Lucy's receptacle, but said, "What did you go there for? Is she with child really, or not?" "Well it's quite true she was so and it was my fault, but she's had a miscarriage and is all right, and we've made it up." "More fool she," said I, "you will serve the poor girl the same dirty trick again." No he wouldn't, he was a thinking of marrying her. "That's like a man," said I. "I'll give you fifty pounds to help you if you do." "Will you sir?" said he. I reflected. "Well, I really think I would." "By gosh I'll marry her in three weeks," said he, "for it would just set us up, and I've saved a little money, and can go home of nights." "Well I must think it over. Come to me tomorrow morning, and if the gentleman writes to me for your character, I will see what I can do for you."

I was really very glad, but did not quite see why I should give fifty pounds. I had done the girl no harm, had given her lots of money, and enabled her quietly to get over her trouble which I had not brought on her. But I had deep sympathy for her, almost an affection seemed springing up in my vacant heart. So thought I, it may do good to her. She is a sweet creature and deserves it; and next morning I told him I would give him fifty pounds, so soon as he was married to her. Not knowing how I might be compromised by this act, I instructed my solicitors in the matter, told them all the circumstances (excepting that I had tailed the girl), and arranged for them to pay the fifty pounds, so soon as they were satisfied that they were married.

He got the place he wanted: soon my solicitors got a letter from her saying the marriage was to take place on a certain day, and subsequently a copy of the marriage certificate. They then paid him the money. He went to service near the village, and so did she for a time, they heard. Two or three months afterwards I received a letter with these words in it: "Sir, God bless you for your kindness, please burn this, I felt that I must thank you. Lucy." — and I never heard of the couple afterwards. It was one of the shortest, but one of the most delicious of my amours, and I look back to it with intense satisfaction.

From first to last I had about three weeks enjoyment of her, for she was only a day past her monthly period, when the accusation came, by which she lost her situation, and I had her up to a day or two before her courses were forced on by the doctor.

I can't explain to myself why I had such a letch for gamahuching her, excepting the extreme beauty of her cunt, and its sweet, inciting smell. I have been always fitful in this taste. To most of the women — including some splendid women — young, beautiful, lascivious, whom I have much liked, I have never done it. I have done it with a half dislike,

[245]

to several lovely creatures who insisted on my doing it to them, and I licked, spitting frequently, and wiping my mouth on the sly afterwards to avoid offence; but occasionally I have liked it much, tho as I write and look back years, I don't recollect one woman to whom I gave such cunnilingual attention as I did to Lucy. The idea of giving pleasure to a woman seems to actuate me more in what I now do, than it used. Once I seem mainly to have thought of my own pleasure. There is a strange feeling of enjoyment comes over me now, when my tongue touches the clitoris of a sweet young woman, if I like her.

Although Lucy willingly kissed my prick and balls, I never even suggested her taking it into her mouth, — do not indeed recollect the idea having ever occurred to me. I was of course curious about James' amatory tricks, but there was little to tell, and what there was, she told me quite freely when I had had her a few days. Excepting at the house, where he shattered her virginity, he had only once had her in another house, the rest of the doings were in my house. When they had brought the dinner or luncheon things up stairs to lay the cloth, he shagged her quickly on my sofa and sometimes on the table. Directly we had left the dining-room, he did the same whilst they removed the things. So very frequently, sweet Lucy waited at table with his sperm both in and out of her cunt, and it is to be hoped that before the dinner bread was cut they washed their fingers, tho I greatly fear they did not. His prick seemed to her about the size of mine, but she had scarcely seen it, and she got with child at the second or third fucking, so she had not had much fun for her trouble. She never had the pleasure with him that I gave her, and that is all she said.

I have had a dozen women with their backs on a dining room or other table, and have found them a most convenient couch. For impromptu coition, tables are just the height for me. I can see, feel, and fuck easily on them, and can save the lady's clothes from inconvenient rumpling. One night in the smoking room of my club, the conversation turning as usual upon women, I alluded to tables, and wondered if every man present had used them. Ten men were present, and each said he had often times done so. One man, since dead, said he had shagged every servant he had on them. He was in the F*r***n office, not well off, and kept but two servants. "It's the safest place in the house," said he, "just before the cloth is laid. Your wife is most likely dressing, the cook cooking, and neither can interrupt you. I expect every man has put a woman's arse on that piece of mahogany."

Then again I sought Camille's society, and for a long time thought her the most charming of courtezans. — She had plumped up still more, took a warm bath every day, and her skin, always good, had the most delicious, velvety smoothness. I use that word advisedly, because having an exquisite sense of touch, I notice that some women's flesh feels like ivory, some like satin, and some like velvet, and some (which is the perfection of all) which seems a compound of all them, and I call that perfect flesh.

Moreover she had a slow, lazy, voluptuous manner of fucking, by which she seemed to prolong my pleasure, and this with her, I think, was art grafted on natural aptitude. She was never in a hurry for me to go, never said she was engaged, or that some one was coming at ** o'clock, or would I excuse her for a few minutes, or similar devices of strumpets with which I am now fully acquainted. Nor did she borrow, nor be dissatisfied with my gifts, nor say she was short of money, that her rent was due to morrow, and so on. She had plenty of friends I know, for her splendid tho quiet dresses, silk stockings, boots, and fine chemises told me that. Indeed she admitted it, showed me various men's cards, saying that she supposed if they left her their cards, they did not object to their being seen, or why leave them. And so I used to sit for hours with her, poking her at intervals, and talking upon sexual matters, as well as all sorts of subjects, and drinking Claret and smoking.

Indeed she was a most enticing creature, for she had among other qualities, a small, soft, exquisitely feminine voice, and a silvery quiet laugh. In cold weather clad in a lovely loose sort of silk wrapper, she sat half fronting the fire, with perhaps one leg just over the arm of the chair, or in some attitude by which I could see half way up her thighs. As it got warmer she would loll about with a chemise so fine, that you could see the hair of her cunt through it, and her rich darkish toned flesh looked exquisite against the white by contrast.

[I had until within a year or two of the period of time now entered on, read but little erotic literature, and that in English. Now I had read much of that written by the French. How coarse and commonplace the average English baudy book is, compared with the French; and the same may be said of the pictures. With certain facilities recently possessed, I must I think (if they exist) have come across English engravings in which the workings of love (called lust), that potent factor of human action implanted in him by nature for his pleasure and the woman's, and for the perpetuation of the human race, are artistically portrayed; yet I have scarcely seen any which, as engravings, are not coarse; designed by those evidently unaccustomed to draw the human figure at all, and quite unable to portray the male and female either in the varied incitements to, or the varied attitudes, in which they copulate. Whilst in the French are to be found copious engravings, true to life in every one of these particulars.]

This literature amused me much, as did the pictures of fantastic combinations of male and female in lascivious play and in coition. Their impossibilities even amused me, and brought frequently to my mind what I had heard of in my now wide experience with Paphian ladies. There is no end of variety in such amusements, and no limits to eccentricities in lewedness, and no harm in gratifying them, either alone with one woman or man, or in society, to whom it is congenial. A field of lascivious enjoyment new to me, seemed opening, and I thought about the out of the way erotic tricks portrayed, and of those I also might play, and that I should like to try them. I began to see that such things are harmless, tho the world may say they are naughty, and saw through the absurdity of conventional views and prejudices as to the ways a cock and cunt may be pleasurably employed.

Why, for instance, is it permissible for a man and woman to enjoy themselves lasciviously, but improper for two men and two women to do the same things all together in the same room? — Why is it abominable for any one to look at man and woman fucking, when every man, woman, and child would do so if they had the opportunity? Is copulation an improper thing to do, if not, why is it disgraceful to look at its being done? — Why may a man, and woman handle each other's privates, and yet it be wrong for a man to feel another's prick, or a woman to feel another's cunt? Every one in each sex has at one period of their lives done so, and why should not any society or association of people indulge in these innocent, tho sensual, amusements if they like in private. What is there in their doing so that is disgraceful? It is the prejudice of education alone which teaches that it is.

Such reflexions for some years had crossed my mind; they tended to sweep away prejudices. And tho I still have prejudice, yet for the most part I can see no harm in gratifying my lust in the ways which the world would say is highly improper, but which appear to me that men and women are intended by instinct as well as by reflexion to gratify. This frame of mind seems to me to have been gradually developing for some time past — and accounts for much that follows.

In these opinions I was strengthened by repeated conversations with Camille. She was one of the most philosophic whores I ever knew, was fairly educated, and had a wonderfully cool common sense way of looking at things. When I had doubts of the propriety of doing this or that, she would solve them with answers which appeared to me irrefutable, at length. We seem to have been on the subject of unusual pleasures whenever we met. — In fact we were constantly talking about varieties in lustful enjoyments. She would sit down smoking a cigarette, and I a cigar, and consider whether there was wrong in frigging, gamahuching, minetting, tribadism, or sodomy. — In men frigging each other, or women doing the same, and other things. Our conclusion was that there was no harm in any of them. With that clear conscience, and aided by my imagination and by the French books and prints, erotic whims began to suggest themselves to me gradually.

I then fell ill for a short time, and during that, arranged some more of these memoirs. Soon after, disappointments, troubles of various sorts, and other considerations made me nearly burn them. Getting well I drowned my sorrows in female society, and had many of the fair mercenary ones, whom I had known before I left England. To their class I owe a debt of gratitude, and say again what I think I have said elsewhere: that they have been my refuge in sorrow, an unfailing relief in all my miseries, have saved me from drinking, gambling, and perhaps worse. I shall never throw stones at them, nor speak harshly to them, nor of them.

They are much what society has made them, and society uses them, enjoys them, even loves them; yet denies them, spurns, damns, and crushes them even whilst frequenting them and enjoying them. In short, it shamefully ill treats them in most Christian countries, and more so in protestant England than in any others that I know.

CHAPTER XXVII

A convalescent amusement. — On copulation, and the copulative organs.

During my illness I was as chaste as men usually are, when they cannot be unchaste; but I thought much about women, and the complicated organs of the sexes, by the agency of which the species is continued. I reflected on the secrecy with which human beings envelop their amours — of the shame which they so ridiculously attach to any mention or reference to copulation in plain language, or indeed at all— altho it is the prime mover of humanity, and finds expression in every day life in some shape or another, by word, or deed; and is a subject which passes thro the mind, almost daily, of men and of women who are in a healthy state of body, and have once fucked, and perhaps before that.

It was a wonder to me that when both sexes feel so much pleasure in looking at each other's genitals — that they should take such extreme pains to hide them, should think it disgraceful, to show them without mutual consent, and penal to do so separately or together in public. — I came to the conclusion that in the women it is the result of training, with the cunning intention of selling the view of their privates at the highest price — and inducing the man to give them that huge price for it — the marriage ring. Women are all bought in the market — from the whore to the princess. The price alone is different, and the highest price in money or rank obtains the woman. Then I wrote what follows, because I never had found it written in plain language elsewhere.

This description of the genitals, and their mode of meeting, has probably in it many errors and omissions, for I am not a doctor, but it was all I knew about it when I wrote it. No attempt is made at anatomical definition or exactitude. — It is what may be termed essentially a popular description, suitable to the smallest capacities, and fit for both sexes — or if you please — instructive reading for the young. It is, to the young, essential knowledge — yet the great aim of adults seems to be to prevent youths from knowing anything about it.

———————

Providence has made the continuation of the species depend on a process of a coupling the sexes, called fucking. It is performed by two organs. That of the male is familiarly and vulgarly called a *Prick,* that of the female a *Cunt.* Politely one is called a penis the other a pudenda. — The prick, broadly speaking, is a long, fleshy, gristly pipe. — The cunt a fleshy, warm, wet hole, or tube. — The prick is at times and in a peculiar manner, thrust up the cunt, and discharges a thick fluid into it, and that is the operation called fucking. — It is not a graceful operation — in fact it is not more elegant than pissing, or shitting, and is more ridiculous; but it is one giving the intensest pleasure to the parties operating together, and most people try to do as much of it as they can.

The prick is placed at the bottom of the belly, and hangs just between the thighs of the man. It consists of a circular, pendulous pipe, or tube of skin and gristle, with a hole through it, by which piss and sperm is sent out. — It has a knob or tip at its end, like a blunt pointed heart, and is covered with a most delicate thin skin, which has the most exquisite sensitiveness to touch. Over this knob or tip is a thickish skin of the same character as that which covers the stem of the prick, and is formed in such manner that it can be easily pulled from off of the tip. It shields the tip from injury, and keeps it moist and sensitive. It is called the foreskin, or prepuce. The prick is usually flabby and hanging down, is about three inches long, and soft to the feel. — The outer skin feels loose all over it as does the foreskin or prepuce, which covers the tip. — But when the man is lewed, that is to say, wants to fuck, it lengthens, thickens, stands up quite stiff, and the foreskin comes a little off the knob, which is then of a fine carmine colour. If the skin does not then move off readily — it is easily pulled back a little. When put to the cunt, it goes back at once, and the knob in its exquisite sensitiveness goes up the cunt uncovered, followed by the rest of the prick, until the whole is up it, to the *Balls*. The balls, or stone bag, is a wrinkled, skinny bag, hanging at the root of the prick and a few inches on its under side from the bum hole. — It contains two stones called also testicles, which feel from the outside about the size of bantams' eggs, and some people call them their eggs. Sometimes this bag feels firmer than at other times — and is always a good handful. If it feels firm and full, and is covered with well defined close wrinkles, it is generally a sign that the man is in fucking order. — This bag is sometimes called a ballocks, but oftentimes when a man speaks of his ballocks, he means his prick and balls all together.

The stem of the prick is smooth, and usually free from hair until towards the point at which it connects with the belly and balls, where it is covered with hair which curls round it. It seems to come out of a hairy thicket, which grows up the stomach towards the navel but stops short of it. There is usually but little hair on the balls, but it grows round beneath them, and sometimes down the inner side of the thighs a slight way, and under the balls' bag to the arse hole, and sometimes even there is short hair round that hole. If there be much it is called hairy-arsed, and is not convenient, for it interferes with the comfortable cleaning and wiping of the bum, after voiding.

The prick is naturally dry excepting the tip, which is usually covered by the foreskin, and which has at all times a tendency to be moist. If a man is randy for a long time and cannot ease himself by fucking, or frigging, or by getting his sperm out somehow, this tip sweats a white pomatum looking stuff, which covers the tip, and collects under the knob, where it joins the stem. This randy exudation called sebaceous, emits strongly a peculiar male smell. A fuck clears it all off. — Inside the body of the male are organs for secreting and forming a stuff called sperm, or spunk, which is whitish, partly thickish, and resembles paste which is thin and badly made, — or thin lumpy gruel. This is spit up the woman's cunt, through the tip of the prick when fucking. — This emission in popular language is called spending, or spunking, and is the period of the highest pleasure of the fuck, and the ending of it. — This stuff, is the male seed, and impregnates the woman, or as it is called in simple language, — gets her in the family way.

The cunt is the woman's organ, and is placed at the bottom of her belly between the thighs. It consists, firstly and outwardly, of a slit about five inches long, looking like a gap or cut, with lips. It begins near the bum hole, and curves upwards towards the lower part of the belly in the direction of the navel, and finishes in a hillock, or pad of flesh, a little above the thighs. This pad gradually dies off into the general

[252]

surface of the belly, and is called a mons, or pincushion. In some women the slit, or cunt gap, is less than in others but in all they begin near the bumhole, and the lips gradually thicken, and then die out again into the mons. In some women these lips are in part of their length, twice as thick as those of a man's mouth. — In others they are thin, and some scarcely have the form of lips at all, but look like swollen flesh. The cunt looks like a mere cut, in such women.

There is hair all over the pincushion, or as it is called the motte, and round the outer lips of the cunt, down to its bum hole end. The hair getting usually less thick, and shorter, as it gets there; but at times as in the man, the hair grows a little round the bum hole itself, and up the bum furrow. The pad, or pincushion, or mons, is placed there to cover certain bones which go over that part of the cunt, and prevent the man hurting his belly, when thrusting up the cunt in fucking. This in his excitement, he might at certain moments do by shoving violently. — The mons, or motte, is more thickly covered with hair than the rest of the cunt, particularly at the spot where the slit begins, or opens.

If the outer lips be pulled open, their inside will be seen to be smooth, fleshy, almost pulpy, and like the inside of a mouth and of pink or carmine colour according to the age of the female and the usage of her cunt. — A little way below the beginning of the slit at the belly end of it, is a little lump or button of flesh called the *clitoris*. This is red, and smooth like the rest, and in some women, is much larger than in others. — When the woman is not sexually excited, or wanting a fuck, or is not randy that is to say, — this is softish, but when randy it gets a little firm or solid, or as they say stiff, but not in all. — It is the chief seat of pleasure in a woman, for tho the prick rubs against it but little in fucking, the woman often gives herself pleasure by rubbing it with her finger, or frigging herself there, till she spends.

This is a description of what may be termed the mouth of the cunt, or its externals, and its inner parts must now be described. Just under the clitoris, almost in continuation of it in fact, but just at the beginning of what I call the prick tube, it being specially made to take the prick, is a little projection in which is a hole. — This is the woman's piss duct. — Both clitoris and piss duct are for the most part covered by the outer hairy lips, the hair curling round in front, and partly overshadowing the gap, hides all of it more or less in most grown women; but when women want to piddle, nature induces them to squat down, so that their bums are within a few inches of the ground. In that position the cunt gapes and opens, the clitoris and piss-vent come to the front, and the piss comes out with force. The hair of the cunt is shortish, opens with the lips but nevertheless it is frequently wetted by the stream. If there is longish hair, you may see drops of piddle, like drops of dew, clinging to it when she stands up after pissing. — Some of the piddle also runs down to the mouth of the vagina, or fucking prick hole, yet to be described, and that part being not unfrequently a little sticky, the piss cleanses it. Thus the outer hair, and the inside of the cunt mouth and lips, are wetted generally by the woman's piddle, — and when she gets up, she usually tucks her clothes for an instant between her thighs to dry it. — This is vulgarly called "mopping her cunt."

Beneath the piddling orifice, the soft red surface slopes down, and inwards, to a hole very near to the bum hole, so near in fact that you may readily put one finger up the cunt and a thumb up the bum hole, and pinch the partition which separates them. This is the vagina, or prick receiver — the hole which goes up into the woman's belly, and in which the operation of fucking is done, by the man's prick.

The opening is in some a little tight, but inside is more capacious. — In all cunts, it easily distends, and will take any thing from a little finger to a rolling pin, — and will gently close on, clasp, or embrace it, with an evenly tightening grip all round, whatever its size may be. — This fucking hole is deep enough usually to take a stiff prick six inches long, without pain to the woman. If it hurts, they have a knack of dropping their buttocks, so as to prevent the prick going too far up. — This vagina, as it also is called, at the top or end, rounds off and contracts, and the tube of the womb enters it. In the neck is a small orifice usually closed but at the proper time during fucking it opens. It is against this opening that the man's prick knocks, and the sperm is shot out in fucking.

From the clitoris, and inside the outer lips of the cunt slit or gap already described, are little thinnish red flaps or cartilage, which descend on each side, and terminate by the prick hole. They are in fact a sort of inner cunt lips, and are called Nmyphæ, or vulgarly often called lapels, or lappets. They are of the same pink or carmine tint as the inside of the whole of the cunt mouth. — In most women these lips are so small that when a woman's legs are closed, or only just slightly opened, the outer and hair cunt lips hide and cover them, or they only just show the thinnest red line between them. — In other women they are large, and hang out even like large red flaps. These lapels are always moist inside, and when large, and a woman opens her legs so that the outer lips separate, the lapels stick together, the clitoris peeping above them. — The prick of course opens and passes between them, and they rub on each side of it in fucking.

In virgins — just inside the tube, prick-receiver, or vagina, and behind the piss-vent, is a little red film or membrane covering the hole, all but a little perforation through which the monthlies, or courses, or bloodies, as they are called, and other cunt juices of the woman escape. This is the hymen, or virginity, which is broken by the prick the first time the women is fucked, leaving the membrane with a ragged edge like a cockscomb, but which raggedness disappears in a year or two after fucking.

The hole or tube which receives the prick, is also pink, soft, and smooth inside, and feels like the kernels on the inside of the mouth. The sides will give ready way to the push of the finger, and being elastic it directly recovers itself when the finger is withdrawn, and therefore closes gently on the prick whether a large or a small one. — This quality makes it a very pretty plaything for the man. — Nothing pleases some so much as putting their fingers up it, or playing as it is called at stink-finger, whilst the woman plays with his cock and balls. — This mutual handling and titillation of each other's privates, makes them both lewed or ready to fuck. — I forgot to say that when the man's prick is randy and the woman squeezes it, that the hole at the tip opens slightly, and a strong smell comes out of it. — Some women when randy like that smell.

The cunt is always wet inside. If anything be put up to dry it, it is wet a minute afterwards. — If a woman wants fucking it gets wetter, and in some women if they have their clitoris titillated, their cunts get very wet indeed. — This moisture is very smooth and slimy, and is salt to the taste, which condition is intended so to lubricate it, and to make it smoother and nicer for the man's prick, the red, fine skinned tip of which is very thin and highly sensitive. It is the seat of pleasure in fact. The cunt has always a peculiar smell, slightly fishy or cheesey it has been called, tho I never detected that sort of smell. This is the case even with the cleanest women, and it is stronger if a women has been very randy for some time, and has not washed her cunt, — or in one who rarely washes it, but depends on her piddle and her cunt mopping afterwards to keep it sweet and wholesome. This cunt smell from a healthy, clean woman, is pleasant and stimulating to most men.

Fucking consists in putting the two organs just described, together. That is, in the man making his prick stiff and pushing it up the cunt as far as it will go, and quite plugging it up. Then pushing it backwards and forwards in it, and gradually quicker and quicker, his prick getting stiffer and stiffer, and her cunt getting wetter, and tighter and tighter, until at last the pleasure which both feel from the instant their privates meet, and which increases gradually as the fuck goes on, gets maddening almost in its intensity, and terminates by the balls shooting out through his prick into her cunt, a quantity of sperm, and the whole surface of her cunt at the same time clipping his prick, and exuding a thinnish milky liquor described before. This done, with intense pleasure to both, they are both quiet, satisfied, and almost insensible for an instant from excess of pleasure. Then the cunt gets lax, the prick shrinks out of it, and the fuck is over.

But before this occurs both of them *should* feel, and the man actually *must* be randy or want to fuck, for without that his prick will not be stiff, and the symptoms of lust or randiness must be understood in the first place.

Randiness in a man shews itself by his prick feeling uneasy, yet with a voluptuous sensation, by its swelling, lengthening, and stiffening. His thoughts go to women who look beautiful in his eyes then, even if they did not before. He longs for them, gets fidgety, and, if sitting, has a desire to wriggle his backside backwards and forwards. — He can scarcely keep his fingers from his prick, but wants to feel it and fondle it. His prick burns, his balls, if he has not recently done too much fucking, are firm and covered with well corrugated, close wrinkles. — If he touches his prick much, it begins to throb, and knocks up toward his belly. His bumhole tightens and squeezes, as the prick knocks, and, when in that state, he is ready to fuck anything, from his sister to his grandmother, from a ten-year-old, to a woman of sixty, for a standing prick has no conscience. — Woe be to the female whom he gets a chance at, if she does not want *him,* for he will have *her* if he can.

Randiness in a woman shows itself in some respects in the same way, but it gives much less outward sign. — She feels restless, has an inclination to press her legs close together, then to open them wide, then close them again. To squeeze her cunt tight by the muscles at the orifice of the prick hole, — the same action closing tightly her arse hole, which thus acts sympathetically with the cunt. — To move her bum about uneasily on the chair, to sigh with a sensation of pleasure, and throw herself about. To put her fingers on her cunt and play with it — and to rub her clitoris. Her cunt feels hot — burning — some times it gets wet — very wet — with a languishing swooning sensation — and yet she does not exude or spend as when being fucked — she is sensitive with men. — If one touches her hand or squeezes it, it gives her pleasure. — Any attention from a man fills her with vague desires of she knows not what. — Her eyes seek his, then drop — and if she has seen or known much of men's nature, — she eyes askant his trowsers, just where his prick lies, and blushes at what she is doing, as if he knew what she was thinking about. If she is of a very sensitive, or warm nature, or what is called "hot arsed" or hot cunted, or "randy arsed" — and this lewedness has continued for a long time without the relief given by fucking, she is subject to hysterics. In young women a good fucking sets them to rights, but this is by the way. — Some girls when randy, giggle and laugh a great deal, and laugh at all a man says to them. — Their eyes brighten and languish, they involuntarily return the pressure of the man's hands. All this is just what incites men to desire to fuck them.

When both the man and woman are randy, they are in the best condition for fucking, but when not so, and nature is impelling them both toward copulation, they make each other lewed if they get an opportunity.

Let us suppose a couple together — he having had women before — she having had it once or twice on the sly, but has been a long time without it, and determines not to risk it again. He knows nothing about this but begins to long for her. — They are quite alone, and there is no chance of being disturbed.

He looks at her, chats pleasantly, draws nearer and nearer, till they sit quite close. — He wonders what her secret charms are, if her thighs are round and plump, her bum big. — Then his mind goes to the cunt. He thinks of its hair, its color, and then his prick stiffens and he longs to fuck her, and wondering if she wants it, or will let him, is impelled to try.

Then under the impulse of intention, his desire to discharge his sperm up her becomes stronger. Reckless, he begins kissing, which is resisted at first by her, but at length permitted once and with protest. — Then his arm goes round her waist — he draws her closer, and so they sit whilst for a time he murmurs love.

Then one hand goes on her knees outside her clothes — and more kisses follow. If not randy before, — the pressure of his arm, and hand now drawn still nearer to her belly, or pressing on her thighs but still outside her clothes, makes her randy now. — He kisses her more passionately and in doing so, his hand pushes against her belly. — She guesses he had done it purposely but says nothing. — Her cunt and bum hole tighten and a voluptuous shiver runs through her. — She fears herself, and threatens to cry out but does not. — Gradually she returns his kisses, but begs him to go and leave her.

Meanwhile he has stooped a little, has felt her ankles, has thrust his hand up her petticoats and it is on her thigh just above her knee. — She resists violently, but lewdness now pervades her system. — She is in a sweet confusion, and overwhelmed with lustful sensations, one moment makes a half cry — then laughs, — then says "hush" as baudy wishes now find utterance from him. — She perhaps kisses him to leave off, but does not wish him, likes what he is doing, knows it is wrong, but makes up her mind that he shan't do the trick to her.

This lasts for a time. She is getting sick with lewed desire. A cry — a struggle — and he has forced his finger between her cunt lips — it is rubbing her clitoris, whilst she with closed thighs is pushing him away with one hand, and trying to pull down her clothes with the other. She shifts her bum back, tightens her thighs together, but he keeps his finger there still. — Then he pulls out his prick, a stiff, ivory, red-tipped rod, with its pendulous, firm balls. — Its look fascinates her. — He tells her to look at it. — She turns her head and eyes away, — but can't help turning them again.

He struggles now to get her clothes up — she to prevent him. — Now he pushes the prick against her hand and a thrill goes through her as she feels the hot rod. — Again and again it knocks against her hand — he snatches her hand and makes her clasp his prick. With a cry, she snatches it away. — In doing this he has for the instant withdrawn his hand from her cunt, and with a slight feeling of relief she thinks for the moment he is going to cease.

Vain hope, if she hopes it, which is often doubtful, for the feel of her hand on his doodle has made him curious. — Seizing her, he pulls up her clothes, — sees her thighs, and the dark hairy shadow above the split, and ere she can prevent it, his finger is pushed further towards the prick hole. — She cries out that he hurts, but he pushes on his fingers. — She entreats, resists, but voluptuous sensations are coursing thro her veins. — The stiff prick dances before her eyes, — and altho she would resist if she could, feels her power to do so going, for lewedness has possession of her body, and desire to let him have his way is taking possession of her soul; and so both panting, they for a minute cease — he keeping his fingers where he had forced them.

Nature has placed the woman's clitoris so that it cannot escape man's fingers. — If a woman closes her thighs tightly, a man cannot from the front get his finger to the cunt hole; and from the back, the arse cheeks close, so that without violence he cannot do it, even when she be standing up, altho as easily then, as from the front. But without hurting her, and do what she may to prevent him, the clitoris can be reached by this middle finger. By pushing it through the closed thighs, — it reaches the upper part of the cunt where the clitoris lies, and was so placed to enable the man to incite and incline the woman to submit to his will in copulation.

In a minute he recommences. — In vain she tightens her thighs — his finger rubs heavier and heavier against it, he holds her close to him with one arm, kissing and beseeching; whilst just under her eyes is the throbbing prick ready to plug her. Her thighs are exposed, she is now too excited to pull her clothes down, and her cunt feels wet. — "Ah! — Ah! — What is this?" A shiver of pleasure runs through her, which makes her, spite of herself, open for a second her thighs — her cunt feels wetter, her face inclines towards his — her resistance is gone, her eyes close, she is nearly spending, she only murmurs, "No — no — oh don't — leave off — I won't," to his earnest entreaties, and the next instant falls back under his pressure, or is partly dragged, partly lifted, lustfully conscious, to the nearest bed or couch, all resistance is gone, she is saturated with lust and is quiet. — Then their bellies meet, his hand insinuates itself under her

[259]

round warm haunches, something stiff and hard, yet smooth and soft, pokes between her thighs and glides quickly down over her clitoris. She feels it at her cunt entrance, — it thrusts, it enters, — it is up her, — she feels it in her vitals and the balls knocking against her buttocks, and then for a minute both are quiet.

Then up to her womb, then down nearly to her cunt lips, backwards and forwards goes the prick. Long shoves —short shoves — quick, quicker, — a sigh from him, a wriggle from her, and then again a slight rest. — A shove again, and then perhaps (tho but rarely) he, curious, withdraws one hand from her smooth bum, and feels the stem of his tool gently closed round by her cunt lips, gently yet firmly, and the hairs of their organs mingling. — His finger gently touches the clitoris against the lower end of which his prick had rubbed. — A shiver of delight goes through her as she feels him, and juices begin to exude from her cunt. — On go the thrusts — quick — quick — quicker and harder, his rigid prick knocks at the portals of her womb. — Now a sigh from her, — her eyes close — her mouth gently opens. — Shorter and quicker are now the thrusts, and his arse wriggles, he thrusts up her cunt as if he would engulf his whole body in her, his balls covering her arsehole, wag and rub, and knock against her bum cheeks, her belly heaves — her thighs open wide — her knees move up gently, her legs stretch out, then close on his again and squeeze his thighs, his prick stiffens more, and begins to throb violently in her, — her cunt juices have wetted it from tip to root — it is running out and wetting the hairs round his prick stem.

Now a more delicious and almost maddening sensation pervades their whole bodies. — Gradually more and more powerful, it usurps their senses in a voluptuous delirium. — If her father were now to come into the room, she would cling to the man. — If he knew his mother was being murdered in the next room, he would not, to save her, withdraw his prick from the cunt.

Now their kisses are moist, their tongues meet, their salivas mingle, — he sucks all he can from her mouth, his hands tighten round her backside, he clasps her to him as if to squeeze the breath out of her; her hands tighten round his waist, or rub convulsively over his buttocks, or up his back. Up go her thighs gently again, and press tightly against his haunches, he grasps her bum like a vice and with a long drawn breath — with a sigh from him — and perhaps a convulsive cry of "cunt," — out shoots his spunk against the portals of her womb which open to receive it, — her cunt at the same moment tightening round his prick and grinding it, and distilling over it on all sides its thin, salt, milky, juices. What sperm her womb does not suck up and absorb, unites with her juices, making a bath in which his prick lies weltering. — Some squeezes out, making still wetter the hair of both their genitals, and then with gentle and gradually diminishing wriggles, and backside movements of both, with gentle murmurs, sighs, and kisses, they lay quiet in each other's arms in luscious Elysium, with limbs stretched out, and every muscle tranquil, — what senses they have left, absorbed in dreamy thoughts of prick, cunt, sperm, and fucking, and in loving delight in each other.

So they lay for a few minutes until he moves again, when the friction of his prick, even in her lubricated cunt, causes it sympathetically to tighten, tho but slightly only, for sated with pleasure that channel to her womb has lost its muscular power for a while. Yet the gentle grip it gives sends a thrill of pleasure through him, and his shrinking prick; this sends forth one drop more of lingering sperm now in its thinnest liquidity. It is the last. — Then his weight oppresses her, she moves, and his shrunken, wet, cock, comes out dripping over her anus, and with a kiss he rises. — In doing so a drop falls on to her thigh, or on the thicket of cunt hair — it is the parting dew. She also rises, pulling down her petticoats and for a minute they are both silent and look at each other. — On his face is a smile of satisfaction. — She blushes and looks abashed at her doings, and is in the dreamy pleasure of a sperm saturated cunt.

If the happy couple have fucked before, and are in bed tranquilly together, the game is slightly varied. Their spend is over; but naked, limb to limb, he lingers on her belly, nestling his balls up to her and trying to keep his prick in its soft, smooth, wet, warm lodging. — He lingers on her long, the hair on both their privates sticking and drying together, so close and intermingled have they got. — His weight, which she did not feel whilst thrusting and moving up her and their postures varied each moment, now oppresses her; and she moves, or has a cough or feigns one, which shakes her belly and his shrinking prick uncunts.

Still he will not get off, and the red wet tip, is still dribbling out a little sperm which drops on her bum hole — or against her bum cheeks. Then following his withdrawal, —

some of their mixed essences which her womb has not sucked into it, rolls out like a great thick tear towards her arsehole. He turns off of her. She turns on her side towards him and the spunk tear changes its course, and lodges on her thigh near to the arsehole end of the cunt. She need not put down her fingers to feel that her cunt fringe is wet, she feels unmistakably that her cunt lips are slabbered, wet, and spermy; and it gives her pleasure to feel it there for it came from out of his body into hers. — She loves him for putting it there. — He also turns towards her, — his prick still shrinking, flabby, and sloppy, falls on his thigh and wets it, and he loves that wetness for it came from her cunt. Then belly to belly — or belly to bum — naked and touching, with soft baudy words of love, and baudy images floating dreamily across their minds. — She thinking of balls, prick, fucking and of the spunk lying in her cunt. He of cunt, spunk, and tongue sucking, they fall asleep — and that is fucking.

But often times something comes of this cunt basting — not quite unknown, but mostly unthought of during the hot fit of lust and pleasure, and certainly unhoped for excepting by married women. Something which, had it been thought of whilst with clasped haunches, wriggling buttocks, prick thrusts, heaving bellies, sighs and murmurs, the couple were insensible to all but pleasure, their souls steeped in Elysium, — would certainly have made the lady at least a little anxious. That second or two's mixed spending, and spunk sucking up of the womb, sometimes causes the lady to be in the family way, and that day nine months, after much fainting, sickness, longing for all that is out of season and out of reason, with a swollen turgid belly — much spewing, five minute pissings, farting, shitting, and the whites: — an infant comes down that cunt, — the result of such fucking, and this is how it comes about.

High up in the belly of the woman and in recesses just outside the womb, are little organs or parts of her body, containing what are called ova — and which common people call eggs — it is a sort of enclosure in which a woman breeds eggs within herself, out of herself, and parcel of her nature. Leading from this egg nest, is a little tube connecting with the womb, and at monthly periods, an egg is squeezed out of it into the womb through this passage, and it only wants to be touched by the man's spunk — when man and woman are both discharging in their spasm of pleasure, and lo! — the thing is done. That which had no life, lives, — the egg is vivified, the woman is impregnated, is with child. Then it will grow bigger and bigger in her, and her belly will swell, until in the nine months, out comes a child through her cunt.

And this is the exact process and time when the egg has life given to it. — As far as is known, the thing takes place at the moment when both man and woman are in the greatest state of voluptuous enjoyment, and at the crisis and termination of the fucking. If the man alone spends in the woman's cunt, it will not do it. — If the woman spends alone, it will not do it. — If they spend some time after each other, it may or may not do it. — But as the fuck goes on, and their mutual pleasure increases — just at the moment that the woman's cunt tightens, just as the man shoves short or merely wriggles his prick as far up the cunt as he can — the egg either being there ready, or being then squeezed out of the bag into the womb — the woman's juices exude from her into her cunt. — The man's spunk squirts, — the womb sucks in the male and female mixture, — the egg is touched, and life begotten. Thus in the delirious ecstasy of the fuck, the job is done.

Such is a prick — such a cunt — such fucking — such the consequence. — The fucking organs excepting to chose who have them, would not perhaps be thought handsome. — No one thinks a dog's prick handsome, or a cow's cunt beautiful, — yet they are not unlike those of the human species. — No one who sees a dog fucking a bitch, thinks that their action is elegant, or their faces edifying, yet their movements are much like those of the human species. — The wriggling of the lady's buttocks when a prick is moving up her, and the up and down movements of the man's haunches, and the saucers he makes in his arse cheeks are not elegant, — their slabbered privates when they have finished not nice, — their faces during the operation not expressing intellect. In fact the motion is somewhat monotonous, is inelegant, almost ridiculous, and the end, sloppy and odorous; yet they both think the operation most beautiful.

And if a woman in stature, form, colour, skin, and in beauty of mouth, teeth, nose, and eye, were perfect; if her limbs were perfection, her breasts ivory — her breath sweet as a honey suckle, her voice tender, her temper perfect, and if in brief she comprised all that we call perfection in a woman; — yet were she without that hairy mouthed, slippery, half slimy, salt, and odorous cunt, a man would sooner sleep with his grandmother or lie down with a cow than with her.

And if a man be tall as a guardsman, formed like Apollo, be strong as Hercules, and a grand model of strength, beauty, and all that is attractive in man — if he even be gentle and kind to a woman — and yet had not that bit of distensible gristle, with its pendant balls, or if having it, it would not stiffen and swell at times so as to enter, fill, and plug up the cunt entirely, and shed into the innermost recesses and end of the cunt — that thickish, semi-opaque, gruelly essence of man's blood — she would not care a far for him, and would sooner sleep with a male monkey.

This is a description of the organs employed, and the object, art, and manner of using them, which is called fucking — together with its results. It is written in this simple, homely, yet classical manner; so as to enable the dullest, simplest, and most unsophisticated to understand it. It is specially suitable for ignorant boys and girls from twelve to fifteen years of age, — at which period they begin to think of such matters, and when they may study it with most advantage, because and at that age the world tries its best to obscure the consideration, and to hinder all real knowledge about it getting to them. It may be read usefully after evening family prayers also, by older members of the family, to whom at times, it may serve as an aphrodisiac, and it will spare many young, but full grown people, trouble and loss of time in searching for knowledge which ought to be known to all, but which owing to a false morality, is a subject put aside as improper.

[At the time I wrote this, I had but little of the anatomical knowledge of the sexes which I now possess, and vulva — vagina — clitoris — and other terms or their exact signification were only partially known to me.]

CHAPTER XXVIII

Thoughts about myself, my skin and prick. — At a Swiss village. — At L***s. — An useful keyhole. — A middle aged couple. — An American family. — Eighteen and naked. — Forty in chemise. — Family jars. — The sponging bath. — Aunt and niece. — At the museum. — The mutilated statue. — Is it male or female? — Are Americans hairy? — The aunt's bed room. — Coy but willing. — Amy undressing. — A voluptuous night. — Fat, fair, and forty. — A mature cunt. — Wise precautions. — To Paris. — To England. — My abstinence from women.

About this time I began to think more of my self than I had done — which seems a strange thing to me. I had to a large extent, though not quite, got over that mistaken notion about the size of my prick, — so many women having asserted it was a handsome sized one. And several gay ladies having shown affectionate attentions to me, from that I inferred they would not have done so had that supreme article of feminine worship been inferior. I might also say the same of a few ladies who were not gay, but whose cunts know pretty well the difference between a prick and a cucumber. For all that, I have been for a short time and more than once, temporarily impotent thro a nervous fit on this point.

I have within the last few years heard much admiration expressed of my face and figure. — I heard this both directly and indirectly, from chaste, as well as unchaste ladies. — "He might with his face and shape have married so and so, and she was dying for him, but he never knew it," — was said of me. Another had praised my face, form, and my demeanour, — Camille told me that her maid always spoke of me as "your handsome friend, madame," when she forgot the name I went by. I had, I know, a skin which for colour and smoothness, was like a woman's — dozens of women had smoothed, stroked, and admired it to my face. — One said it made her spend, directly she rubbed her hand over my back when I was fucking her. Another used to kiss me all over and ask me to turn on to my belly, so that she might kiss my backside, which was equally smooth.

For all that I had but little conceit of myself and fancied I was too thin. — Another stupid fancy, for I never was what could be called thin, tho I was lithe. — When I heard that any woman had mentioned me in a flattering manner, I used to wonder if it were true. Then I had a desire more and more frequently come over me, to see other pricks, and satisfy myself by comparison, whether mine was a full sized one or not, and I wondered if they fucked after my fashion or how, and if they spent as much — and how they looked when spending — much curiosity about males in coition seems to have laid hold of me, and I don't see anything wrong in satisfying that curiosity.

———————

Sick of London, I left in July with a friend, and spent much time in the Swiss mountains. He was married but very fast, and we went to baudy houses together. Geneva, Berne, Lucerne and Zurich saw our pricks. We found it economical, for the regulation price was but about five francs a lady, and also safe (A clap when one is traveling is the worst of ailments.) — for they had just about that time put the Paphians under medical supervision at least in some of the Cantons. — Then he left me, and for some time I remained in the mountains alone.

This tour I became more and more curious about the doings of those in the adjoining bedrooms. I used spy holes whenever I found them, opened others which had been stopped up, and at last even ventured to make some of my own. — But in three rooms out of six, these little peep holes had been made. If I found the bedroom assigned to me had no communication with adjoining rooms, I changed it on some pretext, and again if not then satisfied. I found that second class hotels gave me greater opportunities for satisfying my curiosity, they being mostly frequented by foreigners, who have not the absurd finical notions about nudity and the necessities of nature, which my own countrymen have; but whom I incline to think are on the average as moral as we are for all that.

To use the opportunities advantageously took time and trouble. I had to ascertain what time my neighbours got up or went to bed, or used their rooms. Many a time I have jumped out of bed to peep and saw nothing. At other times when I intended to rise by daylight, and watch (for I was ready for any amount of trouble to see a woman naked, and would have sat up all night to do so), I overslept myself, and lost my chance. — Yet nothing discouraged me, and I saw a lot of women in different degrees of nudity, saw them piddle, wash their quims, and undress, yet the great bulk tho highly pleasing to me, are not worth writing about.

Travelling for the most part quite alone this time favoured me. — When with a friend, we too often had rooms next each other. — This time I often had strangers on each side of me, and tho that meant noise and disturbance, I preferred it.

The oddest thing, as it seemed to me, was that sometimes with holes in doors as big as small peas, the occupants rarely seemed to notice them. — The middle aged sometimes used, but young women rarely. — They were mostly tired or excited, or in a hurry to dress or undress, or to get to food, or move off, or do something, and seemed to notice nothing in the room. — When they had time they almost invariably looked out of the window. This journey was nearly all during warm, light weather.

At the town of L***s in France I had a large room. There were but few travellers. I found not only the entire key-hole of the door dividing mine from the next bed room was free from obstruction, but peep holes were in plenty. — In the morning, awakening, I heard the voices of a male and female, instantly jumped out of bed, and saw a middle aged couple dressing. They were having an altercation, and washing, I think, side by side at the same wash stand, which I could not see. Suddenly the lady stripped off her chemise, put a basin on the floor, and soaped and washed her cunt, talking to the man all the time. She was five and forty quite, had a bum as big as a tub, huge thighs, and lightish brown hair in great quantity, on a cunt which as she squatted, looked enormous. The sausage lips opened till they must have been three inches apart. Great nymphae hung down inside them, and then the red gap looked altogether like a cut in a big bit of meat. — Instantly, — so quickly do comparisons make themselves, I thought of the cunt of my aunt, seen at Hampton Court when I was a boy.

At the same moment appeared by her side a man about fifty-five years old, stout, naked, with a very big prick covered with soapsuds, and there they wrangled close together, she lathering and rubbing her cunt, he his prick. Her cunt got so white and held so much soap, and there was so much hair, that it looked like masses of wool hanging between her thighs. For a minute still squatting, she left off rubbing it, and he holding his big prick in one fist, ceased lathering it whilst they talked. — Then she slopped her cunt and took away the basin. — He went out of sight, and both in half a minute came into sight again with towels, rubbing their privates vigorously, and continued their quarrel. I laughed heartily, but did not care about seeing any more. They were I found from their intonation, Americans. The sight was a comic one.

They must have changed their room or else have left the hotel, for after a midday table d'hôte, it being scorchingly hot, I went to my room for a siesta and was just dozing off, when I heard a young female laugh, and my eye was at the keyhole in a second. I saw a nice girl seemingly about eighteen years of age, naked all but shoes and stockings, laughing loudly with another big fine woman seemingly about thirty-five, who was divesting herself of clothes, but only stripped to her chemise. All the outer blinds were closed to exclude heat, yet such was the brilliancy of the day, that it was quite light in the rooms. They sat down at a table and began to work. The naked one remarked that they had better see to their things than go to sleep. "It gets pretty well as hot as it is down south," said she. — Every now and then she went to a trunk which was out of my sight, and brought back clothes, so I had good views of her body on all sides, and this went on for an hour.

They talked soon about a marriage, and quarrelled. — "Your father will never give his consent," said the older. "He shall," said the younger, "I guess I'll make him." "Why he's brought you here to get you out of Dick's way." "I'll bet Dick will follow me." "There will be a kick up if he does." "I don't care." "He's not good enough and look at his beggarly family, he only wants your money." "He may have it. — He loves me and I love him." — At length they got to high words, and moved to a part of the room where I could not see nor hear them. — In two or three minutes they came again in sight, and the younger one said. — "If father won't let me marry him, I'll have him without marrying." "There! I guess it don't matter much to you so long as it's a man, if you are so hot as all that." "*You* needn't talk about being hot, you let **** do it to you when you were much younger than I am." "It's a lie." "You did, and two years after, mother

[*268*]

caught **** in bed with ****." "It's a damned lie," shrieked out the other whom I heard, but then could not see. "I've heard mother say so more than once, and *** said so before she died." "I won't stop with you, or travel any longer with you, I'll go back," and the elder began to bellow. They both talked together, it was quite a jangle, and they moved. "Don't make that noise, some one is in the next room perhaps," and naked, the younger came towards my door and listened. — I covered the key hole with a coat, but she must, I think, have looked there. Their voices dropped soon after, a door banged, and I fancied one was alone.

Tired of looking I laid down and slept. When I looked again, there was the young lady sitting still naked at the table examining a bonnet. She put the bonnet on, and went to a looking glass, and I had the pleasure for the second time in my life as well as I can recollect, of seeing a naked woman with a bonnet on. It started a letch in me which I satisfied at a future day — and the sight now made my cock stand suddenly. It had not done so before at seeing the slim American lass naked.

Tired of looking, for I neither could see washhand stand, chamber pot, or bed, and so missed the delicate operations the lady performed there, I ceased looking, and hanging a coat so as to cover the keyhole went out. — At the table d'hôte dinner I sat near to the young lady, who was one of a large party, and gathered that the middle aged couple whom I had seen in the morning belonged to the family. He was an American merchant with a branch business at L***s. The woman who had stripped to her chemise when the young one was naked, was called aunt. She had been married, I gathered, and looked a lecherous she. — It was delicious to be talking to the young lady, knowing what I did of her sweet neat body. It was their first visit to Europe.

Next morning I heard a hubbub, and something sound like a gong. Looking, I found that a large sponging bath had been put down, and saw with much pleasure the young lady take her bath, squat and rise, squeeze water over herself in various attitudes, and rub her dainty little bum, belly, and adjuncts dry. Then she shouted out, "Wait a minute," and when nearly dry let in the other lady who was in a wrapper, and she used the bath, which I heard after was their own.

[At the time this occurred such baths were a rarity at foreign hotels — if any, they had but one or two, and you had

[269]

to wait long to get one. — The English mainly used them, and at length forced hotel keepers all over Europe to provide them. At this epoch frequently a bath formed part of an English family's luggage.]

The young one had not put on her chemise when she opened the door. — The elder had not the other day taken off her chemise, as I imagined, out of modesty, — but now she threw off her wrapper and her chemise and stood naked as born, and a very fine made woman she was, with a huge triangular bush of dark hair at the bottom of her belly. She bathed and rubbed her cunt and all dry, delightfully in my sight, and then both had breakfast in the room. — The elder one made my cock tingle, tho the younger had not — and I thought I would try my luck with her, for that she had licked the rolling pin a good bit I was sure, from what I had heard eavesdropping, and what I saw in her face. But I wanted to leave L***s, and go elsewhere, so I must either have her soon, or not at all.

I dined close to home at the table d'hôte and got to a certain intimacy, but there was no chatting after dinner in a garden, nor any means of getting to speak to her alone for long. I saw no chance, but shall have my luck with women I believe, all my life.

There were three men of the party and four ladies. The aunt was the oldest lady. — After breakfast next morning one said — "It's too hot to go out till eventide. — We made a mistake in not coming here later on." The men said they should go by steam to some place. — Aunt said, "I can't stay in all day, I don't mind the heat, and will go to the museum for an hour or two." — In an hour after there she was, and there was I as if by chance. — "My nieces are lazy," said she, "if I come to foreign parts to see, I like to see." — She was well dressed, but of a common breed.

We looked about together, and then sat down. "It is hot." "Not so hot as yesterday, for after luncheon, I stripped to my shirt and sat in it till dinner time." "And I did to my chemise," said she laughing. "I wish I had seen you." "Do you tho?" said she, making eyes at me. "Yes and you might have seen *me,* but we men show too much, our shirts are short." "That depends," said she, chuckling and looking lewed. Then we had a discussion about statuary. — She liked the nude, she said. I ran as closely to the border of decency as I could in talking about it, and she seemed to like it, and my letch for her grew stronger, tho she was middle-aged.

We looked round again after a rest, and came on the fragment of a male bust in marble, the prick of which had been knocked off; but the balls remained, and what is rarely seen, all the hair round the prick had been sculptured and was there.

As we looked, strong words occurred to me, but I hesitated — p'shaw — if she is offended she can but show it, and I leave L***s — if not, I'll go further. — We are really strangers — I'll see if she is game or not, thought I.

"It's a woman's torso," said I. "No," said she, laughing, "where are your eyes?" "Ah — yes — I see where it ought to be, it's knocked off, I wonder what Greek maiden has it." "Oh for shame," said she, leering at me. I took no notice. — "See how rare — I wonder, what is the period of the sculpture?" "What is rare?" "They have shown the hair round — you may see hundreds of pieces of antique sculpture without that." "Oh my — we are getting on I think," and she left me, and sat down. In a minute I was at her side.

The ice was broken, I felt now sure she wanted to hear talk suggesting sexual pleasure, and I followed suit. — "American ladies have a great deal of hair haven't they?" "I don't know." "You have." "How do you know?" "I'm sure of it from the look of you — haven't you?" "I don't know." "Will you ascertain? — but not here." "Oh — it's time to go to luncheon." "We'll go back together." And we did. I felt sure now she'd let me have her.

After luncheon we all loitered a little in the reading room. "Where is your room?" said I. "It looks out on to the back." "Ah you are cooler, mine looks on to **** it is hot, but what a nice view." "What's the number?" she asked. I gave it. — "Why that's next to my niece's." "Yes, I can hear her." She looked hard at me. — The other ladies had just left the room and she rose. — "Are you going to the museum to see if the torso is male or female?" said I.

"No — to my niece, Amy's." "And I to have a siesta in my shirt." — She looked so hard at me that I felt sure some suspicion crossed her mind. We went upstairs together. As we got to my door, — "This is mine," said I, "look, — it is large and so nice." — She cooly walked in and went straight to the door between the rooms, my clothes covered the key hole, but without any hesitation she pulled them aside, peeped thro the key hole, and then looked at me. — "Oh you have been peeping." "Yes, and saw you both naked this morning, bathing," said I boldly. — She burst into a quiet laugh, holding her sides and sitting down. — "We've come to Europe to learn something I guess." "I guess I want you," said I, and gave her a kiss and put my hand up her clothes. — "Hish, she'll hear — don't make a noise," said she. "If we are quiet they can't hear there, my bed is close to the corridor. — Now don't be nonsensical, I saw it all this morning, all the dark hair, and your splendid thighs, and bum," and I pulled my prick out.

She dallied for a minute and did the coy — "I'm surprised at you, — What a shame" — and so on, and squirmed slightly, whilst she whispered her objections, but never dislodged my fingers from her quim, — and laid hold of my prick. — Then she soon got on to the bed quietly, I on to her, and a well fucked cunt received me, — but she was a charming wriggler, and I enjoyed her. — And didn't she like it.

We lay talking in whispers for a time. — "Will you wash?" "No — I'll go to my own room, I'll see if any one is in *her* room." — She peeped at her niece's. — "I can't see her." "Come back to me." "I will if I can in half an hour, but leave your room door ajar then." I did, and she returned in an hour. — "Be quick," said she — and quickly we copulated. "I've passed several times," said she, "but there was always a chambermaid or some one about." "Let me sleep with you to night." "We'll talk about it after dinner," said she. — Then suddenly — "I wonder if Amy's there," and she peeped again. "No. — Could you hear us talk?" "I could not distinguish a word you said, tho I heard you," I replied.

"Not tonight," she whispered to me over a Galignani after dinner — "we are all going out." I was not sorry, for I had fucked rather hard the night before, having been over stimulated by the two cunts. — "Don't stop the key hole." "I will," — but she didn't. I saw both women naked the next morning — but they spoke in a very low tone. I am sure that middle aged lady enjoyed being looked at naked when bathing.

Next day, she said she would leave her door open a quarter of an hour after her niece was in *her* room. — She would not come to my room. — If I was out of my room no one would notice it, but suppose one of their party wanted her, and found she was not in her bedroom, how could she explain that. She was a regular cunning, cock huntress I am sure, and have no doubt that wherever she travelled she got her lower maw well satisfied by fresh pricks. She had lust in her eyes, was baudy to the backbone.

After watching Amy undress at night, I was soon in the aunt's room and passed a lascivious night with her. — She had a beautiful chemise on; her hair was nicely tied up. She was perfumed, had gold bracelets on, and silk stockings and slippers. That middle aged one knew how to excite the male. — She was quite free now. — The other day she would scarcely let me see her cunt, — now she opened her thighs wide to my admiration.

It was one of the largest vulvas I have seen. The mons was like a pincushion, the lips were thick, it opened wide as I clutched it, the whole palm of my hand I laid between the lips, whilst my wrist rubbed her clitoris and my middle finger curved up a little into the vagina. It pleases me much recently, to feel the entire surface of a cunt that way, to grasp the whole, to wriggle my hand over all parts at the same time, it's an unusual mode of frigging and I think it pleases the ladies. — For a minute I lay in that enjoyment with her, our tongues meeting, and, then I mounted her. — Her hole instead of being very large as I expected, seemed delicious. She knew exactly at what level to place her legs to engulf me, not a quarter of an inch of my prick was out of her fat cunt, and instead of thrusting and ramming away, I nestled it close on to her elastic orifice, with a steady quiet pressure, till the upper wrinkles of my testicles were almost in her, and the upper hair of my prick tickled and irritated her clitoris. — So I lay enjoying her, wriggling, not thrusting, and thinking about her large looking, hirsute charms. "Go on dear," she sighed impatiently and fucked me with a cunt movement once or twice. Then, immediately, "Oh — I'm spen-ding." A violent, but momentary oscillation of her buttocks came, and I felt her cunt relax under its own moisture.

"You've spent." "Yes, you haven't — take it out and wait a minute." I pulled it out pretty wet. She kissed me, I turned on my side, she felt my prick, I her wet aperture, and did the old fashioned frig on the clitoris. — "Weren't you in a hurry," I said. "Yes," she replied with all the frankness of a doxy, "I wanted it so to day." The next minute I was up her and never spent in a more delicious cunt, its size and hairiness was a novelty. — She spent with me. — "Let me get up and wash." "No." "I will." She uncunted me and did so. — "Why that?" "Oh you know — to prevent consequences." "But it won't." "Not for sure, but it's wiser." "Have you ever had a child?" "Never." "Are you a widow?" "Yes." — This is exactly what took place — and word for

[273]

word what was said at that minute. I did not know before for a certainty that she had been married, and have only her word for it now.

Then I had a full inspection of her charms, and as I expressed admiration she seemed delighted. She let me bring candles closer to see, and she had all to be proud of. She was a tall, stout woman, with a good looking face, half German in type, fine limbed, and with white flesh, her hair was dark, the thatch of her cunt was large in quantity, and thick and curly. — I have never seen more hair on a woman. It went straight across her belly, half way to her navel, it lay thick and curly down the lips, filling the cavity between the cunt and the thighs. Since my adventure at the railway station, I have rarely looked lower in a woman, but my dislike to the frowsy regions seemed to have left me now, and I looked curiously at her bumhole, and found it surrounded with thick, short, dark hair, crisp, and curly, which went right round the cunt and joined the arsehole edging.

Holding the lips apart, I found that the prick hole looked no larger than that of any full sized matured woman. — Why I expected to find it larger I can't say, but I had. — I put one, two, then three fingers up it, and believe I might have put more. It distended easily, yet the cunt clung to my fingers and tightly. — In her armpits was not so much hair. — "Turn over, love, and let me see those lovely buttocks." She did, and pulling them with difficulty apart, — I saw dark hair from her bum hole to her bum bone. "Are you satisfied?" said she, as I kissed the white marbly flesh. "Yes you are lovely, exquisite," and I laid by the side of her on, alas, too narrow a bed, and we talked till nature made us join our genitals again.

"How old am I?" said she in a conceited manner, when in the preludes of a fuck our hands were employed on each other's privates. — "Thirty-three," said I, wishing to please her. "That's my age exactly." — Aye, I thought, and seven years on to that. I am sure she was forty, tho in splendid condition. I mentally compared her with Mavis, Fisher, Pender, Mrs. O*b***e, and a dozen big women, some of whom I know were thirty-five, — and from face, form, cuntal indications, and others between the bum bone and navel, am sure she was forty. — But I have rarely had a finer night's amusement than I had with her, and I fucked her every hour until six in the morning. We were then both fucked out.

There was the difficulty in getting away — for half an

[274]

hour was I peeping for an opportunity. — At last the coast was clear, the servants had gone off in various directions — out I stepped, and as she closed the door behind me, out stepped from a bedroom opposite, the chambermaid. — She gave an astonished look then turned her head. — I left L***s that night, and never told my middle aged beauty that the chambermaid had seen me leaving the bedroom, thinking it could not be helped and would only make her uncomfortable.

I am beginning to judge of the age of women by the look of their cunts and buttocks. — Age is indicated there, as much as by face and breasts. The growth of hair on the motte, and the state and color of the bum cheeks, valley, declare almost unmistakably when a woman has turned thirty, I think I might bet on it.

After this adventure with the American family, I went straight to Paris. There I had a half dozen women perhaps, at the Rue des M**l**s — but certainly not more, for my stay was limited to a few days — and came on then to England. If I had women on my return I have no memoranda about them — and am under the impression that I had one of the short fits of virtuous abstinence which occasionally overtake me, and to which I attribute having kept my health so well, amidst so much fucking. Then, two or three little lasses fell to my prick, in the most unexpected, exciting, and delightful way — but this result was no doubt owing to a predilection which had been growing on me. — It is by setting one's mind steadily on the object, that so many chances have been found and utilized by me — but how comes it that letches for this and that seem at times to seize me suddenly?

I have often thought since of Aunt W***t*r and her delicious cunt, and recollect that several middle aged women seem to have had the most perfect voluptuous cuntal grip of my prick, spite of the seeming capaciousness of their vaginas. Is it that their cunts grow fat inside, as they increase in flesh generally? — Certainly I recollect many young women, whose small, inviting looking orifices felt loose enough inside, and never gave me so much pleasure.

Aunt W***t*r was by nature lascivious. It pleased her to bathe knowing that I was looking at her, and her niece as well, — "Your seeing her won't do Amy any harm," said she laughing. I fancy they were a hot cunted family, but the demeanour of all the ladies was irreproachable, but the indifference with which an aunt and niece exposed themselves naked to each other astonished me, and their lax notions abut fucking, which the conversation between the aunt and niece disclosed, astonished me more.

CHAPTER XXIX

A letch for juveniles. — On big and little cunts. — In L**c**t*r S****e. — Polly Carter, the young boxmaker. — The brothel. — "Show us yer thing." — Willing for half a crown. — Free, easy, and lewed. — My quick spend. — Her disappointed cunt. — Remedial frig. — Hot cunted. — Her occupation and habits. — Of female box-makers. — A father eluded. — A friend's experiences. — Who first fucks poor girls.

I have now great knowledge of the full grown, full cunted, thoroughly developed woman, my taste has mainly run in their direction, but recently I thought of the younger ones, and that I should like to try those less practised in the art of love, those with forms immature, with smaller and unfledged cunts, and with less cunning and experience in the ways of men, and with a curiosity to satisfy about the male. — For all that, I continued my attentions to the more matured females, and the nascent letch for a juvenile split went into abeyance.

Again the letch for a youthful cunt came on strongly. The idea of seeing a little delicate unfledged slit between two little thighs, instead of the bushy haired, five inch, fat lipped gaps, began to give me a fever of anticipation. I hesitated still a while in procuring myself that voluptuous satisfaction. Why I can not say, but I have been subject to lustful vagaries, hesitations, diffidence and timidity, as well as rash impulses in love affairs, which I cannot account for. So irrational and contradictory at times have they been, that I have been astonished at myself, so will not seek reasons for my hesitation at this time. Moreover my numerous Paphian friends have at times told me of similar male eccentricities, so that I come to the conclusion that many men are as absurd in their behaviour. But chance brought my letch to the front, and to accomplishment.

One night towards the end of November in L**c**t*r S****e, I accosted a lass who looked between fifteen and sixteen years old. She was walking very fast, and I was not quite sure whether she was on the town or not, but know that girls out by themselves at that time at night more frequently than otherwise get their cunts filled for love or money, before they get home.

"Come with me," I said walking by the side of her. She slackened pace, but did not reply. I repeated it, she stopped, hesitated, looked at me, and replied, "I can't stop long." "You shan't, but come." In three minutes we were in a house new to me, but actually at the angle of L**c**t*r S****e, tho with a side door. — (Now covered with a fine building.)

I saw directly we were in the bedroom, that she was a work girl. — "I can't undress, it'll take me such a time to get em on agin." "Yes you must." "Just help us then, it's in a knot behind." — Off her clothes went, hurriedly. She was poorly dressed, and not too clean, I had not expected anything else. "I'll take off my boots cos they'll muddy the bed," said she in a gossiping manner, and was soon on the bed in a dirty chemise only, and was a fairly good looking, dark eyed, and very dark haired girl. I threw up her chemise, and saw a cunt quite girlish in appearance, with a little bush of short, dark hair, about as much as would cover a half crown, surrounding the top of her split, and dying away altogether a little way down the lips, which were fattish and pudgy. Whilst standing and looking at it (her thighs obligingly open without my asking), "Show us yer thing," said she. On producing it, she sat up and felt it earnestly, in quite a simple way, as if it pleased her. "Pull the skin off." I did, and she chuckled. — "Ain't it red?" "Do you want it?" "Shan't tell yer; do it sir," and she fell back laughing. Her manner was funny, lewed, but very natural, and not a bit like a harlot's. — "When were you last done?" "My last overtime night, a week ago." "Are you quite well?" I asked touching her cunt. "Oh I arn't got no illness, yer may see for yerself, sir."

I mounted her quickly, being full of sperm that night. The little cunt excited me — its tightness pleased me, tho I don't like very tight cunts generally — and her manner shewed me that she wanted it and that she was not quite a strumpet. "Let me feel it in," said she putting her little hand down between our bellies when I was up her. Then instantly with-drawing it, and oscillating pleasurably her little backside in unison with mine, all on a sudden I spent copiously in her little cunt, too quickly for my wish, but as I often have done with a fresh girl when I have been three or four days without spending previously.

"Oh go on pushing I was just a commin," said she, pee-vishly, and working her cunt up to me, but my prick shrinking rapidly, uncunted, and I turned off of her. —

"What a shame, and I was just a comin," and she began frigging herself, laying on her back, just as I had got off of her, and thighs open, my sperm oozing from it. And looking hard at me she frigged herself till she spent. There was no sham about it, she had been baulked by my rapid spend, and finished her pleasure by the aid of her fingers, looking at me, and I dare say thinking of my prick.

"It's just as nice that way," said I. "No it ain't, I likes to do it when the man does." And then she told me she worked in the city, left at six o'clock nightly unless busy, and then worked till eight o'clock for which extra she got four pence. — She went there daily unless they were short of work. — She was fifteen and a half, and had been fucked about two months, "on Michaelmas day." A lot of young girls worked in the same warehouse, and they all did it with chaps she believed, tho some of them said they didn't. One of the apprentices did it to her first. He was about sixteen and she would not let him now, they had quarrelled, "Be-sides, he never gived me nothing." — Her father knew the time she ought to be home regular, and kept her in, and gave it her pretty sharp if not home at proper time. But when she worked overtime, he didn't know exactly when she left. — "And then you get fucked." "Yes, if I'm lucky — but not often." — Yes she liked it — "It's such pleasure ain't it?" said she, looking lewed, — "but I must go."

I told her to lay still and I would fuck her if she liked but not otherwise. The edge of my lust being taken off, I could talk coolly about that hot operation, and she amused me. — "Yes, I'd like it, but what's the time?" I told her. "Well do it agin at once then." "My dear I can't yet." — She had not moved an inch during our conversation, which was nearly word for word as written, but lay with her fingers still twid-dling her wet clitoris, and my sperm showing, I leaning on my elbow laying by her side and looking at her. — It was a common baudy house where they allowed young girls to go, the light was poor, the bed dingy, the girl's stockings dirty, her chemise as bad, and my dainty prick seemed for the moment to have had enough of it.

But her youthful cunt, her evident lust, and coarse frankness made me wish for her again.

"Frig my prick up there," said I. — She laid hold of it and frigged so clumsily that her art was useless. — "It won't get stiff," said she, in a disappointed manner. "Well, you don't want it again."

"Yes I'd like it." "Well — I'll try myself," and I knelt between her thighs, pulled open her cunt lips and looked at the thick libation which bedewed its surface, all the time asking her questions about her sensations, and frigging myself briskly. As I did all this I stiffened, forgot about dirty bed, chemise, and stockings, and was soon covering her little belly with mine, and churning up my spunk in her tight little cunt, till the grip of it fetched me, and she spent demonstratively with me. Didn't the young bitch like it?

We washed. Then I put her on the bed and looked at the clean little quim and paid her. She would meet me the next night at the same time, and would buy a clean pair of stockings (I gave her the money for them as I have done a dozen girls), she had none at home clean and she dare not put on a clean chemise till Sunday, her mother would know why if she did. — She reminded me much in her little dodges, and her talk, of yellow haired Kitty whom I knew some years ago, but Kitty was a lady naturally — this one a coarse little bitch — and as hot arsed as ginger.

The first thing she did the next evening when I met her, was to put on the clean stockings before me, and when we had finished love making, she took them off — her mother must not know of them. She had evidently made some attempt to get herself clean and better dressed. — "Yours is a beautiful cock," said she, as she felt it clumsily. — I fucked her twice to her great pleasure. "Oh ain't it nice a doing it," and we parted. There would be no late work the next night she said, there might be next week, her father knew sometimes for he worked in the city too, and sometimes he called at the warehouse to know if his girl was going to work late, he thought to catch her out, but didn't always. She grinned as she told me. Nothing but locking a girl up in a room by herself will prevent her getting fucked, if she means it; and the opportunities of doing it among the humbler classes are hourly — as I know pretty well. You may get any of them, if you don't mind your time and money. — Well — it is what the two sexes were all made for, — to give pleasure to each other.

Then she told me she would be at half past six o'clock in ***** on other nights, that it took her exactly half an hour to walk there. — They left off work as it struck six, and at a quarter to seven if she wasn't in doors, her father "larruped" her, unless she could tell why. Her name was Polly Carter.

My friend L***s has often told me that he has picked up half a dozen virgins in the streets. That a sovereign, offered to lasses looking in at a Linen-drapers, will get them to a house, and that the sight of the gold vanquishes them. He looks out for them quite young, for that turned sixteen they are scarcely ever virgins. He thinks from a large acquaintance with these youthful strums, that their cousins and friends (all boys — mere street boys of their own age), get the virginities for nothing, and before the girls are fifteen years old.

Few of the tens of thousands of whores in London gave their virginities either to gentlemen, or to young, or old men — or to men at all. Their own low class lads had them. The street boys' dirty pricks went up their little cunts first. — This is greatly to be regretted, for street boys cannot appreciate the treasures they destroy. A virginity taken by a street boy of sixteen, is a pearl cast to a swine. Any cunt is good enough for such inexperience. — To such an animal, a matron of fifty or sixty would give him as much, if not more pleasure than a virgin. I am sure of this even from my own experience, for I cared nothing whatever about the virginities I took early in my life. It was cunt alone I cared about, and any cunt for my pleasure then was good enough.

CHAPTER XXX

Big-eyed Betsy Johnson. — Early acquaintance. —
Brothels closed. — Ten years later. — It's you Betsy! —
Her huge nymphœ. — Protuberant eyes. — Witty
baudiness. — My erotic requests. — Her help. —
With Betsy and a man. — Hesitations. — His
offers. — I frig him. — His arsehole offered. — No
erection available. — Pestles and bumholes. — Spunk
and a toothpick. — I poke Betsy. — His thumb on my
bum.

[Before I tell about my acquaintance with this woman, — I
must recall some facts to explain how that acquaintance was
first made.

The London public had a fit of virtue to which it is subject
periodically. It commenced a crusade against gay women,
and principally those frequenting Regent and Coventry
Streets, and others in that neighbourhood. Many nice, quiet
accommodation houses were closed, and several nice gay
women whom I frequented disappeared. Indeed, for a time,
the police were set on with all their brutality. Women by
dozens were taken before magistrates ruthlessly, and altho
mostly cautioned and set at liberty, some were imprisoned;
and the effect was, that for a short time the streets named,
and a few others, were all but cleared of gay women.

Among the women who disappeared was one named
Betsy Johnson, a lovely little creature under twenty, and in
the perfection of her youth. Just before she disappeared, she
said one night to me in her jocular way — "Fucking is done
for here except for love, so I shall take to washing for my
living." — She disappeared, and I was now to meet her
again some nine or ten years after.]

It was in the middle of November, and but about a month
only after I had said good bye to Rosa W***e. — I was
walking along the Strand, one very nasty, muddy, dank, dark
night. The whores were lifting up their petticoats, partly to
escape the mud, but more I expect to show their legs, as
high as they dare, and I was gazing on them with pleasure,

my wind wandering from their legs to their backsides. I passed a female nearly, then stopped — as I seemed to recognize an old carnal acquaintance.

"Why, it's you Betsy." — I turned round, and passed into a side street, followed by the female. "I don't recollect you, yet I know the voice," said she. — I made myself known. Several years had passed since I had seen her. It was Betsy Johnson, whom I had fucked just after she had turned gay, and at about the time I was in love with Sarah Mavis, and had quarrelled with her.

Betsy was a middle-sized female, but her plumpness and roundness were delicious. Her form was lovely then. She had a delicious skin, as smooth as ivory, fine chestnut hair, the same color on her cunt hair, of which she hadn't much. She had two defects. Her eyes were excessively prominent, the clitoris was large, and the nymphæ very large. They hung out when first I knew her, and when she was not twenty years old, full half an inch below the outer lips, and for the entire length of the split. — I did not like that, yet I used to have her, for she was so beautiful in form, so smooth in skin, and fucked so divinely and her cunt fitted me heavenly. She was the wittiest woman of her class I ever met — it was good neat wit — and baudy wit as well at times, for she was fond of baudiness — She enjoyed it. She at that time took a fancy to me, but I did not return it — tho I saw her once or so, when I quarrelled with Sarah, as to the best of my recollection I have already narrated.

We went to a house and she stripped. She was as beautifully shaped as ever — but her genital deformity had increased. — The nymphæ hung down outside the cunt lips, I am sure one inch and a half along her whole split. — We had a long conversation about it and I told her of women having them cut off, I had read of that being done. — She was immensely interested in that, and also had heard of its being done. — She must muster up courage to have them cut, she said. — Men, she was sure, didn't like those flaps — tell her, "Did they?" — Since she had been back in London, she could not secure any regular friends, and kept very poor. "These precious nymphæ must be the cause, they do not please I expect."

She was always lascivious. — "Your fucking is delicious, me dear. You still do it well." — On my preparing to leave. "Why sure, and you're not going after doing it once, and all these years since I've seen you? — I recollect you, when I had to tell you you had done enough for your money. — Ah, I'm older, but sugar me if you go yet," — said she, clutching hold of my prick. So we fucked again, and again, for I could not resist her. — "You'll go home straight me dear tonight, won't you, a fresh cunt won't make it stand again, till you've laid on your back a little, and filled your belly with grub, me dear." — "Won't you see me again?" "Perhaps." — "Ah," said she reflectingly. "You don't like me, I'll go back to S***b**ry. I'm not getting on here — whoring is not my game now." — She was one of those who boldly spoke of whoring for her living — I did not like that. — "Why, it's what it is, isn't it?" she had said when I checked her for her plain speaking.

I did see her again, but her large flapping nymphæ rather turned my lust off. I wanted to go to her rooms. — "You can't, it would horrify you," said the poor woman. — "You see, I've only a gown and chemise on — it's all I've got, but I must show my legs nice." — "My legs are my fortune sir," she said. — She had a lovely leg still, and had silk stockings on, and nice boots, tho almost without under-clothing. "I sleep on the floor on a mattress, there is no bedstead, only a mattress, a table, and a jerry in the room, that's all. I've not even a blind, me darling." — She was not Irish, but affected the brogue.

When we were parting, "Can I do anything for you?" — she asked — what she meant I didn't exactly know, but chaffingly I replied. — "Yes, Betsy. Get me a nice young cunt without a bit of hair on it — and a man to frig." "Och, yer baste, is it a young cunt yer wants, — not for Joseph. But I'll get you a man easy enough if you mean it." — "I do," said I — suddenly thinking I should. — "Well, there are plenty of them." — "But in your room." — "Impossible, you and the sod too, would not stop in it five minutes." When I told her those wants, I didn't mean what I said, but at a subsequent meeting *she* suggested them, and it ended in my arranging to meet her with a man, and we were to go to his rooms together two or three days after, for she had stimulated my curiosity.

I met them in S**o S****e. — He took off his hat respectfully. — "Go ahead, and I'll follow," said I, and on they both went. — She then fell back — I was nervous and told her so. "If I go with you and him is all square?" — "It's all safe, but mind he shan't touch me, he shan't fuck me if that's what you mean — I can't bear the beasts." — "All right, go on, I only want to see what a man of this sort is like." — On the two went, crossed O*f**d St., to a long street, out of which turning up a paved court, he opened with a latch key a door and up we all well went to a first floor over a shop, and into a well furnished sitting-room, and bed-room. As we entered she again fell back, and whispered, — "Mind he don't touch me." — "All right, but no plant Betsy, eh?" — "All square, my pet." — It was a dark night, and I was awfully nervous, but an extraordinary curiosity was on me. I wondered if it was great pleasure to bugger — Betsy had said that men had told her it was.

At last then, the erotic caprice, which I been thinking of at intervals for years, a caprice which had subsided, been forgotten, but from time to time been roused by the sights through key holes, and peep holes, of couples fucking: a ca-price which had got strength, by each succeeding prick I had seen, and specially by the big furnished young man, whom I last saw (poking his wife at Paris) was to be gratified — I had overcome all scruples, and satisfied myself that there was no more harm in feeling another's prick, than in feeling my own. — There was the man before me, on whom I might satisfy all my curiosity — and yet I began to tremble. — Once indeed on the road I stopped Betsy, and said I should not go home with them — but on her laughing at me, I per-severed.

Indeed my heart had palpitated so violently as I followed them, and I felt so afraid of what I was doing, that once I thought of running away — (I have, since that time, had a similar fear) — Pride, bravado, and the curiosity of handling another man's prick, of seeing his emotions in spending, kept me going. — It was nothing but curiosity, for I never liked a man even about me. — But to frig one! — Ah! So many years had elapsed since I had done that, that I seemed to have forgotten all about it.

We went into the bed-room together. She stayed in the sitting-room. — "She is better there," said he. — "Let's see your prick," I said as soon as I had a little overcome my tremor. — He pulled it out, it looked small. I touched it with a sort of dislike. — "Are you fond of a bit of brown?" — he asked. — I did not understand and he explained. — "We al-ways say a bit of brown among ourselves, and a cunt's a bit of red." — I had a feeling of nausea, but went on. —"Let's frig you." — He took off all but his shirt, and seating him on my knee I began to frig him. He questioned me whilst doing so — had I been up a man? — "No." — Then there was no pleasure like it. — I frigged violently but his prick would not stand, I talked baudy and about women. He said "A bit of brown is worth a hundred cunts." I felt quite disconcerted, for his cock remained small and flabby. I had thought that talking about cunts would stiffen it.

The conversation, then led by him, took an arsehole turn. — He asked me to let him feel my bumhole. — I consented. - In for a penny, in for a pound, I began to think. Taking down my trowsers, he looked at my bum, and his prick stood at the sight. "Is it virgin?" said he, and felt it. — Then, standing by my side, my left arm round his waist to steady me, I frigged him, and the little bugger spent, but a very little. I rushed to wash my hand.

When he had composed himself, he washed his tool, and became very curious about me, and most energetically felt *my* prick. — "Put it up me," — said he. — "I can't, my prick won't stand." — "Shall I suck it?" — "You?" — "Yes." — "Do you do so?" — "Lord yes, I have had it so thick in my mouth, that I've had to pit it out of my teeth with a tooth-pick." — I turned sick, but after a time I turned his arse to-wards me, and got my prick stiff by hard frigging, determined to try what buggery was like. But the moment I put it against his arsehole down it drooped — He was kneeling at the side of the bed. — "Wet it well with your spittle," said he, wetting his own hole. — It was useless, and I desisted. — "You will presently," he remarked. — But tho I tried again and again, determined to know everything, and to do everything once in my life, it was useless.

Then he went to a drawer, and produced a small marble pestle such as chemists use, and asked me to let him put it up my bum, extolling the pleasure I should have. — "It must hurt," I said. — "Oh dear no, look." — Going to the side of the bed, he laid down, and cocking up his legs, shoved it up his own arsehole a little way. — That only made me feel more sick, I was so unsophisticated in such matters. I expect he saw that, for he took it out. But then he produced two more of different sizes, one quite a large one, and told me there was a friend he visited every week, who met him in his stables, and he put the larger one up his fundament. — That man said it was not large enough to give him pleasure. "I put it up him to there" said the sodomite marking with his thumb the spot on the pestle. But the description made me feel more modest. — "You should have the small one up

[285]

first, I will do it for you, and I know such a sweet young man who would suck your prick at the same time if you would like." — "Oh, no." — "Do let me sod you," — said he all at once and quite affectionally, "I should so like to do it to you and take your virginity," and he shook his prick, and frigged it a little. — It was not stiff, and was very sharp pointed, but not at all a large one.

I was now quite flabbergasted. His coolness and his tale of picking his teeth free of semen, made me actually shudder. — Then the pestles. — Fancy two men together in a stable, one shoving a pestle up the other's bum. — How curious I thought, yet how abominable — it's incredible. Yet still I felt curious. — "Does it make him spend?" I asked — "His prick stands after I have worked it up and down in the brown for a while, then I go on gently, and suck his prick, till he spends," — he replied coolly.

Again I frigged him, curious to see his emotions, and watched his face when with difficulty he spent slightly. — But my cock would not stand. — So I went into the room to Betsy, determined to try her cunt. — She had been, she told me afterwards, looking thro, and listening at the door all the time. "Don't come near me," said she to to the sod. — After much ado she made my cock stand, I mounted her, and fucked, feeling his prick whilst I did so — that either suggested itself to me, or he suggested it — and it seemed to increase my pleasure.

Then as I rammed up Betsy's cunt, I became conscious he was feeling me behind, and that his thumb or finger was intruding into my bum hole. — "Feel her brown," said he. — I was in the height of my pleasure. "You beast," said Betsy. — Whether I obeyed his advice or not, I can't say. I spent, and fetched her, and then we quickly parted. — I gave him a sovereign, no more, and her two, before each other. — They made no remark. — I promised to see him again, but had no intention of doing so, and never did.

I met her soon afterwards, and she was curious. "Did his arse-hole seem large?" I was unable to tell her, disliked even to refer to it, yet my curiosity seemed unsatisfied and I had a sort of desire to learn more, yet a dislike to myself for desiring it. — When she asked me if she should get him again, I refused point blank, yet all the time longing to try, and dissatisfied at not having put my prick up him, to see if it gave some unknown pleasure or not.

[286]

CHAPTER XXXI

A little virgin wanted. — One found. — At J***s St.
with her. — Another Molly. — Betsy's baudy antics. —
Molly modest, stripped, and liquored up. — Pitching
shillings at cunts. — Molly refuses my amatory
advances. — Betsy's threats. — Molly's virginity
verified. — All three on the bed. — Molly refuses me. —
Betsy's rage. — My prick up Betsy temporarily. —
Molly convinced. — I mount her. — A wriggler and
screecher. — The bed pillow employed. — Stroke
number one. — The bloody sequel.

I spoke to Betsy again about an unfledged virgin cunt. —
She shook her head — did not know where to get one — the
boys had all the girls when quite young. — Didn't she know
what games boys and girls were up to when quite young. —
She had lived at ***** — and there was not there a girl over
fourteen who had not had it done to her — and by the
boys — boys not men — and in the fields, tho sometimes at
home. I had heard similar accounts from women years before, and believed her. — "I'll get you half a dozen little
ones without hair, but they all know as much as I do about
fucking." — That offer I declined, for I knew there were
plenty like that about the streets, whom I could get without
her assistance. — "A virgin, a virgin, and with no hair on
her cunt, or nothing." — Well, she would if she could, but
she shook her head. — Her last words were, "Just a little
hair on it you wouldn't mind, would you?" — "Perhaps if
only just shewing, but mind, I'll have a good look at her
cunt, with thighs open, before I have her. No virgin, no pay.
I won't be gammoned." — "All right, me dear, but you'll
have to wait pretty long."

I met Betsy a little time afterwards by mere chance, and
was going to pass her, but somehow she recognized me and
touched me on the elbow, saying hastily, — "Come here,
come here, I've been looking for you for a week." — We
turned up a side street. — "Oh, if you mean it, I think I've
got such a nice girl for you, but I shall run a risk." — We

had a long conversation, I gave her money to make presents to the girl, and some for herself, but not much. — "I think she will, but if I can't get her, I can't, and then you'll think I've chiselled you." — "No I shan't," and we parted.

I looked for Betsy and a few days after saw her. — "She's a virgin," — said she, "but I don't see my way to it yet." — "Ah, the old game." — "Thought you'd say so, you old fox." — Betsy tried hard to make me go to a house with her, but I would not, tho I made her again a little present, and agreed also the price for her services if they were of use. — "I fear I can't manage it," said she, "tho she is a randy little bitch, and is longing to know what fucking is like, the boys have felt her cunt and she their pricks — she's told me so — ah! she is a regular hot-arsed one, and *you* may as well have her whilst she's got it to give, and you'll give me the money on the night you have her first?" — "Yes, if she be a virgin, not otherwise, and I'll see her cunt well before I do her." — "All right, you old fox, she was a virgin last night, I'll take my oath."

More than a week passed. Then I looked out for and saw Betsy. — I passed her, touched her lightly, said "hish" — and passed on, turning up the next convenient by street. — Betsy followed me and began breathless. — "Oh! It's such a chance, — I've walked up and down here for three nights, and never left the street till midnight, nor left with a man, for fear of missing you."

"She *is* a virgin." — Then she told me that the lass had only the signs of hair on her cunt. — Yes, she had seen her cunt, and had looked at it well. — "Yes — wide — wide open — and you can scarcely get your little finger up the hole, me dear — it's just large enough to let her monthlies through — and she's only had her monthlies twice, —you've got a rare chance — and such a plump, fine, little divel, I'd like to do her myself. But give me a sovereign to rig her out, you'd like to see her look nice. Honor bright — did I ever deceive you? Oh no, not next week, meet us tomorrow night, don't lose a night, or you may miss your chance, she has been sleeping with me three nights, and I don't let her out of my sight. She is such a hot-cunted little devil, that God knows what she'll be up to. — I'll give her boots and stockings, and say you sent the money for them — and you tell her you'll give her a silk dress — and a crinoline —don't forget the crinoline, she is mad for one (they were just in fashion), you'll be pleased, she is as well shaped as I am. — I'm only frightened they won't let her in the house, but they know you well there in J***s St., and that's a good deal. — If they do object you must come to my garret, tho I fear they'd hear us there." — Thus she talked on energetically, without stopping, and saw her ten pounds almost in her pocket.

Next night was dark and cold, and they met me in L**c**t*r S****e. — The girl looked young and a little object. — Betsy told me to say the girl had been in with me before if they objected. — We entered. The door sounded the warning click. I went in first, feeling a little nervous, and had gone up a few stairs, when the door-woman said, — "She can't go in Miss, I can't let her — she is very young." — "Oh, she's not young at it — she has been half a dozen times before with me and my friend — hasn't she sir? — For she is sixteen, tho she looks so young," said Betsy in a low tone.

"She looks very young," said the woman hesitating and standing at the door. I turned round. "It's all right, she's been in here with me before, why object now?" — "She looks very young," the woman said again — just then another couple pushed open the street door. — "Go on, go on," — said the woman — "first floor front," and up Betsy and the young one came with me. — The door-keeper was anxious to get us out of sight of the couple just entering, they helped to settle the question.

The woman soon followed us into the room, and staring hard at the young one, — "If it's all right, I've nothing to say," said she. I put a sovereign into her hand. "We shall stop all night." "Two ladies, sir." I gave her another, shut the door in her face, and bolted it. — Betsy winked at me. "I knew she would if you spoke, and you've stumped up handsome." I had indeed, and had never been charged for two ladies before in that house.

Betsy had made up the girl in the oddest way with a big bonnet, and she looked almost a bundle of clothes too big for her. — It was an error in the disguise I saw at a glance. — But there we were, all three snugly in the best room in the house. Betsy pulled off her bonnet and shawl as quickly as possible. Then she pulled a great shawl off the little one, and a bonnet big enough for a grenadier, and I saw a lovely girl of about fifteen, looking up earnestly from rather deep-set eyes. — "This is the friend who sent you the

[289]

boots and stockings, and he'll give you a lovely crinoline," said Betsy. — "Won't you, sir?" — "Yes," — said I.

I stood staring with delight, whilst Betsy undressed both of them in an agitated manner. First she pulled off her own gown — then the girl's. — Then she stripped herself to her chemise, then the girl. — When the girl was in her chemise, Betsy pulled her slap down on the sofa, and putting her hands under charming plump, little breasts — "Ain't they a pretty pair," said she — "and, oh! she has such a fat bum, and pretty little cunt." — She lifted the chemise, and the girl pushed it down. — She had never taken her eyes off me, nor I off her. "Don't, Betsy." — "Don't you be a little fool, look here," — and Betsy throwing up her own chemise, rolled back on the sofa, threw up her legs; opened her thighs well, and pulled her cunt lips wide open. — "There, look at that, me dear — there's a sight for a stiff prick." — "Oh! — Oh! Betsy, don't," — said the girl. — "Didn't we do so last night my dear." — "Oh, not before a man," — said the girl, colouring up and trying to pull Betsy's chemise down. — "Don't — for shame." — "Shan't — Pough — all my eye, Molly — show him yours." — "Shan't — you're dirty." — "Didn't we look at each other's last night, Molly?" — "Not before a man — don't now, Betsy. — Oh, don't before him." — It was said quite naturally.

But Betsy pulled right off her own chemise, turned to the girl, and in a jiffy had pulled hers off also. — There they were, both naked except their boots and stockings. Then with a laugh, she threw herself back on the sofa, and pulled her cunt lips open again — calling on Molly to do the same. The girl stood timidly looking at me, putting one hand modestly in front of her cunt to hide it, and trying to regain the chemise, which Betsy Johnson had put under her own backside.

I sat down, pulled the little one to me, felt her pretty breasts, her plump round little bum and thighs. She all the time kept her hand in front of her sacred split. I pulled her then on to the sofa, and got my hand between her thighs, talking baudy, and kissing her. — Betsy had got up, and stood naked with her arse to the fire looking at us, letting out baudiness, and inciting the young one to comply with my wishes. — Then I pulled off my clothes to my shirt, and showed her my pego, stiff as a poker and like a burning coal.

"Oh! There's a glory," said Betsy. — "Oh, don't hide it Molly, I wish it were going up my cunt instead of yours," —

and stooping, she kissed it and pulled me towards her by it. — "Kiss it, Molly," — said she — "kiss it before it goes up you. — Oh! Wow — wow — wow" — and she put my prick in her mouth till it was nearly out of sight. The little one stared. "Oh, ain't you dirty?" — "Dirty, you little fool — a prick's nice wherever you put it, nice anyhow, and anywhere. — You'll think so before a week — you'll be ready to eat one a week after it's been up your cunt, Molly." — "Oh — oh," and she went on putting it in and out of her mouth, and kissing it down to my testicles.

I sat down again, got the little one on my naked thigh, and put her little fist round my prick. — Betsy keeping up her baudy patter all the time. Then I pulled the little one to me, her legs apart, mine between them, and my pego rubbed between her plump thighs. I grasped her plump little bum, and kissed her, whilst she kept struggling — mildly tho — "Oh, don't now — oh, Betsy — don't let him — it's dirty — don't" — and so on. Then I got out wine and liqueur which I had brought with me. — There was only a water tumbler in the room, and we all three drank out of it. I would not ring for glasses lest the servant should come in, and see the youth of the lass. The liquor was nice to her for she drank freely, became talkative, and laughed. — Up to that time she had, tho tolerably passive under my handlings, looked scared and fixedly at me, only uttering, "Oh Betsy, don't do so — Oh, I'm — astonished." — Now she was more at home. —

I delighted in talking to her — anticipating the delight to follow. — "You've never had any man's hand between your thighs, have you dear?" — "No sir." "And never put your finger up your cunt?" — "Lord," said Betsy, "you could not get your finger up it. I tried the other night, didn't I Molly?" — "No." — "Oh, you little liar. — I did and I showed her the difference, and told her she couldn't have any pleasure till her hole was as large as mine, and she put her fingers up mine to feel." — "Oh — o-oh — o-oh Betsy, I didn't." — "You did, you little fool, you got your hand nearly up it." "Oh, you beast, you said you hoped you might be struck dead if you told of me," — said the young one, looking quite aghast. — Betsy laughed. — "I said any other girl but not a man, it don't matter to him. — He's a man and going to make your cunt like mine. — Oh, won't your little hot arse shake, where his balls are close up to it. — You'll bless me tomorrow, when you get your new dress and crinoline — and you'll be asking him to put his prick into you again and again."

"Let's look at your cunt Molly," said I, trying. I threw her on her back on the sofa and knelt down in front. She resisted vigorously. Betsy caught hold of her arms and pulled her back, whilst I pushed her legs wide open — the little pink gash widened, but I could not in the struggle and excitement satisfy my curiosity, so desisted for a while. We then drank and talked more, till my lust made me furious to begin.

What strange whims and caprices I have had with women, and usually quite impromptu. I wonder if other men have suddenly thought of such amusements and tricks. — I now had one. I took some shillings out of my pocket, and sitting down on the floor with my back to the fire, — "Open your legs wide Betsy," said I, "as you sit on the sofa, and I'll throw shillings at your cunt. Every time I hit between its lips, the shilling is yours — if I miss, I'm to have three throws more with it and then it's yours." — Betsy screamed with laughter, brought up both heels to the level of her buttocks on the sofa, and spread out her thighs, shewing a wide split, that a half crown could have gone into. I pitched the shillings at her cunt — one on two hit it, and she made Molly pick them up. — The girl stood looking at me — then at Betsy, and repeating, "Well, you *are* dirty," astonishment in her eyes, manner, and voice, but she picked up the shillings fast enough — and gave them either to me or Betsy as she was told. — At length she laughed, and hid her face with her hand. — "Oh, ain't he one," said she.

"Let's throw at yours, my darling," said I. — "Let him," said Betsy, "or I shall have all the shillings." — The girl hollowed, refused, resisted, till Betsy lost her temper, so we had more wine. At length, "Now I'm going to look at your cunt." The wench was now well warmed by wine, baudy conversation, and tricks, yet still there was delay, and she refused. — Betsy said she was not going to be fooled — what she had come to do, she would have to do. — She might go away if she would not. — Go and get a lodging where she could. — "Lay on the steps all night if you like, you shan't come home with me — and *you know*," she said in a significant tone to the girl, which I did not then understand. — With a little more persuasion, the naked lass laid on her back on the edge of the bed, her legs hanging down. — It was at the side of the bed away from the gas, Betsy had pushed her on that side of the bed.

For half a minute I gazed at her with delight as she lay with wonderfully large thighs, and legs, and would never have believed her youth, had it not been for the hairless cunt, and youthful face. She was country born, she had said, and early used to work in the fields, such work soon develops the form, and hence her beauty, but I soon began my investigation into her virginity.

I had doubted Betsy, and thought she was going to sell me about the virginity, spite of her protestations, and spite of my telling her that if not satisfied, I would only give her the price of a fuck of herself, and a little present to the girl: and knowing the room and the way the furniture was placed, and where the gas was, this now occurred to me again. I had to prevent my being cheated, and to get a good look, brought a candle with me which I now lighted, and stood by the side of the bed, — Betsy close to me. — I took one of the girl's legs, Betsy the other. — "Open your thighs and let him look, you said you would — you promised me you would — there's a darling," said she.

The girl's legs opened wide — I gave Betsy the candle, and with the vacant hand pulled open wide the lips of the little cunt, which was of a delicate pink, with the slightest signs of dark hair just on the mons. — Excited as I was, and with a prick throbbing as if it would burst, or spend without a touch, I saw that the cunt had never had anything larger than a finger up it. With an impulse I have always had with hairless cunts, I put my mouth to it, and gave it a little lick. — Such a mouthful of saliva came, and ran out of my mouth at once. — The girl struggled as she felt my tongue, and closed her thighs on my head. The spittle had covered her cunt — I threw off my shirt, pushed Molly straight on the bed, got on it by the side of her, and Betsy got on the other side.

But she would not let me mount her. In vain Betsy coaxed and bullied by turns. — "No — no," — she had altered her mind. — She was frightened — it would hurt, that great thing would hurt her, — it would make her bleed. — Then she burst into tears and cried. I desisted, Betsy quieted her, for fear of the people of the house, and when she had done she spoke to her in a subdued voice as nearly as possible thus.

"You bloody little fool. I had pricks up me twice as big as that, and longer than his, before I was your age — don't I get a living by fucking? — Don't I get silk stockings and dresses by fucking? — How are you going to live? — Who's going to keep you, I want to know? — What did you come here for? — Didn't you promise me? — Didn't you say you'd let him? — Didn't you say you'd like to be fucked if it was nicer than frigging yourself?"

The girl made no reply, and was confused and shaking. "All right, you may go, and you may get home as you can," — saying that, she jumped off the bed and rolled up in a bundle the girl's chemise and petticoat, which were quite new. — "You shan't have the things I've given you, damned if you shall." Then she came to the bed, violently pulled off from the girl both boots and stockings, and rolled up the stockings with the petticoat. — "Now you may go — put on your dress and your boots, and go, you're not wanted here, my friend and I will stop all night."

The girl looked scared out of her senses. "Don't Betsy, where am I to go to?" — "Go to Hell and buggery, go and shit yourself, I don't care a bloody fart where you go to." — The girl blubbered and sobbed out, — "I will then, I will let him." — "Hold your snivelling, and don't make that noise. — Someone's at the door perhaps, — let him do it to you, — if you don't — go — and you know. — You know what," — and Betsy, tho slanging in the foulest way (and I have not told a quarter what she said), — did it all in a suppressed voice.

I got on to the bed again. So did Betsy, who helped the girl to her old place. Again the girl said she should be hurt and refused. — "You do it Betsy, with him — you let him do it." — "Lord," said Betsy, who had recovered her temper, "he may fuck me till his spunk come up into my mouth if he likes — show her how to do it — let's have a fuck, my dear," — and she winked at me — "show her how it's done, and then she will let you, won't you Molly" — Molly made no reply.

I knelt between Betsy's legs naked, with prick stiff, dropped on to her, and put my prick up her — "There, feel, Molly." — She took hold of the girl's hand and guided it between our bellies. — "Feel, his prick's right up — turn a little on the side," said she to me. — We did, keeping copulated. When her arse was a little turned towards Molly, she threw one thigh high up over my hips so that the girl could see the prick as it lay squeezed into Betsy's cunt — "Look under, look Molly — look there, nothing but his balls to see, is there." — The girl put her head down, and curious, touched my balls. — "Oh fuck, fuck, isn't it lovely my darling," said Betsy.

We turned flat again and Betsy began fucking and heaving in earnest. She thought she was going to have the treat for she wanted it. — But I slipped my prick out of her cunt, tho I kept on ramming and driving, as if I was going to fuck her backside up to her blade bones. — "Sham," — I whispered. — Betsy, tho disappointed, took the hint, and we heaved and pushed together, my prick now outside her, and at length screaming out, "Fuck — cunt. — Oh, lovely — ah my spunk's — coming — oh, push hard — dear — fuck — fuck." — We both shammed ecstatic pleasure and sunk quietly down, whilst the lass sitting up naked on the bed by our side, looked at us all the while intently.

"Let him now do it to you," — said Betsy, again coaxing and threatening Molly. — My prick had drooped, just as the girl at last allowed me to get between her thighs — but it sprung up stiff directly I dropped on to her. I worked cunningly, rubbing the tip just outside till I had lodged it. She trembled. I pressed her, and gave a tremendous thrust, and was on the right road. — "Oho — hah — ar," — she screamed — "You hurt — get off — I won't let you — har." — She screeched loudly, and struggled violently. "Hish, you damned howling little bitch," said Betsy, pushing a pillow right over the girl's head. I pressed my head on the pillow, the girl's head was hidden from me, but I could hear her cry. — I had not got up her, was funky about the noise we were making, but in the excitement thought only of my work. — "Hish, they will hear," were the last words I heard Betsy say. — Then I felt my sperm was coming, and with a violent effort, and grasping the fat little buttocks like a vice — my prick went up her, leaving my sperm all the way up as I entered. I felt the tightening of her hymen round my prick, as it went through it with a cunt-splitting thrust.

It was all over in a minute. Then, "Oh, don't," — I heard in muffled tones. — "Have you done her?" — said Betsy. — "Y — hes — y — hes." — She pulled away the pillow, and there I lay with the little naked one palpitating, but quiet in my arms, my prick up to its roots in her. I kept it there, tho it was shrinking, but I kept on gently thrusting, just enough to keep it half stiff. Then I partially withdrew it, the girl winced and murmured. — "Oh, take it out, you do hurt," that stiffened me quite. — "I am fucking again. — I shall spend again," — I said to Betsy, who turned on her side to see better, and in a few minutes of exquisitely prolonged pleasures — I spermatized again the little virgin quim.

[It is the last time but one or two that I recollect doing so without uncunting, for I am approaching a time of life, which makes a pause between fucks usual with me.]

I rose on my knees, and looked at the girl, who lay quite quiet with her thighs wide open, and her hand over her face. — A bloodier mass of spunk I never saw on a cunt. — Her blood had run down on to the counterpane, and lay in a red rim all around my prick near to its root. I was delighted beyond measure. She bled more than any virginity of her age which I ever yet have had, I think.

Betsy chuckled. — "Well, Moll — you've been fucked and no mistake, ain't you? — How do you like it? — It didn't hurt you, did it?" — The girl made no reply, but lay with her nice round thighs wide open, her eyes covered with the back of one hand. — Betsy got off the bed and put a towel under Molly's buttocks and thighs. "You've spent enough and you have spoiled the counterpane." — The girl closed her legs on the towel, turned on one side, and began to cry. Betsy pulled her up and gave me the towel. I wiped my prick, and we all three got up — the girl ceased crying, and then sat on the sofa naked, in front of the fire; and we began drinking again.

Our talk was all about fucking, and we chaffed the former virgin, who sat without answering in a meditative way, seemingly wondering and upset by what had taken place. — At length, looking at Betsy. — "What will mother do if she finds it out?" she said. — "Find it out, how is she to find it out? — You won't tell her, and she does not look at your cunt, does she?" — "She might find it out." — "You little fool, she can't — and if she asks you, tell her to ax your pooper — and come to me, I will get you on to earn your living." — "She might find it out, tho," said the girl, giving her head a hard shake, and looking at the fire and as if speaking to herself. — "Say it's one of the boys in the court who did it, but I'll tell you what to say tomorrow," said Bet.

Betsy had had so much liquor that she was very jolly. The girl was on the sofa between us, when Bet put her hand across and began frigging my cock. "Is the next for her?" said she. — "Look Molly, that's what did it — isn't it nice? — Tell us how does it feel when it's up you? — It didn't hurt you, did it?" — "It hurts me now," said Molly sullenly. — "Wash it, Molly." — I would not hear of that, — I wanted her as she was, I liked to see the bloody smears on her belly and thighs, and know her cunt was full of my semen. "Don't you want to piddle?" — "Yes," said the girl in a whisper. — "Do it then." — "I shan't" — "Why you little fool, you must, we'll all go to bed directly, and you must before you go to sleep. I'm not going to bed with you, unless you do, you'll be pissing over us in the night." — The girl piddled, singing out — "ooooho" in a whisper, as the piddle I suppose touched the torn edges of her virginity.

CHAPTER XXXII

A Rotterdam saloon. — A flaxen-haired North Hollander. — The young Englishman. — An Amsterdam bitch. — A difficult poke and queer cunt. — A Dutch sailor's whore. — Polyglot baudiness. — A pomatum pot. — At B***s**s. — Mrs. W***t*r again. — Acquaintance renewed. — A shallow cupboard. — A cough and a fart. — Four brothels and eight whores. — A larkish maid-servant. — Unsuccessful attempts.

I went on the continent, whilst the weather was yet cold. I saw the dancing rooms at Rotterdam, and poor and cheap as they were, had two or three of the women at them. I had one, really a fine, tall, beautiful woman with flaxen hair, and who wore large silver ornaments like shields, or saucers, on each of her temples. Her flesh was beautifully white — I was cunt-struck and had her within a few minutes after I had entered the saloon, and felt ashamed of going out of the room with her as other couples did with women. But no one seemed to notice the couples retiring, tho all knew what they left the room for. The ladies returned generally alone, the men after their love-making usually going off by a side door, tho I have seen a man and woman come back into the saloon together, tho every one must have well known what they had been doing upstairs.

I didn't like her flaxen-haired motte, it was never a colour

I liked, yet I hadn't left the house a quarter of an hour, when I took a fancy to return to the saloon, and there was the North Hollander, dancing with quite a handsome English youth, well dressed, and seemingly not more than eighteen years old. In another minute he had retired with her, and in about ten minutes more I should think, she returned to the dancing room. She had been fucked, and had cunt-washed in that short space of time. The idea (and what a strange idea it seemed to me) of putting my prick into her after the handsome youth, gave me a cock-stand, and just then noticing me, she came smiling and sat herself by the side of me. At once filled with lust I went upstairs with her again. There I began to wonder at myself, and thought I would leave, but a curiosity sprang up in me about his cock, and in German I asked her if she'd been fucked since I had left her half an hour before.

She said "No." — Then I told her what I had seen, whereat she laughed, and acknowledged it was true. I asked questions about him. His prick was big, "Big, and oh! So stiff." He would not wait till she took off her clothes, but put her on bed-side, his prick went up, and almost directly he spent. — I was specially curious then. — "Ach Gott — he spent wonderful. — Ach Gott, drowned was mine cunt with it, he, was ein English Män."

Then I looked at her flaxen-haired slit, and to make sure of its being free from his sperm, made her wash it well out before me, and then I entered it again and enjoyed her, thinking of his prick having rubbed where mine was rubbing. What strange fancies come into my head now! They never used to run so much on the male, but they seem to do so more, since Betsy Johnson got me the sod — I should like to feel another, and one with a big prick I begin to think. And what harm can there be in doing so?

At Amsterdam I went to the best baudy house, which faced one of the canals, and saw a consequential bitch, who began bargaining with me before I had felt her garters even. To satisfy her I gave her about five times what I had given at Rotterdam, and paid down. Then she shammed modesty till I lost my temper, for I know when a regular whore does that, she is a humbug, and has something to hide. I went in my anger to the door to leave, but calling out for the baud to tell her. That brought the bitch to her senses. Taking about ten minutes to do it, she undressed, and a poor, skinny, bony female she was, and one who could not put her thighs wide apart, or who would not, but I think could not. I have had several women who could not, whose thigh bones seemed nearer together than those of most women. — There seemed scarcely room for my hand between this one's thighs, as I grasped her cunt with my whole hand as I like to do.

The hair of her cunt was dark, and it had two, funny looking, thin, yet fully developed lips. It was an ugly cunt, but for all that I spent in it, and did it standing by the bed side. Unable to get her legs conveniently over my hips, I put them high up, and she then doubled them up till her knees were near her chin. That facilitated my entry, and I fucked her in that attitude. — She said my prick hurt her, which I don't believe, and then she asked me for a further present, which I refused, and did not go to her again.

There was something about this woman's cunt, and the closeness of her thighs, which set me thinking and comparing. I have as before said if I recollect rightly, had women whose thighs did not seem to open wide enough, to let me lie comfortably between them, but this woman's thighs, cunt, and build, seemed to remind me of some woman whom I had had in my youth. At length it occurred to me that she resembled a maid in my mother's service who was named Harriett. The resemblance came into my mind suddenly, and I recollect that I have said a good deal about her. When however I attempt to go into particulars of resemblance, my memory fails me.

A day or two after, going down an alley about five feet wide, I saw a big woman sitting with a low dress at window, showing nearly all her breasts. It was day-time, but giving her about three shillings in English money, I had a very satisfactory poke, in a fully-haired cunt, between a big pair of white thighs, and a stunning backside, and was so well contented, that I had the lady again the next day. Certainly I have had on chance occasions, and for very small money payment, as fine women as a man need desire. — Only they were generally so coarse and vulgar in manner.

This woman spoke German, but in a dialect which I could scarcely understand. But all the baudy words explanatory of fucking, she spoke in good German, and in English, and in French as well. I expect many seafaring men had her. As I examined her perfections whilst she was naked (and willingly) with me, I looked at her bum-hole, and touched it out of fun. Thereupon she told me, and made me understand somehow, that if I wanted to "bougarrr" her, I must pay

[299]

"one Victoria," she never let it be done for less. — "It can't be done," said I. "Yah — yah — hier," said she, jumping up and taking out from a closet a pomatum pot. Then in her dialect, she explained I suppose, but I did not understand, nor did I expend "one Victoria."

At the H*g*e, I got a really splendid woman, and then I fucked my way to Belgium. At B***s**s, the first person I saw at the hotel was Mrs. W***t*r. — We were both astonished, and I think she was vexed at meeting me, but that soon wore off, if it had been so. A hot-arsed widow I expect gets hotter arsed, when she meets a man who has tailed her pleasurably, and certainly we had enjoyed each other well. I also when I meet a woman some time after I have fucked her, nearly always desire her again. I seem to want to see if she is changed in form, cunt, and amourous performance. I long to talk with her, and recall former pleasures. I felt that towards the heavy-arsed, mature-cunted but devilish fine fuckstress, Mrs. W*, and felt also on the instant that I was sure of having her.

She was there with the same party — which now included the young man, whom her niece had declared she would have, whether her father permitted it or not. He seemed a nice young fellow. I used to sit and look at the niece, and it pleased me much to think I had seen her naked, and knew the color of her cunt wig: whilst her intended might have to wait long before he saw as much. I told Mrs. W***t*r my thoughts, when I got a tète-a-tète with her. She laughed at the affair and said, "Yes — unless he gets a look at it on the sly." — Then she turned modest, and said it was really too bad of me, to have been looking at her niece naked through the key hole. But I saw plainer than ever that she was lewed to her very marrow — no whore after twenty years' fucking, more so.

There was great difficulty in getting Mrs. W*r because of the situation of our respective rooms, and circumstances generally. — But cock and cunt won't be kept asunder, if they don't mean it. — I tried to get a room next hers but failed. At length I got one opposite, but two or three days passed without my having a chance. At length we copulated at dinner-time. She shammed being unwell, and staid in her room. I suppose they thought I was out. I hopped across to her, and we fucked three times in an hour and a half. A day or two after, the party went off to Waterloo. — She was to have gone also, but again pleaded being unwell, tho she looked as strong as a horse. I passed the entire day with her, and had a hard ballocking bout. She had food sent up to her room for herself of course, but enough for two was there, and we eat it together. I hid myself in a cupboard when the waiter brought it in, but the cupboard was so small, that the door would not quite close on me, so she pulled some dresses right over me as they hung up there. I had a bad cough, and unfortunately a fit of coughing came on just as the waiter was leaving, and in trying to check the cough, I farted rather loudly. The waiter most likely thought it was she who had let it go.

I felt much annoyed at what I had done, but took no notice of it till we had dinner. Then the comicality of it made me suddenly burst out laughing. — She did the same. "Hish," said she, "they will hear us outside." — "What are *you* laughing at?" said I. — "What are *you*?" Both then recommenced laughing in a suppressed manner. "He thought it was you." — "I'm afraid he did," — she replied, and then we adjourned to the bed, and no further remark was ever made about the flatulent noise. — It was funny, tho — I got away without being noticed I believe that day.

I had Mrs. W***t*r — once again only, and am of the same opinion that I was, about her sexual skill and beauty. For a quite middle-aged one, I don't recollect any woman who gave me more pleasure. Her cunt was perfection tho I can say that of scores. The difficulty of getting her was great.

I had a run at the baudy houses in the town, where the women were both wholesome, and very cheap, both of which conditions for the time were agreeable to me. Altogether I had quite seven or eight of them, my favours being distributed among four houses. — Five francs was then the price at three of them, and at the other (a splendidly furnished house) the price was a Louis. — But not one of the eight women were really handsome, tho half of them had fineish forms, and all were baudy beyond my requirements.

I went on from that town to **** where I nearly got into a servant of a family who were travelling, but did not succeed. I got her out in the dark one night, and felt her cunt whilst she had her back against a wall. I afterwards got her into my bed-room, and there, tho I felt her, and made her cunt sweat with her lust, tho she felt my prick till I nearly spent, tho I am sure from the intrusion of my fingers that she was no virgin, tho she subdued her voice almost to a whisper when refusing me and defending herself, tho I threw her on the bed, and kissed her thighs, yet I never succeeded. I had to let her go, on her saying quite seriously, and sternly. — "Now we've had our fun, but if you're rough I'll cry out — that I will — for you shan't do it to me — and I don't want your money neither, never you mind if I've done it or not, *you* shan't." "I expect you've got the pox," said I, leaving her. I have had others who would go to any lengths, but stop at fucking.

CHAPTER XXXIII

At Paris. — A creole for variety. — Tobacco versus fucking. — A negress for a change. — Amusements with a comb. — A recusant prick. — A determined entry. — Black on white, and white on black. — Fucked at last. — A sudden summons. — Free! Hurrah!

On my way back I stopped at Paris. At a brothel I had a lovely creole, such a tall, handsome creature, but who annoyed me with her smoking. She was naked, all but stockings and slippers, when she came in. After washing her cunt, or as they call it there, making her toilet, she was smoking then. She laid down for my inspection of her cunt and backside, which took me a long time, I was so pleased with her, she smoking all the time, and contemplating me and herself, in the looking-glass which formed the top of the bed. I stripped myself naked, so that I might lay all over her, and enjoy the contact of her lovely flesh with mine, a thing I am fond of doing with women before I fuck them, and there she laid smoking, seemingly quite unconcerned, and I believe was thinking of something else than what was taking place between us. "Put out your cigarette, you don't fuck with that in your mouth, do you?" "I've done so before now," she replied placidly, but she put it down. Then at once she laid hold of my prick, to insert it in her cunt. It was stiff against her thigh touching her cunt, and I was enjoying its stiffness without immediate intention of putting it into her, so I took it away from her cunt, as she put to that orifice "You're in a hurry, ma chère." — "Not at all," said she, stretching out

[*302*]

her hand for the cigarette, which was still alight and within her reach. But I knocked it out of her hand. "Let's think of fucking, ma chère." "Volontiers." Being deprived of her cigarette, she began the proper preliminaries, most voluptuously, and was soon rewarded with a gluey injection.

That over, I questioned her about her parentage, feeling desirous of knowing the breed, for the tone of her flesh was most delicate, and made me curious. Then seeing my curiosity about parentage, "Did you ever have a black woman?" she asked. I never had. She told me then that there was a fine Negress in the house. At once I sent for her, but she had just been engaged by a man, so I fucked my creole again and departed.

A day or two after, I had the black woman, who was, I should say, about twenty or twenty-two years old, and a tall woman. She came in dressed, or half dressed in yellow satin, and with a silk handkerchief of the brightest possible colours, wrapped round her head. She spoke French well, and said she was born at Guadeloupe. Whether that is a place inhabited by a Negro race or not, I don't know.

I was impatient to examine her, and my hand sought her cunt under her single garment without delay. I felt there hair, short and crisp, and close, which reminded me of the vegetable called a loufah, with which orientals rub themselves at the baths, and one of which a friend gave me recently to use, for the first time. He had travelled much in the east and had brought home many things novel to me, loufahs among them.

I stripped her forthwith. She had on white silk stockings, and bright coloured slippers, which made a funny contrast with her flesh, for she was very dark. She was exceedingly well made from her knees upwards, had a handsome round backside, and lovely breasts, but the calves of her legs were miserably thin, and she had very large ugly feet, and her hands were also large. Her face really did not strike me as ugly, and she had splendid white teeth, shewing thro very thick lips. Her face seemed in one perpetual grin, and her teeth shewed incessantly, perhaps purposely.

But her cunt was the most important part to me, I found the split very much like that of any other female, it had smaller inner lips, with a clitoris which stuck out like a very little prick, and seemed to have but little connection with the inner lips, which however, commenced by a junction with it, and enlarged lower down. All this was almost a black red, the vagina looked pink. The outer lips were quite round, and of moderate fullness. The hair every where about her cunt, was quite black, and like horsehair with intense curliness, and laid flat on her motte. There was only a moderate quantity of hair about her cunt and belly altogether. The effect of the deep colored split, with the pink interior, cutting as it were thro the surrounding blackness, interested me but did not stir my lust at all, which surprized me, so I sat to look more closely at her cunt.

The hair interested me. Not only was it crisp, but each hair curled right round, and as it was short and not in large quantity, I could easily trace the curls. I have never seen cunt hair exactly like it before.

[In one or two Negresses since had, I have seen some resemblance, but they had longer and much more hair on their cunts, than this woman.]

I asked her for a comb, and when she had fetched one, I combed, with the finely toothed part, the hair on her mons. Immediately it had passed thro the comb, it curled up and laid flat as before. The Negress laughed her funny laugh, loud and long — never had a man combed it before, she said. When she fetched the comb she thought I wanted it for my own hair.

Then I put her on the side of the bed, and stood holding her thighs. My prick was not stiff, but with some difficulty I made it so. — She wanted to suck it up, but I would not let her. At length it was up to her, and I began the to and fro movement, looking at her handsome breasts as she lay now naked. — But not much fancying her, my prick began shrinking. To stimulate it I relinquished holding one of her legs, which she herself then kept well up in the air without my assistance, and with my free fingers distended her cunt lips at the top, and watched my prick moving in and out of her dark orifice. All was useless, a nervous feeling that I could not fuck her came over me and out my prick came as big only as a walnut. It is always so directly I have such a fear.

It was useless rubbing it against her curly wigged slit. Nothing stiffened it. Saying I was fatigued, I laid on the bed by the side of her. She, cleverer, and I imagine in thinking over the affair, not unaccustomed to such masculine failures, said I had over excited myself, should be all right soon, and so on, and fondling my cock, and lending herself to all my fanciful investigations with my fingers and eyes. In about ten minutes (I suppose) I was stiff again — "Now," said she gaily, and anticipating what I would do, put herself quickly in the same position as before, on the bed side.

Up went my prick again, stiffer now. Shove, shove, shove. A slight thrill of pleasure beginning at my prick tip, running to my bum hole, and from those two centres of lust, right thro my body, passed through me — "A — her — ha —ha — ha," — sighed she, jerking her buttocks, as if about to die with sexual delight, and sob out her life under my thrusts.

But as she sighed, her eye balls turned up, the pupils were nearly hidden by the lids, and I saw that the balls looked quite yellow, instead of white. At once all lust left me, the nascent pleasure in my prick stopped short, quickly as the blood could leave the veins, my prick shrunk, and shrunk, till out of her cunt it came. I had not the power, or the wish, to move or thrust, or to try to keep it up her. Her yellow eye balls had annihilated desire in me, lust had fled — "I can't kiss you," I said, and sat down on a chair feeling my prick, and looking at her naked body with her legs dangling down.

Jumping up "Mais oui, you can, you must — lay down, I will make it stiff again," yielding I laid on the bed, wishing to have a black woman much, and ashamed of my impotency, feeling for the minute that fucking a black was almost as unnatural as fucking a monkey, yet with a strong will to do it, tho without the sexual desire to do it — What was the cause of my prick slinking so I wondered.

Without a word, without a request from me, for I had never thought about it, she pulled off her white stockings, mounted the bed, and naked, laid herself on the top of me. Then as if thinking of it, got up and pulled off my socks (I had only my shirt and socks on) and replaced herself on the top of me — "Regardez — look up," said she.

I did, saw in the top glass my white flesh legs between hers, my prick just showing beneath her black buttocks. "Put your legs outside mine," obeying her as mistress in the craft of salacity, I did. Then I went back to the former position, then I mounted her. Then she laid by the side of me, pulled up my shirt to my neck almost, and placed her body and legs on mine in various ways. At each change of pose she said, "Look at the dark and white, together, oh, the white men are nice." — "Do you like white men!" — "Yes, I love the white man," she cried, and so we moved about. I got excited by the contrast of the colors, and my lust came on.

But my prick didn't stiffen, spite of the sight, and her fon-

dling it. Off the bed she got, with a wet towel wiped my
prick top, carefully wiped her own cunt, threw the towel on
the floor, and mounting, straddled across me, and bending
down, took my prick in her mouth. Her buttocks and cunt
being within a few inches of my face. The play of her
tongue on the gland, the feel of her smooth black bum, the
sight of the cunt (tho I did not admire it, still it was a cunt),
stiffened me. Impatient to consummate, and fearing limpness
again, I turned her on to her back, laid on her, and fucked.
I did not look at her face for fear of seeing the yellow eye
balls, and after a while, fucking far longer than usual, my
pleasure came on and I spent in her.

She retired and came back with purified genitals. Curiously and dispassionately, I looked her over from head to
foot, from bum hole to navel, bestowing most of my attention on her cunt, its intensely curly hair, and the funny little
clitoris like a nut. The inspection gave me no desire to have
her again, and after a conversation about black men's cocks,
which I had heard were very long and big, and which interested me immensely, I left.

Tho I thought over her much, and was interested in what
she told me about Negresses and Negroes it left me with no
desire to have her again, nor did I. Since then I have had desire for another black woman, but have not gratified it. [I
since have.]

Then I sped towards the centre of the continent, till a special messenger overtook me and brought me news. — I had
missed letters at the *poste restante*. — Death had done its
work. Hurrah! I was free at last. I travelled home night and
day, hurriedly arranged affairs, gave carte blanche to solicitors and agents, and with lighter heart than I had had for
years, went abroad again.

CHAPTER XXXIV

My social conditions. — Dainty whoremongering. —
Difficulties in selection of women. — Eccentric fucking
attitudes. — Writing my narrative. — The uniformity
of fucking. — A semi-eastern harem. — Beautiful
courtezans. — A beauty selected. — "I've no hair
there." — Other beautifuls. — A noisy neighbour. —
Male inspection of male erection. — England again. —
Many expensive mercenaries.

Under changed social conditions I now travelled, I was free
from care, had plenty of money (tho getting rid of it fast),
and altogether it was a happy time. I raced about Europe for
two or three months, and had constant change of scene.
When I got to a town, I sought the best brothels, and with
my physique in first rate condition, revelled in female
charms. After perhaps a week abstinence, that time spent in
comfortable travel, how instantaneous my selection of the
woman, with what burning lust I clutched my woman when
I got her, how rapid my thrusts, how maddening in its
ecstacy, as my prick throbbed, and the hot thick sperm
gushed up her cunt copiously as ever. Indeed, sometimes I
think more copiously than it ever did, but that is improbable.

Yet I gratified my sense of beauty largely. Sometimes
when I had fucked a woman, chosen in hot haste, I could
scarcely tell why, I again had the women of the house exhib-
ited to me, and selected another for the second libation of
my prick. More frequently tho, the first one had my second
emission. Then cooled, I left; and waited till the next day,
before I had further sexual enjoyment.

Then I had at times woman after woman to look at,
dressed, half-dressed, or naked to my eyes, so that I might
judge fully of their charms before selecting one for my sexual homage. Then I began to have two at a time, and sometimes three even, in the chamber with me. There, at my
leisure, and without observation but that of my Paphian di-
vinities, I could place them in every attitude, and see every
perfection, before I chose the one to fuck. I had modes of

payment of my own, would give half fees to those whose cunts I had only looked at or felt, and full fee to her whom I spermatized, and so on. At some places they would not agree to this, at some they would.

This contemplation of female charms makes me think I am like Paris, when selecting a Goddess for the golden apple, and I wonder if *he* made a mistake. I often do, and get so bewildered in my choice, that I do not know which to take. This one has such a lovely backside, but has hanging breasts. That one has too much hair on her cunt, and her nymphae hang out too much, but she is otherwise beautiful. That one has a lovely face, but too light a hair on her cunt, and her legs are thin. So I inspected and thought, till my prick would wait no longer, and urged me to let it taste its pleasure. Then when it left their cunts, how different some ladies looked to me, to what they had before. Surely a prick stiff and throbbing, and a prick flabby, wet, and flopping, affect the powers of imagination very differently.

But it was very charming always. At times I paid the full fees for a trio, and placed them as I have seen in engravings, and I invented myself combinations quite as beautiful and exciting. — I discover now, that I have as fertile a fancy as erotic artists, and moreover begin to delight in fucking, in different and oftentimes difficult postures. Postures which give not the voluptuous ease when the prick is in the woman, which the old fashioned way of belly to belly, or belly to backside give, but which nevertheless fire me with a sensation of intense lust, and fill my imagination with ideals of voluptuousness.

During this time I travelled alone, and had no one to interrupt me, or to make demands upon my time for companionship, and so I could arrange my erotic intentions beforehand and surely carry them out. In the intervals of my enjoyment of female society, I amused myself by making notes, or writing the narratives fully. [This I find now by rough perusal of manuscript not yet touched, has a freshness which is not in some of that revised, and which I think I have already said elsewhere, was written out from memoranda (memoranda very copious it is true) many years after and I had at the end of two years a very large mass of manuscript, mostly relating to my frolics with professed Paphians. This I largely abbreviated soon after, and shall do so, still more now. This following paragraph I leave exactly as I then wrote it.]

[*308*]

On perusal I find I think much repetition, much which must have been written elsewhere, tho where, and when, I cannot recollect. Even with my good memory, I cannot at once bring to my mind what I have written in a narrative of the amours of nearly twenty-five years. But I shorten it. The roads to copulation are like the act, very much the same everywhere. Prince and beggar do it the same way. A policeman thrusts and wriggles his prick like a Duke. A milkmaid heaves her buttocks and tightens her cunt like a Duchess. It will be wearisome to tell how I tailed Mary one night, if I have told that I did it the same way to Fanny the night before. Yet when I had women I mostly wrote about my doings with them at great length, described in detail as well as I could our voluptuous movements, and the sensuous ideas which rushed through my brain as I fucked then. That writing indeed completed my enjoyment then. Now my pen may run through the greater part of it.

What is a little odd, is that I got few chances of seeing thro key and spyholes, much worth recording. Perhaps that may be in a degree attributable to spending so much of my time with harlots, and when at my hotel, being usually very tired, and recruiting by repose for my next orgie. Yet I saw one or two pretty sights.

Then I found my way without the aid of a guide to a brothel, where in all my life, I never saw such a selection of beautiful, healthy women. They were not like so many of the flabby breasted, highly got up, yet fucked-out looking women one sees at the houses of certain of the capitals of Europe; but resembled healthy lasses who had just come from the country. — But it was in a country where the women are very beautiful, and I was at a town where the poor women of easy virtue are not used and then abused, kicked, and hooted, and almost branded, but where they often marry and marry well. — A well known traveller is said to have got his wife from one of the houses at this town, and a charming wife and woman she has ever since been, I am told. After a midday meal, walking along in a by, but quite a good street, I heard the merry laugh of women just by my ear, for I was close to the wall in the shade, it being a hot day. Stopping, I could just distinguish female forms thro the close outer blinds, and looking up saw that all the blinds of the house were shut. Fancying it was a harem, I pushed the door, which opened, and I found myself in a fine hall, and mounted a staircase to a very handsome large saloon.

The Abbess of this open-thighed nunnery spoke bad French, but enough for me. Soon trooped in a dozen of the most beautiful women I think I ever saw together in a bagnio, or in any society. I have often been bewildered in my choice at a baudy house, and more so I think when the ladies were naked than when clothed. Here they were clothed, but it was of loose or open make. All were more or less décolleté, their breasts were seen nearly to their nipples, in some the nipples shewed, in some I could see the enticing darkness of the hairy armpits. The majority had the most lovely, tho not flashy or stagey boots on, and the display of calves was fine. They did not all stand up, but most sat down, as if they had taken their places on chairs for the evening. One or two addressed me in a language I did not understand. I spoke then in a language which was replied to by one or two, and I talked compliments and nothings for delay, for I was confused by their loveliness, and a desire to fuck half a dozen of them at the same time.

At length, almost at hazard, and spite of my looking round till my eye balls seemed to ache, I patted a not very tall girl on her lovely shoulders, and left the room with her. She was an exquisite creature, with cheeks like a rose, tho her skin had a darker hue than our English women. She had eyes like a gazelle, and dazzling teeth. In our bed-room, in a second she sat on my knees, and I glued my lips to hers. On a gesture which she understood, she threw off all clothing but boots and stockings, and stood naked, a sight of glorious beauty. She was but eighteen years old. Tho my prick was stiff before I had got up stairs with her, I sufficiently restrained my self to look over, and feel her exquisite form. From neck to breasts, breasts to armpits, armpits to cunt, my fingers ranged, and my lips followed, feeling and kissing, kissing and feeling till I longed to lick her. Then after, opening her lovely cunt-lips, I went on to looking at her bum furrow — for all parts of the pretty creature it seemed, must be pretty to me. To my astonishment she moved herself from off the bed, and turning round with her bum towards me, and pulling the ivory cheeks asunder, so that I could see her anus, "I no hairs there," she said in broken Italian, which with German I found we could best communicate with each other in, tho she belonged to neither nation.

What her object was in informing me of the condition of that part — whether it was an invitation to it — whether its beauty caused it to be often investigated by friends, it never occurred to me to think about, until I began to write this narrative of my visit to the nunnery house, which I did next day. — But the instant she had spoken, so exquisite did her cunt with its crisp dark hair, and pouting lips, look between her buttocks furrow, and lovely thighs, that I inserted my prick, and almost instantly spent the semen in her, which had been boiling in my ballocks, since the time I saw the couple in the bed-room at the hotel: for I did not frig myself there, restraining myself with much difficulty from doing so.

The nymph stood quite still, with my prick in her, satisfied to let it rest there and soak. It showed no signs of shrinking, whilst I stood feeling her marbly buttocks, putting my hand round to feel her clitoris, feeling her breasts and armpits — revelling in her beauty. — Then her cunt clipped it. It was an invitation to go on fucking. But I now wanted her sweet face, her lovely lips towards me. Pulling my prick out of her lubricated cunt, "Get on the bed and lie down, cara mia," I said.

Without reply, and putting her fingers on her cunt, to prevent spilling my spunk out of it, on she got, and smiling, asked for a towel. I gave it to her, and she dried her fingers with it. For an instantly only, I saw between her wide apart thighs, the red slash, covered with the pearly essence of my testicles, and then plunged my wet prick up it again. She met me with ardour in a fuck worth two of the first in duration, baudy thoughts, and voluptuous enjoyment of her spunk filled genital. It ended in her spending when I did, and our mouths overflowing into each other, as the juices of both cunt and prick mingled in her.

Then all is told, excepting that I stopped hours with her, conversing in polyglot, but mainly kissing and feeling her, in delicious, thoughtful, baudy half silence, during the hot afternoon.

The next day I had her again, and thought I should never care about another woman. The day after that, I could not go to the house, but the following evening did. She was engaged I found for the night by a gentleman. Disappointed, I yet saw some of the other ladies. Tho some were then fucking in their chambers, I got one taller, but in every other respect, as beautiful and perfect, as the one I had had. The charm was now broken. I had her again once, but my love of change, the desire to see and know what other women were like, was too much for me. I stayed a fortnight at the

[*311*]

town, and had fucked half a dozen of the women before I left.

I kept to my bed-room, hoping to see some other sights there, but to my annoyance, two officers took possession of it, and walked about as it seemed to me both night and day, with boots and spurs on. There were military doings in the town. They smoked also incessantly, and had a party one night, on which occasion I don't think they went to bed. Being much annoyed by their noise, I asked for another room, tho for many reasons I liked the one I was in. — The manager told me the officers would leave the next day: which they did.

But the same night, two other men connected with the army, tho apparently not soldiers, were put there. They were quiet, and at night hearing them preparing to go to bed, I had the curiosity to get up and peep. To my astonishment one was naked, and the other, in his shirt, was looking attentively at the naked one's stiff prick, and feeling it. What he was doing it for I can't say, for he soon relinquished it, their light was put out, and both almost immediately snored. Who were they — was one a Doctor, but why a stiff prick? All was so solemn and business like, so unlike erotic amusement, that to this day I can't make the affair out.

The day after, I left ***** and went on traveling, but returned to England soon. I had no intrigue on hand, tho I had thought when free that I should soon have one. I had not a servant even to meet. Those nice, little, randy-arsed, well-fed devils, who can only get fucked now and then on the sly, and of whom I have enjoyed dozens in my time, and hope to enjoy as many again. As it was, the mercenary frail ones, of the highest and most expensive class, absorbed my manhood, and my pocket. Cunt, silk stockings, diaphanous chemises, laced night-gown, and jewels, are costly. Then I found one I liked much, and tho I did not keep to her, for I never can to one woman alone, I frequented her for a couple years.

CHAPTER XXXV

Change in social conditions. — Fifteen months'
fidelity. — Virtuous struggles with self. — Fornication
resumed. — Lucubrations on sexualities. — Recurrent
lusts. — Copulative power. — Knowledge of the art of
love. — Girls surprized. — Influence over women. —
Age guessed by pudenda. — Novel lusts. — Female
humbugging. — Men deceived. —Impetuous
stroking. — Camille revisited. —Promiscuity. —
Clapped. — On lubricity in cunts. — My ways with
Cyprians. — Notes on temporary connections.

It is a full quarter of a century since my prick first entered
a woman's cunt. — A great change has now taken place in
my social condition, and full fifteen months passed away
during which I have been chaste — I do not find a single
note or memorandum about illicit amours as they are
called. — Indeed can swear that I never had any, and that all
my sexual worship was given to one woman. Never before
or since have I been so faithful, but *she* is worthy of it. —
Then a change ensued. How well I recollect when I lapsed
into my former habits of sensuality, spite of my struggles
with myself to avoid doing so.

[This change in social life, left me with a limited purse for
free loves — I had generally not the money to enable me to
have the high-priced strumpets of former days, tho at times
I was seduced into such extravagances. — Excepting at intervals, the demand upon my time and my tool elsewhere
prevented my engaging in liaisons requiring time to accomplish or continue them. — But I had varied, fantastic, and
the erotic frolics of mature age, as well as the normal amorous amusement of a sensuous man. The administrators to
my pleasure were content with their gains, relatively small
tho they were, and also were often content with *me,* for I had
not lost the natural faculty (not art, for I never really cultivated the art of attaching soiled doves, and (sub-rosa) frisky

lasses, as well as other females to me; and making them the most complaisant of partners in my pleasures, and even my voluptuous extravagances and caprices).]

For fifteen months, I have been contented with one woman; I love her devotedly, I would die to make her happy. — Yet such is my sensuous temperament, such my love of women, that much as I strive against it I find it impossible to keep faithful to her, to keep to her alone.

I have wept over this weakness, have punished myself in fines, giving heavily to charities the money which would have paid for other women. I have frigged myself to avoid having a woman whose beauty has tempted my lust. I have, when on the point of accosting a lovely frail one, jumped into a cab and frigged myself right off, tho unavoidably thinking of the charms I had not seen. I have avoided A*g**e and C**m***e, and any other place to which whores resort, for fear of being tempted. I have tucked at home with fury and repetition, so that no sperm should be left, to rise my prick to stiffness when away from home; fucked indeed till advised by my doctor that it was as bad for her as for me.

All is useless. The desire for change seems invincible. The idea of seeing the petticoats lifted of some untasted beauty, the disclosure of neat ankles, swelling calves, the garters round white thighs, the smooth belly, and the cunt glowing in its crisp hirsute setting, framed in the smooth white flesh of belly, thighs, and bum globes, fill me with unconquerable wants. — I sicken with desire, pine for unseen, unknown cunts. — My life is almost unbearable from unsatisfied lust. It is constantly on me, depresses me, and I must yield.

I have yielded — Alas — Alas — I am whoring as of old — the charm is broken — my lascivious career recommenced. — Alas — Alas — I ought to feel disgraced. — But what maddening voluptuousness the variety gives me.

Tho I again indulge my voluptuousness with women in whose society I find the greatest charm of life, not only from their possessing the sexual organ which is the foundation of love for *them,* as the male sexual organ is of their love for *us,* but for their faces, form, and beauty, manner, blandishments, and kindness, which are the female attributes. But I must abstain henceforth from those delicious intrigues, which, for so many years, have helped to occupy my mind and to lighten the great trouble of my life. It would be impossible to intrigue, to go cunt hunting as I have done. That involves never giving up a chance, watching for and seizing every opportunity, and giving up all other occupations needful to attain the end — possession of the woman. This now I cannot do, without chance of being found out, and perhaps thus sacrificing the happiness of one for whom I would sacrifice my life.

I must content myself with the pleasures which courtesans can give me. Luckily, courtesans in their ranks have every class of physical beauty to gratify the taste, together with a libidinosity, the idea of which seems more and more to please me. — Luckily also there are those to be found among them willing enough to gratify every taste of mine, — tastes which by experience have now been enlarged in their variety, — tastes to which in my earlier life I was a stranger — tastes which may be aberrations, and of which I have only heard. Thus I see before me endless salacious enjoyments. These are the burning words which express the desires and actions of love. — Love, lust, letchery, lewed, licencious, lubricious, impudicity, salacity, obscenity, ribaldry, smuttiness, baudiness, concupiscence, carnality, fornication, lasciviousness, sensuality, meretriciousness, voluptuousness, lickerishness, ruttish, riggish, stupration and harlotry, all words found in the dictionary, and all of which I suppose may be classed under the term erotic. All are ridiculously used as opprobrious terms, instead of terms of praise and worship, for they are after all, only the charming expressions of the wants, tastes, desires, and concomitants, of the use of the prick and cunt, and for giving to each sex pleasure in some way. The terms should therefore be all gathered together under the word Love, of which they are but the expressions, the signs, and the consequence, and love and lust are almost synonymous.

[It is a quarter of a century since this was written and I have acted in the belief of the truth of them.]

I am forty-two years old: an age when nature should moderate my ardours. — It may have done so, yet I can scarcely find any difference in my physical force, whilst my power of imagination in all things sexual has increased. — This imagination adds infinitely to the charm of coition and makes the woman lovelier than ever to me. — I am in full health and vigor, and am told good looking, more so than formerly, tho I can see no difference in myself. — All agree that I do not look my age. I can fuck once nightly as regularly as clockwork, oftentimes twice, and feel none the worse for the double action. Frequently, even that makes me feed and sleep better, and feel more refreshed and stimulated next morning. — With a fresh woman I can fuck thrice within the hour, but with that have finished my amour for a time. —But so it was with me years ago. [With a little abstinence, and a lovely woman with a fresh cunt, I have many times done my fifth between night and morning.]

I can perhaps for a time control my lustful impetuosity better than I could, which may be a sign of relaxation of strength. Yet at times I have such a strong, hot, fit of passion at the sight of a woman, that nothing restrains me till I've had her, if she can be had. Neither cost (whether I can afford it or not) nor risk deters me. — It seems to me that I then have the same determined aggressiveness which, overcoming a constitutional timidity frequently felt by me with women, tho I have not often told of it, has given me hitherto such success in my amours, — and even with harlots. — Success often times unexpected. My temerity in the attack, so crowned with victory, often times astonished me when my passion has been cooled in the darling's arms, and I have had time to think over what has passed.

Certainly I can now do what years ago I was incapable of, — dally with my lust under the strong excitement of a fresh cunt. I can pull my prick out of it as my sperm begins to rise, await its subsiding, put my prick in again, again postpone the crisis, and get by this husbandry, this prolongation, as much voluptuous delight out of one fuck as I used out of two. I can at times look at a cunt which my prick has never yet opened, and by strong effort of will, contemplate it for a time even with a stiff and throbbing prick. I think at times, even, that I can prevent my prick from stiffening, when looking at a lovely naked woman, but this for a short

[*316*]

time only. — Directly afterwards, when I allow desire full swing, my prick, in rapid throbs, jerks itself up erect. — It seems to me to rise to duty with the throbbing of my heart, when the restraint of my will is removed from it.

I have much, perhaps great, knowledge of sexual matters as it affects both male and female in their daily life, and feel sure that with that experience, coupled with the influence of my age, I can get mastery over women more easily than formerly. — Yet have I not been already sufficiently masterful with them? But my deeper knowledge tells, and adds to my power and pleasure. I can astonish the younger ones, whores tho they may be, by telling them as much as they know, and some of the young practitioners more than they know. — [Many a young pair of eyes I have, since this was written, seen to wonder at my disclosures.] Then finding I know so much of their sex, their mendacity, little dodges, artifices, salacious tricks, and lewed habits, they are frank and tell me much about themselves and of their class. That is to say, some do, — those who naturally are frank. — Those innately cunning liars — but little.

I like to notice carefully, quietly, the difference in cunts; to study the look of cunts. This taste for comparing them has been growing on me for years. But more — I can tell, I think, tolerably closely, the age of a woman by the growth of the hair around, and the general aspect of her vulva. — "How old do you guess I am?" — "Wait till you're naked my dear, and when I've looked at you from your arse hole to your navel, I'll guess." — "You are a funny man, — well look then — now tell me." — That often has occurred, and it pleases me to inspect and to guess.

I can look at a woman's bum hole without dislike, and like pressing it with my finger, when my prick is in her cunt, and, in the ecstacy of the spend, even to intrude it. — Have I not done now nearly everything? Is not everything which two people like to do together, fit and proper for them to do? Besides, some sweet Paphians whom I have had, and enjoyed my embraces, liked that anal plugging.

What often astonishes me is my desire to do again every thing sexual and erotic, which I have done already. Yet many things done, I fancied I should never repeat. I have frigged a man. — My curiosity satisfied, I said to myself, — "I shall never frig a man again." — Yet I want to do so. — After each nearly hairless cunt which I have fucked, I have said, "Bah! she is not so well worth a stiff one as a full grown woman. There's no squeeze in the cunt, tho it be so small and tight — less soft liquidity exudes to meet my sperm, I'll not have another." — But I want another, and seem even to forget the sensation and the distinct pleasure that the small cunt gave me. I still want to compare them with the pleasure from larger cunts. — Nay, I crave for a young, unfledged cunt to lodge my prick in once more, and for the very fact of its being young and unfledged, and without thought of the pleasure of the fuck in it.

I want to do every thing over again. All former gratifications which were a little out of the common, seem to have faded from my recollection somewhat. — I don't clearly enough recollect my sensations, or the quality of the pleasure they gave me. I wish to refresh my memory by repeating the amorous exercises. It is not my lust or powers which want stimulating by variety; it rather seems as if it were strong animal want which is stimulating my desires and exercising my brain to invent even voluptuous combinations. I should like now, I fancy, those amusements I have often objected to. I should I think like my prick sucked by a sweet red lipped mouth. — Many a time I have refused that. What made me do that trick with the three Italian Graces at F**r***e I wonder?

Certainly I should like to gamahuche a pretty, coral tinted, hairless cunt, between young thighs. And a large stiff white prick! — I should like to see the sperm start from it, whilst I handled it. — Big women and little, black and light haired cunts, cunts of fourteen, and cunts of forty, I should like to see and taste again.

And I am middle-aged, and as some would say, should know better. Bah! — why should I not enjoy myself erotically if I fancy it, even if I were a centenarian? — *"Vive le con, vive le vit."* — I will recommence as if I were young and ignorant. — Know better? He who knows how to get full enjoyment of life, be it done how it may, knows best.

I have perhaps arrived at the period of philosophical eroticism, but have I anticipated the period? Camille says that I have, and reminds me that she always said I should, whilst *"beau garçon."* — In fact I know everything about women: their sexual organization, the mysterious influence that the womb exercises upon them, and they upon us from the same source of vitality. — But whilst I flatter myself thus, I know also that I may be, and probably shall be, deceived by them, have their dust thrown in my eyes, — humbugged by them.

Any man may be humbugged by a woman whom he loves. Nay if he only likes her much, he is sure to believe her. It would pain him too much to disbelieve. This my opinion of masculine weakness, for many a year I have held. — It has saved me, I believe, from more than one false step, from several dilemmas. — It may save me from others, but who knows? If I should love, or only lust after, or only like, it will not, especially from gay women. — A gay lady is almost by necessity a liar and trickster — money, money does it. — But in love matters, all women, modest or immodest, are liars, they will lie like a dentist to serve their turn. *Trust them not,* shall be my motto henceforth, but fear it will avail *me* but little, if I love or lust for them.

[Thus ran my thoughts, during the time I was constant and true to one (and to whom I thought I should be constant and true for ever), and the period of hesitation which ensued afterwards. — Thus did sensual cravings surge and struggle with me till I yielded. — They worried me even afterwards, whilst I indulged my lust with cheap Paphians, whom I sighted, longed for, fucked, paid, and dismissed, oftentimes in half an hour; leaving me unsatisfied, almost doubting what had taken place, yet with a desire to see more of their seat of pleasure, which in my lustful impetuosity I had had but a glimpse of. That flash of the cunt before my eyes had a sorcery of its own, for I could rarely help thinking of it and wishing to contemplate it more at leisure, and to think about it when contemplating.]

[Such fugitive pleasures also left me with fear of ailment, not for my own bodily suffering, but for the disclosure of its origin and source, and of the anguish that the disclosure would cause to *her.* Often I vowed that never — never — would I incur the risk again. — Alas for such resolves. — A stiff prick has no conscience. — A lustful throb in mine at a pretty face, a neat ankle, a swinging backside in sight, and all was forgotten, till I saw my sperm rolling out of her cunt, and my regrets and fears returned.]

When I recommended indiscretions (to use the accepted and modest term for going on the loose and fucking others than the legitimate one), I sought Camille. — Years had passed since I had had her, and the look at her was a pleasure to me. — *"Mon Dieu! c'est vous mon ami, je suis enchantée de vous revoir, j'ai cru vous avoir perdu. —* How well you look. — Ah, unchanged — as young and handsome as ever. — Ah, why have you so long neglected me?" — We kissed, in another minute my fingers were on her cunt, hers around my prick — our mouths were glued together in silence, and in a few minutes more, my prick was throbbing out its sperm into her heavenly receptacle, which gave out its tribute to meet mine whilst we sighed ourselves into voluptuous silence.

Camille was unchanged, excepting that she had got stouter, and the hair of her cunt was thicker and covered her motte more. — Her lovely, smooth, satiny skin, her quiet voice, her other perfections mental and carnal, were the same. — But I fancied she had more the manners of a Paphian, more those of a professional fuckstress than when last I had her. We resumed our conversations as of yore. — Fucking and frigging, gamahuching and minetting, sodomy, thumbuggery and tribadism — male with male — woman with woman — man with woman — all the changes were discussed. — All, we agreed, were permissible amusements, and that only fools would hesitate to get any enjoyments out of any parts of their body that they lusted for. It was the same philosophy — a theory of pleasure we had agreed upon years before, and we only reaffirmed it now, after increased experience.

But I wanted other women besides Camille. — Soon she perceived that want, for she asked me if she should get me this woman or that pleasure. She had had now the experience of some years of harlotry, and knew men's natures. — Well, for a short time I accepted her aid, but then went my own way and again ceased seeing her altogether. [Partly perhaps because she left England and partly owing to a change in my residence.]

Then I went promiscuously and took a clap. It was not so serious an affair as the previous one, and luckily, being then temporarily alone in my home, it enabled me to get cured without the ailment being discovered. — It made me more cautious, made me insist on rigorous washing, and cuntal injections, before embracing the ladies afterwards. Occasionally also I then used French letters, but I could not bear them, nor they me. The injections also even if only of soap and water, left the cunts so rough, that my sensitive prick was deprived of half its pleasure. I have lately noticed, more than ever, that some cunts have more natural lubricity than others, and that my pleasure in coition depends on that smoothness. That a sort of soapy, greasy, mucilaginous lubricity, gives me the most pleasure. That is found in perfection in girls about eighteen years old, and afterwards up to a certain age. I think it diminished in a woman after forty.

[Complete lubricity in the woman's cunt has now become a necessity. — Without it at times my prick suffers almost slight pain at the beginning of the fuck. — The second fuck in the spermatized channel is by far the most pleasurable, and on reflexion I am conscious that the liking I had always for an unwashed cunt, or rather for one not recently washed, was an instinct with me, the result of this very sensitiveness of my glans. — I used at the time to think it was purely fancy on my part, yet could not reconcile it with the desire which I had for intense cleanliness in the woman, whilst at the same time I sought lubricity.]

[Finding I could not break away from my sensuality, I gave up the victory to it, tho I never was able to get rid of my moral scruples, and thinking I was unfair to her whom I loved better than my life. But I forgot those scruples, or they troubled me less and less as time went on. — My fears about ailments also grew less, for I reverted to a former habit, and always began my acquaintance by paying the ladies directly I got into the bed room with them. The dialogue was usually this. "Here is the money, don't let me poke you if you have any thing the matter with you." — "I'm all right." — "Ah but if you've been poorly, or are going to be, the least stain will make me ill, my prick's so sensitive, I don't mind paying you a bit, I know you must get your living, so tell my truly, don't let me touch you if you've even the whites."

That has been received in various way. — "You do it, I'm all right. Come on and fuck me," and after the business. — "You're married, I suppose, but don't you fear, I'm all right." — Others on the contrary. — "I'm quite well, but my poorliness was only over this morning. — You mustn't push too deep." — Or: — "Well, I am expecting to be poorly every hour." — Or — "Well, do as you like." — Sometimes "Well I'm a little poorly, but I'm quite in good health" — or — "I'm all right as far as I know." — Sometimes there was an evasive one. Others "Well, shall I toss you off then if you're afraid?" — or, — "A French letter then." A French woman. "Shall I do minette with you?" — and there were other little varieties of meeting my offer, and questions, and result.]

Here from my manuscript are two extracts illustrative of my notes as written almost day by day at that period — many and many a page there was of them. All were amusing, and writing them pleased me immensely at the time. Indeed I think that I had more pleasure in writing my narrative at this period than at any other, tho I had far less to write about. — Of these temporary infidelities I destroy the remaining notes now, excepting one or two curious ones told further on.

Had a woman named Susan ***** seemed twenty-five, a fat arsed, tho she didn't look so in her dress. — Discontented with what I'd agreed to give her, said I give no more, — where on she said. — "All right" and seemed quite satisfied. — Dark hair and eyes, plenty on her cunt, fucked well and, I think, spent; told her so. "Yes I nearly always spend with my first man if he's nice, perhaps I mayn't get another tonight." — She hated frigging herself. — No woman should touch her own cunt, she thought. — A funny one.

21 January. — A funny little bitch about four feet six high, thin. — A modest looking juvenile cunt. — One of the smallest I ever put into — quite tight as I pushed my penis up it — hurt me as I pulled prick out quite stiff — I'd spent, tho I feared — washed. — "You're in a hurry," said she — light haired, squinny face.

23 March — A hairy arsed, low, she. — Wonder I poked her, glad to get away — ten and six — dirty rooms.

A German — long nosed — big — spoke good English, said another woman was in house — would I see her — offered five shillings. — German laughed scornfully so I dropped the subject. — Soon after said she'd go and see — and it ended in having a plump little whore, whose cunt I looked at, whilst I fucked the German, and for five shillings.

If I had any doubts, owing to the woman's manner, I got away as quickly as I could. Sometimes I said, "I won't poke, but show me your cunt." I almost always looked at *that,* and then left, and oftentimes was in a house with another woman ten minutes afterwards. — Once or twice the look of the cunt so excited me that, "Oh, I must fuck you." — "Perhaps

[*322*]

you'd better not," — but they never alleged anything but their poorliness as a reason. — By adopting this mode of dealing with the women, I expect that I often escaped an ailment.

So for some time I had two or three different women weekly — feeling quite sure that I could do duty at home as well, but I had no woman whom I took to as a friend — or regularly visited. It was one continuous change in cunt, which I saw in all sizes, developments, and colors, and this variety largely increased my knowledge of the look, and capabilities of that feminine appurtenance, and the ways and manner in which women used it and permitted it to be used, and their movements, manner, and behaviour, whilst it was used.

CHAPTER XXXVI

Sarah F**z*r. — Form, face, and tongue. —
Micturating frolics. — Spending indications. — Her
dress. — A poke in the open. — Legs in the
street. — A male competitor. — He after me. — A
titanic prick. —Sarah on gamahuching. — Her nose.

In the year 18** I walked up P***l**d P***e at about ten o'clock at night, and saw a tall woman standing at the corner of L**t*e P***l**d Street. Her size attracted me, I spoke, and offering half a sovereign with the understanding that she would take everything off — went with her to a house in L**t*e P***l**d Street.

She kept her word and stripped whilst I sat looking on. — When in her chemise. — "Do you want me quite naked?" — "Yes." Then she slipped it off and stood start naked, boots, stockings, and garters, excepted. — I may as well describe her at once, as for quite four years, she satisfied almost every sexual want, and helped me to satisfy every sensual fantasy.

She was with the exception of the second Camille (the French woman) almost the most quiet, regular, complacent woman I had had since that time, and moreover was most serviceable to me in all my pleasures, ministering to them as

I wanted them — but rarely herself suggesting them. — Ready to undertake anything for me, and after some length of intimacy participating in, and well pleased with, our erotic amusements; never attempting to exact money, but always content, and at length getting so accustomed to me that she let me into much knowledge of her private daily life.

She was I should say five feet nine or nearly ten high, which is tall for a woman. Her hips were when viewed from the front, of the proper width for such a height — but her shoulders somewhat narrow. Altho so tall, she was small boned and plump all over, yet she had not at atom of what may be call fatness; had a small foot, a fine shaped calve, and thighs not quite so large proportionately. Her bum with fine firm round cheeks was not heavy at the back, was rather broad across the hips than thick and prominent behind, yet her backside looked handsome. — In fact she was straight and well shaped from top to toe, but if anything might have had broader shoulders with advantage, to make her proportionate to her height; yet only a sharp critic would have noticed that deficiency.

Her cunt, that important part of a woman, was large, but tight, fleshy inside, and muscular. It clipped my prick as deliciously as if it had been a much smaller one, and it was so healthy and deep, that often as I tried, I never could touch the orifice to her womb, either with my prick or my fingers. Nearly black hair, crisp and in full quantity was on her mons, and down the lips, and almost to her arsehole, but not round that brown orifice. The lips were thick and full, yet if she put her legs apart, they widened at once, showing deep crimson facings, and when shut a thin crimson streak. — Her nymphæ were small.

She had dark brown, bright eyes, dark hair and good teeth — but her nose had been broken. That spoiled her face which otherwise would have been very handsome. As it was it did not make her ugly, but decidedly spoiled her.

She had the longest tongue I ever saw. She could put it further out of her mouth altogether than any one whom I have seen do that trick. — She was somewhat an unusual woman in every respect, and was I think twenty-four years old when I first saw her. — She had been a ballet dancer at some time, altho I only found that out after I had known her some months. — Her name was Sarah F**z**r.

She laid on the side of the bed, pulled her cunt open, knelt on the bed backside towards me, shewing cunt and arsehole together in quick succession as I asked her, and without uttering a word, but simply smiling as she obeyed. It had the usual effect, — a stiff-stander of the first order. It always is so with me. Objections, and sham modesty, a refusal to let me touch, and feel, or see, instead of whetting my appetite for a gay woman, always angers me and makes me lose desire. — With a woman not gay the case is different. The next minute I was enjoying her with impatience, than I lay on her stiff still, and full up her when I had spent. — "I shall do you again." "All right," she replied. My prick never uncunted, but whilst reviving, my hands roved in all directions. She moved first this leg, then that, lifted her backside up, and seemed by instinct to know where my hands wished to go, and they were restless enough. — She was like Camille. — To something I said, she remarked. — "You're fond of it." — As I recommenced my thrusts she said. — "Don't hurry, I want it," — and we both spent together. — I forgot to mention that her flesh was of surprizing firmness, and her backside solid and smooth. — I gave her the half sovereign as agreed — she did not ask for more, and we parted — but not for long.

The readiness with which she complied with all my wishes, together with the recollection of her personal charms, and the pleasure of her cunt, dwelt in my mind. I had her next night, and the night after, and then began to see her once or twice a week, and to indulge in voluptuous freaks which I had not done for three years or more, and which my imagination increased in its powers by what I had seen, read, and done, supplied me. — I am not going to tell of tricks I have done with other women, but only such varieties and vagaries as were newish, and one or two which I had, I think, not done before with any women. If I had, I have forgotten to tell them, tho I am not sure even of that.

My piddling letch, which seems for a time to have been dormant, returned. I began to make her piddle in all sorts of attitudes, first in a pot, then in a basin — at times with her cunt opened naturally, then holding the lips open, so that the little red piddle-vent could be seen almost. — At no time of my life had I such variety of frolics with urine as I then had. — It may be termed my pissing period. I began to piss with her, would keep myself from watering for hours before I met her, so that I might deliver the fullest, longest, and strongest stream of urine possible. — She was famous at it. I have seen the piddle stream of scores of women, but hers was the hardest, and strongest that ever wetted a pot. — I hit on the idea of bringing her to the bedside, laying her back, putting a basin under her bum as close as the bed would permit. Then she would hold the lips of her cunt wide open, and I pointing my tool, would empty my bladder. The yellow stream hitting either prick hole, or broad surface of the cunt, splashed in a thousand little bright drops on her thighs, or lodged in the crisp black hair, then ran down to where the quim nears the bum hole, and dropped into the basin beneath. Directly I had pissed, my prick would stand, I joined my body to hers, and capable no longer of delay, bedewed quickly with sperm the inside of the orifice which I had just bedewed outside with a thinner fluid.

Pissing against her cunt, she declared, no man had ever done to her but me. She enjoyed it, it seemed to make her lewed, and she always spent with me afterwards. — When spending she shewed it plainly, and did not attempt to hide it as some do. — Indeed she could not, for her cunt *would* close so strongly round my prick, that there was no mistaking what it was up to. — Besides that, her face first went scarlet — perfectly scarlet, — a minute afterwards, perfectly white — and then gradually recovered its natural color — I never saw that change in any other woman's face. She always kept my prick up her as long as she could, — twining her long legs round me to hold me up her, whilst her long arms held me firmly round my arse cheeks, as she lay perfectly quiet with her eyes closed. — At other times when she did not spend herself, she took no trouble of that sort, but got up and washed the moment I released her.

The house I went to with her was usually in L**t*e P***l**d Street. — It had some advantages, but there was no looking glass of any size. As I wanted now to see our limbs and muscles move under our embraces, I went to a well known house, — the A*ma in ***** St. (There were several houses in the same street then, in this one there were glasses in profusion.) — It was now my additional delight when looking at her cunt, with her thighs wide open, with the basin beneath preparing for my salt splashing, to glance about and see her long plump flanks and thighs, half hiding the basin, my own nudity, and our erotic tricks.

In the various ways which I amused myself with her, one very large cheval glass increased my pleasure. I mostly managed to get the room in which that particular glass was, for

I soon became known. They gave me what I wanted and never disturbed me however long I stayed.

Two other modes, in which we used to amuse ourselves with our bladders were these. — We used to strip ourselves start naked, shoes and stockings off even, and arrange the cheval glass, so that with other glasses I could see her both back and front at a glance. Then lay on my back with hands under my head on a pillow, so raised as to enable me to see the picture we made. Then she would stand for a minute straddling over me, and the sight of the red stripe peeping out of the black hair would stiffen my penis. Then sitting down on me as she would on a chamber pot, she would take my stiff prick and engulf it in her cunt, the dark hair of her quim meeting mine, her bum cheeks just touching without weighing heavily on my thighs. Then out would come her warm stream, hitting my belly below my navel, and running down in two little streams by the side of my balls, uniting beneath them, washing over my arsehole, and depositing itself on the carpet on which I was lying.

At other times I reversed her, and she engulfed my prick in her cunt with her backside towards me. — Then I could play with her cool, firm, smooth backside, and feel round the stem of my prick just where it was lost, and hidden in her warm juicy tube. I could feel to her bumhole — or back bone. In the glasses I could see my prick rising out from the balls, and losing itself in the dark black thicket on her cunt lips. — "Open the lips, Sarah." — Immediately her two fingers would separate the lips, leaving the broad red surface, at which sight my prick would throb with desire to spend. — "Piss, piss dear, I can bear it no longer." — Then it would fall like a cataract in front of my balls, and partly on my thighs.

At times wrought to an irrepressible pitch, no sooner had the last dribble fallen on my ballocks, than with a few upward shoves I finished my pleasure, feeling her arse, and gloating over the luscious picture we made; holding her on me until my prick slipped out, and drew with it some of my sperm, as it flapped down on to my balls, still wet with her piddle.

By that time the piddle had cooled — my arse used to feel as if it had fallen into a ditch — we both rose, wiped and dried ourselves, and sat down to talk until desire again asserted its empire over me, or over us, for she enjoyed this fun.

Another way I have tried unsuccessfully with another woman. — With Sarah it was practicable on account of her height — for in tall women, the extra length is nearly always in the legs, and not in the body. Stripping ourselves start naked, I stiffened my prick by her incitements, or perhaps by a few preliminary shoves up her cunt, then both standing up before the glass, I used to put my prick up her and she would piss, and the warm stream run dripping round my balls, falling on both our thighs, and descending till we stood in a pond. — Then standing, I would fuck her, watching our movements in the glass.

And all this is practicable, if a man who is lewed as I was takes the trouble, and has a suitable woman. With Sarah I could do this scarcely bending my back, for upright by me my prick was nearly at the level of her cunt. — When the twisting and wriggling of our backsides and genitals had ceased, I have without uncunting, waddled with her back towards the bed, and leaning her on the edge, leaned on her, and took what rest I could in that position, until my prick slipped out. — Such was my force, and the rigidity of my penis, that several times I have done this. But it is a laborious, erotic amusement tho worth trying [I could not do it now].

I used at times, because of the convenience which her height gave for such amatory eccentricities, put my prick up her, and then clasping each other we used to waddle round the room, laughing as we viewed our movements in the glasses. That exciting amusement could not endure long, for there is an involuntary action in a cunt when the prober is in it, which compels the penis to move towards a consummation. After a minute or two, a constriction of her cunt muscles on my prick tip compelled it either to push or withdraw. Then came an involuntary shove or two, and then the sequel came, which was either the perpendicular shag in front of the glass — or an uprighter against the wall — a sloper against the bed side — a horizontal, old fashioned fuck on the bed, or on the floor — or a bum to belly fuck in dog fashion on the bed or on the carpet, bringing their usual crises of pleasure and relaxation of limb, luscious dreaminess, a sensation of cool dampness round the prick stem, and a desire for a doze.

I have fucked and awakened, still finding my prick in her — for she had only to raise her thighs, and bend her knees up somewhat, to bring her cunt in such a position, as to press my balls against her buttocks, and keep my prick in if only the size of a large gooseberry. The same facility enabled me to get my prick up her when limp — I took much pleasure in doing that, and letting it stiffen up her, under the compressive movement or grip of her cunt — I have never known a woman who could give my prick a longer lodging than she could; tho I have known many who could do it well. She knew it was my pleasure, and gave it to me to the full when she got accustomed to me.

I used to be thinking constantly of what voluptuous tricks I could do when we met, but for a time, a preliminary usage of our organs, in pissing some way or another was my delight. — Then it took such possession of me that I thought of nothing else. My letters to her to meet me used to run. "Tonight — seven — keep in P." — By which I meant her to have her bladder full. — So she used — so full at times that she said, "If you don't do something directly, I must piddle, I can't keep it in any longer." Then the evening's amusements began. — The quantity she spouted oftentimes, I am sure, was a quart or more.

There is one thing in these amatory micturating bouts, which I only recollect having done with her and one other woman. — It was pissing when up her cunt. — She told me she had allowed a man or two to try, but that they could not succeed. — Indeed it is difficult. For when a prick is stiff and in the state of nervous strain which fits it for penetrating a cunt, its ejaculatory muscles struggle to shoot out sperm, and so I suppose contract the opening to the bladder, and prevent piddle issuing. — But one night she was undressed, and lying at the side of the bed with thighs wide open, up I thrust my prick bursting, and as I thought with piss so proud, that nothing could prevent the jet. When up her cunt I tried to piss, but my prick began to throb, and her cunt, as I thought, to squeeze it, altho she declared it was quiet. I strained till I farted like a cow after beans, but not a drop would come. — The more I strained, the more difficult I found it to restrain myself from oscillating my buttocks, for an outshoot of spunk.

My prick would not be cheated. Her cunt resented its being treated as a pisspot, and asserting its right to a stronger and thicker injection, closed round my prick, and worked it so, that getting its way, it drew from me its natural embrocation. — As my sperm throbbed out, it caused me such pain that I groaned.

[*329*]

Directly my seminal reservoirs had emptied themselves, with a little effort my bladder opened, and I pissed for two minutes I am sure. — My prick kept gradually shrinking but until it had done its full duty as a sperm spouter and water pipe, kept in her cunt. Pressing out from her cunt came my stream, running over my balls, and down by her arse split on to bed and floor. — At length out flopped my doodle, bringing with it the remainder of my injection both thick and thin. — Up I pulled her, laid down in her place, but sloping off from the edge of the bed and she standing up, I thrust my body between her thighs so that my prick was just under her cunt. — Out came her piddle copiously over my belly and ballocks, and that completed the fun. — She cried out, "Oh, no, I shall wet my boots and stockings," for in our lustful hurry she had kept them on. "Damn your boots — piss — piss." — Out came the stream and I was happy. But we made the bed in such a mess that I was obliged to pay extra for its use.

Then I seem to have ceased eccentric micturating amusements, and erotic pleasures of a different kind took their place; tho as long as I knew her, I made her squat and piddle before me. I shall always I am sure, love to see a well made pair of white thighs, and their oval terminations in rear, whilst from between them the red line opens its hairy lips, and the sherry tinted stream spurts.

She was a scrupulously clean woman, always had the whitest linen on, but it was not of the finest quality, and was without ornament excepting a frill just round the top of the chemise — I never saw her in any dress but black silk. She said it was economical, that one dress helped to repair the other, that in coloured things she looked too big and vulgar — that her friends were mostly quiet men, who did not like women whom every one turned round after. — She usually wore a black veil, which were much worn by women then, lifted it up when she spoke to a man, then dropped it again. — I have watched her several times. — At that time gay ladies were fond of lifting up their petticoats if the streets were muddy, so as to show their legs a little. Sarah rarely did unless as she said she was "hard up." — If she showed her legs she always got a man, yet could not bear doing it. — Odd! — How odd! — She would do anything with me in a room, and perhaps with any other man, yet did not like shewing her legs in the street. — Humbug?

When I came to appreciate her very handsome feet, and

legs up to her knees (her thighs and haunches were scarcely as fat and fine) I found her stockings were sometimes a little coarse, so gave her boots, and silk stockings of the colour I admired. They were then light kid and pink silk — and also beetle-brown kid and white silk. — I gave her also splendid garters and expected her only to wear them all for *me*. I think she did so, for I tried to catch her with them on at odd times, and only found her with them on once. — When we had pissing bouts, she took off both boots and stockings. — Altho fond of a naked woman, I always made her keep boots and stockings on at other times.

Among my delights, was to make her squat at the edge of the bed with her knees up, and heels drawn as closely as possible to her bum. This she did with an ease, flexibility, and completeness which surprized me (the reason will be seen). — Then the dark mass of hair on her cunt, with the red lined lips, shewed up in perfection between her thighs, kid boots, and pink silk stockings. — I used to keep her so for a quarter of an hour at a time, I sitting on a pillow on the floor, so as to be able to look up at her cunt, holding a candle under it almost touching it, and opening, twitching, and fingering the cunt, as the impulse seized me. Then I viewed it from all parts of the room, until my pego would bear it no longer, and I rushed it up her. On several occasions I met her when she had no expectation of seeing me, and she went with me into the first dark plâce, I felt her limbs, and saw what boots, etc., etc., she had on, than I felt her cunt and went my way. I began again about this time occasionally to feel women's cunts in the street. I had not done so for a couple of years. I taught her when I met her, on a signal, to go ahead of me, lifting up her petticoats as high as she dare. — It amused me to see men turn round, follow, and speak to her. — Then she, if I wanted her, turned into the baudy house, I after her. But it was risky, for the sight of her legs used to give me such a cock-stand, that I was always in danger of wanting a fuck in the open. — One night I had her up against the door of a house in a back street. — She refused at first, but at length we did it, after my swearing that if *she* did not, I would do it in the street with *some other* woman. — But I never had her in the street but that once.

One muddy night she lifted up her clothes and walked up P***l**d P***e. — I followed her at some distance, then she turned and went to the house in L**t*e P***l**d St. As she was going there, a man spoke to her just before she got to the door. — In looking at her legs, I had not noticed him till then. In a second I was at the door. The man stood and insisted on going in with her. — She would not let him, and there was quite an altercation. — I slunk off to the other side of the way till it was finished. — The man saw me join her and looked very savage. I went in, had my evening's pleasure, and was there perhaps two hours. When I came out, I saw the same man, and he entered the house directly. — I knew he was after her. She did not come out, and there I waited an hour. — I had begun by laughing to myself at the man for waiting two hours for a woman. Now I waited tho I did not know why. But I thought of what they were doing together. — Now he is perhaps feeling her, now fucking — now she is feeling his prick. Has he fucked her — twice — or thrice? — These and a hundred similar thoughts floated through my brain, until I got as randy as if I hadn't fucked for a week.

The longer I waited, the more impatient I got, yet determined to wait all night if needs be, thinking of nothing but what he was doing with her. — I resolved to see if she would tell the truth or a lie. — At length out I saw him come. I went down towards Ox***d St., — for I knew then the way she went home, — and peeped round the corner of a street until I saw her come along. Then walking I met her as if by accident. — "What you?" said I. — "Yes." — "Where have you come from?" — "From **** — I have never left." — Then she began to tell the truth, and I went back to the baudy house with her.

I am telling this part of my history a little out of order, for it occurred somewhat later on, when I had then got her confidence, and she used to talk to me like an old acquaintance. — In the bed-room she began to laugh. — "You saw the man who followed me. — Well! he waited for *you* going out, came into the house after you left, and asked if a tall dark woman was up stairs. — Of course Mrs. A said — 'No' — He said he was sure she was, for he had seen her come in with a man two hours before, and she had not left. — Mrs. A then came up, and asked me — and I said — let him come up. — He came, I had my bonnet on." "I have waited for you two hours, to have you — how often have you been fucked?" "I told him not at all — that my friend had only looked at me." — "Ah! you frig him, and that is what I want — but I like to be frigged by a woman who has been fucked the same night." "Then I told him you did it to

[*332*]

me once, which *excited* him. He put his hand up my clothes immediately. I asked him what he was going to give me, and he gave me three pounds at once, and said he would give more if I pleased him.

"He made me undress, except my stockings, and stripped himself. — Well — I have seen a good many pricks in my time, but on my soul I think his was the biggest — It was as stiff as a poker when he undressed. — He had not seen me naked then. — Then he asked all about your prick, and what you did — how you spent — I told lie after lie, just as I thought would suit him. Then he laid me on the side of the bed and began to lick my cunt." Sarah often dropped her voice and hesitated when she said a baudy word (women differ in their ways). "Then he turned my bum towards him, and he hit me all over with his prick, as hard as if it was with a stick, and asked if I had ever seen a stiffer, or larger one — then he turned me and said he would put it in — I got ready saying I feared he would hurt me. — He put the tip in which stretched me, gave an awful shove which hurt me, and I cried out. He pulled it out, put me between two chairs, just as you do when you make me piddle (I do that) and sitting down, licked my thing till I could bear it no longer, and laying hold of his head I spent. Then he frigged himself so that his spunk spurted up onto my bum.

"He licked me again, and wanted me to suck him. Then he frigged himself again. — Then he went away and gave me two sovereigns more." — Sarah showed me five sovereigns, together with mine — said she — "I will treat *you* with a bottle of champagne if you like."

His licking her cunt — his big prick — his desire to know all about me — sank into my mind, but as before said, this story is told one or two months too soon. — I fucked Sarah, and departed without the champagne — thinking of his big prick which Sarah never seemed tired of describing to me afterwards, and I quite felt jealous of it.

I had then known Sarah many months, but had never licked her cunt. — Two or three years had elapsed since I had done such a thing. — Sarah altho fresh colored, firm fleshed, and about her cunt a fine woman, had never made me desire that. — Nearly hairless cunts, are those only which I have generally desired (with few exceptions) but *his* licking and *her* description of the effect on *her*, made me curious. — "Why could you not bear it?" "No woman can long — you can't help yourself, — you must make a man

[*333*]

leave off, or you can't prevent yourself spending." "I never did it to you." "No *you* never did, but some men are fond of doing it to me." "Do you like it?" "I like a poke best, yet you can't help liking it if a man begins — and you happen just then to want anything." — Now I will go back, to where I left off about her boots and silk stockings.

Soon after I had known her, I increased and unasked, from ten shillings to a sovereign for her favors — and often stopped later with her. — As she liked champagne, I began to take a bottle which we drank between our fuckings. — When it was warm I used to put her naked on the bed, and sit in a chair so as to look at her cunt and other charms. — When cold we used to sit by the fire both half naked, and talk baudy things — or the news of the day — I used to read the paper — and if there was anything about a woman being ravished — or a fellow showing his cock, — or feeling another man's cock in a pissing place — or an adultery — or anything of that kind, we used to discuss it. — She would tell me her views, and I gained further experience of women in such matters. — She became frank, and told me why and wherefore, in a way that few gay woman had since Camille, and one or two others.

More than once I alluded delicately to her nose. She did not like the allusion, and altho not given to swearing — damned and cursed at *him* about it. — When I asked who *him* was she said. — "No one" — or — "Nothing." — She told me, she was thought a very handsome woman before her nose was damaged, and brought me a photograph [early days of photography] to show me. — In that she looked extremely handsome. — I said so — which set her off swearing at *him* again. — Another night, furiously she said, "If he were here, I would knife him. I'd fuck before his damned eyes. — I'd murder him." Then after a short pause, "But I have served him out." "Who?" "Nobody you know," — said sullenly — and no more could I get out of her — I never knew who *him* was — I have tried to get it from her when half groggy — when ready to spend — and when revelling in baudiness with me, but never did. From chance words dropped from time to time, and the odds and ends of talk, I came to the conclusion that *him* was her *husband*, but it's only a guess.

[Much that I did with Sarah I have done with others, but every woman has a way and manner of her own even in the most simple baudy gambols. That is the charm in having a change in women. The variety gives me exquisite delight. But with Sarah some of my lascivious frolics were the most complete in their performance — and some I never yet have done with other women, as I find in my narrative further on.]

CHAPTER XXXVII

Sarah's agile tongue. — Listening at a brothel. — A hole bored uselessly. — The donkey-hung one. — His letches. — A brothel with a spy-hole. — A hundred couples fucking. — A young couple. — Involuntary onanism. — Five shillings extra. — Sarah's curiosity. — A lady and gentleman. — The lady's fears. — The rickety sofa. — The scare. — The baud's cautions. — Common coitions.

One night Sarah was in a strong fucking mood and put her tongue into my mouth, and I said something which made her remark, "You did it with my friend Eliza, and I have as good teeth as she has." — Altho I had known Sarah so long, I had never put my tongue to hers. Then it was that I found out that she could put out her tongue farther than any one I ever knew. She could reach half through my mouth with it. — When she was being fucked, she used after that to glue my mouth to hers, and I gave way to her. But altho she had a nice mouthful of teeth, I never cared about mixing our spittles — which is curious.

It was just before I had the big Eliza that the man with the big prick watched me into the house, and now I go back to him.

I still went at times to the baudy house in L**t*e P***l**d St. It was dilapidated, the paper partly torn from the walls, and in the upper rooms (it was a two-storey house) the division between them seemed to have been temporarily put up, making one room into two, and was papered and canvassed over; but it was so thin, that you could hear distinctly what was said in the adjacent room. They had been afraid for a long time of the house being indited, so did nothing to repair it. But it was convenient, and why I went there was that I could hear the bed creak when the couples were at their pleasures, and also what they said. On the first floors you could hear, but not so well. The baud somehow found out my taste and told Sarah of the top room. — But altho I could hear, I could not see. The partition was canvassed on both sides, if one side was torn and there partly opened, there was the canvas on the other side.

I bored through it, and tried to make holes as others evidently had tried — and saw, but could not get a good glimpse. The keeper to whom Sarah spoke, refused to allow holes to be made, so I had to content myself with laying on the bed with Sarah, and feeling her cunt, until a couple came in. — Then we listened and it seemed to amuse her as much as me. — When we heard the bed creak, on to Sarah I got, and the delight of my fucking was increased by thinking that close to me was another couple fucking.

The man and woman wrangled about money at times, and I heard many funny things. But one night I slipped outside our door and bored, with a gimlet, a small hole in the door of the back room, and there would stand until Sarah beckoned me to come in. I was not likely to be surprized by the baud, for I could perfectly hear if any one came into the house, and there were no rooms over head.

I could however see but little, could not see the bed, but saw the women washing their cunts, and the men washing with their backs turned to me. Occasionally a woman undressed on that side of the room, then disappeared on to the bed side. I began to crave to watch a couple go thro the amatory preliminaries, and to see the man's prick — But, I was always in fear that some one might come to the door, open it, and catch me.

Just then Sarah met the man with the donkey prick, whom she told me did then exactly what he had done before with her. This recital made me wild with desire. — I told her I would give her something handsome, if she could find a house, where I could see couples fucking. She had heard there was one, but those who knew would not tell, and some time slipped away. — With a smiling face one night she said, "If you don't mind a sovereign for the room, and five shillings afterwards for each couple you see, I know now where you can get what you want." — Off we went the following night to the house, and through a carefully prepared hole beneath a picture frame, I had a complete view of a nice room. — The washing place, bed (no sofa), looking-glass, fire place, were all in sight. In fact only that side of the room in which the eye hole was made in the partition, was not perfectly visible.

I recollect that first night well. — The woman of the house said to me, "You won't tell people will you?" — then — "Put out your light when you are looking." — There was gas in the room. "Don't make a noise — and don't look till you hear, or think they are on the bed." — Then she lifted a picture up on to a higher nail in the partition, which disclosed a small hole. — Then she went into the other room, and did the same to a picture there. It was in a huge, old fashioned, projecting gilt frame, which when hung higher up, just cleared the hole but well shadowed it. — There was one good, strong, gas burner in the room, but no candle to enable people to pry about with.

The hole was so high up, that it was necessary to stand on a sofa placed just against the partition. There was no fire in our room when first I went there, and it was dark at about seven o'clock, Sarah had gone in first. — The woman when she had got my sovereign said, "I don't suppose any one will be there till about eight o'clock."

I undressed Sarah, and sat in excitement feeling her about, and looking at her legs, and talking. — I heard couples going into lower rooms, and the woman saying, "This way, sir" — a gruff voice reply, — "I won't go so high." — At length a couple entered. Sarah turned down the gas in our room, and up I got on the sofa. Oh my delight, — how I wish it were to come over again. There was a fine young man and a niceish young woman — I watched them with an intensity of lust quite indescribable. — I saw him first pay her, she take off her things, piss, and then stand naked expectantly. He took off his trowsers, she took hold of his prick, and he felt her cunt. — Then it was kiss, feel, and frig on both sides. I could hear him ask questions, and she reply. Then he put her down on a chair, and pushed his noble prick up against her but not up her. Then he brought her to the side of the bed, I saw her thighs distended, a dark haired cunt opened and looked at. He pushed his prick up it and had a plunge or two. (His back was towards me then.) Apparently not satisfied, he then pushed her straight on the bed — got on himself, laid by the side of her, and then I saw his prick in all its glory. — She wanted to handle it, he would not let her, but fingered her cunt with his hand nearest to her.

At length kneeling between her thighs I saw it again in all its prominence, stiff and nodding — until dropping on to her belly, it was hidden from my sight. — I watched the heavings and thrustings — the saucers which came in his arse cheeks, and disappeared as he thrust up and withdrew his penis, her thighs move up, and then her legs cross over his, as she heaved to meet his strokes. — Then the shoves became mere wriggles, then were loud exclamations of pleasure, then all was still. His limbs stretched out, her legs came tranquilly down to the side of his, a long kiss or two was heard, then absolute silence. — It was a delicious sight.

Almost before he had finished, I had put the cork in the hole in the partition, pulled Sarah to the side of the bed, felt her cunt, and was about to put up it, when alas I spent all over her outside, on thighs and cunt, then with my cock still dripping I got on the sofa again. — Sarah with me, for she seemed to enjoy looking as much as I did.

He had risen on to his knees between her thighs, and held his prick in his right hand, I could just see its red tip. — "Don't move, I'll fuck you again." "Well, you must give me some more." "I will give you five shillings." "Very well, shall I wash?" "No stay as you are." — Slowly his bum sunk on to his heels — his head peered forward — his left hand went to her cunt. — "My spunk's running out," he said. "Oh you beast." He flopped down on her without another word —and I saw by the action of his buttocks that he was driving his pego up her. — His hands clasped her again, I saw the saucers in his arse — his short shoves — her wriggles and jerks — and heard his sighs and "oha's." Then soon his silence shewed that his pleasure was complete.

During all this I kept telling Sarah in a whisper what I saw — she got as impatient as me and wanted to see as much. — It often was, "Let me have a look." "I shan't." "What is she doing?" "She is doing so and so," — then I let her peep and *she* would tell *me*. — I sat on the sofa whilst she was standing and looking, grasped her arse, put my lips on her cunt, and pulled her towards me, giving utterance to all sorts of baudy extravagances in whispers. — It is odd it occurs to me, that all *she* wanted to see was what the *woman* was doing — what I principally wanted to see was what the *man* was doing. — At all times that I was at that peep hole, the same feelings were predominant in both of us.

The man was pleased, gave the extra money, told her he would meet her again, washed his prick and went off — she leisurely washed her cunt, and off she went — then lighting the gas, I ballocked Sarah — not letting my sperm be wasted outside this time. — "It's exciting," said she, "I have not seen such a thing since the night you had the fine, tall, fair woman — and it makes me as randy as be damned" (her favorite expression). We finished fucking just in time for another couple. We saw three couples the first night.

I am not going to tell all I saw — much of it was commonplace fucking enough — yet some had the charm of novelty, and although I was there perhaps in the course of a year or two, in all fifty or sixty times, and saw nearly a hundred and fifty couples fucking, never grew tired of seeing.

The most amusing thing to me was that Sarah wanted to see so much. — After a time I put her occasionally with her back against the partition, and my prick up her — and then applying my eye to the hole over her shoulder, fucked her, and looked at the fucking couple in the room, until I lost sight of them, in the excitement of my own physical pleasure.

That was a risky thing to do for they could have heard us, as well as we did them. But usually the couples were so absorbed by lewedness, so preoccupied by fucking or anticipation of it, that they rarely seemed to notice anything.

One night a couple came in, she about thirty, he about thirty-five years old. She was not gay, was deeply veiled, and shabbily dressed. — At his request she undressed to her petticoat and I saw she was beautifully white in her linen. She was a fine tall woman. — "We have never been here before," said she, "why did you not go to the old place." "It's not safe to go always to the same place." — They spoke in a very low tone. — Sarah looked, and said she was a modest woman, indeed it was quite evident that she was not gay. She unlaced her stays, and whilst doing so, he knelt and putting his head under her petticoats, kept his head up against her cunt or her thighs. Withdrawing it he said, "Oh! I love you so, I love the smell of your cunt." "Oh darling for shame, how can you?" He took off his coat and trowsers, they kissed and toyed, he got her on to the bed, threw up her clothes, and disclosed as fine a pair of thighs as I have ever

[*339*]

seen. — He kissed her all over and buried his head between her thighs, then rising I saw his prick. He took her hand and placed it round it. — "Feel how stiff it is before I put it up you." — Then he threw himself on her and began his poke.

Their loving voluptuous manner so stimulated me, that making some remark to Sarah, I clutched her round her rump, and pressed my stiff cock up against her thighs. — At that instant a leg of the sofa on which we were standing gave way. — It had, as we afterwards found, only broken off just above one of the castors. — It threw us both violently up against the partition with a bang, or indeed two, for my head went with a second bang against it. — We kept silent instinctively, after we had recovered ourselves.

"Oh my God," said the female voice quite loudly. "What is that." "It's some one under the bed — get up — get off, — I will get up," said she almost with a screech. — After a pause we heard them both walking about for some minutes. — We feared to look. — "Nonsense — under the bed." "Oh look there," I peeped, Sarah holding me for fear the sofa should go worse. — He lifted the bed valance. —"It's in the next room then, I am sure some one sees us." "What nonsense, is it likely, it was over head I am sure." "Well I am frightened," and she got off the bed, and sat on a chair.

They dropped their voices again, but I heard that they settled that it was something over head, and with a little loving enticement, on to the bed they again got, and soon were in each other's embraces. — How they enjoyed it, their kisses and murmurs were quite loud. — They lay when finished such a time with limbs interlaced before he got off. — "Don't she like it?" said Sarah who was much interested in this couple. — I was I suppose unusually randy that night — for I brought Sarah to the edge of our bed — fucked her — and directly afterwards going up to the sofa, which was not now easy to stand on, and which wobbled so that it was not safe for both of us, found him just getting off.

Without washing, they both went and stood in front of the fire, talking about the noise. — "It frightened me," said the woman. "I'm always frightened at these places. — I felt frightened as I came in — as if I should be found out, as if some one would see me. — I know it's stupid — but I never felt like it before — or not so much so as I do to-night." It was said in a low clear voice and I heard it distinctly. — "Who can see you, it's nonsense." "Yes, but I feel as if we were found out, as if some one knows what we are doing in

[*340*]

this room." — It was really wonderful (and I've often thought so since) to hear this. What would she have said, had she found out that two eyes had seen a man between her thighs?

"I must get back," she said. "Wait a little." — He took a chair to the fire, and sat down — sat her on his knee, and his hand went up under her chemise. They faced our partition then. — "Oh don't dear — don't now — I am not washed, it is so dirty of you." "Never mind," he replied and kept her there feeling her, until up came his cock quite stiff. He pulled it from under his shirt and shewed it to her laughingly. Then she felt it, and they sat kissing and toying, and saying how they loved each other, putting their tongues together almost without speaking for twenty minutes, until her thighs moved restlessly under his titillation, and gently he again led her to the bed.

She got on to it cheerfully enough, forgetting her scare. They laid two or three minutes kissing and toying, they scarcely ceased tonguing, they moved in various attitudes, she threw her leg high up over him, he put his prick into her, and then they rolled on to one side clinging to each other, her bum then was towards our partition. "Put your leg up again dear," he said. She obeyed. He thrust for a minute, then pulled his prick out, and pushed his fingers up her cunt. Then in again pushing his pego, they at last consummated their enjoyment, with the utmost love and voluptuous energy. — They spoke so low on the bed that I could not hear much, I only heard murmurs until he got fierce in his lust and spoke louder, but their kisses were loud enough to be heard on the staircase. — They were both as fond and as randy as a man and woman could be. — It was one of the most voluptuous sights I have ever witnessed.

They now dozed, he nestling his balls between her thighs, and keeping one of her thighs up under his arm. Her chemise was just sufficiently up to show where the arse cheeks began to divide at the backbone. — I let Sarah get up and look, then I put her on the bed, fucked her, and went back.

He was putting on his trowsers, she washing her cunt. I could see her head just over the bed and hear the slopping. — Again they stood near the fire whilst she put on her petticoats. They now talked in so low a tone that I could hear nothing. — He put his arm round her waist, and leant his other arm on the mantel piece. — I could see their two faces in the glass, and they were both very plain — but she was a beautiful shape, that is, what I had seen of her. — "Oh, I must go, what will they think?" said she as she broke away from him. "What can I tell them?" — Then they went on dressing and when all but finished, "Let me give it another kiss," said he as she put her bonnet on. — Down he knealt and put his head up her clothes, kept it there a minute or two, she standing quite still just facing me. I could see the bunch his head made under her petticoats, and kept telling Sarah in a whisper what I saw, and was watching the woman, when suddenly she closed her eyes. "Oh don't dear," and she drew her bum back. He got up with his hair in disorder. — "I think he's been licking her cunt," said I to Sarah. "Ah," said Sarah, "she is just as bad as a gay woman."

"I will go out first, you turn to the left when you get into O*f**d St. and get into the cab standing by the kerb. — I will put my stick outside the window, so you will know it's me. — Wait about five minutes after I have gone in case I can't get one directly." He went to the window and looked out (the room is at the back of the house), and said it didn't rain. They kissed and murmured to each other — their faces close together, his arm round her. — Then, "Oh! let's do it again before we go," he said quite vivaciously. "Oh, I can't — I can't — look at the time," said she taking out a watch. "Oh William, I must go, what can I tell them. — Oh, don't now, pray don't," said she, for he had pushed his hand up her clothes again. — "Oh pray don't."

He threw off his hat and pulled off his coat like lightning. "I will — I must. — We won't be five minutes." By the time he had said that, his prick was jutting out in front of his trowsers. — His impetuosity, the sight of his prick (that wonderful persuader) conquered. She pulled off her bonnet, he tilted his backside on to the edge of the bed, threw up her clothes, her belly and thighs came for an instant, and for an instant only into view, and received him; the next instant he was ramming into her, holding her thighs under his arms, and in five minutes was quiet, leaning over her belly. They had taken the foot of the bed and I saw them sideways.

He wasted no time, "mind my chemise" said she as he pulled out his prick, and he did it with care — buttoned up, and without washing went out. — She washed, threw off her cloak, pulled up her chemise, and looked at it in all directions, as if to see whether there was any spunk on it; then dressed, put on a thick veil, and out she went. — "Modest women are worse than gay women, for there is no excuse for *them*," said Sarah.

The baud begged we would not make a noise again for she had heard it, but how could we help the sofa breaking down? We promised and begged her to get in couples, when she thought the woman was not gay. — "I know them," said she, "cause of their veils are down, and they never looks at me; but then your will have to wait, and of course I wants my rooms let." But afterwards we certainly saw many couples, of whom the women were what is called modest, tho necessarily the bulk of the fucking was with strumpets.

I may tell of one or two odd occurrences, but for the most part the couples went through the fucking business much in the same way. If the man was quite young he felt the woman's cunt directly he was in the room, then made her partly or quite undress, and if he did not pull off his trowsers, he pulled out his cock, which was usually stiff by that time (if she undressed). Then she gave his cock a squeeze, or a shake or a frig or two, he groped her cunt, and had a hurried look at it, they got on to the bed, fucked quickly, and then off they went. The middle-aged went to work more leisurely; and carefully looked at the ladies' cunts.

[It is well to mention here that but few vehicles passed through the street, but when they did, their noise prevented me hearing what the couples in the back room said.]

CHAPTER XXXVIII

*Penis in excelsis. — Pride in his Priapus. — A whack
on a bum. — A whack on a table. — Between two
chairs. — Over silk stockings. — A male sixteen and
female fifty. — "My little cunny." — Tooth brush
anus, and suction. — The omnibus next day. — My
letch for minette. — A sodomitic parson and catamitic
harlot. — A bum hole licked. — A bum hole
plugged. — The pains and pleasures of sodomy. — A
digital experiment. — The baud's avarice. — The
couples hurried. — Cyprians remuneration. — A tight
cunted one. — One who knew the spy hole. —
Gossip with Sarah on gamahuching. — Sarah's
letch for gamahuching. — On female cunilingers.*

Two or three weeks after I had used this peep hole, Sarah
said she had again met the man with the titanic prick. — We
had by that time got so intimate, that she told me any funny
adventures she had with men. — He had behaved in just the
same manner to her, and was to meet her that day
week. — "Oh! I long to see him with you — bring him to
the next room," — and it was so arranged. — The spying
room was to be kept for me — the back room I was to pay
a pound for, and it was to be kept for Sarah. The old baud
knew what we were up to. — I told Sarah to keep the man
as long as she could, whether he paid much or little (he gave
her treble what I did), and above all to manage so that I
could see his prick well.

The evening came, I was there before the time, and
thought that they were never coming. — At length I saw
them enter — I had been in a fever lest it should not come
off. — The whole evening's spectacle is photographed on
my brain. — I recollect almost every word that was said. —
What I did not hear, Sarah told me afterwards, tho that was
but little.

"Take off your things," said he. — Sarah undressed to her
chemise. — His back was towards me, his hand was evidently on his prick. — "Ain't you going to take *your* clothes

off, you had better — you can do it nicer." — He evidently had not intended that, but yielded to her suggestion. —When in his shirt he went up to her, she gradually turned round so that *her* back and *his* face were towards me, and her movement was so natural that no one could have guessed her object, altho I did. — Moving then slightly on one side, she put her hands to his shirt, lifted the tail, and out stood the largest prick I ever saw. "Oh what a giant you've got," said she. — He laughed loudly. — "Is it not, did you ever see a bigger?" "No, but your balls are not so big." "No, but they are *big*." "No," she said. "You can't see them," — and he put one leg on a chair, — Sarah stooped and looked under them. — Whilst doing so, he tried to give her a whack on her head with his prick — and laughed loudly at his own fun. — "Why," said Sarah, "if your balls were equal in size to your prick, you wouldn't be able to get them into your trowsers." — He laughed loudly, saying, "They're big enough — there is plenty of spunk in them."

Sarah went on admiring it, smoothing it with her hand, pulling up and down the foreskin and keeping it just so that I had a full view. "You are hairy," said she, rubbing his thigh. — Then I noticed he was hairy on his legs, which was very ugly. — "Yes, do you like hairy-skinned men?" "I hate a man smooth like a woman — take off your shirt and let me see." "It's cold." "Come close to the fire then." — She talked quite loudly purposely, tho it was scarcely needed. His voice was a clear and powerful one. — Without seeming anxious about it, but flattering him, she managed to get his shirt off and he stood naked. — He was a tall man, very well-built, and hairy generally. Masses hung from his breasts, it darkened his arms. It peeped out like beards from his armpits, it spread from his balls half way up his belly, he had a dark beard, and thick black hair. — In brief he was a big, powerful, hairy, ugly fellow, but evidently very proud of his prick, and all belonging to him. Her flattering remarks evidently pleased him highly, and he turned round as she wished him, to let her see him well all over. — His prick which had been stiff had fallen down, for instead of thinking of the woman, he was now thinking of himself; but it was when hanging, I should say, six inches long, and thick in proportion. "Dam it, it's cold, we are not so accustomed to strip like you women." — Then he put his shirt on and began business.

He made her strip and told her to go to the bedside. She

[*345*]

went to the end and leaned over it with backside towards him. — He tucked his shirt well up, came behind her, and with his prick which had now stiffened and seemed nine inches long (I really think longer), hit her over her buttocks as if with a stick. It made a spanking noise as it came against her flesh. Then he shoved it between her thighs, brought it out again, and went on thwacking her buttocks with it. — "Don't it hurt you?" she asked him turning her head round towards the peep hole. — "Look here," said he. Going to a round small mahogany table and taking the cloth off it — he thwacked, and banged his prick on it, and a sound came as if the table had been hit with a stick. — "It does not hurt me," he said. — I never was so astonished in my life.

"I mean to fuck you," said he. "That you shan't, you will hurt any woman." — Again he roared with laughter. — "Suck it." "I shan't." — Again he laughed. — Then he made her lean on a chair, and again banged his prick against her arse. — Then he sat down, and pulled her on to him, so that his prick came up between her thighs just in front of her quim. — "I wish there was a big looking-glass," said he. "Why did you come here, there was one at the other house." — Sarah said this was nicer and cleaner, and he had said he wanted a quiet house. — "Ah, but I shan't come here again, I don't like the house."

"Get on to the chairs — the same as before." But the chairs in the room were very slight, and Sarah was frightened of them slipping away from under her. — So she placed one chair against the end of the bed, and steadied it; and against another which she put a slight distance off, she pushed the large table. Then mounting on the chairs, she squatted with one foot on each as if pissing. I could not very well see her cunt for her backside was towards me, and shadowed it.

He laid down with his head between the chairs, and just under her cunt. He had taken the bolster and pillows from the bed for his head, and there he laid looking up at her gaping slit, gently frigging his prick all the time. At length he raised himself on one hand, and licked away at her cunt for several minutes, his big prick throbbing, and knocking up against his belly whilst he did it.

Said he again, "I wish there was a glass." Sarah got down, and put on the floor the small glass of the dressing table, and arranged it so that he could see a little of himself as he lay. — But he was not satisfied. — He recommenced cunt-licking, and self-frigging, and all was quiet for a minute. — Then he actually roared out, — "Oh — my spunk coming, my spunk, — my spunk, — spunk — oho. — Come down — come over me." — Off got Sarah, pushed away the chairs, and stood over him with legs distended, her arse towards me so that I lost sight of his face, but could see his legs, belly, and cock as he lay on the floor. — "Stoop, — lower, — lower." — She half squatted, he frigged away, her cunt was now within about six inches of his prick, when frigging hard and shouting out quite loudly — "Hou — Hou — Hou," his sperm shot out right on to her cunt or thereabouts, and he went on frigging till his prick lessening, he let it go, and flop over his balls.

Sarah washed her cunt and thighs, and turning round before doing so, stood facing me and pointed to her cunt. His spunk lay thick on the black hair tho I could barely see it. — She smiled and turned away. He lay still on the floor with eyes closed for full five minutes, as if asleep. Sarah washed, put on her chemise and sat down by the fire, her back towards me partly.

He came to himself, got up and went to the fire — then he washed (his back towards me), then stood by the fire, then fetched the pot and pissed. I saw his great flabby tool in his hand, and the stream sparkling out of it, for it was done just under the gas light. — Again he stood by the fire, his tool hidden by his shirt which he had on, and they talked. — Then he strode round the room and looked at the prints on the wall, looked even at the very picture beneath which I was peeping. — "What a daub," he remarked and passed on (it was a miserable portrait of a man), then from the pocket of his trowsers he gave Sarah several sovereigns.

That lady knew her game, and had thrown up her chemise so as to warm her thighs — and after he had paid her, he put his hand on to them. — She at the same time put her hand on to his tool. "Oh what a big one." — nothing evidently pleased him so much as talking about the size. — "Did you ever see so big an one," said he for the sixth time I think. "Never — let's look at it well. — Hold up your shirt." — He did as told. — Sarah pulled his prick up, then let it fall, handled his balls, pulled the foreskin up and down, and shewed him off again for my advantage. — "Why don't you sit down, are you in a hurry?" Down he sat, his tool was becoming thicker and longer under her clever handling, and hung down over the edge of the chair. He was sitting directly under the gas light, and I could see plainly, for Sarah cunningly had even stirred the fire into a blaze. He was curious about other men's cocks — what their length and thickness was. — She shewed him by measuring on his own, and kept pulling it about, her object being to get it stiff again for me to see his performances. — My delight was extreme — I could scarcely believe that I was actually seeing what I did, and began to wish to feel his prick myself. How large it must feel in the hand I thought, how small mine is compared with it, and I felt my own. — As Sarah pulled down his prepuce, I involuntarily did so to mine, and began to wish she were feeling mine instead of the man's.

Then only I noticed how white his prick was. His flesh was brownish — and being so sprinkled with hair it made it look dark generally. — His prick looked quite white by contrast. Sarah must have been inspired that night, for no woman could have better used her opportunity for giving me pleasure and instruction. Repeating her wonder at the size, she said, "Let's see how it looks when you kneel." — He actually knelt as she desired. I saw his prick hanging down between his legs. Soon after in another attitude, I noticed that hair crept up between his bum cheeks, and came almost into tufts on to the cheeks themselves. — I saw that his prick was now swelling. — Sarah taking hold of it, "Why it's stiff again." He grasped it in the way I had first seen him, and said eagerly. — "Let's see your cunt again."

Sarah half slewed her chair round towards him, opened both legs wide, and put up one of her feet against the mantelpiece, as I have often seen her do when with me. He knelt down and I lost sight of his head between her legs — but saw his hand gently frigging himself as before, and heard soon a splashy, sloppy, slobbery sort of suck, as his tongue rubbed on her cunt now wetted by his saliva. Then he got up and pushed his prick against her face. — "Suck, and I will give you another sovereign." "It will choke me — I won't," said Sarah.

Then he began to rub her legs and said he liked silk stockings, that few wore silk excepting French women whom he did not like, — but "they all suck my prick." — Again Sarah put up her leg — again he licked her cunt, and then said she must frig him, which she agreed to on his paying another sovereign.

He told her to go to the edge of the bed and he then went to the side nearest the door, which put his back towards me. — He called her there. — "Come here," said Sarah, lay-ing herself down at the foot. "No, here." "I won't, it's cold close to the door" (she knew that there I could not see his cock). He obeyed, put up her legs (just as I used to do) opened them wide, and I could sideways see her black haired quim gaping. "Close them," he cried. She did and lay on her back, her knees and heels close together up to her bum, "I'll spend over your silk stockings," said he, now frigging violently. Sarah to save her stockings, just as his spunk spurted, opened her legs wide and it went over her cunt and belly. — He never seemed to notice it.

I had passed an intensely exciting couple of hours by my-self, watching this man with his huge fucking machine. Sarah in her attitudes, altho I had seen them fifty times, looked more inviting than ever. My prick had been standing on and off for an hour. — I would have fucked anything in the shape of cunt if it had been in hand, and nearly groaned for want of one. As I saw her legs open to receive his squirt, heard his shout of pleasure, and saw his violent, frig, frig, frig, I could restrain myself no longer, but giving my cock a few rubs, spent against the partition, keeping my eye at the peephole all the while.

He wiped his cock on her cunt hair, washed, and went away seemingly in a hurry. — Sarah came in to me. — "Don't you want me," said she. — I pointed to my spunk on the partition. "You naughty boy, I want it awfully." — Soon after I was fucking her. — With all her care to save her silk stockings, sperm had hit her calf, and while I fucked her at the bed side, I made her hold up her leg that I might look at it. — It excited me awfully. What a strange thing lust is.

I never saw the man afterwards. — She did, but he would never go to that house again. — She thought that he lived in the country. He seemed a gentleman.

———————

One night a couple went in. It was a thin woman about fifty years old I should say, and a youth of about six-teen. — He looked like a Jew. She asked him, directly he was in, for the money; he gave her five shillings, put down his hat, and went up to her. — She had never moved from the door side of the room, and stood with her back to the bed, her face towards us. He seemed shy. She said, "Let me feel your cock." His back was to me, but I could soon see she had hold of his doodle. He was quite quiet, and when he spoke, he did so in a low tone of voice so that I could scarcely hear him. — Her voice on the contrary was that of a magpie, the clack of an old woman. — "Feel my cunny my dear," said she, "it's such a nice hairy cunny." — He put his hand up her clothes and wanted to look. — "Oh, no, you want to know too much, I can't shew it — it's made to feel, not to show, but feel it, it's nice and hairy." — "Oh what a nice cock it is — how it longs to go up my little cunny — how stiff it is — oh what a nice cock," and she stooped and looked at it — I could not see it. — "Oh no I can't let you see it — another time," she said, in reply to something he said. — "Oh put it in, put it in, it's longing to go up my cunny." — Leaning back against the bed, she hitched up her clothes, and I saw a pair of dirty spindle shanks nearly to her thighs. — She never left go of his cock, but pulled him towards her by it. — "Oh it's up my cunny, how often do you fuck, — Oh it is up my little hairy cunny my dear, is it not nice? — Oh fuck it, fuck, fuck, fuck, — Oh isn't nice?" — He had clasped her somehow and was shoving rapidly, and spent almost before he began, for I heard a deep sigh from him and he was quiet; whilst she kept on cackling, "Oh is it not a nice little cunny."

He was in a hurry, or did not like his bargain, for he buttoned up the instant he had done, and put his hat on. — She went across the room, took a towel and gave her cunt a dry rub but did not wash. — "Give me a shilling for luck," said she. — He gave it her. — "I'll give you more pleasure next time, and you shall see my cunny." — Off they went. They had not been in the room ten minutes. — She never took her bonnet off.

Sarah always anxious to see the women, used to say if she knew them or not. — It was, "She is lucky with men," — or, "She used to be about but I have lost sight of her," — and so on — once, — "Oh that woman's been laid up with the pox — I thought she had gone home." — There was always amusement for both of us.

One night a fine looking man with a dark moustache, looking not forty years old, came in with a poorish looking woman. — They talked for some time, then he said, "I will give you five shillings extra if you'll suck me." — After refusal, and a declaration that she had never done it before, she agreed to it. — I told Sarah and let her look. — "I know that woman, let me see her do it, I never saw a man's prick in a woman's mouth in my life." — He gave her ten shillings and said he would give the five when she had sucked him, took off his coat, and feeling in the pocket took out a paper, from which he produced a round handled tooth brush, and put it in his waistcoat pocket. — Then in the centre of the room he dropped his trowsers down. — She laid hold of his tool which was quite flabby, and pulled the skin back, and squeezed it. "Wash it first." — He scuffled with his trowsers down his ankles towards the wash stand, washed and came back. She dropped on her knees. He had refused to lay on the bed as she asked him. — If they had placed themselves so as to let me look at them, they could not have placed themselves better.

She took it into her mouth, and moving her head backwards and forwards fucked his prick so to speak with her lips. Then she spat on the floor, then into her mouth his prick which had begun to swell again went. As it came out it was now quite big.

She stopped, looked up and said. — "You must not spend in my mouth, tell me when you are coming." "Yes I must — there is no pleasure unless I finish." "Oh I can't." She left off and stood up. — After an altercation, he agreed to give her ten shillings instead of five, if she would let him, and she to make sure, had the money first.

She stood besides him for a time, holding his cock and frigging it — for unless a woman loves a man, or is really fond of having a prick in her mouth, as some are, she likes to make the prick suction short, and bring it as much forward by fist-fucking as she can. "Do you never fuck?" said she. "I was wounded some years ago, and have never been able to fuck since." — It was not clear to me why a man whose prick already stood, could not put it into a woman's cunt, as well as into her mouth. — He had then taken the tooth brush out of his pocket. — "What are you going to do with that," said the girl. "I tickle my bum hole with that, it increases my pleasure, you will see."

She dropped on her knees — and his prick which had drooped again, got stiff under her sucking — but she had to go on for such a time, that she rested and said, "Oh you can't spend."

He said he could. — Then I saw him wet the handle of the tooth brush with spittle, and laying hold of it by the bristly end he pulled up his shirt and passing his hand to the rear, began to move it rapidly. — "Have you put it up your arse hole?" said the girl, leaving off.

"Yes — yes — go on — suck — I shan't be long." — On they went, her head bending up and down as his prick came in and out, his hand bobbing from his backside. — He was just beginning to shiver with pleasure, when the landlady knocked at the door. — "Make haste please, we want the room." — I have heard her do this several times when the couples seemed too long — but this couple had been but a short time in the chamber.

Out came the handle from his arse hole, out came his prick from her mouth, up she stood. He called out "I will pay for the room twice." "All right, sir," said the landlady, going away."

"Damn her," said he, "I was just going·to spend — go on." — "Oh what a time you are — you ought to give me another five shillings." "I will, I will," — he said hurriedly.

Sarah who had been looking at intervals thro the peep hole, remarked, "That poor girl will have all her trouble again."

She again dropped on her knees, again engulfed his doodle which had gone to the size of a gooseberry — again the tooth brush jigged up his arsehole, and after much hard work for the woman, he cried out, — "I'm coming, I'm coming," drew out his tooth brush, and holding her head with both his hands, whilst the tooth brush stuck out from one of them, fucked hard in her mouth, till his head fell forward, with eyes closed and his mouth wide open. She slowly mumbled at this doodle for a minute, then emptied her mouth into a towel she had.

Sarah had glimpses, and I told her what was going on. — "Is she still sucking — what is he doing?" were whispers frequently made. — I had never seen her in such a state of curiosity. — "Well! I never saw that before altho I have seen much — I wouldn't make a baudy house of my mouth — or turn it into a cunt for five shillings, or fifty shillings."

I was amused, tho the tooth brush business so disgusted me that I retched, and sent out for brandy. But the cocksucking made a great impression on me, I'd had it done a few times in my life under excitement which left me almost without knowing what I did. Soon after I thought I should like to try it, and I looked out for that very woman, but never saw her — I reserved my want, not liking to ask Sarah. — The sight she said had made her as sick as it had me. — Wasn't she lying? — A desire for Sarah to gamahuche me sprang up that very night, tho I didn't then ask her.

I thought about it repeatedly afterwards for the enjoyment of the man seemed so intense. — His whole frame writhed as he stood, and what struck me was the extraordinary quivering of his thighs; they shook as he spent like an aspen leaf. I noticed *that* more than anything else. He had tucked up his shirt round his waist in a roll, as if quite accustomed to the operation standing.

The girl rinsed her mouth. — He washed his tooth brush and put it carefully up in paper, pissed and began to button up. The woman again asked him if he never fucked, and he made a similar reply; he had not fucked for years. — It is noticeable that he'd never touched or looked at the girl's quim, nor made her undress, nor felt her in any way. — She, curious, asked him many questions. Replying, he said he found no difficulty in getting women to suck him, that some did it much better than others, that he did not often do it, and never twice the same day for it made him ill. Then he drew the girl's attention to something under his balls, but I could not hear what he said for he turned his back, and his belly was to the gas. The girl felt and looked, kneeling to do so. He was an exceedingly fine man and in the prime of life — his prick by no means large.

Next day I got into an omnibus. — A minute afterwards a man got in and sat opposite to me, and I saw it was the same who had the night before tooth-brushed his arsehole. — I was under no error, his eyes, manner, clothes, the ring on his finger, I recognized all. I sat staring until he raised his eyes to mine. I still stared resolving in my mind what I had seen him do, and felt such an aversion to him, that I stopped the omnibus and got out.

Sarah laughed. "Well I have done most things and am not particular, but blessed if ever I had a man's spendings in my mouth and never will." — Yet before a month had passed, she had mine — I expect she lied, but it is never safe to say you won't do anything in love matters. All women I believe have had a man's prick in their mouths, it's human nature.

One night a man of about thirty years old came in with a woman. They had evidently met before, and she knew his ways and wishes. — He was coated and muffled up almost to his eyes. When he'd unwrapped, I guessed by his well-shaven face and long frock coat, that he was a clergyman. He spoke so low until towards the end of his amour, that I could scarcely hear a word. — Before she undressed, he made her kneel on a chair, and throwing up her petticoats exposed her buttocks, and a remarkable plump, well-made woman of about twenty-five she was. Then he walked to the other end of the room and contemplated her. Then he turned her round and made her sit with her clothes up, stand with them up, lay on the floor, backside up, and then belly up, and in fact put her almost into every possible attitude to expose her private parts. — But he never put her on the bed, and as there was no sofa, he placed her always at the corner of the fire place under the gaslamp, so that Sarah and I had the finest view of her. — After having seen her in one or two postures, he, dressed altogether in black, pulled out a stiff cock and his balls, he walked about, still looking at her but without putting his hands on his machine, of which we had a good view. It was rather large, and stood out stiff enough for a time, then it flopped down over his stone bag. — Then he made her strip to her chemise, he stripped to his shirt, and put her through the same postures, but principally with her arse towards him, to which he knelt down and began to fumble about and kiss, and at length to lick.

Almost at the outside Sarah said, "I know that woman, but I haven't seen her for some time," and told me her history which I quite forget. — Then she got anxious to watch her, continually saying, "Let me have a look — do." But it was a sight I much desired to see myself, for the woman looked so nice, that I began to long to have her, and resolved in my mind how I should get her. — Then I got such a stiff-stander, that excepting for losing the sight, I should have put it into Sarah. But there I stood, feeling Sarah's arse and tucking my fingers between its cheeks, and twiddling her cunt and looking.

The man whose prick again got very stiff, began poking it at her. — He pushed it in her face, up against her breasts, her sides, and her bum, but principally her bum. — Sarah looking one minute, said, "He likes her arse better than her belly." Then he put two chairs close together so as to let her kneel with knees wide open, and came close to the partition

[*354*]

thro which we were looking, and stood gazing. Now just beneath her distended thighs I could, tho sideways, see her cunt gaping but it was in shadow in the dark fringing hair, which in quantity in front, was thickish behind.

He went close and pulled open her arse cheeks with both hands, and began licking her brown hole furiously — at intervals leaning back, looking at the hole, and what seemed to us to be thrusting his finger in it, but his head was in the way and we could not be sure.

"He will keep her all night," said I, "let's fuck, my spunk's nearly coming." "Wait, wait, he won't be long now, he is feeling his prick," but Sarah was wrong. — He came back and again stood looking so long, that impatiently I pulled Sarah off the sofa, put her at the edge of the bed, and in a few shoves discharged up her cunt, my seminal libation.

Scarcely waiting for my prick to shrink out I pulled it out of her. — She with cunt full, got on to the sofa before me, and looking attentively for a minute whispered, "Oh! oh! he is going to bugger her — he is greasing her bum."

I could scarcely get her head from the peep hole; when I did, saw he had got a pot of grease and was greasing his prick. — "He's greased her arsehole," said Sarah to whom I kept whispering what was going on. Then he placed her at the bottom of the bed, and their flanks were towards us. — The woman said, "You will give what you did before." "Yes, yes," he replied, but he was scarcely audible. Then she again turned her arse towards him, her legs distended, her face and arms over the bed, he had pulled off her chemise, he his shirt and they were both naked. — His prick stood upright against his belly, with his left hand keeping the bum cheeks open or fumbling, his right hand holding his tool, he put it in her. I saw his arse oscillating and heard her with muffled voice say something which sounded like, — "Oh you hurt so," just as his belly closed on her arse. Then he placed both hands round her haunches holding her tightly. — "He's up her, I wonder if he is up her cunt or her arsehole." "Up her arse or why did he grease it and his own prick as well, — let me look. — I want to know what that woman does, she's cheeked me, and I want to know."

I let her look for a second. — "He is buggering her I am sure from the way he stands." I pushed her head away for she would not move, applied my eye to the hole, and saw him ramming away hard, his bum wag, his thighs shake, his whole form move quiveringly. Beyond "Yes, yes" — when she'd asked him first about the money — I'd scarcely heard him, so low was the tone in which he uttered what little he said. — All at once he drew his belly back from her bum, and looked down, gratifying his eyes, but for a second only; for with a quick shove followed quickly by others — he shouted out in a loud voice, — "I'm up her arse, I'm up her arse, Oh! — oh!," and then still louder, — "My spunk in your arse, my spunk in your arsehole." "Oh! some one will hear, don't," said the woman, lifting her head and turning it partly round. "Don't! hish! don't!" — but he shouted still "arse-hole, spunk," and then was quiet — bending over her, holding her tightly, and gently wriggling his arse about with enervated muscular action.

"He has buggered her, look." "Yes he has buggered her," said Sarah, looking, "a dirty, nasty bitch, she ought to be shown up — dirty bitch, I have a good mind to tell one or two of her friends what I have seen her up to. — I wonder if it hurts her much," said she enquiringly after a pause — I wondered too.

He kept close to her backside, leaning over her and grasping her round her waist. — His head laying on her naked back, his face slightly turned towards me, and I thought he never would get off. At last she moved and I suppose threw his prick out, for he relieved her and threw himself naked as he was on the bed, his arse towards us, and there he lay as if in sleep for I suppose ten minutes.

She took no notice — but opened the door, and asked for warm water, washed, put on her chemise, then put her finger evidently on to her arsehole, and looked at her finger. She did that more than once at intervals of a minute or so. — Then she said I *think* (for she dropped her voice), "arn't you going to get up," — He rose, washed and dressed, and they went away. She was a sweetly pretty woman, had a charming plump figure, and was I should have said a very appetizing fuck, — but she was not well dressed.

Before they went away — he turned her up after she was dressed, looked at her arse hole and kissed it, and they both laughed — but they spoke during the whole entertainment in such a low tone, that I could hear nothing but what I have told.

Sarah and I talked about buggery in general. — "It does not hurt," said she, "to put your finger up, but a big prick must." — I thought it must hurt to put up a finger. — "You can try on yourself." "I would," said I, "if he had left his ointment." She laughed, "We will try it together some day, you shall put your finger up my bum hole and I up yours." "All right you bring the ointment." "I will get some cold cream." We joked about the parson's fun for I was sure he was a parson. — Soon we had another couple to look at, and another, but when we talked we got back to the sodomitical subject — and when I fucked Sarah that night, we both talked as we lay in copulation, of the difference of sensation there might be between arse hole plugging — and cunt plugging. Said I, "The pleasure really must be all on one side." "I have heard that some men and some women too, are fond of the sensation of a prick in their bum holes," said she. This was said whilst I was up her. When in that sensuous, stimulating, lascivious, position, it takes away one's sense largely; all is pleasure, but I know what I have written was said then.

Afterwards I thought of my adventure in my youth, with the fat, squabby, Devonshire woman's bumhole — and wondered if going up that round hole gave greater pleasure than fucking. I longed to try but dismissed it from my mind. Then I wondered if it hurt to put anything up the bum, so greased my finger one day, and to my surprize it slipped up without pain, but with an unpleasant sensation. I asked Sarah about what she had said, and one night she got cold cream, and as we lay on the bed together, I induced her to try on me; and we both poked up each other's arseholes. It rather upset me, and I was ashamed of it. — It gave me no pleasure and gave her none she said, so we never did it again. But from time to time I could not help thinking about it and had a desire to have the woman we had seen buggered.

I have said that the landlady did not give the couples too long a time, especially if business was brisk. — She had an eye mainly to the double fees, for in addition to the pound, I paid five shillings for each couple. They charged the couples three and six pence and sometimes five shillings, never more. It was only a second class house, tho I saw swell women there.

One night she turned seven couples in between eight and twelve o'clock — all of whom we saw copulating — I did not mind the ordinary run being got in and out soon, for they usually went to work with small prelude, and the more petticoats I hoisted, the more cunts I saw, and the more pricks wagged and stiffened in my view, the better. But when a spoony couple were in — or the man had funny letches, — I was annoyed at their being hurried so asked again the landlady to try to put couples of whom the woman was what is called modest (altho every woman is immodest enough to show her own tail, and feel a man's tail at times), and not to hurry them. — The ordinary couples needed no hurrying, for the gay ladies urged on the shagging.

———————

I soon discovered the very unequal fees paid, and what small sums at times were paid even to exceedingly well dressed women. — Many had only ten shillings and often five, although at times they got two or three sovereigns, and from men who did not look very rich. — I once saw a girl come in twice the same night and be fucked for five shillings, and heard her say it was very little. He gave her a shilling more for a glass of wine. — The second time she got a couple of sovereigns. — I chaffed Sarah about the nice cunts to be had for ten shillings, but in my young days I knew that. Yet having for so many years given higher compliments, it came quite new to me, that a clean nice looking woman, would give up her privates for five shillings, yet well dressed women did.

———————

There was a woman looking twenty-two years old, whom I saw many times. — She was well made and had a pretty face. I took a fancy to have her, but did not like to ask Sarah to get her. — One or two men said, "What a little cunt you have," — at which she used to laugh. — I went about this time in the middle of the day and saw the landlady, who made objection, but principally about Sarah knowing of it, but as I vowed I would not tell, I got the spy room by myself, and passed the evening looking — I told the landlady of the girl I wanted but she would not get her for me, few women, knew of the peep hole room, and I should tell the woman, and that would blow the house — I did not see the girl that night and felt not so comfortable alone. — But the small-cunted woman ran in my head. Again I had the room by myself, and that night she came in. I got awfully randy at seeing her fucked, and directly it was over left the baudy house. — The woman shortly afterwards came out, and turned towards **** St. — When she was just in **** St. I spoke to her, and we went to another house. I bargained for half of a sovereign which I knew she had just been paid. — She accepted after swearing she never had less than a sovereign.

She was perfect in shape, and her cunt one of the smallest for a full grown woman my prick ever entered. — Two fingers went in with greatest difficulty, yet the vulva looked as large as an ordinary one. — There was black hair on it. I enjoyed her immensely and fucked her three times, paying her for each fuck. — What amused me was my asking her if she had it done to her before that night, and she swearing that she had not.

I fucked her at the side of the bed at first, to see my prick draw in and out of the small orifice. When I had recovered from my pleasure, I put her legs over my shoulders, and drawing her bum to me, kept my prick in whilst I asked her questions. She did not hurry me. I had noticed she never was impatient with men. — Pulling my prick out, and telling her what I was going to do, I watched my sperm laying at the mouth of the tight hole, and soon began to work again in my own sperm. — "Oh come on the bed, I want it, let's do it nicely," — and on the bed a more voluptuous little devil never wetted my ballocks.

She would make no appointment with me saying I should see her about, but I never did. I asked the landlady at ***** St. She recollected her, said she sometimes came with men often for a week or so, and then did not for a month. She did not know her name nor anything about her. — I never told Sarah.

One night an ordinary woman was on the bed with a man when Sarah, looking, remarked — "That woman knows there is a peep hole, see how she keeps her eye on it." — Certainly she did keep looking, and she pulled her clothes over her thighs as much as the man's lying between them would permit. — She pushed the man away directly he had finished, and got off the bed looking in our direction. — Sarah let down the picture and waited till the couple had gone. — The landlady had told her to do so in case we thought any one looked at the spyhole. — I saw only two or three women out of the whole number, who eyed the spot suspiciously, and never a man, altho I saw a dozen walk up to the picture and look at it — it was most cunningly contrived. [I wonder if it was ever found out afterwards and there was a row, for the house was closed all of a sudden.]

———————

It was shortly before this that I had seen the girl suck the man's prick, whilst he buggered his own arse with a toothbrush handle. — Somewhere also about that time a French doxy — unasked took my prick in her mouth and whom I made desist — I had rarely had it in a woman's mouth excepting in half drunken orgies. Now at once came on a desire for that luxury, it was through seeing this woman's cunt licked. — "Suck my prick," said I. "I'll see you damned first," said Sarah.

I never relinquished a letch till I satisfied it, I talked about what I had seen, what heard, what done that way with women, and got her to admit that she had been asked to suck. I wondered whether it was more pleasure than spending in a cunt. She wondered (I know now it was bosh). We talked about the gamahuching just seen, and prick sucking. Then she said, "Why don't you lick my quim then?" "Do you like it — do you spend with it?" "Of course I like it, every women does, you can't help spending if a man keeps on at it."

"Suck my prick — do." "Lick my cunt then." I have gone thro this talk with other women, but with Sarah it seemed quite novel.

———————

This spy hole amusement was spread over the best part of two years. Many lustful amusements I had between the various sights, which would better have been told in their place, but I shall from time to time refer to them.

After this night I had a letch for being sucked. — When I next met Sarah, we spent the whole evening in talking about that and gamahuching. Sarah confessed to liking it being done to her *occasionally*, and on her undertaking to tell me when she was spending, I did the job for her, and also had the pleasure of spending in her mouth for the extra fee. But I soon grew tired of that pleasure, unless so fucked out that I could not get a cock-stand. Many times after, when looking thro the peep-hole, she knelt on the sofa and gently sucked my prick.

Gamahuching *she* always wanted, when she'd had a drop more than usual, and I believe really had a great liking for it — I did it at times to please her, but couldn't bear the taste of her cunt, and whilst operating used to keep slobbering, so that her cunt was soon much like a spittoon. — "Aren't you coming?" "Yes, stop, lick just there," and with her finger she indicated the exact spot. — I suppose finding that I did not much like it, she ceased after a time to ask me to do it to her.

But we often described our sensations to each other, and she told me very funny stories about women who were fond of having their cunts licked by other women — I was increasing my experiences largely with her, yet did not know what I since believe to be the case, that *she* was a little fond of having another female tongue on her clitoris, and perhaps another clitoris against hers as well.

CHAPTER XXXIX

A juvenile strumpet. — Two saucy little bitches. — One selected. — Sexual manipulations on the highway. — Omnibus riding and jam tarts. — My moral compunctions. — Sarah dissipates them. — An unsuccessful assault. — On the fornicating facilities of four wheel cabs.

I go back a while. — When I had known Sarah some time I wished to go to her house, having to pay heavily at the baudy houses for stopping long there. — Besides I always feel so much more comfortable at a woman's lodgings. J***s St. bagnio was an exception, but that house has been long closed — Sarah objected at first, but as we knew each other better, said that her rooms were comfortable but very homely, that I should not be pleased with them; and moreover her friend was often there, that then I could not, and so on. — On being pressed, she admitted that she lived with a man, had done so for three years, and she showed me his miniature. — I said that nevertheless I should like to go there. — Then she told me the address, but I was never to call. — She would meet me in the street, and if she could take me home she would. He was a traveller for a firm of

**** makers, and often away. For a long time I did not go there.

I had letches for big women. — Sarah was one, and I had other big ones (tho but rarely) who were about town. — Big women, with big arses, and lots of cunt hair had been pleasing to me to see and feel, even if I did not poke them. Now suddenly I desired a little one. At L**c**t*r S****e one night, a group of girls so little that I thought them at first only rude children, spoke to me; and it ended in my going to a house with one about half my height, but who stripped and talked as baudily as if she had been fucked twenty years. — I fucked her, wondering at the little hairless quim my prick was closed up in, and such seemed the difference between the deep, thick lipped, dark, fully haired, large cunts, I had had for a long time, and the thin hairless split, and slim little form I was enjoying, that it roused desires for another.

It was late autumn, I was going along a suburb of London one night at about six o'clock p.m. It was in a dull tho widish road, where the houses lay back from the road in gardens. — A slight fog came on. — On the opposite side of the way, I saw thro the mist two young girls, singing, laughing, and talking loudly whilst walking on. — A man carrying a basket on his back passed them, and I heard him say. — "I should like to tickle up both of your legs a bit." "Tickle us up then," said one in a loud cheeky tone, and then both ran across the road, and down a turning close by me. I heard them laughing loudly when just out of sight in the mist, as if they enjoyed the baudy suggestion.

This stirred my blood. They must be fast young bitches I thought. Soon I heard a shrill voice say. "Come on, he's gone a head a long way." It was one of the two girls. The turning they were up I found was no thoroughfare, altho then I did not know that — I turned at once up it, met them, stopped them, and asked them the way to some place. — I saw the face of the tallest, and as far as the fog would let me see by a lamp, it pleased me. I began to talk, and said they were both pretty girls. — "Give me a kiss and I will give each of you sixpence." — They laughed, said no, but in a minute I gave each a kiss and sixpence. — As I kissed the biggest, I whispered her, "I'll give you a shilling if you will do something for me and get your companion away." "What?" said she boldly. "Send her away." "No, she'll tell, but at **** Street she goes another way — you come back, then."

She said she should not. — "Come on Betsy," and off they went together — I followed just at such a distance as the fog enabled me not to lose sight of them, saw them part, then quickly made up to the tallest, and by degrees persuaded her to stop and listen to me. I know how to deal with young lasses well, having had experience now. — "Now don't be angry — don't be alarmed, it can't hurt you, and if you won't do it there's no harm done. — If you do what I want, no one will know it, and I'll give you a lot of money when I meet you." "What is it?" — Oddly enough, I could not make up my mind what to ask her to do — I wanted to feel her cunt, but guessed if I said so, she would run off as fast as she could go, so went on talking awhile, and at length said, "Here's a shilling for you if you will tell me one or two things. — Have you a brother?" "Yes." "Have you seen his cock?" She began to laugh. "Shan't tell you," and she began to walk away. "Never mind, here is your shilling." She turned round and took it. — "How foolish to go away, you might get more money, and no one but you and I know any thing about it — and directly I ask you a question off you go." "You talk improper," said she. "Never mind, you know you have felt your brother's cock if he is a baby." "He's three years old, and I nurse him when at home." "Then you have felt his cock." — She laughed.

"What are you doing about here?" said I turning the conversation. "Going home from work." "What do you work at?" "Folding up seeds at **** nursery," and she told me where. "What do you get a day?" "Nine pence — we both work there" — (meaning the other girl). "You can get half a crown if you'll do what I wish." "I can't do anything." "Yes, you can feel me." "Feel you, what's that?" — I rattled the money, — "Here are two and six pence, none will see us." We were by a long wall, and the fog was now thickish. "Here is the money — give me your hand."

I unbuttoned my trowsers, my prick was stiff, I put it outside, but under my greatcoat. She gave me her hand in a reluctant way, and I guided it to my penis. — "Lay hold of it." "I shan't, let me go — I'll hollow." "No — feel it, put your hand round it and here is your money." — Her fright got over, she put her hand round it. — Curiosity got the better of her fears, I saw her tho she couldn't in the dark see it, looking down at it. — "You old beast, let me go," — but I kept

[*363*]

her hand on the stem, then put it in my trowsers and under the balls. — "Now let me go." — I relinquished her hand, she turned away, went two or three yards off and stopped. "Here is your money, now you have felt my cock, tell me, is it bigger than your brother's." She broke out into a laugh, turned and ran off — I followed and overtook her standing still some distance off. — "You did not give me the money," said she. "That was your fault, here it is, but come back, people here will see us." — She came back saying, "I must go or I'll catch it." — At the corner I gave her half a crown, and said "Every night you feel my cock I will give you a shilling, and I'll give half a crown if you let me feel your bum." "You old beast," said she again, as the money dropped into her hand. Then she bolted off like lightning.

I went to the spot at the same time next night, but she did not appear. On the third night I saw her and she was alone, there was no fog, but it was between dark and daylight, and the lamps were not lighted. — She recognized me. "Go away or I'll run," said she. "I'm not going to hurt you, give me a kiss and I'll give you a shilling." — I induced her to turn up the same place, and there gave her both. Then she felt my cock again and had another shilling. — She was not in a hurry to take away her hand from my cock as on the first night. I fancied she liked feeling it. "Meet me every night," (it just suited me then). "I can't, cause *she* comes home with me," — meaning the other girl. How cunning young sluts are!

Her feeling of my prick, and the whispering baudy talk in her young ears, took my fancy, but I wanted more. I saw her the next night. She was with the other girl, and like a fool I was going up to her, when they ran off. Another night I caught her alone. I was that night in a frenzy of randiness, put her hand round my prick and my own hand outside hers, and so frigging, I spent copiously. — "What is the matter sir," said she looking up in my face, for I dare say I was sighing and giving evidence of sexual emotion.

Then I missed her, and gave up all idea of getting into her, for that had been in my mind. About two weeks afterwards, by mere chance passing by there, I saw the little devil loitering near the turning where she had first felt me. — Crossing the road, I said in passing, "Come on," — and in two minutes she stood by my side.

She had been ill, her mother said it was fever. But with a chuckle — "I know what it was — I eat too much of them sweets and fruit. — Mother said it was the smell from the privy, and told the doctor so. — He asked me what I had been eating, and I said nothing." — Then I found that she spent her money on fruit, sugar candy and bull's eyes, and in riding in omnibuses. When she felt sick she got some brandy, and she only gave her companion a little bit of sweet. — "Because she'd wonder where I got the money and would tell." — This much amused me, and reminded me of a girl, or rather two girls I had known many years previously. A girl of fifteen riding in an omnibus by herself for pleasure, and gorging herself with sweets out of money got by feeling a man's prick in a street, seems an amusing fact.

She missed the money evidently, and *her* want was *my* opportunity. Said I, — "I can only give you money if you let me feel your bum." "Oh no, not that." "Well, it's no worse than feeling my cock. — If you feel my cock, let me feel your cunt." "Oh! that I shan't," — but she lingered. — "It could not hurt," I said, "and who knows you have felt my cock?" — "Who will know it if I feel your little cunt? —Here is the money." — She looked round (it was dark). — "No. No," — but she stood quite still — I stooped and put my hand up on to her bottom. — "Oh! have done now, let me go, give me the money." "Let me feel properly." "I won't." — With the hand which was on her naked bum, I drew her close to me, and with the other, pushed up her clothes till I felt the top of her cunt. — She struggled tho quietly, and escaped me, but as before stopped till I went to her to give the money; then she went off. — I felt sure that she had come out to meet me that night.

One night soon after it was lighter than usual and some man passing the main road shouted out. — "Leave that girl alone." — I went further up the turning, she with me, and was just stooping to feel her little bum, when some female came out a house and passed us. I stood upright, but soon saw the woman standing at the end of the turning, and seemingly looking back. — No one had ever passed out of the houses during my previous fun. This woman who had eyed us narrowly as she passed, or had certainly turned her head to look, I thought would turn back. The girl was more frightened than me. — "Oh don't again, don't, I won't any more, and I mustn't stop, I'm frightened of mother," — and she walked towards the high road, I following.

A cab passed, few do pass at that spot or indeed much other traffic. — I hailed it. It was empty and stopped. —

"Come into the cab, we'll drive, you can feel me there and I can sit." She hesitated, but I hustled her in. — "Drive to **** Park," and off he drove. — How many times have I got women into a cab for my pleasure, how many times more shall I do so? They like it.

She got frightened and wanted to get out. I pacified her, promised her five shillings instead of the smaller sum I usually gave. — "Where to?" said cabby turning round as he entered the park. — "Go on till I stop you." — On he drove, it was getting darker, I had not yet kissed her that day as I usually did — but in the cab, she stood by the side of me, and I kissed and she kissed again. — Kissing always soothes a female young or old. — Gradually I got one hand round her bum, and the other outside her quim, but directly I tried to insert my finger in the split, she strongly resisted, threw herself on to seat opposite, and cried to get out. — "No, no, I won't — you'll hurt me — yes you will." — So I desisted.

"Well dear, lay hold of my hand — lay hold of this finger — put it yourself there, — just let it go where you piddle from, and no further." — "There," said she, holding my finger so that I just felt the clitoris. Then thrusting away my hand she again sat on the opposite seat, holding her clothes down; but I soon got her by my side again. The baudiness, I know, pleased her.

I was furious with salacity and talked baudy to my heart's content. I had said a little of that sort before, and the little slut had listened to it without uttering a word, but stood drinking it all in with her ears, and as if she knew quite well what I meant, and as if she liked it. — I never liked frigging myself, but now my cock became unmanageable, as I felt her little buttocks, and coaxed her lewedly, and lovingly.

"Frig me my dear," — I had taught her the meaning of that word. — "I can't." Taking her hand I put it round my prick. — "Now I'll lift your clothes — there — it's against your thigh — that doesn't hurt you does it?" — I slobbered my prick with saliva, and taking her hand and putting it round my prick (which she now liked doing), frigged myself with it.

I always frig myself when I commit that wasteful action, with my foreskin nearly up, unless using soap or oil as an emollient; my tip being so delicate. — As the sperm left me, I pulled her hand up so as to quite pull up the foreskin, and cover the orifice, and much was ejaculated into her hand, whilst oscillating my arse, holding her by her bum, and kissing her in my ecstasy. — Trying to relieve her hand, "Let go," said she, "you've done something sticky with your thing. — Oh! let it go, it's nasty," — but she seemed pleased with the fun for all that. — Then she got anxious to go home, so telling the cabman to drive to a convenient spot, I let her out.

. The affair fascinated me. I went again to that quarter of the town at the time the girl left work, but never saw her for a fortnight. — She I believed had avoided me, till she had spent all her money. — Then she only felt my cock, got her shilling and went off. She resisted everything else.

I didn't see now much chance of getting into her, circumstances did not favor me, and I had a long distance to go even to get the chance, so desisted; I had, besides, compunctions, thought it a pity to make the girl a harlot, and so told Sarah all about what I'd done and what I'd thought of doing. — Sarah said I had better leave it alone, but that some one would do it to that girl before long, for she evidently knew more than she should. One of the lads at the nursery would have her. She was more likely to let a lad have her than to let me. Perhaps she'd been fucked already, spite of her resistance. "Those little bitches are so damned cunning that it would surprise you, she'll be gay, whether *you* do it to her or not." — That gave me comfort, and again I thought I'd try to get the girl. — Time had run on, it was now dark at four o'clock.

So a fortnight after, I met her. It was so clear an evening, that I did not like talking to her in the road, and again waiting, got into a cab with her. Familiarity had, I found, removed her fears. I had talked baudy in the street, and in the cab, so far from having to hold her hand on my prick; on saying "feel it," she put her little hand on to it, and grasped and felt about it. — I told her I wanted to feel her cunt, and promised never to move my fingers from her belly to between her legs — I had kept my word before, when she had helped me to frig. — After I had had her some minutes so, she holding my cock, I said, "It twists me so, sit on my knee." She did, but still kept her legs close together. — "Let me put my cock against your leg again." At length I put it against her flank, whilst she still held it. — "Do you know what fucking is?" I said, to which she made reply, "I only knows what you tells me."

I asked her then to come to a house, but got a positive refusal — I got awfully lewed, and by coaxing, at last she stood in front of me and frigged me herself, but she hurt me. — "Hold my cock against your belly, just as it was at the side of your bum." She did. — Then with one hand I pulled her to me, the other was on her naked arse. I'd lifted her clothes, and my prick touched her belly just by her cunt. She was still holding it — I shoved my prick against it up and down through her hand for some time, it was inconvenient, but the lewdness pleased me. — The cab kept slowly jogging on.

My pleasure increased, and with it the desire to fuck. — "Oh! I will give you half a sovereign if you'll do what I want," and I left off frigging. "Ten shillings?" "Yes, ten shillings." — She seemed reflecting. My desire grew stronger, — "I'll give you a sovereign if you'll let me put my prick between your legs — not in your cunt, but only between your thighs, and you shall hold it there."

"Oh no, — none of that," — said she, hastily, "I ain't a going to let you do that — I want to get out of the cab, let me go, oh do." — She was taking fright and beginning to struggle.

I let her talk on. Opening my purse I took out a sovereign. — "Here's a golden sovereign," showing it to her as we passed one of the few gas lamps. — "You shall have it if you let me, you can wrap it up in a piece of paper, then make the paper muddy, and tell your mother you found it." I once taught another girl this.

The girl was silent long, looking me in the face (as it seemed) in the dark. — Then, "No — oh no." — Disappointment in her manner and tone, I saw she would yield. She'd laid hold of my prick again unasked, and I replaced it and my hands as before.

"If you won't I shan't see you again, I can get fifty girls to feel my prick for a shilling." "Has any other girl done it? you didn't tell me so." "A dozen have." "Lor," — and she seemed to be reflecting on the information. "They will all do it my dear if they get the chance." — So we talked. — The cab had gone once round the park, and still drove on. — I expect the driver knew the games we were up to, but never looked round that I noticed. But it was quite dark now.

Little by little I induced her to straddle across me with her clothes up, my legs between hers — I declared I wouldn't touch her cunt, but pushed my body so forward that my knees nearly touched the opposite seat, and holding her close up to me, her legs got more distended, and I more and more reclining. — At length her feet scarcely touched the cab-floor. — She fell half forward on me, her face touching mine. — Promising her more money, she let me with my left hand clutch her little naked backside, my right was at the same spot but outside her clothes. — "Put your hand down, and hold my prick just against the bottom of your belly." "I can't," said she, but she did it, and my prick tip was now near her cunt, and touching her thigh. I began oscillating my backside as well as I could, and got some rough friction against her dry flesh. — "That doesn't hurt you does it?" "No." She seemed amused with the trick.

I slipped further forward, hoping to get my prick against her cunt, then my position was so difficult that I could scarcely jog up and down. — "Let my cock go higher up dear." — I put the hand which had been outside her bum down to hers, and pushed it so that it, with my prick, went nearer to the goal, but bending, its rigidity hurt me. — The idea of its being close to her little cunt then drove me wild — I pushed both hands round her backside, clipped with both; violently oscillated my buttocks, which opened her legs wider, her feet left the floor, she let go my prick, and put her hand on my shoulders to prevent her falling on one side. She was then half lying on me; my prick lodged somewhere in the furrow of her backside, and she cried out, "Oh don't, you're a hurting," and struggled to get away.

Maddened with lustful delight at her cry, now I put one hand round her waist, kept the other on her bum, and grasped her so that she couldn't move her bum, and jerked my arse furiously; my prick left its lodging, and jerked about blindly on thighs, buttocks, and cunt valley, moving recklessly but always rubbing. — I was nearly at the crisis. — "Be quiet dear, I shan't hurt you." "Oho — don't — oh you beast — I'll scream. — Cabman, cabman — let me out," she yelled — and struggled.

Tighter and tighter I held her, and thrust and wriggled in the hopes of finding a soft lodging for my prick tip. — My spunk was rising from my balls when again my tool stuck tight. — Where I don't know, but think it was between her cunt lips. Holding her backside firmly on to it, spite of her struggles, and then wriggling my arse and rigid tool, I spent a flood of sperm, somewhere between her bum bone and her clitoris; felt some of it fall on my hand which was nearest her thighs, and then I relinquished her. She was still yelling. "Oh! you beast — don't — you hurt me — let me go out —

[*369*]

cab — stop," and getting away from me. Yet in the faintness of my pleasure, I was lewed enough to bring my hand round from her bum, and thrust it between her thighs — and in a glutinous state I withdrew it. The driver if he heard took no notice, but she got so vociferous, that I stopped the cab. She got out, ran off, not waiting for her gift, and in a second was lost in the darkness. — A little further on I stopped near a foot bridge, paid the cabman liberally, and went off. — I never saw the girl afterwards, for the scene of my amatory doings was not near my home. I was going to visit a friend when I got this piece of luck, and first met the little stupid, who might have had the pleasure of a fuck, and profit as well. — As it is, I dare say some dirty young boy will open her cunt, and give her a black eye if she upbraids him if her belly swells. That is the course of events in her class. — It is not the gentlemen who get the virginities of these poor little bitches, but the street boys of their own class.

There was sperm on my shirt and trowsers, but no evidences of a shattered virginity. — Was she a virgin, did I hurt her much, how far in her did my prick go, or at all. — What did she think when she had gone, and felt my spunk on her cunt, for certainly I spent against it, if not up it. — A risk I ran, yet missed the mark after all. — That baudy tuition, that titillation of our privates, that spend outside a little cunt in a cab, and all at a cost of a pound or two, amused me, as all chance adventures do. They break the monotony of matter-of-fact hard fucking — yet that I should have taken all that trouble for a dirty little work girl, whose face I never saw excepting by the light of a street lamp, astonishes me often when I think of it.

What convenient accessories to love-making are four wheel cabs. — Some dozens of cunts I have felt in them, some that I should never have felt at all, had it not been for the opportunities the four wheelers gave me. Several women I have fucked in them, as they rumbled along with a discreet cabman. — No doubt other men have found them as useful. — Thousands of women I am sure have fornicated in them, and scores do it in them daily. — Every cabman knows of their amatory utility, and the profit that it gets him, the profit of ambulating brothels. — Dozens are used every night I'm sure. I never spoke with a man yet, who had not fucked a woman in a four wheeler.

CHAPTER XL

My letch for a little one. — Sarah's lodgings. — A new dress wanted. — A virgin proffered. — The deaf little Emma. — The tailor's family arrangements. — The price of the hymen agreed. — Doctor H**m**d. — Sham medical investigations. — Aperiant pills — Sarah's advice. — An aperient Priapus. — Emma leaves Sarah. — The grocer's in B**w**k Street. — On the fucking facilities a little bum gives. — About my remaining manuscript.

When I told Sarah F**z*r this finale, she laughed heartily. — The desire for a youthful virginity seems to have been strong on me. — Sarah said she'd try and find one. Then I became exacting, and wanted one without any hair on her cunt, and I would see her virginity also before I broke it. I told her of the lovely little lass Betsy Johnson had got me, what I paid her, of the little virgin I got at the L**c**t*r S****e brothel, that I'd had both at brothels, and I must now have the girl whom Sarah got, at *her* lodgings, or at some quiet place, not a brothel.

The night we spoke most about this, we were jolly. — Sarah remarked, "I wish I could get you one, for it's cold, I want a new silk dress and warm clothing for the winter, and don't know how to pay for it — but I don't see my way." And it couldn't be at her lodgings. — Then I dropped the affair.

Once or twice after, it was mentioned casually — when my prick was stiff, and a good dinner was in me — for the letch was still on me occasionally, tho I had ceased to expect to gratify it. Sarah began to say as she'd said before, that her lodgings were common, that I shouldn't like them — that she could only let me go to them at particular times, when her husband was not at home — it was impossible — and much more of the same sort. At last, would I promise to tell no one if she let me go to her rooms. — I wondered who she imagined I should tell. — It was ridiculous to suppose I should. For a week or so then, I was mostly at home of a night, and only saw Sarah once. The next night I had her, she said she had got what I wanted, and named the day after for me to go to her lodgings, of which she'd given the address.

I went to her lodgings. — Two rooms on the second floor in G***k Street, Soho. The front looked into the street. — The back into a yard which might once have been a garden, and in which was the watercloset. — The rooms were far better than I expected, they were thoroughly comfortable, and not like those in which courtezans receive friends. The bedroom led out of the sitting room, thro a passage which also had a door on to the landing of the stairs. The staircase went up in the middle of the house. Her sitting room was carpeted, there was a good stove in it with boiler and oven. — She said that was her own putting in. — A large sofa of old fashioned look stood against the partition, there was room to fuck on it and roll off by the side of the woman. — It was really a sofa bedstead, and there were two easy chairs.

The bedroom was equally comfortable. — There was a very large bed with red hangings, and hangings to the windows also. A thick padded curtain across the door opening on to the stairs, which she'd made herself to keep out noise and cold (perhaps to prevent listening). — The rooms looked as if the furniture had been bought at good sales, as I afterwards found it had been. Altogether they were very snug, and when she lighted a lamp and we sat down before the fire, I felt quite at home. I was surprized to find so much comfort. — She had occupied them three years.

She let me in herself. — "I have a new little maid, and don't want her to see that you are strange here — I have told her I expect a friend, a doctor. — If you like her, I will see what can be done. — She'll be in, in a quarter of an hour. Her name is Emma."

The girl who had been sent on an errand was about fifteen, or barely so, short and thickset and had large dark earnest eyes — but not a handsome face. She was rather deaf. — The idea of having her pleased me, I began thinking how I should like to please *her*, hurt her virginity, frig, lick, fuck, and generally teach her the art of love, in a snug private room like Sarah's.

Sarah told me she had no mother and was of German extraction, her father was a drunken tailor. The girl had kept his rooms. There was another girl nearly her age, who he thought now could do this, and he had told this one to get her living in service. — Sarah had taken her, and dismissed her other maid.

I sent the girl out for gin, brandy, etc., etc., giving her always the change, my custom of ingratiating myself. Her face brightened at the gifts. — She sat at needle work whilst we talked. — "This is my friend Dr. H**m**d, he has often attended to me. — Now he shall see to you, if you don't get better," said Sarah, telling me that she had indications of her first poorliness, and that she had advised her to let a doctor look at her when alone. — Then to me when alone, — "And as you are the doctor, you can satisfy yourself." Was she a virgin? — Sarah believed so. — When her husband (her man), was away, she let her servants sleep with her. —When he was at home they slept on that sofa in the sitting room. — He had been away a week, and the girl had slept with her. She had seen her undress, strip and wash. She always made her servant do that every week, or they would not be in the same bed with *her*. — The girl had the slightest sign of dark hair on the motte, but not a bit on the lips. When asleep Sarah had felt her, and so far looked.

Said Sarah, "When we are drinking, *you* give her a little brandy and water, — I can't make her take anything. Make her jolly screwed, and then see her cunt, or we'll do that together." — I let Sarah do it after I was gone, which was a weak caprice of mine.

There was a fire. Sarah sat lifting her petticoats so that the warmth could get up her legs. The girl was told to remain where she was till she was called. — We went to the bedroom, and on Sarah's virtuous bed, I fucked her for the first time in her lodgings.

"I mean to let her know I am gay," said she, — "get her lewed and it will all go right. — Your being a doctor will do it. My poorliness is coming on, and I have told her I have shown you my cunt. — That doctors often see the cunts of women who want advice about poorliness" — only Sarah usually said "my thing," when she spoke of her cunt.

I met Sarah out two nights afterwards by arrangement. — "She is all right, no one has been up her, you can come to night and see for yourself. I have seen her thing, and if you say you must look at it, she'll let you — I have told her that she must have no nonsense with a doctor."

"But she'll expect medicine." "Well, you must give her something which will open her bowels. She'll never think you are going to do her good unless you make her belly ache."

During that evening I made remarks to Sarah of a medical nature. — Sarah said, "I think I must get you to give something to my little maid. — She is not very well, her poorliness won't come on. — It is her first."

"Come here." She put her work down and came. I asked her questions about her bowels, her urine, and felt her breasts, put my hand up her clothes, and pressed her belly, all as nearly as I could in a cool, medical sort of way. — She flinched a little when I said, "Let me feel your stomach," and looked at Sarah. "I must examine her well," said I. — "When next you come — you shall," said Sarah.

How my prick throbbed when my hand pressed the little belly. I could feel no hair, or scarcely any. It is strange, that altho Sarah thought I had better proceed to look at her at once, that I put it off — I can't understand why I did it. We had shrub, the girl disliked spirits, shrub she liked. I have always found young girls will take shrub, it warms the stomach, rises to the brain, makes the cunt heat and tingle, and the girl think of fucking. There is no better term to express a woman's sensation of randiness, and I borrowed it from Sarah.

I again felt her little rising breasts and her belly, and said that in two days I would see her again.

I saw Sarah next night and did not fuck her, said I would not till I had spent up the little deaf maid. Sarah, with the girl in bed, had talked on sexual subjects, had heard that twice men had tried to take liberties with her. — Once a tailor put his hands up her clothes, it was on the stairs. She didn't like to tell, for a tailor had once done something of the same sort to her sister, and she had told her father, who boxed her ears, and said it must have been her own fault. — She had had a sweetheart, who had coaxed her down a yard, kissed her, then pulled up her clothes, and felt her, and she felt for a second, what must have been his cock. — He put her hand to it. She ran away, and had not seen him once. "All poor girls get these chances early," said Sarah. "She says she has frigged herself. — I made her feel what a lot of hair I had, then I felt hers, and I told her it would grow quite hairy when a man had put his thing up her. All girls are anxious to get hair on their things." — Then they got talking about how fucking was done, until, "I believe the little devil got quite randy, I told her that I had had it done to me before

I was her age, that a girl need not have a child unless she liked — that half the girls did it with men but never told." — Sarah strove to fill her mind with desire to be fucked, told of the ease and secrecy with which it could be accomplished, and the benefits accruing. — Any woman I am certain can persuade a girl to let herself be fucked, if she stimulates rising passions, and incites her to compliance both for sexual gratification and interest, and women like teaching them.

Sarah told me she didn't like doing this. "But she will be sure to have some man do it to her, so you may as well have her as any one else, and I shall get my new dress. It will do *me* good and do *her* no harm." To this I quite agreed. It is quite true, and what every gay woman has told me, and is my philosophy.

But if there should be a row? — "I'll chance it — how am I to know anything about it, she might have done it anywhere, when she goes out. I should swear all was a lie, I should say I never had seen you in my life, and no one shall see you if you come at dark, and only when I tell you."

Next night I was there — my prick had been standing as I walked along, and yet I was nervous. I sent her out for shrub and then Sarah said, "I can't get a word out of her till the light is put out, then she talks fast enough, and asks me what the pleasure of fucking is, and if it hurts. — A girl she knows has made her think it hurts. I have told her that it depends upon whether a girl lets a man do as he likes or resists him. — If a girl don't resist, she won't be hurt. She thinks you such a nice kind man, and wonders a man with such a fine moustache, can call her 'my dear,' and speak to her as you do."

"Shall I get into her to night?" "I would rather be out when you do it, I have told her she'd be better if she'd been poked, and she said she supposed she shouldn't be quite well till she married. — I said she might get poked before that, and her husband know nothing about it."

I asked Sarah before the maiden about her own health, her womb, her courses, and so on. The girl looked at me and at Sarah with the appearance of mental strain, which people partially deaf often have. — "Well my dear, and how are you?" — I then felt her breasts and belly, and as I knew her little ailments, the questions were wise enough. "I must see you with your clothes off." "Go with the doctor," said Sarah. "I have told her you'll want to look at her as you have

[*375*]

looked at me." There was such a lot of palaver about the affair, that it crossed my mind I was going to be done.

The girl lighted a candle and went to the bedroom. In the room was a fire. I could scarcely now preserve the gravity of a doctor. — She took off her clothes to her chemise, and a fine little girl she was — I pulled it up, she half resisted, but as if recollecting who I was, stood still.

I asked all the searching medical questions I could. "Lie down, don't be ashamed, I am accustomed to see girls naked — there — so — just so — open your legs a little wider, now put your heel there — that's it, — don't close your thighs when I open the lips — that will do."

There the girl laid on the side of the bed, her thighs distended, one heel up so as to facilitate and keep the legs open, the little thin lips of her vulva gaping, and shewing the pink lining.

I took a candle and saw the orifice which the prick enters, inside it the membrane closing it, excepting down near the bumhole, where was a little opening, that looked as if a little finger would scarcely go thro it. The girl was unmistakably a virgin.

I could scarcely tear myself from her cunt, praised its looks, said what a nice made little lass she was — "And now my dear, tell me, have you ever put your finger up this?" and I touched it.

"No sir," said she faintly. "Are you sure? Tell me the truth, it is no good deceiving a doctor." "No, sir." "Now I know you have," said I, glorying in my baudy treat. "You have tried?" "I tried but it hurts me." "I must try — if it hurts you a little don't mind — it's for your good." — Talking thus, I wetted my little finger with spittle, and pushed it gently through the little orifice and up her cunt, which felt soft and slimy inside. She winced. — "Oh, you hurt me, sir."

Then I turned her bum upwards, and looked at the little cunt from behind, and afterwards saw her naked from head to foot. I laid her on her back, gently rubbed her clitoris with my finger, and asked if she ever did so. — "I fancy you do what so many girls do." — Then I kissed her, told her she was a dear girl, that she would not be better till she had had done to her, what her own mother had had done. I could see her readiness, but had not the cheek to attempt or propose it to her then, which seems funny now, but so it was.

I went back to Sarah in such a state that my resolution left me — I sent the girl out for soda water, and the instant she was out, gushed my sperm into Sarah's quim before my prick was well up it.

When the girl came back she drank shrub. I spoke of her nice limbs, told Sarah of her form, took half a sovereign out of my pocket, told Sarah to buy her boots, and that I felt inclined to give her a new dress. Then on pretence of satisfying myself, took her into the bedroom and again looked at the virgin cunt, pulled out my prick (and didn't she look) and pissed before her. — "You will be better when you let some one use this with you." — She turned away. I don't think she quite heard what I said.

The same things took place between us next time. I asked about the action of the medicine, and familiarised her with talking to me about all the little secrets of her sex. That freedom on subjects usually hidden from each other, paves the way for fucking. Again I saw her little form, from her nascent bubbies to her arsehole — I now put my middle finger thro the hymen and up her cunt — I had cut my nail to prevent my hurting her — but she declared it did hurt badly — I played with the few short hairs which were shewing on her mons, praised her legs, feet, neat boots and stockings — asked if she liked them, and was overwhelmed with grateful replies. — Then I hinted again at giving her a dress, told her she had better not mention about having had a doctor to anyone, and stifling my wants I went into the other room to Sarah.

Sarah said, "Try as soon as you can, for with such a young one now, you never know what will take place. She may be fool enough to tell some one, but she won't if she once gets it done to her — I will then tell her that she will be ruined for life if she mentions it."

Next night Sarah met me out. — Said she, "I will stop out till twelve, make her lushy with shrub if she won't do it without, and then fuck her, but she'll let you. — She is in love with you." — "Didn't the doctor say he would perhaps give me a new frock?" said she to Sarah. — "How could he know I had tried to put my finger up?" — Sarah told her that doctors knew everything about women. — Then I asked her if she had ever seen a man's cock. — Yes her brother's, who showed it her once. He was about fourteen years old, and she used to sleep in the same room with him, and "she had seen it stiff."

"You'll have her — she has had such a talking to. If she

hollows, push a pillow over her face and they won't hear underneath — but the lodger overhead might be coming up stairs, tho he scarcely ever comes in till twelve o'clock. — I'll be in the street for him, and come in when he does, we'll come up the stairs together. — If I hear anything I'll make a noise and knock at the door, so don't be frightened — only you'll have had her before then. — Don't be nervous or you won't get a stiff one." — Sarah had heard from me that once or twice when over excited, my prick had refused to do its duty.

"I have nailed a rug over the door inside and put the chest of drawers against it. — We do that generally in winter to keep out the cold, and go thro the little passage between the bed and sitting room" — which was partly true only. There had been a curtain.

"I told her also you only had an old housekeeper, and were inclined to take her to help. — The girl was delighted." Sarah had given her a pill (I had taken her a box of common aperients). "She thinks you will soon bring on her poorliness, and that she will be quite a woman then." — I sometimes wonder if all this preliminary was needful, and if the girl did not know pretty well what she was about, but this is a narrative of facts, and not of opinions.

Altho the maiden had not been a fortnight in the house, she had been as far debauched in mind as she well could be. — To have been told all about fucking, and by a grown woman, to have confessed to that woman, and to a doctor, all she had done with her cunt, to have got money, new boots and stockings and some other things, see the chance of having a place in the house of a doctor, who twice had looked at and felt her cunt, was certainly enough to upset any girl. — It was a fine preparation.

That night she let me in, said her mistress was out and had left no message. "Never mind I will wait." — I sent her out for shrub, and prepared to try my luck, but felt as nervous as if I were going before a judge for murder — I can't understand myself being like this, for it is only at times that I am so.

She had a little shrub. — "Come here dear and tell me about yourself." — I praised her hair and eyes, which were very good. Taking her between my legs I began feeling her breasts and belly, asking her medical questions all the time, then I lifted her clothes and afterwards said, "Let me see your stockings." For an instant only she resisted as a girl might.

"Why? I gave them you — I have seen your little cunt and your little bum, have I not, and must look at them now." — Then I again lifted her clothes, put my hand up, and a finger on her clitoris, and talking all the while, began rubbing it. "Oh Doctor, don't," said she wriggling her little cunt away from me. "Ah, it's pleasure, but nothing like the pleasure you'll have when a man puts his cock up you," said I, feeling that the ice must be broken. My prick was getting so rampageous, that I felt inclined to carry her to the bed, and ravish her, but I went on talking.

In a few minutes more "I *must* look at you." Into the bedroom we went, she took off her clothes, and again I saw her little virgin cunt at the bedside.

However much I may plan an attack on a woman, — there always comes a time when I follow my instincts and not my plan. — When my prick almost feels bursting, and I am overpowered by voluptuousness, I scarcely know what I do, or what course I take. — Then if the woman is not quite ready in her lewedness, and I make a false move, and startle, frighten, or delay, my chance is gone. But if she be lewed, sayings and doings dictated by nature, infallibly win her. There is a strength of will, and a moral force that a man has when he is furious with sexual want, over any woman whose body is tingling with desire for a male, which make him sure of having her.

Up to this time I know all I did, what followed my excited state only leaves the broad incidents clear — I fell kissing her cunt when looking at her, and sitting at the side of the bed. Then I cuddled her, and told all about fucking. — Then on pretext of looking at her once more, got her on to the bed, and placed a pillow so that her bum was on it, experience had taught me that in case of resistance, my prick would have a better chance of entering if her bum was well up. — I got on the bed, pulled out my prick, and said kissing her, "Let me fuck you love, your poorliness will come on then — you'll want no more medicine, and have such pleasure." — "No-hoh, no, sir — I mustn't till I am married — you'll hurt me. — I mustn't, Doctor!"

I cuddled her as she attempted to get up, promising money and a silk dress, that I wouldn't hurt, and that whoever told her it hurt told nonsense. — "No-oh-no," — but she was nestling in my bosom, and my finger was on the little clitoris. — Suddenly she said, "Will you take me to help as a servant?" — I promised. — In another minute she was on her back. I wetted her cunt with spittle, my prick lay against it, and I feared I should spend before I got it up her. I grasped her bum, pressed her, and drove my prick with all my might. — "Oha-oh-oh," she cried, each cry louder than the other as my prick battered her virginity. — Another cry, another shove, and I was spending up her. Soon, on putting my hand down, I found that not above an inch and a half of my prick was in her cunt, and my desire was to keep it there. She begged me to get off, but I lay soothing her. My prick kept stiff. The idea that my spunk was in her, the delight at feeling the little hairless cunt lips enclosing my swollen gristle, nerved it again. I gave the gentlest push, then harder, and it glided up until I felt it could go no further.

What a delicious, slow, prolonged fuck. The little cunt smooth with sperm, but so deliciously tight and compressive, and I had first moistened that little interior, broken that virgin barrier, thoughts which increased inexpressibly my voluptuousness. I recollect all I did, and what passed through my brain during the second operation. There was only one alloy to this pleasure. Without making a noise, she kept crying, and I spent kissing her, her tears running down her face. But I am not sure that these evidences of pain and nervous shock did not add to my enjoyment.

I lay in her long, pulling her closer as my penis kept shrinking. — It was delicious to hear her say that there was no longer pain, but — "I don't know what sort of feeling" — in her cunt. When I thought of the mischief my prick had done, I delighted in using the words cunt, spunk, prick, fuck, and the whole erotic vocabulary, whilst she lay quiet with my prick still in her, listening but making no reply. What a delicious treat for her also.

I cautioned her against moving, till, "Let me wash you, it will prevent soreness, and your husband won't know what I have done to you." Girls at that age have implicit faith in a doctor, indeed I have found that most women have.

Candle in hand I opened her thighs, and saw the results of my pleasure. — A mass of blood-streaked sperm filled the mouth of her prick-hole, smears of blood lay between the cunt lips and on the thighs. On my prick was blood where the stem joins the balls, but small in quantity. Gently I pushed my largest finger up her cunt. She winced. I revelled in feeling it thick and pasty inside. — Soon my prick gave a throb, and with a movement, almost a jump, came from the droop to the stiff. I longed to be up her again, but feared my prick would droop before I did so. "Lay still, my little darling."

She tried to move but too late — "No Doctor H**m**d, you shan't" — I had lain myself on her and grasped her little bum with both hands and pushed with my prick without guiding it. In a few thrusts it found the right channel, and with one hard shove went clean up her. She gave a little cry and then was quiet. Was the distension now giving her pleasure?

I had spent twice, and to have my prick three times up a cunt in half an hour was a trial — I don't recollect in all my life, having done such a thing in the same time more than once or twice. But now I have had nearly thirty years good fucking and am in early middle age. It was one thing to get my prick up, and another to finish the fuck. After the first burning excitement had evaporated in a few sharp shoves, a desire to be quiet seized me. — Obeying it I talked to her, and my precious prick, thinking it had done enough began to dwindle. — I felt ashamed, forgetting that the girl could not know whether I had spent, was spending, or was going to spend. — So for half an hour, without my cock leaving her cunt, it kept shrinking, then swelling at some effort, and so on. Now I pushed my fingers well under her little bum cheeks, and feeling the stem of my prick wet, I put her hand down to feel it. Then asked how her cunt felt. — All this did not keep me to full rigidity for long, yet I never once got my cock quite out of her. — There was no superfluous fat outside it, and her cunt was easily got at, and my firm hold of her little buttocks kept it close up to my prick, and so I managed it.

At length she complained that I was making her "ache dreadful." I thought of rubbing her clitoris, and putting my finger down did so. The girl felt its effects, and so did I — my prick began to feel voluptuous thrills, and as if sperm was in my balls. No doubt the stretching, pushing, and friction of my cock up her little cunt had inflamed her. The rubbing of the clitoris made the sore little cunt hotter. Gently pushing with cock as stiff now as ever, I heard her sigh and saw her eyes close. She was spending — I saw it in her face, felt it by her manner, and by the sensation her cunt suddenly conveyed to my prick — it was the crisis of my night's enjoyment. — Up her cunt rapidly thrusting before she had recovered, I spent in her again.

I got off of her. She lay seemingly exhausted, did all I told her, and let me do all I wanted — I again washed her cunt, gave her more shrub and she laid down, and went fast asleep for a full hour — I sat down gloriously contented.

It would be an hour and a half before Sarah came back. For an hour during which I read, Emma was still asleep. I pulled up her chemise, and saw the top of the little split peeping out between the closed thighs — I frigged my prick. All I had done, all I meant to do passed through my mind, and at last with much effort I spent, and was done for, for that night and no mistake. What a vagary to indulge in. How can I account for that sudden onanistic letch, I who hate masturbation?

I awakened her — her little quim was swollen and of dark color, the outer lips even I fancied were swollen and irritated. I gloried in the jagged opening made of the little hole of three hours previously, but felt sorry at the depression she was in, for I could now scarcely get her to reply. — Kissing her, promising much, and begging her never to tell any one, I left her.

Sarah was outside. I gave her her money and told her all about it. — Said she, — "The little devil spent! — are you sure?" — Sarah doubted it. — She didn't know whether to encourage her to tell, or to ask no questions, but get rid of her soon, say she was deaf, was not strong enough, or something else. Sarah had her pay and wanted to be quit of the business.

But I wanted to fuck, to frig, to lick her, show her my cock, teach her the art of love, to learn her virgin ideas and sensations; so said she must keep her, arrange how she liked about knowing or not knowing, but I must have her again or we should quarrel. — Sarah against her will agreed — I was positive, peremptory. Sarah was strong in the desire that I should not see the lass again. Perhaps she was quite right, but I had my wishes to gratify, and did not clearly see Sarah's reasons.

On the second night after the cunt rupturing, I met Sarah on her beat. The girl had told her all. Sarah had said she was sorry, but what was done, could not be undone — and it was lucky it was with a wise gentleman like Doctor H**m**d, or bad consequences would come. — She'd be ruined for life if she told any living soul, and if the doctor wanted to do it again, he must. She should turn her out if she thought she'd mention the affair to any one — or allowed any other man even to kiss, or feel her.

I went quietly enough the next night into the bed room with the lass, and had as much difficulty in getting to look at her cunt as before. But I fucked her, and had the delight of seeing her frig my prick, and watch her looks as it swelled. Then I ejaculated the spunk into her. Afterwards I licked her little cunt till she spent, and much trouble I had to make her come that way — I can't understand why I tried to set her to frig herself, which she wouldn't do. — It was a brief honeymoon that and the succeeding nights. — I got her perfect confidence, and this went on nearly every other day for some weeks.

Then I fucked Sarah, and liked her fully developed cunt better than the younger one's. I began to notice that if not very randy, the little one's cunt failed to work up my pleasure, whilst Sarah's big one did. There was indeed but little sympathetic movement in the little one's cunt, and I could only well get my prick two-thirds up her. — At first it delighted me to thrust till she called out, and her, — "Oh don't push so far, sir," — used to fetch my spunk like a shot. — But I grew tired of that, and came to the conclusion, that a good full sized cunt, elastic, fleshy, pulpy, and deep, was the most satisfying to my pego.

Sarah grew tired of keeping the girl for some reason, altho she got two pounds instead of one, each time I saw her. — "The little devil bothers me, she is always asking about you, and about Mr. F**z*r. I have made her sleep on the sofa, for I have found her feeling about my cunt when I awakened. — She thinks of nothing but your coming, bothers me to read your baudy books (I had lent some), and would talk of fucking all day — I am frightened to let her go out. I wish you would let her go." — I had now fucked the lass in every attitude and agreed to it, and told Sarah I would stop away a fortnight.

The girl, I heard afterwards was in tears when she found I did not come. Sarah told her I had gone abroad — I was sorry for the lass, but Sarah had but little pity. — She thought the girl had done very well. — "When she came, she hadn't a rag to her back, now she has more good clothing than me." — I had indeed given the girl lots of good clothes. — "She is set up, and has got a good place as servant, where she will work hard, but what of that. It's better than stopping at home with a drunken father who half starved and ill-treated her. One of his shop mates would have done her business. — Now she can take care of herself, she knows enough."

Her place was at a little grocers' shop in W**d**r Street. — A month afterwards I loitered near the shop curiously, and saw two youths, seventeen or eighteen years old, in it; sons of the woman who kept it I found. Sarah said I was wrong to go near. — "The best thing for you is never to see her again — if any row comes, I'll swear you never were at my lodgings in your life. — No one has seen you come, it has always been dark."

I remarked that the youths would get into her. — "I hope they will, that will shut her mouth. — She won't go long without it being up her, and the sooner she fucks the better," was Sarah's opinion. I never either saw the girl afterwards, nor heard of her.

I don't forget the delight of the girl when her poorliness came on, which it did about a fortnight after I had had her, nor the way she used to burst out into quiet laughter, when she pulled my prick about till stiff, and how she said. — "Oh you do make my legs ache so." All little girls get the leg ache when I lie long between them. — One of my delights was to turn her on her side with her bum towards me, fuck her from behind, and go to sleep so with my prick well in her. It is easier to do it that way with a small bum, than with big buttocks. But pillows must be put under the side of the young ones, to bring their cunts up to a convenient level. Fucking so was one of my delights with Molly, whom Betsy Johnson got for me. At Sarah F**z**'s I never had anything in my pockets to disclose my name. I used to tail the girl whilst Sarah looked on, and have awakened with my tail still in the girl and Sarah tranquilly working in the room, and singing in a low tone to herself.

But I don't understand Sarah's behaviour in the matter; why she wanted to be out of the house when I broached the girl, and so on. — Other women have however acted in peculiar ways under similar circumstances, and the reasons for the dodges of gay women are only known to themselves. Somehow I think that Sarah's man had something to do with her desire to get rid of the girl, but about him I could glean no information; tho at times I was forbidden to go to her lodgings, because she said *he* was there.

[384]

Much as I have abbreviated and omitted, what a quantity of manuscript still remains. — Alas! a casual look through it, reveals the fact that, like much of that written just before this period of my history, it is prolix and copious in detail. — More so even than that preceding it which I shortened with so much trouble. — It is exuberant, because written for my secret pleasure, and I revelled in the detail as I wrote it, for in doing so I almost had my sexual treats over again. — It mattered not to me whether similar pleasure had been mine before or not, whether the erotic whims and fancies, amorous frolics, voluptuous eccentricities, were identical or not. — I described them as they had occurred at the time, and the pleasure of doing so was nearly the same, even had I done them twenty times, and described them twenty times.

But the woman, the partner in my felicity was frequently fresh and new to me, and I to her; and this newness prevents satiety in sexual frolics. There is always a shade of difference in the manners and behaviour of women in sexual preliminaries, and even in final performance. One woman never kisses or sighs, embraces or fucks, in exactly the same manner as another. The broad features from beginning to ending are the same. A coupling of the genitals finishes it all. But there are delicate shades of difference even in fucking which make the variety so charming, and describing them was ever new and amusing to me, when the charmer was new to me.

Yet on glancing through the remaining manuscript, — now in my mature, if not only years — the repetition seems a little wearisome. — What is to be done — abbreviate or destroy — which? — Abbreviation is laborious, and emasculates — the freshness of the writing is gone — nice shades lost. — But destruction saves all future trouble.

Perhaps entire omission of portions will be best, but that will destroy the continuity. In the narrative in its integrity, it is easy to see how in my youth, content with the simplest forms of sexual pleasure, I have gradually with advancing years and experience, been led to strangely erotic whims and devices, and have had the greatest pleasure in acts, and deeds, and thoughts, which in my ignorant youth would have revolted me. — To omit much is to destroy this continuity of idea and action. — No. It must be abbreviation or total destruction. Abbreviation, or else a full stop here, and nearly twenty years' narrative go to the flames.

Another thing — through the suggestions of women, by pondering over those suggestions — by reading works of erotic philosophers — from pictures, curiosity, and opportunity, — I have once or twice done what I regret, what in fact is almost a remorse to me, tho I really see no harm in it. — What a contradiction this, but thus it is. — Shall I destroy those chapters, erase those parts — or leave them — perhaps (for who knows) for some to cry shame. — To omit them is to sacrifice the narrative, and the illustration it affords to myself of my sexual idiosyncrasy — if such a phrase may be used — I know not what to do with this antagonism of thought and intention.

It must remain — written by *myself* and for *myself*, none probably will ever see it but *myself* — therefore why cheat *myself*? — let it remain.

I wish I had begun this revision earlier, perhaps now I shall never complete it — or complete it only in time to destroy it, before I myself am destroyed. — *Tempus edax rerum.*

CHAPTER XLI

Recherché eroticisms. — An outcome of the brothel spyhole. — An abnormal letch. — A man for a month. — Alone with him. — Mutual nervousness. — The ice broken. — Pricks produced. — An exiguous tool. — Unavailing masturbation. — Sarah's participation. — Cuntal incitation. — Prompt rigidity. — Onanistic operation. — Spermatic ejaculation. — Instantaneous copulation. — One on and one off. — A gorged cunt. — Masculine minetting. — A gristly mouthful. — Sucking cum fucking. — After supper. — Sarah's oration. — The end of the orgy.

Then took place the crowning act of my eroticism, the most daring fact of my secret life. An abnormal lust of which I have been ashamed and sorry, and the narrative of which

I have nearly destroyed, tho according to my philosophy, there was and is no harm in my acts, for in lust all things are natural and proper to those who like them. There can be no more harm in a man feeling another's prick, nor in a woman feeling another's cunt, than there is in their shaking hands. — At one time or other all have had these sexual handlings of others, yet a dislike to myself about this sexual whim still lingers Such is the result of early teaching and prejudices.

Twenty-four years had elapsed since my frolics with the first Camille. — Then I had frigged a Frenchman. Then I did the same with the man that big eyed Betsy got me. Then I'd felt the Captain in the dark at Lizzie M***d*n's. Since that I had not touched a male. What I witnessed through the baudy house partition put new inclinations into my head. The handsome pricks which I had seen women play with, the ease with which their doodles were handled, the ready way a girl brought a rebellious prick to stand and spend by coaxing it up in her mouth, etc., raised again desire to feel and play with a prick myself. Other men's seemed different to *me,* and at times I said this to Sarah in some such terms as these. — "I should like for once to feel a man's prick, to see closely his prick standing, see his spunk come out much or little." And so on.

The baudy house sights always terminated in fucking Sarah, and then for a time the desires which arose during my peeping ended abruptly. I talked about them at times when lewed nevertheless with Sarah, who said, "One man's prick stands and spends much like another, play with your own, but if you want, I can get one easily enough, and I'll let him come here for you, if Mr. F**z*r is out of town."

But I thought she meant a fellow who let out his rump and prick, and of that class I had an insufferable dislike and fear. They were I had heard thieves, their pricks used up, and I wanted nothing to do with an anus [at that time, not having found out the pleasure you both take and give by pressing the bumhole of a woman when fucking her] so for some months, altho she described some men as eligible, I would not see them.

At length in the winter she said, "My old woman (a crone who did her charring, and was in fact her servant altho she did not sleep in her rooms) can get a young man about twenty who's not a sod — he is a working man who has been without employment for two months and will be glad

[*387*]

of a sovereign." I thought I was going to be sold, but as I had only promised her a sovereign for getting me a man, I came to the conviction that I had really a chance, so arranged that he was to go to her rooms.

But unpleasant notions came. A poor man! he will be dirty and smelling of sweat — be rough — his linen ragged. — To get over that Sarah said, "Give me a sovereign, he shall have a new shirt, and socks, and drawers, I will buy them" — so I gave that money.

The evening came. I felt so nervous and even shocked at myself that I wished I had never undertaken the affair. — It was in vain that I argued with myself, and spite of my conviction that there was no harm in my doing it, when I came to her door I nearly turned back. I had been trying to strengthen my intention by thinking over my former wishes and curiosities, of the various amusements I should have with him, and how much I should learn of the ways of a man, to add to the lot I knew about women. All was useless, I almost trembled at my intention. I entered, saw Sarah. "He is in the bed room — such a nice young man, and quite good looking, I never saw him till I went to buy the things." I said I felt nervous. "That is stupid, but you are not more nervous than he is, he's just said you were evidently not coming and he was glad of it, and would go." Again she assured me that he was all the charwoman had told, a young man out of work, wanting bread, and not a sodomite.

I followed her into the bedroom. Saying, "This is the gentleman," she shut the door and left me with him. He stood up respectfully and looked at me timidly.

He was a fine young man about five feet seven inches high, rather thin looking as if for want of nourishment, with a nice head of curly brown hair, slight short whiskers, no moustache, bright eyes, and good teeth. He was not much like a working man and looked exceedingly clean. "You are the young man?" "Yes sir." "Sit down." Down he sat and I did the same.

Then I could not utter a word more, but felt inclined to say, "There is a sovereign, good night," and to leave him. All the desires, all the intentions, all expectations of amusement with his prick, all the curiosity I had hoped to satisfy for months left me. My only wish was to escape without seeming a fool.

With the exception of the sodomite whom Betsy Johnson had got me, it was the first time I had been by myself in the room with a male for the clear intention of doing everything with his tool that I had a mind to. My brain now had been long excited by anticipation, and wrought up to the highest when this opportunity came, and every occurrence of that evening is as clear in it now as if it were printed there. Altho the exact order of the various tricks I played may not be kept, yet everything I *did* on this first night, all that took place, I narrate in succession, without filling in anything from fancy or imagination. I could even recall the whole of our conversation, but it would fill quires (and I did fill two or three). — I only now give half of it, and that abbreviated.

I sat looking at him for some minutes — I can frig him, thought I — but I don't want to now. — What an ass he will think me. — Why does he not unbutton? — I wonder if he is a bugger — or a thief. — What's *he* thinking about. Is he clean? — How shall I begin — I wish I had not come — I hope he won't know me if he meets me in the street. — Is his prick large? — These thoughts one after another chased rapidly thro my brain, whilst I sat silent, yet at the same time wishing to escape, and he sat looking at the floor.

Then an idea came. "Would you like something to drink?" "If you like, sir." "What?" "Whatever you like, sir." — It was an immense relief to me when I called in Sarah, and told her to get whiskey, hot water, and sugar. — Whilst it was being fetched I went into the sitting room, glad of getting away.

Sarah, in the sitting room, asked, "How do you find him?" — I told her I did not know and was frightened to go on. — "Oh! I would now, as you have had him got for you, then you'll be satisfied." — Again she assured me he was not on the town, and I need not be afraid. The whiskey was got, and behold me again alone with him. I made whiskey and water for myself and him and took some into Sarah. I began to ask him about himself. He was a house decorator in fine work, such work was it its worst just then, being a young hand he had not full employment, had been out of work nearly two months, he had pawned everything excepting what he had on. This all seemed consistent. He told me where he lodged, where he was apprenticed, the master he worked for last, the houses he worked at. "If you are a decorator your hands will be hard, and if you kneel your knees will." "Yes but I have had scarcely anything to do for two months, and but one day's work last week. Look at my nails." — They were stained with something he had used.

Then he had had one day's chopping wood which had blistered both his hands, for it was not work he was accustomed to. Blisters I saw. There was evident truth in what he said.

This relieved me, together with the influence of whiskey and water. I got more courage and he seemed more comfortable, but not a word had transpired about our business, and an hour had gone. Then my mind reverted to my object, and I said, "You know what you came for." "Yes sir." He changed white, then red, and began to bite his nails.

My voice quivered as I said, "Unbutton your trowsers then." He hesitated. "Let me see your cock." One of his hands went down slowly, he unbuttoned his trowsers, which gaping, shewed a white shirt. Then never looking at me, he began biting his nails again.

The clean shirt, coupled with his timidity, gave me courage. "Take off your coat and waistcoat." He slowly did so. — I did the same, gulped down a glass of whiskey and water, sat him down by me, and lifting his shirt laid hold of his prick. A thrill of pleasure passed thro me, I slipped my hands under his balls, back again to his prick, pulled the foreskin backwards and forwards, my breath shortening with excitement. He sat still. Suddenly I withdrew my hand with a sense of fear and shame again on me.

"May I make water, sir, I want so badly," said he in a humble way, just like a schoolboy. "Certainly, take off your trowsers first." He looked hard at me, slowly took them and his drawers off, and stood with his shirt on. I took up the pot and put it on the chair (my baudy brain began now to work). "Do it here, and I'll look at your cock."

He came slowly there and stood. "I can't water now — I think it is your standing by me." "You will directly, don't mind me." The whiskey and excitement having made *me* leaky, I pulled out my tool and pissed in the pot before him.

He laughed uneasily, it was the first sign of amusement he had given. Directly I had finished, I laid hold of his prick and began playing with it, I pulled back the skin and blew on the tip, a sudden whim that made him laugh, and his shyness going off, I holding his prick, he pissed the pot half full—I was delighted and wished he could have kept on pissing for a quarter of an hour.

The ice was now broken, I took off *my* trowsers, and then both with but shirts and socks on, I sat him at the side of the bed and began my investigation of his copulating apparatus.

"I want to frig you," said I. "Yes sir." "Has any man ever

frigged you." — No living man had touched his prick since he was a boy, he declared. — Then I began to handle his cock with the ordinary first fucking motion.

I had scarcely frigged a minute before I wanted to feel his balls. Then I turned him with his rump to me, to see how his balls and prick looked hanging down from the back. — Then on to his side, to see how the prick dangled along his thigh. Then I took him to the wash stand and washed his prick, which before that was as clean as a new shilling, but the idea of washing it pleased me. Then laying him down on his back, I recommenced the fascinating amusement of pulling the foreskin backwards and forwards, looking in his face to see how he liked it. — He was as quiet as a lamb, but looked sheepish and uncomfortable.

His prick at first was small, but under my manipulation grew larger, tho never stiff. Several times it got rather so for an instant, and then with the desire to see the spunk come, I began frigging harder; when instead of getting stiffer it got smaller. I tried this with him laying down, sitting up, and standing, but always with the same result — I spoke about it. — He said he could not make it out.

His prick was slightly longer than mine, was beautifully white, and with a pointed tip. I made it the stiffest by gently squeezing it — I had had no desire in my own doodle, but as I made his stiff once when he was lying down, my own prick came to a stand, and following a sudden inspiration I laid myself on to his belly, as if he had been a woman, and our two pricks were between our stomachs close together. I poked mine under his balls, and forced his under my stones, then changing, I turned his bum towards me, and thrusting my cock between his thighs and under his balls to the front, bent his prick down to touch the tip of mine, which was just showing thro his thighs. But his prick got limper and limper, and as I remarked that, it shrivelled up. We had been an hour at this game, and there seemed no chance of his spending. No sign of permanent stiffness or randiness or pleasure. He seemed in fact miserably uncomfortable.

Then he wanted to piss again from nervousness — I held his prick, squeezing it, sometimes stopping the stream, then letting it go on, and satisfying my curiosity. That done, I made a final effort to get a spend out of him, by squeezing, frigging slow, frigging fast. Then I rubbed my hand with soap, and making with spittle an imitation of cunt mucous on it, titillated the tip. "I think I can do it now," said he —

but all was useless. "It's no good, I'm very sorry, sir, but I can't, that is a fact. — I don't know how it is."

The last hour had been one of much novelty and delight to me, tho he couldn't spend; but the announcement disappointed me. It came back to my mind that he might be, after all that Sarah had said, but an overfrigged bugger, who could no longer come. For I had heard that men who let themselves out for that work at last got so used up that it was difficult for them to do anything with their own pricks, and that all they could do was to permit men to feel their cocks, whilst they plugged their arse-holes. So I repeated my questions, and he again swore by all that was holy that no man had ever felt him but me; and he added that he was sorry he had come, but the money was a temptation.

I laid him then again on the bed and felt his prick. We finished the whiskey, and I sent for more; and in a whisper told Sarah that there was no spunk in him. She brought in the whiskey herself, and laughed at seeing us two nearly naked on the bed together.

Then I asked him when he had a woman last, if he liked them, how he got them, and so forth. He told me that he liked women very much — sometimes he got them for nothing, and they were servant girls mostly. When at houses if servants were left in them, or even if the family were only for a short time out — young fellows like him often got a put in; or else made love to them, and got them to come out at nights. He warmed up as he told me this, and his prick began to rise, but on my recommencing to masturbate him, it fell down again. He declared that the woman he last had was ten days previously, when he gave her a shilling out of the trifle he had gained, and that he had never spent since. Then he began biting his nails, adding that he hoped I should give him the money, for he could not help not spending, and was desperately badly off — "I have had some bread and cheese, and beer, but I have not tasted meat for six days."

Three hours with him had passed, the frigging seemed useless, but talking about women had brought *my* steam well up, so I began to think of letting him go, and plugging Sarah to finish. "Sarah is a fine woman isn't she? Did you ever have her, or see her naked," I said suddenly, thinking to catch him. — She *was* fine, but he had never seen her in his life, until the day but one previously. — "Would you like to see her naked." Oh! would he not. I knew Sarah would do anything almost, so called her in, told her his cock would not stand, and that we wanted to see her naked, "All right," said she, and began to undress.

He kept his eyes ardently fixed on her as she took off her things — I remarked to him on her charms as she disclosed them. He said "Yes — yes" — in an excited way. Then he ceased answering, but stared at her intently. When her limbs and breasts shewed from her chemise, a voluptuous sigh escaped him, and he put his hand to his prick outside his shirt. Feeling him, I found his prick swelling. "Don't pull off yet Sarah." She ceased taking off her chemise. "Pull off your shirt." Helping him he stood naked with his prick rising. — "Now show us your cunt." Down Sarah lay (after stripping off her chemise) on her back, one arm raised and shewing her dark haired arm pit, her legs apart, and one raised with the heel just under her bum, the black hair of her cunt curling down till shut in by her arse cheeks, the red lined cunt lips slightly gaping. — It was a sight which would have made a dead man's prick stiffen, and mine was stiff at the sight altho I had seen it scores of times. I forgot him then, till turning my head I saw his splendid cockstand. — His eyes were fixed full of desire on her, and he was a model of manly, randy beauty. — "Is not she fine?" said I. "Oh! lovely, beautiful, let me do it," addressing her. "No," said I, "another time perhaps," and I seized his tool with lewed joy.

For an instant he resisted. Sarah said, "Let my friend do it, you came for that." I frigged away, he felt its effects and sighed — I frigged on and felt the big, firm, wrinkled ball bag. A voluptuous shiver ran thro him soon. "Oh! let me feel her — do." "Feel her then." Over he stooped. "Kneel on the bed." Quickly he got there and plunged his finger into her carmine split. Again I grasped his tool and frigged. He cried out, "Oh! I'm coming. — I'm spend — ing" — and a shower of sperm shot out, covering her belly from cunt to navel. I frigged on until every drop had fallen. Then letting go his prick, he sat down on his heels, his eyes shut, his body still palpitating with pleasure and now fingering his still swollen doodle.

The effect on me was violent. Sarah's attitude on her back at all times gave me a cockstand — it had stood whilst frigging him. — There she lay now, a large drop of his spunk on her motte seemed ready to drop down on to her clitoris, higher up on her belly little pools lay. Tearing off my shirt, scarcely knowing what I did, crying out, "Move up higher

[*393*]

on the bed" — which he did, I flung myself on her and put my prick up her cunt. — My prick rubbed the spunk drop on her thatch, my belly squeezed the opal pools between us, the idea delighted me — I fucked away, stretched out my hand, grasped his wet prick, for he was now conveniently near me, and fucked quickly to an ecstatic termination.

The greater the preliminary excitement, the more delicious seems the repose after a fuck — the more it is needed, and I had had excitement enough that night. At length I roused myself. My cock did not seem inclined to come out of its lodging. I felt that I could butter her again without uncunting. So keeping it in, I raised myself and looked at him sitting at the head of the bed, naked and still feeling his prick, which was again as stiff as a ramrod.

"He can spend after all," said I, my prick still up Sarah. — "I told you he was a nice young man." "Should you like to fuck her?" "Just give me the chance." The tale of the soldiers putting into each other's leavings came into my head. "Do it at once." "Lord," said Sarah, "you don't mean that." But I did. "Do it now." — I rose on my knees. — As I took my belly off of Sarah's, they were sticking together with his spunk. It made a loud smacking noise as our bellies separated. — My prick drew out sperm which dropped between her thighs. — As I got off, he got on, and as quickly put up her. The next minute their backsides were in rapid motion.

The second fuck is longer than the first, and I had time to watch their movements. — A man and woman both naked and close to me, were copulating — I could see and feel every movement of their bodies — hear their murmurs and sighs — see their faces. — There stood I with my own prick now stiff again watching them. — My hands roved all over them — I slipped my hand between their bellies — I felt his balls. — Then slipping it under her rump it felt the wet spunk I had left in her cunt, now working out on to the stem of his prick as it went in and out — I got on the bed and rubbed my prick against his buttocks. I shouted out — "Fuck her, — spend in her — spend in my spunk," — and other obscenities I know not what. — I encouraged his pleasure by baudy suggestions. A sigh, a murmuring, told me he was coming. My fingers were on his balls, and I let them go to see his face. He thrust his tongue into Sarah's mouth. — "You are spending, Sarah." — No reply. — Her mouth was open to his tongue, her eyes were closed, her buttocks mov-

[*394*]

ing with energy, and the next second but for a few twitch-ings of his arse, and their heavy breathings, they were like lumps of lifeless flesh. Both had spent. The fancy to do her *after him* came over me — my spunk — his spunk — her spunk — all in her cunt together. I will spend in her again. — The idea of my prick being drowned in these mixed exudations overwhelmed me libidinously. — "I'll do it to you again. — Get off of her." — "Let me wash," said Sarah. — "No.' — "I will." — "You shan't." — He was getting off, she attempting to rise, when I pushed her down. —"It's wiser" — I didn't know what she said scarce-ly. — "No — no — no — I want to put into his spunk." — Her thighs were apart, her cunt hole was blinded, hidden by spunk which lay all over it and filled its orifice. I threw my-self on her, my prick slipped up with a squashing noise — I know no other way of describing it. I think I hear it now.

I felt a sense of heavenly satisfaction. Her cunt was so filled that it seemed quite loose, the sperm squeezed out of her and up, until the hair of both our genitals were saturat-ed — I pushed my hand down, and making her lift up one leg, found the sperm lay thick down to her arse hole — I called out, "Your spunk's all over my ballocks," and told all the baudy images which came across my mind. I told him to lay down by the side of us, and made Sarah feel his prick at the same time I did — I felt my pleasure would even now be too short and stopped myself. Sarah with a sigh cried, "Oh — my God — go on," her cunt tightened, she let go his prick and clasped my buttocks to her — I still held his prick, and tried to lengthen my pleasure but could not, her cunt so clipped me. Abandoning myself to her the next instant al-most with a scream of pleasure, I was quiet in her arms and fell asleep — and so did she, and so did he — all three on the bed close together.

Awakening, I had rolled off close to Sarah on to my side, my prick laying against her thigh. — She lay on her back asleep, he nearly on his back. All three were nearly naked, myself excepted who had on an under shirt next my skin. — She had silk stockings and black merino boots on. My fore-skin had risen up and covered the tip of my prick. In the saucer at the top was spunk which had issued from me after I uncunted. — The lamp was alight. Two candles (they had been short pieces) had burnt out, and the fire had all but ex-pired. The room had been hot all the evening, for there were three of us in it, three lights burning, and the fire. Now it had got cold, and a sensation of chillness was over me.

I got up and looked at the pair. — She a splendid woman, firm and smooth skinned, and of a creamy pink tint — with the dark hair of her cunt in splendid contrast. He a fine young man with white flesh, and with much dark brown hair clustering and curling round his white prick, and throwing his balls into shadow. His prick still large was hanging over his thigh, the slightly red tip half covered by the foreskin pointing towards Sarah, and as if looking at it. Then sexual instinct made me pay attention to her. — She lay there with two libations from me, and one from him in her cunt. I desired to see how it looked and felt it, but was so distracted by my various erotic impulses that I cannot recollect everything accurately. — All I know is that I laid hold of her leg nearest to me, and watching, pulled it slowly so as to leave her legs slightly open. I put my finger down from the beginning of the cleft. It felt thick and sticky, yet but little spunk was to be seen — looking down towards the bum cheeks, I saw the bed patched in half a dozen places with what had run out from her — I thrust my finger up her cunt and she awakened.

She sat up, looked round, rubbed her eyes, said, "it's cold." Then she looked at him. "Why — he's asleep too, have *you* been asleep?" — Then she put her fingers to her cunt too, got off the bed, and on to the pot — looking at me smiling. — "You *are* a baudy devil and no mistake — I don't recollect such a spree since I have been out." "Your cunt's in a jolly state of batter." "It will be all right when it's washed" — and she proceeded to wash, but I stopped her.

He was snoring and had turned on to his back — his prick which seemed large lolled over his thigh. "He's a fine young man and his prick's bigger than yours, and what a bag," said she gently lifting up his prick and shewing his balls. I saw it was very large, as it had seemed to me when I squeezed and felt it before, but then I had been far too excited to notice anything carefully. Now I began to frig him as he lay. "I thought you had done me, for for two hours I could not make his cock stand." "Ah! it was nervousness. — He has never been felt by a man before, some would give ten pounds for such a chance and you are to give him a sovereign." "Do you think he can spend again?" "Yes, see what a lot he spent over me; if he was well fed, that young chap would be good for half a dozen pokes, he's been half starved for two months."

I gently laid hold of his prick, and pulled the skin down. One feel more and it rose to fullish size, and lay half way up his belly. "I thought it would directly you touched it from its look," said she. Said I, "I will frig him," and commenced in the slowest and gentlest manner, scarcely touching it. The stiffening began and the foreskin retired, the tip got rubicund and tumid, an uneasy movement of his thigh and belly began, and muttering in his sleep his hand went to his prick. — I removed mine. Soon his hand dropped by his side again, and he snored and muttered something.

Sarah, who had put on her chemise, then laid hold of his prick and frigged it. — "He can't spend, he's done too much already," said I. "I think he will tho." Then I, jealous of her handling, and lewdly fascinated, resumed the work. — Had he not drunk and eaten heartily, and been very fatigued, he must have awakened, but he didn't. Not spending, I spat on my finger and thumb, and making a moist ring with them, rubbed his prick tip through them. That did it. He muttered, his belly heaved, and out rolled his sperm, as he awakened, saying, "I've had a beastly spending dream, and thought I was fucking *you*." Seeing us laughing he seemed astonished, and was angry when told of our game. We all washed, we men put on shirts, and he got good humoured again.

I had scarcely eaten that day, felt empty and said so — Sarah said *she* was hungry, he that he could eat a donkey, for he'd not had food since the morning — I had never eaten in Sarah's lodgings, for the style didn't suit me, but felt that I must eat now. "Shall I fetch something at once? It's near midnight, and all the shops will be closed." — We had been five hours at our voluptuous gambols, but it did not seem half that time.

I gave Sarah money. She fetched cut beef and ham, bread, cheese, and bottled stout, and also whiskey. — Whilst she was away, he recovered his temper and felt his cock. He said he hated "beastly cheating dreams." "Are you fond of feeling men?" "It's much nicer to fuck a woman," I replied and told him that for many years I had never put finger on a prick but my own.

Spite of dirty knives and a dingy table cloth, we all fell to at the food. — He ate ravenously and told me that the last time he had meat, a mate gave him some of his dinner. I

[*397*]

gave him a cigar, we had more whiskey and water, the room was hot again, we sat round the fire with our shirts only on — Sarah was dressed. — He told me again about himself, and soon the conversation drifted into the fucking line. He had lost his modesty and with it much of his respect for me. Instead of only answering and saying "sir" he began to ask me questions. Just as a woman's manner alters towards a man, directly he has once fucked her, so did his alter now that I had frigged him.

I asked if he liked being frigged. — No he did not like — "spending in the air" — did I? "No" — but I did such things at times. Then Sarah alluded to his big balls, we both felt them, and such a large bag I have never seen before. He said the boys at school joked him about it. Boys know the sizes of each other's pricks.

I wanted to go on. The novelty was so great that I could not see and feel him enough; circumstances which I did not expect had brought Sarah into the fun, which increased the amusement. I am in the prime of life, and altho never attempting such wonders as some men brag of, can easily do my four fucks in an evening with a fresh woman, and sometimes more, altho then used up a little next day. I had now only spent twice and my prick seemed on fire. Wine, beer, and a full stomach soon heat a young man who has not spent for ten days. I pulled his prick about as we sat round the fire, and it readily swelled. He prayed me to desist, he'd had enough that night, but I had not. So I made Sarah take off her clothes to her chemise, and sit opposite. I sat next him smoking and looking at his prick, and feeling it at intervals.

Often in my youth, my prick has stood before my dinner was finished. A dozen times have I got up and fucked in the middle and finished dinner afterwards. — This meal began to tell on all. Sarah raised her chemise to let the warmth of the fire reach her legs, and showed her silk stockings and red garters. — "What a fine pair you have," said he — and down went his hand to his shirt. I saw a projection, and pulling up his shirt, there was his prick as stiff as ever.

"I'll frig you, and you look at Sarah's legs." He objected, had had enough of *that*, he would sooner fuck Sarah. — I had not brought him to fuck my woman — my letch was for frigging him. — Whilst this talk was going on I held his prick. Sarah showed us one of her thighs and told him to let me do what I liked — I had a stiff one and was dying to let out my sperm. I would frig him, and he should fuck her

[*398*]

afterwards. A young man with a standing prick always thinks that there is enough sperm in it for any amount of fucking. — How often I have thought whilst my cock was standing and burning to be in a cunt what wonders I would do, and directly after one coition did nothing more.

I put Sarah on the bed, myself by her, him by the side of us on his back, and upside down; his belly so placed that his prick was near my shoulders, and I could conveniently feel it. His prick was throbbing with lust — I laid on Sarah with prick outside her and began frigging him. He sighed and cried out, "Oh! let me do it to her — do — oho — do." I meant to play with him long, but Sarah was lewed, placed her hand between our bellies and put my prick up her. — Then all went its own way. — If a woman means you to go on fucking when up her you can't help yourself. Without moving their bums, they can grip with their cunt muscles and grind a man's tool so that he *must* ram and rub. I was soon stroking as hard as I could, but holding my head on my right hand resting from the elbow, so as to see his prick which I went on frigging. It was a longer job than before, with all our lewedness and good will, for both of us. At length out came his sperm. At the sight of it out shot mine into Sarah, who responded with her moisture, and all was quiet,

We reposed long, then I got off. "Now you may have her." — Sarah washed. He laid on the bed, and after wiping up his now thin spunk from his belly, began frigging himself up. Sarah laid down by his side and let him feel her clean cunt, but it was useless; and after some violent fisting of his tool, he rose saying, "I'm done up" — and again we all sat down before the fire, smoking and drinking, and talking about fucking, the causes and the consequences thereof.

This talk went on for an hour or so. Sarah said jeeringly to him, "Why don't you have me." — Every ten minutes he frigged his cock uselessly. Then he ate more food. — Sarah went to the watercloset, which was in a yard, and dressed partly to go there, for it was cold. — His prick looked beautiful but lifeless. — My baudiness was getting over and I was tired, but thought then came into my head — a reminiscence of my frolics with French women. But tho I had done everything but one with Sarah, I did not suggest what was in my mind before her — I had a stupid lingering modesty in me. — We were both fuddled and reckless, and Sarah now down stairs. I locked the door, saying, "If you'll promise not to tell her, I will make you stiff enough to have her." He promised. — I laid him on the bed and putting his prick in my mouth began to suck it, first with the skin on, and then gently with the skin off. The smoothness delighted me. I no longer wondered at a French woman, who told me a prick was the nicest thing she ever had in her mouth. I did exactly as it had been done to me as nearly as I recollected; spit out after the first taste, and then went on mouthing, licking, and sucking. It took effect directly. — "Oh! it's as good as a cunt," said he. It was stiffened by the time Sarah came back. I went to the door and unlocked it, he had resumed his seat, then Sarah washed her backside and went back to her seat by the fire. He'd never had his cock sucked before.

We finished the whiskey — it was getting towards one o'clock — Sarah said, "It's time we got to bed — why don't you both stop all night? — it will be cold, for I have no more coals." The lamp was going out, and she went to the next room to fetch candles. When she came back, "If he is going to fuck you, he should begin," said I. "Yes, and I am going to bed whether he does or not." She stripped to her chemise and got into bed. "If you don't have her now, she is not to let you when I am gone, get outside the bed." — Sarah did. — With cock stiff he got on to her in a minute. I saw by a cross twist of his buttocks and a sigh that he was up her — Sarah gave that smooth, easy, wriggling jerk and upwards motion with her buttocks and thighs, which a woman does to complete the engulfment of a doodle — I put my hand under his balls. His prick up to the roots was up her cunt.

Then not a word was spoken. A long stroke ensued, and gradually after hard quick ramming, their last pleasure shewed itself. My randiness increased by watching him, I made him leave her cunt before he had well finished spending and again plunged my prick into her reeking, slippery, slimy vagina. I gloried in feeling their sperm upon me. I was not in the habit of giving Sarah wet kisses, but as I thought, I longed to meet her mouth with mine, and with our tongues joined, and hard thrusts, a pain in my pego, and slight pain in my arse hole, I spent, and Sarah spent. "My God I'm fucked out," said she.

It was three o'clock a.m. — eight or nine hours had I been in one round of excitement — I had frigged him three times and he'd fucked thrice — I had fucked six times — I had fucked in his spunk, and had sucked his prick — Sarah had been fucked quite eight times. How many times I had spent I did not then know, being bewildered with excitement and drink. — As Sarah got up she seemed dazed, sat in a chair, and said, "Damned if ever I had such a night, I'm clean fucked out." Then paying them I left. It was at our next meeting that Sarah said I had fucked her six time. In my abbreviation of the manuscript, I have omitted some of our lascivious exercises, which were in fact but a repetition of what I had done before.

I was thoroughly done up the next day, not only with spending but with excitement. My delight in handling his white prick in repose, half stiff and in complete rigidity, was almost maddening. The delight of watching his prick glide in and out of her cunt was intense. The desire and curiosity of twenty years was being satisfied. My knowledge of copulation and of the penis getting perfected. — Yet I went home in an uncomfortable frame of mind about what I had done with him. There was no one in my home just then to wonder at my being so late, to notice my excitement, or to question me, which was fortunate.

CHAPTER XLII

Unavailing repentance. — Gemini frolics. — Pricks between bellies. — I on him. — He on me — tip to tip. — Boots and stockings. — A lascivious triad. — Gamahuching all round. — A looking-glass got. — Genital manipulations. — Simultaneous fuckings and friggings. — I fuck, she sucks. — Variations on the same tune. — She on my prick sits. — He her clitoris licks. — Three on our sides together. — Amatory exercises with ropes. — Sarah's pudendal capacity. — An assault of two pegos. — Finger and penis co-operating. — Miscellaneous lascivities. — A scare in the street. — A scare at Sarah's. — A suggestive question. — Desires excited. — Heavy pay for an anus. — Sodomy cum onanism. — Fear, disgust, and hasty retreat.

I went home used up, but excited beyond measure. I could not sleep for thinking of having frigged a man. The smoothness of skin, the loose easy movement of the outer skin over the inner rod, and its whiteness — the gradual change in color of its plum shaped tip from pink to a deep carmine, the shooting out of his sperm, the voluptuous shuddering whilst he fucked Sarah, the saucers which came and went in his arse cheeks when he fucked, all danced before my eyes as I lay in bed, and I saw them as plainly as if the fucking was actually then going on. — Again her distended cunt lips, with the thick spunk oozing, my prick pushing between them with a squash, squeezing the spermatic mixture out on to my balls, and up to her motte, and gumming our hair together, my grip of his stiffened cock as I fucked her the second time; all filled me with an incredibly furious, baudy excitement, making my prick stiffen and throb, spite of my fatigue and preventing my rest.

Then came reflexion. — Had I really frigged a man — still worse — got my own prick wetted with the sperm of another man. Above all sucked his prick! — An act I had certainly heard of being done by men to each other, yet all but disbelieved, and looked on as a very foul action — yet I had done it, had enjoyed it all. Much as I had done and seen before, I was not quite easy in my mind, spite of my philosophy that any sexual enjoyment is permissible — that our organs of generation are for our own use and pleasure, and that what men and women choose to do together they have a right to do, it concerning no one else. Such are the results of prejudices and false education. It ended in reflecting that I never had intended to do those things, that opportunity had let me unwittingly to do them, and resolving that I would never do it again, I fell asleep.

Next morning at breakfast I thought, "That debauch will never be renewed." After luncheon, "What was the harm after all." Then I began to think I should like to feel him once more, to watch the phenomenon of the spend more coolly and philosophically. — Once more to make him spend, and to watch his prick from its stiffening to its shrinking. To watch his face and see how pleasure affected it. Why should I not bring him and Sarah naked together as I had done and see his prick rise, let him fuck her, and watch as I did last night — surely there is no harm — or not more than in looking at such doings through a spyhole. — The man is clearly not a sodomite, or he would not be so ready to fuck her. He is out of work, and probably is what he says he is. It is a chance which never may come again to me.

I thought of the double fuck without the washing, of the prick in my mouth, and then felt ashamed. — "I must have been screwed and so excited that I did not know what I was about, I shall never do *that* again, and hope he won't tell Sarah." I then took a gallop, determining again to get him. I had slept so badly on the previous night that on my return I laid down. My mind wandered to his prick and what Sarah called his purse. I wondered if his prick was really bigger than mine and wished I had measured it — I wondered if he spent more or less than me, and many other things; and at last came to the conclusion that I ought to be ashamed of myself, and being empty in stomach and fatigued, said, "I have done with that business." — Then I went to my club, had dinner, desire to see him again then came back, and soon I was with Sarah arranging for another meeting.

Said she, "You'd a pretty good night, I declare that if I were to tell some women what we did, they'd only believe part of it. — He wanted to sleep with me." She dare say he would come again willingly, she would go and see — I gave her money to buy him trowsers, cravat, and collars, said that he was to take a bath, and also gave her money to feed him well — Sarah met me out an hour afterwards. He would be there the following night.

She had done all I wished, and the fellow looked as spruce as possible — I was again nervous, and so was he, but a few minutes' conversation put us at ease. — We stripped, and behold us close together, I holding that handsome tool of his. He asked if Sarah was coming, but I did not want her then, and sat with his balls in my hand, for a time thinking of the size and fullness of the scrotum.

Of the sovereign — he told me that he ˙first paid fifteen shillings for rent, and the rest where he owed money — that Sarah had got him good food, — that he had not spent since that last night. "When I thought of it all, I got to want it," said he.

Then I washed his genitals and made a complete and curious examination of his penis and scrotum, and had more complete quiet pleasure crowding in that than on the previous occasion. Before when feeling his prick it did not make me randy — tonight it did. My examination began to tell on him and when I had pulled the foreskin once or twice up and down, his rod was stiff. Then up stiffened mine. — I began frigging him. — "Now I will look at your sperm as it comes." Suddenly he laid hold of my prick. — "Hullo, don't do that."

He relinquished it begging pardon, saying he did not know what made him do it. — My pulling *his* about seemed quite a proper thing for me, for I paid him for it; but directly *he* touched *my* prick, I felt disgusted. — The mind is an odd thing — if a gentleman had felt me, should I have been equally shocked?

This preliminary was soon over, he was on the point of discharge when I stopped, and making him sit down, watched his stiff prick gradually droop, and then I went at him again and so on. If a copious discharge is to be got out of a man, that is the way to do it. — At length after playing so for long, he said he must and would come — so I frigged as fine a spermatic ejaculation as I had had on the first night. It spurted out a yard, quite.

I had intended not to let Sarah appear that night, but feeling his cock had made my cock stand. "I'll frig myself," I said. But I hated spending in that fashion. — After trying to restrain myself till I could do so no longer, I called Sarah.

[*404*]

She was dressed. Throwing her on the side of the bed, up went her clothes, and I put up her, he looking on. Up came his prick again at the sight. — He asked to have her, but I wouldn't let him, and handled his tool whilst I fucked her.

I carried out my intentions, frigged him four times, and had no end of amusement with him. — I had a taste that night for rolling over him as if he were a woman, when his cock was stiff, and making mine stiff, and laying the two pricks together. I tried all sorts of ways of making his stand. Sometimes by pulling the skin up and down, sometimes by shaking the top — now by giving it a rude pinch — now by squeezing his balls. I tried every way which I could recollect women had used on me, or I had heard or thought of. There was now no difficulty about it, for his cock kept standing after very small handling; and he had still sperm, tho getting at each discharge less in quantity and thinner. At his fourth discharge all was over, but there were still things which I wished to do with him. One was to put his prick in my mouth. Again I rubbed my lips on its smooth white stem, and kissed it, and all but put it in. — But I never will do that again, thought I to myself.

The amusement however seemed incomplete without Sarah. Again I fucked her, and then let *him* do it to her. That was a very long job and finished the evening, and him.

Afterwards. Each meeting I thought would be the last, yet I had him again. Sarah participated in the amusements regularly. The evening did not seem complete without the two. I was infatuated. — Of course four discharges a night could not be kept up, but I did not see him every night. — But as much spunk as could be got out of him I got, pumping him pretty dry with my fist, and myself as well, but into Sarah's cunt. I now tell only some of my amusements, and as near as may be in the succession in which they took place. They could not all be done on one evening.

My baudy imagination being set to work, all sorts of possibilities came into my head. We soaped well our pricks, and under our balls and arse furrows. Then lying on the top of him, we thrust our pricks under each other's balls, and working in the soapy furrows, both spent on each other's backside. — It was not convenient, our pricks rebelled at being so bent and thrust, but the novelty made up for the inconvenience. — Novelty stimulates desire. — I got much amusement from lying on the top of him, when our pricks were not stiff, and feeling the testicles and two cocks in a bunch together. Sarah, then quite delighted, felt our inter-mingled genitals. Then I put him on the top and myself be-neath, Sarah held a looking glass and candle, so that I could see when on my back two ballocks in a heap together. Sarah was delighted with all my lasciviousness and said she never knew such a baudy man as I was.

One day standing up I soaped both our prick tips and we frigged ourselves. We put the two tips so close that they rubbed together, and we spent against each other's glans.

These lascivious vagaries and delicacies did not suggest themselves all at once. Firstly my delight was to watch his face as he spent, then to see the prick stiff, the sperm shoot, the tremulous shaking of his backside, and to hear his quiet murmurs of pleasure. After I had had enough of that, I be-took myself to more fanciful amusements.

Spite of myself, my mind recurred to the feel of his prick when in my mouth, and altho I vowed to myself never to let it go into it again. — Yet why? thought I at length. Have you not licked a cunt? Have you not had the fresh warm piddle squirt against your face from Sarah's cunt? — Have you not savoured the salt liquor which distils from and keeps moist a woman's cunt? Nay. Have you not when moistened till al-most running out, by its sweating (so to speak) under the ac-tion of your tongue on her clitoris, shoved your tongue up her cunt, and brought it back into your mouth with delight and ecstasy at giving her pleasure? Is the putting into your mouth a prick, dry, clean, and smooth as ivory, worse? — But it's a man's. In her mouth a prick is quite proper. He may lick, tickle, and suck her hole, that's quite natural. But a man's! — No I won't.

For all that, one night whilst feeling it, when he had washed after I'd first frigged him, I again washed it care-fully, and laid him on the bed. There hung his prick and his testicles, the tip just covered by the prepuce. As I pulled back the foreskin, I put out my tongue and tickled the top. "Your tongue is on it," said he laughing. — Then I took it in my lips. It was like ivory. I longed to minette with it, and passed the limp, soft, flexible tool entirely into my mouth: not a bit was outside. — It went back towards my gullet and there I held it, till it began to swell. I passed it up and down in my mouth, licked and sucked it, put it out and let it stay till it drooped, then remouthed it, and continued this for a long time. At length his sperm had been so accumulated by the dalliance that he said he could bear it no longer and would frig himself if I did not. I then brought it up to the spending throb, pulled it from my mouth, and finishing with my hand, his spunk shot up. There is nothing like coaxing a prick a long time, for accumulating the spunk in the reservoirs of concupiscence. I'm sure more comes then, than from a hasty frig.

Then I fucked her before him, then sent her out, and again sucked his prick which was in powerful order — I laid him on the bedside in the attitude most convenient to lick a cunt, and so that I might see his face while I operated. It is easy in a man's face to see when his ballocks are about to send forth their juices. — A red Indian, they say, can preserve his features when being tortured. I doubt if he could when spending. — A man's face then is rather stupid, nor is that of a woman's as she is holding tightly to her fucker's backside for the full engulfment of his throbbing cock in her cunt, highly intellectual; but it's much more lovely than that of a man's face.

I offered him money to suck my prick. He would not, and that night's amusement ended. Then much to his delight I began to let him fuck Sarah. Whilst they were doing that trick, I handled his balls, put my hand between their bellies, made them turn over on to their sides and lift their legs in all sorts of ways, so that I might see the movement of the prick and the swell of the lips of her orifice. — I made him fuck her standing up, then on the side of the bed, whilst with a candle I moved round them, satisfying my curiosity. Then I fucked her and made him similarly satisfy himself. He was delighted to grasp my balls whilst my prick was pistoning her. — Modesty and timidity had now left all of us. — Unrestrained libidinous enjoyment was everything to us, each doing the best to stimulate each other's lust. Sarah had become more active, suggestive, and libidinous than we two. She delighted in it.

My libidinosity increased by indulging it. I longed to see ourselves in the various attitudes. — Sarah's table glass was small, and having placed it so as to get a glimpse of ourselves, and finding it unsatisfactory, I bought at a broker's shop, a long, large old-fashioned looking glass in a mahogany frame. We together nailed it up against the wall at the level of the top of the mattress, and so that we could see ourselves from head to foot as we lay. Then our sensual delight was doubled, for as we fucked, or frigged, or sucked, we could look in the glass, and talk about our attitudes.

[407]

One night all three highly strung — I was near her, he by her side on the bed. "Oh look at his prick." "Ah! it's not stiff — he'll spend." "Frig it, frig him, Sarah." She did. "Are you coming, Jack." "Aha." "Yes — my spunk's coming." "Oh fuck me, fuck me," cried Sarah, "or I'll frig myself." "Stop, Sarah, I'll fuck you," and I put my prick up her. — She grasped my rump with one hand, with the other grasped his prick, and so did I. Both Sarah's and my hand were on it. Sometimes she had the stem, I the scrotum. Just before *we* spent out spurted *his* spunk. Then as we felt it, we poured out our sexual tributes, a spasm of libidinous sympathy fetched us both together.

I began then to pay for his baths, his food, and fine linen so that he came perfect from head to toe. He had no hair on his body, excepting on his prick and armpits, and but little on his face. — What with idleness, good living, and baths, he became as smooth as ivory and as nice to feel an the nicest woman. He got in a fortnight plumper, altho I took so much semen out of him; but he was young and strong. — What pleasure for him! — The only annoyance to me was that his prick, when he got randy and it stood, had a strong smell. — The smell of most cunts I like.

After I had sucked him that night, I never repeated it but once. — Altho we had lost all modesty, I did not like Sarah to see all, until late in the evening when whiskey and baudiness told on me. Whatever we did together, I never lost sight of my principal object, which was to frig him, and see either his tool or his face when he was spending. — When Sarah came in, at first we used to sit round the fire drinking and smoking, all as naked as the weather permitted. Sometimes he told his adventures with servants in the houses where he had worked, she about what men had done. The conversation always was erotic. — Until the spirit moved me to action, I usually sat by him in an easy chair, with his tool in my hand. Sometimes he laid hold of mine. "Look at you two feeling each other's pricks," Sarah would say, with a toss of her head. — "Shew me your split, and see if it will give his cock a rise." — She would show it gaping, and his cock would rise. Perhaps he'd kneel in front of her, fingering her cunt, or licking it, whilst she cocked her leg up to facilitate his work. At times both *his* and *my* fingers were up her cunt at the same time, and fifty other baudy tricks we did.

I had now made Sarah suck my prick, but I disliked still

[*408*]

to tell her that I had had *his* prick in my mouth; yet one evening did so. Behold us soon all three on the bed, *she* with *his* prick in *her* mouth, and *he* with *my* prick in *his* mouth. I feeling about *her* cunt and *his* balls, as well as the difficult attitude permitted. Another night we followed it up, by his laying on the bed and she kneeling over him with his prick in her mouth, her backside over his feet, and I at her backside fucking her — I alone could plainly see this in the looking glass, and a most delicious sight it was.

My most satisfactory amusement, I think, was frigging him whilst I fucked her. I used to lay him down so that his prick was well within reach of my hand and in view whilst I did so. At times Sarah laid her head on his chest or his belly, as a pillow, he laying across the bed, and then his prick was just by my shoulder. Then putting my hand up I frigged him. At other times, laying partially on his side with his legs up against the wall at the bed head or near her head, his prick was equally close to me.

Once his tool looked so beautiful that it seduced me entirely — I had again vowed to myself that having had his prick in my mouth and felt it swell within it from flabbiness to a poker, under my lingual pressures, I would never do it again. — But now lying with my prick up Sarah, my left hand under her smooth backside, my right round his prick; my pleasure coming on I could not resist it, and engulfed his stuff cunt-rammer in my mouth. My backside was then oscillating, his hand could just reach my arse and he was feeling my balls. I felt he was near his crisis, withdrew his prick, and at that instant out shot his sperm, just between Sarah's naked breast and mine.

Instantly, for such was the lascivious effect, Sarah and I mingled our mucilages in her cunt. I never had his prick in my mouth afterwards.

He got fond of Sarah and constantly besought me to let him have her. Then after I had frigged him we would all three sit round the fire. "Shew us your cunt, Sarah?" — She'd open her legs so that the article was visible. I watched his prick, which perhaps hanging down lazily between his thighs immediately at the sight of her gaping cunt would gradually thicken until it looked like a short roll of ivory. Then it rolled on one side as if to get away from the big balls. Then with a throb straightened somewhat, its top still pointing downwards, and the little red tipped orifice beginning to show more out of the foreskin. Then it gave a throbbing knock or jump against his thigh and proudly lifted his head, and with other throbs in succession stood grandly stiff against his belly, and the prepuce gently slid off, leaving uncovered two thirds of a deep crimson knob. Then I would gently pull up and down the skin with a slow motion, pleased at the involuntary action of his prick, caused by the mere look of a dark haired cunt. "Let me fuck her — don't frig me this time, you have frigged me enough. — Oh! do let me put into her." Then I let him feel her cunt, and his lust goaded to the utmost, he would sigh and groan almost and lick her cunt. Then I let him have her, or had her myself and frigged him whilst up her. "And so we passed the pleasant time, as well we could, you know, in the day when we were randy arsed a long time ago."

One night, I sat her on my prick whilst I sat on a chair, her bum against my belly, her cunt outwards. — In a looking glass, my ballocks then almost seemed to hang from the arsehole end of the cunt. He knelt down and licked her clitoris whilst I fucked her. Sarah enjoyed the double action, and spent murmuring her lewed sensations; clutching his head, whilst I held her round her haunches tightly, my fingers on the hairy motte. In that position I could only ram gently up her. When she'd spent, he fell back on the floor and frigged himself looking up at her cunt, my prick still up her, and the sperm running out on to my balls, as my cunt plugger slowly left her.

I was slim and supple as an eel. I would on the bed put into Sarah, and then we would both turn on to our sides belly to belly, keeping our privates coupled. Sarah would throw over me her upper-most leg, so as to open her bum furrow, and he laid on his side with his belly close to her rump, thrusting his prick forwards. — The tip would just touch the end of her slit, which was nearest to her bum hole; rub in the furrow, and touch the bottom of my prick as it lay engulfed in her. Then we all began fucking together. I ramming up her, he rubbing his prick up against our coupled genitals, which he had bedewed with saliva. We never hid our pleasures — I would cry out when coming — Sarah would murmur her pleasure, and he the same. The three voices blended whatever baudy, stimulating words fell from us. "Oh! fuck — cunt — spunk — oh — I am coming — I'm spending — spunk — ballocks — aha — ahre" — I spent up her, he against her furrow and the stem of my prick, or over my balls, or against her arsehole or thigh. If the rubbing

[*410*]

against our flesh didn't fetch his sperm, he brought himself to a crisis with his hand, and at the last moment put his prick against her flesh and spent somewhere.

One night as he was tailing Sarah, I felt his hard, wrinkled, full, large scrotum, and slipping my fingers further up, let his stiff lubricated shaft slip through my fingers as it worked up and down her cunt. Then reversing my hand so that his prick rubbed against the back of it, I slowly glided the middle finger up her cunt. "What are you doing," said she. — "Feeling up." — She said no more, the lasciviousness of the act pleased her and him, the whole length of my finger was up her side by side with his prick, whilst he was fucking. His prick glided over my wet finger as they spent together. I had already fucked her, was cool and collected, and noticed the tightening of her cunt as she spent, in a way I never had in any woman; for clear observation of the muscular action of a woman's cunt, at the supreme moment of spending, is impossible; tho my prick is conscious of its constriction.

I did that more than once. Sarah's, altho one of the most delightfully compressive cunts, was undoubtedly largish. — Once she allowed us to try to get both pricks up her together, but we could not manage it.

[It is difficult, even with two very rigid tools to do *that,* for I and another man have tried it since with a woman. But such is the distensibility of a cunt that I'm sure it *will* take two pricks at once.]

Then we reversed our position, and I pushed from behind and spent against *his* balls, whilst he fucked *her.* I liked to vary my pleasures, and when away thought of what I had done, and arranged variations of the fun for our next meeting.

[What whims and caprices lust generates! I have often thought how absurd the following part of my narrative seems, but the deed didn't seem at all absurd to me then.]

Bringing both pricks into use at the same time pleased me much, the difficulty was that our legs got in the way. After thinking how to obviate this, I put a big hook in the ceiling, and a rope hanging from it with hoops at the bottom. Into a loop Sarah put her upper foot, and that slung her leg out of the way. Sometimes he put his foot so. Such ingenious devices voluptuous pleasures led me to. They have seemed ridiculous since, but delighted us all immensely at the time.

Afterwards I put up a second hook and rope, at such distance apart that Sarah could easily put through them her legs up to her knees, and she laid for ten minutes at a time with her legs in the air so distended that her cunt gaped wide. We saw her cunt and anus peeping out from under it. — When in that position I fucked her. Before that we men stood and admired her exposure, feeling each other's pricks, and in the looking glass admiring ourselves in the baudy postures.

I made *him* another time fuck her whilst her legs were slung up, and as soon as his prick was out I investigated her cunt and saw his sperm in it. I find now nothing objectionable in semen — that essence of love.

Whilst I fucked her in that position, I once made him kneel over her with his backside towards me and his prick in her mouth. Then I recollect for the first time that I noticed his anus.

Soon after I had him, I took a fancy to see him in silk stockings. He put on a pair of Sarah's, which so pleased me that I bought him a pair, and a pair of kid boots. I never had him afterwards without them. When on the top of Sarah, with legs together in silks and boots alike, altho the male leg is different from the female, I could scarcely tell which was which, from heels to rumps. But the split and the spindle shewed the difference in the sexes.

Once I made Sarah lay on the top of me and do the fucking, whilst he squatted on her back. So placed I frigged him. Some of his sperm came on to Sarah's hair and made her angry. Sarah didn't mind being spent over anywhere excepting her head. Some of his spunk fell on my face, and I did not like it.

During one period of this erotic frenzy, being as it happened by myself in town alone, I was there nearly every night. My curiosity was insatiable. I would sit on a footstool with my head between his legs, and ear resting against his ballocks — I made the two stand up belly to belly touching, whilst I laid down between their legs and looked up at their genitals, sat with my face against his balls, and his prick up against my nose, whilst Sarah delicately tickled *my* prick with her mouth. I pissed against the tip of his prick, and in brief did every fantastic, erotic, frigging, feeling, tickling, skinning, coaxing, sucking tricks to his rod and balls that I thought of, and always with delight. At last always seeing the tip get redder, the rod stiffen, and the gruelly sperm jet out of it.

Sarah said, — "You've ruined that chap. He can now get

work and won't." — I had then seen all I wanted, and also felt offended with his familiarity; told her I would not see him again, and then he would go to work. "He won't, I am sure." — But I kept away, and whilst doing so recuperated, for I'd knocked myself up a little with the lascivious excitement. I saw one day somebody like him in the streets, which frightened me, although I had never allowed him to see me with my hat on. When I wrote to Sarah and she met me at a house, she said he was sad at not seeing me, and she had told him I was out of town. — "Have you ever buggered him?" she asked suddenly. The question revolted me, such intention had never once entered my head, had never even occurred to me.

Two or three days after I was again alone in town, and awakened with such lewdness that had my grandmother been in bed with me, I believe I should have gruelled the old lady's quim. Tossing about, and resisting frigging myself, the baudy amusements had with him and Sarah kept running through my mind; and altho I had vowed to myself never to see him again, the desire to do so became overwhelming, and I wrote to Sarah to get him.

The evening came, and how strange! I felt part of my old nervousness. — He put on his silks and boots, which Sarah kept. — At the sight of his white flesh, and roly poly pendant, mine stood upright. We stripped. I pressed his belly against mine, grasping him round his buttocks (he was smooth as a woman), and his prick rose proudly at once.

I handled his prick, pleased with the soft feel of the loose skin. — "Fetch me, or I'll frig myself, I shall spend a pail full" — I wetted both our pricks and bellies with soap and water, then putting him on his back on the bed, mounted him. Our pegos were pressed between our bellies, and grasping each other's rumps, and shoving our pricks about as well as we could, the heat and friction drew both our spunks, and we lay quiet till our tools shrunk down over our balls, forming a heap of testicles and pricks.

Then came a dislike to him and disgust with myself that I often had felt recently. But it vanished directly, I felt lewed again and when I felt his cock. It was stiff soon. As he finished washing it he turned round, and I saw it thick and swollen. Just then Sarah rushed in and prayed me to go. "Do, oh do pray, or there will be a great row — for God's sake go." She was much agitated, I had never seen her so before. "You must — you shall go, — or I shall be half

[*413*]

ruined." Yielding, I went as quickly as I could, and he did after me, I heard.

Next night I saw her out, and could get no explanation about her agitation; but she told me I could not go to the house for a week or ten days.

What gave me about that time such hot fits of lust it is not easy to say, but I was in full rut. At times a fellow's prick stands much more than at other, sometimes it is idleness, sometimes stimulating food, sometimes strength. For some days before I saw him again my prick stood constantly, I was again alone in town, and why I did not ease it by fucking don't recollect — Sarah I could not see any where, and I did nothing but think how I would frig him, and tail her, when we met.

When at length we met, he told me he had not spent since I'd made him. Laughing, Sarah said, "The beggar wanted to have me, but I wouldn't let him." Perhaps a lie — I touched his cock which sprang up stiffly at once. He stripped, and his red tipped, white stemmed sperm spouter would have fascinated any woman — I undressed, my cock stiff as his, and libidinous frolics began.

"Have you buggered him" — Sarah's question came suddenly into my mind as I handled his throbbing prick, his rigid piercer. "Fetch me, frig me, then *you* fuck Sarah and let *me* fuck her after — go on — I'll frig myself — I must spend" — said he, and began frigging.

I stopped him. I put him in various attitudes and looked at his naked rigidity — feeling it, kissing it, glorying in my power — with my own prick upright. Both were wanting the pleasure sorely, yet I dallied and my brain whirled with strange desire, fear, dislike, yet with intention. Then I placed him bending over the bed — his bum towards me, his head towards the looking glass — I stood back to look. There were his white buttocks and large womanly white thighs, his legs in silk, his feet in feminine boots. — No one could have imagined him a man, so round, smooth, white, and womanly was his entire backside and form. It was only looking further off that I missed the pouting hairy lips, and saw a big round stone bag which shewed the male. His prick was invisible, stiff against his belly.

I closed on him, put my hand round and gave his prick a frig — his bum was against my belly. — "Fetch me — oho — make haste, I'm bursting" — looking down I saw his bumhole and the desire whirled thro my brain like lightning.

Without pausing or thinking, I felt his prick from under his balls, and whilst he almost shivered with desire — "Oh! make haste, fetch me" — I put both hands round him, feeling his balls with one, his prick with the other; and my own stiff prick I pressed under his ballocks, saying, "Let me put my prick up your bum."

"That I won't," said he disengaging himself and turning round, "that I won't."

Furiously I said, "Let me — I'll give you ten pounds." "Oh no." "I will give you all I have" — and going to my trowsers I took out my purse, and turned into my hands all the gold I had — it was, I think, more than ten pounds.

"Oh no, I can't, it will hurt," said he, eying the money. "It won't." "It will. When I was apprenticed, a boy told me a man did it to him, and it hurt him awful."

I don't know what I replied—but believe I repeated that it would not hurt, that it was well known that people did it, and as I talked I handled his prick with one hand, with the other holding the gold.

"It *will* hurt — I'm frightened, but will you give me ten pounds really?"

I swore it, talked about that of which I knew nothing — that I had heard it was pleasure to the man whose arsehole was plugged — that once done they liked nothing so much afterwards. His prick, which had dwindled under fear, again stiffened as I frigged, he ceased talking and breathed hard, saying, "I'm coming." — I stopped at once.

"Let me." "I don't think you can, it seems impossible — if you hurt me will you pull it out?" "Yes yes, I will."

He turned to the bed again and kneeled, but he was too high — I pulled him off — then it was too low. Again on the bed and I pulled his bum to the level of my prick, I locked the door, I trembled, we whispered. I slabbered my prick and his hole with spittle. His prick was still stiff. There was the small round hole — the balls beneath — the white thighs. — I closed on him half mad, holding him round one thigh. I pointed my prick — my brain whirled — I wished not to do what I was doing, but some ungovernable impulse drove me on. Sarah's words rang in my ears. I heard them as if then spoken. My rod with one or two lunges buried itself up him, and passing both hands round his belly I held him to me, grasping both his prick and balls tightly. He gave a loud moan. "Ohoo I shall faint," he cried. "Ho, pull it out."

[415]

It's in — don't move or I won't pay you, or something of that sort — I said, holding myself tight up to him. "Ohooo, leave go, you're hurting my balls so" — I suppose I *was* handling them roughly — but his bum kept close to my belly.

I recollect nothing more distinctly. A fierce, bloody minded baudiness possessed me, a determination to do it — to ascertain if it was a pleasure — I would have wrung his prick off sooner than have withdrawn for him, and yet felt a disgust at myself. Drawing once slightly back, I saw my prick half out of his tube, then forcing it back, it spent up him. I shouted out loudly and baudily (Sarah told me), but I was unconscious of that. She was in her sitting room.

I came to myself — how long afterwards I cannot say. — All seemed a dream, but I was bending over him — pulling his backside still towards me. — My prick still stiff and up him. "Does it hurt now." "Not so much."

His prick was quite large but not quite stiff. A strong grip with my hand stiffened it, I frigged hard, the spunk was ready and boiling, for he had been up to spending point half a dozen times. My prick, still encased, was beginning to stiffen more. — He cried — "I am coming, I am coming" — his bum jogged and trembled — his arsehole tightened — my prick slipped out — and he sank on the bed spending over the counterpane — I stood frigging him still.

He spent a perfect pool of sperm on the bed. The maddening thought of what I had done made me wish to do it again. I forgot all my sensations — I have no idea of them now — I knew I had spent, that's all. "Let me do it again." "That I won't for any money," said he turning round.

Then I frigged myself and frigged him at the same time furiously. Fast as hands could move did mine glide up and down the pricks. Pushing him down with his arse on the sperm on the counterpane, I finished him as he lay, and I spent over his prick, balls, and belly. In ten minutes our double spend was over.

Immediately I had an ineffable disgust at him and myself — a terrible fear — a loathing — I could scarcely be in the room with him — could have kicked him. He said, "You've made me bleed." At that I nearly vomited — "I must make haste," said I looking at my watch, "I forgot it was so late. — I must go." All my desire was to get away as quickly as possible. I left after paying him, and making him swear, and swearing myself, that no living person should know of the act.

Yet a few days after I wrote the narrative of this blind, mad, erotic act; an act utterly unpremeditated, and the perpetration of which as I now think of it seems most extraordinary. One in which I had no pleasure — have no recollection of physical pleasure — and which only dwells in my mind with disgust, tho it is against my philosophy even to think I had done wrong.

CHAPTER XLIII

Sodomitically complaisant Paphians. — Conversations on sodomy with Sarah. — I suggest. — She refuses. — Mutual incitements. — Mutual consents. — Trials and failures. — Successful at last. — Her sensations. — Effects on her bum hole. — Another trial suggested. — I decline. — A lewed evening. —Fucking, minetting, and masturbating. — Candle and fundament.

I must have been, indeed was, in an almost wild state of mind that night. When I got clear of the street, I saw some gay women, chaffed, and asked them how their arseholes were. My mind ran on anus and nothing else. — A beautiful legged French woman — it was a muddy night — lifted her petticoats and showed nice legs — I went home with her, and turning her bum towards me, looked at her arsehole and asked if *she'd* been *buggered*. She was angry. Then I found I had not money enough to pay her, and we had a row. — I went to one of my clubs, borrowed, went home with another woman, pulled her about, looked at *her* sphincter, and asked if *she'd* been *buggered*. — "No." I offered three pounds to her to let me. I might try, but she thought it impossible. Her bum was towards me, her hole very brown — and the mere fact of her permitting it so disgusted me that I paid the price of a fuck and left *her* directly — I went home yet with another woman, whom I fucked dog fashion, pulling open her buttocks and looking at her bumhole as well as I could, whilst shoving up her. Then I went to my own home, thinking of buggery, and wondering what the sensation was like — for I had no defined notion of it left, such was the state of mad excitement in which I had performed the act. Then I fell asleep.

The next night I saw Sarah in the streets and avoided her, and for a week or so. Then I met her and took her to **** St. for amusement — I never mentioned him, and told her not to do so. At a second meeting the same. But she, — "Aren't you going to see ***? He's every day with me bothering, asking what he is to do, what he's done to offend you. He cries about you almost."

I said that I never meant to see him again, and was sick, sorry, and sad about the affair. — So she told him, I believe, that I had gone abroad. From that day to this I have never set eyes on him, and avoided enquiring about him till once long after. Then Sarah told me that after having spent all his money and pawned his clothes, he had gone to work at painting again.

I cannot describe the effect these frolics had on me. Spite of myself I could think of nothing else — This is the more remarkable because until the few last years I could not bear the look of an anus, and when I fucked dog fashion, I rarely looked at the lady's bum hole. — Now all was anus — anus — nothing but anus. The incidents flashed across my mind repeatedly, and altho the recollection of the thing sickened and even revolted me — altho I felt disgusted with myself — still I desired to try again, to know what the pleasure was — for of that I seemed to know nothing — had not the slightest idea — all was blank.

One night I took woman after woman to a house — and after looking at their cunts, suggested that the other entrance would suit me better. I was unsuccessful at first, and felt abashed, yet persisted. — At length I had a tall dark French woman, and began by fucking her dog fashion — then pulled apart her bum cheeks, and said I should like to put into her bum hole. — "You must give me another sovereign then," said she quickly. — Out came my prick. "Wait a minute," said she. Going to a closet and returning with cold cream, she began to anoint my prick with it, and then anointed her own bum hole — turned round — and the next minute guided my prick there herself.

I refused, left directly, and took a disgust at her; but thought I had had an instructive two sovereigns' worth.

Next night an English woman consented freely, and instantly I paid her and left, my curiosity satisfied. My fancy then turned to Sarah. I thought of our conversations, of the attempt with our fingers, and soon took to fucking her with her backside towards me, and looking at the round orifice when doing so. At length I made the proposal to her, and she said she'd see me in hell first.

The conversation then had a bumhole ramming tendency — I told her what I had tried with the Devonshire woman in my extreme youth, but never about the man. We sat and talked, then lay down and talked about it, till she — "I have a good mind to try." "Do, and if it hurts I'll never do it again." "Did it seem to hurt the woman you did it to?" I told her I could not tell, that it seemed like a dream years, years before. "Try it — I want to try with *you* whom I know, and if we don't like it, we won't repeat it, I half wish to know what it is like," said she.

She came and leant over the side of the bed. I think I see her now — with her bum projecting, the dark haired, full lipped cunt pushing out between her thighs. She was tall, her bum exactly at a level for the work, everything was convenient. "Now if it hurts, promise not to go on." She straddled her legs apart conveniently. With one hand holding open the bum cheeks to see, and with my heart beating, I guided my prick. It began to droop and as fast as I write this, it shrivelled up.

I frigged it stiff, again and again — but the instant the tip touched the brown hole, it shrank. I thrust it up her cunt till almost ready to spend, then pulled it out, and again tried. Down it drooped. Then she sucked it stiff, and again presenting her mark, I again essayed. It was equally useless. All but finishing a fuck in her cunt, to stiffen it for a last trial, I pulled it out and pushed towards the brown circle, when my discreditable prick spent over her rump, and I was unable again to stiffen it, altho I tried my fingers, her fingers, her cunt, and her lips.

I had promised her five pounds if I effected the delicate entry, and she thought I ought to pay it. I did not, and paid fucking price for I had now made up my mind to do it, and when I make up my mind to a thing, like it to come off. — "I have had a stiff prick from merely thinking about your bum hole, and now I fail. When can I try again? — I don't think my prick likes the color."

Next night I went to the spot she usually was to be found at **** and off to the A**a we went. My pego almost lifted me off the ground — I had a pot of cold cream. Hastily we undressed, and turning her buttocks towards me I greased her hole. Then *she* funked it, and turned round. She had been thinking it over and would rather not, altho wishing to try the sensation, she said.

Refusing her invitation to fuck, or be sucked, I buttoned up in a temper to go away. — "The other night I seemed to wish it, but now I fear it, but come and try — give me your word that if I cry out, you will pull it out."

I got a stiff stander of the first order, a little more cream on her hole, a little on my piercer. I gave a push and entered. — "Oho — I can't bear it — take it out — take it out." I drove it up to its limits, pushing her close to the bed — grasping her like a vice — and fucking violently, spent — I had barely done so, when her sphincter tightened round my knob, hurting and ejecting it. She staggered to a sofa and laid down. I threw myself on the bed exhausted with excitement, for again I felt almost mad.

Said Sarah, "Well — I have not a hole left now that a prick can get up that has not been spent in. I would not have believed it but I've done it at last." She washed her anus, I my tool, then we sat and talked.

She said the first sensation was painful, and after that it was a strange sensation, half pain half pleasure. As before — I knew I had been up it and spent, but as to comparing the sensations of the two orifices I could not. — I couldn't realize how I had done it — and didn't recollect any sensation at all. I felt again surprised and shocked with myself, and that's all. This of course was foolish, but my narrative is true.

I took a dislike to Sarah for permitting it and for a time avoided her. When we next met, she told me she was all right. "There is nothing in it after all — I've heard several women say so, you may do it again if you wish, I'd like to try again now without fear." But I didn't wish, I had had enough of the fantasy.

Indeed I liked to think of what I'd done less and less — felt angry with myself. — Spite of my philosophy my act revolted me. But Sarah often referred to it, at first hinted that she'd like to try again, then openly asked me to do it, and was surprised that I refused. "Ask Mr. F**z*r," said I — meaning her husband. "No, I'll never be a whore to him," she replied [singular life, and notions.]

Sarah now with me never disguised her wants, her lusts,

or sensations. — Perhaps the feeling that she need not sham and lie to me was a luxury to her. "You'd better not have me to-night." Or — "I don't want it to-night." Or "I'm just ready to spend, for I've not had a bit of cock I liked for three days, and Mr. F's away" — were phrases, or like those which I often heard. She didn't hesitate to say she should like to be bum-fucked again. "Just to try if there *is* any real pleasure in it. — I wonder *you* don't, as you say you don't even recollect *any* pleasure in spending." But I wouldn't, and never did try.

About three weeks afterwards I went to her lodgings. — She had been out that evening before I called. She said, "I wanted both a man and money, I'm randy be damned to night, and have not fucked for three days — give it me, old man" — and she pulled my prick out of my trowsers. — She had been drinking. I had taken wine with me to her, and when she had drunk two or three glasses, she began talking about her bum hole. "Come, don't be stupid, put it in there, it's my birthday — Mary **** told me that her man often does to her, and both like it. Do it, bugger me and I'll frig myself when you're in." — So she talked and incited me again to open her rectum. I refused resolutely, and didn't like her persistence.

I fucked her soon afterwards. — She sucked my prick as I laid on the bed. She put her finger up my rectum whilst sucking. Immediately after, she threw herself on the bed by the side of me, and frigged herself. "I'm damned randy to night," said she. I raised myself and looked at her whilst she was masturbating, and thrust my finger up her cunt to please her more. In the middle of these operations, she stopped, went to a closet, and got out a wax candle. "If you won't bugger me, push this up," said she — threw herself on the bed, and again began masturbating. — Smitten with the novelty, I did as she asked; pushed it about five inches up, and watched her whilst with distended, quivering limbs and sighs she finished her pleasure, the candle up her arsehole.

"If there's a woman who know more, or has done more than I have, I am damned," said she, "and you — you — of all the baudy beggars in London, I think you are the baudiest." — She did not mind what she now said or did with me.

Thinking of her expressed wishes, and the times when the young man and I used to be laying naked by the side of her, I regretted that we could not give her the double poking simultaneously in her arsehole and cunt, which perhaps we might have accomplished. I never had that delight. — She said she would try to find some one we could all trust, to try it together, but she did not.

Soon after I saw but little of her, yet for a time only fucked *her*. She began again to incite me in the other direction. "Put your thumb up a bit, Doctor, I want to spend, and that fetches me," I did it perhaps once or twice or so, whilst she frigged herself, but disliked it, tho I did it to please her.

CHAPTER XLIV

At a B***s**s lapunar. — Cunt inspections. — The way ladies go up stairs. — A large clitoris. — Flat fuckers. — Gay ladies' letches. — A stercoraceous letch. — Another lapunar and other whores. — My habit of questioning women. — My lascivious questions. — A year later on. — The ocean crossed. — Negro and Negress copulating. — Her cunt and his prick. — I frig him. — A white woman's opinion of a Negro. — About Negroes' pricks.

I was some times that year abroad, and not being much by my self was fairly chaste. — Yet I amused myself occasionally with Paphians, who lodged in flocks in the licensed temples of Venus — I had at times for inspection six or eight of these venal fuckstresses on the same night, I have done this before in earlier years when on the continent, as I think I have told, tho possibly that part of my manuscript may have been burnt with others relating similar fugitive adventures.

I was in the month of *** at B***s**s, a well known town to me, and where as told I have had many amorous frolics. — At dusk I went to the lapunar, No. * in ***** Street. — It was the hour when the women are just got up and dressed for the evening, and before much fucking had begun. — I went at that hour purposely. — "The price of the house is ***** francs," said I. "No," said the abbess of the unchaste nunnery. "It is ****" and she named exactly double the tariff of the charmers, for she saw I was a foreigner.

I rose to go, denying it. "You've been here before?" asked she, seeing that she might lose custom. "Yes, many times." "Très bien donc, restez."

Then I told her I meant to inspect the charms of many, have two at a time to see their hidden beauties but not to fuck; that the ladies would have only the tariff, excepting she who received my final adoration, and who would have her *douceur;* that none need come unless they liked that arrangement. The abbess went out, rang a bell, and soon I heard the rustle of silks and the soft shuffle of feet. Opening the door, I heard the abbess saying something about my being "*drôle*" and the women laughing. — Then in trooped a dozen. "Have you told the ladies?" "Yes, Sir." "Come with me then," and I selected two who pleased me.

We left the room together. "Montez, mes chères." On they went. "Pull your clothes up above your rumps as you mount, and go not too fast." — A pair of naked, broad backsides went up in front of me, whilst I following, looked at their handsome limbs, peeping for the shadow of the hairy valley between their thighs. The girls laughing.

Soon in the bed room I had the ladies naked on the bed, thighs apart, clefts opening. I felt and kissed their flesh all over. — This one had much hair, that one less. — One was hairy to her buttocks, the other smooth and almost hairless to her anus. One cunt with small clitoris, the other with a protuberant. — "Ah! ma chère, vous aimez les femmes." "Hé — Heé — Hé — mais oui, pourquoi pas." Finishing with them. "Au revoir — send me up that tall blonde, the girl with the biggest clitoris in the house." Away they went, saying I was "*un drôle*" and directly after the two women whom I had commanded appeared. — "Non; non, monsieur, not in that room, that is Miss **** room, you must come into ours. — She may get engaged and want her room." Into the room of the tall blonde I went, saw a fair haired cunt, and by its side a dark haired cunt, out of which jutted a clitoris as big as a well sucked nipple, one of the largest I ever saw, with flags falling down from it till hidden by the outer lips. — "You fuck women with that, ma belle." "Jamais, jamais donc — I love men not women." "Why not? — if you like women, all is fair and proper in love. — That is my motto." — But she persisted in her love for men alone.

Then I had the troupe of Paphians sent up to me for further selection, and had another couple, and then another. — Said I, "Jeannette, she with the large clitoris, rubs cunts with you doesn't she? — Tell, and I'll have a bottle of champagne. You stop and I'll fuck you." I sent the other away. I was wrought up with the sight and the smell of so much cunt and female loveliness, and had selected my Venus. "Stop the night with me." "How much?" She told me the tariff, and saying I would stop, champagne was brought and a cake. My Venus began at once to enjoy herself, I drank but little, she much. I sat seeing her eat and drink; and stifling my lust, amused myself by watching and studying so to speak the woman. — More and more I can do that now. I like to sit looking at them, hearing them, encouraging them to talk on, scarcely speaking myself, but thinking and contrasting them mentally with other women I have had.

Two thirds of the bottle had gone, when my Venus unasked, suddenly rose, and pulling her chemise half way up her thighs began to dance a Spanish dance. — "La — La — La — Lala — Lalala — Lala" — sang she. "I can dance — look." "Pull your chemise higher up and show your motte." "Non — non — that will spoil it." Dropping her chemise she sat herself on my knee, put one arm round my neck and kissed me, with the other took my pego out of my trowsers. "Aha — it's stiff — let's fuck." "You've been fucked before?" "Not since yesterday — fuck me — but I shall piss." "No, wait" — I held the basin for the operation, watching the lips open, the stream issue, and then on to the bed with her. I had well nigh forgotten the big clitoris till feeling hers. — "Jeannette has a large clitoris, she rubs cunts with the women, doesn't she." A laugh. "Yes." "Sometimes with you?" "With us all, we have all had her for a caprice." "She likes then women?" "She likes all — men and women. — She's been buggered and fucked at the same moment by two men — she is proud of it." "Une vraie cochonne." "There are three women who like her — I'm not one, but we all have done it with her." — My lass was screwed.

The wine and talk, and perhaps a fancy for the man who had seen eight other women's cunts and had selected *hers* for fucking or perhaps a sudden sting of lust, a recurrence of her daily desires [for gay women have lewed moments, enjoy fucking as much as other women. With them a spend daily is a necessity, and I believe they always spend once daily if not twice], now made her grasp, and squeeze, and frig my prick, kissing me lustfully all the time. — The next minute I was between her thighs, the hair of our mottes entwining, my prick moving in and out and probing her cunt

[424]

to its utmost depths. — Then we died away in each other's arms, and lay tranquilly coupled in spermy slobber, till the prick left her. She washed out the sperm, and again we sat and talked, and both smoked.

I talked about the other women's cunts. My caprice in seeing so many amused her. I must be rich, she thought. Men had strange whims. Nothing surprised her. — There was a gentleman came there, who laid down on the floor, and one of the girls whom he *loved,* and whom he always wrote to the day before, to tell her to hold herself in readiness, then sat over him, and bogged in his mouth. She swore it was true. He always gave her a hundred francs for this stercoraceous amusement. — [I didn't believe it, but now after more knowledge of male whims, think it likely enough to be true. — There is no oddity, no bestiality, no sanguinary deeds that are not pleasurable to the lust of men — each has his letch if he likes women at all — so have women.]

After another poke we parted, for I did not stop the night, tho I paid her the price of one. — No doubt she was just as well if not better pleased with my absence than with my company. It left her free to get others, and more money.

A few nights after I was there again and repeated my amusement. I think I must have seen all the cunts in that establishment, and one or two of them twice, including her with the big clitoris. — [Tho I didn't think much about tribadism then. — I was beginning to think more about it, and its reality came more strongly to me a few years later on, as I grew older, and I grew still more curious about the ways of women with women, and the voluptuous pleasures they could get without the aid of a man.]

It was my letch for the time, I was in the vein for cunt inspection and the night following went to another lapunar, not of the highest class. I had not much want for female aid or conjunction, but an overwhelming, insatiable desire to see all that the women had hidden of their bodies, to compare and note differences, and ask every one of them questions about their sexual tastes, sensations, and habits. I have done that for many many years, have asked scores of times on first acquaintance, expecting more frequently lies than the truth, yet still I asked. — It is delightful in itself to put the lascivious questions, searching for the most hidden thoughts, feelings, and deeds of these lovely creatures. — When I

[*425*]

have known a woman or girl a short time, I have nearly always got their confidence, and then over a bottle of wine, when its generous influence has been felt, I have but little doubt that I got in the main truthful replies.

Long before this period I prepared a set of questions, of which I knew the order pretty well by heart, through repetition. — At about this time I bethought me of additional questions about tribadism, of cunt to cunt rubbing, or as it is called flat fucking; but to which amusement it is only of recent years that I gave attention, or that these feminine games gave me much sensual pleasure to think about, or had roused my curiosity. — From hundreds of answers to these questions, coupled with my own experience in facts, I think I have as good a knowledge of the sexual tastes and habits of men and women as most; excepting old baudy priests, who know all through confession. — The replies of many of the females, particularly of the young ones, I know already have been given in various parts of this history.

I have had many servants. All had been poor, and in their youth had nursed their brothers if they had any. Many had been nursemaids when they left their homes. — Some were nursemaids when I fucked them. They enjoyed my talk on sexualities. It is one of the additional pleasures which servant girls, and women who are not gay, give me. — It adds to the physical pleasure which they always *give* and always *have* with me, for a servant if she will take money, and gifts (and all women will, for that is my experience) have met me, and surrendered to me, for the pleasure of fucking, and not for money.

As before said (often perhaps — I forgot) I always got the confidence and liking of gay women when I visited them regularly. They at times like reminiscences of lust and of their precocious experience, and will often talk freely when there are one or two together, and are a little known to each other. [Two gay ladies of late have often met me together in baudy companionship.] Then over a bottle of champagne or two, they generally will exchange confidences, answer my questions, and tell the truth to each other and to me, tho I have found some manifest liars even when their tongues were loosened by liquor. These were principally the leading questions, which I have put to hundreds, the first mainly to the quite young and youngish, the more searching to females of all ages. — The first twenty or thereabouts I have always asked servants and young girls and nursemaids.

At what age does a little boy's cock get stiff? When do you think a boy first feels pleasure in its stiffness?

At what early age do you think a boy can spend?

Did you ever make a boy's cock stiff?

Did you ever frig a boy till he spent and what was the age of the youngest you made spend?

Did he spend quickly? did it spurt out? was his spunk thick or thin? was there much of it?

How old was the youngest boy, who wanted to put his hands up your clothes, or was curious about your sex or your cunt?

At what age did you know what fucking was?

At what age did you first know that you had a womb, and that children came out thro cunts?

How old were you when you first felt randy?

How old when you first frigged yourself?

How old when you were first fucked?

Did you spend at the first fuck, or if not did you feel any pleasure at all?

Did your first fuck hurt you much, and did you bleed much?

How long was your cunt sore afterwards?

When during a month do you feel most lewed, before or after your monthlies, or whilst they are on?

Does your clitoris get stiffer when you frig yourself, or you feel lewed?

Did you ever frig a girl? What age was the youngest girl you have frigged?

Do many girls frig each other?

Are there any girls after twelve years of age who don't frig themselves?

If girls want the pleasure, do any restrain themselves from frigging?

At what time of day or night do they generally frig themselves?

How often have you ever frigged yourself in twenty-four hours?

Did you ever lick another girl's cunt?

Did another girl ever lick *your* cunt?

Which do you like best, fucking, or frigging yourself, or being frigged, or having your cunt licked till you spend?

Do you like licking a girl's cunt?

Do you like being licked by a man or a woman?

The further questions to the fully experienced women in the *Ars Amoris,* were:

Do you like sucking a man's prick, and have you sucked one?

Do you like the feel of a prick in your mouth best when it's stiff, or when it's limp?

Do you mind or like his spending in your mouth?

Which do you like best — fucking or being gamahuched?

Which do you like best, a man or woman to gamahuche you?

Do you like gamahuching a nice woman?

Do you like a finger up your cunt when you are gamahuched, or up your bum hole?

Do you *generally* spend with men, or with a man who is new to you and fucks you for the first time?

Do you like fucking as much as you did when you were seventeen?

Do you like being dildoed?

Which give you most pleasure, being gamahuched, frigged, or dildoed, or fucked?

Did you ever suck a man's cock while you were being gamahuched?

Does flat fucking give you much, and prolonged pleasure?

Are you longer before you spend that way than when being fucked?

Do the two women flat fucking usually spend at the same time?

Does your cunt feel as satisfied after flat fucking as it does after a man has fucked and spent his sperm in you?

Did you ever see a man buggering another, or one sucking another's prick?

Did you ever swallow a man's sperm?

How does sperm taste?

Does sperm seem a nasty fluid to you?

Were you ever buggered and do you like it?

These are leading questions. The replies suggest others. — The answers given to them by *many* women will, coupled with a man's own wide experience and observation of women, leave him but very little to learn about them; and enable him to form sound opinions about their sexual tastes and habits, and the phenomena accompanying their lust and spending, as well as about the habits and tastes of men.

Now I go back to the regular order of my history, as it followed after my erotic gambols with a man at Sarah's lodgings.

A few weeks after I crossed the ocean, no matter where to. — If any one had before I left Europe told me I would touch another man's tool, I would have sworn that I would not. — But I did — curiosity alone was the cause of it.

During the time I was the other side of the ocean (I must for reasons give not much account of my doings there, they were written but I have destroyed most of the narrative) was where there were many coloured people, and then this incident occurred.

I went to a gay house one day, and was with a white woman, when through talking I took a fancy for a black one. — A Negress was fetched for me, and a very finely formed creature she was. The hair of her cunt was thick, short, and closely curled like the hair on a male Negro's head, but was shorter, and not quite so fuzzy perhaps. It was scrubby to the feel, there was plenty of it, and a couple of crabs would have made a nest there, where they could have reared a family, and defied anything but chemical solutions. Her clitoris and inner lips were smallish and of a very dark mulberry red, and the effect was ugly; but her prick hole was a lightish pink inside the lips, and like white women's in most respects. She spoke broken English.

The white woman was American. We fell to talking about black men, whose pricks I had heard were very big and long; and getting curious, I expressed a desire to see one and to see a Negro poke a Negress. The two women consulted for a minute, the Negress went away, and in half an hour brought back a Negro — a fine young man and well dressed. I had rather feared some bully, or a trick would be played on me, but the white woman assured me whilst the Negress was away that it was all right. That if he would come, which she wasn't sure of, he was quite a respectable man, and very

[429]

fond of the black woman, who would fetch him. *He* would do anything to stroke *her,* but *she* didn't like *him.* At the request of the white I had ordered liquor of some sort, which they all drank when we were together. I did not.

He came in evidently abashed, grinned and chuckled, and showed teeth like snow, but was a little hesitating about showing his doodle. I didn't even like to ask him, for I felt very nervous as usual. — The white woman pulled it out for him. It was limp, but big, and I think it must have hung down five inches or more in its quiescent state. After a time I laid hold of it, for I see no harm in that now. Why should not a man feel another prick, if the two agree? — Then it got a trifle smaller. The white woman helped to pull off his trowsers, and tucked up a shirt made of a linen with big stripes all over it, and I found he had a large ball bag. He stood jabbering and chuckling whilst the woman showed him off. Then the white woman felt it. The man said, "I no fuckar Sar," and shook his head. The black woman who was dressed then stripped and showed her cunt well, and the Negro's cock gave two or three sharp jerks and swelled up in a moment to double the length and size. But it stood out nearly straight from his belly instead of nearly up against it. Then he moved quickly towards the Negress and laid hold of her.

He began playing with the Negress' cunt. "Fuck this white lady," said I. He grinned. — She would not let him, she declared. "Fuck your friend then, and get on the bed." "No, no" said she. "Yars, yars," said he, pulling her. — I promised her more money to let him, which had the desired effect. Before commencing, she laid hold of his tool, shook it, and pulled the foreskin up and down, — said she, "Look, Sar — look. — Nigger man hab dam big cock, Sar, — more big cock than white man cock, Sar." Then she let him fuck her, and I was amused at seeing his big tool, moving in and out of her dark cunt like a piston, and I handled his dark balls whilst he fucked.

The white woman watched them with me till they'd finished, and said, "Aren't you going to fuck me." — Leaving him spent and silent on the top of the Negress, both reposing after their exercise she having spent seemingly, I went into an adjacent room with her and tailed her. She was either hot arsed that day, or I had pleased her, or the spectacle of the two Negroes copulating had excited her, for she wanted me to tail her again almost directly, which I could not do. I sent out for some liquor, which I could drink as well as she. She was a handsome woman, and it gave me pleasure to sit and talk to her, every now and then feeling her cunt, and looking at her as she sat in various nude attitudes. — She had never seen two blacks fucking before, she told me, saying, "Don't they look like beasts." She had been fucked by a black man once but only out of curiosity. She had seen many niggers' pricks. They all had very large pricks, and were fond of exposing them on the sly to white women, whether *they* wanted to see them or not. Their bodies smelt so that she couldn't bear them, particularly that very Negro, who if he met her in the street followed her about, begging her to let him have her, and actually with tears at times rolling down his cheeks. — He was a waiter, and fond of the black woman but not she of him. It was in the hopes of fucking one or both of them, which had got him there. So we talked on. — Again she said, "Don't they look like beasts when doing it." "If they do they've made you lewed." Seeing others fucking always made her lewed, she replied. — Then having heard all she knew, or could ell about the procreating machines of the Negro race, both male and female, we fucked again. — An hour had run away in this pleasing, instructive conversation. Then we went back to the black couple.

I now quite overcame my foolish nervousness, and again handled his great dark tool and pendants; curiously amused at its dark skinned stem, and its contrast with its tip, red like that of a white man's, but perhaps of a little darker red, it was I'm sure nine inches long when it stood. There may be pricks as long as that in white men, but I never saw but one that looked so, tho I've seen many. It was scarcely thick in proportion, tho thick enough. Then I wondered if his sperm was the same as a white man's, and promised him money if he'd let me frig him, he'd only fucked once he said. At first he refused, but persuaded by the Negress he let me, and I frigged him till he spent over the Negress' belly and cunt. She lay at the side of the bed shewing her cunt, whilst the masturbating operation went on. His sperm was like a white man's.

She wiped off his semen, washed her cunt, and for a little time his tool hung down. — Directly he had spent I had quite a revulsion of feeling, neither cared about looking at him, nor his tool, paid him and the woman, and was going away when the Negress ask me if I was not going to see him again tail her. — That again stirred my lewedness, so I waited an hour or more, when she handled his tool, till it stiffened again. — She went to the bed, the Negro following her. He placed her at the side of the bed, and began gamahuching her quite spontaneously, neither having been asked to do so by me, nor by either of the women. — I couldn't resist again feeling his big stiff prick for a minute whilst he gamahuched, for it soon grew stiff again. Then he mounted her, and they fucked like any other mortals; and such are the likes and dislikes which seize me that I couldn't bear now to look at her cunt, when his great black tool had flopped out of it after he had spent. At a glance there still seemed lots of sperm, tho it was his third spend. She washed her cunt, he his prick, I sent out for more strong liquor which the three drank. I did not touch it. We sat a long time. He with his long drooping tool visible, and the Negress quite naked. Out talk was all about white and black pricks, and cunts, and the nigger then asked me to show him my prick which I refused to do, for which I thought myself a fool when I began to write this.

I had been altogether something like three hours at this curiously varied and exciting amusement and was going away, when I thought I'd like a parting look at his big machine. The white woman lifted up his shirt unasked (for he had put it on) and held it for me to see. — It seemed to amuse her very much to show it to me. Then she tucked up his shirt round his waist, the Negress handled his tool, and I asked her to make it stiff if she could. She succeeded. He stood up quite proud of it, each woman then put a hand round it, and at the same time, I also grasped it. The tip was then just showing inside my fist, so it must have been nine inches long, to have lain with three hands at the same time round the stem. It is difficult to guess the length of anything, and that's the way how I came to think it full nine inches long.

I paid the Negress and left the room with my white one who excited me to more amorous exercise. As I was going away after paying my white one, — "I'll just have a look at blackie's cunt again," said I, "if she's there." "I expect she's gone out," said Whitey. But opening the door, there was the nigger on the top of her, ramming away so furiously that the bed shook violently, and both were chattering, gasping, and snorting in such a way as I never heard a man and woman before or since when fucking. They were five minutes at it I should think whilst we stood looking. At last they spent, his prick came out wet and limp, and then I left. I had not paid him anything excepting for frigging him. I rather think as was told me that he came for the poke. — But I don't know how they divided my money. I gave it all to the Negress.

A few days after I had that black woman together with the white one, and put my prick first into one, then the other, to see if my prick noticed any difference. I spent in the nigger but didn't like her. — She told me in broken English all about "Big Negro man" — and it was what the white woman had told me before. She let him do what he liked that day, because feeling my white prick had made her randy, she said. "Me likes white man — not black."

It is the only time I ever felt a black man's tool, or saw a Negro and Negress copulate, but I saw some of their long pricks afterwards in a pendant state, at a bathing place, and also at places where some working in water exposed themselves. It gave me no amusement to do so that I can recollect. All their pricks were I think when tranquil and pendant much longer than those of Englishmen, whose pricks in every condition I have seen many.

What struck me as most peculiar was that his prick, when stiff and hard, did not stand so upright as a white man's does, but seemed to stick out more horizontally from his belly. — Both women said that all black men's tools did. I wonder why. Perhaps it's their length and weight, which makes them bend forward. Negresses' cunts should be deep to take such long procreators up them. I wonder if they are so.

CHAPTER XLV

A light-haired Irish bitch. — Foul-tongued and hot-arsed. — Recondite expressions. — "D'ye loike me." — Her bolt from Dublin. — Baggage detained. — A suspicious tale. — My regrets at losing Sarah. — Camille revisited. — Her brothel venture. — About sodomites and catamites. — Buggers' sphincters. — Her friend's catamitic tastes. — Sodomy cum gamahuche. — Reflexions on the change in my erotic tastes. — An artist in lewedness.

[For continuity of the narrative about Sarah F**z*r, the following little incident was omitted from its proper place. — It occurred about a year before Sarah disappeared. The date on the manuscript proves that. I don't think I ever told Sarah of it.]

I was going along Coventry St. on a muddy evening, and saw a lovely pair of feet and ankles supporting a well grown body — it was a liberal display of leg in silk — looking at the female as I passed, she winked in the lustful whorish way which a woman does when thoroughly lewed at the moment, and looks at a man invitingly. It is my theory that *she* communicates at once some lewedness to *him*. — I don't mean the lewed look of a woman who incites you only to get money, but when she's really randy and wants a male, wants to be fucked badly. — This woman did so, and at once I reciprocated her lust. She followed me up a side street. — "You've a fine leg," said I beginning. — With strong Irish brogue which I can't imitate in writing, nor indeed any way, she said, "Sure and there isn't a foiner in all the town, won't your cock stand for shure if you see a little higher," and she pulled up her clothes to her knees in the dark street. — I can't bear Irish women, having found them liars and thieves, and did not like her manner. — "Com long." "No, I'm poor and can't to night, but here is a glass of wine for you." "Och! to the Divil with the cash — shure and we won't quarrel about that — com — shure an I loike the looks of you — I'm close by — com." I followed her and she went at such a pace, as if either the police were after her, or that she was frightened of shitting herself. We entered a house and a comfortable room with a good fire. — A large trunk was on the floor. — Said she, "Shure and I've not been here an hour and not unpacked — I've been a week coming from Dublin — It's God's truth, may I go to the biggest hell if I've been fucked for a week." — All this rapidly in answer to my questions, and some without my questions. — Then she pulled out my prick. — "It's not stiff — wait a second and it'll be stiff enough, damned if I don't feel as if I'd forgotten what a man is," and in a violent hurry she tore off her things till she was start-naked, boots and stockings excepted, apostrophizing her parts from time to time. — "There's a pair of thighs — haven't I a foine shape — not a foiner by Jasus, and there, feel my bubbs — look at my small waist — and with such a large rump." — By that time she was naked whilst I had only taken my hat off. — Then she grabbed at my prick again (she had pulled it out), then threw herself at the edge of the bed, and opening her thighs, "Put it up me darling bhoy, fuck me chunt — look at the hair on it, it's foine shure, ah! I envy the pleasure yer prick will have in it me bhoy — fuck — com on — fuck." — The slut was hot cunted — boiling with lust — in full rut unmistakably.

I didn't like her manner, speech, or colour, but altho shortish, a more superb form, more lovely white flesh, never was offered to my embraces — I put my prick at once into her. glowing cunt, and directly it was well lodged in its folds, she burst out into such a torrent of baudy words, such obscenity, such ribald screeching, as I never heard before or since from a woman in copulation; tho I have known some gay ladies, when their pleasure was on, pretty frank about it, and have taught a few who were not gay to be warm in their exclamations of pleasure. Of late years I interlard my endearments with lewed words and wishes, it adds much to my enjoyment mentally, for fucking is the sublimest mental as well as physical pleasure. "Aha," she began, "aha — oho — fuck it well — begorra your prick's red hot — it's big. — Ahaa — sure me chunt's as hot as hell — fuck — fuck hard — piss out your boiling spunk into my bloody chunt — sure that will cool me chunt. — Aha God! aha fuck hard yer bugger. — Aha, Holy Virgin my bloody spendings are coming. — Aha — a lovely prick — stiff — push it hard up me chunt — fuck — split me hot chunt into me randy arsehole. — Fuck em both — ahar — fuck — fuck — now —

[435]

now. — Aha, I'm coming — spend — spunk — fuck — cunt — ballocks. — Aha — arseholes — ahra — my spunks — ahaa — ahaa." She was silent, her thighs quiet. She'd spent ere I had half fucked her, for her fierce baudiness and outrageous obscenity at first seemed to stop my pleasure. — It made me think for the instant that she was mad.

I went on thrusting, my lust getting stronger as her lewed words wrought clouds of meretricious images in my brain, when after a short silence, with a sudden effort she uncunted me, and struggling up pushed me away saying. — "Sure and I just wanted a fuck — I hope I'll die a fucking." — Is she mad or drunk I thought? — But excepting for her excitability, libidinosity, and blasphemous obscenity, she seemed sober enough. She smiled as angrily I cried, "Lie down and let me finish," shut her eyes without answering, and seemed to be feeling her clitoris, sitting at the edge of the bed where I stood swearing, my prick standing stiff in front of me.

"Let me finish fucking, what the Devil are you about," and I clutched her as she rose from the bed, but she escaped me. My passion was roused well by the probing I'd had in her cunt. — "Wait a bit me bhoy, thin and shure I'll be after spending agin, by the Holy Mother you're a lovely fucker, you've learned a bit in your time, many's the chunts you've cooled begorra. — No — No — wait a bit and I'll be spending agin with yer." "Humbug you didn't spend, you lie." "Didn't I spend? shure and I did, it's God's truth — look." On the side of the bed she laid down and opened her thighs wide. — "There me bhoy — I'd just have drowned yer prick in me chunt, if ye'd kept it in a minit longer." — Her cunt was wet enough, it had wetted my piercer and my balls before she'd ejected it, and plenty of pearly moisture was just inside, ready to run out as she separated her cunt lips to show me. Suddenly down went her legs, she walked quickly about the room, gave her box a kick, and with both hands slapped her buttocks several times loudly. — "Dam it, lay down and let me fuck you, you bitch," I cried in a rage. — She laughed and continued slapping her backside.

In a minute or so, she laid hold of my prick which had a little drooped. — "It's a fine hot poker, sure and it is — com on then," and she laid down on the bed side again. — I inserted my pego, which stiffened up as its tip touched her lubricated cunt — I drove it up hard, and soon her baudy words recommenced. — "Aha — that's it — aha — my arse

[436]

and chunt are all in one shure — split them with your pego. —Aha. Shove your bloody prick up into my womb — Aha — what a lovely peg — Aha — your spunk a comin — don't — stop — wait for me — I'll spend — Aha — fuck, fuck aha — God if ye'd two pricks ye'd have one in my chunt and one up my arse hole wouldn't ye? — Aha, my bloody hot sphunks comin. — Ahar spunk — spend in my bloody chunt. Ah Jasus — fuck me — now — ahaa — ahaa — prick — ballocks — bugger — aha — aa." I cannot imitate her manner or brogue, it is impossible; nor give accurately her extraordinary quaint, baudy, and blasphemous expressions — I never heard such issue from the mouth of a harlot, but have between some drunken Irish women slanging each other in St. Giles, and also in the lowest quarters of Liverpool.

Tho I disliked her lewed imprecations they now stirred my lust extraordinarily. She kept me up to her as I leant over her, gently working her quim and buttocks. "Kiss me love — don't pull it out — there shure and I'll stiffen it again in me chunt, if your ballocks are close up to me. — Can't you *fuck* just — haven't I spent? the spunks squeezing out. — Begorra ye've spent thick, and lots, and hot, ye spalpeen. — Don't pull it out me darlin — kiss me — you've not kissed me, look what foine teeth I have. — Shove your tongue into my mouth. — Oh keep your prick up me hot chunt — put your finger up my arsehole when you fuck again." "No." "Whoy, whoy won't you? (as I refused) Don't then me darlin. — Don't you never do so when yer fucking? Oh ye spalpeen ye do — I love it, love me both me holes full — chunt and arse hole. — There now it's out — whoy didn't ye keep it up me hot chunt." — Thus she went on as nearly as written without stopping, all being said, and acted with surprizing energy whilst still she was holding me tightly to her, as I bent over her standing at the side of the bed, without uttering more than a word or two in reply to her, and, standing·wondering, amused and almost silent.

It slipped out, the copulation was broken. "Take off your clothes and come on to the bed and lie down wid me, and we'll fuck agin ye spalpeen in foive minutes — we will, be Jasus. Look at me chunt — look at your spunk — it's wet — it is — ain't your spunk thick," said she examining her finger after a feel. — I didn't like that, yet she had made me lewed. She had accompanied words with deeds, and as quickly as she had spoken, she had turned herself in all

[*437*]

attitudes — on to her belly, then buttocks, had opened her thighs, threw her legs quite high up in the air, and other antics just as before, showed me her armpits and teeth, and pulled the cunt wide open to show the libation overflowing from it — all unasked by me; and interlarding her acts, with expressions of strong desire for me.

I now fully excited, stood pulling off my clothes rapidly, and dropping them on the floor by the side of me, silent, unable to resist the fascination of her carnalities and take my eyes off of her. — "Oh look at your spunk in my chunt" said she again. — "Shure and I'm longing for more of it — many a chunt you've filled I'll swear — ain't my breasts beautiful? you shall spend between them some day. — Make haste me darlin — if you don't I'll frig me — I will by Jesus, I'm mad to have it up me agin — come." Then we got on to the bed.

I covered her, I rubbed my tool outside in the overflowing sperm, and was in a few minutes spending with her, with my tongue in her mouth and trying to perforate her bum hole with my finger. After she had shouted out, "Fill me chunt — fuck it — ballocks it well — bugger. — Now. — Shove harder. — I'm spending — ahrr — arsehole." — "Dams and bloodies" in endless combinations she cried, and it had such an effect on me, that I cried out baudy words with her. Never in my life have I heard such a woman. The words from her struck me as abominably foul and obscene, tho some of the words have not, when sweeter, loving women have murmured them with me in our sensual paroxysms — and yet the Irish bitch excited me.

This fuck quieted her — seemed to subdue her — I still laid on her, she still sucking my tongue, or wetting her lips with her spittle, rubbing them on mine, holding my head with one hand, pressing it towards hers, and rubbing her other rapidly, quite rapidly up and down my back and buttocks, as far as her hand would reach; as if she couldn't feel enough of me. — "By me soul and you fuck beautiful — beautiful be Jasus," said she at last. "Sure an we'll do it agin, — a rale man and you are shure. Do you loike me? — your hair's sticking to me chunt." — Smack squash — and moving her cunt a little back, our mottes unjoined, and the glutinous exudations which adhered to our fleshy prominences where they had met so closely made that expressive noise as our genitals partly separated, as she moved her belly when my prick was dwindling out of her split.

Her quick movements, and the fanciful but foul things she

said, had so heated me, so libidinously excited me, that I scarcely knew what I was about. "Yes," I replied, "let's look at your cunt." — I had scarcely seen it in my emotion. — "Look my bhoy" — I rose on my knees, she relinquishing my rump, and I looked. "Your hair's the same color as on your head." "Yes, and are my armpits." — She threw up her arms. — "Don't you like the colour?" — I said — "yes" — but I didn't. — It was a peculiar, sandy red color. — I never before saw an Irish woman with that coloured hair, and told her that most Irish had dark hair. "Shure I'm true emerald." She was, as said, very beautifully formed, and had marvellously white flesh. — I threw up her legs, and saw from her heels to her buttocks. — "I'm beautiful made shure and I am, arnt I?" said she, putting her hands round her thighs to keep her legs up.

I looked and gloated. There was her cunt almost foaming with pearly mucilage. — "Lie down me darlin," — and I did. — She laid hold of my prick and frigged it. — "Oh put it in me — do then. — I'll just take a dale of it to-night — I'm wild just. — A bhoy like you will just make her happy — whoy — I've not slept for two nights, I've left one of my boxes at Birmingham — I ran away — I'd no money — I would not stay to be ill thraited — but the first money I get I'll be after it — I pawned me watch to pay my week's lodgings here this very day, sure and I hadn't enough money to pay me cabman. Pay down the first week says the landlady, or it's no good yer laving your box here. — Wait a minute, ma'am, where's a pawnbroker's? and me and me box and the carman went to pawn me watch."

"You've been drinking," I said, thinking at last that it must be so. — Not she. "By the Holy Mother. — Divil a drap — you're a queer chap, don't you loike me? — now you don't loike me — I'll wash my chunt and you'll like it better." She was twiddling my cock then, but left off, jumped off the bed like lightning, and began washing — I washed my appendages also, and was going to dress. "Shure and yer not going to lave me yet, shure and you shan't till ye've done it agin." "I can't again," said I. — She gave me a rapid push, which sent me on to a chair with such force was it given, and kneeling down began to suck my prick. — "Sure and I'll make it stiff in a jiffey. What a lovely prick, and my first in London — Oh Jesus may it bring me luck — and I haven't had a fuck for a week. By the Holy Virgin I'll have another fuck." Sucking hard, and jerking out these sentences at short intervals with much intensity, and with that and her baudy talk, she in time made me stiff, put it into her cunt herself impatiently, and I gave her another libation. She rattled out the same lascivious cries but less energetically, and I noticed that tho she talked lewedly when we were not in action, that her most outrageous, unrestrained exclamations, were only uttered when she was fucking.

She began again telling her history of running away from Dublin. — "I'd been murdered shure had I staid, it's God's truth I tell ye, and I pawned me watch to pay the lodgings here and me cab." — Then she wanted to treat me to whiskey and water. — What would I have. — Then she mounted me as I lay tired on my back, kissing me, and rubbing her cunt on to my flabby cock, I could not stop her. — She talked the foulest baudiness, and said her poorliness was just coming on. — Wasn't it unlucky, just as she'd come so poor and wanted to get some friends. — She loved a man about her. "Sure God," she did, but hadn't had one for a week, she'd had enough to do to dodge them and get away. "Hide and seek and fucking don't go together." But she was safe now she was in London — I got now curious and tried to learn something more, but she shut up at once. — In her lewed excitement it was pleasure to gabble on and let out a bit of her story, but the cunning jealous secrecy of a harlot returned. — Her fear of being detected, of telling too much, shut her mouth. — I thought, and had no doubt, she'd run away from Ireland to get clear of some scrape.

I couldn't get away from the woman, she sent for whiskey and I drank with her. She frigged and sucked me stiff again, and I fucked her spite of myself — listening — disliking — yet excited. — When fucked out I left. — "Another kiss," said she following me to the door of her room, and pushing her tongue in my mouth. "Feel my cunt again for luck." — I did, promising at her earnest entreaty to see her again. "Never mind the cash me darlin — I loike your fucking — sure and ye'll bring me luck," said she as we parted.

I set myself afterwards to repeat what the woman shrieked out in her sexual ecstasy, for she was thoroughly enjoying me, and the sayings and baudy utterances rang in my ears — I did not like them, but kept repeating them to myself, laughing at them even — I went with another woman a day or two after, and as my pleasure increased when my body was joined to hers, I shouted out some of the salacities — it stimulated me. — "Oh ain't you a going on," said she. — "Say fuck, ballocks." — "I shan't" — then — "oh don't make such a noise, or they will hear you up stairs." — But I would. — That giving way to lascivious utterances helped my fatigued ballocks very much. — I'd been with some woman who was out and out baudy, I told this to this woman. I had no reason for hiding it, and told her all. — "A dirty beast," said she. — Some women are naturally baudy and lewed in talk, others are not. — As among harlots so among ladies. I have known some whom I never could induce to use love words frankly — others soon revelled in them.

I saw the Irish woman once or twice in Coventry Street afterwards, but got out of her way. — She always pulled her petticoats up as high as she dared to show her lovely limbs and walked very rapidly. Tho I did not like her, for all that I went home with her once again. She kissed me in the street when I spoke to her, and talked so loudly, that passers-by stared at us — so calling her a fool, I turned away and went up a side street. — She came to me and then I followed her home. — There she again baudied and shrieked out when fucking, the most original salacities and obscenities, and spent with me, and then frigged me up and sucked me to her heart's content; telling me how she had got on, and what a man did to her, and what he had given her, how she meant still to get her trunk from Birmingham. She hadn't yet. — Altogether she went on almost like an erotic maniac and I was glad when I got away.

I saw her once or twice in the streets afterwards, but she did not see me; then I lost sight of her. I don't think that altogether she was about the West End a month — I must have seen her had she been about longer. I have never met such a foul tongued woman in my life before, she must have been bred and born amongst the lowest. — I haven't told a tenth part of her original erotic sayings, and combinations of baudiness and blasphemy. It seemed to me that when her sensual pleasure came on, that she scarcely knew what she said; that every baudy and blasphemous word she'd ever heard, came struggling up together to describe and emphasize the pleasure she felt in her cunt. — I told her of it. — She said it was my fault, and that she didn't cry out so with other men, it was the intense pleasure I gave. "I'll swallow your spunk and drink your piss if you like," said she. I didn't believe a word she said.

[Once since, at a French brothel, I found an Irish woman,

[*441*]

who certainly was more highly obscene than her sisters
there. One French woman said she was the greatest "Cochonne" in the house, and all the women were afraid of her.

[The disappearance of Sarah was a great loss to me as I
recollect well. She was a quiet woman and handsome,
her form good, her cunt gave me the fullest and most complete
pleasure, she indulged my lewedness, and when intimacy
was established took herself the greatest pleasure in
lascivieties with me. — She procured me virgins whom she
delighted in fingering, and with two of them in flatfucking,
and a man who jointly amused us. In occasional orgies at
brothels, she several times got me other free and easy harlots, but about which orgies I have destroyed the manuscript,
as I did with the women only what I have done with
others. — Her lodgings I could mostly go to, and believe I
was the only man who did, and I missed the means of indulging my tastes in those quiet rooms with a willing min-
istress to them. — Moreover she was not always plaguing
me for money — asking me to pay this, or to lend her to pay
that — which is the common habit and trick of harlots from
high to low — I felt at sea when Sarah was gone, and recollect that for a month or so I was chaste.]

Then I sought Camille — I had seen her thrice only I find
whilst I had known Sarah F**z*r, and had some difficulty in
finding her out. — She was not so young, but was splendidly
preserved. Tho fatter, her soft skin, soft voice and quiet
laugh, in brief all her good qualities were unchanged, and I
rushed my eager pego into her still delicious cunt, and
clasped her exquisitely soft backside with the delight of
former days. She had been away from England two years or
so, having saved money, with which in her native country
she had either bought or set up a licensed house for whoring.
It had not succeeded, she had lost all, and had come back
here to harlotry. — She cried as she told me about her losses,
then began to smoke a cigarette (formerly she did not
smoke). She smiled and said it was fate, that there was always water or charcoal to be had when she was old or tired
of life. — She was seemingly not so well off as formerly, but
said she had a good clientele mostly of married men who
paid well, and didn't stop long. She did not go into the street
much, for her friends expected always to find her at home.
I spent two or three hours delightfully with her talking over
old times. — It was no use disguising her age from me, and
one other Monsieur who also knew her when she first came

to London, the only two, she said; but she took off a few years to new friends when they asked her age. She now spoke excellent English. [Fifteen years later she was alive, and as nice as ever in manner — but she was old and poor, and very often I assisted her.]

Much as I liked, I didn't keep to Camille. I went there when I wanted a quiet chat and information about sexualities (not that I wanted much of that). I find a memorandum of a talk with her, about the effect that continued buggering had upon the arseholes of the buggerees. She thought it detrimental to them ultimately, and had heard so, but the men were reticent on the subject. — About tastes for that abnormal amusement — that there were decidedly those men who enjoyed being operated on — catamites by taste, by nature perhaps; she thought owing to some anatomical difference, or sexual infirmity.

One evening being unusually communicative, she told that she had a friend who came to her rooms at times, and she procured a man to bugger him. When he had had that operation performed, his prick would stand, and he could fuck her and spend. — Nothing else that could be done had that effect; masturbation, suction, flagellation all were useless. — Altho sometimes he shagged Camille after the irritation of his fundament had produced an erection, he preferred being frigged whilst the other man was coupled with him. — It was "vilaine, cochonnerie la plus sale," she said. — "Mais que voulez vous." — "He pay me sometime five — ten pounds sometime. — When I came back to England, he buy me half my furniture. — He send Bordeaux, I cannot such buy — you shall taste. He is good for me and I do what he likes." — Then she fetched a bottle of splendid Château Margaux which he had given her. She had a case of it. — Camille never drank spirits, and didn't care so much about champagne. — I used to take her Claret at times, it was what she habitually drank at her meals.

Then I told her what I had done with the man. She would not at first believe it. — "Fi donc — pas vrai — un beau garçon comme vous." — But she added, "It was curiosity, it is not your taste — bien sur — yet why not if you like — it is for you and him to decide, it concern no one else."

[A paragraph of my original manuscript, without abbreviation or correction, and just as it was then written is retained

[*443*]

here. — It is a clue to my mental condition at that date, and a good introduction to the episode which follows. — An explanation of my tastes.]

My tastes seem for some time past to have been much changed, to be gradually inclining to abnormal pleasures. — Have I seen and done enough with — am I getting tired of common place sensualities — am I on the road to a sensual abyss? — Lustful suggestions come to me more frequently from strumpets, or so it seems to me. — Do *they*, or do I — take more heed of them than formerly? Pleasures which in my youth I doubted as possible, the whisper of which passed by me like the idle wind, others which I did not like even to hear of, I now think about. The tongue and the mouth more frequently minister to my sensuous joys. — Do I really like that or not? My imagination well exercised in sexual pleasures, now suggests strange forms of fornication. — I find women willing to gratify them, nay more — have evident delight with myself in doing so, when I have suggested them. Whether these fancies are indulged in with other men, or others of their own sex, and this not for lucre only, it evidently is to gratify themselves as well as me that they do them.

My lasciviousness has increased by practice and women are similarly influenced. — Is it during the last few years, years which I vowed to consecrate to fidelity, that I have thus changed, or have these tastes been growing on me since puberty? A voluptuous offer from a fair woman, I feel now that I can scarcely resist. — Where will this end, in good or evil?

My knowledge of male and female in sexual matters, in their procreative instincts and sexual vagaries, how large it seems. — Yet there still seems a field of pleasure, of enquiry yet unexplored before me. Shall I yield and gratify it? My former hesitations seem nearly gone, boldly and without hesitation, I now ask women for the satisfaction of letches, letches relatively abnormal. — Perhaps all beyond plain belly to belly copulation may be called abnormal sexual pleasures. Much that is done every hour, every minute by male with female is abnormal. But to what does this lead? — What will be the outcome to this wider range of erotic desires. — Good or evil? — Shall I struggle against it or yield? — Have I not struggled before, struggled against my philosophy, and with what result? — my narrative answers me.

CHAPTER XLVI

*Change in style in writing this narrative. — Reckless
amours. — Nelly L**l*e and Sophy S***h. — Neophyte
harlots. — A first night out. — Madame
S***k*n*us. — Cuntal contrasts. — A lascivious
evening. — Their antecedents and future. — Nelly's
face, form and quim. — Voluptuous complacency. —
Her after life. — My tastes for being gamahuched. —
Externals of sodomites. — Fantastic male
lascivieties. — Champagne and sperm. — Dildo and
arse-hole. — Birching tried on me. — Policemen's
forbearance. — One in plain clothes. — Nelly's
illness and my aid. — Sophy's face, figure, and
colour. —Married, mother, and widowed.*

[It is evident now, altho it did not occur to me at the time
when week by week, or day by day, I wrote these narratives,
that of late years I had a growing habit of giving opinions
on, and reasons for my amorous, erotic exploits. — This certainly was not the case in the early part of this history. — I
suppose the change was the result of experience, and reflexion on that experience, which made me write those opinions.
They were doubtless involuntary, they came in the natural
course of the incidents, and writing them at the time pleased
me as much as describing the events. These opinions and reflexions are an index to my mental state at *that* time, and it
would be well to retain them all. The need for excision and
abbreviation is however inexorable, and few can be kept.
The desires which sprang up, the thoughts or experiences
which led to them, if preludes to my amorous deeds, will
however be retained, where not of too great length.

[Not having been found out in my promiscuous amusements with women, and the ailments of Venus not having at-
tacked me, I became bold, and did openly hazardous things,
which a few years ago I should have never attempted. I
longed for women who had never sold their charms, and
made advances to some who seemed open to them, some
who were as critically placed as I was, and more so, for to

them it might have been utter ruin. — With two or three, I had brief amours which we both enjoyed intensely. The pleasure of eating stolen honey is great, and hazardous, illicit fucking, is the finest of honey. Danger and risks no doubt give its charms to such liaisons, but fucking with eyes and ears open at my time of life, was after all not so pleasurable as fucking with a tranquil mind.

[Altho strong sexually, I thought that at my time of life that the strength could not last long, and seemed to desire to lose no opportunity in indulging with the sex, fearing that indifference which sometimes comes with abatement of virile force. So when I got the chance I had many charming transient amours. Circumstances indeed a little later on favoured me in these, and gave me opportunities of indulging with less risk than before, but what led to those facilities must not be disclosed. Many of my fugitive amours did not exceed the acquaintance of a night or two — nor did I wish them to last — nor perhaps did my female friends. Mostly they were commonplace, and I only tell of those in which was some unusual incident, tho with my habit then, as now inveterate, I duly recorded in my manuscript each amorous adventure.

[The next twenty or thirty pages relate to two young harlots named Nelly L**l*e and Sophy S***h —. I occasionally visited Nelly for many years, the other rarely, tho for as long a time or nearly so. — My libidinous amusement with them were all of the ordinary kind, which I have practised with hundreds of the frail sisterhood, and with many who were not frail in a financial sense. They were as usual, described by me at length in my original manuscript, but the repetition of salacious tricks seems tedious now, so I have carefully weeded out, arranged in some order, condensed, abbreviated this part of my narrative, to about one fifth of its original length; leaving only certain episodes worth retaining for their variety, which I shall put in their chronologcal order nearly.]

Going along L**c**t*r Square one evening I saw a short-ish female in front of me. She had short petticoats (worn then), Balmoral boots, a small foot, and shapely calf. — The movement of haunches and legs told me she had the class of form I loved; I can tell by the pose of the foot, and the swing of the bum, what sort of thighs and rump are moving underneath petticoats — I passed and looked at her. She had a

[446]

quite young, modest face, white and pink complexion, dark
eyes, and looked healthy, fresh and enticing. I stopped,
turned, and she passed *me*. She is modest, I thought. — Bah!
what does modesty do here by itself at eight o'clock
p.m.? — So I accosted her, wondering at her steady bum
swing which looked twenty-one at least, whilst her face
looked but seventeen or thereabouts.

"May I go home with you?" "Yes if you like," and she
looked back. "Where do you live?" — "I live at — oh I forget, but it's just over there." "Go on and I'll follow." — She
hesitated, but turned back. — Up came another female,
taller, with flaxen hair, and a nearly white face. — "The gentleman wants to know where we live, what's the name of the
street?" "Tibble, Tickle, Tish, or something like it I forget,
but I know the way." — They both laughed heartily. —"Well
go on," I said (for we had stopped); "I only want this lady
and not you." — I never like talking long to gay women in
the streets. "It's Pickle Street," said my selected one, laughing. "Cross over." — Both crossed, I following, when a
short, sallow, Jewish looking woman there stopped them. —
"What is it my dear," said she. "The gentleman wants to
know the name of the street." "Oh, it's T***f***d Street,
sair — I will shows the vay," and off she walked rapidly
with the girls, I following a little distance behind them. It
was the baud who was giving them their first lesson in street
walking, and following them in view.

She opened the door with a latch key — "I only want this
dark haired girl," said I, "and I'm only going to give her a
sovereign." "Vel, vel, go in, sair." — I went in and upstairs
to two handsomely furnished rooms — a lamp was already
lighted, and she lit two candles, the girls stood still, silent,
and staring at me, I stood thinking — I hate making these arrangements with second or third parties — a baud, and a
couple of whores are a match for the Devil.

"I only want this lady," I repeated, "and can only give her
a sovereign." "Oh you must give her two sovereigns — it's
her first night in London, she's never been out before. Oh
she *must* have two sovereigns." "No." "Vel dare is no harm
done, sair, you see vat nice young ladies they be, and these
handsome rooms but if you won't, you won't — vel go out
again my dears." — It was all very civilly said. — No
bullying. — She blew out the two candles, not a word had
either girl spoken and she opened the door. Said the woman
as I moved towards the door, "I can't let her for luck's sake

[*447*]

start like that, I brought em both to London the day before yesterday, they've never seen London streets till an hour ago." I paused — I had noticed in the street the girl Nelly staring about in a strange way, instead of cock hunting with the steady glances of a regular strumpet — besides the girl looked so very fresh and so modest, that my prick was standing, and I felt a violent lust for her. — "Well let her stay, I'll give it her, but if I have her another night I can only give a sovereign." — "All right, sair." "But I shall stop a long time." "You may stop as long as you likes, mayn't he Nelly?" "I don't care," said the girl.

The old woman relighted the candles. — "Have Sophy too," said she. I never liked fair haired women. — "No." "Do — it's *her* first night as well — don't make them jealous of each other, they're friends now. — Do, and I needn't go out again tonight." — That struck me as so funny that I laughed. "When you see em both quite naked together, you vil say you never see sich fine gals." "I won't be naked," said one, I don't recollect which. — "Now my dearee, you must please gentlemens if you vants to make friends — Didn't I tell ye now — didn't I tell ye — I'm not a going to keep yer — you've got to keep yourself." Then turning to me, "They will be all right when she knows you, sair; have Sophy, do — she's as white as snow, her thighs and body is, and she is formed beautiful, and her hair's the same color *there,* one's black and the other yaller," and the old woman winked at me again with a leer. The contrast was extreme — "black cunt, flaxen cunt" — thought I. "Well, let her stay too — but I'm not going to pay *you.*" — "Oh! all rights, all rights, sair, you can stop all night vith dem. I knows a gentlemans vhen I speak vid him, all rights, sair, my name is S***k*n*us, and I've been here five year, I'm a dressmaker, sair." (I had some idea that I was going to be bilked.) "Now my dearees mind vot I as tell you, I'm sure he'll be a friend to you both," and nodding her head at the girls she went out. I bolted the door. She was a German woman I found, perhaps Jewish, but who had been some time in England, actually worked with a sister at dressmaking, and let her upper floors to quiet gay women, and had now by some chance got these two young women, to introduce to the *pavé* of London.

"Take off your things, my darlings." — The girls giggling and whispering to each other began slowly to do so; it was perfectly clear that they'd not yet undressed as Paphians before a man for pay. Gradually two pairs of splendid calves and lovely white breasts appeared. "Off with your che-mises." "I shan't," said one, and the other did not obey. — I pulled them both to me, putting my hands on their fat back-sides, and kissed their large white breasts alternately. I hitched up the chemises of both at the same time whilst they struggled a bit, and saw fine round thighs on both; nearly black hair on one cunt, almost invisible hair on the other. "My prick's so stiff," said I, and getting up I stripped to my shirt, pulled it up to my waist, and showed a red headed magnificent erection.

Both burst into laughter, which astonished me. I pulled dark haired Nelly on to one thigh as I sat down, and began feeling her cunt. Flaxen haired Sophy sat down on a low stool opposite us, holding her cheeks and her chin with her hands, whilst her elbows rested on her thighs, like an old Irish woman sitting on a door step. A vulgar, low look the girl had, yet she was of a most uncommon peculiar style of face, certainly handsome, yet of a class I didn't like. Then I noticed that she had white eye lashes, and very light eye-brows, and for the moment she reminded me of an albino, who to me is very ugly.

Now I talked baudy. "Show me your cunt," to Nelly, who had been feeling my prick. — "Ho! ain't he rude," said she giggling and looking at Sophy. — "Do." "Shan't." — I lifted her chemise to her armpits suddenly. She struggled and cried out, "No, no." — I got vexed and swore, for I hate a struggle with a sham modest whore, and hadn't quite arrived at the belief that it was her first night's harlotry. — "Isn't she a fool Sophy?" "She knows best," was the reply made in a coarse, raw, nasty voice. — I had not heard her speak before. I let Nell go. — "Let's feel *your* cunt," said I dragging up Sophy from the stool. — She offered no resistance. Her cunt was reeking wet as my fingers went between the lips, and she opened her thighs to let my fingers up. I pulled up her chemise, her cunt seemed nearly hairless, there was hair, but the color was so light, and it was so small in quantity, that it scarcely showed. Her thighs and belly were as white as milk, her form exquisite. — Nelly rearranged her tumbled hair, for in a small struggle with her it had fallen, came close up to us and said to Sophy, "You seem to like it." "I don't mind much, he's a nice chap," croaked Sophy. [Nelly, I found in after years, was jealous of any woman being no-ticed before her — even when she had brought the woman

[*449*]

herself to me for fucking.] Nelly was jealous now of Sophy's pleasing me by her willingness.

Darkish haired quims were always my delight, so I took hold of Nelly again. Sophy dropping again on the stool not much higher than a chamber pot, looking on stupidly and pulling down her short chemise over her knees as if to hide them. I titillated Nelly's clitoris, made her feel my balls and prick, and lavished obscenity and kisses, till she wriggled her rump voluptuously. I had stirred her lust. She wanted fucking, it was time for emptying my testicles, so I threw her on the side of the bed. — "No, no, let me get on to the bed properly." — I wouldn't, opened her thighs violently, leant over her, and drove my prick up her fat little cunt, till my balls banged against her arse. Feeling the prick up her, she laid still, for pleasure told on her at the first thrust of my pego. I began to look at her quim as I pushed my tool in and out. Then she kept pushing her chemise down. — "I'll slit your chemise up if you do that," said I irritated. — Sophy came up and looked on, for Nelly then ceased hiding her charms, and, I saw, soon had voluptuous sensations; and from the involuntary motion of her belly, the opening of her mouth, the staring look of her eyes, saw that they were getting strong. Soon she gave a voluptuous sigh and I fetched her juices out, as I squirted a shower of sperm up her.

I was in full blood, my prick stood well up her after I had spent, and I bent over her quiet for a time, then rose, gradually pulling my prick partly out of its mucous bath. — "When were you last fucked?" said I. — For a second she lay quiet as if in her pleasure still, at last, "Two months ago," said she. Sophie chuckled, "Ave yer done it Nell with him, ave yer?" said she. — No reply. — "Have yer now? — now I knows yer have, and yer said, yer wouldn't with the chaps." — Nell never replied, seeming to be still enjoying the last sensations of the fuck. "She's spent a cup full," said I drawing my prick quite out. — "Look — it's not all mine." Briskly Nell closed her thighs and pulled her chemise over her reeking cunt, from which a rivulet of thick pearly sperm began to run, and she sat up.

"Do you like seeing your friend fucked?" "Never seed it afore," said Sophy, sitting down again on the stool and tugging down her short chemise. "Well *you've* been fucked." "Why of coorse." "You've seen yourself fucked in a looking glass." "That I ain't, there warn't never a glass in the room

[*450*]

at all — I never war in a place afore with a man and a woman a doin it. — Never with none but my own chap."

"Wash Nell," said I, whilst I was doing so. "When you're gone." "Gone my dear? I'm going to stop hours." — Nellie washed. — I turned to Sophy and grasped her sliggery cunt. — "Shall *we* fuck?" "If yer like." Her cunt was on fire and reeking, as I laid her on the side of the bed. — What a treat the light flaxen haired motte was by contrast, I had not expected such enjoyment from it. I got my prick in her, but the fucking was much longer, and I fetched her before I came myself. Nelly now looked on curiously, it was her turn. — "You've done it with him Sophy." "And so did you." Then both laughed. Getting off the bed, down went Sophy on to the stool again. "You'll wet your chemise Sophy." "Don't care." — But up she got, wiped her cunt outside with a towel, and threw it down on the floor in a low manner.

There was a freshness in manner, and modesty in both of them, and they had manifestly an enjoyment in my fucking, which made me think now that the old woman had spoken the truth. I had thought it all sham. — Neither had ever tasted champagne I found, so ordered some, telling the woman to get it at **** a well known place for food and wine [then]. Madame S***k*n**s fetched it and I gave her a glass. — Was I pleased with the young ladies? — Yes and had fucked both. — "They won't wash their cunts properly," said I joking. *"I have,"* said Nelly — "Sophy has wiped hers." "Oh Miss Sophy, you know what I have tell you." — We had gone into the sitting room which opened with folding doors to the bedroom, and the flaxen motted one now washed her cunt properly. We all drank champagne, the old woman left, I ordered another bottle, and soon both girls were quite groggy.

Then they let out their histories. Many times after I heard both, and they never varied. — Certainly it was their first harlotting night, and most likely neither had been fucked for weeks as they said. I warmed them well up with lewed talk, one held my prick, the other the pot when I pissed. It delights me to make fresh women do those little services. I laid them side by side lengthwise on the bed, and then one on top of the other. The liquor and talk had made them randy. We all stripped quite, and putting the cheval glass to see in it, I fucked one whilst I fingered the other. Then we had more wine, and the girls began to quarrel, which I have often found to occur when I have had two women together and they got lushy.

It really was because I had fucked flaxen motte twice, and Nelly was jealous. I'd fucked Sophy I can't tell why, for I always liked a dark haired cunt, and Nelly's was dark. — I fancy it was that I found Sophy's the nicest of the two cunts, and have since thought so [I sometimes think now that her cunt was the most delicious my prick ever went into] but I never could bear the girl, tho scores of times I have thought of nothing but her cunt, when I have been stroking Nelly and others. I recollect all this clearly because the evening was a memorable one. They now both blabbed and told me all about themselves but the name of the village they came from. — No, they wouldn't tell that. "Don't you recollect that some one fetched me that night, Nelly?" "Yes." "Father said he'd throw him bloody soon into the canal if he came home again with me." "Poor Bet, he never kept her child." "Yes and he made me sleep with him that night." — So that sort of talk ran on, telling me bits of their history as I questioned them, and interrupting and correcting, and helping each other in their tales, both talking sometimes at once. Then we all three turned onto the bed again. I treated the dark haired cunt, and fucked each girl quite twice before the evening was out. When we parted I promised to see them the next day.

[This was their history. Nelly mainly made me her confidant after I helped to keep her during an illness at a future day. Both had been caught fucking without a license. — Sophy by a man of her own class caught in a field by *her* father, who stuck a scythe into her swain's rump. — Nelly was surprized in bed with a gentleman who had promised to marry her, and *her* father had turned her out of doors. — The swains neglected the girls — both had family way sensations in their bellies, and were helped out of the difficulty by a local dressmaker. — Madame S***k*n*us, a German Jewess and dressmaker, knew the village one, who advised the girls to go to London with Madame S***k*n*us. They knew they were going to be gay, tho it was not said so. Uncomfortable at their village, off they ran, and that was their first night in their career of harlotry when I had them. — Both afterwards liked gay life, but neither rose to eminence. — Nell for some years led a comfortable life of indolence, as long as she kept to S***k*n*us. Sophy sank to the lowest depths, was always

[452]

drunk, nearly naked, and would take men home for a glass of gin.]

Nelly was short, beautifully formed and plump, had good legs, small feet, thick ankles, and large bum. — Her skin was a very dark cream color, her hair nearly black, her eyes a very dark hazel, with a heavy expression in them much like that of a cow's. It was a half sulky look. She had thick eye-brows and large mouth but was really handsome. In after years she was often taken for a French woman by men. The hair on her motte was about the thickest I ever saw on an English woman's tho at first there was not much of it. The flesh of the motte could not be seen thro it, and just over the clitoris it formed a thick little clump almost hard, it curled so. Her armpits were thick with hair even at that age. (She was barely seventeen.) She had hair on her cunt, she said, at twelve. Ten years afterwards when I saw her, it was half up to her navel, but it never grew round her buttocks or arsehole. Her cunt was large at seventeen, and some years afterwards was very large. — I could then put a large dildo and two fingers up it at the same time easily, yet she had even then a wonderfully fine cuntal grip on the prick, it was such a fat cunt inside. She had a beautiful steady walk, like a Spanish woman's, looked quiet, and was proud of walking out dressed simply in good black silk, and being taken for a modest woman. — She was relatively modest, when first I had her. In a week I'd taught her much, and modesty was lost. She said she had had more poking in the first fortnight she had come to town than she had had altogether from *her* young man, who had never tailed her more than about a dozen times in all. Her cunt then had all the signs of recent rupture. — In after years she was the most complacent creature, and did with me everything excepting bum fucking. Once when I pressed her to let me do that she nearly yielded, but it was out of kindness. — I was only joking, and but asked as a test. She got me three young virgins, two of whom I poked, a dozen other women, and two men to frig or bugger if I liked — I did not like the latter work. She gradually got poor and ill, and disappeared. Her last stay was in one room. An old gentleman up whose arse she used to put a dildo whist she sucked his cock, she said, then nearly kept her; he was seventy-six years old, yet could spend under that fundamental and labial irritation.

She early made friends among a good class of married men, and was always at home in the afternoon, dressed usually in a blue satin dressing gown, and nice silk stockings and boots. Her foot was beautiful. She for years rarely went out at night or to public amusements, but passed her time in idling, feeding, dressing, reading the newspapers and novels. She said she lost money when she went out at night before ten, so if she went out it was usually very late. She was a very safe woman. Once during what I think was a bad clap, tho she would not say so, and once thro a long illness, I paid her lodgings and some other friend paid for her food. She was on both occasions in the same house (Madame S***k*n*us). She never let me poke her if she had the slightest taint of her poorliness. She was a wonderful frigger. — Her masturbation was most delicate and fetching (some women can never frig), and afterwards she gama-huched equal to any French woman — I have gone to her with my prick as limp as a rag, yet never went away without a spending. She had a wonderful way of pushing my machine if limp into her roomy cunt, and saying "lay still." — Without movement on my part and no perceptible movement to her buttocks, she stiffened me by the compression of her cunt — her gripping cunt seemed to suck my prick up into it. When about thirty years old she began to paint. At rare intervals then I used to talk to her only, and to tip her when I met her, and for years sent her a sovereign at Christmas.

Before I lost sight of her, she used to say that when first out, scarcely any man wanted more than to poke her, but then that half the men wanted to be gamahuched, and some wanted to bugger. She did not allow that, but got them ladies who did. She looked on at the operation at times, and halved the fee paid for their complaisance.

She explained to me the habits of the male sodomites (she had studied and hated them), the way to know them, and how to treat them. It was curious, but I never learned to know them by sight, and never wanted. — To the last of her career so far as I know it, and when she barely had a gown to cover her, she managed to get silk stockings, and tho flabby in her breasts, and with a smaller and flabby bum, never lost her shapely legs. Her heart went wrong, she got dirty, and then I saw her no more.

She rarely drank, tho I have made her tight several times by sipping warm brandy and water with her. With a good fire in the room, her clothes up to her navel, legs so placed that I could see her cunt, we talked and she told me strange baudy fads she had known men to have. One young man, after laying her down with thighs distended and open cunt, used to frig himself into a tumbler of champagne and then drink it, swallowing his own sperm. Another made her run a pin into his balls. One brought small peas, and pushed them down his urethra. — He came with his bladder full — and then pissed out the peas against her cunt, or her arsehole, or her breasts. She flogged some men till they spent, and other erotic whimsies. Many men she said liked a dildo up their arseholes whilst they fucked, or were frigged, or gamahuched. One man only fucked a woman when she had a dildo up her bum; a lady friend she fetched for that purpose. He greased the dildo and put it up the lady's arsehole. It was used for no one else and she showed it me. "That's dildo's my old friend's," she said showing another and larger.

"I don't like it, but do everything excepting bugger, it pleases them and amuses me. If I did not some other would — I should lose friends." Camille has said the same. — She only once let me see her on the sly with a male friend. I looked thro a key hole at them copulating. Once she got a man to fuck her whilst I looked on, and I frigged him afterwards. He was a big fine man, and said he was a carpenter. Once she began to birch me, the only time I ever tried it, but the pain was too great and I made her desist. Twice she played at flat cocks with a female before me, and on one occasion a baudy tipsy night we had, with a second woman.

She used to fuck and spend in a quiet way, never swore, nor raised her voice, nor seemed angry, nor used baudy language unless asked, and chuckled it out then in a quiet voice. She never got into police rows. How she squared the police I don't know. I asked her if she let the constables tail her — "No" — but an Inspector used to have her. He was a married man and came in plain clothes. She never was "run in" that I heard of, when they ran in fifty women a night from the Haymarket and its vicinity.

During one illness I helped to keep her, and meeting then Sophy by chance, went home with her. She was at enmity with Nelly and said Nelly had had a miscarriage, and the father of the child was a labourer. — Nelly afterwards admitted a miscarriage. When she had been launched a few months she got cautious as whores do, and told me nothing; then came her illness, and after as said, she became as communicative as at first. When I was in love with Jessie C**t*s

I did not see Nelly for a year or more. I shan't forget her joy when she saw me again.

Sophy, with the exception of the young lass Kitty with the yellow hair and motte, whom I had in my early manhood, was the only light haired Paphian I ever had more than a few times, rarely more than once. She was full grown tho only seventeen, her hair was like light flax, her eyelashes white. — She was exquisitely made, had the loveliest breasts, and from the nape of her neck to the sole of her feet was as white as snow. Her features were good, her eyes were blue and yet she looked like a fool and when she laughed was like an idiot. — Her laugh was a vulgar, idiotic, coarse, offensive chuckle, she opened her mouth quite wide (it was large with splendid teeth), and she rolled her head about from side to side. — Her hands were coarse. She had slight hollows in her bum cheeks at first, in a few months they were dimples, and she must have put on a stone in weight in time. — Never was there a woman who handled better all over than she, she was delicious to touch, an exquisite piece of flesh.

For a year or two (and in after years she returned), she was in the same house with Nelly and Madame S***k*n*us, who dressed and looked after her. There she did well. Then she went to live by herself having quarrelled with Nelly, and I saw nothing of her for a few years. — Nelly then told me one day that she had married an artisan, who was then dying, had two children by him, that they'd lived respectably and she quietly, but that now having pawned everything to keep them, she was going on to the streets again to live. They literally had nothing in their room but a bed, chair, table and piss pot, and would have starved, if Nelly had not sent them food for some time. She could afford that no longer, but she was keeping one child whom she brought upstairs to show me. — It was flaxen haired, like Sophy.

CHAPTER XLVII

At mid-day on a very hot day, tho towards the end of the summer of this year, I was walking along one of the main highways which lead to the suburbs of London, and was at a spot at some distance from the centre, when I passed two young girls who were sauntering idly along. The taller of the two had her arm round the other's neck, and looked not sixteen, the other perhaps a year younger. They were dressed poorly like the children of artisans. The taller was nibbling a piece of hay, which I saw her pull out of a truss on the pavement by a corn chandler's shop, and staring about her idly and rudely. I was voluptuously inclined that morning, was thinking of the charms of youthful cunts, and gave a loving glance and winked at the taller as I passed them. She returned the glance saucily yet half shyly, and instinct told me at once that if the girl had not had a prick up her cunt, she knew pretty well what a cock and a cunt did when they met. The idea fired my lust.

After passing them I stopped and looked back. They had stopped, and the tall one was looking back, but seeing me stopping they immediately resumed their sauntering. I should like to fuck her thought I, for she has such bright eyes, and turning I followed them quickly, and as I again passed them said aloud, "I'd give a shilling each to kiss you two pretty girls." Again I caught the tall one's saucy inviting eye. When I had gone ahead some distance, I returned and met them face to face again. They were half looking in at a shop window, half in my direction. Encouraged, I stopped at the shop, and looking at the window and askant only at

[457]

them, so as to avoid attracting notice, said, "Come and have a ride in a cab with me." Immediately the tall one said, "I don't mind." The other only stared at me. The taller one then whispered something to her.

I stool without further noticing them, waiting for a four wheel cab to pass, nor they noticing me. At length one came by, I hailed it and it stopped. I half abandoned my intention whilst waiting, for there was a considerable foot traffic, but it was at a part where the road passed through a poor neighbourhood, the traffic was mostly of humble people, poor girls were hanging about, hucksters were in the road, the pedestrians (mostly working people) seemed hurrying and probably to their dinners, none of the well to do were out, nor indeed were there many I expect at any time just there. — Quickly I entered the vehicle, the elder girl needed no further invitation to follow, but the younger hesitated. "Come on Sally, he says he'll gie us a ride," and she pushed the shorter one in, following herself. I shut the door and told the cabman to drive to *****. It was a long way off, but the road I knew would be a quiet one. The girls made no objection even if they heard, but seemed delighted at a ride. The cabman I am sure knew my game, for he grinned.

Excitement and the broiling sun had made me hot, and for a minute I could only wipe off my perspiration, but lust soon stirred up. I looked at the elder, who sat opposite to me staring half saucily, I wondered what was passing in her little mind, but I felt now sure from her saucy look that she was game. "I'm in a sweat." "Ain't yer just," said she. "Aren't you?" "Not much." "You're cunt's in a sweat isn't it now?" "He, he," she giggled. "Here's a shilling, let me feel it." — I offered her the shilling and not waiting for her to take it or reply, pulled her rapidly on to my knee, kissed her, and in a second my fingers were on her split. — "Don't do that now sir," but beyond slightly closing her thighs she made no resistance. My fingers were well between the lips, and her cunt felt quite sticky. — Young girls I notice don't seem to wash their quims much, for I have usually found them sticky when I have suddenly felt them. I rubbed it with my fingers, and she seemed to like it, for her struggling was mere sham, yet she kept exclaiming. — "Oh ain't he a going on Sally. — Don't now sir." — Sally sat staring at my doings.

I felt her cunt for a minute, then gave her the shilling. She held it in her open hand for Sally to see, before she pocketed it. — Then I offered Sally a shilling to feel *her* cunt, but she refused and resisted. "Have you got any hair on your cunt Sally?" "Shan't tell you." — "She ain't, she ain't fourteen, but it's a comin," said her friend. "Feel my cock," and I pulled it out. Both laughed and refused, but Carry soon repented, and felt it, with much gratification. "Isn't it big and stiff," said I. "I don't know." "You do." — Seizing her, I put my mouth to her ear and whispered, "You little devil, you know you've had a prick in your cunt, let me fuck you." "I ain't," and she giggled. — I went on whispering about fucking. "What's he a telling yer?" said Sally, who seemed curious at the whispering. — "I'm telling her I'll give you a shilling to feel your cunt." "Shan't," said Sally. "Feel my prick then." "Feel it, it won't bite yer," said her friend. The girl refused. — "Have you ever felt a man's cock?" "No," said she, boldly and positively. "Oh yer lie — yer have — you've felt Jack's." — Sally made no reply, was shut up, and looked stupid.

In a little time Sally, by my continued requests, and at the advice of Carry, got her shilling, and not only felt my cock, but let me feel her bum. I had Carry on one side, and Sally on the other, both standing up with their backs to the doors of the cab, both feeling my standard whilst I was feeling their little backsides.

It was delightful to handle their buttocks, but I wanted further satisfaction. "Show me your cunt Carry and I'll give you another shilling." She wouldn't, she should be seen, but that at length was arranged. Sally stood looking out of one cab window, whilst I with a little resistance threw up the other's petticoats as she sat on the seat opposite to me, and disclosed soiled underlinen, and stockings dirty enough to have shocked any prick if it had had eyes. — But it hadn't, and stood stiffer than ever, when a very little triangular bit of flossy brown shewed at the bottom of the girl's belly. To get a better view I seized hold of her legs, and pulling them up, tilted her back. She kept laughing but asking me to leave off. Then Sally turned her head and seeing my game, uttered a solemn, — "Hoh! ain't he agoing on."

I had my look and another feel, so got Carry on to my knees again and my finger on her cunt, whispering that I'd give her a crown to fuck her. — "Oh no," — she couldn't. — "She'll tell perhaps, and the people will see us when passing." — But she sat feeling my cock, longing for it to be up her, whilst I rubbed at her clitoris till she wriggled her bum. "You rub this till you get pleasure don't you?" "Sometimes," said the slut laughing. "Oh don't — leave off."

Again I tried it on with Sally, at a length succeeded in feeling her little cunt whilst she kept her legs closed, but nothing induced her to let me look, and as she got noisy — "No I shan't then, I don't care if *she* do — *I* shan't then — leave off" — I desisted.

"Take us back," said Carry suddenly. "If mother goes out afore I get there, I shan't get nothing to eat — and she'll row me tonight when she comes in." — She was much in earnest. — "Let me fuck you then, and I'll go back at once." — We were just then at a spot where there was very little traffic. She refused. Sally might tell — I refused to go back and increased my offer.

At length, promising another shilling to Sally to keep standing and looking out of the window, I pushed my legs well forward to the front seat, and between Carry's thighs, who was standing up in front of me. She was almost too short, her cunt was a small mark to hit, but the little bitch was in heat, and earnestly and silently aided my efforts. My prick was in such a state that it would have pierced a board, and directly it got its tip on her split, with a heave up of my arse, it was fixed as tightly up her cunt as if she'd been pegged. Then I clasped her little buttocks and fairly lifted her off the floor, she came forward, her arms round my neck, her face near mine, and I began fucking with short thrusts; my prick never moved more than an inch backwards and forwards, the position would not enable long strokes, but it was enough. — "Do you like it Carry?" "Y-hes," she whispered. "It's up your cunt." "Y-hes — a-har." "Are you coming?" "Aha — Y-hes — soon," and then with delicious short wriggling movements we both spent, and Carry's head fell over my left shoulder.

I thought my pego would never withdraw, and in meretricious thoughts was content to leave it in its soft luscious compress, holding her still round her small backside close to me. She lay with head on my shoulder, silent, tranquil, enjoying the gentle dilation that my prick still gave her cunt, when floating, dwindling slowly in abundant sperm — in the soft mucilaginous bath we had made together in her temple of love — her feet still scarcely touching the cab floor, her cunt squeezing more and more down on to my ballocks, as she felt the rod slowly receding from her. — Sally looked round. — "You'll lose your shilling if you don't look out," said I just recovering from my pleasure as I noticed her. — The girl then stared steadily out of the window but Carry was roused, I let go her backside, and slowly she sat back on the seat opposite as we uncoupled, looking at me with quite a luscious smile, a smile of delight and gratitude for the voluptuous treat I had given her. Then her eyes settled on my moist pego hanging its head over my balls, for I had still lascivious delight in letting it hang out for her to see, my knees still between her legs as she sat, her petticoats dropping over them could fall no further. Thus for a minute smiling at each other, we sat.

Time was pressing, I covered up my ballocks and sat up, she dropped her petticoats, Sally turned round and sat beside her, staring first at me, then at her companion. The little slut knew, I'm sure, what we had been up to, but never spoke a word as she took my shilling. I told cabby to drive back, and was glad of air, for the sun was beating down, and the cab like an oven, as I had closed both windows to diminish the area thro which people passing should see.

I took Carry on my lap, felt that gluey little quim, kissed her, and kept up a conversation in whispers, much to the annoyance of the other, who every now and then kept jealously asking what it was all about. — I offered a sovereign, if she bring Sally out that night, and induce her to let me fuck her. — She'd try but feared she couldn't. "I knows who will do it to *her* tho." — Her own mother often stopped *her* (Carry) going out of a night but if she'd had a drop she'd be sure to let her go. — Sally's mother wouldn't let Sally. They lodged in the same house, but she would try. — Soon after I got out, paid the cabman, and told him where to set the girls down.

The evening came, I somehow had made up my mind that I should fuck the virgin Sally — if she were virgin — for I couldn't get her to let me feel her closely enough to verify that. I was disappointed. At a little past seven o'clock at the appointed place, Carry appeared alone. Sally's mother wouldn't let her daughter out. "I think she'd a let yer do it to her if she'd come, she told me she would." — Carry went with me willingly to a house, and I stripped her. — She had put on clean stockings and chemise, I had told her to do so when in the cab in the morning. — "Shall I fuck you," said I. "Yes do," she replied quickly.

I mounted the little lass, and gloried in the sweet little pouting, half fledged sheath I fucked when I felt the little lass was having as much pleasure as a grown woman. She was revelling with me in copulation, sighing her voluptuous sighs in that sweetly quiet way which girls do, till they learn to break out into the lewed exclamations of delight, which many do as they grow older. — Then after she'd wiped her cunt outside, and our passions were subdued for a time, we talked.

At first she was reserved, then open, and for an hour I questioned *her* much, and she *me* a little. What sweet confidences between a girl of sixteen and a man not far from fifty. The difference in age gave our conversation an additional charm. It was semipaternal, yet all about fucking. — Of the hour's talk, all worth telling may be soon told.

She had never been in a baudy house before, and had only been fucked two months. Her father died some months ago, her mother was a charwoman and drank. Carry had been a short time a nursemaid, and now did work at home, she did all the cleaning in their two rooms, looked after another sister, and worked with her needle. — She and her mother quarrelled. "Now who fucked you first?" — a young man she knew — "quite a young man" — that's all I could then learn. Sally and her mother lived in the room below, her father was a chair maker, but was a blackguard, sometimes disappeared for a month or two, and her mother got their living principally, and *she* often was drunk. There was a brother nearly sixteen years old and a younger sister, and all three slept in the same bed, and in the same room as their mother and father.

Sally knew all about fucking tho she denied all, and was so demure in the cab. She had seen her brother's cock and felt it, and he had seen Sally's cunt. — "His cock is a good big one too." "Then you've seen it." — Carry didn't deny that. The brother one night tried to do it to his sister "And she'll let him one day I knows, tho she says she won't." Little by little, I got out that these two youngsters had one day frigged the lad, and he'd seen both their cunts. He was a shop boy at a grocer's.

Suddenly a light dawned upon me from some remark she made. "It's her brother who fucked you first." — She broke out in laughter, and denied it. — But I insisted, and at last she admitted it.

Carry had to fetch pails of water upstairs, and the lad used kindly to do it for her — one morning her mother had gone out to work at six o'clock, when the lad knocked at the door as he was going to his work, and asked if he should fetch her a pail full. She accepted and he fetched it. She instead of getting up when her mother left went to bed again, and was in her chemise. He wanted to bring the water in. — "No put it down outside." He said he'd throw the water away. So she let him in, he put down the pail, then began kissing her, she'd already seen his prick, and his spunk, he'd seen her cunt, and a few minutes afterwards, that lucky lad's prick was in her virgin niche, her hymen was but a bleeding split, his sperm was sticking his balls on to her buttocks. — She was in for fucking after that. — When once a female's tasted the sugar stick, it's not long before she gets another taste.

Since then whenever Jack got the opportunity he fucked her, and she let him willingly. — "Why shouldn't I now." She'd never had another man. — But Jack was a blackguard, for tho he'd promised to tell no one — had "took his Bible oath" he wouldn't if I'd let him, he had told a shopman where he was working, and the shopman came after her and told her. But she hadn't and did not mean to let the shopman, she couldn't bear him — and I was the only one except Jack, who had done it to her.

She didn't think Jack had told his sister, but he'd said he meant to fuck his sister, and Carry felt sure she'd let him some day when his mother was out. "She knows all about doing it bless yer. — Why she's seen her father and mother adoing it often, and has seen her father's prick."

That was the history got in an hour's talking, whilst feeling and finger stinking, and by that time my pego being in admirable condition and delighted at its size and look — "Oh yes, it's much bigger than Jack's," — took up her notch again, and again I wetted its little soft interior with my sperm, and she spent charmingly in my arms, kissing me.

I was in love with the little lass, and fucked her once more, but she was in a hurry to get home, her mother would knock her about if she found her out of nights, and unless drunk her mother usually kept at home. She hoped her "mother would be out on the screw." — Couldn't I be where I first met them in the day, then perhaps Sally would go to a house, and let me have her. I couldn't well do that soon, but arranged to be that day week at the same spot and hour if Carry would. She agreed but never came, and I never saw her more.

CHAPTER XLVIII

H*l*n M***w**d. — Our first meeting. — Her physical perfections. — Money differences. — My promise kept. — A year's interval. — Friendship established. — Mutual meretriciousness. — Unrestrained sexual amusements. — Erotic tastes gratified. — Arcades ambo. — Initials. — My age, physical force and adventures. — A carnal paradise. —

One night soon after this, I met at the A*g**e rooms H*l*n M***w**d and was struck with her instantly. My experienced eye and well trained judgment in women, as well as my instincts, told me what was beneath her petticoats and I was not deceived. I have had many splendid women in my time, but never a more splendid perfect beauty, in all respects.

Of full but not great height, with the loveliest shade of chestnut hair of great growth, she had eyes in which grey, green and hazel were indescribably blended with an expression of supreme voluptuousness in them, yet without baudiness or salacity, and capable of any play of expression. A delicate slightly retroussé nose, the face a pure oval, a skin and complexion of a most perfect tint and transparency, such was H*l*n M. Nothing was more exquisite than her whole head, tho her teeth were wanting in brilliancy, — but they were fairly good and not discoloured.

She had lovely cambered feet, perfect to their toes; thighs meeting from her cunt to her knees and exquisite in their columnar beauty; big, dimpled haunches, a small waist, full firm breasts, small hands, arms of perfect shape in their full roundness. Every where her flesh was of a very delicate creamy tint, and was smooth to perfection. Alabaster or ivory, were not more delicious to the touch, than her flesh was every where from her cheeks to her toes.

Short, thick, crisp yet silky brown hair covered the lower part of her motte, at that time only creeping down by the side of the cunt lips, but leaving the lips free, near to at her bumhole, a lovely little clitoris, a mere button, topped her belly rift, the nymphæ were thin, small, and delicate. The mouth of the vulva was small, the avenue tight yet exquisitely elastic, and as she laid on her back and opened her thighs, it was an exquisite, youthful, pink cunt, a voluptuous sight which would have stiffened the prick of a dying man.

Her deportment was good, her carriage upright but easy, the undulations of her body in movement voluptuous, and fascinating; every thing, every movement was graceful; even when she sat down to piss it was so — and taking her altogether, she was one of the most exquisite creatures God ever created to give enjoyment to man. — With all this grace, and rich, full, yet delicate of frame, she was a strong, powerful woman, and had the sweetest voice — it was music.

I saw much of this in her at a glance, and more completely as she undressed. Then the sweetest smell as if of new milk, or of almonds escaped from her, and the instant she laid down I rushed lasciviously on her cunt, licked and sucked it with a delight that was maddening. I could have eaten it. Never had I experienced such exquisite delight in gamahuching a woman. Scarcely ever have I gamahuched a gay woman on first acquaintance, and generally never gamahuched them at all.

As I went home with her in a cab I had attempted a few liberties, but she repulsed them. — "Wait till we get home, I won't have them in a cab." — Directly we arrived I asked what her compliment was to be. — No she had never less than a fiver. — "Why did you not tell me so, I would not have brought you away. — What I give is two sovereigns, here is the money, I am sorry I have wasted your time" — and was going. — "Stop," said she — "don't go yet!" — I looked in my purse and gave her what I could — it was a little more than the sum I'd named — and promised to bring her the remainder of a fiver another day. Then I fucked her. — "Don't be in such a hurry," I said, for she moved her cunt as women either do when very randy, or wishing to get rid of a man. That annoyed me, but oh my God my delight as I shed my sperm into that beautiful cunt, and kissed and smelt that divine body, and looked into those voluptuous eyes. I had at once a love as well as lust for her, as my prick throbbed out its essence against her womb. — But *she* had no pleasure with *me*. — She was annoyed and in a hurry, she had another man waiting in another room in the house to have her — as she has told me since.

What was in this woman — what the specific attraction, I cannot say, but she made me desire to open my heart to her, and I told rapidly of my amatory tricks, my most erotic letches, my most blamable (if any be so) lusts; things I had kept to myself, things never yet disclosed to other women, I told *her* rapidly. I felt as if I must, as if it were my destiny to tell her all, all I had done with women and men, all I wished to do with *her*, it was a vomit of lascivious disclosures. I emptied myself body and soul into her. She listened and seemed annoyed. She did not like me.

Nor did she believe me. Two days afterwards, I took her the promised money, she had not expected it, and then deigned to ask if she should see me again. No. She was far too expensive for me — not that she was not worth it all. — Yea more — but blood could not be got out of a stone. — I had not the money and could see her no more. — "All right," she replied very composedly and we parted. As I tore myself away, my heart ached for the beautiful form, again to see, smell, to kiss, and suck, and fuck that delicious cunt, to give *her* pleasure if I could. Tho I saw her afterwards at the A*g**e rooms — even went to look at her there, I resisted. — What helped me was the belief that I was distasteful to her, why I could not tell, and a year elapsed before I clasped her charms again.

On leaving her that day, I could think of nothing but *her*, went to a woman I knew, and shut my eyes whilst I fucked her, fancying she was H*l*n M. — "You call me H*l*n," said she. "You know a woman of that name I suppose," — I told her it was the name of my sister. Not the only time the same thing has happened to me, and in exactly the same manner with other ladies when fucking *them*, but thinking of *another*.

When I had her again she was in even more complete beauty, had more hair on her motte, and a thick tuft just above the opening of the notch. — Her limbs were larger and finer. I was frank, told her what money I could afford, that I never lied nor broke my word to women. I think began to believe me, but it's difficult to gauge the depths of a gay woman, and difficult for *any* woman who has been gay long, to believe *any* man. — But things were changing, I began to see her for my pleasures, and her only — if I had an occasional letch, a chance fuck with another, I nearly always told her, but that was after I had known her a year or so. — If she then asked what I did not wish to tell, I said I should tell a lie or be silent. — So our meetings were pleasant, and I revelled in her beauty, and tho no longer young, have many a time fucked her thrice within an hour. — Then she began to spend with and enjoy me, which added to my delight; for in later years, giving pleasure to the woman is almost as great a pleasure to me, as my physical delight in her.

But she would not for long afterwards lend herself to my erotic fancies. She had them in her head, in her mind, in her imagination, and wished for many — I believe most. — She was lewed and voluptuous from her earliest childhood, but hid her desires from *me,* only granting a few of my wishes from time to time as the greatest favour. Yet she longed for them at the very time she refused, and in the night and morning by herself in bed, practised them all mentally, her imagination filled with baudy images, whilst with her pretty fingers she frigged her delicate clitoris, for she was sensuousness itself, and a masturbatrix from her childhood. It was only after I had known her three or four years, and she'd disclosed involuntarily almost in our voluptuous conversations the secret desires of her nature, that she practised with me the frolics she never had done with any other man. — Then we studied lasciviousness in all its varieties, for I had conquered all ridiculous ideas she had had as to the sinful usage of her body — of the wrongfulness, of the shame in certain sexual acts. — She agreed with me that cunt, prick, and arsehole, mouth, armpits, feet and fingers, and all parts of the body, men and women might use to give themselves sexual pleasure, and endear themselves to each other — that nothing they did to each other was wrong, that their doings concerned themselves alone, that all sexual instincts were both proper and natural to gratify.

[This will be seen and the lustful amusements we both enjoyed described — nothing I have done with any other woman which I did not do with *her.* One fancy begot another, and erotic conceptions crept on us gradually.]

She said that she'd never done such things with another man — not even with the man she'd once loved, who had kept her, — nor with those she'd lusted for — for she had strong likings — that men had never suggested strange letches to her. I expect she alone indulged with me in them, because sensuously our temperaments were the same. She matched me in lasciviousness, and moreover knew there was not the slightest chance of my divulging our erotic tricks, to either man or or woman.

Many who have not tasted our sexual pleasures will call them beastly. They are not. But what if they are? — What are all the physical functions of man and woman, what are chewing, drinking, spitting, snotting, urinating, farting? — What is copulation? is that beastly? — Certainly it is what beasts do. — They will call that natural perhaps, but it's a purely animal act, tho not specially beastly to me. — What is a woman's cunt? — feel it when not recently washed, or when the prick has just left it and the semen is lying thick inside and out. Is that beastly or not? What is the joining of two tongues, the mixing of salivas, the gluing of two mouths together when fucking? — beastly? But there is no harm in these it will be said, it's natural. — Be it so. — So are other erotic amusements equally natural and not more beastly. — What more harm in a man's licking a woman's clitoris to give her pleasure, or of she sucking his cock for the same purpose, both taking pleasure in giving each other pleasure. So if a man plugs a woman's bum-hole with his finger when they are copulating or gamahuching, and so with other sensual devices and fancies, they are all equally natural tho many may not enjoy them. — All are permissible if a couple do them for mutual delight, *and are no more beastly than simple human copulation,* which is the charm of life, — the whole object of life, — and indulged in by all as much as their physical powers permit — yet it's not thought *beastly.*

Imagination plays a most important part in all acts of *love* and *lust,* which are nearly if not quite synonymous terms. All human affections are generated by the act of copulation and its preliminaries. — It is the dull boor, to whom a woman is warm flesh with a hole for fucking and no more — the man who has no imagination, — who is incapable of highly wrought sensual delights and fucks when his seed makes his cock restive, — only thinking of his woman *then,* and rumps her directly he has done with her — who is the *beast* — *for he only does exactly what the beast, the animal does, and no more.* — The couples blest with imagination, they who by various excitements of which a mere animal is not capable, bring fucking to intellectual height, make it a dream of the senses, make lust and love in its sensuous elevation ethereal, a poetic delirium, — *they are not the beasts.* But reduce coition to the mere act, and the inevitable sequel of the seed laying in the cunt, and the prick

[468]

dwindling out wet and flaccid — at once that couple are brought to level of *beasts,* and of those stupid asses who in their incapability of doing more than the horse, the hog and the dog, those who rut and ruddle like every other animal from a louse to an elephant, — such are the *beasts,* and not those who worshipping Eros, raise fucking by their imagination and sensuous preliminaries almost to a divine level.

H*l*n and I after a time laughed to scorn the crude notions of those animal idiots, who think that all is *beastly* excepting simply putting a cock into a cunt — *which is what beasts usually alone do,* — and amused ourselves erotically as we liked. I wholly for love and lust, she for the same and perhaps also a little for money, — all women are alike in that — but at length she indulged with me in Paphian pleasures for love alone — for our mutual satisfaction.

———————

Henceforth the right initials of my women will not be given always, indeed have not been for two or three years past, as the actresses are probably living. The bagnios will also not be clearly indicated, public improvements and public purity!!! have destroyed most of the best central ones, public morals being seemingly not much bettered. — The cosy haunts of Venus, are now nearer the suburbs.

My casual amours with the mercenary fair ones, were also becoming fewer as my intimacy with H*l*n M***w**d increased, for she satisfied gradually every voluptuous desire. Her desires were in fact as comprehensive as my own, tho for a long time she hid them from me; partly thro the habit and cunning of her craft, partly (tho absurd it may seem) thro a strange dislike to disclose her temperament. She however became a willing partner with me in the most erotic frolics. I did not altogether omit my opportunities with women who were not gay, my sexual strength being still good, tho not quite so strong as formerly, and having always taken care of myself, did not look within ten years of my age, and (it must be said) was thought handsome, tho I never thought so myself. Thus I had still good chances of liaisons, tho only able to avail myself of few of those. After a time she told me of hers. I also had occasional orgies with harlots, all of which freaks I told her of. There was indeed good comradeship between us, that of a man and woman who can freely disclose their *lusts,* to each other, or say *love,* for lust and love are synonymous viewed physically, and whatever morality may say about them. The law defines in a degree their relative meanings, but *law* cannot alter the sexual nature of things, cannot alter human instincts.

———————

Occasional amusements brought me on to late spring, then one night at the A*g**e rooms, H*l*n M***w**d spoke to me. I had several times been there solely to look at her, each time she seemed more beautiful than ever, yet beyond nodding or saying, "How do you do," we held no conversation, for she was always surrounded by men. I used to sit thinking of her charms with swollen pego, then either found outside a lady, or once or twice selected one in the room, so that H*l*n could see, and ostentatiously quitted the salon with her. I felt a savage pleasure in doing so. — A species of senseless revenge.

Sitting by my side, "You've not been to see me again." — "No." — "Why?" — "I'm not rich enough." — "Nonsense, you've got some other woman." — "None." — "Come up." — "No, I'll let no woman ruin me." — We conversed further, she got close to me, her sweet smell penetrated me, and spite of myself I promised to see her next day.

She had changed her abode, had a larger house, three servants and a brougham. I had a sleepless night thinking of coming felicity, and on a lovely spring afternoon, hot as if in the midst of summer, she was awaiting me with an open silk wrapper on, beneath it but a laced chemise so diaphanous, that I could see her flesh and the color of her motte through it. Her exquisite legs were in white silk, and she'd had the nattiest kid boots on her pretty little, well cambered feet. She was a delicious spectacle in her rooms, through the windows of which both back and front were green trees and gardens.

"Say I'm not home to any one," said she to the maid. Then to me, "So you have come." — "Did you doubt me?" — "No, I think you're a man who keeps his word." Then on the sofa we sat, and too happy for words I kissed her incessantly. She got my rampant cock out and laughing said, "It's quite stiff enough." — "Let me feel *you* love," said I putting my hand between her thighs. — "Why don't you say, cunt?" — again I was silent in my voluptuous amusement, kissing and twiddling the surface of her adorable cleft. "Oh let us poke." — "Why do you say poke — say fuck," she said moving to the bed and lying down.

"Let me look at your lovely cunt." She moved her haunches to the bedside and pulled her chemise well up, proud of her beauty. Dropping on my knees I looked at the exquisite temple of pleasure, it was perfection, and in a second my mouth was glued to it. I licked and sucked it, I smelt it and swallowed its juice. I could have bitten and eaten it, had none of dislike to the saline taste which I've had with some women, no desire to wipe the waste saliva from my mouth as it covered the broad surface of the vulva in quantity, but swallowed all, it was nectar to me, and sucked rapturously till, "That will do I won't spend so — fuck me" — said she jutting her cunt back from my mouth.

Quickly I arose and was getting on the bed when, "No — take your things off — all off, — be naked, it's quite hot — I'll shut the window," which she did, and throwing off her chemise sat herself at the edge of the bed till I was ready. — "Take off your shirt." — As I removed it, she laid on the bed with thighs apart, the next second my pego was buried in her, and our naked bodies with limbs entwined were in the fascinating movements of fucking. What heaven, — what paradise! — but alas, how evanescent. In a minute with tongues joined, I shed my seed into that lovely avenue, which tightened and spent its juices with me. She enjoyed it, for she was a woman voluptuous to her marrow, my naked form had pleased her I was sure, not that she said that *then,* she was too clever a Paphian for that.

We lay tranquilly in each other's arms till our fleshy union was dissolved. She then — as she washed — "Aren't you going to wash?" — "I'll never wash away anything which has come out of your cunt you beautiful devil, let it dry on, I wish I could lick it off." — "You should have licked me before I washed my cunt, you baudy beast," — she rejoined laughing.

She then came and stood naked by the bedside. — "Aren't you going to get up?" — fearing her reply. "Let me have you again," — I said. — She laughed and gave me a towel — "Dry your prick — you can't do it again." — "Can't I, — look?" My pego was nearly full size. She got on to the bed, laid hold of it, and passed one thigh over my haunch, my fingers titillated her clitoris for a minute, and so we lay lewedly handling each other. Then our bodies were one again, and a fuck longer, more intense in its mental pleasure, more full of idealities, more complete in its physical enjoyment to me, was over within a quarter of an hour after I had

had her the first time. — Nor did she hurry me, but we lay naked, with my prick in her lovely body, in somnolence of pleasure and voluptuous fatigue, a long time, speechless.

Both washed, she piddled (how lovely she looked doing it), put on her chemise and I my shirt. Recollecting my first visit and her hurry, "Now I suppose you want your fiver and me to clear out." — said I bitterly and taking hold of my drawers, for I felt a love almost for *her* and sad that I was only so much money in her eyes. — "I didn't say so, lie down with me." — Side by side on the bed we lay again.

She was now inquisitive. Hadn't I really a lady whom I visited, she knew that I'd had Miss ****** and Polly **** I had had, she'd spoken about me to them. — Why didn't I see *her*. Hadn't I a lady, now tell her — I only repeated what's already told. — Then the vulgar money business cropped up. — No, she never had and never would let a man have her, for less than a fiver. Going to a drawer, she showed me a cheque for thirty pounds and a letter of endearments. "That's come today, and he only slept with me two nights."

She'd soon again my soft yet swollen cunt stretcher in her hand, and fingered it deliciously, never a woman more deliciously. I felt her clitoris, and kissed her lovely neck and cheeks almost unceasingly. — "Give me a bottle of phiz," said she after a minute's silence — I complied. — "It's a guinea mind." — "Preposterous, I'm not in a baudy house." — "It's my price, my own wine, and splendid." — Of course I yielded, who would not when such a divinity was fingering and soothing his prick? It was excellent, we drank most of it soon, and then she gratified me after much solicitation, by lifting her chemise up to her armpits and standing in front of a cheval glass for my inspection, pleased I fancied by my rapturous eulogiums of her loveliness — and exquisite she was. — "You know a well made woman when you see one," she remarked. — Then quickly she dropped her chemise, — she'd not held it up a minute, — it seemed but an instant, — and refused spite of my entreaties to raise it again. — "You have seen quite enough." — Again on the bed we sat, again our hands crossed and fingers played on prick and cunt, — silent, with voluptuous thoughts and lewed sensations.

Then came the letch — "Let me gamahuche you." — "I won't you beast." — "You did the other day." — "Be content then, I won't now" — and she would not. But I kissed her thighs, buried my nose in the curls of her motte, begging, entreating her, till at length she fell back, saying, "I don't like it you beast." — Her thighs opened and crossed my arms, whilst clasping her ivory buttocks my mouth sought her delicious scented furrow, and licked it with exquisite delight. She at first cried out often, "Leave off you beast." Then suddenly she submitted. I heard a sigh, she clutched the hair of my head — "Beast — Aha — leave off —beast — aherr" — she sobbed out. A gentle tremulous motion of her belly and thighs, then they closed violently on my head, pinching and almost hurting me, — she tore at my hair, then opened wide her thighs — a deep sigh escaped her, and she had spent with intense pleasure. [That vibratory motion of thighs and belly, increasing in force as her pleasure crisis came, I have never noticed in any other woman, when gamahuching them, tho most quiver their bellies and thighs a little as their cunt exudes its juices.]

With cock stiff as a rod of iron, with delight at having voluptuously gratified her, wild almost with erotic excitement, — "I've licked your cunt dry — I've swallowed your spending my darling" (it was true), I cried rapturously. "Let me lick your cunt again." — "You beast, you shan't." — But as she denied it, lustful pleasure was still in her eyes. — "Let me." — "No, fuck me." — At once I laid by her side, at once she turned to me — grasped my pego, and in soft voice said, "Fuck me." — "You've just spent." — "Yes — fuck me — go on." — "You can't want it." — "Yes, I do, fuck me, fuck me," — she said imperiously. I didn't then know her sexual force, her voluptuous capabilities, did not believe her. But I wanted *her*, and she was ready. On to her sweet belly I put mine, plunged my pego up her soft, smooth cunt, and we fucked again a long delicious fuck, long yet furious, for though my balls were not so full, I felt mad for her, talked about her beauty whilst I thrust, and thrust, and cried out baudy words, till I felt her cunt grip and she, "You beast, — beast, — Oh — fuck me — — you beast — aher" — and all was done, I'd spent and she with me.

And as she spent, I noticed for the first time on her face, an expression so exquisite, so soft in its voluptuous delight, that angelic is the only term I can apply to it. It was so serene, so complete in its felicity, and her frame became so tranquil, that I could almost fancy her soul was departing to the mansions of the blest, happy in its escape from the world of troubles amidst the sublime delights of fucking.

Then she wished me to go. But only after a long chat, during which she laid all the time in her chemise, her lovely legs, her exquisite breasts showing, she was curious and I told her more about myself than I'd ever told a Paphian. "When shall I see you again?" — "Most likely never." — "Yes I shall." — I told her it was impossible. "Yes, come and sleep with me some night." — Laughing, I said, — "I can't do it more than three times." — "I'll bet I'll make you." — Then with sad heart, and almost tears in my eyes, I repeated that I should not see her again. — "Yes — you will — look — I'm going to the races to morrow" — and she showed me a splendid dress. — "I'm going with *** of the 40th." How I envied him, how sad I felt when I thought of the man who would pass a day and night with that glorious beauty, that exquisite cunt at hand for a day and night.

She was right. I went after a time to the Argyle solely to see her, and visited her twice more, when she let me fuck her till not a drop of sperm would rise from my ballocks. Then I told her that I couldn't (I was then a little hard up) see her again — yet one *night* (I'd visited her previously in the *afternoon*) I told her I had no money, would she trust me. — "Come along all right" — so I went home with her and a few days after called and paid her in the afternoon, and fucked her. Then for months, I went not near her, not even to places where I could look at her, much as I longed to do so.

CHAPTER XLIX

About flagellation. — A peep thro a key hole at Nelly's. — A lubricious poke in an overflowing cunt. — A little bitch missed. — More manuscript destroyed. — Retrospective and prospective. — Doings at a French lapunar. — Luxembourg Elaine. — The sous-maitresse.

In all my amorous adventures, I up to this time had scarcely thought about the effects of whipping the buttocks of male or female, to excite lust or give sexual pleasure. — About this time, either I had read of, or heard this lustful provoc-

[*474*]

ative talked about, I cannot say which, for there is nothing in my notes to tell, altho I began to refer to birching, and find that of Paphians both of high and low quality, I asked if they'd either witnessed or performed the operation, or had themselves been performed on. All, young and old had heard of it — few had witnessed it — one or two said they'd flogged men, and one that she had been flogged by a woman for a lady's delectation. They had birched her till her buttocks bled, and she was paid handsomely for submitting to it. No man was present, it was a lady's letch, and the lady was masked. — This story I did not then believe, but do so now.

Thinking much of this erotic device I sought Camille. I don't recollect having ever before talked with her about flagellation, tho it's scarcely possible that I have not done so, — having conversed with her about all things erotic. She (now years older) smiled, produced birches, and also bunches of string with knots in them, with which she said she flogged the bums of one or two of her friends. That some of their backsides bled, some not, that they all got good cock-stands and spent freely by this backside punishment. And she offered to try on me if I like, which I declined.

Then not quite satisfied I went to Nelly L**l*e, and asked her. She had clients whom she flagellated with birches, and shewed me the rods. Frank as Camille, she told me all about it, how one of her men never got an erection by any other process but by birching, and that without any act or volition on his part, without his touching, or any one touching his prick, he spent copiously under the operation. He was a man between thirty and forty, — and this I didn't quite believe.

All seemed most incredible, so I visited her again one night solely to complete my information upon the subject, and at length stripped, laid upon the bed, and let her birch my backside — bore a few blows, but the pain became so great that I made her leave off. — Nor did I have a stiff stander in consequence, tho I waited to see what the heat on my bum would do for me in procuring it. After an hour, at the sight of her fully haired quim, up rose my prick at once, and as usual in that receptacle, roomy as it now had become, and as no doubt I have told — I had a complete pleasure, but not thro birching.

[I did not apparently think much more about flagellation then, but in a few years I was to be by chance a witness of many birchings, have seen bleeding male rumps, and have seen the wales on women's bums who had been birched. This will be told hereafter.]

She told me on that night I recollect, that she had seen in her own rooms, a woman, flogged by a man who made wales, on her bum, from some of which blood started. Directly he saw that he ceased birching her, frigged himself, spent over her rump, gave her five pounds and went away. — [That I didn't believe but now believe that lust will breed most extraordinary erotic eccentricities.] That in half an hour after the woman grew wild with lust, the birching heated her buttocks, and then that the heat flew to her cunt, and she frigged herself half a dozen times till exhausted. — If this be true, it shews that birching does stimulate both prick and cunt to action, but it cannot make or store up semen in the male — sperm is the only true source of copulative power.

It was a long time since I had seen a man and woman copulating — nor had I as far as I recollect, thought of seeing any such sight again, when one fine afternoon two or three months after the cunt parade, I called on Nelly, who was still living on the third floor of the house where she had two rooms — a bedroom and another which was her kitchen. — Leading out of each other: each room had also a door on to the landing of the stairs — I knocked. — "Who's there?" — there was a mumbling and a man's voice. "It's I" — a pause. — "Wait a minute and I'll come." — said Nelly who knew my voice, and almost at the same time appeared at the door in her chemise. Seeing me she came right out on to the landing holding the door close.

In a whisper. — "I'm so sorry — I have a friend — can't you come back in an hour?" — "No — send him away." — "I can't till he's had me, he is a married man and so good to me — he was just going to do it as you knocked, and will soon go." — "Let me see him do it to you?" — the desire came thro me like lightning. — "I can't, I don't like." — My blood heated to boiling point at the idea. I promised much money, and she consented after hesitation (all said in a whisper. "Wait here." — Going in and closing the door she went thro the bedroom into the other room, the kitchen, the door of which as said also opened on to the stairs, and let me in. — My brain was now filled with lewdness. "Show me his prick — I won't pay you unless you let me see your cunt full of his spunk after — don't wash — don't move if you

[476]

can help it after he's fucked you till I have seen your cunt — make his prick stiff for me to see, — turn him towards me." — "It will be stiff enough," — said Nell with a grin. — "But don't look thro the keyhole directly, wiat till you hear us talking — go down now a few steps, making a noise as if you were leaving, and then come back here softly." — I went out of the room and returning bolted the door, — Nell went back into the bedroom to her friend, fastening the kitchen door which led out of it on her side — with a small bolt.

I knew the door well and the key hole also, having more than once looked thro it, and asked if any one (jokingly) was looking at me when fucking. — Clothes usually hung over the keyhole on the kitchen side as well as on the bedroom side — I took care always that there was no peep hole, not then liking to be looked at when fucking, but thro the key hole knew I could see the bed and half the bedroom. — It was a fine post for viewing the operation. It was a bright day and the white blinds in the bedroom windows shut out but little light. — Clothes hung over the key hole, indeed almost covered the door on the kitchen side where I was, and had he been suspicious and looked thro would have seen nothing. My lubricity would not let me wait, and the instant almost that I heard the bolt shot, I applied my eye cautiously to the key hole. There were no clothes hiding the hole now on the sitting room side, she knew my eye would be investigating every thing almost before she'd got back to him.

He was sitting on the side of the bed about eight feet from the key hole, and my eye, his trowsers down, his shirt tucked up, his big prick nearly at cock stand size flopping on his thigh, his finger and thumb near the tip of it. He was a handsome tall man of about thirty five, I could hear every thing they said for there was but little carriage traffic in the street.

Said he, "It was a man wasn't it?" — "Yes, he will come back in ten minutes — I'm so sorry dear, but he is such a good friend, and I thought you would not mind for once going soon — he's going off by rail and I don't like him to go without seeing me." — "All right," said the man good naturedly. "If he had been a minute later I should have been up you." — Both laughed then. — "Who's in that room? there is some one." — "Oh, it's the old woman who does my washing — let's do it — I don't want him to meet you as you go down stairs." — She then dropped off her chemise,

[477]

went to his side, and took hold of his prick. He pushed his hand round her bum and between her buttocks. She opened her legs, and I saw his fingers approaching her cunt from behind. She pulled up his shirt which had slipped down, and tucked it up in a roll above his navel. — His prick was now standing up like a scaffold pole, — a big one — feeling her had erected it fully.

Then Nelly pulled the prepuce up and down for my edification. He got up, and his trowsers slipped all down his legs — Nell put herself on to the bed kneeling, and I could see the nick of her cunt in the black hairy setting, as plainly as I could my own fingers, tho but sideways. He opened her thighs more, pulled the cunt lips apart, and looked at it, his prick throbbing violently, rose up and fell a couple inches at each lustful pulsation. — Then up into Nelly's quim he drove it, gave a few quick shoves, then pulled it out slowly just to the tip, looked down, plunged it up again violently and did that two or three times, looking at his prick and opening her buttocks with his hands each time. Then he pulled it out altogether — "The other way," said he — Nell knew, turned on her back on the side of the bed, and up into her cunt went his prick — he holding on to her by her thighs, and pulling her to him. — A few shoves, a very low sigh or two, and he was done, had emptied his ballocks, and was laying over her bending and kissing her, whilst she was holding his shirt up high above his arse for me to see that — I saw all this side ways — saw every wriggle —heard every word — and every sigh — every murmur of pleasure.

He withdrew it still stiff, and came shuffling along his feet encumbered by his trowsers towards the washstand which was quite close to my door. The prick was then within a yard of my eye, and I saw sperm drop from it — Nelly did not get up, but with thighs closed turned herself round so as to lay more easily on the bed, her heels towards the door — "Make haste dear, I don't want him to meet you on the stairs, he said he'd be back in ten minutes — and I want to wash before he comes, you have made me so wet." — He gave his prick a hasty wash — I could not see that, but saw him rub his tooleywag (still stiffish) and a big bag of stones, with a towel. He pulled up his trowsers — he had already his coat on, — gave her a kiss, — said he would see her next week, paid her, and went away. — "Make haste down, I don't want him to see you, turn the key twice — that's it, —

good bye love, shut the door, come next week and write when." — Off he went utterly unsuspecting.

Nelly saying, "Oh I must wash" — as he left, still lay there until the door closed, and we heard the clatter of his feet on the stairs — Nelly let me in then, and immediately laid down again. — Mad with lust I rushed to her. — "Oh lock the door first, in case he comes back." — I ran and did so, and back to her in a jiffy, she on the bed had opened her thighs. — The man's footsteps were still audible going down the stairs, whilst all this took place.

I had seen fresh fucked cunts before, but never but once saw one like this — from her arsehole to clitoris, it was one thick mass of glairy or rather gruelly sperm. — Shutting her legs in getting up to open the kitchen door for me to enter, some had squeezed out and her thighs were wet with it. — It clung to the hair round the lips. — It lay in a large globe at the mouth of the prick hole, ready to drop down or roll down towards her arsehole. I stretched her thighs open wide, the cunt lips opened with them — but the whole mouth of the red avenue was still hidden by the sperm — from clitoris to bum hole, from one lip to the other distended as they were, was one mass of transparent viscosity, mixed greatly with opal lumps. The inner lips, — the nymphæ, — were almost indiscernible — tho they are distinctly developed in Nell now. — She was older and her nymphæ had enlarged since I first fucked her.

My prick was throbbing — I felt as if I must spend even when peeping thro the keyhole, and unbuttoned my trowsers, pulled it out, and gave it ease and play. — "Did you spend with him?" — "No. I was just beginning to feel him when he finished, he was so quick." — "Oh! now don't, — you'd better not — oha — you baudy — beast you." — I had seen Nelly's eyes and knew the look. — Randy and without premeditation, I thrust my pego up her into the man's sperm, and fucking violently, Nelly and I spent together the next minute — I kept questioning. — She ejaculating, "Baudy — beast you — oh — yes — he spends always — spends — a lot — aharr — eher — ah."

When we came to our senses I was anxious and feared consequences, and still up her with prick still stiff, her cunt yet constricting, as if to incite me to continue the exercise. — "I hope he is all right in health," I said — "I think he is so — but I can't be sure, what made you do it." —"You know him?" — "I've seen him regularly for a couple of years, he is married and has a family he says, and comes to town purposely to see me." — I felt then easier in my mind. — Nelly was tightening her cunt still and pinching my prick with it, whilst we were talking. — My pego responded by keeping nearly at cockstand. — "You spent with *me* almost directly I put into you." — "Yes, he'd been tormenting me before and made me want it, he always gamahuches me till I'm nearly mad, and leaves off just before it comes." — "You want fucking again Nell." — She laughed, pushing my prick out in doing so.

Then Nelly shifted herself lengthways on to the bed, leaving a trail of spunk on the coverlid as she did so, then throwing off my coat, I jumped on to the bed — and saw her cunt still flooded with sperm, — now, mine, and his, and hers mixed — fell on her, and was up her cock exhauster with a dash. — "Oh what a baudy beast you are." — "So are you." — "What a lot of spunk's on your cunt." — "He always spends a lot, and so do you. — Oh! oh you beast." — "Is his prick bigger than mine?" — "Oh — same size you — beast — fuck — ahr — fuck" — said Nelly who was unusually hot arsed and lewed tongued, and in a minute we spent together again, talking about her friend's copulative qualities, to the *last* — till our power of talk left us, and we could only ejaculate baudy words, as our seminal juices squirted and oozed and mingled.

Out came my doodle soon — reeking to my balls with spermatic fluids. "You have dirtied the counterpane," said Nell. — I washed my prick in a hurry and Nell did the same to her cunt. — Seeing her black motte over the basin, — "Don't soap it," — I said still feeling lewed — "let's see if the spunk comes out." — Nell did exactly what I asked her, she always did, it was one of her great charms. — She obeyed me unhesitatingly like a French whore, without sham or affectation. There were now very few sperm lumps I recollect, it had got churned up, and came out mixed on to our genital bushes, had rubbed nearly dry on *my* balls and *her* thighs, and all and every where on those surfaces was adhesive. Then for a while we talked and all about the man, his way of fucking, his prick, his balls, his sperm, and everything else about him. — We laid upon the bed whilst we talked. My prick had a soft, lewed irritation on it tho it was not stiff, as if his sperm had left his lust in me as well as my own. Then we moved head to feet of each other lying sideways. — I saw Nell's large, fat lipped, dark haired cunt, under the strong light of the summer afternoon, my head lay on one of her legs, with one hand I propped up the other, which opened the gap, whilst she gently frigged me — she was now a splendid frigger. — Then my prick went into her mouth, and whilst my fingers travelled round her hard smooth bum and thighs, and I gloated on her cunt, titillated the clitoris, twisted the curly thatch, or probed its depth, she gently fetched the sperm out of me into her mouth and at once I fell asleep my head upon her thigh. When I awoke, she was seated at the side of the bed quietly twiddling my cock — she never could keep her hands off of that — and would play with it for hours, twiddling it from the time I first saw her till I left; keeping up voluptuous irritation and desire, even if I had no intention of further pleasure in her charming, soft, pulpy, yet powerful cunt, for its muscularity at the crises merited that description.

There was something in the smoothness of the cunt filled with sperm, a voluptuous lubricity together with the idea of another man's prick having just been up it, which excited me tremendously — I seemed to participate in his pleasure whilst having my own, and as I thrust, could almost feel his thrusts in her — his prick seemed to be up her as well as my own — there was a maddening voluptuousness about it which sank deeply into my mind, and made me desire to taste such pleasure again. — And I have been able to repeat the pleasure, tho I had resolved for many reasons not to do so, after my frolic with the man at Sarah F**z*r's. — It was now some years since I amused myself with him.

I went to see Nell again to talk about it, hoping for the chance of having her after her stalwart friend, but failed — I said I'd wait for another man, but she put me off. Now she went out a night, which she formerly used rarely to do, and that did not suit me. At length she one day said, — "I can't get a gentleman for you to do it after, but there's a man who has begun doing it before gentlemen, will you have him?" — "Is he a bugger?" — "Oh no. He's a poor man, a workman about thirty years old." She did not know how he came to be fucking before gentlemen, a girl had told her of him and that he had a very big prick. — I refused to see him.

Then I went abroad and did nothing worth telling about there. — On my return I found Nell had just got a little servant girl. I could have her if I liked she said, but she'd have nothing to do with it — I persuaded the lass easily enough, and she frankly admitted that several had had her. But the extreme smallness of her cunt was a wonder — I tried to fuck her, but getting my prick in was impossible, to get two fingers up her was as much as I could do. I have had many girls as young as she but none with such a small vagina, tho the cunt in its entirety looked large enough. I doubted if she really had been fucked. Two or three days after, going there to try her again, she had run away, and stolen some of Nell's clothes.

———————

[More manuscript must be destroyed for mere abbreviation will be useless. — Eighty pages must go to the flames. — The narrative thus curtailed cannot show clearly the gradual development of abnormal excentric tastes, and necessitates an epitome of some years to supply the hiatus. Some of the most conspicuous incidents I shall keep as originally written or nearly so, and they will take their place chronologically.]

———————

[Some years before I met H*l*n M***w**d, I had been frequently at ***** and more frequently at bordels than for many years previously. I principally visited one where there were (and still are) about twenty women on the establishment, who sit nightly nearly naked in the saloon, a bewildering, voluptuous sight. Idealities becoming an increasing source of delight to me, and abnormal erotic letches and fancies coursing through my brain whenever I was in rut, variety in form and color of my women, and in their postures, being to me more charming than ever, I sought this lapunar. There I had one, two, or three women, or more at a time and got much voluptuous enjoyment — had all those voluptuous preliminaries which a stiff prick suggests, and never hurried myself to the delicious crisis which for a time destroys desire.

[It is doubtful however whether I got more pleasure, from having three women together, than I got by one alone; so soon as my prick had stretched the cunt, and fucking had begun. But idealities in the preliminaries, and even during the consummation of love, are much — perhaps almost every thing in love. — Is it not the beauty, the taste of the eye, the thoughts, which more frequently than otherwise make the

[482]

sole difference in the pleasure between fucking one woman and another — makes the difference between a cunt which a man thinks pretty, and one which he thinks ugly?

[There was one woman at the lapunar whom I selected often for her exquisite form and sweet face, named Elaine — a Luxembourg woman. She took a fancy to me, and after a time told me much of the inner life of a brothel, of its internal economy, and the habits of the inmates. She told me of those who were much sought after and always had five, six or seven men a night. Elaine saved money, and in three years became *sous-maitresse,* and was then supposed to have ceased fucking *there;* yet I had her there once or twice, on the sly. She then left and set up a bordel of her own. One named Hortense succeeded her, and then Alexandrine.]

CHAPTER L

H. and I get confidential. — Her voluptuous abandonment. — Our erotic philosophy in practise. — My sensitive pego avowed. — My seminal ejaculations. — H. likes a big pego. — A big one up her. — I up after the big one. — Mutual delight in a semenalized vagina. — Reflexions thereon.

H*l*n and I now began to understand each other (tho not yet perfectly). She knew I was not easily humbugged, so abandoned largely Paphian devices, treated me as a friend, and her circumstances compelling her to avoid male friends, and not liking females much, and it being a human necessity to tell some one about oneself, I became to some extent her confidant. She then had a charming well furnished little house, replete with comfort, and her own. I at times dined with her there. She was beautifully clean, you might have eaten off her kitchen boards, and the same throughout the house. She was an excellent cook, cooked generally herself and liked it, was a gourmet. It was delightful to see her sitting at table, dressed all but a gown, with naked arms and breasts showing fully over a laced chemise, with her lovely skin and complexion, eating and drinking my own wine, she passing down at intervals to the kitchen. We eat and drank with joy and baudy expectation, both of us — for she wanted fucking. — Every now and then I felt her thighs and quim, kissing her, showing my prick, anxious to begin work even during our dinner.

Afterwards adjourning to her bedroom, we passed the evening in voluptuous amusements — we had then but *few* scruples in satisfying our erotic wishes. — Soon after had *none*. — How she used to enjoy my gamahuching, and after a time abandoning herself to her sensations she'd cry out, "Aha — my — God — aha — fuck spunk" — and whatever else came into her mind, quivering her delicious belly and thighs, squeezing my head with them, clutching my hair, as her sweet cunt heaved against my mouth when spending, till I ceased from tongue weariness. Sometimes this with my thumb gently pressing her bum hole, which after a time she liked much. Then what heavenly pleasure as I put my prick up her, and grasping her ivory buttocks, meeting her tongue with mine, mixing our salivas, I deluged her cunt with sperm. — Never have I had more pleasure with any woman, with few so much.

Resting, we talked of *her* baudy doings and *mine* — of the tricks of women. — We imagined baudy possibilities, planned voluptuous attitudes, disclosed letches, suggested combinations of pleasure between men and women, and woman with woman — for Eros claimed us both. In salacity we were fit companions, all pleasures were soon to be to us legitimate, we had no scruples, no prejudices, were philosophers in lust, and gratified it without a dream of modesty.

One day I told her again of the sensitiveness of my pego, that with a dry cunt the friction of fucking sometimes hurt me, that my prick at times looked swollen and very red, unnaturally so. — French harlots — more than others — I found washed their cunts with astringents, which my prick detected in them directly, so when I was expected, I wished H. not to wash *hers* after the morning, her natural moisture then being so much pleasanter to my penis. — No saliva put there, is equal to the natural viscosity, mucosity of the surface of a vagina. — But from her scrupulously cleanly habits, I had great difficulty in getting her to attend to this.

That led one day to her asking, if I had ever had a woman who had not washed her quim after a previous fucking. She then knew my adventure with the sailor, that at Lord A's, and at Sarah F**z*r's — but not the recent one at N**l*e L**l*e's. — I told her that I had not with those exceptions. — "I'll bet you have without knowing." She told me of women where she had lived, merely wiping their cunts after a poke, and having at once another man, and of its not being discovered; of she herself once having had a man fuck her, and his friend who came with him, insisting on poking her instantly afterwards.

We talked soon after about the pleasure of fucking in a well buttered cunt, and agreed that the second fuck was nicer if the cunt was unwashed. I racked my memory, and recollected cases where I had had suspicions of having done so. H*l*n who always then washed her quim, again said it was beastly. — I said that if more agreeable to me and the woman, there was nothing beastly in it; nor cared I if there was, fucking being in its nature a mere animal function, tho in human beings augmented in pleasure, by the human brain. "So why wash after, if the two like it otherwise?"

About that time I found I had not quite as much sperm as in early middle age, testing that by frigging myself over a sheet of white paper, and wished to see what a young man spent both in quality and quantity. We chatted about this at times, and one day she told me she had a man about thirty-five years old, who visited her on the sly, but very occasionally; a former lover who had spent a fortune on her (I know since his name, his family, and that what she told me was true). She let him have her still, for gratitude. He was very poor but a gentleman, and now he helped her in various ways. It struck me she liked him also, because he had as she told, a large prick. I found she had a taste for large pricks, and described those of her former friends who possessed such, in rapturous terms. This man spent much, I expressed a desire to see it, and after a time it was arranged that I should see this cunt prober, him using it, and her cunt afterwards, but this took some time to bring about. In many conversations, she admitted that she had not more physical pleasure from a great prick, than from an average sized one. "But it's the idea of it you know, the idea of its being big, and it's so nice to handle it."

I went abroad as said, the incidents there will be given hereafter. On return, I went soon to H. and told her what tricks I had been up to, and our conversation went to the subject of my sensitive prick and semenalized quims, those I'd seen, and what she had promised should come to pass.

One afternoon — this was some months later than what I shall soon tell about — I was in her bedroom as arranged, he

[*485*]

was to have her in the adjoining room. She placed the bed there, so that when the door was very slightly opened, I could see perfectly thro the hinge side. We were both undressed, she with delight describing his prick, repeating her cautions to be quiet, and so on. — A knock at the street door was heard. "It's his," said she, and went down stairs. — Some time passed, during which I stood on the stair landing listening, till I heard a cough, — her signal — then going back and closing my door, I waited till they were up stairs and I heard them in the back room. Opening mine ajar again I waited till a second cough. Then in shirt and without shoes, I crept to their door which was slightly open.

They were sitting on the edge of the bed, she in chemise, he in shirt, feeling each other's privates. His back was half towards me, her hand was holding his large tool not yet quite stiff; but soon it grew to noble size under her handling. Then he wanted to gamabuche her, she complied, being fond of that pleasure as a preliminary. He knelt on the bed to do it, tho he'd wished to kneel on the floor. — She insisted on *her* way, to keep his back to me. So engrossed was he with the exercise, that when her pleasure was coming on, I pushed further open the door (hinges oiled) and peeping round and under, saw his balls, and that his prick was big and stiff — I was within a foot of him. — But he noticed nothing, all was silent but the plap of his tongue on her cunt, and her murmurs. When she had spent once, he laid himself by her side, kissing her and feeling her cunt, his stiff, noble pego standing against her thigh, — she pulling the prepuce up and down, and looking at the door crack. After dalliance prolonged for my gratification, he fucked her. She pulled his shirt up to his waist when he was on her, so that I might contemplate their movements. I heard every sigh and murmur, saw every thrust and heave, a delicious sight; but he was hairy arsed, which I did not like.

Then said she, "Pull it out, he'll wonder why I have been away so long; you go down stairs quietly, and I'll come soon." He uncunted, they rose, I went back to my room. He had been told that she was tricking the man then keeping her, and knew that a man was then in the house, and *he* there on the sly was happy to fuck her without pay — for he loved her deeply — and not at all expecting or knowing that his fornicating pleasures, were ministering to the pleasure of another man.

Then on the bedside she displayed her lovely secret

charms — a cunt overflowing with his libation. — It delighted me, my pego had been standing long, I seemed to have almost had the pleasure of fucking her as I witnessed him, and now to fuck her, to leave my sperm with his in her, came over me with almost delirious lust. "I'll fuck you, I fuck in it," I cried trembling with concupiscent desire. — "You beast — you shan't." — "I will." — "You shan't." But she never moved, and kept her thighs wide apart whilst still saying — "No, no." — I looked in her face, saw that overpowering voluptuousness, saw that she lusted for it, ashamed to say it. "Did you spend?" — "Yes." — "I will fuck." — "You beast." — Up plunged my prick in her. — "Ahaa" — sighed she voluptuously as my balls closed on her bum. I lifted up her thighs which I clasped, and fucked quickly for my letch was strong. "Ain't we beasts," she sighed again. — "I'm in his sperm dear." — "Y — hes, we're beasts." The lubricity was delicious to my prick. "Can you feel his spunk?" — "Yes dear, my prick's in it. — I'll spend in his spunk." — "Y — hes — his spunk. — Aha — beasts." — All I had just seen flashed thro my brain. — His prick, his balls, her lovely thighs, made me delirious with sexual pleasure. — "I'm coming — shall you spend H*l*n?" — "Y — hes — push — hard — ahar." — "Cunt — fuck — spunk," we cried together in baudy duet — her cunt gripped — my prick wriggled, shot out its sperm, and I sank on her breast, still holding her thighs and kissing her.

When we came to, we were both pleased. — "Never mind H*l*n if we are beasts — why say that if you like it?" — "I don't." — "You fib, you do." — After a time she admitted that the lasciviousness of the act, had added to the pleasure of coition greatly — to me the smoothness of her vagina seemed heaven. — I was wild to see all again, but circumstances did not admit of it then, yet in time I did, and one day after he and I had had her, "Go down to him," said I, "Don't wash, and let him have you again on the sofa." — The letch pleased her, he fucked her again, and thought he was going into his own leavings. When she came up, I had her again, I was in force that day. — Her taste for this lubricity then set in, and stirred her lust strongly, — she was in full rut — I gamahuched her after she had washed, thinking where two pricks had been, and half an hour after she frigged herself. Whilst frigging, "Ah! I wish there had been a third man's spunk in it." — "You beast — ah — so — do

I." — She rejoined as she spent, looking at me with voluptuous eyes.

We often talked of this afterwards, and agreed that the pleasure of coition was increased by poking after another man, and we did so when we could afterwards with her friend and others. Sometimes it is true she shammed that she allowed it only to please *me,* but *her* excitement when fucking told me the contrary. She liked it as much as I did, and it became an enduring letch with her.

Whether H*l*n or any other woman — I've known several who liked it — had increased physical pleasure by being fucked under such pudendal condition, it's not possible to say. — With me owing to the state of my gland, no doubt it did. But imagination is a great factor in human coition, and by its aid, the sexual pleasure is increased to something much higher than mere animalism. It is by the brain that fucking becomes ethereal, divine, it being in the highest state of excitement and activity during this sexual exercise. It is the brain which evokes letches, suggests amatory preliminaries, prolongs and intensifies the pleasure of an act, which mere animals — called "beasts" — begin and finish in a few minutes. Human beings who copulate without thought and rapidly *are like beasts,* for with them it is a mere animal act. — Not so those who delay, prolong, vary, refine, and intensify their pleasures — *therein is their superiority to the beasts* — the animals. What people do in their privacy is their affair alone. A couple or more together, may have pleasure in that which *others* might call *beastly* — although *beasts* do nothing of the sort — but which to them is the highest enjoyment, physical and mental. It is probable that every man and woman, has some letch which they gratify but don't disclose, yet who would nevertheless call it *beastly,* if told that others did it, and would according to the accepted notions — or rather professions — on such matters, call all sexual performance or amusements *beastly,* except quick, animal fucking. But really it is those who copulate without variety, thought, sentiment or soul, who are the *beasts* —because they procreate exactly as *beasts* do, and nothing more. — With animals, fucking is done *without brains* —among the higher organized human beings, fucking is done *with brains* — yet this exercise of the intellect in coition is called *beastly* by the ignorant, who have invented a series of offensive terms, to express their objections. — Their opinion of the sweet congress of man and woman —

which is love — is, that it should be a feel, a look, a sniff at the cunt, and a rapid coupling — *very like beasts that!!!*

CHAPTER LI

H.'s protector. — H.'s absence. — Her voluptuous needs. — A donkey prick'd lover. — Caution advised. — Her excuses. — Donkey prick exercising. — The pleasure given by large pricks. —Harry's first sight of a pudenda. — Masturbated by his master. — Protector impecunious. — My visits permitted. — A looking-glass bought. — A garden party. — The swing. — A frisky spinster. — Baudy books lent. — Free and easy conversations. —

Then I saw H. at longer intervals, for reasons of no interest now — and had her after her lover as I must call him, whose name and family I was told, didn't believe, but found by mere chance to be actually true. — Born of wealthy parents, educated at Cambridge, inheriting a fortune, he spent it on women and H*l*n had her share. Beyond this the man had not a vice. — His family allowed him thirty shillings a week, he lived on it as well as he could and would have married her on that. He did also law writing. — He doted on H. — was her go-between, ordered, paid, borrowed, pawned, and did for her anything, everything she asked him. He gave her his money if she wanted any for he adored her, his compensation being to fuck her on the sly for love. — I often felt sorry for the man who was both in voice, manner, and even in dress a gentleman.

Sometimes now she was left alone for a week or two or longer by her friend, tho he idolized her, — but he couldn't help his absence. Then the strong promptings of her carnality placed her in great temptation. Frigging did not satisfy her, her cunt yearned irresistibly for the male. My talk, she averred, so excited her, that when she thought of that alone it led to her giving way to her passions. That I don't believe, tho it might have added fuel to the flames. — She took a fancy after a time to another man. This came about through going to see a dashing gay woman whom she'd not seen since she'd been in keeping. The man therefore was a mere chance acquaintance. He was known in Paphian circles for his physical perfections, and the desire for his very big prick really was the reason of her wishing once to see him, and then for a time her taking to him. But more of this hereafter.

I afterwards witnessed him using his tool. It added greatly to her pleasure to know that I was a spectator. The deed done, he gone away, she came to me, her eyes humid with recent pleasures, still lustful. We fucked, and talked. The idea of my prick being in the avenue his had quitted increased the pleasure of us both when fucking — hers I think more even than mine. Soon after our eroticism entered on even a higher phase of luxuriousness.

When she had thoroughly made the acquaintance of the man with a bigger prick than that of her lover — the biggest she had ever known, she said — she described it rapturously and the delight she felt when it was up her. The gentleman with whom she lived as already said poked her twice daily when there, her poor lover fucked her frequently, I gave her my doodle then once a week, besides gamahuching her which I never failed to do, and in addition to all this she frigged herself nearly every day. — Yet all this did not give her an excess of sexual pleasure, with all her fucking, frigging, and gamahuching, she looked the very picture of health and strength, and had both.

She had met as said this man by chance, was told about him, and it was the idea of his size which affected her sensuous imagination. — He was, she found in the long run, a mean hound, who enjoyed her lovely body yet was often half fucked out before he had her, and scarcely made her the most trifling presents. The size of his prick had made him notorious among gay women, she discovered at last, and he got more cunt than he wanted for nothing. I often advised her to cut him, for she told me all about her affairs with him; not that I preached morality but saw that it was a pity to risk an evidently good chance of being settled comfortably for life. Yet if she wanted another man — if variety was essential, "Have him but beware," I used to say.

I expressed one day a wish to see his pego of which she was always talking. She was proud at that, her eyes glistened voluptuously as she told me of the arrangements for my view. She had long liked telling her letches to me — a willing listener who had no canting objections. — Tho I cautioned her to take care not to be caught by her protector. — She used to reply — "What have I to live for except it. — Philip and I have no society, we can't afford it now — it's a year since I've been to the theatre, — there is nothing but my house, and playing at cards and fucking, to amuse me." — "My darling, fucking is all in life worth living for, but be prudent."

The plan of her house then, owing to the way she and her protector occupied the back bed room, did not favour a secret peep at her with the man, who had become knowing and wary in such matters, by passing most of his times with harlots, and she had a difficult task in humbugging him. It was to come off in the parlour. I at a signal was to go downstairs from her bedroom barefooted, peep thro the parlour door left ajar, was not to make the slightest noise, and retire directly the consummation was effected.

On the day, I was waiting expectant in her bedroom, heard footsteps enter the parlour, went down cautiously to the half landing — heard: — "Ahem" — went lower — heard baudy conversation and then, "It's right up my cunt." Knowing from that that my opportunity had arrived, I pushed the door slightly more open. — She was on top of him on a sofa, her face hid his from seeing me. — She was kissing him, her chemise was up to her armpits, her bum moved slowly up and down shoving a thick prick up her. "It's not stiff," she said angrily. "You've fucked before today." — "I've not fucked since yesterday." — She'd uncunted him as she spoke, and out flopped a huge prick not quite stiff. — There she lay over him thighs wide apart — cunt gaping wide — his prick underneath it. — It was a dodge of hers to gratify my sight, to show me the procreator she was proud of enjoying.

Then she got off, and stood by the side of him, still leaning over and kissing him, to hide his eyes whilst she frigged him. His prick soon stood and a giant it was. She got on him again, impaled herself, and soon by the short twitching shoves of her buttocks, and the movement of his legs (in trowsers) I saw they were spending. — In a minute his moist tool flopped out of her cunt, and I crept upstairs leaving them still belly to belly on the sofa. She had told him that her sister was in the bed room, to which I soon after heard her coming up, and him going down to the kitchen. Oh the voluptuous delight in her lovely face as she laid on the bedside to let me see her cunt, and the delight she had as my prick glided up it softened by his sperm, and her lewed ecstacy as my sperm mixed with his and hers in spasms of maddening pleasure — for now she delighted in this sort of copulation, said it made her feel as if she were being fucked by both of us at once.

This spectacle was repeated afterwards on a bed in the garret — but after a time she sickened of him and saw him no more. — She however still had her large-pricked poor lover, who one or two years after died, and as I have narrated what I saw and did after him, shall tell no more. She had at various times with string measured the length and circumferences of both of these pricks. The way to get proper measurements was carefully discussed by us. I have the lengths and circumferences of the two pricks, and of Phil's all measured when stiff, round the stem half way down — and from the centre of the tip to where the prick joins the belly.

The biggest of the two pricks did not however nearly come up in size, to that titanic cunt stretcher which Sarah F**z*r enabled me to see thro the peephole at the baudy house some years ago. Tho I had no measure of *that*, it was much larger than any I have ever yet seen — there could be no mistake about it — [I have seen a couple of hundred pricks, just before their owners put them into their women].

This big-pricked man was a coarse looking fellow tho stalwart and handsome. He would stop at the house and feed at her expense, and scarcely give her a present, yet he was not a poor man, but a man of business as she knew, and as I took the trouble to ascertain. H*** told me soon all about him. I was certainly the only confidant she could have in this letch. — He was reckless enough to let a youth from his place of business bring him letters whilst at H.'s and she got acquainted with the lad.

H*** told me one day that she was in bed with big-tool, when the youth (then only sixteen years old) brought him a letter. They both lewed, began chaffing the boy, asked if he'd ever seen a woman naked, and pulled the bed clothes down so as to show her naked to her waist. She permitted, nay liked the lark, and admitted to me she hadn't then seen the prick of a lad of that age, stiff or limp. — "Show her your cock and she'll show you her cunt," said big-tool. The boy, glowing with lust approached the bed. H. opened her thighs invitingly, his master got up and pulled the lad's cock out of his trowsers as stiff as a horn, she opened her thighs wider, the man gave the lad's prick one or two frigs, and the

[492]

sperm squirted over H.'s thighs. — This, as I happened to be there, was told me the day after it occurred.

This frigging of the boy led as may be supposed to some erotic episodes. — As a matter of course it stirred H.'s lust, she had never been fucked by one so young, and before long his thin prick and her cunt were introduced to each other. The narrative of a consequent episode in which I was a participator, as written at the time, is reserved from the flames.

A little before this H.'s protector was as I'd guessed in money difficulties. She told him that an old kind friend wanted to visit her, that money must be got somehow or they must part, and he consented to me — and only me — visiting her. She had told him I was too old to poke, and only gamahuched her. Of course I've only her word for that. I never saw him or he me. He was very unhappy about it, but sooner than let her again be gay he would consent to almost anything. — Money and other circumstances, however, prevented my seeing her more frequently, tho I went with greater ease of mind. She was also not under such anxiety, and we had our frolics with increased pleasure — for her lascivious delights with me were greater than ever.

Later on she told me her protector was getting as erotic as I was, tho he was a very much younger man. My impression is that she taught him. — Sometimes it was: — "What do you think? Phil wanted me to do so and so with him?" — or: "We poked in this attitude the other day." — Or: "He likes hearing how formerly I've been poked," and so on. — Then she and I had great pleasure in doing the same things together.

One day I wished we had a looking glass to see ourselves in when fucking. I had told her of the glasses at French houses. — She, excepting in a cheval glass, had never seen herself reflected in copulation, and wished she could. — I offered to buy one, but what would Philip say? "He'd be delighted, we often wish for one when I tell him I've heard of such things, but he's hard up just now — he knows you are the only man who visits me." — He didn't know of her lovers. — Then I paid for a looking glass which she got. It was nearly as long as her bed, was placed against the wall, the bed nearly close to it, and henceforth we could see our every movement.

I shall never forget the day the glass came. We put it up together at the right level, directly we'd done so we rapidly stripped start naked, mounted the bed, and fucked contem-

[493]

plating ourselves, and that afternoon not a drop of sperm was left in my balls. I gamahuched her, and she frigged herself as well, looking in the glass. At my next visit I heard that Phil had done the same, that night after night they couldn't sleep for the rutting state the glass put them in, so hung a curtain over the glass when they wished to excite themselves no more. To see H. frigging herself then was indeed a great treat. Her delight was to make me kneel on the bed naked facing the glass, with my stiff one which she held in one hand, whilst she frigged herself with the other, looking in the glass all the time. It was to me a delight — for her form and face were lovely, — to see her in the venereal spasm — an exquisite sight. — Unfortunately however, the bed was so placed in the room then, that I could not see either bed or reflection from the only door available for peeping, hence the fucking exhibitions were always given in other rooms.

Early in June, one of the most singular liaisons in my career occurred to me — I have thought other events singular, and perhaps they were as much so but they don't seem like this, for I am at an age which made this unexpected. I don't look my age, I am told, nor do I feel my age, and can oftentimes tail an appetizing woman three times in an hour and a half — yet it's nearly forty years since first I fucked a woman.

I was at an afternoon in some grounds near London, and there was a widow with her only daughter who was born in India, her father a colonel. They were in comfortable circumstances, in good society, but there were whispers about the daughter, that her marriage had been broken off mysteriously, that she was a little frisky, had been at a theatre alone with a gentleman, was a bad temper, gave her mother much trouble, — and more obscurely hinted — was fond of a doodle on the sly. I thought nothing about it, it not concerning us, yet it had seemed to me there had been a look in her eye when I conversed with her, which was indicative of desire. I'd found she'd laugh at risky conversation if without frank impropriety, and would egg a man on by questions of assumed ignorance, — then suddenly, "Oh! you're really too bad," and she'd leave — tho her eye gave no signs of her being shocked. Edith H**r*s*n, — not her name tho phonetically resembling it — knows a lot, some men said, and they suggested the possibility of her having been fucked in India.

She was handsome, well grown, and about seven or eight and twenty, had dark eyes and hair, and a remarkably beautiful foot and ankle, which she displayed as liberally as society permitted. — Tho I didn't then meet her frequently, there was something about her which made my pego tingle when I did. Her eyes used to fix on mine with a stare which gradually softened, and then her face flushed and she turned her eyes away — I thought nothing of that tho at times I wondered if she'd been fucked — dismissing the idea at once.

There had been a cold collation and champagne galore, the company were distributed afterwards, mostly sitting about the grounds, when wanting to piddle, I sought a retired corner and passed a spot where surrounded by shrubs was a swing, and she all alone just swinging herself as high as she could. She swung forward just as I approached her, and her white petticoats floating up showed much of her calves. My voluptuous instincts blazed up at the sight of the legs and pretty feet, I bowed my head and tried to look under, involuntarily saying, — "Oh! what a lovely pair, shouldn't I like . . ." — then I broke off recollecting our positions. She tried to stop the swing, I watching till she alighted. All this did not occupy a minute. — She'd taken champagne freely I think — I too much, and with a swelling prick was risky. — She perhaps excited by wine, had at the moment a warmish cunt. — "What would you like?" — said she laughing and looking full at me. — "To have seen a little more." — "Ohoo! oh!" — said she — then both laughed heartily. — "What are you laughing at?" — "At what I should have liked." — "Oh! what a strange man you are, you speak riddles." — "Don't you understand?" — "No." — "You do" — and we looked in each other's eyes again. She looked voluptuous, I fancied.

"You're alone, are you going to run away like Miss *****?" — A lady known to both of us. — "Not with a married man." — "Ah! she *was* foolish, for she might have seen him on the sly." — "Oh! what a horrid suggestion." — "Well — married men are safe flirts, they never tell." — "No, they daren't," said she, and smiled, whilst looking me full in the eyes again, and then colouring up. "I must go to Mamma, she'll wonder where I've been." — "No she won't,

she knows, and I guess." — Laughing, off she went, I piddled, and went back to the guests.

Soon after I was walking with her and talking about the
young lady, she wasn't surprised, the girl was always flirting
with him and had been caught reading objectionable books,
and I asked Edith to describe them. — She'd be very sorry
to do so. — "Oh — you've seen them then." — No she
hadn't, she said in a startled manner, but knew she'd trapped
herself — I harped on the subject. "If I lend you a book will
you tell me if it's objectionable or not?" She would, and
wouldn't tell her mother, nor show it. — "It's all about
love — undisguised love — and pictures some might call
naughty — objectionable." — "Oh, lend it me." — "I'm
frightened — if you're found with it, it will be serious — if
not, only you and I will know it, and oldish men know how
to hold their tongues." — "Do lend it me — no one shall see
it." "It's all about lovers amusing themselves, — but I
mustn't lend it you." — "Oh you're joking I know, — but do
lend it me." — This is only a summary of a long
conversation — for I was cautious, fearing she might be shy.
Now she was wild to see the book, and must have guessed
it was a baudy one. — "I can't send it and can't take it to
you" (I didn't visit them). — "I'll meet you out." — She's
game thought I, and concluded she'd have her avenue fric-
tionized by the male apparatus. — Then she agreed to meet
me two days after, she was going shopping without her
mother.

The party was over, her mother had a carriage, and a seat
in it was offered me — in the carriage in the dusk I squeezed
her hand, she I thought returned it, I pressed my legs against
hers and she didn't move hers away — mine were between
the two women. — I went on talking to Mamma and taking
no notice of the daughter — Mamma asked me in when they
alighted, but I declined, and as I handed Edith out pressed
her hand saying, "I wish the swing had shown more." — She
only said "Thursday" and we parted.

I was at the place, but didn't expect her. — Flirts with
their cunts telling them they are neglected — as they do to
spinsters approaching thirty — are sometimes after food,
champagne, and suggestive gossip, apt to get lustful thrills,
and listen to talk, and to say things which next day they
regret — I took a *Fanny Hill* with me. — Punctual, there she
was, saying she'd not expected *me*. "I've got the book, don't
be angry afterwards with me." — "I won't." — "But I want

a word with you first, get into a cab, for five minutes, we can't talk in the street." — Into a four wheeler we got, I told her more about the book, avoiding baudy words, that the pictures showed "people making love." She put it into her pocket rapidly, I got a kiss, said, "Oh that swing, it's made me want" and we parted naming a day to meet for her to return it. — Afterwards I thought of the risks and wondered at myself — for I'd no defined intentions. The pleasure of lending a real lady a baudy book was my delight — the idea of she and I reading books on sexualities in common — such of course would be the case — delighted me.

She met me and returned the book carefully sealed up. — "What do you think of it?" — "It's disgraceful, you'd no business to lend me such a book." — "You asked me." — "I didn't expect it was one like that. — What must you think of me?" — "Nothing, you've seen such before." — "I'm sure I haven't." — This sham of hers went on a little time in the street. — "I won't lend you any others." — "Oh!" she said eagerly, "have you any more?" — I asked her to meet me somewhere where we could see them privately, but she wouldn't answer, I got her into a cab, kissed her, and I tried a feel unsuccessfully. Would I assure her it was not so improper as the other — a precious transparent sham. — I told her it was not, but was baudier. She took it and another day returned it.

I was on reflexion staggered with what had occurred, so unlooked for, so unpremeditated. The secret baudiness of the affair, my perpetual wondering whether she'd had the doodle up her, kept up my excitement and the lady's also, I suppose. She remarked that she could talk to me as a father, tho few fathers I apprehend have talked to daughters so. Within a few week I'd spoken of the pleasure of frigging and gamahuching and offered to instruct her. She said she didn't believe it, but should wait till she was married, and so on. — She steadily refused to go to a house with me. Then I left town in the belief that she was a cunning bitch, who'd been fucked, frigged and gamahuched, was trying to entrap me into some compromising action, and resolved never to meet her again. For a couple of months abroad I was nearly chaste, and then returned to London.

CHAPTER LII

*In Spain. — Two very small juveniles. — At the bull
ring. — The Count's mistress tailed. — An immoral
family. — Choice of two cunts and one rectum. —
The young lass selected. — The young bugger
rejected. — A little prick felt. — Soldiers' women at
Gib. — Groping at C*d*z. — H.'s lascivity and
confidences. — An evening with Camille and
H*l*n. — A cuntal purse again.*

[To abbreviate, I had retained nothing relating to two months
abroad this summer, but on reading it before destroying the
manuscript, decided to retain it; so interpolate it here.]

In the hot season, wrong for travelling, I went to Spain —
indeed this year was pregnant with erotic novelties to me. In
large towns I always found a bordel of some sort, and saw
there native beauties, even if I did not tail them. My visits
were generally in the evening. I saw some of the poorest, as
well as the high priced "Mujeres mundanas."

At M*d**d I saw two little girls in the street — they had
been walking about in the day like ordinary children of the
poor — so young that I took no notice of them. — That evening not thinking of amatory business, I saw the two, and
fancied one looked invitingly at me. I turned round, they
were looking back and one came back to me. — Was it their
instinct that I needed a cunt and made them come after me?
Certain it was that I had neither sensuous thoughts or sensations at the moment, but now came a rush of lust, a delicious
feeling in my prick, a desire to see them naked, and I offered
a small sum by show rather than by word, which was at once
accepted. I only knew a few words of their language then,
but in every country learn quickly, those which express the
sexual organs, and their pleasure.

Off they went rapidly through several streets, till I had lost
my way, and began to reflect when I found the quarter was
a poor one. Under a huge archway of a shabby looking big
house they turned, I found them waiting, they spoke and
made signs, but I didn't understand, half feared a trap, didn't

now feel sure they were punks — which was foolish — I might be robbed, murdered even, so hesitated. They went to a dimly lighted stone staircase, I didn't stir, they came back, spoke, gesticulated — I was to follow them — then — no one being about — I stooped to feel the tallest one's cunt. Quickly she lifted the only dress she had on, and opened her thighs for me to feel her cunt. — It was hairless. My prick then throbbed, and under its impulse I went up to a fourth or fifth floor, an old woman came out of a room, opened a door, nodded at me, the girls spoke to her, back she went, and in a second I was in a large desolate bedroom with scarcely an article of furniture.

I sat on a chair, felt both their tight little cunts, there was no virginity, made signs that I wanted them naked, and in a second both were so. — They scarcely had any clothing on, one only her frock, one had no stockings, both had no bonnets or head dress. — It was scorching hot weather. The bed looked so miserable that I wouldn't lay down upon it, and put the taller of the two on to a large square heavy table which was in the centre of the room. — There was but one miserable tallow candle, and by its aid I looked well at the biggest girl's cunt, which had plumpish lips and not a vestige of hair. Then I put the other one on the table, and found her cunt as bald. — Then one girl held out her hand for money, and I gave them what I promised — not quite eighteen pence English money — each looked at the other's gift, seemed satisfied, and both got on to the wretched dirty creaking bed — then from their small stature, and the look of their cunts, I guessed they neither were more than twelve years old — I tried to ascertain that but couldn't make myself understood.

Fear of disease came over me — taking up the candle, and out of my pocket a few pesetas, I managed to make known that I needed another light. The shorter girl, naked as she was, took the candle and money, and going across the landing to the old woman's room, returned with a small oil lamp. Left in the dark excepting what light came into the room from the star-lighted heavens, and still half in fear, I felt my companion's cunt, which civility she reciprocated by feeling for my cock. Directly the second light was brought she began to unbutton me. When it was visible, both girls handled it at the same time in a knowing way, smiling and speaking I know not what.

It wasn't quite stiff, but soon became so as I felt their two

[499]

bums during their investigation of my doodle. — Directly its rigidity was complete, the eldest threw herself again on the bed and opened her thighs, but the bed so disgusted me, that shaking my head I pointed to the table, whereon she mounted the table by the help of a chair, then I put the other girl by the side of her, and fetching the dirty bolster put it under their heads — they laughed and seemed to enjoy the position.

Fear of disease again came over me, so as well as I could, I tried to ask whether they were in health, and suppose they understood as both nodded and repeated "Bono — Bono." — Then one held the candle at the other's cunt, and my shrinking cock swelled up again, for the quim looked all right and inviting. The lass pulled open her quim lips wide for my inspection. Both now laughed loud as if it were a capital joke, then both sitting upon the table felt my machine again, and I their cunts with both my hands. — Then one snuffed the candle with her fingers, and wiped them on her hair.

Prudence still prevailed. — Shaking my head I replaced my truncheon, which seemed to annoy the lass at whose split I had actually for a moment pointed it. The one spoke of the "Senora" and I think was going to call her for testimony to their healthiness — "bono," so very often being said, whilst the other officiously got hold of my tool and nodded her head. Then I thought to let her masturbate *me,* laying hold of her hand to indicate my wishes, she began at my tool. I sat down, she got off the table, and then I thought I'd frig *her.* Nothing loath, she sitting on my knee let me, the other silently watching the operation, which went on till my girl I suppose feeling the pleasure, interrupted me, and saying in Spanish, — "No, fuck me" — brisk as a flea she got on to the table again and placed herself there with thighs wide apart.

I'd got my prick now to fever heat — prudence adieu — next minute her cunt was stretched by my pego, and the randy little child spent as she received my injection. I could see it in her face, feel it in her cunt. The other girl stood quite close looking on at the operation.

There was no towel, and she with my libation trickling on to her thighs, ran naked across the landing to the old woman and fetched a dingy napkin. Cooler now, I looked at both their diminutive quims, one only I found had little black hairs just showing on the motte. I guessed and understood them to be thirteen years old, perhaps younger, for hair grows early on the cunts of southerners. Both I'm sure had had plenty of fucking. The one I hadn't tailed then sat on the pot on the table, and I made her piddle. Not knowing my way back I asked them to show me the way. The old woman appeared as I was leaving and I gave her a trifle, I suppose for the room. The girls went ahead of me, an empty cab appeared and giving the girls a tip I got into it, naming the street in which my hotel was.

Some days after at S*v***e when leaving the bull ring, I saw a handsomely dressed, middle-size woman, exquisitely beautiful, come out. Two or three Spanish gentlemen were with her all talking and gesticulating good humouredly. Money was exchanged, and I guessed they were settling bets. She seemed excited and delighted, parted with them, and not finding a conveyance, which seemed to annoy her much, stood fanning herself and hailing every vehicle. I had one and stopped the driver, fascinated by her beauty, feeling sure she was a Cyprian and lust then began to tingle my pego. I felt such a passionate desire to possess her, that reckless of consequences, no knowing more than a few words of the language, I made a sign that a seat was at her service. — The next minute she was sitting beside me.

Then was the difficulty. — She spoke — I shook my head. — She laughed, spoke more, I intimated I didn't understand. — "Holy Virgin" she said tapped me with her fan, told the coachman something and off he drove rapidly, — she chattering to me all the way — I trying to make myself understood. The chariot stopped on the outskirts not far from the ring at a decent looking house. By that time I had reflected, and after helping her down, bowed and was going away tho my prick was erect. But she laid hold of my arm and pointed to the house, making at the same time a movement of her mouth as if kissing. — It was irresistible and I followed her to a suite of rooms on the first floor.

The rooms were elegantly tho not expensively furnished. A maid, well dressed, appeared, then disappeared with the lady, soon returned, and I found to my great relief she could speak a little French. The Senorita hoped I'd stay and eat with her (it was half past five) and I began to fancy I'd made a mistake and that the lady was no common courtesan. — Circumstances, I said, made it impossible for me to stay.

[*501*]

The maid went out and returning, said her mistress would soon be ready, would I wash (the heat and dust was great in the ring). I accepted, not having any idea where I was to go, and astonished, was shown into the room where was the lady in chemise, finishing her toilette She laughed, pointed to the basin, the maid poured out water, left the room, and there was I with this exquisite creature in her chemise brushing her hair, looking ever and anon at me, and smiling.

I now felt sure she was a mistress. I didn't want words, knew that the fee would be high. So when I'd washed I put on my coat — which was all I'd taken off. — She said, — "No — No" — flung both arms round me, and kissing me lusciously, intimated I was to take my things off. The peep at her breasts as she kissed me made me desire her immensely, I kissed her passionately in return, then took out my purse and showed two gold coins, intimating that that was all. She laughed immoderately and nodded, speaking all the time, but I didn't understand a word.

Then she began to undress me, laughing all the time. It was irresistible. — I stripped to my shirt and laid down, she beside me. Then she embraced me in the usual fashion, opened her thighs for me to look and feel, examined my prick, laid down again and squeezed my piercer, smiling at its prompt erection, whilst I felt her cunt. We were coupled immediately, her cunt seemed divine as I spent in it, and in a few minutes all was over. She was energetic in love making and spent with passion. We both washed — then at her cunt I looked more tranquilly, saw her naked form — and a lovely form she had. — She would not let me go, dragged me down on the bed again, made me gamahuche her, then fuck her, and by that time she was satisfied. Laying by the side of me, a thigh thrown carelessly over mine, she called the maid, asked the time, ejaculated, "Holy Virgin," said I must go and began to dress herself rapidly. I the same, we kissed and I departed. The servant told me the Senorita was mistress of the Count **** and told me to go off in a particular direction, which I did. Next day I left M*d**d. A more lovely creature I never embraced. She had crisp short hair round her bum hole and a little on her buttocks — tho she said she was only twenty-one. — Her face was a dream of beauty.

A week after, occurred one of the strangest incidents of my career. Walking up a back and steep lane on the margin tho in the city of G**n*da, strolling with no object excepting to see the city; standing at a sort of cottage door was a lad of about fourteen, who to my astonishment beckoned me and smiled. — I stopped, he beckoned me in, and curious I entered, utterly unsuspecting till well within the entrance, where he exposed his prick. I shook my head, he called out, and a girl of about the same age appeared, together with a stout, bloated yet not bad-looking woman seemingly about thirty-five years old. She spoke, and tho scarcely understanding a word, I found unmistakably that she had come to offer the *girl or herself.* Then to my utter wonderment, by the aid of about half a dozen words, and by gestures, I found that she was the mother of both, that I might have either or all of them, a choice of two cunts and one anus. Whether she was really the mother I cannot of course say, but I repeated in Spanish the words, mother, son, daughter, pointing to each successively, and to all she said "yes" and nodded.

I had had no desire for fucking, nor did the family facilities stimulate me. It really shocked me, tho there was nothing to be shocked at. Shaking my head I gave the woman a few *reals* and departed, she seemed much pleased. He had replaced his pendant tool.

I walked on thinking of this jumble of whores and bugger, (such I now supposed the youth to be) my mind concentrating itself on the girl — a poor sallow creature tho she was. — I wondered what sort of a quim she had, thought I might never have the chance again of seeing that of a Spanish girl of fourteen, my fancy pictured it, I thought till my cock stood, then went back and saw a big common Spaniard talking at the door. I waited in the distance till he went off — he passed and scanned me. Then I wondered if there was danger, but dismissed the idea, for at ten o'clock on a sunshiny morning all must be secure — I entered the house, the little bugger still at the door — thought he was my aim, but shaking my head and saying the single word "girl" — he bawled out, and the two females reappeared smiling. Soon mother and son left, the daughter remained, and in a minute was naked on a miserable bed.

I got out of her somehow, mainly by counting on my fingers, and by signs, coupled with a few simple words, that she was fifteen. She'd three times the quantity of hair on her cunt that an English girl of that age has. She wasn't lewed

[*503*]

in manner, seemed dejected, indifferent. — There was no water, so I made her know by signs that I wanted to wash, and naked she went out and returned with some in a large earthen pan.

She washed her cunt, I my prick, then after inspection of her carnal aperture, and a look at her mouth which had good teeth, I intimated by signs that I wanted to be gamahunched.

She had been as slow and solemn as if at her funeral, but now burst into a laugh, knelt on the bed rapidly, and took my pego into her mouth with quite an air of delight; the next minute it was erect and she handling it with admiration. Then she laid down saying (I suppose) "Come on" but I had fear and kept repeating "doctor, doctor," the only word I could to intimate doubts of her health. — When she understood she ran to the door shouting, "Madre." In came the woman, they both chattered to me at once I know not what, but they understood, for the mother put the girl on the bed, and holding open her cunt lips invited me to see her gap, emphatically repeating "bono, bono." — I nodded satisfied, and off the other went. The I reflected, decided to leave, but again lust came on stronger. I felt and looked at the youthful slit, then yielded and fucked the girl.

I paid her, and when leaving the lad appeared and asked for money. An age had passed since I'd felt or seen a boy's cock. Without a word, without thinking scarcely, a libidinous curiosity sprang up, I pointed to his prick, at once he pulled it out, I handled it and his balls till it stood, but did no more having no pederastic tastes. He like his sister had more hair for his age about his genitals, than we English have.

Shortly afterwards at G**r**t*r, my taste for poor Paphians seems to have revived. [I like always to see all classes of the needful, much abused, pleasure-givers to the male.] Gay ladies of high class I saw not at all, and one evening dressed in my shabbiest to make myself look poor and common as might be, I went up to the quarters where Tommy Atkins gets his sexual solace, and was astonished at the really fine women I saw there. Coarse and common enough in manner, yet good in form I found the two or three whom I stripped for luxurious contemplation at a shilling a piece [it seems incredible to me now that price.] Then at a somewhat better house, having no fear there of Paphian ailments — for Tommy's women are medically cared for well — I fucked a couple at half a crown a piece saying I couldn't afford more. I enjoyed them much, delighted also with the economical instruction.

I fancy they would have taken a shilling for their pleasure from any soldier. Those I had were Spaniards, I noticed a Negress, but whether a punk or servant know not. Then having tailed none of the so called lovely girls of C*d*z tho I felt one peripatetic's grummit on a moonlight evening — a cheap delight, what charm is in a cunt! — I sailed for home, bringing away with me the baudiest Spanish words for genitals and copulation which I made one of the soldier's women spell for me, as I wrote them down. (The others couldn't write or read.) This paper I lost, and the terms I cannot now recollect. Now I take up my narrative on my return to England.

I had told H*** now all the erotic incidents of my life. She, with her fertile brain, voluptuous temperament, and experience in amorosities, both approved, desired to emulate them, and herself to invent. She wasn't — as already said, — at first frank about her letches and lusts, hiding them somewhat and throwing the suggestion of their gratification upon *me* making *herself* but the complaisant partner; but the mask was now pretty well removed — tho probably women in all classes never quite tell their letches or the truth about their baudy wishes — who knows? When guessing her desires, after talking about some luxurious fancies, I passed them over then finding I did not initiate anything, she referred to them again on other visits, and I met them by some such questions as, "Would *you* like so and so to gamahuche you" — or "Like another man or woman with us?" — or "Like me to see you fucked by another?" — "Yes I should" came frankly at last. Then it was, "Let's have a woman to gamahuche me, but *you* ask me to let her, I don't want *her* to think I wish her." Singular modesty, it seemed to me.

Then we got our lascivious tastes gratified and to the full. That kept me from other amours, and to her almost alone, for she had youth, supreme beauty of face and form, was clever, conversable, voluptuous, and enjoyed every lewed device both in body and mind — aye to the extreme. She agreed with me that every amorous trick might be tried, and we gratified our desires to the limits of possibility. I wanted no other woman, excepting when away from town, or on a sudden letch, or out of mere curiosity. These I nearly always told her of. Some of our amorous play I preserve in

[*505*]

this narrative, some will never be even whispered about — the knowledge of it will die with us.

H*l*n soon had great pleasure in talking of her former tricks — would tell what she'd done or had heard of — reserve was utterly gone between us. She pronounced mine to be a most wonderful amatory career, when she had read a large part of the manuscript, or I had read it her whilst in bed and she laid quietly feeling my prick. Sometimes she'd read and I listen, kissing and smelling her lovely alabaster breasts, feeling her cunt, till the spirit moved us both to incorporate our bodies. Her sexual passion was strong, her strength great. I have fucked her thrice, and gamahuched thrice, yet seen her frig herself after that, and all in four hours, without showing a sign of fatigue. — [Five years after she was as strong.]

Having now no harlot acquaintances, it was a real pleasure to her to have some one to talk with on these subjects. — Telling her of Camille one evening and talking of gamahuching, she said, tho the little servant whom I fucked had done it, it was a long time since a *woman* had gamahuched *her*. She liked a fine, fattish woman to do it to her and took a letch for Camille from my description of her. Camille was long past forty yet wonderfully well preserved, and one evening solely to gratify H*** I got Camille to visit her.

We had a lovely little dinner at H*l*n's, then adjourned to her bedroom, both women stripped and looked at each other's cunts — they were so quiet about that — and then Camille gamahuched. "Fuck her, fuck her whilst she's licking me, let me see it," H. cried — But I wouldn't — I couldn't bear my sperm to go into any cunt but her own, and after she'd spent thrice under Camille's active tongue, I fucked her. Then after half an hour's rest Camille again licked H.'s quim till she screamed with the exhaustion of pleasure, and Camille could lick no longer. After repose and wine I wanted Camille to suck *me,* but she refused, telling H. she'd never done it. — A lie, for she has many times minetted me tho she never liked it, and always wanting me to fuck her. — Poor Camille liked me to the last.

Again I then stroked H*** who excited by wine and lewed to her marrow made Camille feel her buttocks whilst fucking, she grasping Camille's motte, or feeling her buttocks whilst she was handling my stones. "What a lovely skin," cried H. as she felt Camille's buttocks. Indeed she had still that exquisite skin and her pretty, tight, deep cunt. Never were two more lovely skinned women together. I then fucked Camille at the request of both of them, which finished the night. Taking Camille home in my cab I paid her handsomely. She could do nothing but talk of the unparalleled charms of H. I never brought them together again. H.'s letch was satisfied, and she did not want gay women.

I told her one evening how I had turned N**l*e L**l*e's cunt into a purse, and she wondered if her own would hold as much. I had doubts, for it did not feel to me as large inside as the other woman's did, but I had H*** naked one day and tried. The silver brought was carefully washed, and the argental cunt stuffing began. I was so delighted and she also with the experiment, that I prolonged the work, not putting in five and ten shillings at a time as I did with the other, when my lustful curiosity was to ascertain a fact, but a shilling or two at a time only, feeling them of her cunt, then glorying in seeing her exquisite form promenading with the silver in her. When about forty shillings had disappeared up the belly rift, I put my prick up her, and felt with its sensitive tip the difference between a shilling which it struck against, and the soft round compressive end of her cuntal avenue. She was as pleased with me at that trick as I was. I nearly spent, excited by my operations, and now with the idea of spending against a shilling up a cunt, but didn't — wouldn't.

I resumed the silver stuffing, she her ambulations, and it is extraordinary that within a shilling or two, she held in her cunt the same number that L**l*e had. She several times walked up and down the room with her cunt so full, that I could see the silver when I gently opened one lip. — The grip and tenacity of her Paphian temple seemed truly wonderful. — What muscular force, what a nut cracker! — But that indeed I knew, for her cunt was perfect in every way, a pudenda of all the virtues, powers, and beauties for fucking, or doing anything voluptuous with — a supreme pleasure giver.

Then over the basin she squatted to void the argentiferous stream. It was beautiful to see her squat, her thighs then rounded into the fullest, loveliest form, it always delighted me to see her in that attitude washing her cunt or micturating. The silver tumbling out of her gaping hirsute cleft, with a clatter against the basin, made us laugh, some refused to quit the lubricious nook in which it found itself, I felt up for it, and she at last by muscular contraction of her cunt aided by her fingers, got it all out. Then with a syringe she purified the receptacle, we went to the bed, and after a little mutual fingering, fucked, — the baudy trick just finished enhancing our sexual delight.

The silver was washed and stored away. "When you pay any one, tell them that the silver's been up your cunt." — "You beast, I will." The servants and a female friend — for she had now a female friend — were told of this. We talked about it all the evening, and she put one shilling well up for me to touch with my prick which I did, but did not spend whilst the shilling was in its lubricious receptacle. [I wish now I had, it would have been something to remember.] Eighty-six or -seven shillings did her cunt hold.

CHAPTER LIII

Frisky spinster Edith again. — Pitch and toss at pudendas. — Naked harlots scrambling. — A Hylas suggested. — Eugêne, the used-up sodomite. — Naked amusements. — Curiosity gratified. — Mutual feebleness. — A masculine sixty-nine. — Sappho. — An erotic triad. — Double minetting. — Eugêne dismissed as not fit. — Pleasant conversation. — Thumb-frigging a clitoris. — My erotic philosophy. — Foolish prejudices. — A demi-mondaine on cock sucking. — Three men to one woman. — An orgy. — About baudy house peep-holes. — A hairy-rumped Spanish equestrienne.

Then I resumed my acquaintance with the frisky spinster, again I met her in the daytime, always lent her baudy books and photographs, and we had free talk. She seemed to desire to know every sexual habit of man with woman, particularly those with harlots. Nothing in my career has been so curious. — With widows and wives I've had *risky* talk, but with a young woman, born, bred, and educated a lady, have I used now the baudiest words, whilst she listened pleased and enquiring, but never once used such words herself. This also was generally in broad daylight and in four-wheel cabs.

It stimulated me at last to try forcibly to feel her, and induce her to go to a house with me. — All was useless. — One day I said if she wouldn't go, I'd fuck a woman directly I'd left her. — "Very well," said she — I never got a feel higher than the calf of her leg and that she resisted unmistakably.

So I refused to meet her or lend her more books, yet there was a novelty, a stinging salacity in the meetings which pleased me much. Once or twice, I met her in society or at places of amusement, but always with her mother. What knowing glances we exchanged!

Then on my way to the sweet south, to get the sun in the months it's denied us here, for a few days sojourn we stopped at **** where again my resolution gave way, and I found myself at the friendly lapunar tho I was tired of it. Change again gave to me an erotic novelty.

Tired, worn out, ill, and alas getting older, I was nevertheless again at the lapunar one night, with my pocket quite full of franc pieces. Entering the saloon, there sat about twenty women, with boots and stockings on, otherwise naked as born — for those who had gauze about them threw it off directly I was seen. — Some lifted up a thigh, some pulling their quims open, all putting themselves into such voluptuous attitudes as they thought best suited to exhibit their charms. Sitting close together as they in the circle were, each tried to entice me to select her for my pleasure in erotic amusements.

I contemplated them for awhile. It was a lovely voluptuous sight, carnal, baudy, but what of that? Then taking out some francs I threw them up in the air. — With outstretched hands, the whole of the naked beauties rose to catch the silver shower, and the next moment were on the floor scrambling in a naked heap.

Such a mass of delicate flesh was there crowded — big bums sticking up, knocking against each other, white breasts flashing glimpses of dark hair in armpits, dark stripes between oval buttocks, hairy triangles of all colors at the bellies, all shewing and moving about in rapid combinations of form and grouping, a kaleidoscope of cunts, bums, and breasts. With chatter and laughter they scrambled till all the coin was grabbed. Then they rose to their seats, ready for another scramble.

Then it was, — "Ici" — "Monsieur," — "Je n'ai rien gagné." — "Voila." — "Ici, regardez." A dozen of them opening thighs wide, pulled open their cunts to entice me. I pitched franc after franc at cunts, sometimes hitting the mark, sometimes missing. The franc was hers at whose cunt I threw it, and another franc if I actually hit the gap. A babel of tongues. — "Ici" — "Ici, monsieur," as each opened her thighs wider in hope of getting a franc pitched well between them. — The mistress and under mistress looked, on, standing at the back of me and laughing.

Then was a pause to chat, and look, — what a sight was the circle of naked women, all exquisitely clean and perfumed, with their hair well dressed and ornamented. — Silk stockings, white, black, grey, pink, blue, and red, mottes, with thatch like flax, and of every shade from brown to black — notches varying from pink to dark crimson, and from a delicate slightly haired slit with an imperceptible clitoris, to gaps with strong protuberances, and nymphæ large enough to frictionise another cunt, and give delight to both the wriggling embraces of tribadism. — On the words — "Open your cunts — catch" — open all went with shouts of laughter, and again the silver coins hit thighs, cunts, mottes and bellies, till with a last shower of silver in the air, all grouped scrambling on the floor. Again, bums, thighs, and breasts in a struggling mass of female form and loveliness, cunts more or less visible in all directions. What a picture it would have made, had it been possible to have fixed the group and photographed them.

Selecting one I went upstairs with her. "I'll make my toilet" quoth she. — "Wash outside, but not up your cunt, I love a cunt with its natural juice — I'll wash it myself" — laying her down, I with a wet towel wiped the face of her vulva from clitoris to anus only, and having told the chambermaid I wished a woman to come to me with her cunt full from fucking, amused myself with this girl — who had got four francs in the scramble out of the hundred I had thrown — till another woman was announced.

About this time in one of the confidential chats I had with my friend the *sous-maitresse,* she told me secretly that a young sodomite could be had there, but notice some hours before must be given, that my countrymen occasionally indulged that way — if known there, not otherwise — and that one had been so amusing himself that night. I declined, having no tastes that way, yet had a long conversation about the subject, for my curiosity was aroused. At times afterwards I had wished I could see this funny product of humanity, yet without any desire to avail myself of his services, passive or active. The matter had for some months passed out of my mind, but this night was evoked again by what occurred.

"Mademoiselle Sappho is engaged, shall she come in after," said the chambermaid entering the room. I refused, being in no hurry, not being yet tired of the woman with whom I was amusing myself — besides my erectile power seemed in abeyance, the young lady having been frigging my tool uselessly. — Then after a minute's reflection "I'll see her, before she meets the man." — Just then the *sous maitresse* appeared at the door, beckoned me, and on my going to her, whispered, there was a young man a "beau garçon" there, awaiting a monsieur who had never come, would I have him, all was quite safe. — With a spurt of lustful curiosity roused on the moment, I accepted, dismissed my companion, and was for a few minutes alone in a curiously excited state of expectation.

Whilst waiting in a feverish state of mind, one minute regretting, the next wishing him, and scarcely knowing what I should do when he appeared, wondering what sort of animal he was, whether if I should ask him to undress or to show me his genitals, how he would behave, and so on, all thoughts tumultuous, the door opened, the *sous-maitresse* appeared smiling, followed by Hylas as naked as he was born, who came in with a skipping, springy step, and a smile on his face like that of a ballet girl. I never was more astonished in my life.

He was a shortish, square built, well set up man, looking about twenty-one or -two years old, and had dark, crisp, curly hair, and dark eyes. His body was well fleshed, well shaped, plump indeed and as white as a woman's. It had not a vestige of hair upon it. He had no moustache, or whiskers, or hair anywhere, excepting on his head, in his armpits, and round his prick, which was set in a neat little, crisp bush. I had expected to be shocked, I scarcely knew what, but had felt sure I should dislike him. In an instant all was changed, and I felt as pleased in contemplating his nude figure, as I have at seeing the Apollo Belvedere, and other glorious examples of Grecian skill in portraying the naked male. — Nor had I the slightest feeling of any other sort, all erotic notions had for the moment vanished. That soon changed, he stood for a minute staring at me, then without word or summons addressed to him, came and sat on the divan by the side of me, and put his arm round my neck. That instantly I dislodged and moved away, and for a minute we sat looking at each other.

Gradually, all sorts of lewed ideas arose in me. — Many a prick had I seen of late years, some of which I had longed to handle — a fugitive desire, gone as soon as formed — but then there were no opportunities. — Here one was. — Within a few feet of me sat a man of perfect form, indeed every way "beau garçon" and hanging out from the crisp little hairy thicket a nearly white, thickish prick about three inches long, with a "leetle" bit of red tip shewing.

Then desires rushed tumultuously through my brain — I longed to feel it, to frig it, stiffen it, see it spend, watch the sperm flow, see his vibrations of pleasure, hear his murmurs, watch his face as the ecstatic crisis overwhelmed him — and at once I grasped his prick, uncovered the tip and squeezed his balls. — Yet not a word had been spoken till he said, "Won't you take your clothes off like me?" Obeying his suggestion, rapidly I put myself as naked as he was, eying him all the time whilst undressing but not speaking. — He laid himself along the divan, and gently pulling his prepuce up and down, smilingly watched me till I sat myself naked by his side, and seized again his prick. Then he seized mine — all dislike, all repulsion had gone for the minute, I seemed to be doing the most commonplace thing in the world — curiosity had me.

"Let's go on the bed," said he. Obeying, we placed ourselves side by side — our flesh touching everywhere — feeling each other's cods — with seeming curiosity he *mine* — I *his* with curiosity mingled now with strange voluptuous wants. Then I mounted him as reminiscences rose up in my brain of doings with the young man at F**r*rs years ago. — Belly to belly, breast to breast, we were, I clasped his buttocks, laying between his thighs as if fucking a woman — our pricks and balls touching, laying in a heap together, neither prick stiff — then I moved with a fucking motion. "Look in the glass," said he. — Turning both side ways, our genitals in a heap, the sight overwhelmed me, yet lust, a desire to Socratize him — as nearly as I can define my sensations — scarcely entered into the confused and lustful combinations, caused by my clasping him as if he were a woman.

Then I recovered my sense, had clear intentions of doing things, and by his side I played with his prick, frigging it gently, lifting up his thigh to look at his balls, and then again went on frigging, but his prick remained limp. Then at my command he frigged himself — and seemingly to stimulate himself felt my pego — but all was of no avail, there it lay like a sausage.

Then curiously I looked him all over, stood him up, turned him round as I should a woman, saw that his feet were white and clean, his toe nails carefully trimmed. Never in my life before had I so inspected a naked man and it pleased me much, and to my astonishment. Then we talked, he suggested this and that, knelt and turned his rump to me, shewed me how he stooped to be sodomized. — "I will suck your prick, and you shall suck mine — it is delicious," said he.

After washing our pricks we laid down together head to tail, and taking his prick in my mouth I minetted it. The smoothness pleased my palate, nothing ever seemed more delicate in my mouth, it excited my saliva, it felt like a jujube between my tongue and palate, and so we played long with each other. But I couldn't make his erect, nor he mine, tho we lay enjoying our mouthfuls for a quarter of an hour perhaps. Then I told him he was frigged out, and not worth his money. I wished to feel and frig a stiff one, and had no intention of doing anything else, tho he politely suggested his anus. He said he should be better another night and could not account for his condition then. — "You have been frigged before tonight" — he denied it — and still we sat feeling each other's pricks.

Then a knock came at the door. — Opening it, there stood a little dark-haired woman — Sappho — who had just been fucked. — "Yes full of sperm" — a fine young man had had her — "full of *fat* sperm" — Glad of the change, I laid her on the bed and tired to insert my little machine. The sight of her cunt filled with healthy issue pleased me, I saw in imagination the man enjoying her and ejaculating his semen, but all failed to rouse me, I was done for and wild. — "Shall I minette you?" she asked. — Hope rose again at the proposal — hastily I washed my cock, laid down, and she kneeling with her rump towards me, began the delicate exercise, she licked round the glans, tickled the frenum, ran her tongue lightly up and down the stem and over my balls, and then engulfed it in her mouth. — At times it softly rubbed her palate, then came out of her mouth immediately to disappear, then rubbing it gently between her tongue and palate, sometimes she gently squeezed my balls, sometimes the

tongue ran quickly just over the delicate little tip slit, sometimes she pushed finger on to my bum hole, whilst I looked
at her plump round buttocks, and the black haired, red split,
now gaping and dividing — its colour spoiled by the glaze
which covered it.

It wouldn't stiffen, tho faint pleasure began to steal
through my refractory tool. "I'm too fatigued — you can't
make it." — "Mais si, si, j'en suis sur — soyez tran-
quille — ne pressez pas" — and again my penis was hidden
in her mouth — Eugêne stood looking on, then placing his
finger under my balls, gently intruded one into my anus. —
A voluptuous shiver ran thro me — fancies whirled through
my brain. "Kneel over me and put your prick in my mouth,"
I cried.

He sprang on to the bed smiling, delighted with the invitation, knelt over me, and in a minute his limp prick met my
lips — Sappho had to move slightly to let his legs come over
me. His body then hid her head and breasts and I could see
her no more, but by turning my head could see her buttocks
and sperm-slobbered cunt, now half hidden by the left bum
cheek, I felt the delicate movement of her mouth on my
prick which began swelling with pleasure, then feeling under
his balls and guiding it, his prick dropped well into my
mouth, I clasped him round his smooth buttocks with my
left hand, pushed my right hand fingers up her glutinous
cunt, he began fucking my mouth, I clipped his pego with
my tongue, her bum began to wriggle as my three fingers
stretched it, and vigorously she worked at my penis which
was swelling fast. Imagination played its part in me, all was
soft movement, and the two pricks and two mouths worked
silently.

Suddenly my prick throbbed, a painful pleasure crept
along it, I groaned, still his prick in my mouth. He cried
out, — "Foutre — foutre" her buttocks wiggled, I twisted
my fingers about in its lubricity and my spunk ejaculated
into her mouth. — Now faint with pleasure I noticed nothing
more but the lubricity of her vagina, the swelling of his
prick between my lips, and the soft squeeze of her mouth
still minetting out the last drop of my libation, whilst my
pego slowly dwindled.

All was tranquil for awhile. Artists in eroticism, they perfectly well knew when to move. — Then all rising, quickly
she left the room, Eugêne threw himself by the side of me
feeling his own prick not yet stiff. My prick shrinking to a

bag of skin, had a chilly sensation on it, due to the evaporation of her saliva. So I lay speechless till she returned smiling, with her mouth and cunt purified.

I spoke. "You are frigged out Eugène, you have no spunk in you." — "Ah yes — tonight so — but another night, Ah! you shall find me strong." — "Go now." — These were the last words spoken, I paid him and he departed naked as he came.

Sappho now stood by the bed side, wetted a towel and washed my prick and balls, I pissed, and we both laid down. — The pretty little damzel was curious, talkative, and very communicative. Almost directly I reversed her, placing her head at the foot of the bed, keeping mine at the top. So placed she laid hold of my prick and I felt her cunt conveniently placed both for feeling and seeing.

She not being dressed had not been present at the money scramble, and was sorry. How much had I thrown, every girl had got some thing but four. — She of course not — did I often do that sort of thing? — I was talked of in the house as good to the women — that I liked spermatized cunts. — She was sorry I had not stiffened, for she had never had it done her when full by another man. — She would have liked it, like to try, did I always like it so? Our talk ran then about the funny letches of men and women — she evidently liked the conversation and had only been in the house six weeks, this was her first house. The chambermaid afterwards told me that what she had said was true, that she had come there "an innocent." — The *sous-maitresse* said the same thing to me also. — "Have her, you will find her charming, she is fresh."

We talked thus for half an hour in the warm room. Her clitoris was a large one, and I had, with the usual restlessness of my hand when on a cunt, rubbed her clitoris continuously with my thumb. After I had fingered and satisfied my curiosity about the innermost parts of her sex, I ceased thumbing, tho laying hips touching, side by side, it was quite easy. — "Go on rubbing," said she. — "What, softly like that?" — "Yes, don't leave off." "Do you like it?" — "Yes." Replacing the thumb I rubbed on and we went on talking. She hadn't spent *that* night, once a night she always spent, and often twice, it depended on the man, she told me. — Soon after she lent her head back on the pillow, then rose and sucked my prick for a minute, relinquished it, fell back, and saying, "Go on," closed her eyes.

I watched her carefully, voluptuously curious, but not too much excited — for fucking alas, was not for me any more that night. I rubbed gently with my thumb a long time in unbroken silence. Then her breath shortened, her belly heaved, her thighs twitched and still she lay with eyes closed. "Quicker," said she, and laying hold of my thumb she placed it in a little lower down — quicker and harder I rubbed till her thighs and belly became agitated, that indescribable jogging, heaving, wriggling came on with sighing and murmuring soft sounds of pleasure. "Her — er. — He — her" and clutching my prick, she subsided into quietness, and half sleep. Thus we lay without speaking some minutes, I looking, watching her tranquillity, pleased at having given *her* a spend, voluptuous fatigue of body on *me* — mind tranquilly voluptuous. — "Aha — a — a — a — a" — said she at last, with a prolonged sigh and rising. — "You haven't spent," said I. — "Yes yes — feel me — look." — Her cunt was running over with her juices it was wet outside as well as up — I saw, felt it, and was delighted. — "I never frigged a woman before with my thumb and lying in that attitude" I remarked. — She laughed. — "I've never been frigged so before — I did want it." — "Why?" "Don't know, seeing his prick in your mouth I think — I never saw a man do that to another. — Ah! polisson — it's not nice — a woman and a man may do anything together — but two men — no 'tis villainous. — Ah! — I like it not." — "But it made you hot cunted." — "C'est vrai — mais," — and she shrugged her shoulders — other gay women have said the same.

There can be no indecency, or impropriety in women or men amusing themselves any way they like in private — objections arise from prejudice and custom. — Yet I was glad to get Eugêne out of the room. It annoys me to think that I had him, as I write this — which is absurd. — What is the use of my philosophy if it leaves me thus minded.

A French lady of whom I shall tell nothing more — a lady lewed enough but not gay — told me that she thought the loveliest mouthful any woman could have, was a nice soft prick. That no woman and man ever lived together a year and loved each other, without the man putting his prick into her mouth, or that she could love him without sucking it — she didn't say let him spend in it. This has been told me by more than one French "dame galante," when I have been long intimate with them. The lady also said that no woman had enjoyed the sublimity of voluptuousness, till she'd been fucked by one man whilst she sucked and palated another's pego.

Mademoiselle A**l*e also — not quite gay — told me that the most voluptuous evening she ever passed was when the man who kept her brought home three male friends with him. All five stripped naked, she laid on the bed edge a man laying on each side of her, and one kneeling over her head. Then her "mari," standing and tilting up her thighs, fucked her, whilst another's prick filled her mouth, and she frigged the other two. Four pricks had she in keeping at once, one in her cunt — one in her mouth — and one in each hand. — Semiramis or Messalina could not well have had a much greater treat.

Every man fucked her that night, and all felt each other's tools — they were friends, and Frenchmen. All of them got drunk. — If true, I should like to have been one of the party. But was it true? I am quite prepared to believe that it was.

She said that *she* should never forget it, and would *pay herself* to get such a treat again. Her "mari" (who kept her) brought the men home with him from a club. Their principal regret was that there was not another woman. Her "mari" suggested that he should fetch another, but she wouldn't have it. She said — "Mon ami, respectez moi — je ne suis pas putain." I fucked that lady several times, she had a fancy for me. — [Ultimately she went to a French colony with a general officer. — She may be living now.]

Then I grew tired of the erotic spectacles, and of taking pleasure in lubricated channels, so resolved to go no more to them. — Many a day elapsed before I did.

Erotically maddening as the sights were, they were one and all with courtezans, with whom satisfying love and lust is a trade. — In my whole experience there I never saw a woman who was not a baudy Cyprian, and contrasting what I saw *there* with the snug house at **** St. where, years ago, Sarah F**z*r and I had our evenings and where at every other visit I saw love making with women not gay, but with servants and others of better class — I preferred the sights *there* to those at the lapunar.

A month later I was some hundreds of miles further south, through December and January, and all but chaste. One night I went to a circus, an hour afterwards met a woman in the streets, went home with her, and found her to be one of the circus riders, and a Spaniard. In a slovenly bedroom, in a little cot slept a child a year old. — A "love child," she said. — Doubting her and not recognizing her, she described the horse she rode. — The next night I saw her riding it. — All she got a night for her equestrian skill, she said was five francs. — Her cunt I fancy paid her better. — I stripped her, she was shortish, plump, had an exquisite shape, and flesh solid as ivory, her face was handsome and pure Spanish. — What astonished me, was to find so much hair on motte, cunt and buttocks; four inches all round her anus was quite black with crisp, shortish hair which was not handsome to me but she seemed proud of it. — Tastes differ. — I fucked her and gave her ten francs, for which I might have her again, she asked me to — I repeated this another night when I had seen her riding a white horse. — My God! and all that skill for five francs. — I wondered as she whirled round on the horse, now throwing this leg up, now that — if many there knew of her hirsute buttocks besides myself. — It pleased me to think about her cunt whilst she was riding.

[This reminds me, that perhaps the hairiest women whom I have had were Spanish. I've had them at two or three French border towns, in Paris, and several in Spain, and the cuntal regions of all were unusually hairy.]

CHAPTER LIV

Nationalities of the women I have fucked. — The beauty of cunts. — Their fucking qualities. — Ignorance on this head. — Ages of the women I have fucked. — How the sight of cunts affects men. — Physiognomy of cunts. — Their classification.

In my travels in various parts of the globe, I have never failed to have the women of the various countries passed through, as well as many of the women of the provinces, countries, and nationalities, which in some cases make together what is called an Empire. Thus women of Croatia, Styria and Dalmatia, and those of Vienna and Pesth, altho all belonging to the Austrian empire, are of absolutely different physical types. — A Dalcarlian and a woman of Gottenburg differ greatly, yet both are of the Swedish kingdom. — In Great Britain, the English, Irish, Scotch, and Welsh are of different types, and there is even a great difference in face and form between a Yorkshire and Devonshire woman — both English.

I have tasted the sexual treasures of all these fair creatures in their capital cities, and many of their large towns; not only in Europe, but in lands and countries away over many oceans. I have sought abroad variety in races and breeds at the best lapunars, where they keep women in different nationalities to suit the tastes and languages of travellers. Thus I have had women of all parts of the world, and from parts in which I have not set foot. They may differ in face, form, and color, but all fuck much in the same manner, their endearments, tricks and vices are nearly the same, yet I found great charm in the variety, and always voluptuous delight in offering the homage of my priapus to a woman of a type or nationality unknown to me.

Looking thro diaries and memoranda, I find that I have had women of twenty-seven different empires, kingdoms or countries, and eighty or more different nationalities, including every one in Europe except a Laplander. I have stroked Negress, Mulatto, Creole, Indian half breeds, Greek, Armenian, Turk, Egyptian, Hindu, and other hairless-cunted ones, and squaws of the wild American and Canadian races. — I am but ***** years old, and the variety I have had astonishes me. May I live to have further selection, and increase the variety of my charmers.

I have had of course women in most parts of the United Kingdom, but fewer Irish women than others; having generally found them the lowest, baudiest, foulest-tongued, blarneying, lying, cheating, as well as the dirtiest of all the harlots I ever had.

[In the manuscript the names of the various places where I had the women, together with dates were mostly set forth, but to do so here would disclose too much.]

———————

I have probably fucked now — and I have tried carefully to ascertain it — something like twelve hundred women, and have felt the cunts of certainly three hundred others of whom I have seen a hundred and fifty naked. My acquaintance with the others beginning and ending mostly in the streets, with the delicate operation of what is called stink-fingering. Many incidents connected with these fugitive sexual amusements have been briefly described already, and on revision I find but few others worth noticing, tho some of them at the time struck me as novel. I expect that for the most part they were but such, as every man who with an amorous temperament has behaved in his secret life much as I have done, has met with. So to the flames with these short histories of amatory, fingering, &c. &c.

My sense of the beautiful in all things, which makes me now more than ever look to form in a woman more than to face, has shewn to me distinct beauty in some cunts compared with others. For many years — tho perhaps it did not absolutely determine my selection of the woman at first, I still must have been conscious of it — it must in a degree have determined afterwards, whether I had the woman a second night or not (gay women). Altho the reasons why I selected the lady for the second night's amusement are mixed and difficult to analyze, my recollection dwells pleasantly on those women whose cunts pleased me by their look, whilst the externals of those whose slits lacked attraction and looked ugly to me, I think of even now with some dislike. For years past this perception of the physiognomy of cunts has been ripening by experience and reflection, and now when I lift a woman's chemise, my first impulse is to see if her cunt is pretty or not.

I have in fact become a connoisseur in cunts, tho probably my taste in that female article is not that of other men. There are perhaps many who would call those cunts ugly, which I call handsome, and vice versa; just as they might differ from me about what is beautiful in form, face or color of a woman; and even about her style of fucking, her manners, language, or other particulars.

Not only is beauty, or want of beauty, to be seen in the externals of a cunt, but it is to be noticed when the fringed covers are opened. Many a woman looks well enough as she lies on a bed with thighs nearly closed, and the triangle of hair — be its color what it may — shadowing the top of the rift which forms her sex at the bottom of her belly, but whose vulva looks plain enough, seen when the outworks are opened wide, and large nymphæ growing from a clitoris

[*520*]

protrude, and the opening to the avenue of love looks large and ragged. — Other cunts with small delicate inner lips, which merge into the general surface before they reach the small looking opening at the lower end, are pretty, and invite the entry of the prick beneath the little nubbly red clitoris. — The charm of color also enters into the effect. The delicate pink coral tint of a very youthful virgin, is much more pleasing than the deep bluish carmine — the color of many matured, well fucked, or well frigged quims, or of those which have let through them several infants.

The saying that every woman is the same in the dark, is the saying of ignorance. It implies that every cunt gives equal pleasure, an error which I think I have exposed before, and combatted with several men. The pleasures which cunts give men in coition vary greatly. Scores of women I never seem to have properly entered or enjoyed. In some my prick seemed lost, in others felt an obstruction. In some it seemed to move irregularly, meeting obstacles here and there, as if the cunt resisted its probing, or when a snug place was found for the tip — wherein lies all male pleasure — at the next thrust it was lost and difficult to find again. Up others my prick has struck their end before half its length was sheathed in it. Sometimes a pretty looking little orifice leads to a capacious tube inside, and is wanting in gentle pressure on the prick when within its folds. I have had some women, up whose cunts I have thrust a finger by the side of my pego when within it, tho it was swollen to full size, and seemed large enough to fill any cunt, and yet the vagina seemed a cavern to it.

There are cunts which fit me to perfection, in which my prick revels in voluptuous delight, from the moment it enters till it leaves it; in which it cannot go wrong, whether lying quiescently within its warm lubricious folds, whether the thrusts be long or short, quick or slow. Such cunts make me feel that I have an angel in my embraces. Others do their work of coition uncomfortably, making me almost glad when the orgasm is over, and leaving me indifferent to the woman when my prick leaves her. What my experience is, must be that of others.

I have either fucked, felt, or seen the cunts of a child in its cradle, and those of females of all ages between six and fifty, have seen them of all sizes and developments, and in color from pale coral to mulberry crimson — I have seen those bare of hair, those with but hairy stubble, those with bushes six inches long, and covering them from bum bone to navel. It might have been expected that I was satiated, that all curiosity, all charm in this female attribute had gone from me.

Nevertheless the sight of this sexual organ pleases me as much as ever, sometimes I think more. Little intrinsic beauty as it may have, little as it may add — artistically considered, — to the beauty of the female form in those parts wherein it is set. — Nay, altho at times I may have thought it ugly in a beautiful woman, it has still a charm, which makes me desire to see the cunt of every young female I meet.

This is the reflex in the brain of the joy that the penetration of the cunt has given me, of the intense mental and physical pleasure of fucking, pleasure which for the time makes the plainest woman adorable, and her cunt a gem which the mines of Golconda cannot match.

There is no more exquisite, voluptuously thrilling sight, than that of a well formed woman sitting or laying down naked, with legs closed, her cunt hidden by the thighs, and only indicated by the shade from the curls of her motte, which thicken near to the top of the temple of Venus as if to hide it. Then as her thighs gently open and the gap in the bottom of her belly opens slightly with them, the swell of the lips show, the delicate clitoris and nymphæ are disclosed, the enticing red tint of the whole surface is seen, and all is fringed with crisp, soft, curly, shiny hair, whilst around all is the smooth ivory flesh of belly and thighs, making it look like a jewel in a case. Man's eyes can never rest on a sweeter picture.

Then as the thighs widen for man's embrace, and the cunt shows itself in all its length and breadth, red and glistening with moisture and lust, all seen but the lower end where lies the entrance for the prick, which is partly closed by the ivory buttocks, and seems of a darker red, by the shade in which it lies, telling of the secrecy and profundity of the tube which the prick is to fathom, and in which it enters, stiffens, throbs, emits, and shrinks out whilst its owner almost faints with the pleasure it receives and gives, is there aught in this wide world which is comparable to a cunt? How can any man cease to have curiosity, desire, and a charm in it?

At such moments my brain whirls with visions of beauty and of pleasure, past, present, and to come. My eyes embrace the whole region from anus to navel, the cunt seems invested with seraphic beauty and its possessor to be an angel. Thus even now I can gaze on cunts with all the joy of my youth, and even tho I have seen fourteen hundred, long to see fourteen hundred more.

Of the physiognomy of cunts, and of their pleasure-giving capabilities, perhaps I know as much as most men. Physiognomically they may be divided into five classes, but a cunt may partake of the characteristics of one, two or more, and particularly in respect of development, of clitoris and nymphæ. I classify them as follows. — Clean-cut cunts. — Clean-cut with stripes. — Lipped with flappers. — Skinny lipped. — Full lipped — and Pouters.

Clean-cut cunts. — Are those resembling a cut through an orange; the flesh on each side is full, thick, swelling up, turning upwards slightly, and forming a fattish pad rather than lips, altho a tendency to the form of lips may be seen. Neither clitoris nor nymphæ are seen in some, tho in all the flesh seems reddening as the sides turn inwards and meet, showing the slightest coral stripe, a mere hint of the red surface inside. This sort of cunt is most beautiful in girls up to about fourteen years of age, just before the hair begins to grow on them, tho they are to be seen in much older females. The pads of flesh are firm yet elastic, and that of the motte — which is full — is equally so. This class of cunt generally alters by age, but I have seen it in one thirty-five years old. There is usually ample space between the thighs where there are these cunts in full grown women, so that a man's hand can lay comfortably between them, and grasp a whole handful of vulva. Perhaps the bones of the thighs are set widely apart in the pelvis, but I have seen and felt this width of cunt in short women.

Straight cut cunts with stripes. — These cunts are much like the former, but the nymphæ are slightly more developed, as well as the clitoris — not largely, but sufficiently to give a visible red stripe between and seeming to open the outer lips. Sometimes the red shows largely only when the thighs are widish apart — in others it shows even when the thighs are closed. — In some the little clitoris (not an ugly big one) just protrudes itself under the dark hair which thickens just about the split, and an inch below it the nymphæ are lost to view unless the thighs be wide apart. I have seen this cunt in women up to thirty, and it is to me certainly the most delicate, most refined, handsomest, and most exciting cunt. I have nearly always found it in the finest modelled, plump, and loveliest woman. — It is indeed the only class of cunt which can be said to be handsome. A cunt is perhaps not a really handsome object at all, tho sexual instincts make its contemplation exciting and charming to a man.

Lipped cunts with flappers. — These have the lips usually fully formed, the clitoris sticks out and the nymphæ hang out from it nearly the whole length of the split down towards the vagina. — Women towards forty have mostly this cunt, and if they have fucked or frigged themselves much, the color is a very dark pink or carmine. I have seen it in women of nearly a mulberry red. The nymphæ I have also seen hanging out of or projecting beyond the lips, from three quarters to an inch and a half in depth, it was so detestable to me, that it quite spoiled my liking for a really well made pretty woman of thirty-five whom I once knew. Many French gay women in the baudy houses get this sort of cunt, I expect thro excessive venery. They grow thus oftentimes in women if they have children. — It is a cunt nearly as ugly to me as the pouting cunts. [Years after writing this I had a girl under sixteen years of age and looking fourteen, with nymphæ hanging an inch and a half outside the lips and a quite large clitoris. The nymphæ on one side was much larger than the other, and her vagina would have engulfed the prick of a giant. I saw and fucked her a second time, out of sheer curiosity.]

Skinny lipped cunts. — These may be either with or without the nymphæ shewing. Poor slim, youngish, half starved women with thin thighs and miserable rabbit backsides, have this form of cunt. It is not ugly actually, unless the nymphæ are too obtrusive, which they frequently are, for many of these poor thin women have had a child, and you may see the signs of that on their poor flat bellies lying in a hollow between their ill covered hip bones — [women with this class of cunt usually sham modesty, put their hands over their gaps, say they don't liked it looked at and giggle in an affected manner. I suppose they are conscious of the want of beauty in those parts.]

Full lipped cunts. — These are usually mature, they puff

[524]

out like the half of a sausage, then die away into ample flesh on each side under a fat, fully-haired mons veneris or motte. Women fleshy and well fed have them, and they look well and handsome between the large white thighs and the big round buttocks below, between which they are enclosed and lay. They were the cunts which I loved most in my youth and long after. Mary, one of my first loves, and Louisa Fisher had such cunts in perfection. — I expect they are most attractive to quite young men, for they realize the cunts which all boys — as I very well recollect — figure to themselves before they have seen the sex of a woman. The general effect of the cunt is that it is capacious. Women with this class of cunt usually allow them to be looked at and fingered freely, and smile voluptuously at the man whilst the inspection is going on, as if proud of their notches, and they like the men to look at and to appreciate them.

Pouters. — The lips of these cunts are like half thin sausages, and almost seem to hang down from the belly, so that they leave a furrow between the outer sides of the lips and the inner side of the thighs. It is the ugliest cunt — and is still uglier if the nymphæ show much, as they often do. They look as if the owners were in a consumption. The hair on these cunts I have found often look straggling and thin — or if thickish, the bush is weak, long, and with but little curl in it. — Several times when I have found myself with a woman who had this ugly sort of genital, I have been unable to stroke her. — Pouters, like the thin lipped cunts —usually belong to women, lanky, thin, poor, ill fed and not too young, poor, short, skinny arsed seamstresses, those whose bum bones you can feel. I fancy it is largely through want of nourishment in their case and frequently through ill health. — Middle aged, needy whores — those who wear veils and try to pass themselves off as thirty when they are nearer fifty — have them. — I have in my youth many a time been taken in by them, but never now go after a woman who wears a veil.

All classes of beauty may be found with one or other of the defects, for the variety in combination of outer lips, clitoris, nymphæ, motte, and hair in quantity, size, and shape is infinite. No two cunts are exactly the same in look, hence the charm of variety, and the ever recurrent desire for fresh women by the male. There is always a charm in novelty, it is born with us.

CHAPTER LV

*Luck. — Harry masturbated. — An orgy. — Two males
and one female. — Bum-fucking intentions. — H.
gamahuched by both. — Simultaneous masturbations. —
Confession of sodomy. — Anus and pudenda
plugged. — Sphincter and thumb. —Fucking cum
cocksucking. — H.'s unsated lust. —Champagne and
repose. — Amorous exercises resumed. — Baudy
ejaculations. — Fucked out. —Voluptuous eyes. —
Balls handled. — Prolonged conjunction. — Finger
and bumhole. — More repose and more champagne. —
Erotic fury. — All exhausted. — Finis. — Reflexions.*

In August I went abroad, returning in October. — Beyond a
visit to a lapunar, there was nothing worth relating. —
Indeed my fidelity was remarkable.

I had been but little to see H****. Going there towards the
middle of October on my return, she had much to tell me.
She had quarrelled with the "mean cur" (Donkey prick) yet
had not absolutely broken with him. Her other lover was
dead. With a little pressure — for she was really longing to
tell me — I found she had gratified Harry and herself by letting the lad fuck her, and was frightened of Donkey prick
knowing it thro the possible indiscretion of the lad in keeping silence about what he must have been proud of — lucky
beggar. — She described his prick to me, compared it with
the donkey tool and her protector's, told me laughing how
the lad behaved at his first fuck, and whilst we were talking
this over, a letter came from Donkey prick which was
brought by the lad who was waiting for a reply. With that instantaneous letch, and recklessness of consequences which
when they come, come more rapidly than ever, "Show me
his prick, let me see him," — I said hastily.

The idea pleased her. "But I don't want him to know *me*."
"Keep your hat on." — She would go and see him. I rubbed
some black off a stove with my finger, darkened under my
eyes, and made my eyebrows also darker and wider with it,
put on a skull sleeping cap which I happened by mere

chance to have in the pocket of my traveling suit, and also a pair of tinted glass spectacles which I had used on glaciers. Really I scarcely knew myself when I looked in the glass.

She laughed when she saw my disguise. She had written a letter to the Donkey whilst down stairs, and now thought for a minute. Donkey prick was going out of town. — Harry was to take the reply to him at the station, and dare not wait long to fuck her as I now suggested, or he perhaps might lose his place — Donkey prick being a hard master. — "I'll make him show his prick and make it stiff." — "All right." — On the landing she called him up into the bed room. — "Never mind this gentleman." He was scared at seeing me. — Then what followed took place as quickly as I write this narrative of it. — All was unpremeditated by either of us, one letch leads to another, I follow blindly the promptings of instinct when in this concupiscent state.

"How's your prick, Harry?" said she. He seemed perfectly flabbergasted for a moment, looked at me, then at her. — "Is it stiff?" — "No it ain't," said he — shamefaced in manner. "Show it me." — "No" — said he very solemnly and looking but for an instant only at me. "Why? you know I've seen it." — He grinned. "Do" — said I speaking in a husky voice "and I'll give you five shillings." — H**** said. "There, show it, and I'll show you my cunt." — He reflected — "I can't — if I don't catch him before the train, he'll sack me perhaps." — "I'll give you a cab fare and here is five shillings" — shewing it. — H. then without more ado laid hold of him and pulled his prick out, he unresisting. "When did you fuck last?" — "Not since *you*," said the lad getting bolder. — "Have you frigged yourself?" — "No." — "Would you like to see my cunt." — "Oh yes." — She went to the bed and lay down on the edge. — "I'll give you half a sovereign if you'll let me frig you" for that letch now seized me. — "There's luck, Harry." — He never looked at *me*, was engrossed with *her* and made no reply — his prick was not stiff.

H. pulled up her clothes. — At the sight of her lovely cunt quickly up rose his prick erect — a longish but thin article, perhaps to thicken, in a year or two — I seized and felt, then frigged it, he making no resistance and she inciting him. "Let me fuck you — do," — said he piteously, as I found by a certain vibration of his belly that he felt the pleasure. "No. You get the half sovereign." — "Open your thighs wider," said I, "pull open the lips" — for I wanted to make him

[527]

spend over her cunt. She saw my game. — "Is it nice?" — "Yes" — "Shall you spend," said she. — "Yhes" — and his bum jogged. I felt him coming. "Bend forward, put your prick nearer her cunt." "Oh let's fuck," he cried as his sperm shot over her vulva, and I frigged till not a drop was left in his balls.

He put his hand to feel the lovely receptacle, but she arose and I gave him the money. "You take the letter and be off, or you'll catch it," said she. — In a minute he was out of the room, buttoning up his trowsers as he went. She laughed. "Fuck me, dear," said she going on to the bed, and shewing her mucilaginated vulva. — But I'd fucked her twice and couldn't again then, so without further word she frigged herself. — "Ain't we beasts?" said she as she washed her cunt. "No; I'll gamahuche you." — "Do. I've not been fucked for a week. Phil's away, and I've quarrelled with Donkey" — as we now named him. — "But you've frigged yourself." — "Of course, every night — I sleep by myself and read in bed till tired, then frig myself and go to sleep."

[It was a great piece of luck this to me and the next time I saw H*** we talked over this masturbating frolic with the lad. She had been fucked by him twice, and the letch gratified, desired no more of him. But his youth and inexperience started in me a wish to see him fucking, to be in the room and then for us all together to do what we liked erotically. Before I left it had all been planned. The baudy episode — tho so long and prolix — is one of the remaining evidences of how this manuscript was originally written. It is too much trouble to abbreviate and I retain it nearly as it was written. It's the narrative of one of those erotic frenzies, which come over women and men when together, and they are heated by wine and lust.]

On the evening about a fortnight after, H. looked lovely in laced chemise, crimson silk stockings, and pretty slippers. — As she threw up her legs shewing her beautifully formed thighs and buttocks, the chestnut curls filling the space between them, relieved by a slight red stripe in the centre, never had I seen a more bewitchingly voluptuous sight. Rapidly my cock stood stiff and nodding, tho I was a little out of condition. — What a lovely odour it had as I gently licked her clitoris for a minute. But we had other fish to fry. "Harry's here," said she. I stripped to my shirt, then he came up, a tall slim youth now just turned seventeen. Quickly *he* too stripped, for he knew the treat in store for him. I laid hold of his long thin tool, which was not stiff, and he seemed nervous.

How strange seems the handling of another's prick tho it's so like one's own. "Show him your cunt." — Back she went on the bed exhibiting her charms. The delicious red gap opened, his prick stiffened at once, and after a feel or two of his rigid gristle, I made him wash it tho already clean as a whistle. — I'd already washed my own. Then a letch came on suddenly, for I had arranged nothing — and taking his prick in my mouth I palated it. What a pleasant sensation is a nice smooth prick moving about one's mouth. No wonder French Paphians say that until a woman has sucked one whilst she's spending under another man's fucking, frigging, or gamahuche, that she had never tasted the supremest voluptuous pleasure. Some however had told me that they liked licking another woman's cunt, whilst a woman gamahuched them, better than sucking a prick in those exciting moments. But erotic tastes of course vary.

I laid him on the side of the bed alternately sucking or frigging him. — H. was laying by his side, and he put his left fingers on her cunt. — I had intended to let him have his full complete pleasure in my mouth, but changed my mind. Then we laid together on the bed — head to tail — making what the French call sixty-nine or *tête-bêche,* and we sucked each other's pricks. — He was pleased with the performance. — H. laying by our side said she should frig herself. Whether she did or not I can't say, being too much engrossed with minetting his doodle. — He did not irruminate me with skill, and after a little time we ceased and his prick drooped.

Then I mounted his belly as he lay on his back, and showed H. how I used to rub pricks with Miss F**z*r's young man, and putting both pricks together made H. clutch them as well as she could with one hand. — But two ballocks were too large for her hand. — Then came on a desire of long standing, that of feeling the sensation of a prick up my own bumhole. — He consented to operate without hesitation. These erotic tricks will give H. something new to think of when she frigs herself in the morning — as she says she usually does before she gets up. Her delight in our performance was immense, she felt us about everywhere, looked everywhere and gave herself gentle frigs at times as well.

His prick was much smaller than mine, and according to

H.'s opinion what would be called a small prick. It was in size like a longish thin beef sausage, and as I thought just the size for me. So wetting my bum hole and feeling nervous, I laid down on my backside on the edge of the bed lifting up my thighs, choosing that position so as to watch his face whilst he spent. — We could not manage it that way, I turned my rump round, H. delighted guided his prick to the orifice, and at one thrust he went half way up. A revulsion came instantly, "Pull it out," I cried. — Out it came, she laughed and there it ended. — I did not feel pleased with myself at all. — What is the good of my philosophy?

H*l*n's fingers had been feeling her own quim, almost the entire time since we had all been together, and her face now looked wild with voluptuousness. — She cried out "Fuck me, fuck me" and threw herself on the edge of the bed, thighs distended, cunt gaping. But I knew my powers were too small that night to expedite my pleasure crises, and wished to prolong the erotic excitement, so would not fuck her nor let him. — But I gamahuched her. Then he did the same. She lay full length on the bed, he knelt between her legs, and whilst he plied his tongue upon her vulva, I laid on my back between her legs and his, and took his prick in my mouth. I felt her legs trembling and heard her sighs of delight, she was entering into the erotic amusement with heart and soul, cunt and bum hole as well, as I knew by her movements, ejaculations, and then tranquillity. She spent just as a rapid ramming of his prick between my tongue and palate, told me he was about to spend also. So I rejected his tool quickly.

With rigid prick and incited by H. he continued licking her cunt till she spent again. Then I laid them both side by side on the edge of the bed, he began frigging *her,* and I frigging *him.* — "It's coming" said he, and at the instant out shot his sperm in four or five quick spurts, the first going nearly up to his breast. — How the young beggar's legs quivered as his juice left him. Nelly leant over and looked as he spent. — His sperm was thinner than it should have been, tho he said he had neither fucked for a fortnight, nor frigged himself for a week. I believed he lied. — My sperm would have been at his age thicker after a week's abstinence. The last time he had fucked her before me it was much more and thicker. He reaffirmed that he had not spent for a week, and she declared he had not fucked *her,* so I suppose it was true.

He washed and pissed, again I played with his doodle and

questioned him. He had he said buggered a man once, and frigged one. — Now he had a nice young woman, who let him have her for half a crown when he could afford it, but he only earned a pound a week and had to keep herself out of that. His prick was soon stiff again. — He gave her cunt another lick, and then we went to work in the way I had arranged with her when by ourselves. He did not know our game.

H. in our many conversations on erotic whims and fancies, had expressed a great desire to have two pricks up her orifices at the same time. She wanted to know if it were possible, if sexual pleasure was increased by the simultaneous plugging of cunt and bumhole, and wondered if it would increase the pleasure of the man. I had shewn her pictures of the positions in which the three placed themselves for the double coupling, and we arranged to try that evening. He was not now to know what we were at, his inexperience coupled with his excitement at being fucked by a most lovely creature, were calculated to leave him in the dark as to the operations at her back door. But we were obliged to be cautious.

He laid on the bedside his legs hanging down, whilst she standing with legs distended and enclosing his, leant over him — I watched the operation from the floor kneeling, and saw his doodle going up and down her cunt. Then when we knew his pleasure was increasing, I lubricated her bumhole with my spittle, and rising pressed my pego between her buttocks and against his prick, touching it from time to time as she moved her cunt on it. I did this as a blind. Soon after. "Do you feel my prick?" said I. "Yes." — He didn't, for I was then putting my finger against it, but he was too engrossed with his pleasure to notice it. Then she backed her rump artfully, and his prick came out, and she pushed her buttocks towards me, and she kept on talking to him whilst making a show of introducing his pego again to her pudenda.

At the first push my prick failed. It was right in direction — for I had tried the orifice with thumb and finger — all inconvenient nails removed — and, knew the road was clear. — Push — push — push with still failure, and then came nervous fear. There were the loveliest buttocks that belly ever pressed, or balls dangled against, smooth, sweet-smelling flesh, an anus without taint or hair, a sweet cunt and youthful prick, and a woman wanting the supremest voluptuousness. Every erotic incitement to sight, touch, and imagination was there, but all was useless. My nature rebelled. Tho I wanted to do what she and I had talked of and wished for, my recreant prick would not rise to the needful rigidity — the more I strove the less my success.

I was mad not for myself but for *her* disappointment — it was *her* letch. — We had discussed the subject many times, and I longed for her to have sperm shed in her cunt and fundament at the same time. Further trial was useless, his prick was again worked by her, and I knew by her manner that she was near her crisis, when anxious to give her other orifice, the pleasure, kneeling I licked her bum hole then thrust my thumb into it, took his balls in my other hand and thumbuggered her whilst I squeezed his cods. She cried out. "Oh — bugger, fuck," — when madly excited and both spent. Then his prick flopped out wet and glairy from her cunt into my hand which was still beneath his balls — I arose and so did sweet H. looking with bright voluptuous eyes at me. — He lay still on his back with eyes closed and prick flopping down, with a pearl of spunk on its tip. Then too late my damned, disgraced prick stood stiff like an iron rod, and could have gone into a virgin's arsehole twelve years old, or slipped into H.'s with ease. Sheer nervousness stopped it from doing duty, aided I think by a natural dislike — much as I desired the novelty, — novelty *with* her and *for* her.

The strongest fuckstress, with unlimited capability for sexual pleasure, the most voluptuous woman, the woman with the most thirsty cunt I ever knew, guessed my condition and state of mind. — "*You* fuck me, dear," said she, and falling back on the bed opened her thighs. Her cunt was glistening with what he had left there. — He'd not uncunted two minutes, nor she finished spending four, yet she wanted my prick — either to gratify me or herself.

Randy enough I went near and pulled open the lips, saw the glistening orifice, pushed fingers up and withdrew them covered with the products of *her* quim and *his* doodle, and looked in her voluptuous eyes. — "Fuck — come on — fuck me." — "You can't want it." — "Yes — do me — do it." — Harry then roused himself, I caught hold of his tool still thickish. "Wash it, piddle, and she'll suck *you* whilst I fuck *her*." — He who only had spoken the whole evening in monosyllables, did that quickly. I laid him on the bed and she leant over him standing and bending, laid her face on his belly, her bum towards me. — "Suck his prick dear" — "I shan't." — She wouldn't, entreaty was useless, I could not wait, so opening her lower lips for a final look at the sperm, put my prick up her. — Oh! what a sigh and a wriggle she gave as I drove it hard against her womb. Her liking always was for violent thrusts, she liked her cunt stunned almost. — It gives her the greatest pleasure she often tells me. [When at a future day I dildoed her, she liked it pushed violently up her.]

I husbanded my powers, urged her to gamahuche him, hoping she would. — Her refusals grew less positive, and at last into her mouth went his prick but only for a minute. — "There I've done it," said she. — His doodle had stood, but drooped directly her lips left it.

She'd do it no more, but laying her face on his prick, wriggling her backside, saying, — "Oh fuck me — fuck harder — go on dear." What a fetch she has when she tightens her cunt round my prick and wriggles her lovely bum, it is almost impossible to stop thrusting!

But I would not finish, pulled out my prick and felt with pleasure its now spermy surface. I turned her round on to her back at the edge of the bed, and put him standing between her thighs. Then belly on belly, cock to cunt, all sorts of postures suggested themselves to me whilst they posed so, and I varied them till I could vary no longer.

Then I made him kneel on the bed over her head, his belly towards me. His prick hung down still biggish just over her head, whilst into her cunt I drove again my stiff stander and fucked, bending my head towards him to catch in my mouth his prick. She laid hold of it and held it towards me, I took it into my mouth and fucked her, holding her thighs and sucking him. — The young beggar's prick soon stood again — went half down my throat. — "Is his prick stiff again?" said she, spasmodically. — "Yes" — I mumbled. — "Oh, we're beasts — fuck me, fuck." — But as my pleasure came on her mouth pleased me best, I let go his prick, and sinking over her put my tongue out to meet hers, and with mouths joined we spent. — He had slipped on one side when I relinquished his doodle, and when I raised myself and severed my wet lips from hers — our pleasure over — he was looking at us, and she with closed eyes had found and was clutching his doodle stiff still. What a treat for the young beggar. — Thousands would give a twenty-pound note to have seen and done all this. He had the treat for nothing. — All was her device, her lecherous suggestion.

Then we all washed, drank more champagne, and after a slight rest we both felt Harry's pego. Taking it into my mouth it stiffened. — "Can you fuck again?" — "I'll try," said he.

Ready as if she had not been tailed for a month, her eyes liquid and beaming with voluptuous desire, she turned at once her bum towards him at the side of the bed, and gave him free access. I guided his pego, and the young chap began fucking hard again. — Then I laid myself on the bed, her face now on *my* belly, but spite of all I could say she would not suck *me*. Was she frightened that *he* would tell Donkey prick of her? Annoyed I arose, and slipping my hand under his belly, frigged her little clitoris whilst he was fucking her at her back, I could feel his prick going up and down, in and out her cunt, and felt even his balls — which are small. — From time to time I left my post to view the operations from afar, to see his bum oscillate and her thighs move. — It was a long job for him, but *she* spent soon. — The more she spends, the more violent at times seem her passions. — "Ah — don't stop, Harry — fuck — let your spunk come into my cunt," she cried as she spent. He didn't spend but worked on like a steam engine. — "Spunk — Spunk" — she cried again. Flap, flap went his belly up against her fat buttocks, the sound was almost as if her bum was being slapped by hand. — I thought he'd never spend so long was he in her, till I saw his eyes close. — "Are you coming?" — "Yhes." — "Ahaa — fuck fuck," — she screamed again, her whole frame quivered, then action ceased, she slipped a little forward fatigued, his belly and pego following with her, and there they still were in copulation both silent and exhausted. — Soon after she uncunted him, and without a word turned onto the bed and laid down — I looked at her cunt and squeezed his prick, felt madly lewed but had no cockstand — I dare not excite myself too much now — I was envious, dull at not being able at once to fuck her again.

She lay with eyes brilliant, humid with pleasure and a little blue beneath the lids, and very red in face. She looked at me intently. "Do it again," said she. — "I can't." — "You can, I am sure" — leaning on one elbow she raised her upper knee, her cunt slightly opening, and I felt it. He was washing. — "Put it in for a minute." — "It's not stiff." —

Reaching out a hand she gave it a grip. — "You *can* fuck," said she edging herself to the bedside again and opening her thighs. "Do it this way just as I am lying." — I could not resist and put my pego where she wished it — would do anything to bring my prick to touch her cunt. — It was not three inches long — but directly the tip was on her vulva and she rubbed it there, it began to swell. Stiff, stiffer it grew as she nudged it into her cunt. "It's quite stiff," said she — I feared a relapse and set to work vigorously, sucked her sweet mouth, exhausted it of spittle which I swallowed and then we spent together, *he* now looking on. — It was an exciting but killing fuck to me — my sperm felt like hot lead running from my ballocks, and the knob felt so sore as I spent, that I left off thrusting or wriggling, and finished by her repeating cuntal compressions and grind, in the art of which she is perfect mistress. — When I first knew her and her cunt was smaller, she never exercised that grip even if she had it — now her lovely avenue tho certainly larger to the fingers, is fatter inside, and has a delicious power of compression.

Harry now was silent, and she at last seemed fatigued, yet sitting by his side began again restlessly twiddling his cock. There were evident signs of its swelling — I felt it, but my lust was satisfied and I cared no more about feeling it. We chatted and drank awhile, and then she laid herself along the bed as if going to repose. Not a bit of it — her lust was not sated yet. She put a hand on to his tool and said, "Fuck me, dear." He said he could not. "Try — I'll make you." H.'s eyes when she wants fucking have a voluptuous expression beyond description. — It appeals to my senses irresistibly — It is lewedness itself, and yet without coarseness, and even has softness and innocence so mixed with it, that it gives me the idea of a virgin who is randy and seeking the help of man, without in her innocence quite knowing what she wants, what he will do, and that there is neither shame nor harm in trying to get the article of which she does not know the use. Her voice also is low, soft and melodious — I was sitting when I saw that she was now in furious rut. — I've seen her so before — and she said to the lad "Get on me — lay on me dear." — "I can't do it." — "You shall," said she impetuously. "Lay on my thigh." The slim youth turned at once his belly on to hers. *He* had now no modesty left — we had knocked that out of him quite.

Wildly almost, she pulled his head to hers and kissed him, her eyes closed, her bum jogged, down went one hand be-

tween their bellies, a slight movement of *his* buttocks, a
hitch of *her* bum, a twist, a jerk, then up go her knees and
legs, her backside slips lower down, and by a slight twist she
had got his prick into her. Then she gave two sharp heaves,
clutched his backside and was quiet — her eyes were
closed — I would give much to know what lewed thoughts
were passing through her baudy brain just then, a flood of
lascivious images I'm sure, whilst her cunt was quietly,
gently clipping his doodle. She opened her eyes when I
said, — "Fuck her well." — "Fuck dear," said she to him
and began gently her share of the exercise. He began also
shagging, but quietly. "Is your prick stiff?" said
I — "Yhes." — A strong smell of sperm, prick, cunt, and
sweat, the aroma of randy human flesh now pervaded the hot
room — the smell of rutting male and female, which stimulated me in an extraordinary way. I got lewed, my prick
swelled, and for a moment I wanted to pull him off and fuck
her myself, but restrained myself and put my hand under his
balls to please my lust that way.

If he was a minute upon her he was forty. — Never have
I had such a sight, never assisted at such a long fucking
scene. She was beautiful in enjoying herself like a Messalina
all the time — I squeezed his balls and gently encouraged
him with lewed words, she with loving words till she went
off into delirious obscenity. With her fine, strong, lovely
shaped legs, thighs, and haunches she clipped him, he
couldn't if he would have moved off of her. Every few minutes she kissed him rapturously crying, — "Put out your
tongue, dear, kiss — Kiss. — Ahaa — fuck — fuck harder —
put your spunk in my cunt." — Then came prolonged loud
cries. — "Ahrrr — harre" — and she violently moved her
buttocks, her thighs quivered — and after screeching. —
"Aharrr" — beginning loud and ending softly, she was quiet
and had spent. But a minute after she was oscillating her
bum as violently as ever, and crying, "Spend Harry,
spend — kiss — kiss — put out your tongue — kiss —
you've not spent — spend dear, kiss" — and her kisses resounded.

I moved nearer to her, and standing, slid my hand under
her raised thighs and gently intruded my middle finger up
her bum hole. — Her eyes opened and stared at me baudily.
"Further up," sobbed she in a whisper, her bum still moving.
Then she outstretched her hand, and grasped my prick, and
I bending to her, we kissed wet kisses. His head then was

laying over her left shoulder hidden, he was ramming like a steam engine, and neither knew where my finger was, nor thought of aught but her cunt, I guess.

Again he put his mouth to hers, their tongues met, and she still holding my pego, on went the fuck. The ramming indeed had never stopped for an instant. My finger was now well up her bum, his balls knocking against my hand, and each minute her baudy delirium came on. — "Now — spend Harry — spend. — Oh God — fuck — fuck — bugger. — Aharrr — aharrr." — Again a screech, again quietness, and as languidly he thrust again she stimulated him. — "Fuck dear, that's it — your prick's stiff — isn't it?" — "Yhes" — "Your spunk's coming." — "Y — hess." — "Ahaa — spunk — fuck. — Ahharr" — she screeched. The room rang with her deliriously voluptuous cries, and again all was quiet. So now was *he* for he'd spent, and out came my fingers as her sphincter strongly clipped it and *she* spent.

I thought all was over but it was not, her rutting was unabated. "Keep it in dear — you'll spend again" — "I can't" — "Yes, lie still." — Again her thighs clipped his, and her hands clutched his backside. I felt under his balls the genial mucilaginous moisture of their passions oozing. His prick was small and I slid my finger up her cunt besides it. — He never noticed it. "Don't you beast," — said she. — "Give me some champagne." I withdrew my moistened finger, gave her a glass, filled my mouth with some and emptied that into hers. She took it kissing me. She was mad for the male tho she murmured after her habit. — "Ain't we beasts?" — "No love, it's delicious, no beast could do what we do." — He lay now with eyes closed, almost asleep, insensible, half only upon her, his face half buried in the pillow. — She raised her head partially, not disturbing his body, I held up her head, and a full glass of champagne went down her throat. — Then she fell back again and put her hand between their bellies. "Is his prick out?" said I.

No reply made she — I put my hand under his buttocks, touched his prick which was still swollen, found she was introducing it to her quim and it touched my hand in doing it. — I saw that heave, jog and wriggle of her backside, her legs cross his, her hands clamp onto his buttocks, the jog, jog gently of her rump, then knew that again his pendant doodle was well in her lubricious cunt, and that she'd keep it there. — "How wet your cunt is, H*l*n," said I. — "Beast" she softly murmured and began fucking quicker, tho *he* lay quite still. — Her eyes were again closed, her face scarlet. "Feel his balls," said she softly. — "Do you like my doing it?" — "Yes, it will make him stiff — do *that* again." — Her eyes opened on me with a fierce baudiness in them as she said that. — The exquisite voluptuous look, the desire of a virgin was no more there — delirious rutting, obscene wants in their plenitude was in them, the fiercest lust. — Up went my finger in her bum, — "Aha. — Aha — God" — sobbed she in quick staccato ejaculations. — "Fuck me dear."

He roused himself at that, grasped her buttocks, thrust for a little time then relaxed his hold and lay lifeless on her. "I can't do it, I'm sure." — "You can, lay still a little." — Still he laid like a log, but not she. — An almost imperceptible movement of her rump and thighs went on, ever and anon her eyes opened on me with a lustful glare, then closed again, and not a word she spoke whilst still her thighs and buttocks heaved. — I knew her cunt was clipping, was nutcracking his tool, — often times I've felt that delicious constriction of her cu   as in baudy reverie I've laid upon her, half faint with the voluptuous delight of her embrace. — Some minutes ran away like this, whilst I was looking at their nakedness, feeling *his* balls withdrawing my finger from *her*, then gently, soothingly replacing it up her bum, frigging my own prick every now and then — none of us spoke.

Then more quickly came her heaves, he recommenced his thrust. "Fuck dear, — there — it's stiff. — Ahaa — yes — you'll spend soon." — "Yes" murmured he. — "Yes, — shove hard — give me your spunk." All was so softly murmured and with voices so fatigued, that I could scarcely hear them. Again I took my finger from her bumhole (for the position fatigued my hand), on they went slowly, again he stopped, again went on, each minute quicker, and soon furiously rammed hard whilst she heaved her backside up and down, thumping the bed which creaked and rocked with their boundings, and the champagne glasses on the tray jingled. Up into her bum hole went my finger. "Aharr," she shivered out. — "Bugger — fuck — fuck Harry — quicker — aharr — my God — I shall die — y'r spunk's — com — com — aharr —God — I shall go mad." — "Ohooo" groaned he. Her sphincter tightened and pinched my finger out, another bound up and down, one more scream, then both were squirming, another scream from her, a hard short

[538]

groan from him, and then she threw her arms back above her head, lay still with eyes closed, mouth wide open, face blood red, and covered with perspiration, her bosom heaving violently.

He rolled half off of her, his prick lay against her thigh dribbling out thin sperm, his face covered with perspiration and again half buried in the pillow and laying nearly a lifeless mass at once he slept. Her thighs were wide apart, no sperm showing: his spend must have been small. Both were fucked out, exhausted with amorous strain.

My strength had been gradually returning, and prick stood like a horn as I felt again his prick, and thrust my fingers up her lubricious cunt. No heed took either of my playing with their genitals. — I forgot the pains in my temples — cared not whether I died or not, so long as I could again penetrate that lovely body, could fuck and spend in that exquisite cunt. Pouring out more champagne I roused her and she drank it at a draught. "Am I not a beast?" said she falling back again. — "No love, and I'll fuck you." — "No, no. You cannot, I'm done and you'd better not." — "I will." Pushing the lad's leg off hers — he fast asleep — and tearing off my shirt, I threw myself upon her naked form and rushed my prick up her. Her cunt seemed large and wet but in a second it tightened on my pego. — Then in short phrases, with baudy ejaculations, both screaming obscenities, we fucked. — "Is my prick larger than his?" — "Ah, yes" — "longer?" — "yes — aha, my God leave off, you'll kill me — I shall go mad." — "Ah, darling — cunt — fuck." — "Aha — prick — fuck me you bugger — spunk in me arsehole fuck — bugger — fuck — fuck." — With screams of mutual pleasure we spent together, then lay embracing, both dozing, prick and cunt joined in the spermy bath.

"Get up love, I want to piddle," said she. I rolled off of her belly. — She rose staggering but smiling, kissed me and looked half ashamed. Her hair was loose, her face blood red and sweaty, her eyes humid with pleasure, and puffy and blue the skin under her eyes. She sat on the pot by the bedside looking at me and I at her, and still with voluptuous thoughts she put up her hand and felt my prick. — "You've fucked me well." — "My God! aren't we three beasts — I'm done for." — "So am I."

I'd fucked her thrice, he thrice. — She spent to each of our sexual spasms and many more times. During their last long belly to belly fucking *she* kept him up to it for *her* whole and sole pleasure, for she was oblivious of *me*. — She must have spent thrice to his once, for her lovely expression of face, her musical cries, her baudy ejaculations during the orgasm — I know them full well by long experience — were not shammed. That would have been needless and impossible. — The tightening of her bum hold on my finger told the same tale, for the sphincter tightens in both man and woman when they spend. — She'd also frigged herself, been gamahuched by both of us, and spent under all. For two hours and a half, out of the four and a half I was with her that night, either finger, tongue, or prick had been at her cunt and for one hour and a half a prick *up* it.

Impossible as it seems even to me as I write it — absurd, almost incredible — she must have spent or experienced some venereal orgasm — something which gave her sexual pleasure, which elicited her cries, sighs, and flesh quiverings, with other evidences of sexual delight, from twelve to twenty times. She may not have spent always, her vaginal juices may have refused to issue, their sources may have been exhausted after a time, yet pleasure she had I am sure. There was no need to sham, why should she, for she gained no more. The amusement was planned by us — so far as such a programme can be, jointly for our joint erotic delight. — Harry was but a cypher tho an active one, a pawn to be moved for our mutual delight, and nothing more — tho of course much to his delight — lucky youth.

I thought of the orgy perpetually until I saw her again three days after. I couldn't get to her before. — She looked smiling and fresh as ever, not a trace of fatigue was on her face, but she admitted she was quite worn out that night, and had spent as nearly as she could tell, twelve or fifteen times, had laid a bed all next day, drank strong beef tea, and that such another night would almost kill her. — Never had she spent so much, never had had such a night before and should recollect it to the last day of her life. She hadn't seen Harry since and didn't want. — "We mustn't be long, Philip is coming to town tonight and will stop a fortnight, he'll be here in two hours, so get away soon." Her cunt had got its cherry red on it again, its delicate scent filled my nostrils and excited my brain, I gamahuched it, fucked her twice and left. — As I drove off I saw a cab with portmanteaus on the top going in the direction of her house. — Instinct again helped me, and stopping my cab, telling the driver to follow me, I walked slowly back, and when in sight saw the cab

stop at what I suppose was her door. — It was, I found afterwards, her protector, and I'd been nearly caught there.

[Lascivious orgies I've had of various sorts — maddening,
exciting, all — but for a refined voluptuous evening none
ever came up to this. — To the last day of my acquaintance
with her I shall recollect it. — We often talked about it together for some years after.

[I altered but very slightly the wording in places of this
narrative, omissions were not needed. Would that I could illustrate it by pencil.]

CHAPTER LVI

*Fucking on chairs. — Condoms tried. — Blowpipe,
condom, and cunt. — My ill health. — H.'s sexual
strength. — A sea voyage. — A young plain-faced
widow. — Masturbation of a circumcized. — A
harlot's naked street antics. — Fucking against
bamboo. — A comedy of donkies. — Lewed effect on
the widow. — An aperient applied to her pouters.*

For sometimes I hadn't seem H. at all, and when I did told
her all. She said she didn't care but was evidently angry. We
had champagne. Neither Donkey prick nor her protector had
had her for about ten days (so she said when sitting on my
knee, feeling my prick and I her vulva). She said she'd contented herself with digital movements on her cuntal bud, —
which wasn't all *she* needed — and before I'd been in the
house a quarter of an hour she was manipulating my love
staff. This shows how the recital of any amorous trick affects those whose lust is rampant. — I'd said that I'd fucked
Phoebe whilst sitting on a chair, she sitting on my prick with
bum against my belly. — "Fuck me so," said H. Next minute
I did. — She put a glass on the floor with lights by its
side — as L**l*e used, — so that both could see the movement of my prick in her cunt, as she fucked me by rise and
fall. We were delighted, she enraptured. — "Do you see your
balls?" "Yes dear — frig your clitoris." — She obeyed. Then
sobbing out our carnal chorus, looking in the glass whilst
fucking and frigging, we got repose in concupiscent

Elysium. — Afterwards we varied it by fucking whilst sitting face to face and tongue to tongue, — that luscious lingual junction, a delicious addition. — It pleased her to know I had fucked Phoebe in *that* posture. — Said she as we began, "I can't see your prick moving when face to face, *you* can," — then she put the glass at the back of our chair, and looking over my shoulders was gratified, tho she could only see herself moving.

A day or two after, there again, meretricious inventiveness was on us both. It was an age since I'd had a condom on my prick, and she long since one so sheathed had been put up her. We had talked of that before. I took condoms with me, we began operations with one on, but not liking the sensation — which cheats the sexual pleasure of both, — I took my prick out, well greased the condom outside, put it on and up her again. We compared sensations, but both agreeing that the pleasure was largely lessened by the intervening skin between prick and cunt, I took it off and fucked without one.

I took another day with me a condom tied on to a little bone tube, which I took out from an india rubber bottle or injector, and with that could inflate the condom. — Wetting the condom she pushed it — a gutty little string — up her cunt as far as she could with her fingers, leaving the mouthpiece hanging out, and laid herself at the edge of the bed. Then taking it in my mouth, I tried to inflate the condom by blowing into it, but with all the force of my lungs failed to do so effectually. It might have been done perhaps with a pair of bellows, but with my mouth I could do nothing more than inflate it a little. Directly I ceased blowing, the squeeze of her cunt drove all the wind out again. She could feel the dilation, which gave her cunt what she called "a tickling squeeze out" but nothing more. We both thought it good fun, which shows what infinite variety of amusements reside in cock and cunt. A trial on another day, when the condom was pushed up her dry, was equally unsuccessful.

Then I blew up her cunt thro an india rubber tube — my breath blew against her womb, which we thought at the time good fun. — Indeed any absurdity (as it may be seen afterwards) will amuse a meretricious couple fond of playing with each other's genitals. Then as she had a pretty bum hole, I introduced the india rubber tube up that and blew up — "I'll put a fresh fart into you," said I — "Beast," —but she liked the fun.

Inventions multiplied. I blew a condom out, tied the end to keep up the inflation, then pushed it up her cunt. It was larger in circumference then any prick I have seen — so far as I can judge, — but up it went, and I moved it very gently whilst she frigged herself. There were pleasant chats about this, and we agreed that a cunt full grown would take a much larger prick than ever man yet had.

Then I fell out of health and was ordered to a warmer climate for the winter. — Before departing, H. and I had a frolicksome evening, in which we invented postures and modes of pleasure, in which we both got tight, and her lasciviousness had full play. With great regret we parted, as much exhausted with lecherous amusements as a couple could be. Her wonderful strength showed itself that night, for under my prick, finger, and tongue, she spent eleven times, and at that last gamahuche, during which I added to her pleasure by inserting my middle finger just through her sphincter, she gave such a long, loud screech as she spent, that it must have been heard throughout the house, and she nearly tore the hair off my head. — "Aha — my — God — suck — bugger — quicker — haa — spunk," she screeched in ejaculations, pausing between each word. — I wrote an account of all next day, this is but an abbreviation.

———————

A longish sea voyage, no incidents worth noting, excepting that of a healthy and very plain-faced, tall woman, seeming about twenty-five, traveling with her mother and father to the East, was seasick close to me. I led her to her cabin and comforted her on the way. "How very kind," said she next day, and then to my astonishment I found she was a widow. The sea air and extreme rest soon made my prick voluptuous, and I thought of the widow whose cabin was only a few yards from mine — I like talking to widows, they know all about fucking, they want it, and will take any sly allusions to it, whilst I am wondering how they assuage their passions, and how their cunts must tingle with want of the male. They tingle much more than virgins' cunts who don't know the stretch of the prick. There were her "Pa and Ma," and I also had friends with whom I was travelling in my way. But walking on deck after dinner one fine evening with her "Pa and Ma" about — we leant over the bulwarks talking about sea sickness. Was I sick? she asked. — "Sometimes qualmish but soon over, and it was a very

[543]

peculiar effect on me." — "What?" — I hesitated, then — "It makes me want to be in bed with a companion." "Ohooo," she said giggling and went off to her Ma — I didn't fear, knowing that a widow wouldn't tell of that. — Half an hour later sitting at cards, I noticed that every minute she looked across at me. I fancy her cunt was stewing.

Once or twice on the voyage I nearly frigged myself, after I'd been standing at a place where I could see the women's feet as they went up to the decks, and I'd let the young widow see that I looked at hers. I fancied she let me see as much as she dare, and a beautiful foot and ankle she had — her sole charm — complimenting her on it, — "You've no business to be looking" said she laughing. "Why not, what are pretty feet, and legs etc. etc. made for but to be seen?" I thought what a hard case hers was, to be deprived of the male after three years regular fucking, which I ascertained was her case.

At an Oriental city I found perpetual blue sky, hot sunny days, and coolish nights. — All the delights of novelty in climate, vegetation, architecture, food, customs, dress, and where colored skins from the blackest to the whitest, were seen, and where among the peasants prick is king, no shame in showing it, whilst the women would sooner shew their cunts then their faces. I landed with a fortnight's sperm in my balls.

Two nights after on a blue-sky'd yet darkish evening, I wandered about the streets in the city, delighted with its wild, half-savage, irregular beauty. A few women flitted by me, their faces covered with the yashmaks, men turbaned and with flowing robes, others with baggy trousers and a fez. — Negroes and Negresses mixed with others of tawny hue, whilst at rare intervals an European was seen. In a widish street near a café chantant all was bright, yet within two minutes walk from it, were poor houses, ragged, unkempt gardens and waste grounds. At the corner of a cross street, stood a short young man wearing baggy trousers, and on his head a fez. I stared at everyone that night for the novelty, and stared at him as I passed. He gave a significant jerk of his head and turned down the street. I followed, thinking he would show me a brothel of which I stood in need, as I had heard that pimps of whom no fear need be had, were always about. In two minutes we were by the ragged waste ground and almost in the dark, tho there were there some street lamps at long intervals. I was hesitating to follow further, when he turned round and exposed his prick, I could fairly well see it for it was not very far from the last gas lamp. Then he turned, went on further, and in greater darkness stopped against some bamboo railings enclosing some waste grounds.

At once surprized, as I was for a moment, it occurred to me that he must be circumcized. Such a prick I'd never seen, so closed on him and felt it. It was soft, thick, and grew big under my handling. Then said he "Turko fuckee" and pointed in the distance. Scarcely a word of the language knew I, but guessed somehow that he meant a sodomitic den of which I had heard there were many there, and to which the Orientals openly went. I shook my head, he gesticulated persuasively, but it was of no avail.

Then he pointed to his prick which I'd relinquished. I had not satisfied myself about the circumcision, and by signs intimated I wished to see it again. He understood, pulled it out again in the half light, and I saw he had no prepuce. He advanced across the road nearer the light to show it, guessing from my manner what I wanted. He seemed quite indifferent whether he was seen or not by others, but I retreated, and he came back to me and towards some miserable bamboo railings. A man and woman passed on the opposite side but took no notice of us. The old letch came on with force, and naming a coin (about two shillings) I intimated by gesture that I wished to frig him. He nodded, I paid, he stood sideways so as to aid my operations. His prick grew stiff, then solid as a horn and very large yet smooth. I felt the glans which no prepuce covered, pleasure signs came on him and he tried to feel *my* prick, but I refused and frigged on slowly till he spent. My fun was over and off he went. It seemed an unnaturally large prick for his stature, but his race have large cunt rammers.

I walked away wondering at myself. I had not struck the whores' quarters which I'd sought, and was lusting strongly from long continence, when again I came across him accompanied by a girl. It was in a main road with feeble lights also a long distances apart. The girl immediately pulled her single garment right up to her neck and was all but naked, for she had neither shoes or stockings on, and holding them up she walked thus by my side accosting me, I guessed asking me to have her. The man who knew me again went on the other side of me chattering — some natives came towards us but took no notice. Then, two Europeans passed us and the girl turned back and went after them, but soon after turning round I saw her coming to me, and again she'd pulled up her clothes. — I pushed her off and she disappeared in the darkness.

Resuming my stroll and motioning him off, in a minute the girl was again with me, again exposed herself and under a lamp, for there were still fewer people about. She looked about sixteen, had lustrous eyes and was very handsome tho copper colored. — I was quivering with want of a woman, and thought I'd just feel her cunt and nothing more.

A darkish, silent side road being close by, I turned down it. She took me by my hand, led me into the semi-darkness, where impelled by lust which had become too strong for prudence I felt her hairless cunt, and put my fingers up the warm avenue. Fear of danger then left me, I had heard that no European was ever molested there, that women for a mere trifle would let men fuck them, and within a short time I was fucking her, my concupiscence making me oblivious of all the chances of ailment, indifferent whether I was seen or not, tho I knew that my friends might be about.

Cooled by fucking I felt mad with myself. The risk I had ran when on the eve of a long journey where medical aid could not be had, astonished me. My having frigged the Oriental on a public road surprized me — yet strange inconsistency, marvellous power of concupiscence, who can withstand it? I longed to feel the woman again but only to feel her. My feeling and fucking had not I guess occupied three minutes, and the moment I had spent I ran off. Would she piss over my hand as harlots have done in the streets of Europe? So ran my thoughts, my prick stiffened again, and with half an hour I was fucking her in the same place, and at the same time feeling the youth's prick with one hand — for he had suddenly appeared and produced his tool —whilst I held her naked rump with the other. That night's amusement cost me only about eight shillings.

These incidents astonished me, but I soon found that they were usual enough everywhere in Oriental cities, and that the satisfaction of the senses carried no disgrace. But the nude exposure, the hairless prick and cunt, the singularity of the incitements, I thought of all next day. A rutting fit came on me and I thought of and longed for the cunt of every woman who passed me.

After a midday meal, travellers sat in front of the hotel with parasols up, digesting and talking. I thought of the cunt of each woman I looked at, then moved my chair to talk to the widow who with her parents was there. My friends had gone for a stroll. — Soon her parents went and we were alone, but there were other travellers sitting about. I looked in her eyes, thought of her cunt, and my cock stiffened. "What a lovely climate etc. etc," she said. — "Yes and it's having the same effect on me as sea sickness." Her eyes opened wide, she colored up, made no reply to the observation, but drew my attention to a finely clad Turk who was walking by. Shortly after I looked her full in the eyes and laughed. — She laughed, and I felt sure she was thinking about my words.

We had slightly moved our chairs the better to avoid the sun, and then were overlooking the street sideways. We were talking about the hotel bedrooms, and found that mine was near hers tho at the back of the house. Suddenly the violent braying of a jack ass was heard, and turning to look, there was a splendid nearly white donkey, with a prick a foot long, getting into a very small donkey, one of several standing in the street for hire. Just as we looked Jack made a successful lunge and his big prick disappeared in the small donkey's cunt, and he rammed with energy, whilst the little female with her tail obligingly turned aside, stood still enjoying it. A donkey boy with yells and blows pulled Nanny away from Jack, by her ears and bridle. — The owner of the stallion, who rushed out of a shop, belaboured it with a big stick, pulling its head at the same time quite round, and at length the two got separated, but Jack's sperm was issuing as his big tool withdrew from the Nanny. By that time a group of Orientals with one or two Europeans who had collected thro the violent braying, seemed delighted, and witnessed the scene laughing. I looked on, the widow at my back I caught looking on when I turned round, tho she'd turned her parasol down in the direction of the street, as if to shut out the view. My procreator, hot before, was now burning and throbbing. — "I shouldn't like to be disturbed like that," said I. — "It's hot, I shall go in," she answered and quickly rose up. — Instinct I suppose made me reply that I should do the same, and we entered the hotel together. — "Didn't the master twack the poor jackass," said I when we were indoors. — "I didn't see anything," said she, — her face as red as a poppy. Then she burst out laughing. — "You did,"

I replied, laughing heartily too. — "I don't know what you mean. — He — He — He." — "You fib," — replied I. Then both grew serious.

We stood talking in the hall for a minute, I smiling, she scarcely restrained from smiling herself. We each knew well what the other was thinking of, and I wish I could have felt the sensations in her cunt, for I saw from her eyes that she was lewed. We both went upstairs together, and when in the bedroom corridor, "That's my room, they are lower this side but larger than yours." "Really?" — "Look." — I opened the door, she half entered it, I laid hold of her arm quite gently, and without any resistance, pulled her in and shut the door. — "Oh! I mustn't stop here." — "Give me a kiss — I will have one." — She didn't resist the kiss. — "I mustn't stop here." — "Yes do — I'm dying for you — let me see that sweet foot and leg which I saw on the steamer." — "I shan't" — I pulled her down on to the bedside and put my hand on her calf. — "Oh you shan't" — next second it was on her thigh. — "Oh now — no, you shan't." Next minute my fingers were between her cunt lips, and I was titillating her clitoris, and kissing her. "Let me have you, my darling." — "Leave off now." — "Let's fuck." — "Oh, I'm sorry I came in, what will the servants say if they see me leaving?" The lovemaking then ran its course — how commonplace but how delicious, tho the same, and the same, and ever will be the same. — Frigging her first, then baudy words, then pego erect, dazzling and fascinating her, next her hand is round it, and I've a finger up the warm moist avenue. — "Hush dear, don't make a noise, they can hear thro the partition — I will have you, don't be foolish. — Hish." — "Oh — now — don't get me with child then." — "I won't, I'll spend outside. — Hish." — I pulled her bonnet off and threw it on the floor, then pulling her back onto the bed, the mosquito curtain tore down in all directions, then she was laying on the bed silent, her cunt thirsting for the soothing lifegiver. I see a dark-haired motte for an instant, then my belly covers her. — "Ah — Herr" — she sighs as my prick is buried in her. "Aha — err" — and I'm rapidly fucking her. "Aha" as my tongue meets hers. "Oh don't — ahr." — My spunk was coming, was throbbing out into her, she spending, our pleasure was complete, her cunt full of my libation, *my* promise was forgotten, she'd forgotten *her* request, but both were happy.

Then came the wash and the usual regrets — the modest

[*548*]

look — the fears. — "Oh if I'm seen." — "Wait longer — now let me see it." — She made no sham, she knew she could give no more than she had, and waited till she'd seen my prick erect again, till I'd seen her charms from bum hole to navel, and we'd fucked again. — Then smoking, I promenaded the corridor till the coast was clear, whistled loudly, and she escaped safely, nor did I see her until with Pa and Ma seated at the table d'hôte. — Then how we looked at each other. — A widow I'm perfectly sure can't help getting fucked on the sly, and they know somehow, I find, how to take care of possibilities to themselves afterwards. — There were two other widows at that hotel, and also two soldiers' wives who had been without their husbands for months. — Had they done without sexual solace long? — Perhaps — most likely not.

CHAPTER LVII.

An Oriental bagnio. — A circumcized cunt. — Terpsichorean bum-vibrating whores. — Cunts in the street. — Penis sine præputium. — The physiognomies and sizes of pricks. — Female admiration of big ones. — The time consumed in a fuck. — The number of thrusts. — Quantity of sperm injected. — Amorous ejaculations whilst fucking. — Abnormal erotic whims and fancies.

Then I found out the locality of the whores. My friends had already done so, and we walked in the daytime there together. Evening found me there alone. Many an Englishman had been in the house, and the women had learnt a few English words explanatory of copulation — "Me fuckee prick," said one — I saw two dance naked their national dances. The quivering of their buttocks raised my pego in no time, whilst the novelty of hairless quims finished my excitement. I had a woman, and afterwards looking at the other's cunt it did not seem to have a clitoris and that the nymphæ were also partially gone — all in fact of that on which women frig themselves, and looked what much like a scar, — tho reddish like the rest of the vulvas — was in their place. I pointed to it hoping some explanation by

[549]

gesture or pantomime. But the girl looked sulky, then savage at me, got up and left the room, nor would she return. — Cautiously I mentioned this to a married one of our party whom I knew to be without prejudices, and had several times been in the East. He laughed. "You've been at **** I knew you would. She's been circumcized, they cut off the clitoris of some girls to prevent them frigging themselves and flat fucking, but what objection they find to their amusing themselves that way, I can't guess." — When I returned after a month or more, I sought the brothel again and fucked the circumcized one (if that be the term and it were the fact). — She laid quite sulkily whilst I fucked her at the side of the bed, never helped me, laid like a log, and looked away from me, I cannot imagine why.

Then master of myself, I yet was unavoidably chaste. Hundreds of miles away from the great city I got no opportunities, but saw bathing and at other places, men naked or partially so, with big pendant tools which would have made the average Englishman's look small. They are a big-pricked race. — Of cunts I saw none, but often felt wild with desire to raise the clothes of the women, garments which shrouded their forms so much, that one only guessed them as women from that.

At the end of some weeks, one night I saw the dancing women, saw them dancing naked. There were two — a copper-colored woman and a sweet little dark-colored girl about fifteen years old, a Nubian with the most exquisite form, with faultless breasts, teeth white as snow, a sweet little plump creature who danced wriggling her body, quivering over belly, and breasts and buttocks, till I thought her lovely little dark bum would drop off. — She ceased, smiling, showing teeth exquisitely shaped and whiter than snow and demanded backsheesh which she liberally got. — Her companion dancer, a brownish copper-colored woman about twenty I guess, did the same, and both got well rewarded. The little one looked in my eyes voluptuously, invitingly, and tho two male musicians squatting on a carpet were there, I couldn't restrain myself, and turning my back to the musicians, grasped my buttocks, pouted my lips, protruded my tongue. She understood. At a sign the men left the chamber, her female companion remained.

The next instant, I had her on a dirty divan, on one side of the room, and wide enough for fucking, and was inspecting her little gap round which not a hair was visible from motte to bumhole. She was Mahomedan and *they* all divest their quims of nature's clothing. My inspection was quick, I looked at her bright handsome face, her smiling mouth, and snow white teeth in a slightly prognathus jaw, and the next minute we were one in body. Five minutes after, our union was dissolved and her cunt white with sperm. How strange it looked, that pearly white film over the dark red oval, in the dark and nearly black surface of cunt lip, and thigh. She was a Soudanese and almost like ebony, tho a nice fleshy tint ran underneath the black. Her skin was satiny, ivory. — No white woman's skin ever felt more delicious to me.

As my belly left hers, I became conscious that the other dancer was in the room, in my erotic excitement I had not noticed it before. — Standing naked she had watched our coupling. — With a very much larger mouth, with fuller lips than the little Nubian, there she stood smiling at me lewdly, as the little Nubian got up with her cunt full. — Then unasked she laid down at once upon the divan, and opened her thighs just as if it were the custom of the house to do so, and that at once I would begin to enjoy her. Shaking my head I pointed to my pendant tool, but still she lay there making Ghawazee signs, opening the doors of the temple with one hand, and pointing to it with a finger heaving, jerking her belly, quivering her body from thighs to breasts, in much the same manner as when dancing.

The Nubian got me water and I washed my prick — fearful of consequences — I pissed, then shook my head. The dancer got up from the divan, fell down on her knees, and minetted me. The little black lass rose from the floor where she had squatted on her haunches after washing, and placing herself in front of me, — having snatched up a tamborine — commenced the wriggling, belly and bum shaking dance, and the copper-colored woman sucked me, till what with her labial exercise and the jellylike quivering of the little black's haunches, my prick rose stiffly, and at once on the divan I opened her cunt with it. But it was too soon after the first, it slunk out from it. Then I laid on my back on the divan, and my pego went into her mouth as she knelt and gamahuched me, as whores do everywhere in every clime, whilst the little black continued vibrating her buttocks close to me. At last I stopped her by feeling her cunt and groped till my libation sped into the other's mouth, which completed my evening's pleasure.

[*551*]

Another enforced chastity of weeks and again I was in the big city. I saw the short fellow whom I'd frigged in the street and shook my head as he approached me. I found that in other streets and places besides that where I'd seen it done, women lifted their clothes up as an invitation to their charms, and I felt one or two smooth-lipped quims. Then I had curiosity to see if another native's standard was like those seen by chance and which seemed so big in repose. — It was not lust but simple curiosity. — Seeking a brothel I had a smooth-cunted harlot, and having learnt of the language enough to enable me to say I wished to see a prick, when there I'd forgotten half, yet by the aid of two or three words and baudy signs the girl at length understood, and called an ugly, hook-nosed woman, whose nationality I guessed was Greek, and who spoke two or three words of French and English. It took me long to make her even understand my wants, but at length she did, and in a quarter of an hour in came a young man about five feet nine high.

He stripped at once and shewed a dark brown skin, and hairless, large pendant tool as brown as the rest of his body, and without a bit of prepuce; all having been cut off. He began feeling for my prick and jabbering all the time. I didn't understand a word and pushed his hand away. Saying something which sounded like "hicke" he threw himself face downwards on the bedside, his rump towards me, and pulled open his buttocks. I pulled him round and frigged him till his prick became very big, and his semen fell in front of me. My curiosity was satisfied and I left very rapidly, — glad to get away.

In another city wandering thro a cemetery, I saw a girl seemingly about fifteen with a white child who could just toddle. The girl was of the brownish copper tint, but so handsome that I couldn't help noticing her. She followed me leading the child, so that I met and met her again, and each time she fixed her big dark eyes on me till my prick swelled and I lusted for her. — What was she, that she was unveiled at her age, and with a white child? Surely not a Moslem — and yet her color! — It was in the afternoon. A party of English strolled through the cemetery and disappeared. Again I met the girl and child in an obscure part, it was hot, I sat down on the ground, she squatted near me. — She'd rings round her ankles.

Then my sperm began seething in my balls. I smiled at her, she smiled in return. Going closer I touched her gar-

[552]

ment, and at once she lifted it up to her navel, laid down on the sand, and intimated that I might fuck here there. Tho alone and nobody near, I shook my head, not being equal to lying down with a girl in a cemetery in broad daylight. With a little gesticulation and showing some coin she understood me, and leading the child she left the place — I following slowly in the distance, to a cottage just outside, — there were a dozen or so cottages — and she entered one. I hesitated and stopped. Soon her head peeped out beckoning me to her, and with prick erect I entered it.

In the miserable chamber were one or two articles of furniture, and a divan covered with a wretchedly shabby carpet. After she'd closed the door, without a word she threw off her only garment and laid down start naked. An exquisitely beautiful shape she had, such breasts, such thighs and arms. I pulled out my stiff prick which she at once started up to look at and kiss, as if in extreme delight. Then she laid down again and I mounted her, but finding the divan too narrow for easy fucking, got up. She seemed to understand, got up, pulled the carpet onto the floor, put a cushion for her head, laid down and opened her thighs wide, showing a pretty, pouting-lipped, hairless cunt, and in five minutes I had filled it with my semen. Never had I a more delicious fuck. She wanted it again, but I gave her money and departed quickly, tho I no longer feared the ailments of Venus, being about to sail for Europe soon.

I visited other towns without whoring, then left the East. A longish sea voyage followed, and landed me at a great French seaport. Never in four months had I done so little fucking. The opportunities were few, and when they occurred, I thought of my health, restrained my desires.

During my voyage on a sea as calm as a mill pond, I wrote an article about pricks and what I had seen and done with those carnal tools in the East. On my return home, I looked out scraps of manuscript written at different times on that and the cognate subject of fucking, and thinking they would be better together than distributed, placed them here under the Ægis of the rod of life.

I have seen a great many pricks in a state of erection as well as repose, tho I've felt but few. I suppose that there are pricks which may be termed handsome or ugly, and that women see beauty or ugliness in them, just as I do in cunts.

The greatest number seemed to be of about average length and thickness, but the difference between the largest and the smallest was very considerable; certainly quite two inches in length, and in thickness proportionately.

No two look quite alike. There are those very long and thick, those long and thin, short and thick, and short and thin, those equally thick throughout their length, those which taper a little from root to glans. There are those with tips or glans flattish, round-topped, or pointed. Some tips are like a heart, others like a plum, some with little, some with big tips, with big knobs some. Some look quite straight when stiff, others have a well-defined curve. Some have a little scrotum, others a big bag of testicles, and there are no end of combinations of all these features, endless varieties in size and shape. Moreover some are brown skinned, some white, some of which the tips are never covered with the foreskin, others covered wholly or but partially. — Some tips are of a pink tint, others of carmine even when in repose and lust not rampant.

Women according to their tastes, I remark, call them fine, big, noble, splendid: rarely do they say, lovely, pretty, or beautiful. They express admiration of size alone. I've not heard them say. "A beautiful shape, a pretty knob" and so on. But no doubt women are not insensible to beauty in the article, and indeed some pricks have pleased *me* more than others. But size is the only feature which is worthy of remark about them here.

To me a prick only looks well on a man when smallish and pendant, then it seems in fitting pose, and neither adds to nor detracts from his physical beauty. But when it is stiff and the man naked walks about with it projecting like a bowsprit, and nodding with its weight and his movement, it makes the man look ridiculous. It would make the Apollo Belvedere look absurd. Yet it has when in that state of erection a special charm for the woman, it fascinates her, and few can handle it for a minute, without lying down and opening their thighs to receive it into the realms of Venus, whether the man is eager or not for the conjunction.

This I have discussed with many Cyprians, many a time also with H*** Indeed of late we never meet without talking about the sizes and capabilities of pricks, in which subject she takes the greatest interest. We had at various times arranged how pricks ought to be measured. She measured mine one day with pieces of thin string carefully cut off to mark sizes, and subsequently she did the same to her protector and to both of her large-pricked lovers. How we laughed when we compared them with mine. The strings were given to me and I noted the lengths and circumferences. The following dimensions of the pegos were all taken when stiff. The lengths were measured on the upper sides from the tip to where the prick joins the belly, and not underneath where it joins and is lost in the balls. The following measurements show how much smaller the two large pricks were than she had supposed them to be. She had often spoken of both as seven or eight inches long or more.

No. 1—Donkey prick 6 3-4 ins. long 5   ins. circumference
No. 2—Poor lover   6 1-4 ins. long 4 3-4 ins. circumference
No. 3—Philip   5 1-4 ins. long 4 1-8 ins. circumference

The measurements of my own I omit out of modesty, but it's neither so short or so long as the extremes. — Once I was ignorantly ashamed of its size — I knew no better then.

The biggest prick was under seven inches long but looked *very big* and far above the average of those I have seen through peepholes, with one exception. You hear gay women say, "Oh, his prick was seven or eight inches long." I have talked with dozens of women about this, have discussed it in conclave with three harlots and a baud. I cut bits of wood, six, seven and eight inches long and projected them from my belly to show them what a six, seven and eight inch prick was, and what a little they knew of length — I should say that six inches is more than the average length of stiff pricks measured in the way described. That titanic doodle which F**z*r showed me some years ago must however have been nearly eight inches long. *She* had never seen such a tool before, she told me. There was also one very big prick which I and a woman handled together, the narrative of which I think is preserved, but cannot at this moment recollect.

What is the superiority of the big doodles? Six inches is the utmost that the ordinary female can take up her cunt with pleasure. A vigorous hard rammer of even six inches hurts many women, and a moderate-sized one they all admit gives as much pleasure as the largest — yet all seem to admire — to be fascinated — by the idea of huge cunt stretchers, and always speak admiringly of them. Somehow even *I* seemed to have more pleasure in looking at the large ones than at the others.

[555]

Some women have told me they preferred a good thick prick to a long one, that the sensation of stretching was nicer. But perhaps that was mere imagination, for a cunt is big enough for the biggest, and involuntarily closes on and grasps a prick, fitting itself to the size whether it be a large or small one, directly it is lodged within its folds, and I believe the smallest cunt will take the largest prick.

I have collected many notes made principally at lapunars, of the time a man takes in fucking, and how many times he thrusts up the cunt before spending. From my experience at the baudy house in **** S^t. I knew it varied immensely. Then, I never had made observations watch in hand. — I have asked harlots without any satisfactory reply. They ought to know, but they didn't, and only said. — "About so and so." — It was not that they didn't want to know or tell, but they didn't know. — "You *are* a queer man," said one to me when I questioned her, and who became immensely interested in the subject.

At the lapunar in after times, this inquisitiveness arose in me, and being older and with less urgings from my ballocks to get rid of its accumulation, cooler in fact with advancing years, on some evenings at the lapunar with watch in hand I made observations, having first fucked a harlot to cool my carnal promptings and leave my brain clearer, but keeping her with me — gaining her experience by questions.

One youngish man whose prick was stiff as he washed it spent in three and a half minutes. In *my* youth I have spent at the moment my glans touched the cunt.

One man, seemingly forty, who turned the lady's bum towards him, was six minutes in her cunt including the time his prick lingered in her before and after spending. From the moment he began his thrusts to the moment he uncunted was five minutes and he averaged a thrust a second. Allowing a minute for the repose of contemplation at his entry, and half a minute for repose after he'd spent, he was four and a half minutes thrusting which makes two hundred and seventy thrusts up the lady's pudenda — I don't know why it should be called "pudenda" or that there be anything to be ashamed of in it, since she was born for the sole purpose of using that pudenda, cunt, gap, quim, notch, split, slit, thing — to put names alphabetically — or whatever else it may be called.

Then I timed a man who perhaps was forty-five years old,

but a fine, vigorous, big fellow. First he fucked the woman standing as she lay on her back at the bed edge. In about six minutes he turned her bum towards him, and re-inserted his prick, fucked, spent and withdrew. He was leisurely in all his preliminary movements, and in the change of posture of the lady, and from first to last occupied sixteen minutes. I held my watch in my hand all the time, timed his thrusts in the middle of his fucking, and found that each was as nearly as possible a second, perhaps a very little less.

Allowing a minute for repose after insertion and two minutes for change of pose of the lady from belly to bum and his re-insertion, and his quietude when contemplating the beauty of her buttocks, and of his own prick as three or four times he drew it out slowly to the tip, and put it up again equally slowly, and also a minute's repose before he uncunted after his spend, that man was twelve minutes fucking. — He was slow and luxuriously contemplative at his work. I timed him at various stages and found after the lady's rump was towards him — the last posture — that he was somewhat quicker in movement than at the first. Allowing on the average that he was a second and a quarter at each thrust, or say fifty thrusts a minute — then he made six hundred thrusts up that woman's cunt before he spent. He was always slow, she told me.

I timed three or four youngish men who put into their women without much preliminary dalliance. They varied from three to four and a half minutes before they spent and their thrusts from two hundred and fifty to two hundred and ninety-five.

One French harlot told me she thought that most men were, if young, about six minutes in their cunts altogether. An English harlot years ago said seven minutes. — "But lor, I have had some who have fucked a quarter of an hour without spending, then pulled it out and began again after waiting, and some spend directly." — H. told me her men were up *her* and over in no time and that some spent directly they entered.

I have seen men begin and finish in three minutes and often have done so myself. I saw once a man who must have been half an hour up a woman before he spent, and kept ramming hard at intervals all that time; he was a feeble man. Many others pause long with prick in the lady talking all the time, but these are exceptions.

My impression is that from the time the man first feels

the pleasure of the contact of his glans with the cunt, to the time he spends in it, that he fucks at the average of forty-five thrusts a minute — this average excludes hot full-ballocked young men, and lewed, experienced, philosophically fucking, middle-aged men, and old men; tho perhaps if these extremes were included the average might remain about the same.

I think that on the average, men between twenty-five and forty-five, and in full strength, are at their first fuck no more than four or five minutes in the woman's cunt, which includes the lingering of the prick for a short time after the seminal discharge. The second fuck occupies a longer time, but of the second operations I have seen fewer. I have myself I am sure kept my prick in for twenty minutes at my second poke, ceasing to thrust, nearly withdrawing it, checking the spend when pleasure became strong, then keeping it up a few minutes after spending.

If a woman has three men on one night — and many do — and each on the average thrusts his prick four minutes only, and at the rate of fifty thrusts a minute, she would have six hundred thrusts up her cunt. — What a fine material a cunt lining must be!

I don't think any man could make such observations if his spermholder was full, and he himself wanted to fuck. — He must be cool, and collected, which means empty ballocks. This was my case when most of the observations were made on special nights, but on others the results were about the same. Few of the men were more than half an hour with the women altogether, including amatory preliminaries, dressing, and undressing.

In my youth I fucked women in silence excepting the sights and murmurs of pleasure. When older, with softest words of love and endearment, mixed at times with expressions of rapturous adoration of the cunt I was enjoying, and with the ideal beauty of which and its owner my mind was filled as: — "Darling — lovely cunt." — Pleasure evokes voluptuous thoughts and reminiscences most varied. I now ejaculate the most obscene words and phrases. This stimulates my passions, increases my pleasure, and affects, I find, my partner in fucking, who sympathetically responds similar words, heightening her pleasure and mine as well. Of the many men I have seen fucking, few have cried out such lust-

[*558*]

ful, stimulating words as I now do — when I could hear them, which was not always the case.

The language of love is always exaggerated, hyperbolical, full of flights of fancy. A standing prick and a stiffening moistening cunt cast a glamour over the genitals and all their operations. The glowing terms of lust and love seem almost ridiculous when fucking is over and one is cool, yet they represent the exact feelings and sentiments of both sexes *when* fucking.

Curious to know the quantity of sperm spent at the first fuck, many a time I have frigged myself during my career. I have also frigged men, and seen a hundred cunts with recently injected semen in them. I fancy that a *large tea spoon* full is about the quantity spent by a man at his first fuck, when in the vigor of life. Harlots have told me the same, but one told me she knew a man who spent about a dessert spoonful. In the decline of life the quantity falls to beneath a tea spoon full — it is a steadily diminishing quantity with age — the quantities spoken of in baudy books as spent are quite figurative.

Among the hundred and fifty pairs I have seen copulating I have scarcely seen any of those fanciful, *outré* amourous tricks, which I have myself played with women. This sometimes makes me think that I am somewhat exceptional in this. Nearly all of my tricks have however been played at the houses or lodgings of the women, and after I have known them sometime. Perhaps this is the case with other men.

CHAPTER LVIII

At the lapunar and peephole. — Alexandrine's
advice. — Katie's instruction. — Marguerite's
fornication. — Profits and losses. — A hairy arsed
harlot. — About the propriety of seeing and feeling
other men's pricks. — A double cunted strumpet. —
Katie's eventful history. — England again. —Alteration
in the arrangement of my narrative. — The
philosophy of fucking virgins and juveniles. — H. lost
and found. — Mutual friggings in a cab. — The snug
accommodation house. — Baudy books and prints. —
H.'s pleasure in meeting me. — Minetted by Misses R
and Black. — Baudy triads. — A flagellation
spectacle. — Three women and self. — An orgy. —
Black becomes favourite — Epitome of voluptuous
amusements with H. — Termination of narrative.

Taking rest tho travelling, I reached the city of pleasure and
was welcomed with open arms by Alexandrine, who still retained her post. There was much change in the woman-kind in
the bordel since last I was there — a longish time ago — but
enough of the old ones left to know me. — "C'est lui," —
when I appeared in the salon. Marguerite was there as beautiful as ever, indeed still *more* beautiful in form. A
wonder — for there she certainly has been seven years and
more and Alexandrine tells me, never has less than five men,
and frequently seven, in each twenty-four hours. "She makes
much, as much as any three women. — But. Ah! — it all goes
outside to some one." — "Un homme?" — "Je le suppose,"
and she shrugged her shoulders. I fucked Marguerite and told
her she'd made a fortune. "But I spend it." — "How
then?" — "In pleasure." — "Ah there is *un amant de*
cœur." — "Peut-être," — and she smiled. — She was a lovely
creature.

I saw also about a dozen couples fucking, saw the Cyprians before it, enjoined them to shew off the men's pricks
well, and was obeyed. The sight of a handsome stiff pego, I
sometimes fancy now excites me more than the sight of the

more secret female organ. — Why? — Is my desire to see this procreating tool improper or not? Prejudice and education in false principles would make answer. "Yes." — If it be so, then man made in God's own image, is in his nudity a thing to be ashamed of, and his pego obscene, filthy, abominable. Yet the creator has made him with that tool for the great purpose of peopling the world, of creating beings whom he then endows with souls. Strange that it should be thought abominable and immoral for a man to show it, or other men to see and touch it — simply ludicrous. — All males at some time have both exposed their own, and felt other men's pricks — perhaps only boys' pricks — but the act is the same. — Powerful organ which all love and women worship — why art thou called filthy and obscene?

One evening a nearly black haired woman came in to me, with a copious overflowing libation in her quim — fat spunk and lots of it. — I looked, investigated, said she might go, and proffered payment. "Mais baisez moi donc." — "Ah no I want it not." "But you must, you shall, you have not kissed me for three years." I had quite forgotten her, then recollected her hairiness which had displeased me then, and displeased me now. She was one of the hairiest in the region of cunt and bum hole I ever saw. From navel to arsehole, it was black, long, curly, thick, and hid everything. The gap was hidden by it quite, her buttocks were covered with hair up to the bum bones, gradually thinning off to those ossifications, but still black and thick. It must have been an inch long round her anus, and all jet black. It filled the hollow between cunt and thigh. As she knelt, it looked like the arse of a black bear and was ugly, yet such was her almost angry persuasiveness — such the excitement of novelty — that I fucked her, tho against my will as I did it, but I verily believe to her great delight.

"There is a fresh woman and she's two cunts," said Alexandrine to me as I entered one night. "Impossible." — "It's true, she comes from Marseilles and has been stopping at the F*r*y's and now is here." — I asked for Katie, and had a chat with her. — "Yes it is true, and she is in society now." — "Better and better," I said. "Let her come to me after." Awaiting her, I amused myself with Katie, who told me all about the woman till she entered.

I put her on to the bedside quickly. — She had heard of

[*561*]

my letch — and opened her thighs. There was much thick sperm outside, what looked like any other cunt, and I said the *two cunts* was a joke. But Katie coming to my aid pulled open the lips, which so far resembled an ordinary quim, but down the center of the cunt, was a membrane or diaphragm looking like one of the nymphæ, extending from the clitoris to the lower end of the split. The two proper nymphæ were in their place. I put my finger up. — "There is no sperm in there," said Katie, "look here" — and putting the central division on one side, there was the opening with sperm in it. I rapidly looked all over her two quims randy in mind, but was just then not strong, not well, and my prick would not stand. — Katie sucked it to a slight rigidity and I put it with difficulty up the spermy orifice. — It would not remain there, her cunt fell away from me. "There is not much spunk in you," — said I. — "Not much," said the Marseillaise, "it's all run out, but the Monsieur is waiting for me to go back." — So I let her go. She came back soon after with her cunt or cunts washed. — Excited and lusting for her, yet I now couldn't get my prick stiff at all so tried Katie's quim which didn't rise it, and in despair I left the house.

Next day I had the same two women. Kate, because being English she interpreted for me when my French failed me, and I learned all about the double cunted one. I saw her piss, felt one then the other vagina, felt to the top or bottom of each, rubbed the womb entrances, put two fingers, one up each cunt at the same time, and felt and pinched the gristly or fleshy division between the two. Every enquiry I made was answered with frankness. Katie gamahuched me, and so did *"double cunt."* — All was again useless, I wanted the woman, yet had a dislike to her. So tipping handsomely for the trouble I had given, I departed again with flaccid tool, and without having this time even got the tip up either of the double cunts, or the single cunt, for I tried Katie's — I had done for myself by recent amours I suppose.

The third time I was better, and had had a cock-stand when thinking of the funny fucking apparatus of the Marseillaise. It was in the afternoon after a good luncheon that I went to see her, and had her to myself for a couple of hours.

She was a well grown woman say five feet six high with firm fleshy large buttocks, scarcely any waist, good shoulders, large firm breasts, and full sized thighs. From knees to ankles the legs were hairy and ugly. She had dark hair on her head, and a slight darkish moustache on her mouth, and dark eyes. Her face had a somewhat sad expression in it. — The hair of her motte had the growth of a woman of thirty and was very dark. She said she was twenty-three. — There was scarcely a sign of hair by her anus. Her cunt may be likened to one of the short leathern purses like a bag, which opens with a clasp, and shews inside a division or central pocket, with a pocket on each side of it. The cunt had the central division only and two pockets only, that is, a cunt — on each side. The central division looked like one of the nymphæ, but there were nymphæ of the ordinary size and usual place, just within the outer lips — I am certain that a man not knowing of the peculiar physical conformation of the woman, might have put his prick up one of the cunts, fucked and finished, without knowing that another cunt was by the side of his penis — always supposing that he had been lewed and full of sperm when he began feeling, looking, and fucking. In brief, in the usual physical condition of a healthy man when wanting a woman.

From what she told me on this and another occasion, she did not seem to have been conscious of her peculiar conformation till her menses began to show. She had them now from one cunt after the other — never at the same time from both. Each lasted about three days — under her true clitoris, but lower down and on either side of the central division of the two vaginas, were two little piss ducts, and she pissed first from one and then from the other. — These piddle openings were not just inside and near to the vaginas or prick holes as in most women, but higher above them tho both were hidden partially by the diaphragm dividing the cunts and by the nymphæ and outer lips. I am sorry I did not see her piss.

She had pleasure she said in fucking, but could not say the pleasure was more from one cunt than the other. — She seemed from her description to have had the usual alloverish voluptuous sensation from both cunts when fucked. She had been in the family way on her left side womb, and when four months gone and her belly much swollen, the doctors told her parturition probably would kill her, and so she procured abortion. — The central division where it joined the real clitoris, protruded like a *second clitoris,* the piddle vent holes a little lower down were on each side of it. She could frig herself to pleasure and a spend on the lower as well as the upper clitoris. Sometimes one cunt spent, sometimes the other, she didn't know which would spend when she frigged herself.

The doctors said that she had two bladders with two distinct wombs and adjuncts. How they were connected with her breasts for milk, they did not know. They warned her again breeding. — A person, a doctor, had offered her a large sum to go to America to exhibit herself, but she was frightened and refused. She liked whoring in her native land best. The doctors had passed implements and drawn off the water from each of her bladders as an experiment, to settle the point whether she had two bladders or not.

I forgot to ask her about her virginity. She liked fucking she said — and when she frigged either clitoris she seemed to spend from one cunt or both, she could not control it, *but both cunts did not wet.* — Two friends once had her together. She stood over the one with the shortest prick, and the other pushed up her other quim from her rump side — the one she was on was well up her, but the other got his prick only a little way in, for it was difficult. Both spent up her and she spent — all three nearly at the same time — but she never could tell *which* of her cunts, or if *both* did, but she spent certainly. She was made so lewed when they did it she couldn't tell. Then both fucked her twice again, one after the other, both looking on alternately. "Yes, once in the other's spunk, the other time in different cunts." — "One liked fucking in the foutre?" — "Oui, *like you,*" — said she with a smile. — She'd heard of me. — They were Frenchmen. — She was all the evening with them.

I saw her again some months after. She had then gone to another lapunar — all the clients at **** had had her. *She did not take,* few men had her more than once for curiosity. She didn't like them not to fuck her but many did not. — I went thro all the examinations again and heard the same story. — I got my prick first up one cunt then another, but could not spend, and after trying in every attitude came away without spending. — She this time told me that she'd had two virginities, one her lover took — the doctor who examined her subsequently had the second.

I was resolved to fuck her, visited her again, heard all over again and a lot more. My cock stood so I mounted her, I pushed my prick up her left avenue, then exchanged it for the right one. I wanted to compare differences of sensations — if any — and whether the cunts gave the same sort of feel to my tool as a one cunted woman gave me — but

[564]

over-excited again, my tool to my annoyance began to dwindle and came out flabby almost suddenly. — The abnormal nature of the female's organ in fact gave me a slight disgust, but really tho curious, there was nothing in the slightest degree — as I now think of it — disgusting about it. Again by the help of her fingers and her mouth I rallied, and bringing her to the side of the bed, I first looked at her quim from behind her bum, then reversing her and lifting her heavy thighs up, I asked her to put in my prick for me. — "Which cunt?" — asked she. "Your left, the side you bred it." She placed it there, up went my prick, and I left my sperm in the favoured avenue.

Her cunts did not seem as nice and smooth as the ordinary female article — but somewhat fatigued, not much wanting it, and over-worked before — for my cock had recently gone into quite a dozen cunts and mostly smooth with sperm and I had seen thirty couples copulating — I was rather done up — I'd had difficulty also in finding where this woman had moved to, so I was not in a good state for judging, and felt all the time that I was fucking out of mere curiosity.

A few months after I sought her at the same house. — She'd left. — Then I asked Alexandrine, who under pledge again (she'd told me before) gave me another address — but she had left, had gone abroad they told me. — Perhaps so, and all Europe may see this lusus naturæ.

[I have always regretted not asking more and precise questions of this double cunted woman — but the excitement caused naturally by talking on the subject, and having the cunts at hand and the naked owner of them there ready and willing to fuck made me forget asking much which I intended. I should have written down my questions, and asked them seriatim. — But that might have scared her, and she would most likely have lied more than perhaps she did, but as far as I narrate I think it is all true about her. — I had Katie — the only English woman in the house, — to interpret and aid me. But above all, Alexandrine, who had been for a few years my friend, aid, and adviser in erotic business told me a great deal.

[Katie had a wonderful history. From being an ordinary harlot there, and first in London, then at Lyons, she married the nephew of the mistress of the bordel, and was for a time practically mistress of the establishment — and would with her husband have inherited it, with an income as far as I could make out of quite three thousand pounds a year. Good behaviour in her lodgings got her that marriage and that position, prosperity upset her. — She became a drunkard, quarrelled with the women, and caused rows in the house (never permitted in a French "maison de tolerance"), was rejected and dismissed — of course still married — and as far as I could learn, she was afterwards sent to England a confirmed drunkard, her husband keeping her here. — Her name had occurred in the original narrative, but in the abbreviations those incidents had been destroyed — hence the need to preserve this short memoir of her here — an eventful history.]

My narrative is nearly finished, my amatory career ending. My sexual powers lessen tho still strong, but as the urgings of concupiscence are less powerful, opportunities seem not to occur so frequently and my sins against chastity grow fewer. The actors and actresses will henceforth be nameless or named wrongly for they are living and about. — The houses which gave me shelter exist, but must not be named. The amatory episodes were for the most part more briefly written by me than formerly, and need but little abbreviation. Their chronological order will not be quite followed in the interest of all the actors, actresses and self.

[Here is placed a loose paragraph — I fancy I have written a similar one before — but lest not so, it's well to preserve it.]

[How similar for the most part have been my temporary amours. How similar the behaviour of the women who have procured me the virgins. Whether L**l*e, F**z*r or others, all were similar. All the virgins were got for money. What pleasure also the Paphians had in enticing the lasses, and for their own lust in seeing the hymens taken — in inducing the girls to fuck. — What complete unanimity in opinion, that their little protegés would soon be fucked by some one if not by me. What tales they told me of the nascent desires, lewed wishes and erotic knowledge and habits of the girls at that early age, and the encouragement they gave to the males — mostly lads a little older than themselves and of the same class. — Verily a gentleman had better fuck them for money, than a butcher boy for nothing. It is the fate of such girls to be fucked young, neither laws social or legal can prevent it. — Given opportunities — who has them like the children of the poor? — and they *will* copulate. It is the law of nature which nothing can thwart. A man need have no "compunctions of conscience" — as it is termed — about having such girls first, for assuredly he will have done no harm, and has only been an agent in the inevitable. The consequences to the female being the same, whoever she may first have been fucked by.

The first week of my return I telegraphed a meeting with H. Getting no reply I went to her house which was empty. I telegraphed the scout, got no response, went there and *she* had flown, but I found that her letters were sent to a neighbouring chandler's shop — I wrote there naming an appointment in the dark near **** and there found H. waiting. All was changed, she lived in the country, was not sure if she could meet me, but if so at great risk, didn't know when or where but in a week would let me know. We drove through a park which was on the road to her station and felt each other's carnal agents, I besought her to get out and let us fuck against a tree. She was indignant at the proposal, and it ended in our frigging each other in the cab, face to face, kissing and tonguing, to the great injury of her bonnet, and a little soiling of her silk dress and my trowsers. Who would care where sperm fell in such an entrancing ride.

A week after, a place of rendezvous was found, at a convenient snug little house where we met generally. — Before she'd taken anything off but her bonnet and I my hat, we fucked on the bedside with intense mutual delight. Directly I'd uncunted, we both stripped start naked and got into bed, drank champagne there, and fucked and fucked again till my pego would stiffen no longer; fucked four times, a great effort now for me, but not for her. But frigging and gamahuching always satisfied her as a finish — luckily.

Then our meetings were at longer intervals apart, which only made them more delicious. But I alas, am obligated to husband my strength more than formerly, so the long intervals suit me better.

When next we met, we found that the mistress of the establishment had voluptuous photographs, pictures, and engravings by hundreds, and one or two chests full of the best and baudiest books in English and French. — We revelled in them that day for all were placed at our disposal. — We sat feeling each other's genitals between our fuckings, looking

[*567*]

and commenting on the artistic display of nudities and erotic fancies, and wishing we could participate in such performances ourselves. They awakened ideas which had slumbered in me certainly. She said in her also, but she always declared that I had put desires into her head unknown before. We were well matched.

Living far off now, without a male or female friend with whom to talk about sexualities, more than ever now she looked to our days of meeting, and hours of unrestrained voluptuousness. After hearing all she had done at home even to domestic details — which she was fond of telling as showing her domestic comfort, — lust and love in all its whims and varieties we talked about. "Did you ever do that?" "Do you recollect when I showed you ***'s prick?" — "When did so and so occur?" So ran our talk. How often he'd fucked her or gamahuched her, how often she'd frigged herself, the sperm *he* spent, and all the domestic baudy doings were told me with delight, and similar frankness exacted from me. — Then came wishes. "Let Mrs ***** get us another woman, you fuck *her* whilst she gamahuches *me*," was a request made whilst after fucking, we laid reposing in the bed. — I agreed. — "Let her be stout, I'd like one as stout as Camille," — these are the very words said funnily enough in a half shamed faced way — for absence and the change in her circumstances, at first seemed to impose some stupid modesty on her. — But both of us liked to call a spade a spade.

All was accomplished. The abbess as I shall call her, we ascertained would procure us every pleasure, tho only cautiously and from time to time she disclosed her powers. A very plump and almost fat, handsome woman of two and twenty was our first companion. — "Don't let *me* ask her, *you* say that *you* want her to lick my cunt — I don't want her to think that *I* wish it," — said H. So it was done, we had champagne, I stripped the plump one, then asked H. to look at her quim — which she was longing to do — and then incited her to the gamahuche. Baudy talk and wine raising our lust made us friends soon, and Miss R. jumped at the idea of gamahuching the other. Then naked all three (warm weather now). Looking-glasses arranged so that H. could see all, she laid on the bedside whilst R. gamahuched her. On the bed by H.'s side I also laid, she frigging me during her pleasure. "Aha — God — lick, quicker. — I'm spending," — and she spent nearly pulling my prick off during her first ecstasy.

Pausing for a minute, R. recommenced, for H. likes to

continue uninterruptedly at that luscious game, till she has spent at least twice. It was a lovely sight to see H. with her beautiful thighs, and the coral little gash set in the lovely chestnut hair, which R. held open for a minute to admire. Then her mouth set greedily upon it, her hands under H.'s buttocks, the dark hair of R.'s armpits just peeping, her big white buttocks nearly touching her heels. I stooped down this time and peeped along the furrow past the bumhole, and could just see the red end of her cunt with the short crisp hair around it. Then straddling across her waist, my prick laying on her back between her blade bones, I watched the lovely face of H. which in her sexual ecstasy is a lovely sight. "Fuck, fuck her," she cried to me. But I wouldn't. Next minute saw H.'s lovely eyes fixed on mine, whilst with soft cries she spent.

A rest, more champagne, a discourse about the pleasures of woman cunt licking woman and of men doing it, and H. again was on the bed. — "Oh, I'm so lewed I want a fuck so," said R. — "He'll fuck you, won't you?" — I complied. Further back on the bed now the better to reach her cunt with her tongue, with pillows under her head lay H. when R. recommended her lingual exercise on the sweet and fresh-washed quim. I standing up now at R.'s back. — "Fuck her, and spend when I do," said H. — R.'s bum towards me was almost too fat an one as she bent, so I made her bend lower, and then between the buttock went my prick, dividing two well haired, very fat lips of her sanctum of pleasure. She adjusted her height to the exercise when my tip was well lodged, my balls were soon against the buttocks, every inch of my prick up a cunt deliciously lubricated by its owner's randiness. — "It's up her cunt love," I cried, began fucking and R. began gamahuching. All now was silence but the lap now and then of R.'s tongue on H.'s cunt. "She's coming darling — I shall spend," — I cried at length. — "Oh — God — fuck her, fuck, slap her bum," cried H., writhing and sighing. — My slaps on the fat arse resounded, as R. writhed and shivered with pleasure whilst licking on, and both of us spent as H. spent under the tongue titillation. Then with slobbered prick and wet cunts we got up. Soon after standing by the bedside I fucked H. whilst she frigged Miss R. Never were there three baudy ones together who enjoyed the erotic tricks more than we did.

These delightful voluptuous exercises were repeated with variations on other days. R. sucked my prick and took its libation whilst I was lying full length on the bed, H. kneeling over my head, I licking her clitoris the looking glasses so arranged that H. could see all. Another day I fucked R. whilst she frigged H. Then I put my prick into both women and finished in R.'s cunt, which completed that day's amusement.

Soon afterwards we noticed wales upon R.'s capacious white buttocks. It was from her last whipping she said. That disclosed what in time was sure to have become known to us. That the abbess was an expert in flagellation, that swells both old and young came under her experienced hand. Questioned, the abbess told us all, was indeed proud of her performances, shewed us the varied apparatus with which she either tickled or bled the masculine bums, and women's as well, or superintended men flogging female bums. Such as the fat arsed R.'s were preferred, tho some she said liked younger and thinner buttocks. Some brought and birched a woman whom they liked and fucked, some a special woman to birch them. They all paid very handsomely for bleeding a fair pair of buttocks.

R. told us that flagellation *of her* backside made her lewed an hour after or so. She liked the birch just to hurt slightly the cunt lips. Then if she couldn't get a man, she frigged herself — that some girls said it did not affect them lewedly — others that it did. — We talked quietly with the abbess about this. Both H. and I desired to see the operation, and heard that some men liked to be seen by other men when being flogged. If we would on a certain day, there would be then a gentleman who had a taste for being made a spectacle, and she would arrange for us to see — for pay of course.

We went on the day but the man didn't appear. Two ladies were ready waiting to flog him. The abbess said it didn't matter, something had detained him, that when he disappointed he always paid the money for all concerned. One of them was dressed as a ballet girl, the other only in chemise, such were his orders. — She in chemise, was a sweet faced, dark haired shortish girl of nineteen, with fine teeth. We asked her to our room to take wine, and it ended in H*** frigging her and my fucking her, then in my fucking H., whilst she looked at the other's quim, and we agreed she would be better for our amorous games than R. — I will call this dark one "Black." She had one of the most delicate, refined, cock stiffening, slightly lipped, slightly haired cunts I ever saw: it resembled H.'s cunt years ago. Black took at once a frantic letch for gamahuching H. — and who

[*570*]

wouldn't? — When *my* mouth covers it, I can scarcely tear it away from it.

At our next visit the flagellation came off. As H., who'd only her chemise on, and I my shirt and wearing a mask, entered the room, there was a man kneeling on a large chair at the foot of the bed, over which he was bending. Over the seat and back of the chair was a large towel to receive his spendings. He had a woman's dress on tucked up to his waist, showing his naked rump and thighs, with his feet in male socks and boots. On his head was a woman's cap tied carefully round his face to hide whiskers — if he had any — and he wore a half mask which left his mouth free. — At his back, standing, was one youngish girl holding a birch and dressed as a ballet dancer, with petticoats far up above her knees, and showing naked thighs. Her breasts were naked, hanging over her stays and showing dark haired armpits. Another tall, well formed, tho thinnish female, naked all but boots and stockings, with hair dyed a bright yellow, whilst her cunt and armpits' fringes were dark brown, stood also at his back — a bold, insolent looking bitch whom I one day fucked after she'd gamahuched H. — tho I didn't like either her face, cunt, form, or manner — but she was new to me.

What he had done with the women before we entered we were told afterwards by yellow head, was very simple. He'd stripped both women naked, and saw the one dress herself as ballet girl, nothing more. Neither had touched his prick nor he their cunts. When the door was closed after we entered, he whispered to the abbess that he wanted to see my prick. Determined to go thro the whole performance, I lifted my shirt and shewed it big but not stiff. He wanted to feel it but that I refused. "Be a good boy or Miss Yellow (as I shall call her) will whip you hard," said the abbess. — "Oh — no — no — pray don't," he whispered in reply. He spoke always in whispers. Then he said H. was lovely and wanted to see her cunt, which she refused. He never turned round during this but remained kneeling. Then after childish talk between him and the abbess (he always in whispers), "Now she shall whip you, you naughty boy," said the abbess — and "swish" the rod descended heavily upon his rump.

"Oho — ho — ho," he whispered as he felt the twinge. I moved round to the other side of him where I could see his prick more plainly. It was longish, pendant, and the prepuce covered its tip nearly. — Swish — swish — went the birch, and again he cried in whispers. — "Ho, ho." — H. then moved round to my side to see better. — Yellow head from behind him felt his prick. — The abbess winked at me. — Then he laid his head on the bedstead frame and grasped it with both hands, whilst very leisurely the birch fell on him and he cried. "Ho — ho." — His rump got red and then he cried *aloud*. — "Oh, I can't" — then sunk his voice to a whisper in finishing his sentence. — Yellow head again felt his prick which was stiffer, and *he* sideways felt *her* cunt, but still not looking round.

Then was a rest and a little talk, he still speaking in whispers. The abbess treated him like a child. I felt Yellow head's motte, she looking at H. to see if *she* permitted *me* the license. Yellow head then took up the birch, and H. and I moved to the other side of the bed. Both of us were excited, H.'s face was flushed with lust, I felt her cunt, and she my pego, now stiff. "Look at those two," quoth the abbess. We, and both the women laughed. — The patient had turned his head to look, but could see nothing but us standing. — Swish — swish, fell heavily the rod on his arse, now very red indeed. — "Let me lick her cunt," whispered he, nodding at H. — She refused. — "I'll give her five pounds," he whispered. H. hesitated, but short of money as usual, at length she consented, beside she was lewed to her bumhole — "I shall spend," she whispered to me as she got on to the bed and saying aloud, "Five pounds, mind." — "He'll pay, he's a gentleman," murmured the abbess.

Then was a spectacle such as I never saw before nor shall again. H. settled on the bed, thighs wide apart, quim gaping, legs over the bed frame, cunt close up to the victim, but too low for his tongue to reach the goal. The abbess, Miss Yellow head and I, pushed pillow after pillow under her lovely bum till it was up to the requisite level, and greedily he began licking it. I moved round him again, looking curiously at his prick which was now stiff. — "Let *him* feel it," he whispered more loudly than usual. I felt and frigged it for a second. Whilst I did so, swish — swish — fell the rod on his rump, which writhed. — "Um — um — hum," — he murmured, his mouth full of H.'s cunt. "Ahrr," sighed H., whose lovely face expressed her pleasure, for she was lewed. Yellow head laid hold of his prick, gave it two or three gentle frigs, and out spurted a shower of semen. Then he was quiet with his mouth full on H.'s open quim, whilst still Yellow head continued frigging his shrinking organ. — "Have you spent?" — said I. "Damn it, I was just coming," said H., jogging her cunt still up against his mouth, wild for her spend. But he was lifeless, all desire to lick her had gone.

At a hint from the abbess we went to our bed-room. — "Fuck me." — On the bed she got, her cunt wet with his saliva, my prick nodding its wants and lust, up I plunged it in her wet cunt, thrust my tongue into her sweet mouth, our salivas poured into each other's, and we spent in rapture, almost before we had began the glorious to and fro of my prick in her lubricious avenue.

Neither of us had seen such a sight before, never had either of us even seen any one flogged, and we talked about it till the abbess came up. The man had left, but only gave three sovereigns for H.'s complaisance. "No doubt she's kept the other two," — said H. afterwards. The young ladies were still below, would we like to have a chat with them? Our passions were well roused, H. at once said "Yes," and up they came. We had champagne, giving the abbess some, then all talked about flagellation. The younger woman showed marks of the birch on her bum, and when the abbess had gone, we heard more about the rich victim, whom both had seen before and who was between fifty and sixty. He always had two women, but not always they two, they'd never known him allow strangers to be present when he was flogged, and he wanted to know if H. would whip him some day. (She never would.) Then we all four stripped, both women gamahuched H. and whilst the younger one was doing *that* I fucked Yellow head, whose cunt I couldn't bear. Then *she* gamahuched H. and I without any effort fucked up the other girl and found *her* cunt delicious. — In the intervals we laid pell mell on the bed together, topsy — turvy, — arsy — versy, and any how and in all sorts of ways, looked at each other's cunts, the two women both sucked my prick to stiffness but no further and Yellow head put her finger up *my* bum as I fucked the younger girl at the bedside feeling H.'s lovely sweet cunt whilst I did so, and as *her* rump was towards me I paid the finger compliment to *her* bumhole. — We had champagne till all were tight, and gloried in most unrestrained baudiness in act and talk. We all pissed, and I felt their amber streams whilst issuing, and pissed myself against Yellow head's cunt, H. holding the basin. — Then fatigued with lustful exercises — H. excepted — we had strong tea, and went our ways. A veritable orgy, and an extravagantly expensive one.

Now it was very clear and frankly avowed by H., that our

[573]

meetings were the delight of her life, that tho happy at home they were friendless nearly, and she looked forward to meeting me with the greatest pleasure, not only to tell me all, but to indulge with me in reminiscences, and have baudy afternoons with other women. "And it's your fault, you've told me more than all the men and women together whom I've known." — But there were hindrances. Sometimes two or three weeks intervened between our meetings at the abbess'; tho each meeting brought some baudy novelty.

When next we met we had little Black and not Miss R. for our companion, and Black and I together gave H. her complete dose of pleasure. Two fucks, a frig, and three or four gamahuches, some by me, some by Black, seemed the quantum which she called a jolly baudy afternoon. All were pleased, for B. loved gamahuching H., and being gamahuched by *me,* and tho so young, willingly sucked my pego to its liquid culmination. — H. still refusing to do that, or to touch B.'s quim with her tongue. — What with conversation about fucking in general — of the erotic caprices of men, of money gained and spent, sexual incitements, etc. etc. — in which conversations the abbess joined now at times — we passed most voluptuous afternoons or evenings. — But the cost was heavy — for the abbess' house was quiet and expensive, and champagne and a second gay lady added much to the sum total of the expenses of meeting H.

The abbess was the most kindly woman of her class I ever knew and superior to her business, her house the nicest and quietest.

Now for brevity sake I epitomize the narrative of my doings with H*** during this year and years after. At intervals we met and indulged in every lascivious caprice. I had taken home from *** a fine dildo which squirted liquids, and which it amused her to be fucked with. Then I fucked her with it, licking her clitoris whilst I did it to her. Then Miss Black licked her clitoris whilst the dildo was working up H. — Then with the dildo strapped on to her, H. dildoed Black. Then she dildoed Black whilst I fucked her from behind. Then I fucked the pretty little black cunted lass whilst she gamahuched H. — Another time I dildoed H. whilst laying on her back, and B. licked her clitoris, and at the same time and unknown to B., — for H. objected to any woman knowing that I played with her bum hole — put my middle finger up that tight anal orifice, and H. spent in ecstacies during the dildo fucking, finger buggering, and cunt licking. I could feel whilst up her bum the dildo moving up and down in her cunt, and H. grew a little fond of that double insertion. — We kept it to ourselves, tho often talking about it when alone, with her never failing remark, "Ain't we beasts?" and my reply, "No, beasts don't do that."

After that she dildoed R. who was fattish and big arsed. — H.'s taste was for fat women to gamahuche her. — Then she frigged R., whilst standing in the rear I fucked the fat arsed one. Then we had R. and B. together, and I gamahuched H. whilst she frigged both women who lay one on each side of her. Then the two quiet strumpets — they were not street walkers — gamahuched each other whilst I fucked H. All these pranks were reflected in large cheval glasses, so that we could see every posture. At intervals of rest we drank champagne, eat cakes and sandwiches. Every woman as she pissed I made to mount the bed, and squat over a basin, whilst I kneeling on the floor in front of her, contemplated the amber jet from the crimson gash. How we laughed one day when B. let a little fart when piddling, and how annoyed she was, how modest, how she blushed — harlot tho she was — but it's a fact.

I now gamahuched H. as much as she liked it done to her: the broad lick of her sweet vulva, the plunge of my tongue up the soft avenue was delicious to me, but *her* great pleasure was in frigging another woman whilst I was titillating her clitoris with my tongue. Then I had a whim which she didn't like but to which I made her yield. I laid on my back on the bed naked, H. naked knelt over me, a knee on each side of my head, her cunt on my mouth so that I could lick her clitoris easily, whilst I grasped her satiny buttocks. Then one of the women — either R. or B. — gamahuched me and took my libation into her mouth. In the glasses H. could see all this. I with mouth on her cunt, and head enclosed by her lovely thighs could not. I could tell always when H. was about to spend, by the trembling movements of her thighs, and shiver of her belly and bum, and her cry. "Oh — I'm coming — suck his prick — spend dear — aha — spunk." — She used these licencious ejaculations always now. She'd spend twice before I did once for I'd usually fucked her once before, and was longer in coming than she with her lustful capabilities. Indeed this double minetting was usually the termination of the day's amusements, when all three had been fucked, frigged, or gamahuched.

Of course as said all these amusements were not had on the same day, this is an epitome of what took place from time to time during this and a few years after. — Each day's amusement was noted down by me soon after, but are condensed here. Our meretricious tricks were nearly always played in the afternoon in broad daylight, beginning soon after luncheon, and in a room on which the sun shone brilliantly most of the day; often times on prick and cunt fell the warm sunbeams. The room was one where none could see or hear us, and where the amiable assistants got for us were mostly young and handsome, and who could bear any amount of light, any inspection of their secret charms, and who full of hot blood and the voluptuousness of youth, and stimulated by champagne, loved the baudy tricks and spent freely.

And to complete this catalogue of letches, and delights, — it occurred two years later when I first dildoed H. — I had an umbrella with a smooth handle of peculiar shape, and H. was delighted to let me fuck her with it till she spent.

Indeed most things that a man, and three women could do together we did. What was wanting to complete the variety was H. to gamahuche me, but she'd neither do that, nor gamahuche the other women tho she'd frig them till they could spend no longer. — In after years once under pressure of circumstances H. took my libation in her mouth, and once sucked me up to rigidity only.

———

The narrative in its chronological order of events I finish. Many more incidents might have been told of varied delights, of whims and fancies normal and abnormal, yet tho the places, participants and actresses were different, the amatory amusements were similar to others played elsewhere, and their repetition in the narrative would be tedious.

I break with the past, my amatory career is over, my secret life finished. My philosophy remains the same. My deeds leave me no regret — with the exception perhaps of a very few. — Would that I were young enough to continue in the same course — that all might happen to me over again. — But age forbids, duty forbids, affection forbids — Eros adieu.

Here abruptly terminates the narrative. Some years after the writer died and the manuscript came as already told into the possession of him who arranged and abbreviated it. A wonderful narrative of something like fifty years of secret life.